The Evil Men's Book Club

The Evil Men's Book Club

T. C. Schueler

Peebles Press
2024

This is a work of fiction. Any resemblance to real persons, places, or institutions is coincidental.

First Printing: 2024

ISBN 979-8-32004-235-0

Peebles Press may be contacted through the site listed below:

www.tcschueler.com

Cover art: Robert DiFiore

Author photo: Douglas Scott May

Dedication

To the original evil men—
you know who you are.

Chapter 1: The Alley

Friday Night, 13 November 1998
Silver Spring, MD

SO I PEED behind a dumpster—sue me. But before you do, hear me out. Getting to a restroom tonight was out of the question. Sure, there's a Gents inside the bar, but I couldn't go near it. This goon named Mullet came looking for me earlier, see, so I had to bail out to the alley.

Mullet.

Am I scared of an angry man with a stupid haircut and an even stupider nickname? Yes, I am! See, due to a recent financial misunderstanding, Mullet wanted to have a "chat" with me. Luckily for yours truly, however, the "mullets" of our world abide by the age-old axiom: *dead men don't pay,* so I knew if he grabbed me, something unpleasant might happen, but I wouldn't be killed.

But out in the alley, there was an actual *killer,* a guy who bumped someone off not twenty feet from my dumpster *baño.* Did you hear me? Twenty feet! One moment I'm tending to my own business, the next I'm running for my life! I'd caught the attention of this murderer, see, who proceeded to chase me down the alley. I'm pursued to the rear of St. Paul's Church, down its cellar steps, down into a crowded basement where I'm currently hiding.

Just relax, catch your breath—I'm talking to myself here, not you—*and stop panicking, or you'll look like the winded idiot you are.*

Okay.

Now I'm not safe yet, but it's better in this basement than being chased through the dark, so I guess I have time to introduce myself. My name's Trevor, Trevor Pug. Think pug as in "rug" or the crumple-faced dog from *Men in Black.* Got a wife, a kid, a job . . . which isn't important right now. The alley killer chased me a block and a half, see, and now he's down here in this crowd somewhere, too, looking for me. I didn't see him clearly in the alley, and I'm pretty sure he didn't see me either—it was dark, my back was turned—but I can't be sure.

So, the basement: it's large, crowded with hundreds of folding chairs and all sorts of people. It's one of those twelve-step meetings—everyone's finding their seat. I don't have a drinking problem myself, but like my dumpster wee-wee, this is an emergency, so thank God for drunks and their well-attended AA meetings, 'cause that means the alley killer's got a couple hundred folks to sort through.

Got my breath under control now—that's the good news—but I'm still shaking. Have you ever tried to stop shaking on willpower alone? Try it sometime, tell me how you do.

Okay, the murder. I'm sure you're curious.

Picture this. It's 9:30 p.m. and dark, the kind of dark making my any-port-in-a-storm alley stop completely secluded, or so I thought. I was whizzing away behind this eight-foot-tall BFI dumpster when suddenly I heard voices, loud ones, so I closed my floodgates so as not to be caught urinating like some asshat. That done, I stuck my head around the dumpster. I was curious; I get that way when I drink. Just beyond the dumpster, there's a break in the alley wall, a twenty-foot cutout for a loading dock. There's a six-foot-tall chain link privacy fence in front of it, plus a door that's normally chained shut. I remember carefully stepping over an empty Blockbuster VHS sleeve to quietly get closer.

The voices were coming from behind the fence. I couldn't see through the mesh because it had those plastic slats weaved through it to block prying eyes—like mine, I guess. There was an unlocked padlock hanging from the fence door. I've never seen it unlocked. (I use this alley a lot.)

More on the alleyway: At one end of it there's a couple of no-pay parking spots along Loraine Boulevard, and at the other it's Georgia Avenue. Nelson Street, with its front-facing businesses, runs between them, paralleling the alley. I usually park in one of the Lorraine Blvd no-pays so I can walk up the backstreet to the rear entrances of my two favorite bars: Shorties and Hell.

And yes, you heard right. "Hell" is the official name on the liquor license—no fooling. It's where I usually start my Friday nights, like tonight. I'd arrived earlier through Hell's rear entrance. This was about 6:45, so still some daylight. (When it's full dark, I take the longer way along the well-lit Nelson St sidewalk to avoid the mugging I'd otherwise deserve.) I'd meant to get a quick beer before heading to Shorties for the book club, but I lost track of time—to be honest, three hours' worth.

But back to the unlocked gate. The fenced-off cut-out's maybe fifteen feet wide by thirty feet deep. Behind it is an elevated loading dock with a rolldown door. The business, Nelson's Paper Supplies, went belly-up five years ago, so no reason for anyone to be there. Well, no *good* reason, anyway. Yet here two guys stood, arguing. I eased up to the chain link. I still couldn't see them, but I could hear better. One guy had a high, nasal voice. This guy—turns out his name is Mark—sounded desperate, so it was easy to catch what he said. The other guy had a deeper, harder-to-hear voice. Between the two, this was what I heard:

"C'mon, man, I need it!" said Mark. "That's why you carry it, right?"

The thick voice: "For emergencies only."

"This *is* an emergency! My skin's crawlin'!"

"No, Mark," said Thick Voice. "You know what needs doing, you just aren't doing it."

"Sure I am!" Mark insisted. "Just need it for my nerves, then I'll go the distance."

"I wish you would, but we both know you won't."

"Sure I will!" Mark again insisted. "C'mon, man! Give it here!"

"No," said Thick Voice. "It stays in my pocket."

After a short silence, the Mark guy gives this enraged yell and a struggle begins. Someone grunted, then someone bounced off the chain link fence, flexing it loudly. I couldn't make out anything through the privacy slats, so I stepped closer to the fence gate—not because I was brave, but because Budweiser makes me curious—and I knew the slats on the fence door stopped a foot above the ground. If I crouched next to it, I could look underneath the door, so I did. Now I could make out footwear: dirty Nikes and a pair of scuffed work boots. I watched the shoes shuffle as they fought. Mark kept yelling "Gimmie! I need it!" and Thick Voice kept answering, "No you don't." The scuffle intensified. One of them got slammed hard against the loading bay wall, and . . . there was a fleshy, cracking noise. The one wearing the sneakers dropped, hitting the pavement with this awful *wunk* sound.

Thick Voice exclaimed, "Mark!"

Though the light at foot level was poor, I knew it was Mark of Nike shoe fame lying on the asphalt. He was badly hemorrhaging. Without help, he would surely die. I could also make out the killer's rawhide-laced boots. Seeing all this, I stood up to get away. Unfortunately, my clumsy foot kicked a bottle (*cau-clink-clink!*) and the bootman heard it. I began running. He rushed to the door, flinging it open and yelling, "Wait!"

I remembered thinking, *I don't think so, pal.*

The Bootman wasted no time pursuing me, his heavy boots clomping. I desperately wanted the well-lit freedom of Lorraine Blvd (and my car), but the Bootman blocked that direction, so I juked the other way toward Hell, back to where my dumpster adventure began.

As stupid as this sounds, I knew I needed to go to Hell as quickly as possible (haha)—Hell may be a sketchy bar, but it's crowded on Friday nights, so I'd be safe there. Then I remembered: Mullet! He was probably playing eight ball at the table near the backdoor (the one I'd vamoosed through earlier) keeping an eye on it just in case I was stupid enough to return. Now, running straight into a cue-wielding Mullet was a terrible plan

B, but it beat being caught by the murderous Bootman, so I went to Hell. (Haha again.) My reasoning: Mullet and his goon buddy, Rocker, wouldn't expect me to burst back inside like a bat out of . . . yeah, yeah, sorry. Once inside, I planned to swoop past them—please forgive me—through the Gates of Hell. Seriously, that's what the front doors are called.

Unfortunately, the weak light over Hell's back entrance revealed that the Bad Luck Express had just pulled in: a bored-looking Mullet stood in the alley, smoking. I flew toward him, involuntarily making eye contact. Surprised, he dropped his Winston to lunge at me. He was too slow, however, but with Hell blocked off, I had to keep barreling down the alley. "Wait!" Mullet yelled. My pursuer also blew past him, boots clomping hard.

Despite my need for self-preservation, I began slowing, Budweiser competing with adrenaline. In another hundred feet it wouldn't have mattered—I'd reach Georgia Avenue's well-lit six lanes of freedom. From there, I'd double back to Lorraine Blvd and my car.

The last building before the alley ended was St. Paul's Church, or more accurately, its rear basement steps. In front of them, blocking me from freedom, however, were a couple dozen smokers.

My choices: turn and face Bootman the Alley Killer or dive into the crowd. I dove, mumbling apologies as I forced my way to its center, supposedly the safest part. Just then, some bell I couldn't hear must have begun ringing. The smokers heard it though, 'cause they suddenly heeled their cigarettes, then began moving down the basement steps like livestock. It came to me then: *They're going to an AA meeting*. I thought about fighting my way back to Georgia Ave, but starting a shoving match with these people, some of them Mullet-sized, didn't seem wise. Plus, I figured this AA crowd should keep me, you know, *anonymous*. Once inside, I'd find another way out.

As the crowd moved along, I saw the figure of the Bootman behind me in the alley. Too many people to get a good look, but it must've been him—he was out of breath like me. To my horror, he too joined the herd. We entered the basement, trundling through a hallway like satisfied concertgoers, all small talk and laughter (them, not me). Somebody said hello, nodding like she knew me, but I just looked down, which made me unhappy because there were tons of boots. (Most of these people must work with their hands. Perhaps the Alley Killer does too.)

We passed by a kitchenette holding a huge coffee urn and a big candy bowl. Several people stopped for coffee, filling Styrofoam cups and pocketing Jolly Ranchers. There was a buzz—everyone was talking. We then entered a very large room, the one I'm in now—rows and rows of chairs with an aisle down the middle—seating for hundreds. The front of this room was higher than the rest, like a stage. On it, a wooden lectern was flanked by folding tables; people were sitting behind them like contest judges. Kinda felt like a middle school assembly.

Which brings me to the present, as in right now. *Where do I sit?*

"Your first meeting?" asks an older African-American man. Picture Alex Haley, the guy who wrote *Roots,* then add wrinkles and thick glasses. "No, not my first," I say. I don't know why I lie—I've never been to an AA meeting in my life—but I do. "Not seen you here before," he says, extending his hand; his eye wrinkles tighten as he smiles. "Welcome. My name's Reggie." I don't know what to do, so I shake his hand and *boy* does he have a grip. I don't want to tell him my name.

Now I'm freaking out 'cause if I don't sit down soon, I'll be the standing, out-of-breath, easily identifiable guy. (Perhaps the Bootman's picked me out already! I can't express how much that possibility sucks.) Meanwhile, Reggie politely steers me to the last row where two middle seats remain. People graciously move their feet as we step past them. We sit.

Mouth to ear, Reggie whispers, "I can smell the alcohol." I panic—he's gonna throw me out! That kind of attention, hell, *any* kind of attention, is the last thing I need. "Don't worry, it's okay," Reggie says. "I wasn't sober my first meeting, either."

I'm confused; I'd already told him I'd been to an AA meeting before. How does he know I'm lying?

"Why don't you and I keep a low profile here in the back row," Reggie suggests.

"Really low, sir," I say. He chuckles. I look at my watch. It's almost 10:00. A few people in the row in front of us turn to acknowledge Reggie. They nod to me as well with this weird friendliness. I don't like it. Thanks to my brother Willie's exploits, my cult radar begins pinging: *The hard sell cometh.* But I tell myself, *Don't worry about what flavor of Kool-Aid's being served, just keep it together.*

"Figure you don't want to give your name," Reggie whispers to me.

"That's right."

Reggie smiles again. "I'd like to call you by something, though," he says. "How about I call you 'Bud?'"

"Sure," I say. "I've been called worse." I slouch in my folding chair, ball cap low over my eyes. I'm sneaking looks at people's feet, trying not to be obvious. Bad news: boots are everywhere, at least three dozen pairs.

I take a closer look at Reggie. I told you about the wrinkles, so add to that a wedding band, short-cropped gray hair, a paunch, a collared shirt, and a pair of navy slacks. And the Buddy Holly glasses. From his wardrobe, I imagine he's got mid-level responsibility, maybe a cab dispatcher or a head clerk. Cult member or not, Reggie's not wearing boots, so he's not the Alley Killer. I love him for that.

There's some announcement I don't quite catch, but everyone simmers down hearing it. One of the table sitters, a mousy-looking woman, gets up and goes to the lectern to begin reading from some book. At certain points during her reading, everyone in the audience, Reggie included, chants along with her, which is creepy. After she's done reading, she introduces herself and everyone says "Hi, Janice!" She begins speaking.

"This place got a side entrance?" I ask Reggie during a pause.

"An escape hatch?" His smile says *yes*.

"Can you show me?"

"Afterward," he says, pointing toward the podium.

"How long's she gonna take?" I ask. In addition to escaping, I still need to pee.

"Is there somewhere you need to be, Bud?" Reggie whispers.

I shrug my shoulders.

"The meeting's an hour. Starts at ten, ends at eleven—strict about that. Listen to Janice. You might learn something."

I'm not here to learn anything, I'm here to hide, but since everyone's intent on Janice, I feign interest too. I silently review my problems. The first is Mullet's wanting to chat with me about money. The second, obviously, is having to hide from a murderer. Oh, there's a third problem: I've totally missed book club—Loo Spicotti, my co-chair, will be furious.

Some guy two rows forward has just turned around to stare at me. He's wearing scuffed boots with rawhide laces.

Bootman laces.

Chapter 2: Shorties

Friday, 13 November 1998
Silver Spring, MD

IT WAS NOW 7 p.m., two and a half hours before Mark would be killed in the alley behind The Short Round pub, a bar that everyone called "Shorties." Loo Spicotti, a mid-size man with powerful shoulders, jogged toward the pub's entrance. A homeless person sitting next to it asked him for a quarter. Loo, late, ignored him, rushing headlong down the pub's stairway instead.

Shorties was a basement two-room *ratskeller*, not so much a hole in the wall as one in the ground. The smaller of the rooms was the rear space where the club met—a poorly lit twenty-by-fifty area crowded with tables. To reach it from street level, one first descended narrow stone steps as Loo had just done, then crossed the front room, carefully lifting one's feet over the four-inch threshold dividing the spaces. With no rear exit, the back area was a fire marshal's nightmare. Backroom patrons, however, were less concerned with safety than ambient light. If you wanted to see your date, you wanted the larger, better-lit front room with its Anglo pub décor. If you wished your date were more attractive than he or she actually was, however, then the darker, Bavarian-themed back room was for you.

And this room did resemble a beer garden. One wall held shelves of ornate steins. Another was covered with posters of old-timey European beer ads where buxom, blue-eyed *fräuleins* served frothy ale tankards to felt hat–wearing accordion players. The third wall featured a large poster of Pele scoring a goal. It was flanked by the logos of the Manchester United and Arsenal football teams.

It was a busy Friday night—the bar was crowded and therefore loud. The front room also held tables and a full-length bar which Shorties' proprietor, Poland Manchester, now stood behind. Poland, a squat bald man, was currently using meaty fingers to punch up the volume on his TV remote. Channel 4 was dropping a tease he didn't want to miss: Silver Spring's very own scofflaw, the Deerslayer, had just added two more animals to his "Bambi Count," which now stood at seventy. Some patrons booed hearing this, others whistled. The tease turned into an ad for Gillette Mach3 razors which Poland tuned out.

Loo pushed up his Ben Franklin-style glasses to take in tonight's floor servers: Vicky and Randy, the fabulous Vee Sisters, and unfortunately their moody cousin, Brian. The trio was bustling back and forth to the cook counter, dropping off orders and picking up plates of food. *I hope Eeyore's not serving us,* Loo thought, by which he meant Cousin Brian. Seeing his six buddies already seated, Loo sat down in one of two unoccupied chairs, then poured himself a beer from a half-full pitcher.

"Who's our server?" he asked.

"Eeyore," someone sketching on a napkin said.

Damn.

"You're late," the sketching man continued.

"Trevor's not here yet?"

"Nope."

"Then I guess I'm in charge, again," Loo said, thinking, *Trevor Pug—derelict in your duties.*

He looked at his compatriots. To his left sat Henry "Splashdown" Takahashi wearing a *They Killed Kenny!* t-shirt. Splash, the intent napkin doodler, was drinking some formidable dark ale.

"Whatcha drawing, Splash?" Loo asked him.

"Don't bother an artist while he's working," Splash said without looking up.

"Did you read *Pulp*?" Loo asked him. *Pulp,* Charles Bukowski's 1994 novel, was this month's book selection.

"Another question means you're still bothering me," said Splash, continuing to sketch.

"You delivering tonight?" asked Loo, by which he meant pizzas.

"No," said Splash, finally looking up. "Got the night off on account of this important scholarly exercise we go through each month." He snorted contemptuously. "It's Friday night. Of *course* I'm delivering."

"Taking Make My Day?" "Make My Day" was the name of Henry's massive five-chambered revolver.

"Always," said Splash.

Loo nodded. "How go gallery rentals?"

"What rentals?"

"Keep up that positive attitude, samurai," Loo said.

"Sure thing," replied Splash, returning to his drawing. Most would agree: the well-kempt man had the frame to pull off looking like a shogun.

Next to him sat a man wearing a starched shirt and a loud tie. Though his Def Systems photo ID identified him as Darius Kay, he went by D-Kay, pronounced like *tooth decay,* a disgusting but effective mnemonic. D-Kay caught Loo's eye. "What's up, Loo, Loo, Loo-ser?" Loo flipped him off. D-

Kay, a supersized version of Danny DeVito, served as the club's ego check and distributor of nicknames. In Spicotti's case, he'd shortened Luigi to *Loo* "in honor of British bathrooms worldwide."

Next to him sat Reymond Perkins, whom D-Kay had christened *Death Rey* "in honor of crappy science fiction movies worldwide." Club nicknames sometimes mutated. Henry Takahashi had gotten a particularly large dose of rads, starting first as "Henry the Eighth," then "Henry the Eighth Track," then "Henrique," then "Re-Hentry Vehicle." D-Kay finally landed on *Splashdown* "in honor of Apollo programs worldwide" which admittedly made no sense whatsoever. D-Kay did not care. If you didn't like your nickname—or in Henry's case, nicknames—too bad; find another club.

Opposite Rey sat Gary Graft, as of that evening the club's newest member, in a collared shirt, muted tie, and a sports coat. Gary had short-cropped, receding hair and light stubble. Everything about his appearance was professional but subdued, as if he didn't want attention. He could not hide the intellect in his eyes, however.

To Gary's left sat Ken Ert, who, so as not to be confused with his nearly identical cousin of the same name, was called *Original Ken*. Original, in a white Oxford and lime green bowtie, was showing Gary a *Washington Post* sports article with Ert's byline. Gary was nodding, impressed.

Next to Original sat the unnicknamed Phillipe Gallois, pronounced *fil-eep gal-wah*. He was a large-framed man in a work shirt with *Southwest Airlines* emblazoned across its front pocket. Between him and Loo, who was wearing a Baltimore Orioles gimmie hat and a F**K THE YANKEES sweatshirt, sat Trevor Pug's empty chair.

Seven total members, eight if you counted the missing Trevor.

"Before Loo officially gets us started, guys," said D-Kay, "I need your help. I'm writing an opera about four Italian brothers. Got names for the first three: Buttholio, Assholio, and Cornholio." From the table: laughs, groans, and a *whatever, Beavis*. "I need a fourth brother. His name must end in *oh*. Splash, why don't you start."

"Opera?" Splash asked. "If you're singing in it, then I'm passing on it."

"No help from Splash," said D-Kay. "How about you, Loo?"

Loo said, "Prego, it's in there . . . Ee-oh."

"Is that your final answer?" asked D-Kay, Regis Philbin-like, "because it sucks. Death Rey, got anything?"

"There once was a man from Nantucket—" began Rey.

"You're out," said D-Kay.

"But I didn't even get a chance to finish—"

"Correct, you didn't. Original, care to give it a go?"

Original Ken pondered, then shook his head disappointedly. "I have nothing."

"How about 'Uh-oh, Spaghetti-oh?'" Loo offered. "That ends in *oh*."

"Not bad," said D-Kay, "but it doesn't follow my 'butt' theme, and besides, you're double-dipping. Phillipe?"

"How about 'Uh-oh, *Spicotti*-oh?'" Phillipe offered, riffing Loo's last name and making everyone laugh.

"Love it," said D-Kay, "but guys, remember my *butt* theme? Death Rey of Nantucket fame, care to try again?"

"You're the Babble King, D-Kay," said Reymond. "Why can't *you* come up with something?"

"I am the Babble King. I can do anything," D-Kay responded, then snapped his fingers. "Which includes getting inspiration here from Rey's general asshattery. Thank you, asshat. Here it is, boys: 'Sphinctolio,' my fourth brother. Rey, I'll think of you when I'm selling out Broadway." It was a good dig. The guys laughed.

Gary, the new guy, spoke up. "So it's *Buttholio, Assholio, Cornholio, and Sphinctolio—The Opera*. Will it be any good?"

"Given the theme, it's sure to be shitty," Loo said. More laughs. "All right guys," he continued, "let's get going. First, our motto." Together, the men, all in their early thirties, spoke in unison, "Stop illegitimacy, read a book."

Gary, who'd remained silent, looked confused. "It's supposed to be 'illiteracy,'" explained Phillipe. "Our little joke."

"Oh, gotcha," said Gary.

"Okay, for the benefit of Gary the newbie," said Loo, "the rules: one, the Evil Men's Book Club must always meet in a bar." The old hands looked around overdramatically, then nodded. "Two: do members have to read the book?"

The regulars: "No."

"Alrighty then," Loo said, "housekeeping's complete. Original Ken, great job on last month's *Lolita* minutes. Your spelling out the legal difference between child endangerment and enticement was particularly enlightening. So, who'll take tonight's notes?"

"I will," said Phillipe. He took a hefty, oil-stained book from his coat pocket and began tearing pages from it for scratch paper. The manual's title: DC-9 Landing Gear Operations and Maintenance.

"Um, Phillipe," said Loo, "isn't that sort of manual . . . important?"

"Sure is," he responded, ripping away. "But I don't bother reading them." Phillipe, who worked maintenance for Southwest Airlines out of their Baltimore hub, now had everyone's attention. He began smoothing out his torn pages, "unmindful" of the anticipation he'd created.

"Okay, I'll bite," D-Kay finally said. "Phillipe, *why* don't you read the safety manuals? I might be going out on a limb here, but isn't a functional landing gear, like, important?"

Phillipe explained with a smirk: "Typical plane's got north of a million parts. Nobody knows them all. The wheel mechanic looks at the wheels. I'm a skin mechanic—I look at the hull. That's it."

"Okay, Phillipe," Loo said. "Thanks for that confidence-building aviation update. Someone let John Denver know. Moving right along, tonight's selection was *Pulp* by Charles Bukowski, a warm, sensitive, dare I say *loving* treatment of the detective genre. Gents, who read the book?" All hands but Gary's went up.

"Thumbs up, thumbs down?" asked Loo. Five thumbs up, with Rey dissenting. "Evil score?" The finishers gave numbers to Phillipe, who tallied, announcing, "An average of five."

Gary leaned toward Phillipe, asking, "Evil score?"

"One to ten," Phillipe answered. "One means not evil. Think *The Three Little Pigs* or a government pamphlet on weatherproofing."

"And ten?"

"Think *Mein Kampf*," Phillipe said.

"Really, *just* five?" Loo exclaimed. "With all that talk about nailing Jeanie Nitro's ass? Come on, guys, I may only be an unfrozen caveman lawyer, but even I know you're lowballing." No one, however, was willing to change their score. "Fine, you're all cretins, especially you, Death Rey."

Brian, a morose-looking man wearing Robert Smith eyeliner, arrived at their table bearing burgers, fries, pizza slices, onion rings, and one order of hummus (Loo was vegetarian). They began eating. Loo continued grousing about the low scores, particularly Rey's "3." Rey wouldn't budge, saying, "The book was a waste of time. I hated it. If it was alive, I'd give it the finger."

"Duly noted," Phillipe said, scribbling this down.

"Didn't Bukowski die after writing this?" Splash asked.

"He died *because* he wrote it," said Rey. "And I don't buy that it's a crime story parody—this piece of crap represents an existential threat to the entire detective genre."

Phillipe leaned toward Gary to whisper loudly, "Rey's pathologically serious."

"Then should we drink every time he says something like 'existential threat?'" Gary suggested.

"Good call, new guy," D-Kay said approvingly.

"'Gary the New Guy,'" said Gary. "That my club name?"

"Unless I come up with something better," affirmed D-Kay. "Problem with that?"

"No," said Gary.

"Good, because speaking of problems," D-Kay continued, loading up a non-sequitur, "I got one: all the stans confuse me."

"Stans?" Gary asked.

"Yeah," D-Kay replied, "you know, after the Commies broke up the band, they left all those little 'stan' countries. I can't keep 'em straight and I definitely can't pronounce them. Is it Kak-kak-istan?"

"No, it's 'Kazakhstan,'" said Rey.

"That's my point," replied D-Kay. "Stan countries: completely unpronounceable. Another one: 'Uzi-becky-stan.'"

"*Uz-bek-eh-stan,* you idiot," said Rey slowly.

"Well, maybe it *was* Uzi-becky-stan and they just shortened it," said D-Kay. "And don't look at me like that."

"I'm with Death Rey on this one," said Original. "Even crappy Eastern Bloc countries should be pronounced correctly."

"Perhaps we should rename the stans," said Loo. "Easier names, like Kick-istan or Fruit-istan."

"That's brilliant!" cried Splash.

"Fruit-istan?" said D-Kay. "I don't get it."

"You don't *under-stan*?" asked Rey. The guys snickered.

"No, I don't understand," said D-Kay, sounding defensive, but it was hard to tell with him.

"Yes," said Rey, smirking, "we under-stan that you don't under-stan." Laughter.

"Oh!" said D-Kay. "Under . . . *stan*. Got it! I made a 'stan' country without even knowing it. *God,* I'm good."

"You're a real genius, Darius," declared Original.

"A real dumb ass is more like it," said Rey. D-Kay blew Rey a kiss.

"Other suggestions?" asked Loo. "Think outside the bun."

"How about American-ban-istan?" offered Original.

"*Eastern Europe,* imbecile," said Rey.

"Maybe my stan's a U.S. territory," Original said defensively, "like Guam. And if you don't like 'Ban-istan,' sue me, but don't take the *stan* without a good lawyer." More laughter. For the next few minutes, the club created fictional stans to replace the hard-to-pronounce ones, better attempts being Stan-by-your-man-istan, the country of supportive women; the no-tell motel country of One-night-istan; and Custer's-last-istan, popular with Native Americans. "Okay, this has gone too-far-istan," said Loo, getting up for the bathroom. "Don't pinch my hummus while I'm gone." Everyone scoffed. "Don't worry, Tree Boy," said Splash. "No one wants your rabbit food."

Loo made his way to the Gents, a two-urinal, one-stall affair with a 40s-era sink and a condom vending machine. The wall mirror above the basin was missing. In its place someone had cheekily written *Just assume you look like shit*. The towel rack was also missing; a gigantic roll of Georgia-Pacific industrial-grade paper towels sat precariously on the basin.

A year before, Poland Manchester had the old graffiti in his pub bathrooms painted over. The freshly blank walls, however, proved irresistible to a new generation of high school desk defacers now old enough to buy beer. Much of their work was still traditionally themed: oversized genitalia, sexual promises (with names and phone numbers), maternal disparagements, and chestnuts like *Don't look here, the joke's in your hands.* Loo read what was new. Someone had written *Four stars, would pee here again.* Someone else scrawled *Was gonna rite somethin, but got nothin,* to which a third man had sympathetically responded *Happens to everyone—just draw a big dick next time.*

Amused, Loo returned to the table. "What the hell, guys!" he shouted. Someone had drawn a happy face in his hummus.

"Don't worry, Loo, the culprit used a clean spoon," said Splash. He got up. "I'm off to work now, gents. Got a studio to pay for. See you next month."

The table bid him adieu. After Henry left, Loo looked at the napkin he'd left behind. "Holy crap! Look at this!" Henry had drawn "EMBC" in impressive Gothic letters on his napkin, intertwining them with thorned roses held by tiny, mischievous-looking demons.

"Now *that's* metal," D-Kay declared. Everyone agreed. "Splash Takahashi," D-Kay continued, "the fourth member of Motörhead. Who knew?"

How perfect this evening is, thought Loo. *Nothing can spoil it.*

Chapter 3: The Curse

Friday, 13 November 1998
Silver Spring, MD

DEFILED HUMMUS ASIDE, Loo was having a great time. His eyes wandered about Shorties, pausing momentarily on Victoria Manchester, then toward the front room bar. All ten of its stools were taken, including one occupied by Prophet, the homeless man Loo had encountered on the way in. Prophet's presence was unusual, and it looked like Poland Manchester, Vicky's father and bar owner, was denying him service.

Prophet didn't interest Loo half as much as Christian Luntz, however, the imposing man now talking to Poland. Luntz wore a cutoff denim jacket emblazoned with the outline of a musket-wielding Continental soldier. The Minuteman logo stood for the Old Line Biker Club.

Something's up, thought Loo. Manchester, who'd previously barred the entire Old Line from Shorties, in deep conversation with its head hooligan? Loo watched Christian hand an envelope to Poland, who ran his fingers through its contents, then nodded toward Loo's table. *Oh crap, he's coming over!* Christian ambled across the front room, then stepped over the threshold, coming to rest behind Trevor's empty chair. Close up, their visitor looked a weathered fifty—creased forehead, salt and pepper hair, the beginnings of flab. In addition to denim jeans, he wore work boots with rawhide laces, and despite the pub's poor lighting, oval sunglasses.

"Evenin' boys. Where's Trevor?" he asked.

The table looked at Loo to answer for them—he was one of the two club founders, after all. "Don't know where he is," Loo replied.

"That so?" asked Christian, drumming his fingers on the absent man's chair. "Hmm. In that case, tell him Old Line's lookin' for him." Stiffly, Loo asked why. Christian smiled, revealing two gold teeth. He leaned close to him, whispered something in Loo's ear not meant for public consumption, then asked everyone, "Enjoyin' your little club?" No one answered. Christian let his question hang in the air a moment longer, then recited, "'To betray, you must first belong'—Kim Philby." Then he laughed and walked away.

Loo looked at his friends' concerned faces, all guys who'd signed up for a monthly airing of their Y chromosomes, not ominous biker peril. Once Luntz was safely out of earshot, D-Kay exclaimed, "What the fuck was *that* about? What did he say to you, Loo? Is Trevor in trouble?"

Thank God I'm buzzed, thought Loo, *because lying doesn't come easy*. "No more trouble than usual," he said. "Something to do with Trevor's brother." All except Gary knew Trevor's big brother Willie was once an Old Line member, so Loo's answer made sense.

"Hope Trevor's okay," said Original.

"I'm sure he's fine," said Loo, thinking, *Trevor, I'm covering your ass—again.*

"By the way, who's Kim Philby?" asked D-Kay.

"A double agent for the Soviet Union," said Gary.

"How do you know that, New Guy?"

"I read a lot," Gary said.

Vicky chose that moment to stop by the table, immediately lightening the mood. Victoria, along with her twin sister Randy—short for Veronica—was one of Poland Manchester's daughters. Shorties was a family business. At first glance, Poland's daughters looked identical, so it was natural to think these young twenty-something women purposefully dyed their hair to avoid confusion. A closer look, however, revealed fraternal differences. Vicky had naturally reddish-blond hair and her father's light blue eyes. She was also a touch shorter than her sister. Randy was a slim brunette who'd inherited their mother's much darker eyes. Though sometimes confused with each other, everyone could agree that God built the Vee Sisters to get attention.

"How's it going, boys?" Vicky asked, beaming, putting her hands on D-Kay's and Rey's shoulders. "I miss you guys, even these two jokers," she said. "Especially this fiscal conservative." She tweaked D-Kay's cheek to emphasize his well-known stinginess.

"We miss you too," Original said.

"Is Brian taking good care of you?" she asked.

"That sad sack Eeyore's got a name?" asked D-Kay.

"Now Darius Kay," Vicky chided, "be nice to Brian. He's family."

"Sorry, Vicky."

"And besides," she continued, "you guys look smart enough to sit in my section next time, right?" Heads bobbed. She smiled again before returning to her side of the room.

"She must paint those shorts on," Original observed.

"Yes," said D-Kay wistfully.

It was 9:15 p.m., which was when the club usually wrapped things up. Loo cleared his throat. "Okay, before we get the bill, which you cheap bastards better be good for—especially you, Darius—there's the matter of next month's selection. Any suggestions?" At the close of each meeting, anyone attending could volunteer a book, then the top two vote-getters would be rematched to determine a finalist. In the club's four-month existence, they had polished off *Junky, Lolita, American Psycho,* and as of tonight, *Pulp*. Original threw out Henry Miller's *Tropic of Cancer.* Phillipe offered Hunter S. Thompson's *Fear and Loathing in Las Vegas,* and D-Kay lobbied for Hubert Selby's *Last Exit to Brooklyn.*

"Can I vote?" Gary asked.

"I don't know," said Rey. "Can you hold up your hand?"

"Gary the New Guy, you most certainly can vote," said Loo, looking sharply at Reymond.

"Yeah, don't mind him," added Phillipe, companionly putting an arm around Gary. "The Evil Men's Book Club is alive, see, and like every living thing, it's got an asshole." Phillipe pointed at Rey. "He's our asshole." Laughter at Rey's expense.

The two finalists that night were *Fear and Loathing* and *Last Exit,* with *Fear and Loathing* winning out.

"What do you do to break a tie?" Gary asked.

"Rock-paper-scissors," said Original Ken.

"I thought it was one-potato, two-potato," D-Kay said.

"Shouldn't it just be a coin flip?" asked Phillipe.

A tie, yet to happen, suddenly became a hot topic, something fun to squabble about. As they debated, the table received another visitor: Prophet, the street person whom Manchester had earlier refused service. The man, resembling an anemic Gandalf the Grey, was soliciting beer money—now it was their table's turn.

"It's the book club!" he exclaimed. "Surely one of you scholars will buy a fellow bibliophile a drink?"

"Beat it," said Rey, speaking for the table. Prophet's reputation as a part-time psychic and full-time panhandler was well established.

"Come on, guys," said Prophet, looking sincerely desperate. "I'll read your palms, tell you your fortunes. One beer each. Who's first?"

"Read this," said D-Kay, grabbing his crotch.

"God, the halitosis," added Rey.

Prophet stared at the table's drinks intently, then licked his lips. "Guys, they don't call me Prophet for nothing! I've got a reputation for *seeing* things. I'll give you a special—one beer and I'll do all your palms."

"That does *not* sound right," said Phillipe.

"Seriously, Prophet, beat it," said Loo. "Poland will have your ass if he sees you begging."

"I am *not* begging," Prophet said defensively. "I'm providing a service. Come on, these never lie," he said, pointing to his eyes.

No one knew what to say. Poland allowed Prophet into Shorties provided he had money, but soliciting was always forbidden. "How about half a beer," Prophet said, pointing a tremorous hand toward an unfinished pint in front of Gary.

"Leave him alone," said Phillipe, shifting Gary's glass aside. "Move along before—"

From the front room came Manchester's thunderous voice: "Prophet!" Bar-wide, conversation stopped.

"I told you to never bother the customers. *Never*. Congratulations, you're banned." The barkeep put down his sop rag and started toward their table. Prophet looked crestfallen but then drew himself up to glare at the table.

"You!" he said loudly, pointing at the club, "You're all worthless! Weak! You're selfish a-holes who've never known what it's like to suffer."

"I've known suffering, trust me," said Rey smoothly. "So piss off, you alcoholic geezer."

Prophet, eyeing the approaching Poland, said threateningly, "You're gonna get arrested, all a' you."

Poland arrived, putting two beefy hands on Prophet's shoulders. "Let's go fortune teller," he said.

"And you're gonna lose your jobs," Prophet continued, pointing an authoritative finger at each man at the table. The bar was quiet enough that his words seemed to echo. Poland started dragging him away, but the man continued to curse them. "And your women are gonna go bad. Gonna go *south* on ya!"

"That's a good thing, isn't it?" asked D-Kay.

"No, it's not, you idiot!" Prophet yelled as he was dragged over the threshold separating the front and back rooms.

"Any other predictions, jackass?" called Rey.

From halfway across the front room, Prophet formed a gun with his fingers, pointing. "Yeah! You're gonna die! How do I know? *'Cuz I'm a prophet!*"

Poland pushed him up the entrance stairs, admonishing him, "Don't wanna see you any closer than a block from the door, ya hear me, or I'll give you worse."

Prophet grimaced, yelling back at the club, "I'll show you! Just you wait—it'll start with dreams!" So forceful was his energy that the guys involuntarily shuddered. But as quick as it came, the energy left, and Prophet's shoulders drooped. He looked around, confused, then began dejectedly climbing the steps to street level.

Poland reached to close the door, but an odd gust of wind forcefully swung it shut on its own. With a harumph, Poland announced, "Show's over, folks."

Bar buzz slowly resumed.

"What's wrong with that guy?" Gary asked.

"Just another bum," said Rey. "Don't worry about him."

Rey was right—the club needn't have worried about Prophet the "bum" bothering them again, for he would die within the hour. But Rey was also wrong. In the future, the guys would come to learn just how uncanny Prophet's augury would be.

Chapter 4: The World's Biggest Coffee Urn

Friday, 13 November 1998
Silver Spring, MD

HEY, IT'S ME, Trevor. It's halfway through this AA meeting I'm hiding in that I notice the Alley Killer two rows in front of me, his head twisted *Exorcist*-like to see me. Two hundred people looking one way, one scary dude looking the other. He's huge, a quarterback sacker with small eyes. "Who's he?" I nervously ask Reggie the Alex Haley impersonator.

"That's Thumper," he says. "Just ignore him."

Ignore him? Ignore a Randy Savage-looking dude staring at me as if I've offended him in some way, like witnessing him murdering someone? And he's got boots, *scuffed* boots, the Bootman's boots. He's found me, so soon I'm gonna die, and you know what's sad? The last thing I will have done here on God's Green Earth is attend some cult meeting, just like my brother did. That's just depressing.

"You don't look so good, Bud," Reggie whispers. "You need to get sick?" Honestly, until he asked, I'd had no urge to ralph, because I'm not a puker. But now, since it's obvious Thumper the Bootman won't let me leave this church alive, puking is all I can think about. "Oh boy," Reggie says, pulling me up. "Let's go." He hustles me past the gigantor coffee urn into a bathroom, one with blue and white tiles—not that I care about tiles because Thumper the Bootman's following us!

"No, no!" I'm saying loudly to Reggie. "Take me outside!"

"Bud," Reggie says, "let's not vomit on the sidewalk for everyone to have to step over." He opens the stall door. I don't make it in time, barfing on the floor, the seat, the tank—everywhere except the bowl. (Mark McGwire at the plate I'm not, but I've got more pressing concerns.) "Reggie," I croak, wiping my lips, "he's after me!"

"Who?" he asks.

"That guy, Thumper! He's gonna kill me!"

"Thumper? No way. He might bore you to death, but that's about it." Reggie points to the bowl. "That's your target, Bud."

Just then the bathroom door opens, Thumper filling its frame. As I mentioned, he's large, easily six-two and at least 250, mostly in his shoulders. He's got a look in his eyes that says *we have unfinished business.*

"He's gonna kill me!" I scream, and—I'm not proud of this—I cower behind Reggie. Thumper pulls something out of his coat pocket. Not a gun or a knife, thank God, but a book with a blue cover. I don't think you can be beaten to death with a book, but the guy looks large enough to try.

Thumper sniffs and says, "Not Chanel No. 5 in here."

"Nope," says Reggie. "Thumper, this here's Bud. Keep an eye on him while I get a mop."

"Don't leave me alone with him!" I plead.

Reggie patronizes me: "You'll be fine, Bud. Just aim for the bowl."

"Yeah, take it to the rim, Shaq," Thumper adds.

I grab at Reggie's slacks desperately. Unknowingly, he's gonna leave me with a guy who slammed another guy's head into a wall!

"Please let go of me, Bud," Reggie says patiently but firmly. More gore rises in the back of my throat, so I jerk my head into the bowl and vomit again.

I hear Reggie leave. Oh God, now I'm alone with a murderous ape named Thumper! I start crying, sick with terror. Oddly, this is what I'm thinking: *At least ol' Thumper's being a gentleman, waiting 'til I'm done puking before he strangles me. Perhaps he'll even let me clean myself up first?* Not profound, I know, but thinking this BS seems to be extending my life.

"Bud, you're a mess," Thumper says. "You got a problem."

Yeah, my problem's you're gonna kill me! "Didn't see you do it," I tell him from the toilet bowl.

"Do what?" he asks.

It takes everything I got, but I turn toward him. It's actual curiosity on his face, not panic, not rage. I certainly hadn't expected that. "Nothing," I say.

"You got a higher power, Bud?" he asks me.

"A what?"

"A higher power," Thumper continues, "because, Bud, you ain't special. 'Less you got a higher power, here's your choices: jails, institutions, or death. Take your pick. My higher power's God, see? *I* got choices." His eyes brighten. He holds up his book, thumping it enthusiastically. "You need the program of Alcoholics Anonymous. It's all outlined here in the *Big Book*. You got your copy yet, Bud?"

"Um . . . no?"

"Well, here you go, then," says Thumper, putting it into my coat pocket. "You read every word, son, *every word*. Underline what's important, then go back and underline everything else, because that's important too."

Wow, he's a true believer. But if I've heard the pitch once, I've heard it a thousand times: (1) you're doomed; (2) we're not; (3) we have the cure/answer; (4) to get it you must join us; and (5) by the way, it's all spelled out in whatever our version of *Dianetics* is.

Reggie enters the bathroom again. He's got one of those wheeled mop-bucket combos you see janitors pushing around. "How about a courtesy flush, Bud?" he asks.

"Sure," I say, and push the toilet handle, watching the water spin.

"I can clean things up, Reggie," Thumper says.

"That's okay, Thump," says Reggie, transferring warm water from the sink into his mop bucket with a coffee cup.

"I really don't mind—"

"I got it, Thump," Reggie says.

Thumper looks disappointed. "Come on, Reggie, it's not my first rodeo."

Reggie politely ignores him and turns to me. "You get rid of all your Budweiser, Bud?"

"Yeah," I answer. I'm curious: "How'd you know it was Budweiser?"

"Trust me, I know," says Reggie. He starts mopping.

"But *how*?"

"Well, I drank Budweiser for eighteen years," he says. "I know what it smells like going down, and I know what it smells like coming up."

I look up at him. He's got a big grin, and Thumper does too. *Oh, Budweiser! Hence the nickname "Bud." Hardy har, fellas.*

"Seriously, Reggie, I'll take him," says Thumper.

"Good of you to offer, Thump," says Reggie, "but he's best suited for Cisco."

Suited for what? I ask myself.

"You *always* give the newbies to Cisco," Thumper complains.

"That's not true, Thump," Reggie responds, mopping. "And you know better. 'Let 'em come to you.'"

"It's just I'm good with the pukers—"

"*Thump,*" Reggie says firmly.

"Okay, okay," the large man says, hands up.

"Guys," I say, "I'm not a puker, okay? It's just stress."

The look in their eyes—it's embarrassing how much they don't believe me. "Stress, huh?" asks Reggie. "Never found drinking stressful myself. Now *between* drinks, that was stressful. Thump, what about you?"

"I drank around the clock," he says. "No 'between.'" He gives Reggie a knowing look and that's when I decide they're both bastards. But at least Thumper's not the Alley Killer, so that's a win. But the Bootman is sitting on one of the metal chairs in the other room, no doubt suspicious about the guy—*me*—who'd been rushed out to the can. I ask if the church's front door is open. Reggie says they rent the basement only, no upstairs access. That's understandable—who wants drunks wandering the pews? He mentions the side door again and says he'll show me.

Thumper says, "I wrote my number in that book. Call me if you want to live."

Call me if you want to live? What is this, *The Terminator*?

Reggie notes my confusion, saying, "He wants to sponsor you."

"What does 'sponsoring' mean?" I ask.

"Shepherding new guys through the program," Reggie answers.

Program? *Program* doesn't sound good. In fact, it sounds terrible, like a Christopher Reeve equestrian safety class. Anyway, don't these guys get it? I'm not a drunk, I'm just trying to leave before I get murdered. Of course, I can't say that. I start thinking maybe I should look for that side door myself when Reggie asks, "Bud, you're not done drinking yet, are you?"

I spit out the tap water I'd been gargling. "Done with drinking?" I respond, bewildered. "Whatever gave you that idea?"

Back in our seats, the meeting goes on like before—someone talks about drinking too much, then everyone says "thanks for sharing," like they're passing around donuts or something. Finally, someone at a table up front says, "Time to close," and everyone stands up. "It's over now, right?" I ask Reggie. "How about that side door?"

"Wait," he says. "This is the best part." He leads me to the room's perimeter where, apart from one elderly man, everyone is joining hands. We all face inwards like the Whoville Whos at the end of *How the Grinch Stole Christmas*. Reggie takes my left hand. An older heavyset woman with Betty White hair takes my right, her eyes starry, like she's about to be raptured—my cult detector's pinging so loudly I'm surprised everyone can't hear it. If standing in a giant circle keeps these people from drunkenly calling their exes at 2 a.m., then I'm all for it, I guess, but I'm uncomfortable, feeling like I'm participating in some rite I shouldn't be.

Everyone stands in silence, giving me one last opportunity to check out the footwear. Discouragingly, there are more work boots than I originally estimated. Someone begins the Lord's Prayer, and everyone joins in. It's weird, but I join in too. I don't want to be the odd man out, drawing even more attention to myself, plus I've had eight years of Catholic school. I look around some more. Everyone's eyes are closed. The only other man looking around is Thumper. He's staring at me again but this time I'm more annoyed with him than afraid.

The prayer concludes and everyone drops their neighbors' hands. Spontaneous talk erupts, filling the room with sound. Reggie's socializing, too busy to show me the side door. In fact, no one has left yet, so I wait. Finally, people begin leaving in ones and twos. I could make a temporary friend and walk out with him, but what if it's the killer? More people filter back toward the basement steps now, and I begin panicking. This version of musical chairs is, I decide, very important to win. I gotta time my departure right, otherwise I'm easy pickings. With my luck, I'll be the *last* guy out and the next-to-last guy will turn around and say, "Hello, I'm Bootman the Alley Killer," then stab me to death.

The older woman who'd held my hand in the circle introduces herself as Alice. I tell her my name (Bud), and then I eyeball Reggie, looking antsy. Alice asks, "What did you think of your first meeting?" In a room with so many people, how can everyone tell I'm new?

"I was just about to show Bud the side door," Reggie interrupts.

"Need an out, huh?" Alice asks knowingly.

Yes, Alice, I very much do.

"Well, let's not keep Bud waiting."

On the way, Reggie grasps the arm of an older man, saying, "Hey, Cisco." The man nods wearily. Arkin looks early seventies. He's got one of those shiny foreheads that men with male-pattern baldness get. He's wearing a peacoat, jeans, and boots. Boots! Jesus H. Christ, another guy with boots! He's holding a handkerchief.

"Sorry guys, I have a cold," he says, then blows his nose.

"You poor dear," Alice says. "That's why you were outside the circle tonight! Cisco, you should be home in bed."

"Right as usual, Alice," says Cisco somewhat distractedly. "Hadn't planned on coming, but something came up with a sponsee."

"I know how that goes," says Reggie. "Cisco, this is Bud."

"Bud, huh?" Cisco says, looking like he's in on the Budweiser joke too. "Hello, Bud."

"Say, Cisco," says Reggie, "Bud needs a sponsor. I think he's your kind of guy."

"I don't need a sponsor," I say. And I surely don't. Even if I did, it wouldn't be any of these codgers.

"Can't take on anyone new right now," says Cisco in the labored way people with stuffy head colds do. "What about Enrique M?"

"Enrique's doing some Chesapeake Bay bed and breakfast tour with someone he met on something called Match.com," says Reggie. "I have no idea what that is."

"Bill R?" asks Cisco.

"Manning the hotline this month," responds Reggie.

"How about George C?"

"Back surgery."

Irritably, Cisco asks, "Well, Reggie, why can't *you* sponsor him?"

"As it stands, I got six knuckleheads, one over my limit," says Reggie. "But I bet Bud will keep for a few days until you feel better."

I realize I'm being haggled over by the Senior Mod Squad and nobody wants me. Should my feelings be hurt?

"What about Thumper?" Cisco asks. The question sounds like a Hail Mary, even to me. I may be scared and sick, but I've gotten the message: Thumper's not the A-team. Reggie shakes his head, indicating *Nice try, Cisco.*

The last stragglers are heading down the hall. It's now just the four of us: Reggie, Alice, Cisco, and me, plus two guys breaking down chairs who at least aren't wearing boots. I keep thinking about the Alley Killer, wondering what his plan is, and I have this deranged thought—he *and* Mullet are outside sharing a cigarette while they wait for me. Okay, sounds stupid, but dodging a shakedown from Mullet *and* a witness-hunting murderer? That's a pooch screw.

Meanwhile, the Mod Squad has reached consensus. "*Fine,* I'll sponsor him," says Cisco. He absently retrieves his wallet, handing me a card with his name and number on it. "Call me when you've decided alcohol's no longer working for you, Bud. Good night." He offers no handshakes, which is fine—no one wants his cold.

"Goodnight, Cisco," Alice cheerfully says as he leaves. "Come on Regg," she continues, taking him by the arm. "Onward to the escape hatch."

"Escape hatch?" I ask.

"Yeah," says Reggie. "That's what we call the side door, 'cause it leads to two bars and a liquor store." He chuckles good-naturedly saying this.

"And also to a world of pain," Alice adds, smiling but not chuckling. They escort me again past the world's largest coffee urn, now unplugged, down a short hallway to a door with a window. "The escape hatch is right through here," says Reggie.

"Good night, Bud," Alice says encouragingly. "Keep coming back!"

"Sounds good!" I say, thinking, *Lady, I will never be back.*

Through the door's window, I see another door with an EXIT sign above it. Reggie grins, giving me the nod. I nod back and go through the first door. As it closes, I'm feeling uneasy. I just *know* the Bootman knows the church's layout, has guessed my plan, and is waiting patiently outside the hatch. Instead of exiting, I crouch down, putting my back against the door I'd just gone through, trying to ride my cowardice out. I look at my watch—it's 11:15. I'm normally a night owl, but between Mullet, the Alley Killer, and barfing my brains out, I'm dead tired.

Through the door, I can hear Reggie and Alice talking. They think I've already gone.

"What do you think of Bud, Regg?" Alice asks.

"I think getting sick at his first AA meeting isn't a stellar start."

"How bad was it?" she asks.

"He didn't make it to the stall."

Okay, Reggie, tell everyone *why don't you.*

"Oh dear," says Alice. "Well, thanks for handling the situation. 'There but for the Grace of God go I,' right? Still, I don't like it when they show up drunk. I know, I know, we accept everyone, it's just—it's disrespectful, distracting. But he seems nice enough."

"You saw the wedding ring?" asks Reggie.

"Yes. His wife probably needs our other fellowship," says Alice.

What other fellowship is that?

"Could be," says Reggie. "What brought you out for such a late meeting tonight, Alice?"

"Supporting Whitney, one of my sponsees. With her job, tonight's the only meeting she can make."

"Aren't you a saint."

"No halo, please," replies Alice. "It would just be something else to clean. Say, Regg, your slate is not as full as you'd have Cisco believe, and the poor man looks like he's on death's door. Does he *need* another sponsee?"

"Probably not. Heck, he's sponsored half the men in the room tonight, or their sponsors, and in some cases, their grand sponsors. Don't have to tell you that he's AA gold. But still, he's been saying 'no' a lot lately. I'm concerned."

"Well, he is getting up there."

"We're all getting up there, Alice." They laugh. I guess because they're old too.

"You think it's something else besides Maggie's death, Regg?"

"It's been two years already. Sure, the first six months were tough, but he came through it well enough. Must be something else."

"He's sure thrown himself into the program since then," said Alice, "but there is more to life than AA. Is he burned out?"

So the guy that's offered to sponsor me, whatever that means, is a burnout?

"Maybe," says Reggie.

"Then how will another sponsee help?" asks Alice.

"Don't know. Just a feeling. Bud looks stubborn, *Cisco's* kind of stubborn."

"Maybe you're right, Regg," Alice says. "Now be a gentleman and escort me to my car."

"You got it." They begin walking back through the basement toward the rear steps.

A minute later, I suck it up, open the escape hatch, and run two blocks to my car.

Chapter 5: A Ride Home

Friday, 13 November 1998
Silver Spring, MD

DAMMIT, THOUGHT REY. *I can't believe this!* And Rey really couldn't believe it. His '97 Acura was barely a year old and had never given him a lick of trouble, nor had his last one, nor the one before that.

After leaving Shorties, he'd returned to his car in a parking lot three blocks away, having walked past several mostly Latino small businesses to do so. He'd unlocked his Club steering wheel lock, then turned the ignition but his Integra didn't turn over. *And the lights aren't working,* he realized. He tried the engine again, but nothing, not even a sputter. *It's 10 p.m.,* he thought, *and my car's in downtown Silver Spring where vehicles go to get stolen.* Rey began beating his steering wheel in frustration, then stopped, hoping no one had seen him. No one had—he was alone. *Relax, Rey, it's just a dead battery.* He got out to pace around while he called Triple-A. *Yet another club I belong to.* He got through and was told it would be seventy minutes. *And on top of everything, it's cold.*

He heard polite honking. There on Nelson Street was Gary Graft, idling in a nondescript, no-frills '95 Concord, his head out his window. "Need help, Rey?"

"My battery's dead," Rey responded.

Gary pulled into the lot, parking between Rey's Integra and an ancient, adhesive-shedding Plymouth whose bumper sticker declared MY OTHER CAR IS ALSO A PIECE OF CRAP. Rey stopped pacing long enough to read the large decal on the back right panel of Gary's Chrysler: PROPERTY OF THE US GOVERNMENT. "I called Triple-A already," Rey said. "They're on their way."

"Hey, why don't I give you a jump, and you can call them back and cancel?" Gary offered.

"Okay," said Rey, embarrassed with having to accept help.

Gary asked him to pop the hood. When he did, the hood didn't make its usual *ka-wump* release noise. "Rey," said Gary, "your hood's already open." Gary opened it fully, then said, "Rey, ah, your battery. It's missing."

Christ on a cracker! Thought Rey.

"Good news is Triple-A will probably have a new one for you," said Gary, "but they may charge a premium." Gary's brow furrowed. "Wait, there's more. Your distributor's missing too."

"You're kidding me," said Rey, exasperated.

"I kid you not."

"I guess I'll just have Triple-A tow it. No way am I leaving it here, not after someone's started stripping it."

"You want me to wait with you?" Gary asked.

"No, that's okay." And Rey didn't want him to. Gary had presented as an eager beaver at the meeting, going into detail on obscure subjects no one else cared about—it had been a little frustrating. "I'm sure Triple-A will be along shortly."

"You're probably right," said Gary, "but I don't mind. Let me just call my wife. Besides, it's cold."

Rey tried begging him off again, but Graft wouldn't hear it.

A wrecker arrived an hour later—none too soon for Rey since Gary had been boring him to death. The operator hopped out, apologizing, "Sorry, busy night." Rey summarized the situation, speaking slowly to ensure the man understood him.

"I got a battery that'll work," the operator said, "but we don't carry distributors. Is there a service station you'd like me to tow it to?"

"Take it to my dealership," Rey said, giving an address.

"You sure you want to hassle with the dealer, sir?" the man, *Manuel,* according to the patch on his shirt, asked. "My cousin owns a shop, give you a much better—"

"The dealership," Rey replied curtly.

"You're the boss," Manuel said. After some paperwork, Manuel positioned his truck, securing the Acura's rear wheels. "The dealership's closed but I know where to leave it," said Manuel. "You can call them in the morning, sir, okay?"

"Fine," said Rey.

Manuel paused before saying, "You can come with me, sir, and I'll drop you home afterward."

"That's okay," said Gary. "I'll take him home."

Before Rey could protest, the operator agreed, thankful to avoid having to drive the impatient man home.

"You sure, Gary?" Rey asked.

"Yes, of course. Hop in."

Do I really want a ride from him? Rey asked himself. Gary had made the wait for the wrecker interminable, going on and on about Phoenician dietary habits, of all things, but at least his Chrysler had been warm. Rey got in. He assumed the ride back to his condo would involve another lecture from the professor, but instead, Gary asked questions.

"So, how did you join the club, Rey?"

Rey explained that he knew Trevor Pug through work. Trevor had invited him to the group's second meeting. *Of course, the main reason I went was because my therapist said I needed to socialize,* he added mentally.

"So who knows who?" asked Gary.

"Loo, Splash, Trevor, D-Kay, and Original Ken all went to school together. Virginia Tech. Class of '87 or maybe '88. Phillipe's a high school friend of Trevor's."

"So adding in you and me makes eight," said Gary.

Your point being? "Hey Gary, who invited *you* to the meeting?"

"I went to VMI myself. That's short for—"

"Yeah, I know," said Rey, "Virginia Military Institute."

"Where did you go to school, Rey?"

"Undergrad and master's at Brown. Computer science. Your major?"

"History."

Well, no surprise there. "What do you do with your history degree?"

"Doctorate," Gary clarified.

No surprise there, either.

"I work for the government."

"And what does Gary do for our government?" Rey asked. *Christ, I can't believe I asked, because now he'll tell me!*

"I make myself useful," said Gary. "Say, Rey, I couldn't help but notice you were a little frosty to Manuel."

"Who?"

"Manuel, the Triple-A operator. His name was on his shirt."

"Didn't notice, plus I don't care for illegals."

"How do you know he's illegal?" Gary asked.

"Gary, they're *all* illegal."

"That so?"

"Yeah, that's so." *One of the many things Mr. Jacobson and I agree on.*

"Oh, well, okay then," Gary said uncomfortably. "Hey, looks like we're here." They pulled up to Rey's building. "Again, sorry about your car."

"I'm just glad they didn't finish stealing it," Rey responded.

"Who?" Gary asked.

The brown hoodlums, Gary, thought Rey. *I mean, have you* seen *the neighborhood?* "The thieves," Rey said diplomatically.

"Right, well, I don't mean to be rude," said Gary, "but I do need to get home to the missus."

"Of course," said Rey. He got out, stepped toward his building, but then turned around. "Hey."

"Yes?" Gary said through a window he'd opened a crack.

"Thanks. And sorry for being a jerk at the meeting."

"How?" asked Gary.

"You know, 'I don't know, can you hold up your hand?' Pretty childish."

"That's okay. I don't remember that," said Gary, who did remember. "See you in a month."

"Yeah, see ya."

Rey watched Gary drive away.

Reymond Perkins was the first club member to dream that night. The vision was a familiar one—darkness, firelight, confusion, someone tugging at him. A girl with a gun, a girl who was supposed to kill him but seems uncertain about it. Waiting for her to decide was the worst part of the nightmare, but as with previous versions of his dream, she finally decided to let him live. Still, Rey never knew if *this* time would be the time she decided differently.

Despite the coolness of his condo bedroom, Rey woke up perspiring. He'd not had the nightmare since—how long had it been? June? July? *Damn.* In the morning, he placed a call to his therapist's answering service, asking to have his next appointment moved up.

Splash Takahashi also dreamed. After coming home from work, he hung his Domino's Pizza shirt up, put Make My Day on the table next to his bed, then watched an episode of *The Simpsons.* He brushed his teeth and went to bed. After a repetitive anxiety dream—delivering pizzas to unhappy people who never paid—he slept more deeply.

Just after Rey dreamed about the bandit girl deciding his fate, Henry began dreaming again. He was flying down a four-lane highway in a black 1970 Dodge Challenger, one with blue stripes, air spoilers, and a chrome air intake. Open desert flashed by him on either side of the empty highway as he drove. His speedometer read 90 mph—the car's V8 engine was purring like a tiger. Henry fed it gas, pushing it to 95, then 100, then 105. The engine roared louder but didn't labor. He knew it wouldn't top out until at least 140, possibly more with that shiny intake.

This is excellent.

In the distance, the sun winked off the windshield of an approaching vehicle. Something wasn't right about it. For starters, it drove on Henry's side of the highway—the wrong way—straight toward him. *How did it get across the median?* On Splash's side—*well, both their sides now*—was a guardrail, a narrow shoulder, two twelve-foot-wide pavement lanes, and a Jersey divider wall. *Plus white lines down the middle,* Splash mused. *We're playing chicken. Cool!* He sped up to 110. The other vehicle, a large truck of some kind, accelerated too. *But not as fast as me. No way a semi beats a Challenger.*

The approaching truck was wider than one lane, which shouldn't have been possible, and if it continued coming, there'd be no escape. Time grew short. Henry considered slowing down to take an off-ramp. *No,* he decided, *I'm not going to.* He sped up: 115. *This guy's a trucker, a working man, so he'll be practical and get out of my way.* But if that were true, why was he barreling down the *wrong* side of the highway in the first place? Splash passed one last off-ramp. In five seconds, they would collide.

Henry shifted from the right lane to the left, hugging the Jersey barrier wall. The truck shifted into that lane as well. *This guy will flinch,* thought Henry, *in three, two, one—oh no!* Splash veered back to the right lane just as the truck, a gaudy red Peterbilt, rocketed past. Without the narrow shoulder, Dream Henry would have been killed. Splash had glimpsed the driver—it was a man who looked a little like Prophet, the street hustler who'd bugged him for change before the meeting.

Henry awoke thinking, *Guess I shouldn't have told Prophet to eff off.*

Chapter 6: The Siberian Barbecue

Saturday, 14 November 1998
Wheaton, MD

TREVOR LIT HIS Kingsford briquettes, then looked through his slider door at his wife, Carol, sitting inside on their living room couch. It was 4:30 p.m. and getting dark. Carol, who'd been prepping food since early morning, was taking a well-deserved break before their friends arrived for the Pug's impromptu "Siberian" barbeque.

You look pretty, honey, he thought. This was an improvement on what he'd previously been thinking, which was, *Did I really witness a murder last night?* Of course, that answer was yes, but he didn't know whether anyone had found the body yet, and he'd felt too punk all day to watch the news or read the paper, which he felt guilty about.

Trevor grabbed a beer from his cooler and went inside with it pressed against his forehead.

Carol looked up, asking, "Are you okay, Trev?" He nodded. *Good,* she thought irritably, *because our friends will be arriving any minute.* "Kitty Batman," Carol said to the cat in her lap, "your hungover father's gonna set the table now." This meant nothing to the cat, who arched his back into her massaging hands.

"You're babying him," Trevor said, still holding the beer to his head.

"Until I have another baby, this one will have to do."

"Another baby?" Trevor playfully answered. "I'd be *happy* to arrange that."

"I'm sure you would, Trev, but right now all I need is napkins and forks on the left, knives and spoons on the right. It's a buffet, so don't put the plates out."

"But hon, I need to grill."

"You should be done by now," said Carol. "Isn't that right, *wittle kitty*?"

Kitty Batman, a glossy black tabby whose white chest, chin, and cheeks gave it a caped crusader look, arched his back even more. Trevor sighed, then headed into the kitchen. From her couch, Carol and the cat watched her husband set one table for the adults and one for the kids, enjoying his struggle to remember what went where. Their daughter, Reesie, joined Carol on the couch to pet Kitty Batman.

The doorbell chimed with a cheerful *ding-dong!*

Carol took pity on her husband and got up to answer the door. Friendly hellos from the Spicottis filled the entranceway—it was Loo, his wife, Cindy, and their two children. Loo, who had their nine-month-old son, Joshua, in a BabyBjörn, came over as Trevor put out the last of the utensils. "Hello, Loo," said Trevor. "'Sup, Little Man?" Pug asked the infant, declaring, "Would you look at that? He's got his entire hand in his mouth! Wow!" A ropey tendril of spit began dripping from Joshua's wet wrist.

"Loo, for Pete's sake!" exclaimed Cindy. "You've got one job tonight—keeping spit off your son." She produced a handkerchief, wiping the boy clean.

"Hey, Cin," Loo said, looking down at the salad and the twelve-pack of IPAs he carried, "I'm transportation, not sanitation."

"You can't multitask?" Cindy asked.

"You normally don't like the results when I try."

"That's true," she admitted, adding as a sidenote to Trevor, "Joshua's teething." At the mention of his name, the baby removed his fist from his mouth and chortled. Carol walked over, taking the salad from Loo, who then handed Trevor the IPAs. "Ah, yes," said Trevor, "the price of admission. Come on in, guys."

The minute Reesie saw the Spicottis' five-year-old daughter, she shrieked, "Hanna's here!" Hanna, wearing bright white Keds, screamed just as excitedly as they sprinted toward each other.

"Good God, Reesie," said Trevor, watching the girls embrace, "keep it down. Daddy's got a headache." *Daddy's also worried he might get killed by some boot-wearing murderer, but best not to tell you that.*

"Another headache?" Carol mock scolded. "Maybe Daddy needs to see a doctor."

"I'll get right on that, hon," Trev said.

"Grill first," she responded. "And don't burn the buns."

Trevor wasn't finding grilling in November particularly pleasant, and since Channel 4 had predicted frost by midnight, he wanted back inside.

His patio was small, as was his front yard, but his backyard, surrounded by a palisade fence, was sizable for the neighborhood. The fence was strung with multi-colored holiday lights, creating what Reesie called Christmas Land. Tonight, however, the lights didn't cheer him. *I shouldn't be so hungover*, he thought. He'd consumed less than usual the night before and, thanks to the Bootman, had thrown all of it up, so why the after-effect? He carefully put Loo's Sierra Nevada Pale Ales into his cooler. He looked at them, feeling conflicted. *Hair of the dog,* he finally decided, opening one.

The decision to have the day's first beer had at least proven easier than *not* thinking about Mark's murder, a thought seemingly wedged in his head. Luckily, his small grill required shift cooking, which helped take his mind off things. He started half his burgers, glancing occasionally through the slider door at the arriving partygoers. He could see the adults talking voicelessly while the girls attempted to lure Kitty Batman down from the Pug's china cabinet, something the Caped Crusader was having none of.

Loo emerged through the slider into the backyard. The door made a tired, pneumatic-sounding *weesh* noise when opened, and a *thunk* when shut.

"Dude!" said Loo.

"Dude!" Trevor answered, brightening. "Which way's it hangin'?"

"To the left, like my politics."

"Good ol' Larry Lorax," Trevor said, checking his burgers.

"Guilty as charged," said Loo. With manly salutations out of the way, Loo cleared his throat, watching his breath mist. "Hey, missed you at last night's meeting."

"That so?"

"That's two no-shows in a row, champ."

"Something came up," said Trevor. *Boy did it ever.*

"Did that something have to do with the Old Line?" Loo asked.

"Why?" Trevor asked warily. "What happened?"

"Christian Luntz swung by Shorties last night looking for you."

"Really? What'd he want?"

Loo hesitated, looking inside to make sure no one was within earshot. "Says you owe Old Line money . . . Some twenty thousand dollars."

"Jesus!" Trevor exclaimed. "He said that? In *front* of the guys?"

Since twenty grand was well north of chump change, Loo found it strange that Trevor cared more about embarrassment than about the amount and to whom he owed it. "Luntz was a gentleman about it," he said. "Told me, not the guys. They *were* curious, of course. I told 'em it had to do with Willie."

I guess my dead brother's still worth something. Trevor drank more of his beer.

"Sorry, man," said Loo. "Best I could do under the circumstances."

"No worries," responded Trevor, looking like a man calculating something. Loo waited, listening to the background hum of Beltway traffic. "I can't possibly owe those knuckle draggers that much," Trevor finally said. "I owe Poland a grand, maybe two. Twenty thousand? No way."

"Luntz said Old Line bought up all your bar debt, Trev, not just Shorties—Barnaby's, too, and Hell and The Royal Mile. And that's just Silver Spring.

Throw in downtown and Northern Virginia and it apparently adds up. Wants to discuss terms." Loo, concerned, thought, *Surely that'll get his attention.*

Trevor went quiet again, flipping his patties, turning them ninety degrees. Seemingly ignoring Loo's remarks, he said, "Clean grill marks are essential."

Loo reacted. "Jesus, Trevor, who cares about grill marks! You owe bikers money!"

"Technically they're a fellowship of motorcycle enthusiasts," said Trevor, "not a biker gang." *An important legal distinction Willie used to make.*

"Whatever," said Loo. "The interest alone will kill you."

"No it won't," said Trevor. *At least I hope not.*

"Why not?"

"As you know," replied Trevor, "my brother ran books for Old Line, back before the Gate got him. He's an alumnus, so to speak, so I'll get the 'friends and family rate.' Five points, tops."

"Five percent? Well, I guess that's not bad," agreed Loo.

"Monthly," Trevor added.

"Geez, Trev! That *is* bad!" Loo declared, genuinely disturbed. "What are you gonna do?"

"Keep saving America from the Y2K apocalypse so I can pay 'em, that's what I'm gonna do. Things are a little tight right now, I'll admit, but with Carol's two days at Hallmark, we'll be okay. Besides, Frankie says I'm looking at a promotion."

That's good, thought Loo. *Hope all those Y2K jobs don't disappear after you geeks fix everything.*

Darius and his wife, Sandy, came to the slider. Loo opened it with a *weesh,* gave a beer to Sandy, let D-Kay out, then closed it with a *thunk.* "'Sup, gents," D-Kay asked, watching his breath fog. "Is Splash attending this tundra extravaganza?"

"No," said Loo. "He's got a showing tonight."

"And we weren't invited?"

"He'd rather have 'wallets' show up than his schmuck friends," Loo said.

"Schmucks we are," concurred Trevor, "and rich we're not."

"Good point," agreed D-Kay. "But the wallets rarely show. It's always just starving art majors and homeless guys. We should've sent someone."

"We couldn't," said Loo. "Tonight's a private showing."

"Sounds promising," responded D-Kay. "You think he ordered real *hors d'oeuvres* this time? All the cheap bastard ever served us was day-old pizza."

"Hey, the guy's sunk every cent he has into that gallery," said Loo defensively, "so don't bitch about the stale pizza. Besides, you'd be no help, anyway. Unlike our fine friend, Henry Takahashi, you don't speak Japanese."

"Sure I do," responded D-Kay. "Listen to this: sake, hara-kiri, and thanks to Styx, *domo arigato*."

"Don't stop there," encouraged Trevor. "There's kamikaze, karaoke, karate, and, um . . ."

"Teriyaki, tofu, typhoon," D-Kay added.

Loo grimaced. Trevor and D-Kay had started playing Babble, a stream-of-consciousness word association game rewarding assonance and alliteration. Unlike Trevor, who was good, and D-Kay, who was brilliant, Loo's game was mediocre.

"Whatcha got, Loo?" D-Kay prompted.

Loo knew he'd never string three Japanese words together under pressure, so he purposefully fouled out: "Godzilla, uh, gopher . . ."

"Errrt!" exclaimed D-Kay. (*Errrt,* a bastardization of Ken Ert's last name, meant disqualification.) "I forgot how much you really suck at this, Loo. You're out. Trevor, your turn."

"Sumo, sushi, and . . . um . . . wait . . . samurai. Ha! Beat that."

"Well played, Trev!" exclaimed D-Kay, "but prepare to lose." His next words fell like piano hammers: "Sensei, tsunami, shiatsu! Kimono, koi, katana! Judo, miso, dojo!"

It was impossible to beat D-Kay, so after a few more back-and-forths sprinkled with gibes and insults, Trevor threw up his hands, saying, "Fine, you win."

"Once you've sold your soul to the Babble god," D-Kay gloated, "you win every time."

"What a dumbass thing to sell your soul for," said Trevor. They all laughed.

"So turns out," said Loo, wanting to get back to the art event, "Henry knows someone who knows someone who knows a curator connected to—get this—the Japanese embassy! The ambassador's daughter is big into anime—you know, *Akira* and *Ghost in the Shell*. Sounds like showing her work is gonna be Henry's big break! So he doesn't need his knucklehead friends effing up protocol tonight, bowing at the wrong time or whatever."

"That does sound big," agreed Trevor. He, along with the entire club, wanted Henry to succeed.

"Yeah," said Loo. "Embassy dudes are checking Henry's gallery out tonight, seeing if it's the right fit."

"Right fit? It's a gallery in a sketchy neighborhood is what it is," said D-Kay. "Well, at least he won't get robbed again, not with Make My Day in his pocket." D-Kay let out another foggy breath, watched it for a second, then said, "Hey, it's goddamn cold. I'm heading in."

"No you're not, Babble Man," said Original Ken. He'd just opened the slider door (*weesh*). He handed D-Kay a platter of hotdogs and two bags of Safeway buns. "Sandy said to tell you that Carol said to tell you to stay out here to make sure that he"—Original pointed at Trevor—"doesn't burn this stuff. Oh, and hello."

Ken stepped through, closing the door behind him (*thunk*). "Hey Original!" Trevor exclaimed, looking his friend over.

Given his high cheekbones and subtle New England accent, the guys had once voted Ken Mayflower's Man of the Year. It was a title he didn't mind since his sister, Sylvia, told him every woman had a WASP crush. *Unless, of course, those women don't like men,* he thought.

"Did you bring your lovely sister, Original?"

"Yes," said Ken, "but Sylvia and the hellions drove separately."

"Hey guys!" The new voice belonged to Gary Graft, who had just emerged (*weesh*).

"Gary! Good to see you," Trevor said, thinking, *Did we invite him?* "Hey New Guy, be a pal and take these in." Trevor handed Gary a platter of grill-lined burgers and perfectly toasted buns.

"Sure!" Gary said cheerily, returning inside (*thunk*).

"Nice guy, but he talks a lot," D-Kay said. "Anyway, Pug, I guess I'm now out in the cold having to monitor your sorry ass."

"So you're some kind of bun burner, Trevor?" asked Original, fishing a beer out of the cooler.

"Yes," Trevor said, enjoying himself now, thoughts of the Alley Killer temporarily banished. He waved his spatula over the grill as if conducting a symphony. "Clinton's impeachment, Phil Hartman's murder, erections lasting more than four hours. We all got our problems—bun-burning's mine. So, what'd I miss club-wise?"

"Next book's *Fear and Loathing in Las Vegas,*" said Loo.

"But that's not the big news," said Gary as he re-emerged (*weesh, thunk*).

"What's that?" Original asked, handing him a beer.

"Haven't you guys heard?" Gary asked. The three other men shrugged. "It's all over Channel 4. You know that guy, Prophet?"

"The street psychic?" Trevor asked, still waving his spatula. "What's he done that the TV people care? *Correctly* predict something?"

"What he did is get himself murdered," Gary said.

Trevor's spatula stopped midair. Memories of last night's violence returned, as did his fear of being killed. He began moving the spatula again, hoping the guys hadn't noticed.

"Really?" asked Loo. "Wow."

"It happened after our meeting in the alley behind Shorties," Gary went on. "But that's not the creepy part, Trevor. We saw him, Prophet, last night—*before* he was killed."

"That so?" asked Trevor, feeling ill, hoping Prophet and Mark weren't the same guy.

"Yeah," said D-Kay, "he tried bumming drinks from us, *at* the table."

"You're shitting me," Trevor said, no longer having to feign surprise.

"I'm not," said Gary. "I got a transistor radio in my car, I could bring it out here, we could—"

Trevor interrupted: "And Manchester didn't stop him?"

"He did, but not before Prophet 'cursed' us," D-Kay added luridly.

"What does *that* mean?" asked Trevor.

"He said our luck, *all of us*, is gonna 'turn bad,'" D-Kay said.

"And we're all gonna get arrested," Gary added.

"Plus our women are gonna leave us," said Original, "and get this: one of us—or was it more than one?—is gonna die. But it looks like Prophet's the one who's dead."

"Probably for giving shitty prophecies," Trevor said with snark to cover his uneasiness. "What else do you know, Gary?"

"Prophet's name is weird—two first names: Mark Marks. They found his body behind that fenced-off portion of the alley behind Shorties."

What? No! thought Trevor. "You said 'Mark?'"

"Yep. You know him?"

"No," Trevor answered. "Prophet was just 'Prophet' to me." He changed the subject swiftly. "So how did *Pulp* score?"

"All thumbs up except for Rey," Original answered.

"No surprise there," D-Kay said, looking pointedly at Trevor since he was the one who originally invited Rey.

"And sadly, only a five for evil," Original continued. "Did you read it, Trev?"

"No time this month."

"That's what you said *last* month," complained Loo.

"Hey, you know the rules," said Trevor, "you don't have to read the book."

"True," agreed Loo, "but you could at least show up for the meeting. The club was your idea after all."

"*Our* idea, Luigi," said Trevor. "And I'll be back. Right now, I'm keeping all the plates spinning at work. Promotion time, cetera-cetera." To lighten the mood (and avoid discussing Prophet's death), Trevor turned to one of his amusing but useless talents: belching like a Klingon.

"Oh, *that's* professional," said Loo, laughing despite himself.

"Bring it up again and we'll vote on it," added D-Kay. More cackling.

"So, his royal highness, Sir Reymond of Death, made the meeting?" asked Trevor carefully, knowing by now his workmate was largely disliked.

"Yeah, brought his full arsenal of dick behavior," responded D-Kay.

"Oh, you just hate competition for being lead asshole," Ken teased.

"The guy had a bit of bad luck last night," said Gary. "Somebody messed with his car. I was driving by, gave him a ride home after the wrecker came."

"Well aren't you Sammy Samaritan," D-Kay said snootily.

Gary, who'd not yet figured D-Kay out, responded, "Well anyway, I did. And I don't think Rey's fond of Hispanics."

"That's odd," said Trevor, "'cause he's great with our Spanish clients. Totally fluent. That's why Sim 2K hired him. Our Madrid customers *love* their Reymond. He makes fun of their siestas, but he's always yacking it up with them, BS-ing about soccer. He's the reason why Sim 2K *has* Spanish customers."

D-Kay asked, "Spain's got a Y2K problem?"

"Yeah," said Trevor. "They still use a lotta legacy Fortran and COBOL. The background code's in English, with a Spanish interface. A bilingual guy like Death Rey is a big deal. And since the Spaniards want their toasters to continue working into the twenty-first century, that's money. Still, Sim 2K's best coder? You're looking at him." Trevor puffed himself up, letting out another Klingon boarding announcement.

"Jesus, Trev, see a doctor already," said Ken, laughing.

"You sound like my wife," Trevor said, scooping dogs onto a plate alongside perfectly toasted buns. "Time to go inside."

Chapter 7: The Pink-butted Monkeys

Wednesday, 9 March 1977
Colombia, South America

WALTER PERKINS WATCHED the pink-butted spider monkeys swinging through the trees. The tiny primates were screeching and hollering, worked up about something. Exhausted as he was, Walter imagined—or possibly dreamt—that the angry monkeys were miniature protesters waving signs reading YANKEE GO HOME! The thirteen-year-old American, swallowed up by Colombia's backwater wilderness for over a week now, couldn't have agreed more. Walter wanted badly to go home to Raleigh, or for that matter, *anywhere* in America. As far as the teen was concerned, the pink-butted monkeys, whose freedom he resented, could keep their gloomy jungle. Walter was a hostage. The only thing he wanted was rescue.

Perkins, who seven days ago had been kidnapped by a platoon of pimple-faced freedom fighters, grew tired of watching the monkeys. There was little else to look at, however, besides the trunks of huge trees tied together by ropey vines. He spied a sleepy-looking macaw, but macaws were common in the jungle, like pigeons. He could have looked at his captors, *los camaradas* (the comrades), of course, but chose not to. If stared at, the gun-toting guerillas, barely older than Walter himself, would swear at him in incomprehensible Spanish. The meaner camaradas, like Sebastian and his rabid little brother, Gustavo, would also shove him.

Earlier, Camarada Sebastian had parked Walter unceremoniously between two roots of a massive ceiba tree, motioning him not to move. It was nearly 2 p.m. (stripped of most everything else, he had been allowed to keep his watch), but it felt more like twilight because the intertwined crowns of the trees, including those of the giant ceiba he now sat beneath, allowed little light to reach the jungle floor.

Miserably, Walter turned his eyes back toward the noisy primates. The spider monkeys couldn't understand Walter's lamentable circumstances, of course, but even if they could, they had their own problems. Previously, soldiers with slingshots had forced the monkey troop from its spot in the ceiba tree, the one Walter now sat under, and they wanted it back. The simians' current plan, furious posturing, had been successful so far—the bulk of the slingshot-using bipeds and their terrifying dogs had moved further down the trail. However, two men remained: prisoner Walter Perkins and guard Camarada Sebastian Ruiz. Since the squawking hadn't discouraged these last two, the primates upped the ante, taking matters into their own hands. Each monkey—there were dozens—was now lustily scraping his own butt crack (and sometimes his neighbor's) to extricate feces, packing it together into flingable balls.

Initially, luck was on Walter's side. One of the root walls afforded him cover from the poop throwers, its mossy surface blocking their volleys. The spider monkeys, however, with their seemingly endless supply of excrement, kept it up. Working together, the troop members continued throwing their dung balls, arcing them higher and higher, feeling out the range like a mortar crew. They eventually found the sweet spot, plinking Walter consistently on the head. As they did, Camarada Sebastian, from the safety afforded by the ceiba trunk, chuckled snidely. He'd have laughed louder, but to avoid counterinsurgency militias, jungle travel was completed as quietly as possible. This near silence, along with loyal guard dogs and well-placed spies, protected the guerillas from attack. As well, the thick, light-robbing tree canopy protected them from their other threat, the helicopters of the Colombian Army. The fusillade continued—*plink, plink-plink*—and Sebastian kept chuckling. For his part, Walter minded neither the poop balls nor Camarada's contempt; he'd fallen asleep.

In Walter's home state of North Carolina, it was the dregs of winter, but here in semi-tropical Colombia, the jungle air was humid. Walter Perkins, taken hostage by the *Fuerzas Armadas Revolucionarias de Colombia,* a separatist group of child soldiers better known as the FARC, slept poorly. The FARC, who many rurals lauded as champions of Colombia's oppressed "peasants," had been hustling Walter through the wet jungle for days, considering themselves heroes for doing so. Other Colombians—wealthy landowners, urbanites, and anyone associated with the government—held the opposite view: the FARC were a loose band of armed criminals specializing in extortion, kidnapping, and illegal drug production.

Camarada Sebastian Ruiz, a lean, formidable-looking man, poked Walter awake with the butt of his Galil rifle. He spoke tersely to him in unfathomable Spanish, except for the last word: *vámanos*. Walter opened his eyes, suddenly becoming terrified. Camarada Sebastian Ruiz and three other guerrillas, including Sebastian's girlfriend, Bruna, his kid brother, Gustavo, and Ruiz's buddy, a soldier nicknamed "Jaws" after the American shark movie, were standing in a half circle, pointing their weapons at him as he sat curled between the ceiba roots. Were they waking him up just to kill him? Couldn't they have had the decency to shoot him in his sleep?

Something bounced off Walter's forehead. As frightened as he was, he ran a hand through his hair. No blood—just monkey shit! He couldn't believe it, but then again, his life was so upside-down that he could. Worse, Sebastian's cronies were now tracing imaginary bullseyes around Walter's head with the tips of their rifles, as if helping the monkeys with their aim. *Haha. Very funny, assholes.*

As glum as he was, a tiny smile now crept across Walter's face—the three goons had inadvertently exposed themselves, and now the monkeys had switched targets in response. Sebastian's thugs, teens a few years older than Walter, quickly shouldered their guns and retrieved their quieter slingshots. Walter envied the FARC's slings. His sling, a Magnum Wrist Rocket hidden somewhere in his Carolina bedroom, couldn't compare. The FARC was sparing with most supplies, but it provided good weapons.

The turd pellets were no match for lethal ball bearings. The spider monkeys scattered, their pink butts swishing as they vanished. One of the three thugs, Camarada's younger brother, Gustavo, fetched the sole casualty. "*Para nuestra Madre!*" he proclaimed proudly, holding the dead monkey by its tail. Camarada Sebastian hadn't joined the fun. "Vámanos," he repeated, more to his goons than to his prisoner, who had already stood up. Walter brushed the remaining pellets from his hair, massaging the shoulder that the Camarada had "poked." He looked at his watch: 2:20 p.m. Twenty minutes of sleep—a drop in his exhausted bucket. *Time to follow the boots again*. He began walking.

Sebastian, Gustavo, and Jaws walked ahead of Walter, leaving the other guerilla, Bruna, a sixteen-year-old, to trail the *Americano. In case I run off,* thought Walter. *Yeah, right, and go where?* He had no clue where he was. For the past week, he'd mechanically followed the boots in front of him, knowing he'd never survive on his own. The rainforest needed no razor wire; it was already the perfect prison. If Hernandez and Jacinto, two Colombian soldiers the FARC had captured eight months ago, wouldn't attempt escape, why would a terrified kid from *Los Estados Unidos* try?

Walter stared sullenly at Camarada Sebastian's feet. The sound of his green gumboots made a rubbery *wurt wurt* noise when the tops of the boots struck the soldier's legs, and it annoyed him. He was envious. *Waterproof rubber with good tread . . . Much better than my disintegrating Pumas.* Walter hated Sebastian's assault rifle and his sharp machete, he hated his crisp *campesino* hat and his sturdy pack, but most of all, he hated the wretched squeaking of El Camarada's well-made boots.

Comrade Sebastian Ruiz's powerful legs made him a boot-wearing wall of energy, and his severe features were striking. A dark neck supported a prominent head with short black hair and a strong nose between suspicious eyes. Muscular forearms emerged from the rolled-up sleeves of a fatigue shirt that camp followers kept well-mended. That afternoon, El Camarada also wore his favorite undershirt, a Black Sabbath tee filched from a Goodwill mission bin. Based on budding crow's feet, Walter guessed Ruiz was somewhere in his late twenties or early thirties.

Walter didn't know whether El Camarada's vitality came from laboring on farm fields or years of jungle work, and he didn't care. He did know that Ruiz, the oldest man in this group of FARC revolutionaries, was a strapping Communist who detested him. Beyond being an Americano, Perkins knew El Camarada also hated Walters's height. Though only thirteen, the American boy towered over his captors, which wasn't an advantage. None of the FARC soldiers liked looking up at Perkins, who'd quickly learned to stand downslope whenever possible.

Walter continued listening to the monotonous singing of Ruiz's rubbing boots while watching the man's tall pack sway back and forth. Walter, Sebastian, and the others were marching at the back of a twenty-man platoon that included several freedom fighters (one with a badly hurt leg), two captured government soldiers, another Anglo prisoner named Jack Sparks, and the platoon's leader, a formidable woman named *La Madre,* currently breaking trail with a machete.

Camarada Ruiz's rucksack was enormous, yet neither he nor any of his fellow soldiers complained about the weight. Walter found the endurance of these low-altitude "Sherpas" amazing. And the amount of gear they carried! On their persons, they bore Galil rifles (an Israeli blend of the Finnish Valmet and the Russian Kalashnikov), bandoliers, machetes, pistols, and in one case, a grenade launcher. In their packs? Sundries: ropes, radios, tarps, medical kits, hammocks. Food: sacks of rice, pasta, cornmeal, beans, bottles of cooking oil, aluminum pots, cans of fuel, jugs of water. Individual items: clothes, candles, cards, canteens, and for those lucky enough to have them, extra boots. Prisoners got off relatively light, carrying garments, perhaps a poncho, and their share of the food.

Back in the rear, Gustavo and Jaws—a guerilla whose large, crooked teeth mimicked Benchley's villain—passed a lit cigarette back and forth. The boys, both fourteen, wore hand-me-down sweatpants, rubber boots, and American tee-shirts taken from the same bin El Camarada had liberated the Sabbath shirt from; Gustavo's promoted 7UP, Jaw's extolled the need to Keep on Truckin'. Like Camarada Ruiz, they wore campesino hats, a wide-brimmed cross between a fedora and a sombrero. In their hands, Jaws carried a chicken in a woven basket and Gustavo carried a petrol can.

The acned Gustavo said something to Jaws, who looked back at Walter, sniggering. Walter had no idea what they'd said, but since Sebastian sniggered too, it was obviously an insult. *Real funny, guys,* he thought.

Bruna, the trailing guard, wore her pack over a bandolier of bullets, keeping her rifle ready in the off chance that Walter proved stupid enough to run. Like the boys, she wore the FARC's standard outfit of gumboots, sweatpants, and a campesino hat, plus a snug fatigue shirt with the top buttons undone. She wore no bra, but Walter didn't care: a week of marching, hunger, and poor sleep had crushed his adolescent libido. On top of that, bare flesh lacked novelty in the rainforest. FARC life was primitive and therefore intimate. Whipping it out to pee was so commonplace soldiers sometimes accidentally urinated on the next revolutionary's foot. Also, it wasn't wise to ogle El Camarada's lover, so Walter, who hated all his "little brown bastard" captors, even the stacked sixteen-year-old ones, kept his eyes to himself.

Hate 'em all you want, mate, Walter imagined Jack saying, *but keep following the boots.*

Jack Sparks, the FARC's other English-speaking prisoner, had drilled the mantra *follow the boots* very deeply into Walter's head. "Just follow the boots," Walter mumbled to himself as he watched El Camarada's pack move rhythmically in front of him.

Walter may not have been looking back at Bruna, but she looked at him. It was her job to do so, of course, but *Rafa,* a nickname derivative of the word *giraffe* the girl soldiers had given him, was interesting to look at. First, Rafa was a very tall, black-eyed prisoner boy, one with large hands supporting long, slender fingers. And he was pale. Given all the time the FARC spent in the jungle gloom, no platoon member was particularly bronzed, but the Americano was exceptionally pallid. "Rafa's white, like a wedding dress," Tatiana, Bruna's boyfriend's sister had observed wistfully that very morning.

"Of *course* Rafa's dress would be white," Bruna had told her. "He's still a virgin."

"How would you know?" asked Tatiana.

"The same reason I know you're still one, Tatiana," Bruna had answered with a worldly look. Bruna smugly remembered Tatiana's jealousy.

Each FARC platoon of fifteen to twenty soldiers had a nickname. The platoon that had kidnapped Walter called themselves *Los Jaguares Verdes* (the Green Jaguars). Besides Bruna and Tatiana, the Greens had other female members, which wasn't unusual—women and girls made up a third of the

FARC's thousands of freedom fighters. The Greens were led by a woman, which at the platoon level wasn't unusual, either. They were commanded by Annabel Ruiz, a stocky woman of forty-two, a semi-venerable age for the FARC. The Greens referred to Señora Ruiz, the mother of Camaradas Sebastian, Gustavo, and Tatiana, as La Madre. The platoon's five other females ranged in age from Tatiana, who was thirteen, to Bruna, nearly seventeen. Except for Tatiana, each young woman had a boyfriend within the platoon or the larger hundred-man company to which the Greens belonged. Tatiana, however, by virtue of being Señora Ruiz's only daughter, was begrudgingly maintaining her virginity; La Madre had spelled it out to her men long ago: "Whatever is done to her, I will do to you."

They believed her. No one touched Tatiana.

Sebastian Ruiz was a proud young man. All the Greens were, but he was especially proud today because they held not one, but *two* valuable captives: Walter Perkins, a *Norteamericano,* and Jack Sparks, an *Australiano.* The soldiers called them *los niños* (the boys), not caring what their actual names were. True, los niños weren't the Greens' original targets, but that was okay. The unlucky pair were as good, if not better than, their intended victims, oil executives. The foreign boys' families, and certainly their deep-pocketed governments, would pay handsomely for their return.

The Green girls understood the importance of ransoming but were more interested in the prisoners' exoticness—particularly Walter—than the money. Jack wasn't unpopular—his nickname, *Guro,* a derivation of "kangaroo," was established right away, but the ruddy Australiano had a frame the girls were used to, short and stocky. The giraffe boy, on the other hand, was different—striking. Rafa said he was only thirteen, yet he was taller than all the rebels, including Camarada Sebastian, whose gait had taken on a competitive, matador-like strut since Rafa's capture. On the night of Walter's kidnapping, the Greens had measured him: Rafa was 180 centimeters, a meaningless number to Perkins, who would only understand its English equivalent (five feet, ten inches). As tall as Rafa was, however, it was obvious to the young women, particularly the boy-starved Tatiana, that the good-looking Walter was still growing. It would be a shame to have to kill him.

Lost in his thoughts, the exhausted Walter realized he'd come to a stop in the middle of the game trail the FARC were following. Bruna poked his backpack with the butt of her Galil: *Keep up, Rafa.* Rifle or no, before moving again, he gave her the ugliest look he thought he could get away with. (On top of being miserably scared, Walter was also resentful at being bossed around by a girl.)

Bruna smiled condescendingly back at him.

Chapter 8: Uninvited Guests

Saturday, 14 November 1998
Wheaton, MD

AT THE WINTER barbeque, the men all re-entered Pug's 50s-era bungalow (*weesh, thunk*). Inside, Trevor put the hotdogs on a warming plate on the kitchen counter. Other guests had arrived, including Ken Ert's sister, Sylvia, and her nine-year-old twins, George and Gregory, wearing Ren & Stimpy t-shirts. A neighbor, David Chin, and his boy, Sunny, had popped over as well. Carol greeted everyone with hugs, taking their potluck items to the kitchen. Sylvia called out to her brother: "Kenny, *please* take Gee and Gree out back."

"Of course," said Ken. "Boys, coats stay on. Straight for the backyard—don't touch anything." The twins came forward with matching *Who, me?* faces. Other children, including Sunny and Reesie (holding Hanna's hand), raced to the slider as well. "Let's play Red-Light, Green-Light!" yelled Reesie.

"Hold it, kids," said Carol commandingly. "Coats."

As Reesie put hers on, she said to Hanna, "Uncle Ken's a *fun* adult." Then she announced to all, "Let's go to Christmas Land!" Out they went, followed by Uncle Ken.

"Trev, don't abandon him to the wolves," Carol said. "Go out and supervise."

"Honey, I just got back inside—"

"Go host, Trev." She then said in a lower, conciliatory voice, "Keep the hellions from breaking anything."

"Ha-ha, host," D-Kay said, smirking, but then Sandy, his wife, said with her own smirk, "You too."

"*Me*?" reacted D-Kay. "Why do *I* have to go? I'm not qualified. I don't even *have* kids."

"You're almost as mature as they are, so it's a good match," Sandy responded. D-Kay gave her a stink eye, then went out.

"I'll head out too," volunteered Gary, and David offered as well. They emerged to see Trevor placing beer bottles into the Coleman's ice water like delicate trout hatchlings. "Can I join?" Gary asked, eyeing the laughing children.

"Heck yeah!" said Trevor. "Go for it."

Should have brought the kids, Gary thought. *And the wife.* But that was a non-starter. *Remember,* he told himself, *this is a work assignment, not play.*

Gee, Gree, Reesie, Hanna, and Sunny ran around Christmas Land chaotically until Ken and Gary organized the Red-Light, Green-Light game. The children elected Ken to be the first traffic cop, and Gary scooped up Sunny, putting him on his shoulders to play. The remaining men watched.

"Nice lights, Trev," said Loo, looking at the festive bulbs. He pointed to a string of lights around a tree, adding, "And that's a nice-looking elm, though Dutch elm's disease is gonna kill it."

"Well, that's depressing, arborist," said Trevor. "Any other predictions, Tree Boy?"

"Nope, that's it." Loo shouted to Ken, "Is Cousin K coming tonight?"

Ken, at one end of the yard, the children at the other, yelled: "No, he's at Seneca Rocks, climbing. *Green light!*"

"So he's spent all day clinging to some cold cliff face like an idiot?" Loo asked.

"*Red light!*" Ken shouted. The children all tumbled to stops and laughed, including Sunny atop Gary's shoulders, who repeated *idiot* multiple times.

"Kids, don't say, 'idiot,'" said Ken. To Loo: "What can I say? My cousin's an adrenalin junkie. That side of the Ert tree's all 'Hold my beer' people. *Green light!*"

"Hence the infamous missing Ert fingers," said Loo. The edgy adventures of Ken's extended family were well-known to the group.

"*Red light! Gree, take five steps back you little cheater.*" To Loo: "Frostbite, farm accidents, an uncle who forgot he was holding a lit M-80 . . . *Did I say 'green light' yet, Gee? No, I did not. Five steps back.*"

Out of the blue, D-Kay asked impishly, "Gone on any dates lately, Original?"

Oh fuck off, Darius, thought Ken. "*Green light!*" He cleared his throat. "No dates, Tooth D-Kay."

"Why not?" pressed Darius.

"*Red light!* You know why not, you jerk. Sorry kids, don't call anyone a jerk, *and George, I saw you move. Ten steps back! You too, Gary—I mean what the hell! You're an adult. Set a better example.*" The reprimand got the kids howling, as did Gary's innocent expression. Sunny started chanting "What the hell! What the hell!" His father on the sidelines cringed.

"Oops," said Ken, embarrassed. "Don't say 'hell,' either."

"Come on, Ken," said D-Kay, not letting him off the hook, "fourth time's the charm."

"After I sent the first three over to the other team?" Ken asked rhetorically. "No thanks, Tooth Decay. *Green light!*"

D-Kay added, "It's not like they hooked up with each other . . ."

"Then drove off together in a Subaru," Trevor added, piling on. It was a good quip, but poking fun at Original hadn't been Pug's goal; keeping his mind off last night's murder had.

"Hardy har, boys," Ken said. "Sylvia's husband is still in the wind, so I got no time to date. *Red light! Okay, all you cheating ingrates, especially you,* Gary, *back ten steps!*"

They played three rounds with different traffic cops before Carol cracked the slider (*weesh*) to yell, "Time to eat!" *Thunk.*

"You heard the lady," said Gary. "Everyone inside."

The children were herded in, de-coated, then sent down the buffet line. The adults went next, loading their plates, bringing them to the dining room. When D-Kay sat down, Kitty Batman made a beeline for his legs.

"Aah! Someone rescue me from this allergy bomb!" he exclaimed, shooing him away with his foot.

"Don't hurt my cat, Mr. Kay!" Reesie exclaimed, running over.

"Reesie, Honey," said Carol, "put Kitty Batman in the basement."

"Mr. Kay," said Reesie, annoyed but sage-like, "why can't you get allergy shots?" She scooped up Kitty Batman and huffily carried him away.

For once, D-Kay had no rebuttal. "It takes a child to shut up another child," said Sandy.

"Anyone heard from Phillipe?" asked Loo.

"He's coming with Estelle, fashionably late as usual," Carol replied.

As if waiting for this announcement, the doorbell rang. Phillipe Gallois and Estelle Largo had indeed arrived, bearing an expensive bottle of wine and a three-bean salad from a chic Adams Morgan eatery. Carol couldn't help gawking as they came in. Estelle wore a cashmere coat over an undoubtedly elegant dress, but as usual, her face, with its long lashes, full lips, and snub nose was her best feature.

You two belong on a wedding cake, Sylvia thought unkindly.

Ken thought, *You're too damn charming, Phillipe.* It was hard to compete with the rugged man who looked like the Brawny Paper Towel Guy. *On top of his good looks, he's a freakin' pilot too. He's got no problem attracting teammates, so of course he gets someone like Estelle. Me? I make women* change *teams.*

After she and Carol hugged stiffly, Estelle declared, "Hello all! Did you hear the news? Phillipe got a promotion!"

"Estelle, I thought we agreed not to talk about—" began Phillipe.

"Nonsense, these are your *friends,*" Estelle continued. "Don't you think they deserve to know?"

"Not right out of the gate, hon," said Phillipe, looking awkward.

"He oversees the whole maintenance crew now," continued Estelle. "He's the new . . ."

"Hanger 18 Supervisor," Phillipe finished.

Affirmative clamor erupted. "Whoa!" said D-Kay. "That's awesome!" declared Loo.

Estelle continued layering it on. "And he's the *youngest* man to ever hold that position. How many people do you oversee now, Phillipe?"

"Thirty, but it's not about—"

"And it's more money," Estelle interrupted.

"Yes," said Phillipe, thinking, *Hon, please stop talking.*

Estelle's bragging, however, wasn't Phillipe's real issue. It had been two days since the promotion, but only now were his new responsibilities sinking in: there would be more of what already made his job difficult—more overtime, more paperwork, more union issues, and worst of all, more responsibility for delays. *And accidents.* An imaginary scenario had been plaguing him all day: a fatigued mechanic missing one checklist item for one small but very important system on a 757. The consequence at 36,000 feet? One very catastrophic plane crash and one very messy, career-ending National Transportation Safety Board investigation. Plus the mass casualties. And this wasn't paranoia—Gallois was now responsible for things he would not be inspecting personally, including the remaining ninety percent of the plane he was unfamiliar with. *I don't think I'm ready for this.* He thought about silk instead.

"Darling, don't stand there spacing out," said Estelle, "hang up our coats."

The impromptu nature of the Pug's "Siberian Barbeque" hadn't stopped Estelle Largo from dressing to the nines. She unfastened her overcoat, dropping it for Phillipe to catch. Underneath she wore a green dress, a tight affair held together by brass snaps along its seams, with a leg slit revealing pantyhose and three-inch heels.

The men stared. The women looked as well, no longer hating her "reveals," which were common now, but still annoyed by them. "Would it kill her to wear a pair of jeans?" Carol whispered to Cindy. Then, louder, "Such a lovely dress."

"Yes," said Estelle, "perhaps too much for a barbecue, but you only go around once."

"The dress is a Versace," Phillipe proclaimed. "Wonderful stitching."

"You notice those details, Phillipe?" asked Carol, surprised.

"*Maman* was a seamstress," he replied, shrugging sheepishly.

"Well, come in," Carol said, placing Estelle's salad purposefully behind everything else on the counter. "We've already started."

The new arrivals went through the buffet and sat down to eat. Conversation grew louder, drowning out Kitty Batman's despondent cellar-door meowing. When it became apparent that Gee and Gree, who'd already netted a broken plate and a dropped burger between them, were vibrating with dessert sugar, the women ordered the children and the men outside again.

As everyone got up to move, Estelle and Phillipe excused themselves, apologizing for having double-booked that evening. (Phillipe looked more chagrined to be leaving than she did.) Sylvia had been grumbling about a migraine, so Carol kindly offered her the guest bedroom to lie down and rest for a bit.

Once the dishes were cleaned, Cindy, Sandy, and Carol sat down in the living room to relax, enjoying some freedom from responsibility. They watched the backyard activity through the slider as they drank Estelle's fancy wine. "Baby Joshua's out like a light, Cin," said Carol. Joshua, in Cindy's arms, slept motionlessly.

"Yes, this is when they're the most beautiful, right?" said Cindy, looking down at him fondly. "How's managing childcare, Carol?"

"Great! I watch Reesie and Sunny—look how cute he is on that guy Gary's shoulders out there—Monday-Wednesday-Friday here at the house and David watches them Tuesday-Thursday while I'm at Hallmark. He's only two houses away, you know. Their house is a tear-down, by the way—palatial inside. You wouldn't believe the size of the romper room."

"Really?" asked Sandy. "How can they afford that?"

"His wife Angie's a divorce attorney. High-priced."

"Is there any other kind?" asked Sandy. "What's she like?"

"Angie? A type-A nightmare. An okay looker, but no Estelle."

"Thank God," said Sandy, who felt like Phillipe's soft-hearted nature was being ruined by his ostentatious girlfriend. "You two are saving each other a fortune in babysitting costs. What does David do when he's not watching the kids?"

"He appraises houses when he has time, but he's mostly finishing his dissertation."

"Really? In what?"

"Bugs of some sort," Carol responded. "Ants, I think."

"Does Angie ever watch the kids to help him finish?"

"No, she's hardly ever home—always traveling. Sometimes I think I'm more Sunny's mom than she is."

"Why don't they just get an au pair?" asked Sandy.

"They can't afford one. She put out her own shingle last year, borrowed a ton to do it." *And au pair or not,* thought Carol, *she'd still be a second-rate mom.*

"What I don't get is why she's with David. With her career and need for control, you'd expect a trophy husband, which David certainly isn't."

"I suppose he's cute in an ugly puppy kind of way," said Sandy diplomatically.

"But he's such a good guy," Carol continued. "Really thoughtful, and great with the kids. Angie's overbearing as hell. He's really too sweet for her."

"Jeez, sounds like you're sweet on him. Should Trevor worry?" Cindy asked wryly.

"Psh, David's nowhere near George Clooney, so I think not," Sandy said, and all three laughed. Trevor wasn't George Clooney either, but he was handsome and charming, and everyone knew how committed the Pugs were to each other.

Sunny screamed in celebration as he touched Ken, winning another round of Red-Light, Green-Light. Gary put him down.

"New Guy, tag in," said Ken, and Gary happily switched. The kids had taken to Gary instantly; it was obvious he had kids of his own.

"Channel 4 says the Bambi count's 70 kills now," said Original. "What motivates that guy?"

"Can't be a vigilante thing," said D-Kay. "I mean, deer-on-human violence just isn't a thing."

"It is when one wrecks my Grand Cherokee," said Phillipe. "I say more power to the guy. What do you think, Mr. Pacifist?" he asked Loo.

Loo looked uncomfortable. "I can't condone somebody using a weapon in public like that, but he's keeping the deer population in check. Last week, I saw seedlings for the first time in ten years in Aspen Hill."

"Seedlings?" asked D-Kay.

"Baby trees, dumbass," said Original. D-Kay, out of sight from the kids, flipped him the bird.

"Hundreds of 'em," continued Loo, "'cause the deer aren't eating them anymore."

"It's kinda weird he uses a crossbow though," Trevor contemplated. "Seems more work. Maybe he couldn't get a gun."

Gary, who had come to deliver a tearful Sunny to his dad because he'd skinned his knee, commented, "It's easy to buy a gun in the District, actually. DC's overflowing with them. All illegal, of course."

"So, how's the book coming?" Cindy asked Carol.

"I should really be done by now, but I've been stuck on this one frustrating scene—you know the one I've been complaining about, between Laura and Bill—I just can't find the right dialogue for their argument." Carol frowned, then crossed her arms. "It feels like I'll never figure it out."

Cindy said, "We all know how good of a writer you are. You'll get there—just give your creative mind some breathing room." She shifted Joshua to one arm so she could squeeze Carol's hand reassuringly.

At that moment they were briefly interrupted by a *weesh* as Trevor darted inside to use the bathroom, then darted back out shouting, "Love you, hon!" *Thunk*.

"Say, how's the sex streak?" Sandy asked roguishly.

"Every week for eight years," said Carol, cheeks a little pink. "But you know, earlier this week he actually turned down a blowjob."

"You're kidding!"

"I'm not. I used to be able to lure him away from the Super Bowl. *The Super Bowl*. 'First down and inches' is what we called it."

"Is something up?" Cindy asked, attuned to her friend's well-being.

"He's just been watching TV and drinking beer a lot lately," said Carol, her smile fading. "All that bucking for his promotion is getting to him."

"You think it's a trend?" Sandy asked.

"Oh, no!" Carol said. "He offered to impregnate me just before the party. I'm not worried."

"That sounds like Trevor," Sandy said, laughing. They continued lamenting—pressure gets to everyone.

Conversation shifted to Cindy's part-time job: shopping for rich clientele to spare them the mundanity of buying their own groceries. She had plenty of gossip to dish about who bought what, and what kind of fad diets the Bethesda "elites" currently favored.

Gary returned to the guys after ushering cold, breathless children inside. "Hey, friend," he said, turning to David, "I'm Gary, by the way." David, who'd been on the edge of the conversation the whole time, shyly introduced himself.

Trevor realized they'd been completely ignoring his neighbor. *Even if it's only Chin-chin*, he thought, *that's a hosting foul*. "Say, David," he said, "how's that thesis of yours going?"

"Oh, what's it about?" asked Original.

"It's called 'Suppression Strategies for *Solenopsis Invicta*.' It's coming along slowly."

"I'll bite," said D-Kay. "What's solenoid-us invita?"

So-len-op-sis in-vic-ta, David enunciated mentally to himself, looking happy someone had at least asked. "Fire ants."

"There money in it?" asked D-Kay.

"Hopefully," said David. "Though it's definitely not as exciting as fixing the Y2K bug. Right, Trevor?"

"Yeah," Trevor responded. "Sim Systems has every man they've got working on it. It's a huge deal."

"What's the biggest problem?" David asked.

"Back in ancient times," Trevor explained, "meaning the 70s, computer coders wrote years as two digits, like now it's 1998, soon to be 1999, but coders would use 98 and 99."

"Why not all four digits?"

"To save memory, which in the Stone Age was at a premium. I mean, remember the Commodore 64? That was 64 kilobytes. Big whup when disco was dying, but nothing now. Anyway, come Year 2000, all those old programs will assume '00' means 1900."

"But who cares if some nerd code fizzles?" asked Ken.

"You do realize our nukes are automated, right?" Trevor responded. "*Lots* of industries run on old software: banks, insurance companies, manufacturing. Hell, *elevators* run on it. All that stuff's gotta be checked for calendar sensitivity."

Weesh! The slider flew open and Reesie screamed, "Daddy, Daddy! Come see what we found!"

Realizing they no longer needed to stay outside, the men came in to find the children and other adults clustered in the kitchen. "What's going on, Reesie?"

"I found one of your secret notes, Daddy!" she said, proudly holding up a scrap of paper.

Outside, loud, rumbling vehicles stopped nearby.

"Reesie, honey," said Carol nervously. "Where did you find that? You know Mommy and Daddy's room is off-limits—"

Reesie, too excited to listen, read loudly: "Your ta-tas are tar-if-ic!"

Everyone erupted in laughter. Trevor grabbed the now scarlet-faced Carol and said, "Well, they are, honey. I do really love them. And you, of course."

Carol whacked him playfully, then admonished Reesie, "Honey, we don't go through people's private—"

The doorbell rang.

"Reesie, be an angel and answer it," Trevor asked. "It's probably Mr. Gallois coming back for something."

"Come on," Reesie said to Hanna, "It'll be fun!" They ran to the door, opening it quickly.

The adults heard a low, grumbling voice that definitely wasn't Phillipe's. There was a tense moment of silence, then the door suddenly slammed shut.

"What's wrong, Reesie?" called Carol.

"B-bad m-men," Reesie called from the hallway.

"Oh, don't be silly," Carol said, walking to the door as the doorbell rang again.

"No, Mommy, no!" Reesie pleaded. "Don't let them in!" Hanna, scared mute, bobbed her head in agreement.

Carol paused, deciding to look through the peephole first. Then she backed away, stunned. The doorbell rang a third time. "Trev!" she yelled.

He walked over, confused, cracking open the door as the girls all backed away nervously.

A large, big-faced man with long hair and two gold teeth stood outside on the stoop. Trevor's jaw dropped. Christian Luntz, the leader of the Old Line bikers, stood on his porch. Behind him was Mullet, Rocker, and at least twenty-five more bikers.

"We were drivin' by and saw the cars," said Christian. "Decided to drop in, see how Willie's little brother's doin'."

"Yeah, uh . . ." Trevor said, stepping outside and closing the door hurriedly behind him. There was barely room for him on the stoop because neither Christian, Mullet, nor Rocker had given way.

"You know, a welfare check," said Christian, smiling wryly. Mullet chuckled. *Good one, boss.*

"Not gonna invite us in, Trevor?"

"Just tell me the points, Christian," Trevor said nervously.

"Twenty."

"Twenty percent?! That's the 'friends and family' discount?"

"No discount on account of how rudely you treated my man Mullet, here," Luntz said, clapping his arm around his lieutenant's shoulder. Mullet beamed grotesquely. "You dodged him when all he wanted was to talk to ya. Four thousand by the first, payable in Hell. And a' course, we'll break your hand if you don't pay. Can't type a keyboard too good with only one hand, can ya?" Trevor swallowed.

"Right or left?" asked Rocker. "We like to establish that early." Trembling, Trevor held out his left.

"Popular choice," said Luntz. Mullet giggled childishly at this—the boss always cracked him up. Christian leaned into Trevor until their faces almost touched, then said quietly, "Don't go runnin' to that Hale-Bopp asteroid like Willie, hear me?"

Trevor barely resisted shrinking away. "It was a comet, not an asteroid."

"You get the point." Christian turned to his followers. "Well gents, looks like we're not gonna be invited in." A chorus of boos. "I know, I know. It's okay. Onward to Hell. First round's on Old Line!" Loud *yeahs* and whistling. "Okay, boys, say 'Nighty-night, Trevor.'"

As if responding to a pep rally cheer, two dozen plus men called out: "Nighty-night, Trevor." A wisenheimer added, "Don't let the bed bugs bite!" With that, the bikers pushed their hogs off Trevor's lawn, mounted, punched their starters, and loudly roared away. When Trevor stepped back inside, all eyes were on him—except Reesie, whose face was buried in Carol's stomach.

Chapter 9: The Reservoir

Friday, 1 December 1950
North Korea

HE DREAMED OF the reservoir.

Private Cisco Arkin was wounded, weak, and cold, but by comparison, his buddy, Jamie Took, was much worse off. *Jamie, pal, worried you'll soon be paying the ferryman.* The hypothermia wasn't surprising. For two weeks, the nightly mercury had fallen below zero. They were all cold: Privates Cisco Arkin, James Took, and John Wendell, of Wichita, New Orleans, and San Diego, respectively, and Corporal William Biloxi of—well, Biloxi never said where he was from. The four men crouched behind the remnants of a shot-up three-quarter-ton truck avoiding rifle fire. They were hiding behind the tires, listening to the truck's torn tarpaulin cover snap in the wind. To the left, back up the road, the Chinese were pursuing the fleeing Americans. To the right, further down the road, the enemy was flanking the column, attempting to cut it off. In front of the soldiers was an icy, unclimbable rockface with Chinese riflemen atop it, and directly behind the four GIs was a precipitous drop.

The foothill in which the road had been carved was one of many bluffs surrounding the Chosin Reservoir, a manmade lake in the northeast corner of the Korean Peninsula. In Cisco's dream, it was late afternoon on 1 December 1950 and bone-chillingly cold. Dusk was beginning to claim the narrow mountain road and the RCT-31 vehicles now stopped on it.

Regimental Combat Team 31, originally two thousand and five hundred men strong, was now, thanks to multiple wave attacks over four nights by the Chinese People's Volunteer Army, at twenty percent strength. The US Army RCT-31 remnants, which had taken most of that cold December day to punch through a tightening Chinese noose, were now evacuating five hundred wounded men down this mountain road, fleeing the PVA. The PVA was in pursuit, having been ordered to annihilate the Americans. They were gleefully doing so. Chinese snipers lay atop the rockface in front of them, pinning down the US troops from above. The men behind the three-quarter-ton truck were cut off; if they weren't shot dead by the up-slope snipers, the Chinese soldiers advancing down the road would push them off the hillside.

"This is it, Arkin," said Took. "We ain't makin' it home." Arkin nodded at his shivering buddy. Their situation, being the rearguard of the retreating RCT-31 column, was untenable.

RCT-31 was a hastily assembled mishmash of GI units sent to push scattered, retreating Chinese troops back into Manchuria. After initial success, on November 27 the combat team encountered something far worse than the freshening Siberian wind: six regiments of General Song Gilun's twelve-division army. RCT-31 had been initially overrun, but the men had rallied, forming a defensive perimeter, an irregular Alamo surrounded by an enemy eight times their number. This morning, December 1, RCT-31 had sustained heavy losses breaking through the Chinese ring and was currently retreating down a winding road toward the relative safety of Hagaru, a small village still under NATO control. The caravan of GI trucks, jeeps, and ambulances—each vehicle packed with wounded—had been snaking its way along the snow-covered road, pursued by twenty thousand Chinese.

Marine Corsairs had been dropping napalm all day to buy RCT-31 time to retreat, but the caravan had hit a roadblock, which now allowed the Chinese to pick off the truck drivers. In the rear of the caravan where Arkin, Took, Wendell, and Biloxi were crouching, the remaining drivers had just abandoned their vehicles—anyone who could run, walk, or hobble was fleeing on foot. The advancing Chinese soldiers, cold and miserable themselves, pursued them, robbing, beating, even killing abandoned American wounded along the way.

All four American soldiers were injured. Cisco had shrapnel in his back plus a round lodged in the meat of his calf. The bullet hurt like hell, but he was better off than Jamie Took, who'd taken Chinese frag across the temple, a wound festering under a three-day-old dressing. Took's second injury was far more serious, however—a perforated bowel now swollen with peritonitis. John Wendell, a 105 mm howitzer operator whose artillery piece had been destroyed the first day of fighting, had a missing hand and a right knee that would not flex. He was currently mumbling the Lord's Prayer repeatedly to escape the pain. The semi-able-bodied Biloxi—just a bullet graze to the shoulder and frostbitten feet—had refused to leave Wendell under any circumstance. Arkin understood; he wouldn't leave Took, either.

Their wrecked truck was a refuge with no future. They needed to flee, but where? If they followed their retreating comrades, the cliff snipers would shoot them like pigeons. Escaping back up the road toward the advancing PVA soldiers was out of the question, as was scaling the wall on the other side of the road—something not even possible for the able-bodied. (Even if they could, they'd end up in the laps of the PVA riflemen currently pinning them down.) That left the steep talus drop-off behind them, a descent that looked deadly.

A rifle cracked twenty yards up the road. The Chinese had discovered a terrified GI; the man's desperate cries hadn't forestalled his execution. Hearing him, the four mutually agreed: it was the slope behind them or death. Biloxi took charge. He, the only man with a functional M-1—the gun oil in the others' rifles had frozen—would go last, providing cover fire. Arkin, aided by gravity, would drag Took and Wendell down the rocky slope, the logic being the Chinese would home in on Biloxi, letting the others escape. Biloxi gathered their remaining cartridges—five bullets.

The sun set, leaving a perfect twilight, the transition time between day and night vision. *The time you bugle-blowing Chinks always charge*, thought Arkin, *'cause you're damn near invisible then.*

"Now or never," said Biloxi.

He provided fifteen seconds of cover fire, then flung his M-1 away, plunging down the icy scree to follow the others. Two flares shot overhead, bursting into intense balls of light, allowing the PVA soldiers to see the escaping GIs. The Chinese along the upper ridge as well as those just arriving at the truck opened up, and the snow-covered rocks around Biloxi snapped with bullet strikes. He twisted an ankle and stumbled, descending so quickly that gravity nearly swept him past the others. Arkin grabbed him but had to drop Took to do so. Biloxi's momentum now carried Cisco Arkin and John Wendell, who Cisco still gripped by his collar, further downslope. Took was left behind.

The PVA soldiers, aggravated that Biloxi's foursome was escaping, tried picking them off, but that proved difficult; the escapees were already midway down the scree, sliding between boulders serving to screen them. Grenades, however, didn't need precision aiming and soon the air was filled with the sound of burning fuses, the clatter of hand munitions bouncing off icy stones, and finally, explosions.

The Chinese were equipped with good firearms, particularly their rifles, *Zhongzhengs,* but their grenades left a lot to be desired. Only half exploded fully, with one being a complete dud. The fusillade, however substandard, still managed to punch Wendell's ticket. There was no time to grieve—Arkin yanked his dog tags while Biloxi scrambled back upslope to grab Took. The remaining three plunged downhill again, desperate to reach the frozen reservoir at the bottom of the talus. The boulders and cobble gave way to loose gravel, the three slipping and falling like novice skiers. One determined PVA soldier up on the road set up his light machine gun, firing it spiritedly, its tracers seeking the GIs like pencils of angry light. A bullet nipped Biloxi's buttocks. He grimaced but continued dragging Took, both men tumbling toward Arkin, who'd already reached the reservoir's frozen edge.

New flares exposed the three Americans again, luckily now at the very limit of Chinese rifle range. They hid behind a squat boulder protruding above the surrounding gravel. Arkin looked at his comrades—Biloxi had made it down in one piece but Took's helmet and the field dressing covering his head wound were both gone, and the man clutched his middle like something vitally important had seized inside him.

Corporal Biloxi evaluated. Despite his previously damaged shoulder, frozen toes, and a new divot across his buttocks still burning with tracer phosphorus, he was mobile. Arkin said he could move if he used his gun as a crutch. Took, however, needed to be carried. Biloxi and Arkin prepared to leave the stingy cover of their squat rock to drag Took across the reservoir's crusted surface, the water body's enormity revealed by overhead flares and flashes of distant artillery.

What Chairman Mao didn't spend on grenades he spent on flares, as the sky above the three men remained unnaturally bright orange. Worse, the Americans now heard voices—a few enthusiastic Chinese were sliding down the talus in pursuit. Once, again, it was now or never. As they braced to leave—"On the count of three, guys!"—Private Arkin quickly stooped to retrieve Wendell's dog tags, which had fallen from his pocket. Inexplicably, when Biloxi counted "one," Took stood up. Arkin distinctly heard a bullet travel over his head to hit Took. He and Biloxi jerked Jamie down to assess his condition. The good news: the spent bullet hadn't penetrated Took's bare skull. The better news: one of the pursuing Chinese soldiers had gone down hard, slowing down pursuit.

Despite the wicked lump forming on his head, Took gave Cisco a loopy half-wink, saying, "Can you believe my luck, Arkin? Gonna leave a mark." Despite his fear, Arkin began sniggering. *Gonna leave a mark* was the platoon's default joke. "Here's a match for you," said Biloxi, holding his wounded buttock and pointing at Took. "Your face and my ass." All three sniggered now. When they settled back down, Took grew serious. "Fellas, just drag me onto the ice some, away from the Chinks, then you two get gone."

The uphill voices were closer now, but the sky above had gone dark, which was the break they were looking for. Arkin and Biloxi grabbed Took, pulling him across the snow-blown ice, but after a minute, Jamie asked them to stop. "Far enough, boys," he said quietly. A moment later, Private Jamie Took of New Orleans died. Cisco looked at Biloxi, who nodded. They continued dragging him south toward Hagaru. Hagaru and the US Marines that protected it, however, were still three miles across the reservoir. As the night wind swirled hoar-frost around Took's body, matters worsened. Arkin and Biloxi—wounded, frostbit, suffering from five days' insomnia—now watched sourly as the Chinese once more launched flares overhead. If they kept dragging Took, the PVA soldiers newly arrived at the rockslide bottom would see them and finish them off. Arkin looked at Biloxi, who reluctantly nodded. They pulled Took's dog tags and left him. Hours later, as the pair finally reached Hagaru, yelling out lest anxious Marines behind machine guns slaughter them in the dark, Cisco wondered, would the Chinese take Took's body or leave him for the spring thaw to claim?

Sunday, 15 November 1998

Aspen Hill, MD

Cisco Arkin, now a seventy-year-old veteran of the Korean War, lay in bed, having just awoken from his Chosin Reservoir dream, the same one he'd been having on and off since returning from Korea forty-seven years ago. Sunshine shone through his windows. He could smell the coffee and bacon Maggie, his wife, was preparing in the kitchen. It was Thursday, half past six, time to get up—retirement was no excuse to loaf. A man could forget the day of the week doing that. With a heave, he got out of bed.

"Coffee smells good, honey," he declared, coming downstairs.

"Good morning, dear," Maggie said. "Your cup's on the table. Sit and talk to me." He sat. "You don't look rested, Cisco. The dream again?"

"Yes," he said, sipping his coffee. Strong and black—the way he liked it.

"Did it turn out the way it always does?"

"Yes."

"And you're still here," she said smiling, putting her hand briefly on his shoulder before turning back to the stove.

Since he could never articulate how *vivid* the dream was—the sight of endless, dirty snow, the smell of cordite, the chafing of his GI boots—he never discussed the details with Maggie. The vision still terrified him, of course, but through repetition it was familiar, bringing him a sort of solace—*Korea happened, I'm still processing it, and I will do so until my last day.*

This morning, however, Cisco mulled the dream over more than usual. Unlike previous occurrences, last night's version *was* different. He began comparing his memories against the dream, searching for out-of-place details, looking carefully, but finding none. The dream contained the same grey rocks, the same holes in the truck's shot-off door, the same dirt in the creases around Biloxi's eyes; the groans of the wounded were the same as well, as was the labored snick of Arkin's half-frozen M-1 and the droning of those cursed Chinese bugles. The same Hail Mary rifle shot from the highlands above the road had flown over Cisco's crouched form, hitting his army brother, James "Jamie" Took of New Orleans in the head. In traveling thousands of feet, however, it was more a boxer's punch than a gunshot, but was still nearly enough to do Took in. Because of this, Cisco had always felt guilty. If Took had retained his helmet, that mostly-spent round might have bounced off, and he and Biloxi could still have dragged the semi-conscious Took to safety. But wishing didn't make it so. During five days of battle, the air was constantly thick with lead and steel; getting hit or not often came down to luck and Cisco knew this—second-guessing was useless.

The dream of that frigid night was accurate . . . up to the moment Biloxi declared that they flee across the frozen reservoir on the count of three. In last night's dream, Cisco had *not* dropped Wendell's dog tags. Last night, Cisco was the one to stand too early, not Took. Yes, the bullet still went over his head and still hit Jamie, but it came closer to Cisco than he knew to be true. In last night's dream, had he stood completely up, *he*, not Took, would have been hit.

But that had never happened.

The sounds of breakfast, the bubbling of frying bacon and the tumbling of three-minute eggs, soothed him. Cisco turned to his sixty-eight-year-old wife, Maggie Arkin, seeing not an old woman but the vivacious girl he'd married. He read her a corny joke from the funnies and she pantomimed laughter. Not to be outdone, she asked if he might *finally* consider sponsoring someone. He smiled at the joke. At seventy, Cisco Arkin was one of southern Montgomery County's AA elder statesmen, having sponsored, as his friend Reggie put it, more men than a mutt had ticks. Today, like every other retirement day, he would work other men through the Steps.

He looked out the window. Oddly, the sunny morning sky had turned dark. "But I can't sponsor on an empty stomach, Maggie," he said, turning back toward her, but Maggie, his wife of forty-two years, no longer stood at the stove by the egg timer. She lay on the floor instead, half her face limp, the other half spasming. He reached for the phone, an indestructible Ma Bell that had hung reliably on the kitchen wall for decades, but it wasn't there. He looked again through the window, hoping to flag down a neighbor, but his neighborhood had disappeared. All was dark. He couldn't breathe.

Cisco woke up again—this time, for real—with the sad knowledge that his wife, Margaret Arkin, was dead and had been so for two years. This second dream—talking with his wife, then re-witnessing her massive stroke—was the true nightmare.

He lay in bed until guilt finally motivated him. After the bathroom, he returned to his bedside, carefully going to his knees. His first prayer was succinct: "Dear God, I am a grateful alcoholic. A grateful alcoholic never drinks." He then launched into a pair of memorized devotions: the Sick Man's Prayer and the Prayer of St. Francis. He also prayed for his son. As he stood to head downstairs, his knees popped. After cold cereal and hot coffee, he retrieved the paper from the front porch, read the headlines, then folded it under one arm. He unbolted the cellar door and descended wooden steps to check if anyone was in the "drunk tank," Cisco Arkin's finished basement with a couch, a tiny dinette, a small bedroom with a bathroom, a washer/dryer, and storage shelves. The basement had its own entrance with a buzzer that chimed upstairs. The cellar was kept locked, but several copies of its key floated around the greater Wheaton AA community; it wasn't unusual to find someone who'd let themselves in.

The tank was empty this morning. With no one to feed, Cisco felt disappointed; he liked cooking a hot breakfast for overnighters. Next, he examined his "cubbies." (Years ago, he'd mounted two apartment-style US Postal row mailboxes to a wall.) All the boxes were closed and each was numbered: 1 through 24 on the larger units; 25 to 32 on the smaller ones. Many of the boxes were labeled with names. He dug a key out of his pocket, inserting it into Box 7, which had no label. Inside were several folded pages of barely decipherable hand-written pencil. He took them out, then headed to the cellar door, up concrete steps to his well-maintained backyard. He placed the papers under the grate of a handsome brick barbeque, then ignited them with a lighter emblazoned with the 7th Infantry insignia: two tip-touching black triangles on a circular field of red. Beneath them were the embossed words KOREAN WAR VETERAN 1950-53. As the papers curled to ash, he cried briefly, then said a prayer for the man who would no longer need them. When he was satisfied there was nothing left, Cisco returned to his cellar and closed Box 7, leaving the key in the door. Upstairs, the telephone rang.

Chapter 10: Make My Day

Saturday, 14 November 1998
Wheaton, MD

HENRY WAS THE first to get arrested. It happened the night of the Pugs' barbecue. That evening, Splash had been at his studio nervously awaiting the Japanese ambassador's visit, praying he'd remember the greeting rituals correctly. Introductions ended up going smoothly, but not all communication did. Henry, who only spoke Japanese with his parents, found himself using too much English. Luckily, the ambassador's daughter, Juri, interpreted when needed.

It was obvious Juri, a mischievous-looking sixteen-year-old artist, liked the space. It was also obvious the ambassador's bureaucratically faceless four-man entourage did not. Juri's passion to "slum it in an American ghetto," however, carried the day. It helped that Haru Takahashi—*Henry* to everyone outside his family and *Splash* to the book club—impressed the ambassador, who recognized an earnest young man when he saw one. Still, he did not appreciate the unnecessary praise Juri showered on Henry, her self-declared *koneko* (kitten). Henry, twice her age, blushed whenever she did this, as embarrassed as her father was.

Now that the ambassador's party had left, Henry beamed with pleasure. The exhibit of Juri's hand-sketched anime would open the second week of January. The particulars, including a fee, would be discussed during a Monday appointment at the embassy. Henry, who had never had a studio rental longer than a weekend, now had to decide what to charge for a full three weeks! He worried about readiness. Given the upcoming holidays, would two months of prep time be enough? Despite his anxiety, Henry felt on top of the world: his dream, one built on four years of sacrifice and the delivery of hundreds of Domino's pizzas, was being realized.

It was 8:15 p.m. Henry thought about closing the gallery to head to Trevor's barbecue to share the good news but stayed instead to begin constructing the mock walls that would be needed to showcase Juri's copious collection. Wall construction was a labor of love, and time passed quickly. It was Henry's rumbling stomach that finally convinced him to look at his watch: 11:13 p.m. A stop at Roy Rogers on the way home was in order.

He turned off the studio lights, locked the squawking front door, lit a cigarette, and carried two boxes toward his car.

The Gate of Heaven Studio was located in a shabby industrial district next to the CSX tracks. Henry scanned the parking area, having been robbed at gunpoint a year earlier while delivering pizzas. His car, an '86 Taurus, was the only one left in the lot. *No black '70 Challenger with blue stripes,* he thought sadly. The strip mall was far from residences and restaurants and therefore abandoned on a weekend night, which was one reason why Henry could afford to rent there. Still, he worried about theft. But the theft of what? His gallery was currently empty of everything, including art. Better breaking-and-entering candidates were the next-door upholstery shop and a tile wholesaler, both having cash registers.

He saw no one, but since he'd parked farther away than usual to leave the well-lit spaces for his embassy clients, prudence made sense. He had Make My Day with him, but he wasn't wearing it; the gun rode in one of the boxes, along with his copy of *Pulp* and next month's *Fear and Loathing in Las Vegas.* The Taurus sat a hundred feet away, next to a grove of scrubby-looking pines.

Surely you can make it thirty yards without your gun? he asked himself.

Uh, remember that muzzle in your face?

He put the boxes down and placed the gun in his coat, then made his way toward his high-mileage vehicle, popping its trunk. After putting the boxes in, he closed it.

"Got a cigarette?"

A young man had suddenly appeared in the space the upright trunk door had momentarily blocked from view. He was thin, practically a reed, wearing a Washington Bullets sweatshirt with its pull-up hood obscuring his face. Despite the cold, he wore basketball shorts, his knobby knees floating over rawhide-laced workman's boots. In addition to scaring the crap out of Henry, the oddly dressed guy confused him: Reedy was already smoking a cigarette.

"You got one lit already," Henry answered.

"Yeah, well okay then, what time is it?" asked Reedy, stepping around the Ford's bumper. More confusion: Splash could see Reedy wore a watch. The skinny dude wasn't physically imposing, but the ease with which his hands moved toward his pockets frightened Henry, reminding him of the two holdup men who'd asked to buy a pizza before mugging him.

"Wait!" Henry blurted, reaching into his coat. "You want a cigarette? Hell, you can have the whole pack." Before Reedy could say anything, he pulled out Make My Day, pointing it at him. A half second later, he remembered to disengage the hammer block.

Reedy's disposition changed immediately. He threw his hands up, saying, "Ah, yeah man, this ain't what it looks like. Don't want no cigarettes, nothing. Sorry."

Reedy's eyes shifted quickly to the scrubby pines behind him, then back to Henry. There was a rustling in the brush. From the scrub, a voice called out, "Pull yours, Spencer. Don't fuck this up."

No! thought Henry.

Reedy quickly looked behind him again, then reached one hand inside his shorts.

Panicking, Henry shot him.

Montgomery County Police responded to Henry's call within minutes, as did an ambulance. Reedy, a seventeen-year-old minor whose real name was Spencer Washington Jr., was pronounced dead at the scene. Initially, things went okay for Henry. He readily provided proof of business ownership and hence a reason for being there that late at night, and he learned that Washington Jr., who'd been carrying a knife/brass knuckle combo, had a rap sheet. Henry's gun was confiscated, which made him nervous, but the responding officers stated he'd eventually get it back if it was legal and if there were no charges filed against him. Henry nodded hearing this. Detectives arrived. After an hour of questions, Henry was told to go home—the police would follow up with him in the morning.

Which they did promptly at 7 a.m., arresting him for illegal firearm possession.

Henry's father posted bail the same day.

On Monday, the police reviewed footage from the tile distributor's video camera, which had recorded a distant view of the confrontation. Though the unit's dirty VHS tape head caused dropouts, including the time just before Spencer was killed, it had recorded the gunshot flash—a reasonable viewer might believe that Washington's hand (or possibly hands) were still in the air at the time of his death. This interpretation of the video sent the emotions of Spencer's father, a well-known local councilman, into the stratosphere. Henry was ordered to attend a hearing as soon as one could be scheduled.

"Don't worry too much about it," the lead detective told Henry and his father. "Illegal gun aside, you have a clean record and had business being there that night. Young Mr. Spencer did not."

Chapter 11: The Deerslayer

Monday, 23 November 1998
Kensington, MD

LATE ON A cold fall night, the Deerslayer watched his prey walk quietly up a trail to their bedding-down site—several large clumps of inedible stilt grass. He lay still, watching their vapory breath rise between moonlit poplars. The man wore a scarf that ineffectively hid his scent, but that was okay—tonight he was downwind. This was necessary since, though the animals had comfortably adapted to city life during the day, sometimes browsing right next to speeding traffic, they were far warier at night, in large part because of this man. As the herd moved, its leader scanned the narrow woodland ahead for danger. The stag could not smell or hear him—at least not yet—and he couldn't see the Deerslayer, cloaked as he was by a cut-up Value Village thrift store blanket and lying prone on a tree-mounted board above the forest floor. The buck proceeded. The Deerslayer quietly scratched his nose. The herd worked its way up a woody ditch between two cul-de-sacs toward the thick stilt grass clumps behind the hunter. Looking through his scope, he thought, *I am here to cull you.*

The herd was now thirty feet away. The buck was closer, but a poplar blocked a clear view of him. As well, it would have to be a head shot, and since the man had learned the hard way how difficult those shots could be, he let the buck pass. The second, a doe, presented a better target. *Lung shot,* he thought. *Or a headshot if she gets close enough.* His nose itched, so he forced himself to wait. The doe hesitated, flicking her ears, then drew closer, her head now clearly visible. The man squeezed and his bolt flew. She dropped where she stood, her body bouncing once on the forest floor. The herd scattered.

"Seventy-two," the Deerslayer said, finally scratching his nose.

He dropped the blanket to the ground, then the board, then himself. He retrieved his bolt, dragging the body for ten minutes down the hollow, back into the park proper. There, he broke the dead doe's leg with a rock and cut the animal's belly open, the first action meant to mimic a deer/vehicle collision and the second to attract vultures faster. *Though neither trick's working like it used to.*

All of this he did methodically, and though the Deerslayer didn't enjoy killing, he would admit to liking the routine, and of course, the result: the end of destructive overgrazing. *It's necessary,* he told himself, because all the deer's natural enemies were absent—wolves, cougars, coyotes. Deer removed thousands from the state population each year, but this close to the nation's capital hunting was prohibited within one hundred and fifty yards of homes and roads. Since most urban forests were at best fifty yards wide, this was tantamount to a ban, which the whitetails seemed to know.

By June, he'd cleared out twenty-five animals within a mile of the copses surrounding his neighborhood. The difference by August was evident: seedlings were surviving and the browse line, the vertical limit of a deer's reach, was disappearing. There were more birds and mammals; native plants were starting to hold their own against invasives. The average jogger might not find the change striking, but the Deerslayer did.

The man, who wore no blaze orange and didn't know how to dress a deer, had purposefully chosen a crossbow over a rifle. Guns were too loud, too unsafe. His bow was high quality, bought with cash. His scope was powerful during the day but marginal at night, the only time he hunted, so close range was critical. What he did had to be done right—heart, lung, or headshots only, since he didn't want any of Montgomery County's eight hundred thousand citizens waking up to some poor wounded animal in his yard with one of his bolts stuck in it.

He used solitary evening strolls, ones meant to "clear his head," as cover. The strolls weren't new behavior. That spring and summer, his wife thought nothing of the hour-long absences, walks producing a calmer husband upon return. And most nights, a relaxing walk through the neighborhood was all that occurred. But one, two, sometimes three nights a week, the Deerslayer quietly purged the forests.

In the beginning, it took two months to save for the bow, scope, and bolts, a week of scouting the woods for where to bury it lest his wife discover it at home, and then another week observing his prey. *Should I start with a small one?* he'd asked himself. *Or a big one? A buck? A doe?* He'd been a complete novice, knowing nothing about hunting other than reading a few library books which he couldn't check out because his wife would surely ask about them. He remembered his initial practice and how his first shot went high, lodging ten feet up a tree next to the Rock Creek Trail. At least a thousand people trooped by it before he could return the next night with a ladder and a pair of pliers.

He'd been an anxious mess on his first night's hunt. "Honey, you haven't touched your meatloaf," his wife had asked beforehand. "I didn't burn it, did I?" He'd answered, "No," then watched *Jeopardy* with her, their weekday ritual. "I think a walk might help settle my stomach, hon," he said. "Maybe a long one." Between the darkness and his nerves, he almost missed the footpath to his buried gear. After retrieving his weapon, he'd circled back to the drainage hollow behind his house to wait, the smell of musty leaves and wet clay from a nearby ditch making his nose itch. *I hope they don't come*, he'd thought.

But they did come. At that time, they were still desensitized to humans, even at night. That evening, a herd had proceeded tamely toward him, habitually giving him a wide berth as they had done all week during his "practices." These were early days—no camouflage blanket, no assessing wind direction, no boards in trees. He saw the troop leader clearly, a large buck with flared nostrils. It stopped, standing sentinel between the man and the rest of the herd as they passed. Even in the darkness, he could make out the stag's large, blinking eyes. How could he possibly slay it? He'd never killed anything larger than a cockroach before. Now, not fifteen feet away, stood something thin and malnourished, sure, yet regal, unaware of the ecological damage it was doing. Hell, it was trapped in this forest remnant, hemmed in all directions by asphalt and speeding cars. *Perhaps I'm aiming at the wrong enemy*, the man had thought.

He felt miserable, imagining what would happen once he released his tri-head bolt. Would he hit the wrong part of the deer? Would it flee and bleed out, dying miserably due to his incompetence? Maybe he *wanted* a bad shot, a reason to be so nauseated that he would just bury his bow for good. His hands were shaking, his breath quick. It was too close to miss, but could he *guarantee* he'd kill it? *Where am I supposed to hit it again? In the chest? No, low, behind the shoulder.*

Am I really going to do this?

In the end, it was a look the stag gave him that did it. Once all his charges were safely past, the stag turned back toward the man derisively: *Don't you have anything better to do?*

The bolt went flying before the man knew it, striking exactly where the library books described. The stag's eyes went incredibly wide. It inhaled harshly, reared, pranced two paces, then fell to the scrubby forest floor, shaking before going still. The man stood, awed, first by revulsion for taking a life, then by the pride of living his convictions, and finally by the amazement of how *final* death was. Then he doubled over and puked.

The deer vigilante had not vomited since. He killed two or three animals a week, a rate that cleared out his corner of parkland without drawing undue attention, at least at first. After all, multiple deer died nightly on DC's exurban streets—what were a few more? By mid-summer, however, storage became an issue; the illegal carcasses were stacking up. There was no room left in the now corpse-crowded hollow behind his house. Smell was a problem; just like the ones that rotted on highway shoulders, his carcasses stank. Burial? Out of the question. Too much effort and the graves would be obvious.

One day he asked himself, *What happens to roadkill?* DPW eventually collected them, taking them God knew where. If he started plopping his bodies roadside, the county would pick them up, but eventually they, too, would become suspicious. The only practical option was dragging the bodies further into the park, letting the scavengers—ugly black vultures and carrion crows—eat them.

The birds grew fat and populous that summer; the powerlines of the man's neighborhood began hosting hundreds of shifty-looking blackbirds. It even made the news—Channel 4's local affairs reporter Trixie McPhane nicknamed his neighborhood Hitchcock Heights.

Presently, with that November night's work done, the Deerslayer cached his weapon and returned home. "That was more than an hour, hon," his wife said. "Should I be worried about another woman?"

The man moved across the bedroom floor, grasping his wife playfully from behind. "Don't need one since I got the best one God ever made right here."

She sighed, then told him to skat as she'd things to do before bed. "It's like Poe moved from Baltimore to our neighborhood," she added, looking out at an array of blackbirds backlit by the moon. "Hon," said the Deerslayer's wife, "be a dear and make sure the cat's inside."

Chapter 12: We Kept This Safe for You

Friday, 28 November 1998
Wheaton, MD

PHILLIPE GALLOIS VISITED Dalia's Drycleaners to see his *maman,* the proprietor. After hugs, he rolled up his sleeves; Dalia's was chronically understaffed and Phillipe, who'd worked high school summers for his mother, didn't mind helping. Maman asked questions, mostly about Estelle, dropping not-so-subtle hints about matrimony until he groaned, "Maman!" Though thrilled to be teasing her son, she acquiesced, leaving him alone to launder a particularly fancy ballroom dress. As he did, a yellow business card dropped from it. On one side of it was an image of a man wearing a dress, and on the other, *Men's Lounge: Thursdays,* listing a local number.

Dalia's had a strict policy—items found were placed in small opaque bags, then attached to the owner's garment. "No treasure hunting," Maman told new hires. Not everything found was kept—illegible receipts and wadded Kleenex, for example, were trashed. Most other items, including the mundane—pens, tubes of lipstick—as well as the sentimental—funeral Mass cards and rabbits' feet—went into bags labeled *We Kept This Safe for You,* as did what Phillipe called real loot—stripper club matchbooks, condoms, fake IDs, lighters, and "folding" money. Phillipe examined the card thoroughly, finding the dress-wearing man particularly intriguing. He reached for a baggie per protocol but stopped, thinking, *I really like this, and it's just a business card.* He wrestled with his principles—*Hey, just write the number down and bag it*—but the item's thick cardstock fascinated him. For the first time, something he found went in Phillipe's pocket. Once there, the card felt important to him, like a talisman. *I'll keep this safe for you,* he thought.

That night, after back-and-forth anguish, Phillipe called the number.

A man with a gruff voice answered, "Men's Lounge. Who's this?"

Phillipe hesitated. "Uh, Phillipe?"

"'Phillipe.' That your real name?"

"Yes, sir."

"Jesus, pal, we don't *ever* use our real names, understand?"

"Sure," said Phillipe, "but why?"

"You should *know* why. What's your stage name?"

Stage name? thought Phillipe, confused.

"Give me one or I'll make one up for you," said the gruff man, "and believe me, you don't want that."

"'Johnny,'" said Phillipe.

"How original. Where'd you get this number, 'Johnny?'"

Phillipe felt like hedging but told the truth. "On a card I found."

"Where'd you find the card?" asked the gruff man.

"At the dry cleaners."

"Was it left for you?"

"Um, no," said Phillipe.

"Then we can't help you." *Click!*

It took two workdays at Hanger 18 and two nights of repeatedly squeezing his Washington Redskins 1992 Superbowl Champions stress ball before Phillipe built up the nerve to call again.

The same gruff voice: "Men's Lounge. Who's this?"

This time, Phillip was more prepared. "Johnny," he said.

"Just Johnny?" the man asked.

"Yes."

"Well, we got a half-dozen Johnny's," said the man. "You sound like Johnny Bomb. That you, Bomb?"

This took Phillipe by surprise. "No, um. Say, look. I called two days ago, said my name was, well, I gave my real name and you told me not to, and—"

"Yeah, yeah, I remember," said the man. "You're the dry cleaner guy, 'Johnny Laundry.' But since you weren't invited, Laundry, we still can't help you." *Click!*

Phillipe called back immediately.

"Men's Lounge. Who's this?"

"Johnny Laundry," Phillipe answered.

"Jesus, kid, I just got done explaining—"

"How do I *get* invited?" blurted Phillipe, thinking, *I can't believe I just asked that*.

A short pause. "Do you know what we do here?"

A longer pause. "You wear . . . women's clothes?" *Wild-ass guess on my part,* thought Phillipe, squeezing his stress ball firmly.

"Maybe we do, Laundry, maybe we don't. If we do, then why?"

Maybe we do. Phillipe had never discussed crossdressing, let alone admitted doing it, with anyone, *ever. And "we?" He said we?* "Because it makes us feel good?" he ventured.

"That it does. So tell me, Laundry, are you a cop?"

"No," said Phillipe.

"Are you gay?"

"No," Phillipe said.

A male voice in the background said, "Ask him if he's a gay cop."

"Are you a—"

"No, not a gay cop," answered Phillipe anxiously. "Look, maybe this was a bad idea—"

"Have you ever been arrested, Laundry?"

"Never," said Phillipe.

"Have you ever been arrested for solicitation?"

"No, I said I'd never been arrested—"

"We're *thorough*, Laundry," said the gruff voice. "Do you do drugs?"

"No."

"You sure?"

"Yes, I'm sure," Phillipe said. *Jesus, is this some horrible, complicated prank?*

"How old are you?"

"Thirty-two," Phillipe answered, then switched to offense. "Are you guys pervs?"

"No." If the question affronted the man, his voice didn't reflect it. "Wait a sec, Laundry." There was a pause. The background voice, a man with older intonation said, "Why not. Got a feeling."

"Okay, Laundry. You live alone?" Phillipe said yes. "Gimme your address." Phillipe hesitated, then gave it. "We'll be in touch, kid." *Click!*

What am I thinking, Phillipe thought immediately. *Should I book myself on The Jerry Springer Show now and avoid the rush?*

In touch the two men were—that very night, in fact. Phillipe answered his door: two unexpected men stood there, one middle-aged, one elderly.

"Johnny Laundry, I presume?" asked the middle-aged one. Phillipe nodded. *Your voice matches the phone voice.*

"My name's Mr. Pendous," the middle-aged man said. Pendous was of average height with male pattern baldness and a five o'clock shadow Richard Nixon would be proud of. He wore a thick suit, slightly scuffed shoes, and a large wedding band. "And this gentleman," Pendous said, pointing to his elderly companion, "is Mr. Waldorf."

Mr. Waldorf also wore a suit, an impeccably tailored three-piece number complete with a neatly folded silk handkerchief protruding from the pocket and a matching tie. He held a glossy wooden cane with a diamond in its pommel, and his gold-rimmed glasses gleamed. Waldorf was a class act, a wealthy elder statesman plucked from some portrait-crowded drawing room. By contrast, Pendous's suit made him look like a 70s movie extra.

"Well, young man," said Mr. Waldorf, "will we be invited in?"

"Um, sure. Come in. Welcome."

Despite Phillipe's professional orderliness, his Wheaton apartment was not particularly tidy, which normally wasn't a big deal. Estelle infrequently visited, preferring that he stay over at her more well-appointed apartment in Chevy Chase. Waldorf sat in a chair Phillipe offered, and Pendous stood slightly behind the man who was obviously his boss. "Can I get you something to drink?" asked Phillipe.

"Mr. Waldorf will take water with ice," said Pendous. "Nothing for me." Phillipe grabbed the cleanest Diet Pepsi glass he could find and brought ice water to Mr. Waldorf. Looking at the glass, Phillipe thought, *Mr. Waldorf's probably the least likely man to ever sing, 'You got the right one, baby, uh huh.'*

"Interesting choice of reading," Mr. Pendous said, eyeing Phillipe's copy of *Pulp*. Without thinking, Phillipe stole Loo's description. "It's a warm, sensitive, dare I say 'loving' treatment of the detective genre. Have you read it?"

"Well, I have to now," Pendous said, sounding intrigued.

Seeing an opening, Phillipe asked. "So, ah, Mr. Pendous, how does the Lounge work?"

"How does one join? Quite easily. But first, Johnny, show us a dress."

"But I have questions—"

"So do we, kid," said Mr. Pendous, "so do we."

"Relax, Pendous," said Mr. Waldorf. "Young Laundry here looks safe enough to confide in."

"Of course, Mr. Waldorf, but preliminaries are preliminaries," answered Pendous. "We need to know if he's on the level. So go on, Laundry, grab a dress," Pendous said. "Chop-chop."

Phillipe warily went to his room, thinking, *What the hell am I doing?* He kept his eye on the odd pair through an opened door. He retrieved a heavy opaque Southwest garment bag from his closet, putting it on his bed, which, miracle of miracles, he'd made up that morning with clean sheets. Unzipping it, he removed a blue dress, bringing it to the living room. He shook it, fluffing it out.

"Nice," said Pendous. "That your favorite?"

"Nah, just the first thing I put my hands on." This was true; the dress wasn't his best, but it *was* the one he'd been wearing before jumping into jeans because Pendous had unexpectedly called from the lobby. "How long have you been wearing?" asked Pendous.

"Dresses?"

"No, burkas. *Yes*, dresses."

Phillipe hesitated, looking at Mr. Waldorf, who smiled back amicably.

"If you mean publicly . . . never."

Pendous looked at Phillipe, motioning toward the bedroom. "First time for everything, Johnny. Go on, kid, put it on. Time's money."

What the hell am I doing? thought Phillipe. He entered his room, closing the door this time, stripped to his skivvies, and donned his blue taffeta dress. He was nervous, almost nauseous—he'd just left two strangers alone in his apartment to do God knows what. They could be thieves, pervs, or worse, sick maniacs ready to laugh at him. He emerged quickly, half expecting his Kenwood stereo to be missing. Mr. Waldorf and Mr. Pendous, however, had not moved.

"Looks good on you, son," Waldorf said. "Really does."

Pendous nodded, agreeing, then asked, "Undergarments?"

"None," said Phillipe.

"Don't have 'em or don't want 'em?"

"Sir, ah, I don't have an *identity* problem," Phillipe said. "Plus, panties are just too tight. No room for the . . . uh . . . rod and tackle."

The two men erupted in laughter so genuine that Gallois found himself joining in. "Pendous," said Waldorf, guffawing, "I like this kid. I really do."

Settling down, Mr. Waldorf took a photo out of his pocket. "Here, son, check this out." It was a photo of Waldorf and another old man in drag. "That's my brother, Statler," he explained.

Phillipe carefully examined it. They weren't attempting to look "pretty," which was good because that wasn't a possibility. They posed like captains of industry, each sitting in matching highbacked leather chairs—substitute suits for their dresses and they could be Rockefellers. Suddenly it hit him: for the first time, Phillipe was talking with men who might *understand* him. Emotion, bottled tightly since bullies discovered that a school-aged Phillipe *liked* helping his mother sew dresses threatened to burst, but he bit his tongue.

"At the Lounge, we require undergarments," said Mr. Pendous. "Men's, women's, we don't care. Just secure the aforementioned rod and tackle." This set Waldorf laughing again.

"Understood," Phillipe said, smiling.

"You got money, Johnny?" asked Pendous, looking around doubtfully.

Phillipe stopped smiling. "What do you consider money?"

"Hmm, if you have to ask . . ." began Pendous. "Initiation's twenty thousand, monthly dues are four-fifty. Social engagements, particularly the New Year's Eve Ball, are extra."

Phillipe was crestfallen. The other shoe, an obviously unaffordable one, had dropped.

"Another scholarship, Mr. Waldorf?" Pendous asked, seeing Phillipe's long face.

Waldorf looked around curiously. "I see a lot of pictures of planes on the wall, young man."

"I'm an airline mechanic," said Phillipe, smoothing imaginary wrinkles from his dress. "And I own a Cessna."

"A bona fide *pilot*, huh?" asked Waldorf. Gallois nodded.

"The usual, sir?" Pendous asked Mr. Waldorf. "Two thousand entry fee, then fifty monthly?"

Mr. Waldorf nodded, saying, "Yes, Stu, a working man like Pilot here—I like Johnny Pilot better than Johnny Laundry as a stage name by the way—doesn't need complete charity."

Nothing says real like requiring money, thought Phillipe. *Unless it's a scam.* "What does two grand buy me?" he asked.

"Come to the Lounge next Thursday with a check and find out," Mr. Pendous said. He handed Phillipe a card, one with a downtown address on it, then helped Mr. Waldorf up from his chair. Phillipe escorted the two to the elevator. When it dinged, he shook their hands, wishing them well as the door closed.

Good God! Phillipe suddenly thought. *For crying out loud, I'm standing in the hallway in a dress!* He ran back to his apartment, looking up and down the hallway—the coast appeared clear. He locked his door and ran to his bedroom, collapsing. The sluice gates opened, releasing his tears. After a half-minute's crying, he calmed down enough to puzzle something out: Mr. Waldorf had called Pendous "Stu," so assuming that was a first name, he was *Stu Pendous.* "Stupendous!" Phillipe declared out loud, laughing. Now *that* was a stage name.

Chapter 13: Naughty Notes

Tuesday, 1 December 1998
Silver Spring, MD

CAROL PUG TOLD Cindy Spicotti she was managing, and by "managing," she meant the austerity necessary to cover the mortgage, utilities, two car payments, three credit cards, and her idiot husband's bar debt, debt now "owned" by the Old Line. Carol was shocked to learn the bikers expected four thousand a month in interest alone, regardless of principal, until the entire debt was paid. After they roared away the night of the barbeque, Carol sent Reesie home with Cindy so the child wouldn't hear the fireworks. "Trevor, you irresponsible asshole! You drank us—us, *your family*—into debt!" Trevor got defensive, chest-thumping about the size of his salary, but eventually admitted that all their debt, plus Old Line's usury, would consume every penny of it. The fight ended with Trevor moodily surrendering his cards. There were to be no frills for the Pugs anymore: no restaurants, no movies, no Domino's, no cable, no beach vacation. They sold his car the next day, applying what they got for it against the worst of their debt. Trevor griped about everything but mostly about losing cable.

"But honey, it's hockey season!"

"Too bad, Trev. Go read one of your 'evil' books."

Carol determined they would make their minimum payments, chip away at Old Line's extortion, keep the lights on, put food on the table, and that was it. "Given time," Carol told him tetchily, "it will work. And it's not like we're on food stamps, Trev. There'll be an end to it. With luck, we'll be out from under Old Line's thumb in twelve months, maybe fourteen. We'll finish tackling the cards after that. Sorry if this upsets you, but humility's good for the soul. Plus you can't be half as humiliated as I am for not even knowing this was going on. If Mother ever finds out about the loan sharks, I swear I'll crawl under a rock and die."

At Hallmark, Carol asked for more hours, and since people were snapping up Beanie Babies for Christmas like crazy, she got them. But more time there meant less time to write. *And now David is doing most of the childcare.*

"Oh honey, it sounds like you're managing," said Cindy, bringing Carol back to the present. "Really, you're handling this well. Who knew how much Trevor was drinking? Twenty thousand dollars! That's so extreme—oh Carol, I'm sorry! I didn't mean it *that* way."

"It's okay, I know what you meant," Carol responded. "You know, last night I brought up AA to Trev."

"What'd he say?"

"He said he wouldn't go. 'AA's for drunks,' he said. 'I'm not a drunk.'"

Carol hadn't had a counterargument as, on the face of things, she agreed with him. Drunks lived under bridges. Drunks stood around fires in barrels. Drunks (and perverts) wore dirty overcoats. Trevor had never lost a job, never wrecked a car, never got a DUI. He suffered his hangovers well enough, which was good because hungover or not, she was driving him to the office now in their remaining vehicle, encouraging her hubby to get that promotion.

"Do you think he's a drunk, Cin?" Carol asked seriously. "Tell the truth."

"Well," said Cindy, "he's got a good job, he comes home at night, and he's not violent, right?"

"Of course not." Carol hadn't considered violence, relieved at not having had to.

"So he's not a drunk," said Cindy. "He just needs to cut back. Tell me . . . what does Gladys think?" Gladys was Carol's mother.

"'You married him,' Mother says, 'so fix his drinking.' I didn't say anything about the loan, obviously." *Fix his drinking*. Carol mulled over her mother's marital philosophy: women maintained marriages because men were too stupid and selfish for it to be otherwise. "God, Cin, Mother hates Trev, like he's personally wrecking her golden years."

"Well, that's Gladys for you," said Cindy, who knew Carol's mom well. "Always take her with several grains of salt."

"More like the whole mine," said Carol, and they laughed.

"Trevor just needs to slow down, maybe stop," continued Cindy. "At least for a while. He'll do it for Reesie, right?"

Stop? Trev had cut down before, but he'd never stopped, and Carol, a wine fan, wasn't sure she wanted him to. Plus, Trev had a new plan—only drinking at home—which she supported because she now bought the household alcohol: cheap beer for him, and unfortunately, cheap wine for her. *That's control*, she thought.

"Even before Old Line destroyed our lawn," Carol continued, "I'd been telling him to drink like a gentleman. We're not in college anymore."

"So maybe the motorcycle 'loan' is sort of a blessing in disguise," Cindy reasoned.

"It's *extortion*, Cindy, not a loan. And it's not a blessing, either."

"Yes, of course you're right. So, how's he taking the belt-tightening?"

"He's sulky. You should hear him: 'No wheels and a fifth-grade allowance . . . Can't get into trouble *now*, can I, Carol?' Sure, he's around more, but I'd hoped he'd spend the time, you know, helping Reesie with her homework or straightening up his toolshed, anything productive. He just sits around watching network TV, bitching 'cause we don't have cable."

"He still gets out," said Cindy. "He watched the game with Loo the other night." *And drank a lot of beer, come to think of it. 'Course, with the Skins' 3 and 9 record, who could blame him?*

"Yeah, it's not like I put an ankle bracelet on him. He's seeing the other guys, too—D-Kay, Phillipe. He tried getting up with Henry, but after what happened, that *shooting*, the poor guy's laying low."

"Is this the beginning of some midlife crisis?" Cindy asked.

"Trev?" asked Carol. "Cin, he's thirty-two, not fifty-two."

Carefully, Cindy asked, "Do you think there might be another woman?"

"No." Carol was sure of this. Trev never returned home smelling like he shouldn't.

"You know, enough about Trevor. Have you all done any Christmas prep?" asked Cindy, ready to pivot.

"Pretty easy this year," said Carol, "because we've scaled back—*way* back. But the inside lights are up and you saw Christmas Land out back. It's still my favorite time of year." Carol smiled, then frowned. "Guess who's coming for Christmas, *again*?"

"No!"

"Yes! My sister has once again bailed on hosting Mother for the holidays. Three years in a row. So much for the fifty-fifty split."

Carol continued venting about her mother's impending stay since she and her mother crowded each other, but the "crowding" Carol really cared about now was her underfoot husband. There had been the usual tension over the years that any marriage experienced, *but this Old Line mess is different*. Would they be able to go back to "normal" after she cleared the debt?

Though not the best how-I-met-your-father opener, Carol had met Trevor playing Scrabble. It was Spring Break '84. Carol remembered sitting across from Trev at a beach house, the pair of them surrounded by dozens of people cheering. Before that moment, the break had been typical—parties at night, sleeping late in the mornings, afternoons spent watching TV, drinking every time soap opera stars kissed, slapped, or hugged each other—but midweek, a bored girl grabbed the house Scrabble game, asking for players, and before long the random games formed into an intense NCAA-style, single-elimination tournament. The spoils: bragging rights, plus going home with their house's street sign, SEA BREEZE LANE, which someone had stolen on the first day.

In the competitions, Carol—an English studies major at Virginia Tech—had several showy successes in clearing three hundred points, even using all seven tiles from her tray occasionally to score fifty extra "bingo" points. Trevor did decently well in his own games, not employing many big or complex words, but utilizing good placement strategies. In the game before the final round, Carol had used her extensive vocabulary to clobber a snobby Wahoo by sixty points. (Trevor had barely squeaked by his last challenger.)

Squaring off in the final round were Carol and Trevor, strangers then. Carol was confident she would win, having noted Trevor's lower totals and the fact that by 11 a.m., he was already buzzed. The spectating crowd was attentive and energetic for this championship showdown, and Carol relished the attention.

Scrabble success boiled down to letters: good tiles, good score; bad tiles, bad score. Carol drew well and smiled. Trev, who had not drawn well, scowled. Scowl or no, however, Carol found the charmer easy on the eyes. There was also added spice because Carol knew Trev had been checking her out all week. Still, competition was competition and she felt confident: between his buzz, her good looks, and decent letters, the road sign was as good as hers.

Carol couldn't resist laying out words like SPECTER, FLUNKY, and WINNOWS, playing for flash, while Trevor played monosyllables that weren't fancy but scored respectably. Seeing that Carol was casually showing off, the onlookers began chanting "Bingo Queen! Bingo Queen!" She was playing it a bit risky for the show but was still clobbering him.

They'd all been calling Trevor "Poker Joe" because of his confident use of fake words, and at one point he produced a bogus-sounding secondary word, AA. She challenged him. The tournament used a tattered Merriam-Webster dictionary to settle disputes. Lo and behold, AA was a word (a type of lava), which meant a lost turn for the Bingo Queen. Still, she was comfortably ahead, and even Trevor joined in the bingo chants.

After that, however, Carol's tiles turned cold. In the meantime, Trevor continued plodding on with his monosyllables, having dropped COD on a triple-word score. Too late Carol realized that playing to her vocabulary might have cost her the game. Desperate, she gambled, placing EAU (meaning water) with exaggerated nervousness, hoping he would challenge her and lose a turn.

At first, Trevor looked like he would, but after stroking his chin with unnecessary slowness, said, "That's not a word, love, but I'll allow it."

"You're gonna let me get away with that?" Carol said, shocked.

"Of course," Trevor said. "I'm a gentleman."

The arrogance!

She remained five points ahead, but people were cheering them both on now. The final scoring came down to the negatives from the remaining tiles, and Carol was sweating.

Luckily, she went out before Trev, winning by one point and the crowd erupted: "Bingo Queen! Bingo Queen!"

When everyone settled down again, Trevor asked, "As the vanquished, may I have a kiss?"

The spectators took up his cause, shouting "Kiss him! Kiss him!" over and over. After extended goading, she kissed him chastely on the cheek. The crowd went wild. Later that night when there was no crowd, her kisses weren't chaste at all.

Back home from the beach, Carol overheard Cindy bragging to their mutual friend, Sandy: "Trevor's five-eleven, cute. Got a great smile—when he's not smirking, that is. Nice bod! He's funny, smart, and *gawd*, Carol's *so* into him!" Carol blushed because it was true. Trev was what girls in Carol's league aspired to. After the "perfect" girls like Estelle and the alphas like Angie claimed the quarterbacks, second-round girls like Carol snapped up second-round guys like Trev, getting them as quickly in front of their mothers (and an altar) as possible.

Despite their current financial woes, Carol's love for her man remained strong. It helped that Trev unquestionably loved and cared for Reesie. Last summer, he'd built a backyard treehouse, spending hours on Saturdays with his daughter pretending to be pirates, "avasting" Carol while she delivered lunch to her buccaneers.

The notes helped too. Trev left handwritten messages for her all around the house—a *lot* of them. There were to-the-point requests, like the Post-It affixed to the last Yoplait: *Yo—gurt me some more, please*, and subtler ones, like the one attached to their owl-shaped junk dish: *Who, who, who forgot her keys?* The bathroom fair game—*You make me flush*—as was the garden—*I love you from my head tomatoes.* It wasn't unusual to find notes weeks later, sweet nothings like *I've got felines for you* (under the cat food bowl), *I love you a latte* (behind the coffee maker), and *You're warm and fluffy* (written on an orphaned dryer sock). Trev amazed her with these. He repeated themes, but it was never the same note twice. She scrapbooked the best ones.

Then there were the sex notes. "Shall I oil your love machine?" or "Roses are red, violets are blue, you have a fantastic ass, and this doesn't rhyme." In addition to being naughty, these less discrete notes were risky since they could be found by anyone. It was one thing if your best friend discovered *Sometimes I'm too blunt* on the knife block, but it was something else entirely when your mother found *To hell with spooning, let's fork* in the cutlery drawer. But it had been two weeks since Reesie found the *Daddy loves Mommy's ta-tas* note, and at least three months since Carol had found anything before that. Even courtesy notes like "I'll be back at 10 p.m." were few and far between lately, and these days *back at 10 p.m.* really meant *back at 3 a.m.* She worried. Gladys kept insisting that husbands sometimes "withdrew" from marriages. Was Trev withdrawing? Was family life too much for him? Were her hips too wide? Was it—Heaven forbid—another woman? *No.* Trev could be an idiot, but her nose told her he was a loyal one. The truth had started becoming obvious even before the Old Line rolled up unannounced to park on her front lawn: *My husband drinks too much.*

Chapter 14: The Cerrejón Mine

Wednesday, 9 March 1977—Day 7
Colombia, South America

IN THE 1977 backwater jungle of eastern Colombia, women understood they were second-class citizens. Most weren't glum about this, finding fulfillment in the time-honored roles of wife and mother. Patriarchy in the form of heavy-handed fathers and drunken husbands, however, failed these women. In the jungle, for a girl or woman trapped by abuse or neglect (or whose ambition, like La Madre Ruiz's, rivaled a man's), the FARC was a way out.

Girls escaped to guerilla life, but boys chose it, joining because the FARC were badass and, in terms of manpower, far outnumbered the other rebel options: the Maoists and Castroists. More importantly, the FARC were winning their war with the Colombian government, at least in the south. The FARC entrance price was very steep, however: lifelong membership. Considering the *chicos'* other choices—herding cows or picking coca leaves from dawn to dusk—boys signed up in droves. Food was consistent and the guns were free. What wasn't to like?

The Greens stopped that Wednesday at 6:30 p.m. to bed down, promising the prisoners, Walter and Jack, they would be reaching a permanent encampment with "facilities" the next day.

Jack watched the guerillas ready that night's camp, then said dryly to Walter, "That might mean something if they hadn't been promising the same rock-up for the last four nights."

He and Walter sat back-to-back on a small knoll above the forest floor, waiting for permission to hang their hammocks. "We're gonna be marching forever," Walter said despondently. "Jack, I don't think I can take another day."

"Don't worry, Bruce," Jack said. He called Walter *Bruce*; Walter never questioned why. "We'll be ransomed. And you're an American. They'll get a pretty penny for you."

"Who's gonna pay? My dad? He sells speakers on commission."

"Compared to these clowns, Bruce, he's got money."

"How about your parents?" asked Walter.

"My old man runs a two-thousand-head sheep station in Victoria," said Jack.

"Is he rich?"

"Hardly. Sheep ranching's demanding. Lots of worries. Lots to go wrong."

"He's got to be worth more than my dad the stereo man," said Walter.

"Yeah, when you put it that way, you're plum, I guess," answered Jack. "He owns our land outright. A thousand hectares."

"How big's that?"

Jack looked at him quizzically, then remembered his American buddy thought in imperial units. "I don't know exactly but more than a thousand acres, that's for sure. Maybe twelve hundred?"

"That's two square miles," said Walter. "That's huge."

"Huge?" Jack pridefully questioned. "Well Bruce, my fine American mate, you have obviously never been to Australia."

The guerillas made short work of bedding down. The niños were marched through hellish terrain twelve hours a day, forced to carry their own food and whatever personal items they could scrounge—to Walter's envy, Jack had traded his leather slouch hat for a worn pair of gumboots—but they weren't expected to help set up camp. Next, the FARC soldiers assembled a crude sleep platform for La Madre out of *tablas,* hacked-down jungle saplings cut lengthwise, before stringing their own hammocks up. Walter had to hand it to the rebels—the rag-tag guerillas might be uncouth crotch scratchers, but they worked magic with their machetes, and very quietly. It wasn't just camp craft they were good at—during the day the guerillas cleared trail efficiently, their blades whistling softly, not a swing wasted, carving through jungle that had been impenetrable only moments before.

That night, everyone ate rice and a mash of toasted yucca flower called *farina,* with gravy rendered from the fat of several *capybaras* (large, trappable jungle rodents), plus Gustavo's dead monkey. Dubious the first day, the boys now salivated when any sort of stew was brought to them, eating it quickly, licking their bowls clean. The previous seven evenings' meals had been similar, sometimes with the fibrous hearts of small palm trees instead of yucca, or fish instead of capybara meat. Breakfast and the midday break featured *arepa,* a fried bread served with wedges of *panela,* an unrefined brown sugar. For all meals, the FARC served a Kool-Aid-type drink called Frutino spiked with additional panela. The sugar rush was potent but short-lived, so the guerillas supplemented meals with candy bars, canteen coffee, and cigarettes.

It had been a godsend that Jack Sparks had entered the same contest Walter Perkins had months ago, otherwise, in his present circumstances, he would have understood no one. Walter, who hated travel, had won his trip to Colombia through an essay competition sponsored by the American energy conglomerate, Exxon. Each year, Exxon sponsored four spring break trips to worldwide locales like Alaska, Jordan, and Namibia. This year's ad: "Colombia, South America: See firsthand the latest coal-mining technology!" At first, he'd tried dodging the competition. "But Walter, you love science!" his mother pleaded. "Take a chance. Write an essay. Learn about, I don't know—chemicals? If you win, it's a free trip to Colombia! How exotic!"

"But Mom, I don't wanna see some dumb coal mine," Walter had asserted, "and anyway, they cover chemicals in chemistry class."

"Honey, you're a good student, sure," his mother insisted, "but this is a once-in-a-lifetime opportunity. We could never afford to send you overseas."

"Well, I don't want to *go* overseas."

"Nonsense, of course you do. Don't you want to see new things? Eat new cuisines?" Walter, partial to segregated portions of starchy foods, thought not. "And you'll learn about coal."

"I don't care about coal, Mom. I'm not entering and that's final."

But it was final only if Mr. Perkins said it was. Perkins, a direct man, particularly at the end of a day without sales, put it plainly to his son: "Write the essay." As always, there was an implied "or else," and in the Perkins household, *or else* was never good.

His dad wasn't all stick, however. Mr. Perkins sweetened the deal, offering a tempting carrot: "If you win, kiddo, there'll be a new set of Cerwin Vega speakers for you when you get back, and who knows, maybe money for a Tower Records run."

Walter, an audiophile who'd recently discovered progressive rock groups like Yes and King Crimson, welcomed the potential expansion of his record collection, but still thought it was unfair. Good at mathematics, he understood probability, recognizing a sucker's bet. Winning writing contests took actual writing talent, which he had in short supply. *What a waste of time.* "Or else" was still "or else," so with the help of his mother, the eighth grader cobbled together something good enough to get his parents off his back. He wasn't worried about winning—Exxon's contest attracted thousands of entries each year, only taking the top eighty. *I'm not gonna get in*, he thought, so after mailing his submission, the contest slipped from his mind.

What Walter didn't know was that Exxon wasn't interested in his ability to write *per se*. Instead, the company believed that any science nerd (grades were also submitted) who could string five hundred reasonable words together about visiting an open pit coal mine in another country might be the type of well-rounded self-starter their college co-op program would be looking for. Three thousand essays were typically submitted worldwide; it was a low-cost recruitment tool with positive PR that a soulless corporation could easily benefit from. The top eighty essay winners (twenty students, four separate trips) were offered an all-expenses-paid, one-week excursion. Due to conflicts and illnesses, however, not all original winners could make it. Walter placed eighty-seventh. Seven winners couldn't go, so Walter was chosen for the last slot of the last tour.

"Walter, I'm so proud of you!" his mother exclaimed when the award letter arrived. "It'll be so *exciting* going down into a mine!"

"It won't be exciting, Mom," Walter said. "It'll be terrifying." But Walter needn't have worried. Actual mining operations hadn't started yet.

The seven-day trip boasted a polished schedule organized by some dedicated admin assistants who knew what Exxon wanted out of this. There would be convenient but long travel by plane and bus. There were glamorous locales. There was a sprinkling of local cuisine alongside more typical American food for the pickier students and plenty of icebreakers and "inspirational" games to vet children with leadership potential. Exxon execs took pride in these itineraries, basking in the positive reviews from the parents. Be it Bismarck, Berlin, or Barcelona, the trip organizers could boast that every child had made it back home in time for school. They were confident the fourth and final week, Walter's week, would follow suit.

The first day of the trip was Saturday, 26 February 1977, a tiring one with long flights, the lengthiest being Jack's nineteen-hour trip from Victoria, Australia. Walter was a terrible flier but managed not to vomit. The winners arrived at the airport in Colombia's capital, Bogota, where they were greeted by a middle-aged man named Señor Campeón and his young assistant, Señor Barro. Tired or not, the kids perked up once they saw a balloon-festooned banner reading WELCOME EXXON PRIZE WINNERS with each of their names inscribed on it. The *señores* beamed as they shook hands with each arriving child. Señor Campeón was a cheery man with a well-groomed white beard matching his crisp white suit. In his lapel was a large INTERCOR OIL stick pin, Intercor being Exxon's in-country Colombian subsidiary. Once ready, the winners boarded a chartered bus for the ride downtown to Bogota's National University. After an informal dinner at the university's main dining hall, Señor Campeón ingratiated himself by reciting entertaining stories told in lightly accented English, with a smattering of Spanish and French thrown in. As he had done with the last three groups, the Señor began uniting an otherwise awkward troupe of teenage strangers into Intercor Oil's fourth and final batch of "mine" campers.

The second day was another travel day, going from Bogota to Santa Marta. It started with air travel in a large prop plane—again Walter would amaze himself by keeping his cookies—and then a bus ride. The bus was an old but very clean Bluebird model with its own bathroom. Jack noted there being a separate Land Rover that Señor Campeón and three men in understated Intercor uniforms would ride in. "They have guns," Jack observed about these men. "From the looks of them, real dinki-di rifles."

"Why are those men armed?" Walter asked the Señor as the man watched Barro load the children's suitcases.

Señor Campeón looked at the Rover. "There is a little trouble very far south of here. Some thugs, so-called guerillas. Nothing to worry about. We're going north."

"So why do you have them?" asked Walter. Conspiratorially, the Señor asked, "Can you keep a secret?"

"Yes, Señor."

"We like to keep people employed," Campeón said, winking. "That's *our* revolution. Now if you would, please hop aboard."

During the long bus ride, Señor Barro was seemingly everywhere at once, directing attention through various windows to identify different trees, local animals, the stunningly azure Caribbean Sea, and the ice-covered *Sierra Nevada de Santa Marta* mountains. He was prideful of his country's natural beauty, and the kids were easily caught up in his passion. The views truly were impressive.

The rest of the days were spent at the *Cerrejón* mine site, where there was, in fact, no mine yet. However, there was an impressive tent city erected in a huge expanse of cleared forest. The children were awed by the seemingly endless lines of survey flags, the massive machines tearing down trees, and the resulting gigantic log heaps. The students were very impressed by it all, and truth be told, a little overwhelmed.

For the next three days, Señor Campeón continued to entertain them, helping them feel at ease while also showing off all the new machinery and the miners in their preparation work. There were presentations, hands-on learning experiences, and of course one thrilling detonator demonstration. They were served dinner every evening around a campfire where Campeón told more funny stories while Barro exaggeratedly pantomimed, and they all learned some simple songs in Spanish to sing together. Late in the evening, the exhausted campers would trundle off to their canvas tents to sleep, warmed by the fire and new friendships.

Now, a week after the kidnapping, here Walter and Jack were again bedded down in the jungle, but were neither warm nor secure. They were in darkness so total Walter could not see Jack in his hammock two feet away.

He could hear his beginning snores, however, and exhausted as he was from following El Camarada's boots all day, Walter soon joined him.

Chapter 15: The Muppet Room

Thursday, 4 December 1998
Washington, DC

THURSDAY, MEN'S LOUNGE day, finally arrived. Phillipe drove to the address on the card Stu Pendous had given him, a downtown hotel called Winsor Heights. He skipped valet parking. Based on the size of the check he'd written—two thousand dollars—he couldn't afford it, plus he wanted his keys handy should he need to flee. He parked at a public deck a block away from the hotel. Its lower levels were full, so he made his way to the structure's rooftop, a platform giving a full view of Winsor Heights' fourteen stories. The building, designed in the 1920s modern architectural style with a stone façade that blended old money, prestige, and civic pride in equal parts, lit up the skyline.

It was a cool December evening. Phillipe wore wool slacks and an Oxford shirt under his leather coat, carrying a silk dress in a gym bag. He descended to street level, walked a block, then paused nervously in front of the hotel. Drawing a breath, he passed through doors opened by a uniformed doorman. The lobby was high-ceilinged with multiple chandeliers, and smelled like perfume and wood polish. Conversation hummed. Phillipe approached a long check-in desk.

"Can I help you, sir?" asked a smartly dressed concierge.

"I don't need a room. I, um—"

"Perhaps you're attending one of the functions this evening, sir?" suggested the man helpfully, whose nametag read *Cleveland*. He pointed across the lobby toward three sets of ballroom doors.

"Uh, yes, I am. Thanks."

Phillipe traversed approximately a mile of plush carpet to reach the ballrooms. Each one was named after a Native American tribe—the Cree, the Cherokee, and the Seminole. To get to them, one had to pass a registration table manned by two middle-aged women. The happenings within each ballroom were printed in fancy lettering on a placard behind them: the National Realtors' Association Conference, the DC Area Shriners' Awards Dinner, and the American Petroleum Institute Offshore Opportunities Seminar. Nothing with the word *lounge* in it. Phillipe seriously considered leaving when one of the ladies (*Doris*, according to her nametag) asked if he needed help.

"Well, ma'am, I don't know if I'm in the right place," Phillipe answered uncertainly. He presented the card Stu Pendous had given him.

"Oh, you definitely are," Doris replied. "Name, please?"

"Uh, Johnny. Johnny Pilot."

"Here you are, young man," she said assuredly, checking his name off a list. "Do you have payment, Mr. Pilot?"

Phillipe fished out the two grand check. *Maybe I should rent a "dressing room" in some self-storage facility instead,* he thought as he handed it over. *It would be cheaper.*

"This is an anonymity agreement," said Doris. "Please sign here."

"Is the lounge in one of the ballrooms?" Phillipe asked, signing.

"Oh, gracious no," said the other woman, whose nametag read *Jeannie*. "It's upstairs in the Iroquois Room. The elevator is that way, toward the gentleman at the end of the hall."

"Thanks," said Phillipe. He continued after a pause: "Say, how do you know I'm the real Johnny Pilot? I could be, I don't know, *anyone*."

Both women laughed good-naturedly. "You're you, Mr. Pilot, no doubt about it," Doris responded, pointing to the check-in list and the pencil rendering of Phillipe's face next to his name.

Wow, these guys don't mess around.

"Mr. Waldorf took up sketching five years ago," said Jeannie, reading his mind. "He's getting good, don't you think? Now off you go, Mr. Pilot," she said, not waiting for an answer. "You don't want to be late."

Phillipe approached the far hallway elevator. A very large man whose nametag read *Teddy* stood in front of it. Teddy, muscles bulging beneath an expensive suit, looked him over.

"I, ah, don't have a ticket—" Phillipe began, thinking that *Bruno* would be a better name for this wall of meat.

"Relax, friend," said Teddy. "The ladies have cleared you, so once I check this, you're good to go." Teddy took the gym bag, asking Phillipe if it contained anything Teddy wouldn't like. Phillipe assured him it didn't. "First-time jitters?" Teddy inquired, handing the bag back without opening it.

"Yes," Phillipe affirmed.

"Not to worry," said Teddy assuredly. "Thursday's not human sacrifice night," he continued, winking. "Please proceed to the fourteenth floor."

"The penthouse?"

"No, the penthouse is private."

"I thought this hotel only had fourteen floors."

"It does, but it was built in 1927—superstitious times—hence no thirteenth floor, so twelve, fourteen, then the penthouse. When you get off the elevator, the changing room is the first door on your right. The Lounge is straight across from there. You can't miss it."

"Okay, thanks," said Phillipe.

The changing room was right where Teddy had described, across from two tall chestnut doors emblazoned with the words *The Iroquois Room.* Inside the changing area were hundreds of large lockers, including one labeled *J. Pilot*. There were no locks. *Teddy's probably hell on thieves anyway,* Phillipe thought. *Am I really going through with this*? he asked himself. *And what, exactly, does 'going through with this' mean?* His heart beat rapidly.

Out of nervous curiosity, he opened the lockers to each side of his. The one labeled *T. Wife* was empty, and in the other, labeled *S. Struck,* hung a well-tailored men's suit like what Mr. Waldorf had worn to his apartment. *So far, my slacks and Oxford aren't cutting it.* He opened a random locker labeled *W. Bang*. It held an outfit like Phillipe's—good pants, a collared shirt, and a Members Only jacket—making him feel better. He was moving Mr. Bang's clothes aside to look at his shoes when a voice behind him said, "Sir, that's not your locker."

Phillipe spun on his heels. A young woman stood there, eyeing him. She wore men's clothes—some sort of hotel costume—with the words *Winsor Heights* sewn below fancy-looking heraldry on her vest pocket, and below that, the name *Steve*. A black mustache was tastefully drawn above "Steve's" lips. She wore a white shirt beneath the vest and tight riding pants, topping everything off with a ringmaster's stovepipe hat. "I wasn't stealing anything . . . miss," Phillipe responded. He'd said the word "miss" questioningly, struggling with what to call a woman dressed as a man.

"Mr. Bang will be relieved to hear that," she said. A pause, in which Phillipe stared at her in fear. "Are you okay, Mr. . . . ?"

"Gallois—I mean Pilot. Johnny Pilot."

"Oh, Mr. Pilot! We've been expecting you. Welcome. I'm Steve."

Wow.

Since arriving, Winsor Heights had been overwhelming Phillipe, everything from the ostentatious lobby to Doris and Jeannie, the gracious hostesses, to the humongous Teddy guarding the elevator, and now this twenty-something looker calling him *mister*. He felt lightheaded. *But it's not just the hotel, is it?* There was also the pressure of his promotion, his hot but demanding girlfriend, Estelle, and his almost sexual obsession with silk. *I'm spinning too many plates.* And of course, the mysteries of the Iroquois Room still awaited.

"Mr. Pilot, you're staring," Steve said, her cheeks turning pink.

"I'm sorry!" Phillipe said, first looking away, then looking back again because Steve, or whatever her real name was, was Estelle Largo's opposite. Estelle was a tall, full-figured, dark-eyed bombshell. Women like Estelle (and the Vee Sisters, Randy and Vicky) stopped trains, or at least trains of thought, but Steve was a train-stopper in her own right: diminutive, but with an athletic torso accentuated by her blackjack dealer's outfit. With animated eyes and glowing cheeks, the P. T. Barnum hat-wearer was a beauty.

He began asking questions nervously: What really went on in the Iroquois Room? Was it a con? Some sting operation? Or his worst fear, a lair of old men waiting to bugger him?

Steve's eyes widened. "You're obviously new to the Lounge, Mr. Pilot."

"Did I really say, 'old men waiting to bugger me?'" asked Phillipe, blushing.

Steve nodded, suppressing a laugh. "Mr. Pilot, there's nothing to fear. It's just men wearing dresses, smoking, drinking. Older men, usually," she said thoughtfully, looking at him a little more intently. "So, Mr. Pilot, Mr. Waldorf invited you tonight, yes?"

"Yes," said Phillipe.

"That's quite an honor."

"I'm beginning to think so, but an honor for what? I mean, you're *sure* there's no buggery?"

Steve laughed out loud this time.

"You can call me Phill—I mean Johnny," Phillipe said, wanting to emphasize their similar ages. He was thirty-two; she was in her late twenties.

"Sorry, but that's frowned on." She eyed his gym bag. "So, what did you bring this evening?"

Phillipe looked around. They were alone. He took out a red and black checkered dress—each square edged with gold.

"Well, Mr. Pilot, it's beautiful," Steve said. "Who's the designer?"

"Um, you're looking at him."

Steve eyed Phillipe, impressed. "May I ask what you do, Mr. Pilot?"

"I'm a mechanic for Southwest," he answered, then added, "and a weekend pilot."

"Hence the name," said Steve, pausing. "This is a stunning dress, sir, but let me do something about those wrinkles." She took it to an antechamber labeled HOTEL STAFF ONLY. Phillipe sat on a comfortable bench to wait, snapping the fingers of one hand while simultaneously tapping it into his palm—a man with no idea what to do with himself.

Steve returned. "Here you go, Mr. Pilot. Wrinkles gone. Also, I took the liberty of getting you these." She handed him a pair of large red slippers which complemented his dress far better than his loafers would. "The loungers, as we call the patrons, end up leaving a lot of things behind. Consider them yours."

"Gee, thanks."

"Do you need any help getting that on?" she asked.

"Ah, no, I'm good from here, Steve. Thanks."

"Some of the loungers are quite elderly," she explained.

"I'm not," said Phillipe.

"No, you're not," Steve said, smiling. "Please leave your phone in the locker. They're not allowed in the Lounge."

Phillipe tried handing her money, but she wouldn't take it. "Your dues are all-inclusive, Mr. Pilot. Tipping's not necessary. Don't worry—I'm well paid." She walked to the staff-only door, saying, "I'll be here if you need me."

Phillipe put his Nokia phone in his locker and changed, then went out to the hallway to stand before the double doors of the Iroquois Room. Cackling male voices could be heard behind them. He imagined men in tuxedos all set to laugh at him. *And why not? I'm in public, for Christ's sake, wearing a dress!*

He took a breath, his deepest of the evening so far, then opened the tall doors hoping that men in dresses, not tuxedos, would greet him.

Roughly a hundred men in women's attire stood around cocktail tables or sat in overstuffed leather chairs. No tuxedos. The clubroom was a saloon backlit by the flames of a large hearth; it smelled of tobacco, whiskey, and rich food. Two dozen attendees gathered around a large, wood-paneled bar set in the middle of the room. Steve had been right; the cross-dressers were mostly middle-aged and older.

He could see right away that at the Lounge, there were two types of dress-wearers: guys who tried, and guys who didn't, and unfortunately the ones who tried were outnumbered by victims of some dinner theater costume room explosion—poorly fitting bridesmaid dresses, hideous pantsuits, plastic Mardi Gras beads, ratty stoles. There wasn't enough beer in the world to confuse any of these Python-esque men for actual women.

Although the attire was feminine, the conversation was not. Phillipe had entered a proverbial boys' club of smoking, drinking, laughing, and backslapping. Outside, it was the decade of Alanis Morrissette and Mortal Kombat. Inside, apart from the apparel, it was yesteryear's Tammany Hall.

Two young women tended bar while others circulated with drink trays. There was an hors d'oeuvres table with an attractive woman serving large pieces of aromatic brisket to a line of waiting transvestites. All the help dressed like Steve: quasi-blackjack dealers' outfits with top hats and penciled mustaches.

At the back of the ballroom stood a cluster of chairs and side tables on a thick rug next to the crackling fireplace. Mr. Waldorf was sitting in a high-backed armchair in front of it. He waved Phillipe over. Mr. Pendous was there as well, standing behind Waldorf's chair as he'd done at Phillipe's apartment. In a matching armchair across from Waldorf sat another elderly gentleman. Both men wore dresses. Stu Pendous did not. Phillipe approached the men.

"Well, if it isn't Johnny Pilot!" Mr. Waldorf exclaimed. Waldorf sported a knee-length green dress, pantyhose, and a pearl necklace. It wasn't a bad getup. Aside from the skin wrinkles and abundance of body hair, he was "trying." He rose, shaking Phillipe's hand.

The other gentleman shook his hand from his seated position. "Smashing dress, kid," he said. "Name's Statler. So, you're the boy Waldorf here's been gloating about all week." Statler pointed to a chair, motioning "Johnny" to sit.

Unlike his brother, Statler, who wore a brown polyester mid-length skirt, a faded cotton blouse, worn flats, and an overly colorful headscarf, wasn't trying, unless trying meant looking like a haggard TV housewife. Waldorf produced a cigar which Pendous clipped, then lit for him. Statler already had one going.

After two initial puffs, Waldorf eyed his brother. "Johnny, what do you think of Statler's 'Madge' look? Atrocious, right? Hell, it's vulgar. Go clean a bowling alley, Brother."

Statler shrugged his shoulders. "Brother, I wear what I feel."

"With that outfit, *I feel* you should be turning down beds for housekeeping," Waldorf said with mock disdain. Phillipe caught Pendous smiling and relaxed, knowing it was okay to enjoy the old men's banter.

Statler tapped his cinders into a Winsor Heights ashtray, then waved around. "Welcome to the Muppet Room, Johnny, the Lounge's 'club within a club.' What do you do for work, son?"

Phillipe explained his profession, mentioning his recent promotion.

"Congratulations!" Statler said. "Bet it's stressful, yes?"

"Yes, sir."

"You should try running a hotel," Statler continued good-naturedly. "You're obviously in need of a drink. Gordon! A scotch for young Johnny here."

A female waiter with a "Gordon" name tag appeared, placing a tumbler on Phillipe's side table. He wafted in its warm aroma, then drank it. It was remarkably smooth. Phillipe, aka Johnny Pilot, continued listening to the two old men chew the fat, understanding them now as David and Adam Winsor, the hoteliers who owned Winsor Heights.

Suddenly, he smiled and chuckled to himself.

"Cat got your tongue, Johnny?" asked Waldorf, waiting for an explanation.

"Your stage names, sir. 'Statler' and 'Waldorf.' I get it now. The two old hecklers from The Muppet Show."

"Who are you calling old, Sonny Jim?" groused Statler, but Waldorf smiled back, saying, "The kid's sharp. Some of the regulars still haven't put two and two together."

Phillipe asked how the Lounge got started. "The Lounge is about costumes and stage names," said Statler, "though there's no stage. For fifty-one years, I'd been wearing my *other* costume—a three-piece suit, which, believe me, gets old."

"Fifty-*two* years, Brother," corrected Waldorf, "not counting the war years, of course."

"Fine," said Statler. "Fifty-*two* years running a five-star hotel—"

"Plus our other ventures," added Waldorf.

"Yes, yes, Brother, plus our *other* ventures. Now shut it, I'm talking."

"Then get on with it." Waldorf turned his chin toward the crackling fire, clearly pleased with himself.

"I will if you stop interrupting me. So, Johnny, me being captain of this enterprise, which is understandably stressful—"

"You think *you're* the captain?" exclaimed Waldorf. "Hah! That's rich, Brother."

"Put a cork in it, Waldorf," said Statler, irritated. "He's impossible, Johnny. *Impossible.* Anyway, I told him one night that, after being in the hotelier business at that point for twenty-six years—"

"Plus our other ventures," said Waldorf.

"Shut up, old man!" exclaimed Statler. "Anyway, one night in 1972—"

"Specifically, the twenty-fourth of June, a week after Nixon resigned," interjected Waldorf.

Statler gave his brother an ugly look, then rushed on to avoid further interruption. "I just wanted one day a month—it was once a month at the beginning, you see—where I didn't have to wear a suit and make decisions for hundreds of idiots, including my own brother. One day a month to hang up my spurs like Howard Hughes and *lounge*. You know, as a lark. We wore robes at first—"

"Hotel robes," said Waldorf, "which we incidentally sell in the gift shop."

"Yes-yes-yes, Waldorf, now shut it. At first, we kept on one-upping each other—robes, then boxers, then briefs. We agreed early on—thank God—that birthday suits were the Maginot Line." Here Waldorf nodded. "Then Waldorf got particularly drunk one night and stole some poor woman's dress—"

"Borrowed," Waldorf clarified.

"Keep telling yourself that, thief. So that spurred a drag competition. Some of our old school chums joined in, and it went on swimmingly for months until we were 'outed' by some yellow journalist from that afternoon rag, *The Washington Star*. We worried the story would ruin our father's good name, but the account of our secret club"—here, Statler air-quoted *secret*—"turned out to be good for business. People like their rich to be eccentric, you see."

"Save me! Save me!" interjected Waldorf in a high-pitched, mock feminine voice, hand across his brow. "My responsibilities are just *too* stressful."

"Get thee to the Lounge, my good man," Statler added. "Cross-dress that stress away!"

The two men chortled and even Pendous laughed. The brothers continued reviewing Lounge history, going out of their way to correct each other, and Phillipe listened politely, fascinated. By his second scotch, he realized that he could now live a dream he didn't even know he'd had: membership in a club where men, *in drag*, talked smack.

"Statler's wife wasn't supportive at first," said Waldorf. "Mine either. Came as sort of a shock to our better halves. But after some initial handwringing about what the mahjong set might think, they came around."

"Waldorf's wife didn't come around," Statler said. "She divorced him."

"That had been in the works for some time, dear Brother."

"True," said Statler. "For my part, it took some doing, but eventually my wife, Edith, accepted our 'club.' She knew I wasn't light in the loafers—"

"Your philandering *proved* that," Waldorf needled.

"No tales out of school, Brother," Statler said, bringing his stink eye to bear. "So I finally told Edith, 'Look, honey, it's just one night a month. There's no hanky-panky, and the lunatics run the asylum for a day. It's mad fun.' There's a picture of me in a swank Christian Dior outfit in my office. People think it's *grand*. It's the cigar, see? A man wearing a dress is weird, perhaps pathetic, but put the same man in front of a cabinet of top-shelf liquor, give him a stogie, and put his hand on top of an Irish Wolfhound, and he's balls! Hell, Edith enjoyed it. She started choosing outfits for me. We even went to fashion shows once she realized I wasn't just there for the jubblies."

"None of this stopped my brother's philandering, however," Waldorf clarified.

"Oh God no," responded Statler. "That got worse because Edith thought a man in a dress couldn't attract women. Well, I'm here to tell you the better I got at wearing dresses, the better I got at taking them off!"

The old men cackled like magpies, saluting each other with their drinks.

Suddenly, the mood changed. "God, I miss that woman," Statler said. "May she rest in peace."

"You didn't deserve Edith, Brother," Waldorf said. Statler shook his head in agreement.

To fill a developing pause, Phillipe asked about the first thing that came to mind, which was the Deerslayer. His exploits were being discussed everywhere: Channel 4 News, WTOP News Radio, even the syndicated shock jock Howard Stern and DC's own Greaseman had opinions. It seemed like a safe topic to bring up.

Statler swirled the ice in his drink, scratched at his kerchief, then responded, "I don't know the man, of course, but I *like* him. The goddamn deer eat everything, including the estate's azaleas. Rats with antlers is what they are."

Waldorf grunted in agreement. "The county forbade hunting, and now the chickens, or should I say the deer, have come home to roost. This slayer fellow? Hat's off to him."

Statler scratched at his headscarf again as a man started making his way toward the fireplace. "Good Lord," Statler said, "here comes what's his name. The man's dress is so ugly he makes *me* look good."

Stu Pendous whispered to Statler, "Sir, Mr. Star Struck is Councilman Washington. His son was killed a few weeks ago."

"Oh, then I'd better be polite," Statler said.

"Yes, dear Brother," Waldorf agreed.

Struck arrived, sporting a three days' beard, slumped shoulders, and darkly ringed eyes. "Messiers Winsor," Struck said.

"Mr. Struck, I must insist you adhere to the house rules," Statler said.

With a trace of peevishness, Washington said, "Mister *Statler* and Mister *Waldorf*."

Waldorf looked at Statler reproachfully, saying, "Never mind my rude brother, Washington. Sorry to hear about your loss. You've been coming here for years, paying at the highest level, I might add, so please call me David. May I call you Spencer?" Spencer Washington, aka Star Struck, nodded. "He's Adam," Waldorf said, pointing to his brother. "Have a seat. What can we do for you?"

"Thank you, David," said Washington, sitting. "Well, I'll get right to it. I would never ask you to use your influence," though his face implied that that was exactly what he was asking, "but the county DA and I aren't seeing eye-to-eye on the dirty son-of-a-bitch who killed my son. He should be throwing the book at the foreign bastard." The man's fatigued eyes grew angry. "Junior was my son. My *only* son. Seventeen years old."

"Foreign, you said?" asked Waldorf.

"Yeah, a Jap named Takahashi." Phillipe cringed hearing this.

"Really?" said Statler. "After the thrashing we gave them in '45, I'm surprised our yellow cousins could work up the nerve to kill an American."

"Like you would know," Waldorf said. "While you were busy pushing papers in North Africa, *I* was island-hopping, actually *fighting* the Japanese."

"Fighting? Really?" challenged Statler. "I'll give you a new set of pearls if you can prove you stepped on one beach the Seabees hadn't already groomed like a golf course."

The two brothers began arguing about who had faced more actual danger during WWII, and Washington, clearly concerned with the rabbit hole the Winsors were digging, spoke up. "The DA's balking about pressing charges. Anything you can do would be appreciated," he continued, hands bunching the fabric of his ugly dress. "Not just by me but by thousands of voters."

The tone of gravitas arrested the old men's war story spat.

"Sure, Spencer," said Waldorf, sounding sincere. "Can't have Japs murdering Americans again. We'll look into it." He patted the hand of Star Struck, aka Spencer Washington Sr., County Councilman at Large for Montgomery County, Washington DC's wealthy neighbor to the north. It was a gesture of compassion. And dismissal.

"Thank you, gentlemen," Washington said, getting up. "And both your outfits are divine," he added.

"Thanks, Spencer," said Waldorf. "Now why don't you get yourself a drink." Washington left. "The man looks miserable," Waldorf continued. "But he's right, my Brother: my outfit is divine. You, on the other hand, look like a Mexican prostitute."

"I'm channeling my inner housewife, *señor*," answered Statler, "and anyway, Washington's dime store outfit makes me look like the belle of the ball. Now Johnny, where were we? Yes, yes, tell us more about that nail-biting vocation of yours. Peril in the sky!"

Phillipe, surprised at how quickly the man could pivot from Washington's grief, answered his questions as best he could, but even though the freedom to carouse with like-minded men while wearing silk had put fire in his eyes—*he'd been searching for the Lounge his whole life!*—the "foreign bastard" talk troubled him.

He excused himself after a bit more conversation, escaping to the changing room to call Henry, but Splashdown's voicemail was full. It had been full all week. *Well, it was clearly self-defense,* he told himself. *Everything's fine.*

He returned to the Lounge for another hour before leaving to retrieve his car. He called Estelle on the way home, asking to come over.

"Gotta warn you, coming in hot, hornier than a shipwrecked goat!" Estelle was delighted and cooed naughtily.

"Come on in, man-rocket," she said when he arrived at the door, "you've been cleared for landing." She nuzzled his neck passionately, aroused by the scent of cigarettes and scotch, presumably from Phillipe's Thursday Night Hanger 18 poker game.

He felt bad about lying, but the Lounge was anonymous, as spelled out in the legally binding hush documents Doris had given him to sign. That was okay, though. Phillipe didn't *want* anyone to know his secret—the Hanger 18 crew would crucify him if they ever found out. And Estelle? *That* would be ugly. No sir. In her book, no self-respecting man-rocket ever wore a dress.

Chapter 16: Tori Bora

Thursday, 10 December 1998
Silver Spring, MD

KEN ERT, AKA Original Ken, sat in Mrs. Nigel's waiting area as he'd done every week for the last month. Mrs. Nigel, his cognitive therapist, rented space in a downtown Silver Spring office that was an apartment building remodeled for corporate use. Her waiting area was furnished professionally, with a coffee table displaying a mint bowl, stacked coasters, and a vase of intricately folded origami flowers. On an end table stood a lamp and a small transistor radio tuned to a classical music station at low volume. Magazines hung on a rack on the wall (*Time, Psychology Today, The Washingtonian Magazine, Highlights*).

Ken Ert seeking mental health support was a carefully guarded secret. No one knew except his sister, Sylvia, who was the one mandating it in the first place: "Kenny, it's been seven years." He trusted her discretion. His nephews George and Gregory, on the other hand, were told Uncle Ken had to "work late" on Thursdays. At first, they keenly felt his evening absences. *Mom, Uncle Ken's coming home later, right?* Knowing full well the boys feared losing their uncle like they'd lost their father, she'd respond, "Of course he is." Relieved, Gee and Gree would then return to chasing each other with wiffle ball bats.

Why was Ken seeing Mrs. Nigel? In large part, to escape the jokes about not attracting straight women. *What did the first lesbian have in common with the second one?* Answer: *They both dated Ken. Har-har!* For years, he'd pretended the jokes didn't hurt, but they did.

To accommodate working clients like Ken, Mrs. Nigel started at 1 p.m. and stopped at 8:00. Sessions went forty-five minutes, giving her a quarter-hour between counselees to jot down notes. Original was always timely for his 7:00, but tonight he was purposefully a half hour early. A week previous, he'd misread his watch, mistakenly arriving a half hour early as well. To kill time then, he'd read the children's magazine, *Highlights*, noting how much more wholesome it was compared to *Fear and Loathing in Las Vegas*. A minute later he'd heard laughter, peals of it, coming from behind Mrs. Nigel's office door. She and her client were obviously having a good time. Their mirth was contagious; Original couldn't help smiling. When they wrapped up their session, a woman emerged from Nigel's office, a shapely one with large eyes.

"Goodbye, Tori," Mrs. Nigel said happily. Tori, a woman in her late twenties with hair teased like Virginia Hey's in the movie *The Road Warrior*, smiled back.

Ken should have been using the wait time to finish his article concerning the market woes of the underperforming Montreal Expos; it was his opinion that if they didn't get their act together in the next three years, some other city, perhaps DC, would buy them. *But instead, here I am reading friggin'* Highlights.

Tori regarded him with a look about as far from *You had me at hello* as one could get, then stepped past him. Did he hear her scoff? At first, he'd thought his perusing a magazine meant for six-year-olds was the problem, but it wasn't. Yes, she had beautiful eyes and that 80s perm he so loved, but a third of her hair was shorn very short and the woman wore an unflattering nose ring. *Three Lives* by Gertrude Stein protruded from her enormous handbag, which had an upside-down pink triangle on one handle and a rainbow button on the other. Ken assumed he knew the reason for the scoff—*Oh look, another man who wants to watch me mud-wrestle my girlfriend. And I don't think she liked my bowtie.*

Despite her rebuff a week ago, here he was, early again. Was it just his biological imperative? Perhaps. Nose ring or not, Tori physically appealed to him. *Or maybe I just need help identifying lesbians in the wild because I'm so bad at it*, he thought. *Maybe she could help me.*

Even though there was a brand new *Highlights* hanging from the rack this week, he ignored it, not wanting to look unnecessarily foolish when Tori emerged from her session this time. He thought about removing his baby blue bowtie, this year's Christmas gift from the hellions, but decided not to. A moment later, the building's HVAC went silent, allowing him to hear Mozart on the waiting room radio. Suddenly, from behind Mrs. Nigel's closed door, Ken heard Tori clearly declare "Girls! Girls! Girls! That's what I want!" She and Mrs. Nigel burst out laughing as they'd done the previous week.

Seems we have something in common, Ken thought. Befriending someone from the other team now seemed like a dumb idea. *Jesus, I hate this jinx*, he thought.

To hell with it. He picked up the new *Highlights* magazine off the rack just in time for Tori to emerge from Nigel's office. He'd remembered her proportions correctly—not a small woman, but not a big one, either. Wide-ish hips, breasts which gravity would eventually claim but not without a fight, and intelligent, gold-flecked eyes. She wore black jeans, pumps, and a blue blouse under a smart-looking coat. She still had her two-thirds of a good perm, the LGBTQ-festooned handbag, and her nose ring.

Tori hugged Mrs. Nigel, who hugged back warmly. (Mrs. Nigel was big on hugging.) As Tori turned to leave, Mrs. Nigel nodded to Ken, mouthing "five minutes" before gently closing her door. Tori advanced toward Original, first staring at his bowtie (another one!), then at what he held—*Highlights* again!

He dropped his eyes, pretending to study it carefully as he proudly announced, "I read it for the pictures."

"Good, because there's no editorial section," she said, eyebrow raised.

Stodgily, Ken replied, "Yes, it's unfortunate they can't post my op-ed demanding that Elmer's make their glue taste better. *Someone* needs to speak for today's toddlers, don't you think?" He stood up, extending his hand. "Introductions are in order. I'm Ken."

"Tori," she said, taking his hand grudgingly.

"Sounds like you and Mrs. Nigel have a lot of fun. All that laughing. I want *your* problems."

"Oh, I assure you—Ken, is it?—that you don't," Tori said.

Original pointed his *Highlights* toward her bag. "That's quite an impressive knitting hauler you got there, but you're a bit too young to be a grandma, aren't you?" Ken, usually reserved to the point of repression, couldn't believe what he'd just said.

Apparently, Tori couldn't, either. "My sister *made* this bag."

Ohhh . . . shit.

"What are you here for, terminal smugness?" she asked. Ken, embarrassed, said nothing. "You really don't like my bag?" she asked after a beat of awkward silence, tugging at its handles, looking a little hurt.

"It's a fine bag," he offered.

"Don't lie."

"Seriously, it's not ugly, it's just—"

"Something Granny would haul around?" Tori challenged. "You already mentioned that."

(And he thought she'd looked at him coolly *last* week.)

"On that note," she continued, "good day." She looked at him expectantly. "*This* is where you say, 'Good day,' and I walk off in a huff, just like the book."

"The book?" Ken asked, totally confused.

"*Go Dog Go.* Surely a man of letters such as yourself," she said, tapping his copy of *Highlights* for emphasis, "is familiar with *Go Dog Go.*"

"Never heard of it."

"Oh, you'd like it," she said. "It's a children's book. A *simple* one. Lots of pictures. Okay, so say it now."

"Say what?" asked Ken.

"Say, 'Good day, Tori.'"

"Good day, Tori?"

"Good day, Ken." Tori walked to the door with a huffiness that Ken could only hope was exaggerated. "And unless you have barbershop quartet practice later," she added before leaving, "you should know that Pee Wee Herman bowtie says it all."

Chapter 17: The Coventry Lane Christmas Carnival

Saturday, 12 December 1998
Reston, VA

YOU DECIDED TO live at the edge of the world.

Five months ago, D-Kay and his wife, Sandy, a pair of Virginia Tech sweethearts, had become owners of a large house in a Reston subdivision called Governor's Landing. It was in the Northern Virginia boonies but was affordable and reasonably close to Def Systems, the defense contractor where Darius worked as an engineer. The home was built as a faux colonial, one of three building plans available, which made it almost indistinguishable from every other house along Coventry Lane. Nonetheless, D-Kay and Sandy, DINKs (double-income, no kids), were proud of their new home. They moved in on the fourth of July, the perfect holiday to celebrate freedom from rent. Every lawn had an American flag, courtesy of the Girl Scouts, and later residents gathered outside the neighborhood clubhouse to watch Reston's colorful fireworks. That evening was perfect—a slice of summer about as far removed from Christmas as one could get.

So when their next-door neighbors asked the following day, "Do you know about the Coventry Lane Christmas Carnival?" Darius and Sandy were mystified. The inquirers introduced themselves as Halle and Ben Horowitz, middle-aged empty nesters. "Well, our street, Coventry Lane, particularly this block, is sort of famous for Christmas lights."

"Like the 'Miracle on 34th Street' in Baltimore?" Sandy asked, sounding thrilled. "That's where I'm from—Baltimore. Every Christmas, there's this strip of rowhouses lit up like Vegas."

D-Kay wasn't as thrilled, picturing an electric meter spinning out of control. "Sounds expensive," he said. "Is this carnival mandatory?"

"No, no, of course not," Ben Horowitz answered.

"Just neighborhood spirit," Halle added, a bit nervously.

"Heck, we're Jewish," Ben continued, "but Santa's Santa, plus Halle and I put up what's likely the largest menorah on the Eastern Seaboard."

Halle nodded in agreement, adding in a voice meant to be reassuring, "Don't worry, it's not so bright that you can't sleep."

"Well, Christmas is a long way off," said D-Kay. "And we just moved in."

"Of course," agreed the Horowitzes.

Fu-tat!-Fu-tat!-Fu-tat! went the sound of a nail gun.

"Who's that guy?" D-Kay asked, pointing to a man in the backyard of the other home abutting theirs. The man, standing on something allowing his upper torso to be seen above an eight-foot privacy fence, put his nail gun down when he noticed the Kays, then began waving energetically.

"That's Kent Ruger," Halle answered, waving back.

"He's a good neighbor," added Ben, waving. "Just a bit enthusiastic." With that cryptic description, the Horowitzes left the Kays to continue unpacking.

The nailing started up again. *Fu-tat!-Fu-tat!-Fu-tat!*

Kent, a man in his early forties, came over later that afternoon to introduce himself, speaking quickly, as if time were of the essence. "Kent Ruger. You must be the Kays. Great to meet you. Sorry I couldn't come over sooner. Finishing the first stage of my platform. Making two. Real doozies! I'm sure you've already heard about the Christmas Carnival, right?"

The Kays introduced themselves once he gave them a chance to speak. Ruger was affable but intense, loading the conversation from that point with neighborhood trivia, opinions on local schools, and a lengthy discourse on the Coventry Lane Christmas Carnival, something he took seriously since he was already working on it in July. Sandy asked him how he had liked the Rinaldis, the former homeowners.

"Alright, I guess," Ruger said guardedly, "but they had trouble pulling their weight." With this mysterious remark, Ruger beamed at them and invited them to his house for dinner the next Saturday. Sandy was on the verge of reluctantly accepting when D-Kay interjected that there was simply too much unpacking to do, so could they get back to him? "Sure," said Ruger, a bit disappointed.

"Hey there, hi there, ho there," D-Kay said after Ruger left. "I believe we've met the neighborhood Ned Flanders." Sandy agreed, thanking her husband for the save; Kent Ruger seemed nice enough, but somehow a little off. They avoided Ruger's second invitation as well, D-Kay promising him a round of golf instead. A few Saturdays later, Kay and Ruger were paired with two vacationing Scots at the local course. The Scots were good golfers, Ruger was very good, D-Kay was a duffer. Kent was characteristically chatty, not letting the Scots' brief attempts to speak stop him from lecturing them about the origins of golf, the weather patterns of Northern England, and the best way to ensure that azaleas got off to a good start.

By the back nine, the heat was taking a toll, yet Ruger kept at it. "So Darius, it's only July, but I gotta ask 'cause Thanksgiving will be here before you know it. Will you be ready?"

"Ready for what?" D-Kay asked, teeing up. *Whack!* He watched his first decent drive of the day fly straight.

"The Coventry Lane Christmas Carnival light show, of course!" Ruger answered as if D-Kay were Forrest Gump.

"Sure, I guess," D-Kay answered, hopping into their cart, pleased to have finally landed cleanly on the fairway.

"Well, I hope you are, my friend," Ruger continued, getting in. "Starting the day after Thanksgiving, *Black Friday*, people from miles around will drive to Reston, to Governor's Landing, right down Coventry Lane to see the lights. It's spectacular! There's pressure to keep it fresh every year, of course, but five years in, we keep pulling it off."

"Does everyone do it?" Darius asked.

"Oh yes!" Ruger exclaimed as they drove along the fourteenth fairway, the Scots following them. "Two solid blocks of it, both sides of Coventry Lane. Your house and my house? Smack dab in the middle of it, neighbor. We're the linchpins!"

Being a linchpin sounds expensive, D-Kay thought.

Ruger continued: "The Rinaldis, God love them, weren't really what I would call team players if you know what I mean. Didn't take it seriously enough. It's a serious deal. We even have our own website! Coventry Carnival dot com."

"Pretty large power bills, then?" D-Kay asked.

"Mine sure is," Ruger answered pridefully.

Great, thought Darius.

After finishing the fourteenth hole, the foursome arrived at the next tee. "Listen, Darius," Ruger said quietly as the Scots teed off, "what lights the Rinaldis did put out you'll find in your crawlspace. Take my advice: get the good deals on lights early. Lowes, Home Depot, Target, Walmart—buy all you can. Christmas will be here before you know it." Ruger teed up next, and with a *whack!* drove an excellent drive straight down the fairway, one of many that day. "*Tempus fugit,* Darius. November 26, rain or shine."

"Thanks for the head's up, Kent," said D-Kay, teeing. *Whack!* "Dammit!" Ruger's motivational talk had caused him to slice left.

"Hard luck, Darius!" exclaimed Ruger. The Scots agreed.

Yeah, yeah, I get it, thought Darius. *I'm Happy Freakin' Gilmore.*

July turned into August and, like every August before, D-Kay didn't think about Christmas. But Kent Ruger, possessor of four cats, did. He brought over a large box of "extra" light strands (thirty-eight to be exact) for D-Kay. In combination with what Darius had discovered in the crawlspace while stashing some infrequently used items, he now possessed fifty light strings, plus a worn, inflatable snowman. *A shit-ton more than I plan to put up*. Ruger continued hammering away—*fu-tat!-fu-tat!-fu-tat!*—weekends and evenings through early November. The privacy fence made it impossible to see what he was building, but now that the leaves had dropped, he and Sandy could get a glimpse from their second-floor bath. The man was creating siege machines of some sort.

Two weeks before Thanksgiving, D-Kay chatted with the Horowitzes again about Ruger. "Kent really takes the whole carnival deal seriously, doesn't he?"

"Oh, yes," said Ben, "you don't know the half of it. Each season he builds something larger. The Post prints a picture every year, plus Trixie McPhane from Channel 4 does a segment. It's a big deal."

"But you guys just put out that menorah you talked about, right?" asked D-Kay.

Halle Horowitz began rummaging through her handbag. "Our sons will be over this weekend to set it up," she said, finding what she wanted. She showed him a nighttime picture: the Horowitzes' front yard was a sea of white lights surrounding an eight-foot-tall blue menorah with yellow bulbs for flames. There were lights on the house as well, but what really concerned D-Kay were the carloads of gawkers lining Coventry Lane.

Wow, better not have a heart attack in December, he thought, *'cause no ambulance will make it through that.* "That's a lotta lights, Halle."

"Not according to Kent," she said. "Are your lights ready, Darius?"

No, why would they be? he thought. *Turkey Day's two weeks away.* When he did put up his lights, it'd be at least a week *after* Thanksgiving, and even then, he'd no intention of putting up all fifty strands—that would be tacky. Stupid, in fact. *I'm not gobbling up gigawatts just so the unwashed masses can trap me in my own driveway. If the neighbors wanna follow Ruger the Yuletide Piper, that's great, but not me.*

But it really wasn't great. Though D-Kay was an intelligent man with many gifts, handiness wasn't one of them. If it couldn't be fixed with duct tape, he called the repairman. The ease at which Ruger flitted about his house exterior, bounding up extension ladders like a mountain goat, pissed him off. *Ruger showing off his siege machine blueprints. Ruger leaving 20%-off Ace Hardware coupons in my mailbox. The fu-tat!-fu-tat!-fu-tat! of Ruger's effing nail gun. And those jolly ho-ho-hos. Jesus, Ruger, you started that happy crappy the day after Halloween!*

Ruger pestered his neighbors, including the Kay's, to make sure "the Lane" would be ready in time, and the closer the calendar got to November 26, the jollier his ho-ho-ho-ing became. At last, Black Friday, the official start of the Coventry Lane Christmas Carnival light show, arrived. With Ruger's insistence, the neighbors had responded dutifully—though some, particularly D-Kay, groused at his henpecking. Everyone hung up their old standbys, with many adding new ones. To Ruger's glee, a dozen more homes had joined Carnival Row. It was now three blocks long, centered on the property line between his yard and the Kays'.

As colorful as everyone else's decorations were, they were small potatoes compared to what Ruger had created. Kent had constructed a huge Disney-esque spectacle—a surprisingly accurate miniaturized version of London Bridge and the Tower of London, each smothered with lightbulbs. *Jesus H. Christ,* thought D-Kay. Ruger's thousands of multi-colored lights blinked on and off, racing up and down the strands like squirrels. D-Kay had hired a neighborhood kid to put up a dozen strands and the worn snowman, nothing compared to Ruger's UFO beacon. To make matters worse, Ruger's lights were so powerful that Darius had to tack blankets over their bedroom windows just to sleep.

By December 1, traffic began clogging Coventry Lane. D-Kay complained to the police. "We're eating our Quaker Oats, but still, what if someone has a coronary?" The situation was deemed unsafe, but someone, probably Ruger, had pull with Reston's superintendent; police officer volunteers began controlling traffic. This helped, but it was still slow going, and now trash and frozen dog turds appeared on the Kays's sidewalk each morning, compliments of the gawking crowds.

Now it was a cold December Saturday afternoon and D-Kay had been on the phone for ten minutes arguing with his friend about the difficulty in heading north for tonight's EMBC meeting.

"Loo," said D-Kay, "all I'm saying is why can't the book club meet in Alexandria? The commute's killing me. Silver Spring's practically the other side of the planet."

In truth, Alexandria wasn't a whole lot closer but was at least on the Virginia side of the Potomac. Meeting there would save him from crossing the dreaded American Legion Bridge. But so far, Darius's complaining had done nothing but wind Spicotti up.

"Look dude," Loo said defensively, "you decided to live at the edge of the world 'where there be dragons' and shit."

"Well, *dude,*" replied Darius frostily, "the edge of the world's the only place I could afford to buy a house, so thanks for making fun of that!"

The cause of Kay's woes were two Eisenhower-era superhighways: I-95 and I-495. The first one, I-95, ran north-south along the eastern edge of the Nation's Capital. The second, I-495, budded out from the first like a pregnancy, surrounding the District of Columbia to the south, west, and north. The two combined formed the sixty-six-mile, six-lane loop known worldwide as the Beltway.

Darius Kay lived eighteen miles as the crow flew from his Maryland buddies. Traffic-wise, however, Maryland might as well have been Canada. To attend meetings, D-Kay had to cross the American Legion—a bridge whose resident trolls didn't eat commuters but consumed their time instead. When Loo was a teen, the loop was never as clogged as it was now: Dodge Caravans, Honda Accords, Freightliners, Yellow Cab taxis, and taco trucks. Loo knew that if D-Kay didn't hit the Beltway soon, he was screwed; a glowing sea of red taillights would separate him from tonight's meeting.

"Do you think the guys would read David Lee Roth's autobiography, *Crazy from the Heat*?" asked Loo, trying to lighten the mood. "Wouldn't that be great?"

"I dunno," D-Kay answered. "Still working on *Fear and Loathing*. Ten pages to go."

"You really do sound miffed, D-Kay," Loo said. "It's not just the hell traffic, is it?"

"No," Darius said begrudgingly.

"Want to talk about it?" asked Loo.

"No," said Kay. In addition to his problems with the real Ruger, he'd had a dream where Ruger felled a large tree on his property, sending it crashing through his privacy fence to land ten feet from where Darius stood. The dream had been very lifelike and unpleasant.

"Look, I gotta take care of something with my pain-in-the-ass neighbor. God and traffic willing, see you tonight at Shorties." They hung up.

Geez, Kay, Darius thought, *you really didn't need to give Loo the what-for. He's not the enemy. You know who the real enemy is—Ruger. You gonna do something about him or just whine? I mean, you've had enough, right? Enough of the Battle of Britain blackout curtains? Enough trash and doggie biscuits?*

"I've suffered this bastard too long," he said aloud. "And I know what needs to be done."

Darius went outside and deflated his snowman, putting it away in the crawlspace. He turned his Christmas lights off and went to the street to look back at his home. He was satisfied: his house was now a black tooth in Coventry Lane's otherwise festive grin.

Ruger knocked on his door shortly thereafter, asking if Darius had blown a circuit.

"You could say that," Kay answered.

Ruger gave him a measured look. "You turned your lights off on purpose, Darius, didn't you?"

Though he was no churchgoer, D-Kay said with complete equanimity, "Just keeping Christ in Christmas, Kent," then closed his door.

"The Lane won't stand for this, Darius Kay!" yelled Ruger. "It most certainly will not!"

Chapter 18: Say It Again!

Saturday, 12 December 1998
Wheaton, MD

THE ALLEY KILLER sat in Wheaton Regional Library's reading room perusing Saturday's papers. Per *The Post's* crime beat section, the Montgomery County police still had no lead on Prophet's killer. A re-hash article stated that a month ago Mark Marks had died from blunt force trauma to the head. This occurred during a late-night altercation inside the abandoned loading bay of the defunct Nelson's Paper Supply in Silver Spring. Initially, the police had canvassed the local businesses for witnesses—a man's shoe print was discovered outside the enclosure, different than the two sets identified inside, indicating a potential witness. But no one had come forward in the last four weeks, so though the investigation was still listed as "ongoing." The Alley Killer presumed correctly that the authorities had moved on.

He also knew that the witness really did exist. The killer started leafing through *The Washington Times* for updates, thinking, *I need to identify him.* In chasing the man down into St. Paul's basement, it seemed oddly lucky that the witness had been able to disappear into that large group of recovering alcoholics. Had the man, who'd run so fast that the Alley Killer almost lost him, *known* about that meeting? Was that why he'd headed there? If so, was he an AA member—a "regular" as it were?

As Trevor Pug believed, the Alley Killer had not gotten a good look at him, only knowing that he was young, or at least relatively young, and fast. But even in a room full of people that night, the Alley Killer was able to rule many of the attendees out, including women, men over forty, the infirm, and overweight. That still left a large number, however. *But I'll figure it out.*

Assuming the witness was an alcoholic, the killer had been returning to the same 10 PM Friday night meeting, each time eliminating more "suspects," shortening his list. For now, the as-of-yet unidentified man was maintaining the anonymity Alcoholics Anonymous was known for. He thought: *That anonymity needs to be permanent.*

Silver Spring, MD

The viciousness Rey would display later that evening had much to do with Mr. Jacobsen's inflammatory chatroom post. Rey wasn't mad at Mr. Jacobsen about it, however—heavens no. Mr. Jacobsen was a saint. He'd put up the article as an example of what was wrong with the country—it was the simpering liberal cocksucker who'd written "Bloodshed on the border—ICE uses unnecessary force" who Rey was mad at. What a joke! Violent criminals (illegals are, by definition, criminals!) needing protection from the under-funded, out-gunned American Border Patrol? Ha! The wetbacks weren't nice people, no-no. *I understand this better than anyone.*

Before December's EMBC meeting, Loo and Rey had by chance arrived in downtown Silver Spring at the same time, 6:45 p.m., at the same parking lot. They helloed and together walked toward Shorties up Nelson Street along a sidewalk lined with small businesses, including a pawn shop, a Vietnamese nail salon, and an El Salvadorian bodega. An ancient pickup with a bumper held together by bleached REAGAN '84 stickers was parked in front of the bodega.

Three Latinos wearing coats over spotted painters' outfits lounged in the bed of the tiny truck, a case of beer at their feet. Loud mariachi music played from the old Datsun's radio; one man with a thick grey mustache was holding forth in rapid Spanish. Loo saw them first and turned his head to avoid staring. Rey, displeased by the music's volume, glared at them. The men laughed loudly at something the man with the mustache was saying as Rey and Loo walked past. Loo thought nothing of this until realizing that Rey had stopped.

The energetic storyteller ceased speaking and regarded Rey pleasantly. "Hola, señor."

"What?" asked Rey. "Speak English."

The man's face became cautious. "Amigo," said the storyteller, "help you?"

"I'm not your amigo, pal," Rey replied.

"Let's go, Reymond," said Loo.

Rey ignored him, looking at the beer bottles. "So, you guys got jobs? You know, *jobs*. Employ-oh-*muuundo*."

Storyteller now looked worried.

"Rey, this isn't necessary," said Loo, concerned. *Why are you being a jerk?*

One of the two other Latinos said something to Storyteller along the lines of *don't make trouble* while the other became very interested in his own paint-splattered pants. Storyteller carefully hopped out of the bed, then reached into the cab to turn the music down. Pointing first to himself, then his compatriots, he said, "Paint. You need?"

"No, I don't *need*," Rey said. "Are you even legal?"

Storyteller again gestured to himself and his buddies, saying, "Green card."

"Sure, pal, whatever," Rey said, walking away, Loo gratefully falling in step with him.

Storyteller turned the music up again, muttering something Loo didn't understand, but whatever it was, Rey sure did. He immediately turned round, exclaiming, "*Dilo de nuevo!*" then returned to the rusting Datsun to tower over Storyteller. "*Dilo de nuevo!*" Rey repeated, then in English: "Say it again!"

Storyteller froze. Rey eyeballed him, then really let go, dressing the painters down in Spanish, mincing nothing, berating their immigration statuses, their work ethic, their mothers' fidelity. Storyteller and his friends look bewildered. Who was this tall, fiery gringo who insulted them not only in Spanish but in Castilian from the old country?

Loo understood none of this but knew that the tall, thin Reymond was built to change lightbulbs, not duke it out; he was going to get his ass kicked, or worse, Loo's. Rey continued yelling, challenging the other two men in English to get out of "their rusting piece of crap" truck and confront him. Loo nervously looked around the twilight-lit street: no witnesses. One of the Latinos in the bed jumped out, opening the passenger door quickly to leap inside and turn the music off. The second one followed, slamming the door behind him. Storyteller, who'd recovered from his initial shock, stood his ground, however, and began arguing back.

"Let's go," Loo said nervously, grabbing Rey by his bomber jacket, but he shrugged Loo off. Storyteller was now almost as heated as Rey, gesturing at Loo dismissively. *Listen to your friend! Move along!*

This incensed Rey, who pulled his wallet out to flash at Storyteller, screaming, "I-N-S! I-N-S! *Policia! Policia!*"

The tide immediately turned. Storyteller blanched, changing his tune. Looking desperate, he dove into the driver's seat, turning the engine over. The Datsun started up roughly, belts complaining, tailpipe belching smoke. As it sped away, it backfired.

Which Reymond found hilarious.

"Jesus, Rey!" declared Loo. "Was cussing out a bunch of Mexicans *necessary*?"

"*God* that was funny," said Rey, still laughing, "and yes, it was. And they're El Salvadorian, not Mexican."

Loo, flustered, said, "Rey, it's rude letting people think you can't speak their language when, in fact, you *can*."

"Got news for you, Luigi. These little brown bastards *assume* we don't understand them, so they talk trash behind our backs. Hell, sometimes in front of us, like that guy. He called me a stork with a stick up my ass. And he called *you* my girlfriend. If you wanna be insulted by government tit-sucking illegals, that's up to you, but I won't be."

"So, you feel good about that?" Loo asked pointedly.

"Sure do," said Rey, who began walking again.

Loo followed him reluctantly to the entrance steps down into Shorties. *Okay,* he thought, *though Rey seriously egged the guy on, that "girlfriend" reference stung.* No matter how badly addressed, did Rey have a point? In his interactions with Latinos—Loo managed crews of Park and Rec laborers, many of them Hispanic—were any badmouthing him under his nose? *Maybe. Maybe not.* The guys Rey had just insulted were possibly, okay, *probably* illegal, but to believe Loo's workmates, they were just escaping the crap economies and dangerous conditions of their homelands (being willing to work cheaply in the American shadows to do so).

Perkins, thought Loo as he watched a grinning Rey walk over to the club table, *you really are a stork with a stick up your ass.*

Rey mentally critiqued that night's meeting.

First and foremost, Tree Boy hadn't found his encounter with the El Salvadorians as funny as he had. *Thus, Loo, you threw mental daggers at me all night.*

Trevor had been a no-show—again. D-Kay brought up Prophet's "curse," which everyone laughed about. They were all supposed to get arrested, lose their women and their jobs, not to mention their lives, but so far, except for Splashdown's illegal weapon charge, none of that had happened. *Some curse. And old news.* Rey did learn something new that night; Splashdown was the "Takahashi" that had shot that thief in self-defense, something which impressed him.

Rey had dutifully read that night's selection and was happy when *Fear and Loathing* got all thumbs up. It had only received three for evil, however; the guys, Rey included, had expected more drug-fueled rampaging. Still, he'd enjoyed it much more than that detective travesty, *Pulp*. Next month's book would be *Crazy from the Heat*, David Lee Roth's autobiography. Rey didn't think it would be good, but he'd read it anyway.

All in all, not a terrible meeting, and Loo's daggers aside, yelling at those wetbacks had really made his evening.

Loo's restlessness woke Cindy up, something she resented as she was responsible for the bulk of Baby Joshua's night feedings. It was 2 a.m. and she had just fed and put him down, hopefully for the rest of the night, *so Mr. Husband, if you can stop thrashing about, Mrs. Wife, who is exhausted, would very much appreciate it.*

Loo continued moving, so she elbowed him, knowing it would wake him up and not caring. But something seemed wrong—Loo wasn't waking. He was muttering and sweating. *Do you wake someone up if they're having a nightmare?* Cindy wondered, but then Loo suddenly came to.

"What's wrong, baby?" she asked, concerned. Loo, gripping his sheets tightly, breathed loudly for a few seconds, then began settling down. "Nothing, Cin—just a bad dream."

"What about?"

"Me and my guys at work were, ah, clearing around one of the pavilions, and our woodchipper, it, well, sorta went wild and chased me."

"Scary, huh?" she asked.

"Yeah."

"That's what you get for watching *Fargo*, babe."

"Got me there," Loo acknowledged.

"You're back here with me safe and sound in the real world, Tree Man. No woodchipper."

"Good," said Loo, sounding much calmer.

The baby monitor started squawking. Joshua had not gone down as well as Cindy had hoped.

"I got it," said Loo. "I'm up anyway."

"Thanks, dear."

Loo went to the nursery and picked up his son, who struggled with gas. Loo walked him around, patting him soothingly until the child, looking vulnerable in his reindeer onesie, finally burped. *Like a champ*, thought Loo. "Uncle Trevor would be proud." The gas was now gone but Joshua's teething kept him unsettled, even after two renditions of "Strawberry Fields Forever."

Loo looked at himself in the nursery mirror: a tired-looking Italian-American man with brown hair holding a small infant with an adorable cowlick. *Future fat Sicilian geezer* was D-Kay's cut-to-the-bone physical description for Luigi, which was funny because the squat "DeVito" looked more Italian than Loo did, but that didn't mean Kay was wrong. One day in the not-too-distant future, Loo knew he would wander around family gatherings like his uncles did now, pinching babies' cheeks, asking "How 'bout this heat?" But for now, he still had cannons for arms—catching a throw from him was still a bruise waiting to happen. "Yes, I'll be a fat old man, one day," he told his son. "But not yet." He put Joshua down and watched him until he fell asleep. Relieved, he returned to bed to do the same.

Loo hadn't been the only club member to have a nightmare that week; they'd all been dreaming since Prophet cursed them. Henry still dreamed of playing chicken with the Peterbilt driver and Rey still waited anxiously as Gun Girl counted down his fate. D-Kay still dreamed of Ruger felling a tree "at" him; Darius was taking longer and longer to step out of its way. Phillipe dreamed of plummeting from a thirty-foot ladder while inspecting the hull of a Boeing 737. Luckily, he was falling toward some piled cartons and not the BWI tarmac itself. Gary had been dreaming that a bearded man was drowning him in his own bathtub. Ken had dreamt of standing in a row of aluminum bleachers watching a local high school game for *The Post*. During the imagining, a disagreement between a father and a ref turned ugly, with the angry dad shoving the ref into Ken, who lost his balance. As he fell, the angry man, who looked strangely familiar, yelled, "Told ya, starts with your dreams!"

Chapter 19: Keep Christ in Christmas

Saturday, 12 December 1998
Reston, VA

ON HIS WAY home from that night's EMBC meeting, D-Kay finalized his plan to further annoy Ruger. *A come-to-Jesus sign,* Darius thought. *Fantastic idea.* The task took two nights and three trips to Home Depot to complete. During this time his lights stayed off, and Ruger left messages: "Darius Kay! Don't disappoint the children! They come from miles away! They send Christmas cards thanking me, thanking *us!*" D-Kay erased every one.

When Kent's individual efforts failed, the "block boss" enlisted other neighbors to nag on his behalf. D-Kay, relishing the role of Scrooge, challenged them. "What's wrong with you people, are you fascists? Follow Herr Ruger if you want, but don't expect me to. I never signed up for this! If Ruger jumped off a cliff, would you dumbasses follow him?" D-Kay's abrasive taunts, sometimes delivered megaphone-style through an orange traffic cone, didn't endear him to his neighbors.

On Monday the 14th, up went D-Kay's crudely constructed sign: CHRIST, NOT CONSUMERISM, lit by one lonely spotlight and surrounded by cheap nativity figures he'd bought at Costco. The sign was seen by some as an unwanted lecture about how Americans overdid things, but others saw the Kays as courageous Christians, bravely tilting against godless consumeristic windmills. Still, even these people had a hard time accepting the semi-profane Darius as some sort of disciple, and anyone with active neurons had the question: if Kay had such a holy hair up his ass, why wasn't he venting his spleen at the light show puppet master, Ruger, instead of the good citizens of Governor's Landing? So, despite implied damnation, popular opinion swung back toward Kent Ruger. After all, hadn't Ruger brought fame to the block? (This year it was three blocks!) And what was a little electricity (okay, a *lot* of electricity) when the resulting light show brought with it TV's shapely Trixie McPhane? D-Kay was seen as a humbug, a Christmas curmudgeon too cheap to turn his lights on.

The Kays became Governor's Landing pariahs, but there was a small core of neighbors, including the Horowitzes, who supported them. After all, no one had elected Ruger grand marshal; there was no such position in the first place, and Ruger wasn't even on the HOA board. His zealous, Flanders-like manner embarrassed these people, as did his annual mugging for the Channel 4 cameras. Plus, wasn't Darius Kay saving the environment and defending the true meaning of Christmas, albeit with insults?

Ruger, a regular churchgoer, bought none of D-Kay's newfound piety. Neither of the Kay's cars ever left their driveway on Sunday mornings. *The nerve of that man . . . that pagan. Invoking the Savior's name like this means war!* To Kent Ruger, D-Kay's false witnessing and humbuggery guised as anti-consumerism was a call to arms, a battle between light and darkness, specifically between his glowing London light set-up and the dark eyesore of D-Kay's blacked-out house.

The next morning, Tuesday, December 15th, D-Kay's sign was gone, something he reported promptly to the police. Officers questioned Kent Ruger, who swore up and down that he wasn't responsible and seemed genuinely upset at being suspected. After fuming at his Compaq because it took forever for the dial-up whir to connect him to the internet, Ruger blogged about the incident on the CoventryCarnival.com website, describing it as an affront to the whole subdivision. This further pitted the neighborhood camps against each other, ardent Coventry Lane Carnival supporters versus the strange bedfellows of real Christians and environmentalists (of which D-Kay was neither). The poor Horowitzes supported the Kays, knowing Ruger for the Christmas bully that he was, but felt powerless to confront his cohort of supporters.

Luckily for all involved, the Kays left town on the 17th for a long-planned trip to visit Sandy's parents in Maine. The trip was usually a grueling affair sapping D-Kay's spirits—Dan and Gwen, his in-laws, were conversationally exhausting to the point that he took up "vacation" smoking just to have an excuse to leave the house.

Between the public rift with Ruger and the nightly carnival traffic, D-Kay figured ne'er-do-wells might be tempted to mess with his darkened house, so he installed a cheap security camera and posted a sign on his door: THE ELF ON THE SHELF IS WATCHING YOU, printed over the silhouette of a CCTV cam. He also asked Ben Horowitz to feed a non-existent cat as an excuse to come over twice a day to check on things. The night before leaving town, he installed another yard sign: KEEP CHRIST IN CHRISTMAS, proud that his printing skills were improving.

D-Kay's stay in Maine was made bearable by smoke breaks and dives into David Lee Roth's autobiography. The daily call to Ben Horowitz also helped. Ben had reported no issues—neither the Kays' home nor lawn was defiled in any way even though it was kept as dark as a tomb to continue sticking it to Ruger. Mother Nature provided additional security by snowing on

Governor's Landing midweek, a rare event for DC. In addition to lifting spirits, the snow meant that any would-be infiltrators would leave tracks.

Ben came over to the Kays' an hour before dark on Monday, December 21, to check on the house again. He never arrived later than 4 p.m.; with neighborhood feelings running as high as they were, even "feeding the cat" might prove risky after dark. There were no tracks from the night before, and the poorly lit sign still stood, surrounded by Darius's cheesy nativity set. Ben entered the house with the Kays' mail and did a quick walkaround. As he finished up, the front doorbell rang, scaring the bejeezus out of him.

It was Ruger.

"Hi, Ben. Heard the Kays were visiting out-of-town relatives. Collecting their mail, huh? Just my opinion, but two trips a day seems excessive. Is there something else bringing you over?"

Is there something else bringing you *over?* Thought Ben. He mentioned the need to feed the Kays' fictional feline, feeling guilty about lying.

"Feeding the cat? Good of you, neighbor. Funny, I heard Darius was allergic to the suckers." Kent leaned around Ben to examine a house he'd never been invited into. "So neighbor, took me a few days to learn the Kays were gone. Do you know when they'll be back?"

This wasn't top secret information, so Ben told him: tomorrow evening. Ruger chatted him up a bit more, smiling when he learned the Horowitzes would be away tonight as well visiting one of their sons. "I do hope the cat doesn't starve. I'd be happy to feed him since you won't be here in the morning. Say, why don't you give me the key?"

Ben built on his earlier lie. "I just put out extra food for him. I'm sure he'll be fine."

"Well, hope Fluffy stays off their Christmas tree!" said Ruger, not believing him. "My four are murder on the ornaments!" With that, he left, leaving Ben standing at the door, fingering the Kays' housekey uncomfortably, not liking the look in Kent's eyes.

The Horowitzes arrived home the next day, December 22, an hour before dark. After passing a Channel 4 News crew setting up cameras on Ruger's lawn, something happening every year now, the elderly couple pulled past the Kays' lot, only to be shocked: there were hundreds of tracks around their neighbor's house!

Gone was the second sign and gone was D-Kay's Costco plastic nativity scene. (Strangely, the figures had been replaced with larger ones of higher quality, along with a wooden background shed façade and haybales.) Gone too were D-Kay's anemic light strands. In their place, thousands of red and white bulbs, sure to make the house look like a giant peppermint candy if turned on. Ben traced the strands to their power source: snarls of cords plugged into the Kay's outside outlets, along with light sensors meant to trip when it got dark enough. *It'll be pretty, but it's still vandalism,* Ben Horowitz thought, *and Darius will go bananas!* The Horowitzes worried; should they call Sandy's mobile and break the news? (Calling Darius directly seemed unwise.)

Ben knew this was all Kent's doing, and since Ruger wasn't the kind of guy who could bus in out-of-town "help," other neighbors must have assisted. He hoped Darius's camera had recorded the offenders. (Later review revealed that the "helpers" wore Santa masks.) Removing the new light strands was out of the question—they'd been placed high on the house, so two old "elves" like the Horowitzes couldn't possibly undo what an army of presumably younger elves had done overnight. The situation seemed so unusual (and wrong), yet Halle hesitated to call the police: what would they say? Was it a crime to wrap your neighbor's house with Christmas lights? Should they confront Kent? They instead left a message for Sandy, which she didn't retrieve in time.

Sandy and Darius returned an hour later, just before dark. She had enjoyed herself well enough in Maine, but despite smoking as much as possible, a week of his father-in-law's political insanity had taken a toll on Darius. Although he'd sped the whole way, the return trip was still an exhausting nine hours. But matters were to worsen. At 5:15 p.m., trapped a block away from their house by looky-loo carnival traffic, the Kays watched their home suddenly light up like a neon candy cane.

"What the hell!" D-Kay yelled. His back spasmed, forehead veins bulged. Suddenly Darius desperately needed to kill someone, and at this point, pretty much anyone would do. Then he remembered his real enemy—Kent Ruger. "Sandy, stay here," he said, pulling over.

Darius burst from the car in search of the object of his derision. He took everything in, the tracks around his house, the new high-end Mary and Joseph collection, the strands and strands (and strands) of lights spun over his house like webbing, the second missing sign, the concerned look on Ben Horowitz's face as he emerged from his own house, and finally, Ruger, merry fucking Ruger, chatting it up with that curvy but annoying McPhane woman from Channel 4 News.

"Ruger, you bastard! You did this! I *know* it was you!"

Ruger gave D-Kay a beaming smile, one full of holiday cheer (and not a little impishness). He called out: "Darius, the devil didn't make me do it, Father Christmas did!" Then he laughed his annoying Ned Flanders laugh, as if everyone on Coventry Lane, Darius Kay included, was in on the joke.

But as his brain tried reconciling the good-naturedness of his prank with the fury in Kay's face, Kent Ruger's cheer changed to concern. As Kay got closer, Ruger began backing up.

"Darius, *buddy*, your neighbors were just trying to bring some holiday—"

D-Kay slugged Ruger, knocking him backward into one of the supports for the London Bridge, forcing the structure to involuntarily take a knee. Ruger collapsed, unconscious. For the benefit of family viewers, Trixie McPhane exclaimed "Dear God, is he alright?" but then stepped out of shot, mouthing "Tell me you got that" to her cameraman.

The man nodded, giving her a thumbs-up.

Chapter 20: It's My Cooler

Friday, 24 December 1998—Christmas Eve
Wheaton, MD

HEY, IT'S ME again, Trevor. If I sound subdued, it's because I'm in county lockup hurling my brains out. It's something I need to do very quietly—a real challenge. What happened? That bastard I invited to book club, Death Rey Perkins, is what happened, but I'm getting ahead of myself.

This all happened yesterday, Christmas Eve.

So my boss at Sim Systems 2000, Frank Deguzman, gives out bonus checks the day before Christmas—his holiday tradition. We're doing well, and though Frankie can pinch pennies, he's generous at the end of the year. Everyone, from team leaders like me down to the lowliest intern, gets one because hysteria about the pending Year 2000 meltdown's been quite profitable—clients are tripping over themselves getting through the door, all saying the same thing: *Don't explain the technological apocalypse to us, just save us from it.*

My team's been writing code like madmen—sixty-hour weeks—and after the New Year, the pace will pick up again. Carol's been dropping me off at work early. Frankie hasn't seen me so punctual in months—my bonus should be very good this year.

So it's the morning of Christmas Eve, and Frankie's donned a Santa hat to make the rounds through Cubeville to drop off checks for the rank and file. Big dogs like me, however, don't get *those* checks. Instead, we get invited to his office, which is great because in addition to getting the largest bonuses, this is how Frankie gives promotions.

So Frankie's finished distributing checks to the happy coder elves. It's taken a while, which is a good sign. It's now 11 a.m. and most people have already left for Christmas Eve. Six guys, however, including yours truly, are waiting outside Frankie's office. He invites us in based on bonus size, least to most. At first, I'm sweating, worried I'll be called in right away, but four other guys go in ahead of me. That leaves me and Death Rey to battle for first place. Frankie calls Rey in. I mouth "Ha-ha, sucker" and he mouths "Bite me." Fifteen minutes later, Rey emerges from Deguzman's office beaming like some maniac. *Okay, Rey, a big bonus for you—great. But not as big as mine's gonna be!* Deguzman calls me in.

"Merry Christmas, Frankie," I say. "How's it going?"

"Great, Trev. Merry Christmas. Have a seat."

I sit. Gone is Frankie's Santa hat. He looks normal now, which is to say a bit formal and stiff—think Al Gore trying to do the macarena. "Well, Frankie, you called me in?"

"I did, Trev. I have something for you," he says, briefly touching an envelope on his desk. I smile. "But first, I need your help with something."

"Okay, Frankie, you got it."

"Take a look at this." He hands over a green and white sheet of dot-matrix output. "Tell me what you think."

It's not unusual for Frankie to get a last bit of "added value" out of an employee before dropping a big promotion. It's a way for him to, you know, *remind you* who the boss is. I look the printout over. It's our own code, obviously the work of one of our new hires—guys not used to adhering to protocol, so it doesn't take long to find fault.

"Well, Frankie, there's some dupe code," I say, pointing. "There's a clunker subroutine here and half the stuff's not annotated, at least not correctly. After Christmas, you want me to talk to the mental midget responsible?" Overseeing smart but poorly documenting new guys is the responsibility of the Chief Coder, which happens to be the promotion I'm bucking for. I smile at Frankie again, waiting. He hadn't returned my first smile, and he doesn't return this one, either.

"Trevor, that's your code," Frankie says.

"My team's code?" I ask.

"No, your personal work."

If I was chewing gum, I would have swallowed it. I mean, there is *no way* this is my code. I wouldn't have written this crap even when *I* was still a newbie. There must be some mistake, or maybe it's just a joke. Deguzman's sense of humor can be perverse.

"That's not my code, Frankie. I code great. Hell, I'm your *best* coder. If this is a gag, Frank, it's not funny."

Deguzman looks out his window, then back at me. He says, "Take a look at the time stamp." I do. It was written four months ago. "Now take a look at the assembly log." Frank hands me a thick, three-ring binder. The assembly log's a 24/7 master list of what's being written, by whom, for whom, and on what machine. The data's generated in real-time, but Deguzman likes his three-ring binders; he's lined his office walls with them. According to the log, I wrote the code for Burtonsville Glass, one of my clients. I reexamine the printout and my stomach rolls because now the work's starting to look familiar.

"Did someone fake this?"

"Nobody faked it," Frankie says.

I'm stunned. I try to recover, be more honest. "Frank, maybe I've dropped the ball once or twice—"

"More than that, I'm afraid," Frank says. "And this isn't the worst example. At least the code you're holding works."

This is not good. "Well, Frank, I'll admit I was a little slack this summer," I say, "but lately you've seen me here what, ten, sometimes twelve hours a day?"

"True, Trevor," Frank says, looking out the window again, my envelope now in his hand. "You've been more punctual and that's great." The comment is positive, yet he still isn't looking at me. "Trev, the problem is your code's held together with spit and glue. We do alpha work here at Sim, and your work's not alpha, not anymore. Our product's alpha because we use QAQC procedures you helped develop, procedures you're not following anymore."

"Frank, I can talk to my team, push them harder—"

"Trevor, it's not your team I'm worried about, it's *you*. Yes, your work's improved recently, but honestly, not a lot. And the clients are complaining. The Burtonsville Glass guys say you haven't returned a call in weeks."

I hadn't seen this coming, but I can tack quickly when I need to. It's time to promise to knuckle down and bust my ass, not to mention my teammates' asses, to get back on Frankie's good side. I can do it. The way my finances are, I have to.

"Frank, *buddy*, look at me." But he doesn't look at me. He continues staring out at our parking lot. "I know we're slammed," I continue, "but I'll put it in high gear."

"Normally I would appreciate that, Trevor," Frankie says, head still turned.

I don't like where this is going, so I try humor. "I guess it's a no-go on that Chief Coder promotion, huh?"

Frankie turns back toward me with a small, pained smile. "I gave it to Perkins."

Well, that explains Rey's shit-eating grin. As the "Spain Guy," I didn't think Rey would even be considered for domestic management and I voice this.

"Yeah, it'll be a stretch," Frankie says, "but his new guy, Gonzales, a native speaker, will pick up Madrid." He turns back toward the window.

At this point, I'm starting to worry about my job. Not a lot, mind you; coders are the Red Bull-drinking, work-hard, play-hard types of the digital world—without actual physical labor. Programmers regularly push it too far, then crash and burn. When that happens, we send them home for a few days, maybe a week, to get their heads back on straight. We baby them 'cause we have to—retention's an issue. Since we can't brand our guys or make them wear cowbells, keeping them comes down to more money and, when necessary, sucking up to them.

"Okay, Frankie, Rey's got drive, I'll give him that. And it's totally your call, of course. So . . . I'll be his assistant?"

Frankie turns toward me, handing me my bonus envelope, which has a little snowman superimposed over the company logo, then turns away again.

"Am I gonna like this?" I ask. I presume it'll be a low-ball "punishment" bonus, the message being *Get back on the straight and narrow*. A small bonus sucks but I'll still take it, of course. Carol, back at the house with my monster-in-law (who at least drove her to work today so I could use the car), has given me strict orders to return directly home, no stops, so she can run the check to our ATM. I worry that a smaller bonus might dampen our Christmas Eve tradition—holiday "action"—but I'm not too worried as we've got a killer streak going. Cal Ripken's streak was 2,632 consecutive games so we're going for 2,632 weeks of nookie! Anyway, just as the Old Line parked their hogs in my front yard to get my attention, I will explain to Carol this is Frankie's way of doing the same. I open it. Inside are two pieces of paper. The first is the bonus check and *wow* was I wrong about good ol' Frankie! It's the biggest bonus I've ever gotten.

"Gee, thanks, Frankie!"

"Read the other paper, please."

"Okay."

It's brief and to the point: I've been terminated. The check isn't a bonus—it's a severance. "Now hold on, Frankie. What gives? I'll admit I'm having, well, a bit of a rough patch, but I helped build this company! No *way* you'd be where you are without me. You know that!"

"That's why the check's so big, Trevor," he says.

I continue protesting, but before I can really crank up the righteous indignation, Frankie cuts me off. "Trevor, the real problem's your drinking on the job."

"What? No! I mean I *schmooze* the clients, take 'em out for happy hour, which is what the guys at Burtonsville Glass expect—"

"That kind of drinking, in moderation, is fine. Here at the office, it's not fine."

"But I've never drunk on the job, Frankie," I insist.

"So, you've never drunk alcohol, here, at the office, during work hours?" asked Frank.

"Of course not."

Frankie looks away again toward the parking lot, then back at me. "You sure about that? Not even once?" The air in Frank's office now feels chilly. "I mean specifically here, onsite, just you," Frank clarifies.

"Frankie!" I plead, "I'm not a bottle-in-the-drawer guy!"

"I believe you there," he says, "because I've checked."

Great, I think, glossing over this invasion of privacy. "Then why are you asking?"

"Trevor, just stop talking for a minute and listen. This is important. Yes, or no: have you ever drunk here, on the job, by yourself?"

"No," I say authoritatively. And in the narrowest sense, it's true.

Frank's nostrils flair. "I say you have, Trevor," he says, "so that must make me a liar."

Oh no—the worst thing you can do is call Frankie a liar. He's *really* sensitive about that. I need to fix this because the discussion is no longer about my current job, which I've lost. This is about my *next* job. The IT world is smaller than you think. Guys talk—word about boozing will certainly get around. The smart thing to do, and I know it, I just *know* it, is to come clean, then do something theatrical, like ripping up the severance check. Or just get on my knees and bleat like a goat, promise to go to rehab, say whatever it takes to avoid getting blacklisted, because *c'mon, it's Christmas Eve for Christ's sake!* Frankie's not a monster—I might even keep my job if I grovel well enough, so the sooner I fall on my sword, the better.

But I don't fall on my sword. Here's why—I've been damn careful. I've never brought alcohol into the building. Ever.

"Now Frank, sure, there's been some beer at lunch—off-site—but drinking on the job? No way. I'm not a drunk. I mean, who would *do* that? If I did that, my work would suffer." The irony that my work has in fact suffered, which is why I'm in the principal's office in the first place, is lost on neither of us.

He sighs, then says, "I was hoping to avoid this." He rotates his screen so I can see it. He types briefly, pulling up a photo taken from the very window Deguzman's been looking through the last twenty minutes. It shows yours truly emerging from some bushes near my usual parking space. Something's in my hand. It's not the best picture; *I* know I'm holding a beer, but a jury could be convinced otherwise. Not that I'm on trial, but I sort of am. "Here's another," he says, tapping the keyboard. It's a photo of my Coleman cooler, the one I normally keep next to my barbecue. It's open: Pabst Blue Ribbon cans are floating in it. "I found that hidden in the bushes," he says. "Going to deny it's yours?"

How can I? It's got PUG written on the side. But still, it's not like I'm going out there three times a day or anything. I swear it's just for emergencies. I can't go out with the guys for lunch anymore, not on my Cub Scout allowance, see? So I eat my lunch at a nearby picnic table—maybe have a beer, maybe not. No big deal, but Jesus, Frank sure thinks it is.

"No, it's my cooler," I say. "I have a beer at lunch. *Occasionally*. I'm brown bagging it these days, Frank, so there's no time wasted driving to lunch and back. That means more office time, better for the company." It sounds lame, even to me.

"Drinking in the parking lot, in *December,* where anyone, including clients, can see you . . . that doesn't work for me, Trevor."

There's a long pause, as obviously Frankie's not buying what I'm selling. What's the saying? *When you're deep in a hole, stop digging*. Unfortunately, it's time to bow out as gracefully as I can.

"Can I have an hour to pack up my desk?" I ask.

"That's fine, Trevor. I'll help you."

Oh, that's swell of you, Frankie. Really swell.

I head back to my desk to find my computer gone. Not just the tower but the monitors, the mouse, the keyboard, the speakers, the *second* tower, and the knot of cords connecting everything together. Yeah, so it all officially belongs to Sim Systems, but Christ, what did Frankie think I was gonna do? Grab a tower and make a run for it? Adding insult to injury, someone has put cardboard boxes next to my chair. Seeing them, I wonder if there'd really been a chance of saving my job.

It's 2 p.m. on Christmas Eve, so everyone else is gone. He insists on helping me carry my boxes out to my car. We pack everything up, including my copy of *Crazy from the Heat*, as of yet unread. Is he helping me move my crap because he's a nice guy, or am I now just another disgruntled employee to be escorted around so I don't launch a virus? I carry out my last box; he follows me, locking the door behind us.

"Anything on the system you need, email me, and I'll burn it to a disc for you," Frank says collegiately. "Just ask." He shakes my hand, wishes me a Merry Christmas, of all things, then gets in his Beamer and drives away.

I put the last box in the car and wait for his taillights to disappear. When they do, I retrieve my cooler from the bushes. I'm completely on edge. *Just need something to settle my nerves.* The sentiment sounds familiar, and I realize it's what Prophet said to the Alley Killer before the poor guy got whacked. Some small voice in me, one I can barely hear, says I should be glad that unlike Mark Marks, I'm alive, but I don't listen to it. I down a Pabst. Then another. Then another.

Before I leave—security cameras be damned—I piss on the door.

The trip home sucks because all I can think about is how Carol will cook my balls when I get to the house. It'll be the complete show—tears, yelling, various renditions of *My mother was right.* And, oh joy, the monster-in-law will be there, too, smiling like a vampire!

I feel ashamed, stupid. *Why* hadn't I come clean? Surely all Frank wanted was for me to 'fess up so he could do something boss-like, like drive me to rehab or something. I mean, yes, I've been an eff-up, but I've been a *loyal* one. Surely, he appreciated that. The one thing he doesn't appreciate, of course, is being bald-faced lied to. I'm driving, fixating on my lie, repeating the conversation over and over, pretending I gave Frankie the non-career-ending *right* answer.

Well, Trevor, ol' pal, at least there's this fat severance check. It'll surely take the sting out of things with Carol.

I'm a mile from home and I see the ATM we use to do our banking. It's sandwiched between a Chinese restaurant and a liquor store. I pull in to deposit the check to make it a little easier on Carol. The least I can do, right? I get out of the car with it in my hand.

I don't remember anything after that.

Chapter 21: Camp Mimada

Wednesday, 9 March 1977—Day 7
Colombia, South America

THE REASON WALTER was still a miserable FARC captive on Day 7 was because of the bus trip he'd taken on the final day at the mine site when he was still a free man. The contest-winners had woken up for the return trip to Santa Marta and their flight back to Bogota, most of them genuinely sad to be going home. The departing vehicles left the Cerrejón mine site led by Señor Campeón and three security men in a Land Rover. Behind it came the Blue Bird bus with the children and their minder, Señor Barro. A second Rover with four more men followed the bus. Unlike the men in the front SUV, the men in the second Rover wore black fatigues instead of Intercor uniforms. Their Rover was covered with road grime, but Jack, up on his cars, pointed out its extras: a bull-bar, tinted windows, and a snorkel. "Big Oil springs for the best," he told Walter. Walter agreed, feeling safe: if one security vehicle was good, two were better.

Everything was fine until mid-morning. After the caravan had navigated a particularly tight turn in the road, the children riding in the front of the bus, including Jack, Walter, and Rosa, their friend from Madrid, were first to see the wreckage. The Rover-bus-Rover caravan slowed, then halted. A beat-up International Harvester truck coming from the opposite direction had slid into a roadside ditch, spilling its contents—large, water-filled plastic barrels—across the road. The locals present looked like all the "rurals" Walter had seen seeing since leaving Bogota—thin men and women wearing homespun clothes or mission donations. Four more locals were fiddling with a jack, trying to replace a blown-out tire.

Sr. Campeón and his head of security emerged from the lead Rover to assess the situation. The two guards accompanying them stood by the Rover, weapons lowered; breakdowns were common, and waving guns around unnecessarily wouldn't be helpful. Two of the locals, a young husband and wife, were yelling at the truck driver, upset at the loss of their barrels. They wanted him to help with the flat, but the man sat stone-faced, refusing to budge. The couple stopped harassing the driver once they realized strangers had arrived. They approached Sr. Campeón and his security man with relieved faces. *These authoritative men will put things right.*

Meanwhile, the weapon-holding guards stayed with the Rover, looking back toward the bus, waiting for two of the four men from the trailing vehicle to come forward. (Campeón's security chief had radioed them to do so—standard operating procedure for these situations.)

The husband, hat in hand, apologized profusely to Sr. Campeón in excited Spanish, not a word of which Walter understood. Rosa, having gotten close to him and Jack on the trip, interpreted for him. According to the apologizer, a well-built man with a handsome but severe face, the accident had occurred ten minutes ago. The husband explained that he and the other locals had paid the truck driver to haul much-needed water to a nearby farm. According to them, the driver had fallen asleep, crashing the vehicle.

Sr. Campeón listened intently, appeasing hands raised, trying to calm the man down.

But something seemed off to Walter. Liquid was still flowing out of several of the loose containers as if the accident had happened seconds, not minutes, ago. And if their water was so precious, why weren't they righting the containers, saving as much as they could, instead of letting it *glug-glug* onto the hardpan? Rosa looked anxious too.

Just then, something behind the bus exploded and everyone's ears popped. The Bluebird's body rocked, and its metal skin rang with gritty *pings*, sounding to Walter like a crashing beach wave. The children were terrified. In front of the bus, the husband produced a large pistol, jabbing it into Campeón's throat. He began yelling into the señor's face while his wife pushed a matching pistol into the security leader's chest. The forward Rover's armed guards, whose attention had been diverted by the explosion behind the bus, turned back again, finding their superiors' hands in the air. The four locals who had been changing the tire were moving forward, waving machetes. An unspoken agreement passed between the two guards; they slowly put their guns—what Jack would identify later as MP5 submachine guns—down on the hardpan and were surrounded.

"What's he saying?" a terrified Walter asked Rosa.

"He asked Señor, 'Who's on the bus?'" she interpreted.

"And?" asked Jack.

"He said just students, but the man says Sr. Campeón is lying . . . That the bus is full of oil people."

With his pistol still buried in the Señor's fleshy neck, the bandit shoved him toward the bus door, demanding the driver open it. Campeón shook his head at the driver—*No, do not let him in*. The bandit punched Campeón in the ear, and he cried out in pain. The bus driver, a bald, fat-faced man, eyed the outlaw coldly, then looked back behind him toward some commotion.

Barro had briefly heartened the children by pulling a gun from his own pocket. However, he'd immediately dropped it to the floor and was now trying to crawl out of an open bus window, completely ignoring the children's cries for help. The driver looked at Barro disgustedly, considered his options, then slowly opened the bifold door, letting the Pistol Bandit and his hostage in.

One look from the bandit said it all: a busload of children wasn't what he'd expected. He gave them a confused, angry look, then asked, "*Quien habla Inglés?*" Campeón, holding a bleeding ear, shook his head again. Pistol Bandit rapped him a second time, then parked him next to a dejected Sr. Barro, who'd sat down after realizing he couldn't fit through the window.

The air tastes smokey, thought Walter.

"*Quien habla Inglés?*" Pistol repeated.

"He wants to know who speaks English," Rosa said, raising her hand tremulously. No one else did. Pistol took one look at Walter and motioned him forward. Jack begged him not to go, and for this, he was called forward as well. Pistol led both boys off the bus and into the arms of his "wife," then began grabbing other light-skinned children, leading them forward toward the bifold door. He stopped to look down at the driver, whose eyes dropped in submission, but only just. Before Pistol could push another child off the bus, loud, rapid gunfire began, and a rural bandit in front of the bus collapsed.

"*Tomarlos!*" yelled Pistol to his "wife." She rushed Walter and Jack to the relative safety of the roadside ditch, then grabbed the collar of her wounded companion, pulling him in. More gunfire broke out and the children on the bus crouched, ears covered, screaming in fear.

The gunfire briefly paused. The driver swung unexpectedly into action, first shoving a surprised Pistol off the bus with his boot, then slamming the bifold shut, grinding his gears, launching the Bluebird backward (and everyone in it forward). The bus's back bumper smashed into the wreck of the rear Rover which Walter later learned had been hit by a rocket-propelled grenade. The Rover, whose tires were burning, squawked angrily, resisting movement, but the driver continued flooring it, praying that he wouldn't ride the Bluebird up over it and stall out. The Rover's burning frame finally began shifting. A barrage of gunfire erupted again from where the bus used to be, along with heavy-throated shouting. Bullets pocked the Bluebird's grill.

"Well fuck me dead," Jack said to Walter as they huddled together in the ditch, "we're defo in it now, Bruce." Walter, sheet white, was too scared to reply.

It was now a week later: Day 7. While the boys continued watching the FARC assemble that night's camp, Walter told Jack about the earlier incident with the poop-throwing monkeys.

"My God, Bruce, that's ace, simply ace!" declared Jack.

Despite the beginnings of an adult's barrel chest, fourteen-year-old Jack was short, barely eye to eye with his captors. All week long, the Australian had been walking the line between respect and submission, and submission was winning. The jungle, as well as the teen soldiers' bullying, had battered his normally can-do spirit.

Jack ran his hand through his bristle-brush hair. "Bruce, do what they say. This isn't *The Great Escape*."

No kidding, thought Walter, who'd been hearing this from the Aussie all week. "I'm *terrified*, Jack. I'll do whatever they tell me. Problem is I can't understand a word they say."

This wasn't entirely true, but seven days and nights into what his parents and future counselors would call the "ordeal," Walter barely understood any Spanish.

Jack Sparks, on the other hand, had a gift for languages and was picking it up quickly, asking repeatedly for *las palabras nuevas* (new words). Walter asked him why he was so determined to learn "the enemy's" language.

"They won't kill someone they've bothered teaching to speak," Jack answered. "You should try harder." It was an excellent point, but Walter resisted; the weeklong ordeal had taken its toll, pushing his mind back to a childish, sulky state. *The marching's endless*, he thought, *and on top of the snakes, scorpions, cockroaches, mosquitoes, tarantulas, and biting flies, I have to learn a new language? And adolescents with guns, of course—can't forget them. And the ants. Oh my God, the ants! They're everywhere!*

The FARC finished the boys' sleeping area, a plastic sheet strung between two trees, then moved on to other tasks. Jack and Walter hung their hammocks underneath and crawled in, falling quickly asleep. Jack's sleep was dreamless, but Walter found himself following the boots, following the boots, marching forever.

The boys were awoken the next morning with rifle prods. After brushing insects from themselves and peeing, they were given cups of sugary Frutino the Green Jaguars brewed each morning, plus a piece of bread and a plantain each. After eating, they shouldered rucksacks for the day's march. Walter feared Day 8 would be no different than the previous seven: march—lunch—march—collapse.

The day, however, turned out quite different. First, there was an incident involving Gomez, the guerilla who'd been shot in the leg during the bus attack. The sixteen-year-old was being carried on a lashed-together *tabla* stretcher by four rebels. A week of infection had finally broken what Walter would learn was called *machismo*; Gomez began crying so loudly that Camarada Sebastian (the attack's pretend husband) had to gag him.

Then about midmorning, Walter witnessed a particularly large, poisonous *riacha* (snake) surprise the two guerillas clearing trail, biting the foot of the first, Gustavo, Camarada Sebastian's brother. The other guerilla was Sebastian's flirty but vexing thirteen-year-old sister, Tatiana, who immediately and emotionlessly chopped the snake's head off. After determining the riacha's fangs had not completely penetrated her brother's rubber boot, she held the headless animal up, smiling—*just another day in the jungle, boys*—then looped it around Gustavo's neck.

"*Muy bien, mis hijos,*" said La Madre proudly as she pushed to the front of the column; anything remotely edible would go into tonight's dinner. Gustavo ignored his sister's posturing, looking put out. From body language alone, Walter understood Gustavo's next words as *Why do I have to carry it?* For Walter's benefit, Tatiana pantomimed her response to Gustavo: *Because it bit you, not me.* She smiled slyly at Walter, then began cutting line again.

At noon, La Madre's group met up with another FARC platoon, *Los Jaguares Rojos* (the Red Jaguars). La Madre spoke with their leader while his Reds stared curiously at the captured gringos. Jack caught enough to piece together that the Rojos had recently skirmished with a local paramilitary group, *Los Fantasmas* (the Ghosts), who were competing with the FARC for regional control. The Rojos were putting on a brave front, but Jack could tell that whoever these Los Fantasmas were, the guerillas were afraid of them. Before parting, the Reds gave La Madre's Jaguars a crate of rocket-propelled grenades to hump back to basecamp.

Despite the news of the paramilitary "ghosts" and Gomez's painful, muted cries, the Jaguars' mood was lifting. Today they would finally reach *La Finca Mimada*, the "Pampered Estate"—the FARC basecamp where the boys would be held until ransoming could be finalized. Arrival at the oft-promised camp brought tears to the Caucasians' eyes. Hernandez and Jacinto, two captured Colombian soldiers who the Greens were also escorting, were less enthusiastic, having been to this camp twice before.

They looked at the wet-cheeked gringos fatalistically, knowing well their government's policy on ransoming soldiers: it was never done.

The Mimada, as the boys called basecamp, was indeed luxurious compared to the drop-and-sleeps of the previous seven nights. There were over a hundred other soldiers based here: the Red, Yellow, Blue, White, and Black Jaguar platoons, who, along with La Madre's Greens, made up the complete Jaguar Company, *Los Seis Jaguares* (the Six Jaguars), plus a half-dozen captured Colombian Army prisoners of war, including Hernandez and Jacinto. With the addition of the Green Platoon, Jack estimated Camp Mimada's population at a hundred twenty men. The camp was laid out in pods, one per platoon, each with its own collection of *coletas*, permanent thatch-roofed platforms with no sides (only latrines had actual walls). Walkways of hand-cut tablas linked the pods to a large common area housing a small water tower and an outdoor kitchen, what Jack called a commissary, complete with foodstuffs and butchered cow carcasses. *Javelinas* (wild pigs) and dogs roamed freely. Mimada quietly bustled behind protectively thick vegetation, every part of the camp carefully constructed to blend in with the saman, ceiba, and rubber trees.

"We're invisible from the sky, Bruce," Jack said, looking up. Walter nodded dejectedly. If government helicopters were looking for the boys, they wouldn't be seen.

Camp Mimada was run by a squat, pot-bellied man in his late forties named Lt. Buscar. The lieutenant debriefed La Madre and Camarada Sebastian, then inspected the prisoners, starting with the POWs, turning a cold eye toward Jacinto and Hernandez. "*De nuevo?*" he asked. (Again?)

He'd forgotten that the FARC's eastern commander, an imposing man named Mono Jojoy, had ordered him to house these two POWs again. It was routine to rotate prisoners between camps; this would be the army POWs' third stay at Mimada. The lieutenant flicked his eyes toward Camarada Sebastian, who led them away, then looked speculatively at Jack and Walter, his two fair-skinned cash cows. *Unplanned cows that should have been industrialists, not children.* Buscar cleared his throat, beginning a short monologue about la Finca Mimada's rules, translated into passable English by a young woman named Camarada Luciana Cruz standing beside him.

"We are here to protect you. Negotiation underway for your release. You will be provided clothes and personal things. Stay quiet. Behaved prisoners get fed, bad ones, no. Stay in coleta unless told to move. You will be under guard always, and at night, chained. Try escape—you will be killed. If *Los Jaguares* attacked, you will be killed." After a pause, the lieutenant added, "You will get education."

"Bruce," Jack said afterward, "we're still defo screwed, but less so now I think."

Walter nodded, asking, "Did the lieutenant say *chains*?"

23 March 1977—Day 21

The boys spent the next two weeks playing by Camp Mimada's rules. Daytime quickly became routine: release from leg irons by 6 a.m., escort to a foul-smelling latrine the boys coined "Big Stinky," then another escort to the commissary area to eat. They looked forward to breakfast—variations of fried bread, eggs from local farmers (fish soup if there weren't enough eggs), and charred bacon butchered from pigs who hours before had been happily grunting. The boys passed on the FARC's bitter coffee in favor of Frutino, the trail juice the guerillas made even more enamel-destroyingly strong at base camp. The food tasted okay, some of it actually quite good, but there wasn't enough of it. Breakfast—all meals, in fact—never quite filled their bellies. They would remain skinny through their ordeal, becoming markedly so by the end.

The next stop was school for "correct political thinking." It was held in a ten-by-twenty coleta in the middle of the common area. Like all coletas, this one was an unwalled platform with a thatched roof. On it sat several rough-cut benches. Buscar or La Madre (referred to as Camarada Ruiz—the "comrade" title was mandatory in camp) gave the lessons, short speeches which Camarada Luciana Cruz interpreted for the boys. Other than their physical attendance, the "indoctrination" (Jack's word) wasn't forced, and the boys, who the Lieutenant referred to as *los reys gringos*—the white kings, by which he meant powerless chess pieces—were encouraged to ask questions, which they sometimes did. No matter how odd the boys' inquiries were, Lt. Buscar and Camarada Ruiz tried their best to answer, treating the young capitalists as if there was still some hope for them. Their informational talks included outlandish pronouncements—for instance, Americans were being irradiated by their own nuclear warheads—and made for interesting discussion.

More often than not, however, Buscar and La Madre were busy with camp matters. During these times, Camarada Luciana Cruz read communist tracts to them instead. Cruz's English was only fair, but the boys didn't mind this. She seemed more interested in improving her English than teaching Marxist theory anyway, so the three spent time polishing their respective second languages.

A week in, with her mother's reluctant permission, Camarada Tatiana Ruiz, Sebastian's young sister, was allowed to attend "school" to improve her English as well (under the assumption that two frightened, heavily guarded gringos weren't likely to molest her). Despite the public setting, Tatiana, sexually untested and unhappy about it, enjoyed getting handsy with the gringos, sitting behind them, rubbing their backs. She paid special attention to Rafa, the tall American boy, whispering breathily into his ear, making him blush.

"Hard to learn when you're cracking a fatty, isn't it, Rafa?" Jack later teased.

"Yes, that's true," answered Walter. "And call it a 'boner' like normal people." Their assigned guards, the entire camp, in fact, found Tatiana's boy torture highly entertaining.

The Anglo and the Australian continued learning Spanish. Jack absorbed everything like a sponge, including the bane of junior high English, conjugation. Walter struggled but made progress.

After morning lessons in *pensamieto político correcto*, they were returned to their coleta where Jack walked circles around it. Walter sometimes joined him. At lunch time, sides were predictable, bread and plantains, but the entrees weren't. Fish head soup, roasted javelina, and beef stew were commonly served, but there were outliers. On Day 21 of captivity, for instance, the boys ate buttered ocelot. Lunch stretched for two hours. Off-duty guerillas played cards or napped or listened to AM radios set at low volume. Since Walter and Jack were technically hostages, not prisoners of war, they weren't forced to work like the POWs were and therefore had their afternoons free to sleep, tread the rutted trail around their coleta, play checkers, or write letters home. Lt. Buscar encouraged letter-writing as a form of propaganda and possible ransom enhancement, mailing the boys' letters every few weeks.

17 April 1977—Day 46

Sometimes in the afternoons, the captives watched the FARC play shirts-and-skins fútbol in a small clearing reasonably shielded from aircraft. The FARC soldiers had fast feet, artfully moving a ball back and forth between two crude goalposts. Today, Day 46, the off-duty guerillas found themselves short two men. On a whim, they motioned for the captives to play. The uncoordinated Walter hated sports and tried begging off but was unsuccessful. Jack, on the other hand, joined without hesitation. They were put on the "shirts" team.

Walter was bad from the get-go. Rafa (everyone called him that now) found himself quickly assigned goalie duty where his five-eleven body might do some good. Jack's frame, however, a short but stocky torso on muscled legs, served him well. He was a good player who spun easily, reminding Walter of the Looney Tunes Tasmanian Devil character. For Jack, the game was fun; for Walter, it beat the monotony of swatting at flies. Within minutes, Jack's prowess earned him a promotion to forward where he did well, scoring against the "skins," putting the shirts up by one.

With ten minutes to go, Camaradas Sebastian and Gustavo walked by, not pleased to see hostages playing fútbol. The Camarada said something to his younger brother, and Gustavo promptly removed his shirt, replacing one of the skins. From then on, the skins, led by Gustavo, played harder, but more importantly, dirtier. Any shirt supporting the Australiano was shoved or tripped. Jack dug in, rising to the challenge. Despite being stiff-armed and kicked in the Achilles by Gustavo, he continued playing well.

When it became apparent that no amount of rough-housing on Gustavo's part would intimidate the more skillful Australian (who by this time had scored again), he sucker-punched Jack in the face, then began yelling curse words that by now even Walter understood. Walter helped Jack up, horrified by the boy's broken nose. He led him quickly back to their coleta, away from the savage, gloating Gustavo. Gustavo kicked the ball into the shirt's now-vacant goal, demanding the game continue. The remaining players, however, walked off the field, disgusted.

Before that evening's dinner, Lt. Buscar walked swiftly to the boys' coleta, barking the Spanish equivalent of "No fútbol for gringos," then strode away.

Chapter 22: Twenty Questions

Saturday, 25 December 1998—Christmas Day
Wheaton, MD

HEY, IT'S ME. After last night's blackout, I ended up here—here being the Wheaton Precinct headquarters of the Montgomery County Police Department. Specifically, I'm in its holding cell where I'm trying to barf quietly into a steel toilet because I feel awful, like ten pounds of crap in a five-pound bag. There's only one commode for twenty of us, by the way, and the only thing more difficult than barfing quietly is doing so with an audience.

The others with me think I'm slacking because I'm hunched over the bowl instead of manning our "human wall." See, we've been blocking the guards' view of the back of the holding cell so a guy with a Sharpie can finish the mural he's working on. They pat the prisoners down pretty good. I wonder where he hid the Sharpie.

A guard has just announced that my bail's been posted, the first good news in the last twenty-four hours. This holding cell smells like vomit and anxiety, and I'm certainly ready to leave it, but I take a quick look at the mural the Sharpie guy's putting the finishing touches on: it's Santa wearing sunglasses with an old-time Western kerchief over his mouth. St. Nick's holding up a liquor store, pointing a massive .38 at a scared-looking clerk. Through the store's window, Rudolph can be seen sitting in a getaway sleigh. It's really quite good.

"Let's go," the guard says impatiently, letting me out. The remaining cell occupants continue blocking Bad Santa from view.

After getting my wallet, cell phone, belt, and shoelaces back—but not my license—I ask what's next. The guard hands me a gym bag. "Your wife and your mother-in-law left that for you." Inside are clothes, toiletries, and a brief note:

I'll tell you when you can come home.

Oh boy. Carol's surely pissed about me being charged with a DUI, no doubt about that, and Gladys Edock, my monster-in-law, must be *thrilled* I've effed up so badly. I've taken the guards' word about the driving under the influence charge, by the way, because I don't remember anything after the ATM. Nothing. If you can believe the police, I was involved in an accident. The cops say I hit a car. Luckily, it was a parked car. Unluckily, it was a parked *police* car. They say I hit it so hard it slammed into a second parked vehicle, also a police car. That car, in turn, hit a *third* car, which was—wait for it—another police car. It gets better: the third vehicle had an actual police officer in it. In addition to spilling his coffee, he may have whiplash. I'm being arraigned Monday.

This information about the three-car pileup—four if you include my wife's vehicle—was conveyed to Carol at about two this morning. As you might imagine, she took a dim view of things. Apparently, according to a sniggering jail mate, I had called her from lockup, telling her the last thing I remembered, which was trying to deposit the check. "How?!" she'd screamed. "I have the ATM card, you idiot!"

I'm outside the police station now. Had to duck behind some bushes to vomit again. God my head hurts. It's Christmas Day and I have two dollars to my name. No credit cards, no license, and no home to go to. "Fuck me" doesn't seem to cover it.

I start calling my single buddies, looking for a place to stay, though I don't call Rey. That promotion-stealer can suck it. None of my buddies pick up. My cell phone dies, so I walk to a 7-Eleven to get change for its payphone. I call every remaining single guy I know, but no one answers. It's Christmas—where *is* everyone? I'm down to my last thirty-five cents. There are two pieces of paper in the billfold of my otherwise empty wallet, plus the severance check. The first has the phone number for Old Line's clubhouse in Waldorf written on it. Calling Old Line's an idea that can also suck it, and *why* do I have that number, anyway? The second is a card with the name *Cisco Arkin*. The guy from that AA meeting.

I'm desperate, so I call him.

"Hello."

"Cisco?"

"This is Cisco Arkin. Who is this?"

"Uh, my name's Trevor, sir. We met at St. Paul's." There's a pause like maybe he doesn't remember me. I add, "Reggie called me 'Bud.'"

"Yes, I remember now. You in trouble, Trevor?"

"You could say that."

I explain my situation. Cisco agrees to pick me up. I'm relieved. He pulls up outside the 7-Eleven an hour later. He lets me in but doesn't say anything, just looks at me. I stare back, fully remembering him now from that crazy AA meeting that Reggie coddled me through.

Mark Marks' murder suddenly comes to mind. I keep thinking about him and how violently the poor bastard died, and how I heard his skull . . . cracking. This will sound bad, really bad actually, but I wish I'd drank more that night, then maybe I would've blacked it all out. But no, I remember everything.

Cisco asks, "You done throwing up?" I say yes, but he's dubious, handing me a plastic bag. "Puke in that, not in the truck. Got it?" I nod. "Stay here," he says, then he goes inside the store, returning with a six-pack of Budweiser, handing me one. *Well, this is a surprise,* I think. Without further thought, I pop it, down it, then throw the can out my window.

"Pick that up, Trevor," Cisco says sternly. I look at him like littering isn't the most heinous crime I've committed recently, but the truck doesn't move, so I get out and put it in the trash. "Now we can go," Cisco says, flipping his headlights on.

We talk. I bring him up to speed on the last twenty-four hours. Apparently, I've been making some poor life choices (perhaps the understatement of the year). He listens, nods. He says that if I can follow some simple rules, I can stay one night in his basement. I'm out of options, so I say yes. My stomach spasms, I clutch the bag, but it passes.

We arrive at his house in some neighborhood I've never been to, but we don't go through the front door—we go around to the cellar entrance, down some stairs lit by a yellow bulb. Inside is a modest, finished basement: a worn but serviceable-looking couch, a coffee table, a small kitchenette with a table and two chairs, a minifridge underneath the kitchenette counter, and an old AM/FM radio on top of it. Low pile carpeting everywhere. There's a shelf with self-help books, mostly AA-themed, plus a bunch of mini-magazines called *The Grapevine,* and dog-eared paperbacks, mostly Westerns. There's also a door to what I presume is a bedroom. I've seen worse, but without a TV, stereo, or pool table, it's no man cave. Oddly, there are also two sets of aluminum letter boxes mounted on a wall like you'd see in the lobby of an apartment building. Most have name tags.

Cisco sees me staring. "My sponsees use them. Think high school gym locker."

"Oh," I say.

"Have a seat," he says, motioning to chairs tucked under opposite sides of the kitchenette table. "Need another beer?"

"No, I'm fine," I say, but my hands are shaky. They've been shaky since leaving lockup. He takes a beer, opens it, and puts it in front of me, and the aroma of hops overwhelms me. A voice inside me says, *You must drink this.* I don't like this voice, but I listen to it. For appearance, I drink as slowly as I can. Cisco goes to the minifridge, retrieving soft drinks for us.

"Curious about the Budweiser, Cisco. You're an AA guy, right? Why do you still buy beer?"

"So guys suffering from acute alcohol poisoning don't die in my basement," he says.

I look down at my now empty can of beer. *Pretty sure he means me.*

Cisco gives me a contemplative look, then asks, "So, Trevor, who put you in lockup?"

"Uh, the police?"

Cisco looks disappointed. "Did you have anything to do with it?"

"Sure, I guess."

"You guess?" he asks. "Let me understand this. Your boss fires you for drinking on the job. You get blackout drunk and blow three times the legal limit. That's after wrecking not one, not two, but *three* police cars—one with Montgomery County's finest still in it—plus your wife's car. Correct so far?"

Well, you don't have to be a prick about it. "Yes."

"Naturally, law enforcement being down three Crown Victorias is displeased, so they arrest you. Your wife posts bail, then throws you out. As you sit here, you're so hungover you've got *delirium tremens,* and need alcohol so that you don't shake apart. Do I have any of this wrong?"

You're batting a thousand, I think, hating it.

"And that's just the last twenty-four hours," Cisco continues. "So tell me, how was everything before that?"

Hey old man, stop being so heartless! But he waits for details. Grudgingly, I relay the highlights of the last several weeks, ending with how Old Line now owns me.

"Old Line?" he asks. "Small world." He continues asking gap-filling questions: *How long have you been married? First marriage? Kids? Been arrested before?* It's not an interrogation per se, it's more like going over a job description (my life) that I realize I might not be qualified for. When he's done, he sucks in his breath, saying, "Trevor, your butt's on fire. Agreed?" I nod. "You want help putting out the flames?"

"Sure," I say, looking at the aluminum mailboxes. "Will I get one of those?"

"Depends," says Cisco.

"On what?"

"On whether you think you're an alcoholic or not. Are you?"

It's a trick question: do I say *no* and risk getting pitched out in the night, or do I say *yes* and have to listen to a bunch of AA shrill? "Do *you* think I'm an alcoholic?" I ask.

"Makes no difference what I think," Arkin says. "It's what you think that matters."

"But you're an expert," I say. "You got an opinion, right?"

"My opinions aren't your business."

What kind of answer is that, Captain Conundrum?

Cisco goes to the bookshelf and returns with a pamphlet and a pencil. "This might be helpful."

There are twenty questions. Here's a sample: *Do you ever drink more than you plan to? Has alcohol affected your friendships? Have you lost work due to drinking? Have you ever had a blackout?* I give myself the benefit of the doubt, but still have to mark *yes* several times. "So what's bad?" I ask. "Fifteen yesses?"

Cisco cracks a smile, the first one I've seen him use. "Rule of thumb is six or more and you may have a problem. How'd you do?"

"I'd rather not say."

"Fair enough," Cisco says. "First time I took it, I had twelve yesses. My sponsor said six was bad, so I changed seven answers." He takes the marked-up pamphlet without looking at it and puts it in an unused mailbox, closing it, giving me the key. "That's yours. If you decide you're an alcoholic, you keep it. Decide you're not one, return it. Deal?" Seems straightforward to me, so I say yes. "That pamphlet," he says, "any one question concern you more than the others?"

"'Have you ever been in trouble with the law while under the influence?' I think my 'accident' qualifies." Cisco nods. It's a *been there, done that* look I find annoying.

"What? Don't tell me you can beat that, Cisco," I say.

The old coot's still smiling. "Your three-cruiser hattrick is colorful," Cisco says, "I'll give you that, but you're still bush league."

"Really," I say, insulted. "I probably put a cop on disability. What beats that?"

"Vehicular homicide," says Cisco.

Okay, that very much does beat it. Now I feel like a jerk.

Cisco looks at the wall clock: 9:30 p.m. He yawns. "It's late," he says. "I'm going upstairs. No TV down here, but there's plenty to read. Listen to the radio if you want, just keep it low. There's tap water plus sodas in the fridge. I put another beer in there. Suggest you drink it right before bed. There's a bathroom off the bedroom. We'll talk more in the morning. Goodnight, Trevor."

"Okay, goodnight," I say, then watch him ascend creaky wooden steps.

As soon as the upstairs door closes, I fish the beer out and drink it. I think about turning the radio on, but don't. I think about reading something, but I don't do that, either. I examine the bedroom and bath. Both are clean, but it's not the Ritz. I think about brushing my teeth, but pass on that as well, instead collapsing onto the twin bed.

I missed Christmas for crying out loud! What's Reesie going to think? What excuse did Carol give her? "Grandma got run over by a reindeer. So did Daddy."

I sleep okay at first, but then I start dreaming that I'm Mark Marks, collapsed in the alley behind Shorties, dying. I can feel his terror. It's . . . what's the word? *Visceral.* The nightmare wakes me up. A tiny voice inside me says, *Better him than you.* Another voice says, *Are you sure about that?* I'm shaking, from the dream, the DTs, or the little voices—I don't know. There's no more beer but maybe a soda will help. I go to get one and lo and behold, there's another beer behind the sodas! Cisco must have miscounted, or perhaps he hid it on purpose, so I'd pace myself. I don't care how it got there; I down it.

Saturday, 26 December 1999

In the morning, I still feel rough but have stopped shaking. Cisco brings down some breakfast. I manage to eat a little. When I'm done, he says, "Okay, it's the day after Christmas. What's your plan, kid?"

Pissed or not, I tell him I need to get Carol the severance check.

"We'll drop it off after a meeting," he says.

"Sure," I say, "that'd be great." Going to a meeting won't be great, but I've got no wheels and no home at the moment, so I don't have a lot of choices. I don't even know where I am.

"You're gonna need a lawyer. Got one?"

I say no. He recommends a woman named Janice Bees, giving me her card. "Follow her directions *to the letter*. First thing she's gonna tell you: go to AA meetings every day and get signatures." It's an excellent idea, but I tell him I don't know where or when any AA meetings are. From the shelf, he grabs another pamphlet. This one is titled, oddly enough, "Where and When." It's a listing of local meetings, organized by day of the week. "Go to meetings with an *O* by them," Cisco says. "The *O* stands for an open meeting—anyone, non-alcoholics included, can go. Don't go to *C* meetings yet. Closed meetings are reserved for folks who can admit they're drunks, so unless you're comfortable saying 'My name is Trevor and I'm an alcoholic,' don't go. Understand?"

That won't be a problem, I think, as I'm not a drunk.

"The meeting we're going to is at noon. Be ready in an hour. If you take a shower, hang the towel back up. I don't want to find it on the floor."

He takes the dishes upstairs. I shower. My phone is charged now, so I call around again, this time getting a hold of Phillipe. I'm relieved: he says I can crash on his sofa. I leave a message with Janice Bees the Lawyer's answering service. She calls back, instructing me, among other things, to attend daily AA meetings and get signatures. Cisco yells down, "Ready to go?" I say yeah, thinking, *Let's get this over with.*

On the way to the meeting, which is called "High Noon"—each meeting apparently has its own name—Cisco asks more questions, but not the important one, which is *How am I gonna patch it up with Carol?* All he wants to know is what I'll be doing for the next twenty-four hours. I tell him that other than this High Noon meeting, my schedule's pretty clear. He talks more about the program of Alcoholics Anonymous and my "cult" radar begins pinging. Truth is, it's been pinging since last night. Color me paranoid, but this "program" stuff sounds a lot like what my brother Willie latched onto before he died. Too late we saw the signs: an isolated, controlled environment (like Cisco's basement), specialty literature (like "Twenty Questions about Your Drinking"), and a charismatic leader (probably not Cisco—Captain Conundrum's not a smooth talker). The last step for any cult victim is surrendering your money and possessions—all of it and all of them. When will they ask?

Okay, so AA's probably not like those Heaven's Gate whack jobs who "cleansed" Willie. But a nice cult's still a cult, and they all start nice.

"So Trevor, do you believe your life's unmanageable?" Cisco asks.

Well duh! Between bikers, a lost job, a four-car accident, plus two turtle doves and a partridge in a pear tree, I've had a lovely Christmas.

He asks more questions. He doesn't ask me *how much* I drink, which I'm sure I would lie about, but does ask me *where* I buy my alcohol. Until recently, bars, I tell him. Carol's running the books now and buys swill beer for me at Safeway. I don't have access to real money anymore. *But that's not true, is it?* I've been squirreling away my golf bet winnings in my bag—my friends, particularly D-Kay, are pitiful golfers. Mixed in with my tees are a hundred bucks. Not a lot, but it's cash I can use without having to recite the Cub Scout Pledge. A few weeks ago, I bought six cases of cheap beer, even cheaper than what Carol gets at Safeway. I stashed them in the toolshed, something neither Carol nor Captain Conundrum needs to know about.

"Do you drink anything besides beer?" he asks. I say no, which happens to be true. "Me," says Cisco, "I liked the hard stuff." There's a glint in his eye. He sounds nostalgic, like he's ready to hit happy hour after the meeting. I think, *Really, this guy's an AA guru?*

Later, I will learn how completely wrong I am.

"Trevor, do you have the power to choose how much you drink?" asks Cisco. I say of course. "Good for you," he continues. "Must be nice. I no longer have that power, kid. Lost it sometime after Korea. Anyway, once I take that first drink, I'm powerless over what happens next." I tell him I'm sorry to hear that, and I am, because he makes it sound kind of sad, like he's a cripple or something.

"Oh I'm not sorry, Trevor," he says. "Becoming powerless is the best thing that ever happened to me. It took a while, but I finally learned that my life, run by me, was completely unmanageable. Worse than yours."

Is he bragging? Can he *really* beat no license, no job, no home to return to, plus potential jail time? I feel insulted, but I keep my mouth shut. He did imply earlier that he'd run someone over.

"You know what AAs call powerlessness over alcohol and having an unmanageable life?" he asks me. I shake my head no. "They call it the First Step."

We arrive at the High Noon meeting. Cisco gets me a signature sheet, sits me down in a chair, and tells me not to say anything. Specifically, he says, "Take the cotton out of your ears and stick it in your mouth." That's fine—for the next hour, I'm just along for the ride anyway. He also gets me a cup of coffee from a giant urn, almost as big as the one at St. Paul's. What's with AA and these gigantor coffee urns?

The meeting's an "OD" meeting, which means open discussion format, the same format at that very first meeting I "hid" in. *You hid there instead of calling the police about Mark Marks' murder*, a tiny voice says. *I mean, the church did have a phone. Maybe he was still alive. Maybe he could have been saved.* I hate my "little voices," I really do.

I turn my attention to the front of the room. There, a woman named Cheryl with a long red ponytail is moderating, allowing people in the audience to speak, something AAs call sharing. Like Cisco, she doesn't seem like cult leader material. (I understand AA's worldwide now—it may be months before I meet the top guy.)

Just like on TV, people say their first names and call themselves alcoholics. The shares include testaments and advice and expressions of gratitude, which on the surface seem genuine. There's a few good stories, like the guy who couldn't hide his bottle in the toilet tank because his wife's bottle was already there.

Things slow down toward the end of the hour. Cheryl says, "We got time for one more." No one volunteers. "Does the businessman"—meaning me,

I'm still wearing a tie from two days ago—"have anything to share?" she asks. I look at Cisco, who looks back at me. *Well, kid, how you gonna handle this?*

Not by calling myself an alcoholic just to fit in, that's for sure. I go with the first thing I think of. "Can someone sign my paper?"

Cheryl smiles at me. It's a *knowing* smile, one that says *Oh, aren't you a hard case!* "See me after the meeting, hon," she responds, clicking her pen twice.

Next, they do something called *chips*, again like on TV. The first chip, the white one, is for anyone who is twenty-four hours sober. The chip guy says, "Does anyone want to walk with us one day at a time?" Some people turn toward me. I stare so intently at the head of the guy sitting in front of me that I worry it might explode. I'm panicky; are they all gawking at me? *We've all drunk the Kool-Aid, kid. Now it's your turn.* But the Chip Guy moves on to the next chip, which is for thirty days, and so on. Someone receives a nine-month chip, and everyone claps enthusiastically. I do too. It can't hurt.

No other chips are given out. Then, just like the meeting the Alley Killer chased me into, everyone gets up in unison—still feels spooky—forming another giant circle. Hands are held and, just like last time, Cheryl leads everyone in a prayer. Also, like last time, the second the circle is broken, dialogue erupts; handshakes and hugs are given out liberally. After Cheryl "Two Clicks" signs my paper, I help Cisco put chairs away. He's my ride, and I don't have anything better to do, anyway. On the way back, Cisco asks, "The group circle at the end makes you uncomfortable, Trevor. I'm curious why."

I answer, "Willie." This confuses him some, which I enjoy. *I, too, can be cryptic, Mr. Conundrum.*

"Who's Willie?" Cisco asks.

"My dead brother."

"What'd he die of?"

I'll give it to the old man—he gets straight to it. No *sorry for your loss.* I inform him, "He died from group circles."

Hearing this, Cisco nods that annoying *been there, done that* nod, even though he can't possibly know what it's like to lose someone to a cult.

We arrive at my house to drop off the severance check. The monster-in-law's Audi is in the driveway. Ack! I hope to God she's not home. Cisco's body language says, *Stay here while I run this to the door.* I feel ashamed. What kind of idiot has to stay in the car while some stranger drops money off for his wife? Cisco knocks twice, but no one answers. He scribbles something on the envelope, puts it through the mail slot, then returns to the truck.

"Where to now?" he asks. I give him directions to Phillipe's apartment building. On the way, he noodles through radio stations. I get a snippet of "Iris" by the Goo Goo Dolls before he lands on WTOP—twenty-four-hour news. Per the announcer, there's going to be more of everything: more cold weather, more Middle East violence, and more Deerslayer drama. Apparently, he left two carcasses near a children's playground and moms are freaking out.

"What do you think of the Deerslayer?" I ask Cisco. "Some of my buddies think he's a vigilante."

"Vigilantism's dangerous," he answers firmly, as if knowing firsthand. "You got an opinion?" he asks.

"Not really. Got a friend, Loo. He's an arborist. He says deer eat up the forest. Thinks the Deerslayer is some sort of ecoterrorist."

On the radio, there's more about the Deerslayer, including a "Bambi" count now estimated at 80, then the announcer moves on to the death of Councilman Spencer Washington's son. Even given its sensational nature, a stick-up gone wrong, it was old news, but now there's a twist—a murder charge is being brought against Henry Takahashi, originally thought by police to have shot Washington's son in self-defense.

"Oh no, I know that guy," I tell Cisco.

"The councilman's son?" he asks.

"No, Henry Takahashi, the . . . shooter."

"Friend of yours?" Cisco asks.

"Yes." *And hey, watch that judgmental tone.*

"Well, I hope it all gets straightened out for him," the old man says sincerely. Perhaps I imagined his tone.

I point out Phillipe's building. Cisco pulls over. I thank him for the lift and the overnight stay. He nods, then cocks his head to take one more run at me. "For what it's worth, Trevor, you could benefit from the program."

I'm just doing this to satisfy some judge, I think. Reading my face, he adds, "You have my number if you change your mind." I wave as he drives away.

I buzz Phillipe's apartment and he greets me at his door. "Welcome, dude."

It's been a while since I'd been to his place, but it's still 90s-budget bachelor chic: IKEA furniture, nubby track lighting, a two-man-carry Toshiba TV, and several posters, mostly airplanes, plus a few hotties: Claudia Schiffer, Elle Macpherson, Uma Thurman on a *Pulp Fiction* movie poster. There's one item, however, that doesn't match: a large blue dress hanging over the back of a chair—it's huge. *What the heck, Phillipe?*

"Really sorry to hear about the accident," Phillipe says. Over the phone, I'd told him that I'd wrecked, but not the full circumstances, other than Carol being pissed and kicking me out. "You okay?"

"Yeah," I say. "Hurt nothing but my pride."

I don't know much about dresses, but the blue one's no size 2. Maybe it's a 22—do they come that large? I ask him why the dress is there. He seems embarrassed, says his mother made it for Estelle. I say that's cool, which it is, but think, *Since when did your girlfriend become a cow?*

"Anyway," Phillipe continues, "you're welcome to the couch as long as you need it. Carol will calm down eventually." I nod. (It would be a week before she would let me return home.) "Can you believe what happened to Darius?" Phillipe asks. I know he means the Christmas Carnival incident, but since I've been out of pocket for two days, he fills me in on the latest: the guy D-Kay slugged, some clown named Kent Ruger, is threatening a lawsuit. "Meanwhile, the putz is hogging the limelight, doing multiple interviews, milking his sore jaw for all it's worth."

"I just heard on the radio they've arrested Splash," I say.

"What for?" Phillipe asks.

"The police now think *he's* the aggressor!"

We both believe he's innocent and bat the subject around, wondering what we can do. Phillipe calls Henry unsuccessfully, then calls his parents, getting his dad. Yes, Haru has been charged with second-degree murder. Phillipe tells Mr. Takahashi that he's willing to do anything to help his son. Mr. Takahashi says there's nothing for him to do right now, and thanks him.

I eye Phillipe's copy of *Crazy from the Heat*. It's on the coffee table, bookmarked halfway through. My copy is, well, destroyed, like the rest of my car.

Your wife's car, a little annoying voice says.

Well, my friend, you need to shut up, I tell it. "Phillipe, given Splash's circumstances, could I trouble you for a beer?"

"Sure thing," Phillipe says, fetching two from the fridge.

Chapter 23: Mrs. Nigel

Thursday, 7 January 1999

Silver Spring, MD

MRS. NIGEL HUGGED Ken Ert as he entered her office, then sat, placing a teacup and saucer on her end table. The table—all her office furniture—was elegant, and on her walls hung safari trophy photos: leopards, gazelles, elephants. The largest picture, featuring two lounging lionesses, was the most striking. "So how are you, Ken?" she asked.

"Still jinxed," he answered. "'Hi, my name is Ken and I repel straight women.'"

Mrs. Nigel smiled.

The way she did so emulated another happy therapist, the famous Dr. Ruth Westheimer, and Ken felt compelled to smile back. There were three differences, however, between Nigel and Westheimer: Mrs. Nigel's accent was British, not German; she wasn't a degreed doctor; and unlike the renowned diminutive sex therapist, Mrs. Nigel was nearly six feet tall.

"Ken, jinxes are not real."

"They're not?"

"Of course not," she said. "You're good-looking, well-mannered, and employed, plus you don't live with your mother. You are a straight woman's dream. You just don't think you are."

Ken's smile tightened. *Ma'am,* he thought, *it's been weeks and I'm still not getting through to you.*

In his life so far, Ken had attracted three of the most engaging queer women the planet had to offer. His first love was Melody, his high school sweetheart—smart, pretty, wholesome. She'd been head-over-heels for Ken, doting on him, giving him time, attention, praise—everything a high school boy could want. Except sex. She was very shy on that subject, which was A-okay with the equally virginal Ken. When she did promise to go all the way the night of their senior prom, he was surprised and a little shocked, wondering, *Will I have the nerve to reciprocate?*

By prom night, he'd worked up plenty of nerve but came home disappointed. The event turned out to be an awkward affair with Melody dancing stiffly with him, barely touching him. Ken sensed her cold feet, and when he whispered that she needn't keep her promise, she'd cried, hugging him gratefully.

Melody wasn't just suffering neophyte jitters. Ken knew something deeper was going on, and later that summer he found out what. In a parking lot, of all places, Melody tearily admitted that she "wasn't sure which way she was wired." Ken was crushed by this news. He never mentioned the conversation to anyone, but word unfortunately got out. The taunting from the high school asshats for having "driven Melody to the other side"—*Hey Ert! Only queers date queers!*—humiliated him.

Ken's cousin of the same name, Cousin Ken, supported him, however, saying, "Ignore those cheese dicks. You're going to college, you'll never see them again." Clapping a hand on Original's shoulder, he continued: "Besides, time to lose that cherry, Cousin, and I got the perfect ticket for that. Two tickets, in fact! Dude, we're goin' to see Slayer!" Original, who hated heavy metal, balked, but Cousin would hear none of it. "We're going to Hammerjacks Friday night and you're getting laid. Why? I'll tell you why. Because we're family!"

Family seemed an odd card for Cousin to play, but it worked. Ken went to the show, losing his virginity in the back of a rusted Pontiac to a large Slayer groupie named Vertigo. Sweaty vinyl seat *wham-bam, thank you ma'am* (one eye nervously scanning the parking lot) wasn't how Ken, a romantic, had pictured his first soirée, but Cousin had been right—the event served as a badly needed ego boost, and once word spread (Cousin tactfully leaving out Vertigo's size), the cheese dicks moved on.

On their way home that night, Cousin declared, "So Melody's gay, big deal. Just a fluke, Ken, and now that you've been 'vertigoed,' you're ready for college!"

Cousin ended up being right about that, too, more or less. University of Maryland started off reasonably well: a few dates freshman year, but nothing serious until becoming a sophomore and meeting Joanne, an easy-on-the-eyes blonde. Jo was loud and adventurous, Melody the Wallflower's opposite. "A bit on the wild side, Kenny," was Mrs. Ert's cool observation at the time. Jo was quite mischievous—4 a.m. nooky on a darkened athletic field being an example of this. At first, Ken was thrilled with their romps, but as the weeks went on and as Jo started missing her own high-risk rendezvous, giving him no reason, Ken worried. Like Melody, something was again off.

He followed Jo one night as she supposedly headed to the library to study. Instead, he watched her arrive at one of College Park's many off-campus housing apartments. After hemming and hawing for a half-hour, he finally rapped on the door. It was then he came face to face with Jo and her other lover, a woman she happened to be holding by the waist. "Ken!" Jo declared, shocked with embarrassment. She began explaining: "You see, I'm bi . . ."

Jo's girlfriend processed who Ken was and was now equally shocked. "Though I mostly like women . . ." Jo painfully reassured her. "Did I not tell you guys that?"

No, Jo, you most definitely didn't.

Ken took the revelation hard. At least with Melody, an honest, upright young woman, he'd accepted the bromide *if you love something, set it free.* With Jo, however, there was no freedom to grant because there was no doubting her enthusiastic heterosexual abilities. The woman was a total minx in bed. No, this was crushing infidelity, plain and simple. In Cousin Ken's words, a "bi slut betrayal."

Again, Cousin Ken, heavy metal, and a parking lot came to the rescue.

"Dude, you'll never believe it!" Cousin declared. "I got Anthrax tickets!" Original still detested loud music but accompanied his cousin again. His backseat date this time—a groupie who hadn't volunteered her name—was just as enthusiastic as Vertigo had been. Once again, Cousin bragged, "Wow, look at you! Vertigo, Jo, and now . . . whatever her name was. Listen up, Cousin, 'cause I'm tellin' you: lesbian-wise, Melody and Jo were just coincidences. Third time's the charm!"

But the third time wasn't the charm. It was much worse, as Mrs. Nigel was learning.

"Ken," she said gently, "can you tell me more about Rosalita?" She treaded lightly; it had taken weeks for Ken to open up about his ex-fiancé, and he'd only recently turned the corner on this subject. "Where did you meet her?"

"On the job," Ken said, crossing his legs. Personality-wise, Rosalita, the supposed third charm, split the difference between the wallflower that was Melody and the party girl that was Jo. "Rosy and I were freelancers. I wrote, she took photos. Rosalita was, still is, a wiz behind the camera."

"Did you hit it off right away?"

"No, it took time," said Original. "But it was the real deal, Mrs. Nigel. We were happy. I mean *really* happy."

This is good, thought Mrs. Nigel. "Go on."

Ken paused, then continued. "She's from this huge Hispanic family, see? When I popped the question, she was thrilled. *Thrilled.* Her *madre* too. We moved into this tiny apartment in Northwest DC near the embassies. Madre didn't approve of that, but boy was she excited to be planning a wedding."

"Did that make you feel good?"

"Yes, it did," said Ken. "God, Mrs. Nigel, Rosa couldn't *wait* to get married. We set the date for the following summer . . . But then Rosy met Sonya." Another pause. Ken's body language stiffened.

Keep going, thought Mrs. Nigel.

"I should have known better. I mean, they met at one of those gay pride marches downtown for Christ's sake." Ken clarified: "Rosy was there photographing for *The Post*."

"Tell me about Sonya."

"Sonya and her girlfriend, Katie, were two of the march organizers. They seemed committed, *old-married people* tight. I wasn't worried. Anyway, Sonya and my girl Rosy shared an interest—photography. Rosy was teaching her the craft. Seemed innocent enough."

"Then what happened?" asked Mrs. Nigel.

"Well, you know what they say," Ken continued. "Love is blind, deaf, and dumb. And apparently in my case, very stupid. Though this time there was another casualty—Katie. Like me, she'd been totally blindsided. Later we talked. We'd both sensed something might be wrong with our partners, but not *that* wrong. I mean, according to Katie, Sonya had sworn off straight women ages ago, and Rosy had never had a homosexual thought in her life." Ken examined the large photo of the lounging lionesses. "To my knowledge, anyway."

"Ken," said Mrs. Nigel, "sounds like you had empathy for Katie. That's great!"

"The poor woman was shell-shocked. And Rosy's madre was beside herself, furious with her daughter. Me, I was numb at first, but when Rosy returned the ring, I felt everything at once. I immediately drove out to Great Falls and threw it in the Potomac. That *Titanic* stunt cost me two thousand dollars." Ken laughed ruefully, rubbing his eyes.

Mrs. Nigel smiled supportively. *Keep going.*

"My cousin told me, 'Once is a fluke, twice is coincidence,'" continued Ken, re-crossing his legs. "Well, I'm here to tell you that three times is a *trend*." He let out another weak laugh, looking at the lionesses again. "Cousin offered me Motley Crüe tickets this time, but I passed. No more parking lots."

"Did you feel like Rosalita was 'the one,' Ken?"

"I mean, I loved Rosalita, *really loved her*, you know? But it doesn't matter. Got no time for dating anyway, with my sister's kids and all." Ken forced a weak smile. He had no intention of abandoning his sister or her troublesome twins. Besides, faux fatherhood suited him, especially since he believed actual fatherhood wasn't in the cards; any future Mrs. Ert would either be a secret lesbian or be stolen by one. In Wendell the Deadbeat Dad's seven-year absence, life with his sister had been good, and despite recent media downsizing, Ken's sportswriter duties at *The Washington Post* had expanded.

But being the 'family hero' keeps you from facing your personal losses, doesn't it? thought Mrs. Nigel. "Any dates since Rosalita?"

"Early on, my friends' wives tried setting me up," Ken said. "'Oh, you've *got* to meet my friend, Ken! He's great with kids!'"

"Did you go out with any of these potential jinx breakers?" Mrs. Nigel asked, sipping her tea.

"No."

"Why not?"

"My cousin said it best: 'My emotions are like Elvis—they've left the building.'"

Emotions never leave the building, thought Mrs. Nigel. "Tell me more about your cousin."

"Cousin Ken? Well, for starters, he's dangerous."

"What makes him dangerous?" she asked.

"Mostly he does."

Despite the opening rabbit hole, Mrs. Nigel let curiosity get the better of her. "How?"

"Where do I start?" asked Ken. "There's the skydiving, then there's the free-climbing—that's rock climbing *without* a rope. Oh, and the chainsaws."

"Chainsaws?" asked Mrs. Nigel, intrigued.

"Yup. Cousin juggles 'em."

Mrs. Nigel's brow wrinkled. "You've seen him do this?"

"Oh yes. And believe me, not only is it scary, it's loud."

"He sounds like a thrill seeker."

"You're right," said Ken.

"How does that make you feel?"

"What, your being right or my cousin juggling chainsaws?"

"Your cousin's juggling act," Mrs. Nigel said, not laughing. "I don't want you to take this the wrong way, Ken, as I know he's pretty important in your life, but he sounds a little unstable."

"Oh, he's not a little unstable, Mrs. Nigel, he's *a lot* unstable. It's a quality that unfortunately George and Gregory love."

"Does that, your nephews idolizing him, make you jealous?" she queried.

In her asking, Ken realized the truth of this. "I'm not jealous of Cousin's antics or the way the hellions worship him. By the way, Cousin's saws don't have actual chains, their motors just rev. And they're small saws. I mean, he's not a *complete* idiot." Ken paused again. "No . . . I think it's his freedom I envy, but I don't want to be him 'cause he's got a screw loose."

"Doesn't everyone?" Mrs. Nigel joked.

"No," said Ken. "He *literally* has a screw loose. The guy's got eight broken bones and three titanium pins. He worked one loose last month. He's getting surgery—that is to say *more* surgery—in two weeks to reset it. He doesn't care, though, 'cause women love an Evel Knievel."

"Is he good-looking?" asked Mrs. Nigel.

"Not particularly. Plus, he's crazy."

"Well, you have him beat there," Mrs. Nigel said.

"What, you think I'm crazier than he is?" Ken asked.

Mrs. Nigel's brow furrowed again. *Sometimes, Mr. Ert, your object clarification game annoys me.* "Your *looks,* Ken. Let's say women actually do 'throw' themselves at your cousin—do you really want the kind of woman who's attracted to, as you put it, a crazy man?"

Ken envisioned Vertigo and Anthrax Girl making out with Cousin. "No, I guess not."

"Does your cousin's popularity make you feel left out?"

"No," said Ken. "If I just felt *left out,* I'd do something about it. But I'm jinxed, see? Big difference."

"Ken," Mrs. Nigel said, "there's no sign on your forehead reading 'Lesbians only.'"

"No, but there may as well be."

Okay, at least we're back on track, thought Mrs. Nigel. "Is it really a jinx, Ken, or have you created some sort of self-fulfilling prophecy?"

"Not a prophecy," Ken answered, briefly thinking of Prophet.

"No?"

"No, okay?" Ken said defensively. "There's something fundamentally *wrong* with me and women can smell it."

It was now Mrs. Nigel who paused. "I don't buy that," she said, starting again, "but I buy your anger, and Ken, you should be—you've been betrayed three times. That would make anyone angry." She let this sink in.

Ken looked at the lionesses again.

"My question, Ken, is who are you angry with?"

"Uh, the lesbians?" he asked.

I won't let you wiggle off the hook, Mr. Ert, Mrs. Nigel thought. She went for it: "No, you're not angry with lesbians, Ken. Try again please."

Ken hadn't expected her to sidestep his snarky comment so easily. "Well, who else does that leave?" he asked. Mrs. Nigel regarded him and a moment passed. "No, I'm not mad at *myself,* Mrs. Nigel. *I'm* the victim here."

"Ken, answer me honestly: are you throwing yourself at your job and your sister's family to avoid emotional pain?" Ken sat silently. "And will that avoidance work in the long run?"

"It's worked so far," said Original, looking at the lionesses again.

"Hey," he said suddenly, "I don't want to cross an ethical line, Mrs. Nigel, but that woman, Tori Bora, your client before me, is she here because she's coming out?"

"You are."

"I'm what?" asked Ken.

"Crossing an ethical line," said Mrs. Nigel. "Would you want me to share your personal information with other clients?"

"No, I guess not," said Ken. "Kinda stupid I would ask." But he didn't think it was stupid.

"I'm curious, Ken," she said, "why bring Tori up?" She thought she knew why, but she was pretty sure Ken didn't, at least not fully.

Ken answered honestly. "I'd like to talk to a lesbian. You know, one I didn't personally create."

Interesting, thought Mrs. Nigel. "Why a lesbian specifically?"

"To get pointers," he answered. "You know, to avoid sending the wrong signals or whatever I'm doing."

"You want some sort of 'coach?'" she asked.

"Yes, that's it."

"That's a novel concept, but I'd advise against it in Ms. Bora's case," she said, finishing her tea in a very "topic-closed" manner. "We still have ten minutes, Ken. More on Rosalita?"

"Actually, Mrs. Nigel, I think I'm done with personal discovery today."

I'm a little done in myself, she thought. "How about something lighter, then? How's that club of yours?" She found the Evil Men's Book Club concept quite novel as well.

Ken recalled the mid-December meeting at Shorties and how the Vee Sisters had worn Santa hats in addition to their normal short shorts and tight tops. Rey had arrived late, something about "an obligation in La Plata." Loo had run the meeting solo, as Trevor was once again AWOL. The meeting had given the guys another chance to size up their newest evil member, Gary Graft, someone who could opine intelligently on virtually any subject. As erudite as he was, however, his uber-knowledge proved exhausting to listen to. By the end of the evening, the guys started changing the subject to things he couldn't possibly know, like the most chainsaws Cousin Ken could juggle (four) just to shut him up.

But none of this is worth relating, Ken thought, answering, "The club's fine."

"Want to discuss anything else?" asked Mrs. Nigel, sensing he was holding something back.

Well, there's that dream where two men argue, then my head gets shoved into a bleacher. "Well," Ken began, "there was this guy named Prophet." He explained the basics of the murdered man's predictions: lost jobs, lost women, lost freedom, lost lives.

"Poor Mr. Marks!" declared Mrs. Nigel. "And what a dreadful-sounding curse."

"It is, and guess what? Some stuff's started happening! First Henry got arrested, then D-Kay, and now Trevor. You might have seen D-Kay on the news—he's the one who slugged the Christmas Carnival guy."

"Oh my!" declared Mrs. Nigel.

"And Trevor lost his job too."

Curious, Mrs. Nigel asked, "Did any women leave their men?"

"No. And we're a little fuzzy on the whole death threat deal. D-Kay's sure we're all meant to snuff it, but Phillipe's convinced it's just one of us. Also, there was this weird thing with the new guy, Gary. We take "joke" meeting minutes, see, writing down our best bits. We had Gary play secretary to slow down how much he talks. Didn't work. Anyway, the funny thing was that he started writing in English, then suddenly changed to Spanish. When he saw me looking, he changed back to English."

"Wow," said Mrs. Nigel, intrigued. "What does this Gary do?"

"For a know-it-all who can't shut up, he doesn't talk much about himself. Government, I think. Maybe he's a spook, but honestly, I can't picture that."

Ken started describing all the arrests in detail, explaining the councilman's son's death last. "Even in self-defense," Mrs. Nigel said, "it must have been a shock to learn that your friend Henry killed someone."

"That's the problem," said Ken uncomfortably. "The police are changing their tune and calling it murder now! I want to support Henry, but he's making it tough. He won't answer his phone. I tried his apartment. His car was there, but he wouldn't come to the door. His studio's chained shut."

"That must be frustrating," Mrs. Nigel said. "Well, you at least have the knowledge that your friend Henry didn't kill someone on purpose."

"Yes," Ken said. But this wasn't totally true. More than once Henry had told him, flippantly perhaps, how cool it might be to shoot someone if he could get away with it. Had he tried but gotten caught?

"You're a good friend, Ken," Mrs. Nigel said, smiling warmly. "You know that, right?"

Ken said nothing. Mrs. Nigel realized they were ten minutes over, so she stood, indicating it was time for their session-ending hug. Ken's book club members' stories were very . . . *'Lurid' is the word you're looking for,* she told herself.

"Oh, Ken, I almost forgot," she said brightly. "Before you go, I am assigning homework."

"Homework?" said Ken. *That's new.*

"Yes, I want you to ask someone out. By Valentine's Day. Any available woman will do. Will you do that?"

Ken looked uneasily at the lionesses. "I'll have to think about it."

Chapter 24: The Angry Hornet

Saturday, 9 January 1999
Aspen Hill, MD

THE BULLET FLEW past him like an angry hornet, startling Cisco awake.

Arkin had dreamt again about the night-time retreat across the ice-covered Chosin Reservoir and the bullet that had punched Jamie Took's ticket. The vision was always vivid, always true to memory, except that now there was this new ending, an ending where it wasn't Private Took in danger but Private Arkin. In this version, Cisco hadn't fortuitously ducked to retrieve Wendell's dropped dog tags. In this version, the angry hornet sped toward *his* temple, not Jamie's, and in tonight's dream it had missed him by inches.

Shocked awake, the seventy-year-old Cisco pondered this incorrect dream. In real life, the bullet had struck Took's helmetless head and not his—Cisco was alive to prove that. Since his wife Maggie passed, this Korean dream, one he'd been having since he'd left the service in 1951, was coming more frequently. This in and of itself wasn't cause for alarm; the familiar version of the dream hadn't disturbed him for years (not deeply, anyway). But this new version, with its nasty ending, did.

Since he'd started sponsoring Trevor two weeks ago, however, this was the new nightmare's first recurrence. *Fewer dreams,* thought Cisco, *is the kid some sort of good luck charm?* He didn't think so. After all, what made him special? Arkin sponsored eight other men—Trevor was just one more knucklehead in a long line of knuckleheads, and not a particularly promising one, either.

Some newcomers adopted the program from their very first meeting. Others struggled but were at least sincere in their desire for another way of life and got it eventually. Then there were the Trevors, "smart guys" who sponsored themselves, white-knuckling it for days, weeks, even months until whatever hailstorm their drinking had kicked up blew over. But when the ice finally melted, they'd keenly theorize, *Since I was able to stop, perhaps I overreacted. With better planning and more willpower, I'll be able to drink successfully again.* These men invariably "went back out," as AA folks called it, to kick up larger and larger hailstorms. Some limped back into AA, but most didn't, ending up in jails or institutions if they were relatively lucky, or dying if they weren't.

Trevor Pug's efforts over the past two weeks *seemed* sincere to anyone with, say, less than a year's sobriety, but there was no fooling an old-timer like Cisco. *At least the kid has a sponsor—me,* he thought. Odds vastly improved with sponsorship, and on the surface, Trevor was a sponsor's dream; the consequences of the kid's drinking couldn't be more obvious: a lost job, loan shark trouble (involving Cisco's 'pals,' the Old Line, no less), and legal concerns, though calling his blackout DUI a "concern" was putting it too mildly.

Trevor had been arraigned the Monday after Christmas at the courthouse in Rockville, Maryland, having been strongly advised that, apart from AA meetings, he should stay home. Admitting powerlessness over alcohol, the first half of the First Step, however, was something else entirely. Sure, Trevor was ready to swear off booze for as long as it took to navigate the legal system and get out from under Old Line's thumb, but after that?

To his credit, Trevor was back home with his family and looking for work. Though his exploits hadn't made the Channel 4 News highlight reel (as D-Kay's slugging his neighbor on live TV had), word still spread rapidly through the DC IT community. Though he presented himself as a penitent "ex-drinker" with very affordable coding skills, neither the startups nor the corporates would touch him.

"The Y2K-fix-it market's on fire," he'd complained to Cisco, "but even the contractors are turning me down." One did take pity on him eventually, giving him piecemeal assignments mailed to him on disc. "It hardly beats minimum wage," Trevor had grumbled, but Carol warned him: *Don't turn anything away*.

At least AA meetings represented "release" from home detention. Cisco sometimes picked Trevor up, and sometimes he had another sponsee, Chico, do it (taking alcoholics to meetings was considered good service work).

"Between potentially going to jail, avoiding getting my hand broken, and giving all my severance money to Janice the Lawyer," Trevor had told Cisco, "I'm officially scared straight. My trial's in March. But Janice says I got a good chance staying out of jail: clean record, first-time offense, long list of meeting signatures. Sounds like a plan, doesn't it?"

Want to make God laugh? Cisco had thought. *Tell Him your plans*. Aloud he'd said: "Worry about the present, Trevor. Let the future take care of itself."

"That's your plan, huh? *Not* worrying about the future?" Trevor had asked.

"Not *my* plan, kid. God's plan."

"God's plan." It was an answer Cisco repeated now while standing in front of his bathroom mirror. It was 4 a.m. He was up for good now; he'd no intention of dreaming about the angry hornet again.

Yesterday, he remembered saying to Trevor, "Step Two is *Came to believe that a power greater than ourselves could restore us to sanity.* You got a higher power?"

"Sure," Trevor had said.

"Okay, who is He?"

"God, Jesus, Buddha," Trevor had answered. "Looking for someone in particular?"

"I don't care who your higher power is, kid. That's up to you. It can be a doorknob if you want. Don't laugh. Right now, a doorknob would run your life better than you can."

"Hey, I believe in God and He's a few steps above a doorknob," Trevor had said, miffed.

"Great, kid. Me too."

To the kid's credit, his belief in a higher power would save Cisco from waiting until Trevor resigned from the *Does God Exist?* debate club. It wasn't disbelief that killed alcoholics, it was ego. Atheism, or not believing beyond the rational, worked just fine in AA because whether God existed wasn't the point. The point was that the alcoholic realized he or she *wasn't* God. Cisco's business analogy was cut and dried: *Fire your CEO—you. Put someone else in charge before you run your company into the ground.*

"So tell me, is God an active partner in your life?" Cisco had asked.

"Like the 'Jesus is My Copilot' bumper sticker?"

"Yes."

"Um, sure," Trevor had said.

"What's wrong with having a copilot, kid?"

"Nothing, I guess. Just don't want someone pulling my strings because, they're, you know, *my* strings. Free will and all."

"Free will?" Cisco had asked, smiling obliquely. "Trevor, most faiths believe free will is a gift from your Creator. You have it, it's yours, and it can't be taken from you, though you can choose to give it up. But remember that it's a gift. When God made man, free will didn't have to be a standard feature. The point is you should be thankful. Another question, Trevor: Your god, *God*—do you trust Him?"

"I'm not sure." The question had confused Pug.

"Fair enough. Let's take a step back. What's the purpose of a god?"

"To make the Universe?"

"A Creator, like in the Bible?" Cisco had asked. "Or is he some sort of cosmic record keeper, punishing those with too much red ink? Or an avenger, a smiter of enemies? What do you think?"

Trevor remained mute.

"*My* higher power, dear boy," Cisco had continued, "is potent. He's mysterious and unknowable, so don't ask me anything like 'If God's so powerful, can He create a rock so large He can't pick it up?' Stuff like that's the reason why 'smart guys' land in AA in the first place. Trevor, how powerful is your higher power?"

"Powerful, I guess."

"*How* powerful?"

"Very." Trevor had paused, then emphasized, "*Very* powerful."

"Great," Cisco had said. "So why don't you trust Him to run things?"

"Because I guess I don't want him to have *all* the power," Trevor had honestly replied.

"If there's power to be had, *you* want it, right?" He'd let Trevor's silence serve as acknowledgment. "Relax. We all want to be gods, but none of us are, not even remotely." Arkin had smiled genuinely. "Not happy about that? Welcome to AA."

With men like Trevor, Cisco had learned to work slowly. The boy had a toehold, at best, on the first two steps, and on Step Three (*Made a decision to turn our will and our lives over to God as we understood Him),* had no hold at all. As far as Cisco knew, Trevor was staying away from booze, but he credited the kid's wife for this more than Trevor himself because he recognized "wife-ordered" when he saw it: in Trevor's case, either the booze was going or he was.

From experience, he also knew that spouses like Carol (and lovers, parents, children, buddies, bosses—everyone affected by the alcoholic's drinking) fell into one of two groups: those that didn't need Al-Anon, AA's sister program meant to help the victims of alcoholics, and those that did. Having met Carol, he was sure she could benefit from Al-Anon, but was she willing to go this route? He'd certainly suggest it, but thinking about her right now wasn't his immediate concern, Trevor was. Would the kid "half-measure" it until he was out from under the judge's gavel, then chase the lie *I can once more drink like a gentleman* again? Or would he buckle down, do the hard work?

"Time will tell, Maggie," he told his dead wife. "Time will tell."

Having gotten up early, Cisco was productive. After prayers, coffee, breakfast, and reading the paper, he paid bills, fixed a leaky faucet, and fielded morning check-in calls from several sponsees. He then made calls to Chico and Trevor that went something like this: "Shave and get dressed. Wear a tie—you're going to a funeral. If you want to keep me as a sponsor, then *no*, you don't have a choice. See you in an hour."

It was cold and rainy when Cisco's truck pulled into the Pug's driveway. Trevor, who'd been standing at his door, got in without a word. He sat next to Chico, a young, rail-thin Puerto Rican wearing a heavy coat over a light summer suit. Trevor had dressed opposite: a light coat over a thick wool two-piece. Cisco's S-10 had no backseat, so they drove three-wide.

Twenty minutes in, Chico broke the silence. "Who died, *Jefe*?"

"One of us. His name was Mark."

"Did he die sober, Jefe?" For some reason, Chico liked calling Cisco "Jefe."

"No," said Cisco. "But that doesn't matter."

They drove west for another hour through Maryland's foothills. The rain abated but the wind picked up, at times pushing the small pickup sideways.

"You guys eat breakfast?" Cisco asked. Headshakes. "No? Good. There's a roadhouse at the next exit. Hope you boys like peanuts." Cisco pulled into a parking lot for a restaurant called Skipper's. It was 10:45 a.m. on a Saturday and the lot was packed. They waited briefly before being seated. "No menus, guys," Cisco said, pointing to a wall-mounted chalkboard listing entrées and specials. Surrounding them were tables of happy families. Those who hadn't been served yet were grabbing handfuls of boiled peanuts—each table had a large bowlful—eating them and throwing the shells to the floor. Trevor was taken aback by this but Chico loved it. "Jefe, I *like* this place," he said, munching away.

"Mud strong today, miss?" Cisco asked their waitress. The fifty-something woman responded, "It'll clean your sparkplugs. Want some?" Cisco said yes, indicating his sponsees would as well. "What else can I getcha?" she asked.

After they ordered, she returned with coffees as dark as engine oil. The boys looked at their cups dubiously, then liberally added cream and sugar. Cisco drank his black. All three ate peanuts while waiting for their food, pitching the husks to the floor. A man in overalls came by every so often to sweep them up. Their food arrived and they began eating, watching people from various tables accost one another in loud, friendly voices.

Toward the end of their meal, Trevor thought about how every meeting he'd attended had at least one colossal coffee urn. "What's with AA and java, Cisco?" he asked. Other than his breakfast order, this was the first time Trevor had spoken beyond affirmatives that morning.

"What do you mean?" asked Cisco.

"Why's an organization—"

"AA's not an organization," Cisco corrected. "It's a fellowship."

"Yeah, okay. Fellowship. Why's a fellowship dedicated to abstinence—"

"It's not a program of abstinence," Cisco corrected again. "It's a program of recovery."

Trevor continued, annoyed: "Okay, fine. Why is a fellowship, the AA *program,* in this case, one dedicated to recovery—" He paused to ask, "Am I good so far, Jefe?"

"Pray continue," said Cisco.

"Why's AA dedicated to recovery from one drug, *alcohol,* but it pushes another—*caffeine?*"

Cisco chuckled. "It may seem like we're singlehandedly supporting the coffee industry, but the two aren't comparable."

"They feed coffee to drunks to sober them up, right Jefe?" Chico asked.

Cisco chuckled again. "Bad idea. The only thing more dangerous than a sleepy drunk driver is a wide-awake one."

"But coffee's cheap, right?" added Chico.

"*AA* coffee's cheap," Cisco agreed, waving for the waitress. "Let's get going. Gotta be there by 11:30. We don't want to be late for Mr. Marks's funeral."

"*Marks* is his last name?" asked Trevor.

"Yes, 'Mark Marks,'" Cisco said solemnly.

Mark Marks, the guy I witnessed getting murdered, realized Trevor. *And now I'm going to his funeral.* Trevor shivered, no longer curious about AA coffee. Peanut shells popped underfoot as the trio made their way to the register. Cisco paid, then the S-10 once again headed toward Cumberland.

Chapter 25: Casseroles

Saturday, 9 January 1999
Cumberland, MD

MARK MARKS WAS of two municipalities. He was born peacefully in the western panhandle city of Cumberland, Maryland, and died violently back east in Silver Spring, just north of DC. A contest of wills between Winnie Marks, Mark's mother, who wanted her son's casket interred in her Cumberland parish's graveyard, and Reverend William Kristee, who did not, had delayed the funeral almost seven weeks. The reverend, a persuasive clergyman, had had his reasons. First, available plots within Christ the Redeemer's cemetery in the heart of Cumberland's historic district were dwindling, something he apologized for. Second was the cost of the plots, particularly the full-sized one Mrs. Marks wanted, as it was above her means, something he politely talked around by mentioning more than once that a smaller, more affordable urn plot was available. Finally, there was the third unspoken reason: even dead, Markie Marks, a parish pariah whose last act, leaving town, was the only popular thing he'd ever accomplished, wasn't wanted.

Despite Reverend Kristee's verbally sweet roadblocks, Mrs. Marks, a lifelong Christ the Redeemer congregant, wasn't taking *no* for an answer. "Jesus wants a casket service for my son, Reverend, *not* cremation, so if you want to argue, argue with Him."

Reverend Kristee could only smile painfully during these discussions. The contest of wills proceeded through the holidays until Winnie implied (because Christian ladies never threaten) that passing a description of her problems to the editor of *The Cumberland Times* might speed things along. Reverend Kristee, imagining an op-ed titled Christian Widow's Son Denied Burial Plot, finally relented, giving her the full-sized space for the cremation price.

Markie's nefarious adventures in the big city, as the locals called DC, weren't nearly as well-known as his boyhood exploits were. Markie Marks (he was always "Markie" in Cumberland, never Mark), a child of an overprotective widow, lived fast and drank hard, as back copies of the *Cumberland Time's* weekly crime report could attest to. His ignominious end—a big city murder—surprised no one.

Winnie made her way to her son's service that cold Saturday morning on foot, carrying a mental barbell: grief on one end, the town's judgment on the other. The previous evening, she'd fielded condolences from a dozen wake attendees. However, with each set of kind words—*The Lord has called him home* or *He's in a better place*—she imagined the recriminations of those purposefully absent. *That drunk was so lazy, someone had to help him die,* or *Shame 'bout Mrs. Marks' quarter-beggin' boy dyin' like that.*

Didn't these people understand she'd outlived her only son? She wiped a tear away. These imagined voices would break her heart if she wasn't careful. *Despite your pain, Winnie,* she told herself, *you will attend Markie's service with your backbone straight. You may be a mother of a delinquent, but you will not be pitied.*

She walked on.

It was six blocks to Christ the Redeemer, and, as she used an umbrella to fend off sleet, Winnie Marks wondered who would be there. The reverend, of course, and none too happy about it, but who else? She assumed that the cadre of her fellow Baptists, the older, more duty-bound ones who'd attended the wake would probably show up for the indoor church service. She could forgive them for skipping the final rites, which were sure to be cold and miserable. But when an image of her and Reverend Kristee graveside, *alone,* filled her mind, she stopped walking. The scything of her only son by Demon Alcohol felt completely overwhelming. It took conscious effort to move again, one wet boot in front of the other, until her feet finally consumed enough sidewalk to arrive.

The building's burial ground was much older than the church and looked it. In several places, the roots of massive oak trees had buckled its ivy-covered privacy wall. The cemetery's cluttered headstones leaned intimately toward each other—one could be forgiven for thinking the corpses beneath had been put away sloppily, like jangled spoons, but this wasn't the case. As Old Charlie the groundskeeper knew, the dead just didn't have much elbow room, which meant the few remaining plots at the center of the graveyard (burials having occurred from the walls inward) were valuable, since everyone assumed, morbidly, that the oaks' powerful, fibrous roots were prying open the older caskets.

As Mrs. Marks looked over the uneven stone wall toward the graves, the recriminating voices began again: *A bum like Markie Marks doesn't belong in a nice cemetery like this.* "Too bad you think so," Winnie said. "I'm buryin' my only son here and there's not a thing you people can do about it."

As expected, the inside church service was sparsely attended—ten people, including her two friends, the "hens": Mrs. Ripple and Mrs. Beacon, also widows. In anticipation of the final rites and with the help of his grandson,

Young Charlie, Old Charlie wheeled the simple casket outside, depositing it on the machine meant to lower it into the grave. To Winnie's relief, the sleet had stopped and the day, though still cold and blustery, was turning bright. She and her small troupe, which included the reverend and the hens, approached her son's grave, watched on by Old Charlie and his grandson. She pinched her lips with her teeth, thinking, *This is it. The last prayer, then throwing the dirt. It won't take long.*

But it did. There was some mechanical issue with the contraption meant to lower the casket; Old Charlie, a codger making Mrs. Marks feel young, kept hitting the LOWER button, but nothing happened. Young Charlie tried with the same result. *You incompetent idiots,* thought Winnie. The cold began seeping through her coat; the sunshine, though pretty, wasn't warm. Charlie whispered something into Reverend Kristee's ear, who turned red, then looked at Mrs. Marks. *Don't you tell me Charlie's contraption won't work,* she thought. *Get it fixed this instant!*

Both Charlies scurried to the toolshed to somehow redeem the situation, which, as dreadful as it was, was now even *more* upsetting—weirdly, late arrivals were appearing, strangers wearing dresses and suits under winter coats, approaching her son's open grave. Who were they? And why so many?

Oh God, Winnie prayed, *forgive me my selfishness, but deliver me from this embarrassment.* Ruffled as she was, she stood stoically. If Providence had chosen to flood her son's service with mourners who hadn't yet realized they were at the wrong service, then she would endure it. But where were they parking? (Christ the Redeemer's lot was notoriously small.) An older man seemed to be their leader. Winnie watched as he whispered to the reverend, who pointed toward her. *Oh Lord, what now?* The man approached, introducing himself as Mr. Cisco Arkin, giving the names of the two young men with him. He then apologized for their late arrival.

"Honestly, Mrs. Marks, I misread the service time. I thought it was 11:30, and therefore everyone you see"—he pointed to the others entering the graveyard—"is late because of me."

A look of speculation overcame Winnie. "No need to apologize, Mr. Arkin, but who *are* all these people?"

"Members of Alcoholics Anonymous, Mrs. Marks. We all knew your son." As he said this, Mr. Arkin's "other thing" began rumbling inside him, but he wasn't worried about it that morning. *If I can ignore the angry hornet, then I can ignore you.*

"I see," Mrs. Marks said uneasily—her son had never mentioned AA—"but you're much too late."

"Ma'am, I meant to say that your son was a member, which sounds like news to you."

Mrs. Marks looked confused. *AA? Something else my son failed at?* She knew little about Alcoholics Anonymous, but at least these people looked non-threatening. One person walked with a cane, another one, a mother, approached holding the hands of two small children. *She must be the wife of one of these abstainers*, thought Mrs. Marks. *A mother knows better than to drink too much.*

Meanwhile, both Charlies returned, looking nervous. They began tinkering with the lowering machine again; they had made calls for help, but apparently the cavalry wasn't coming. More people arrived, including two people Trevor remembered from the night of Prophet's murder—the older Black man named Reggie, and his friend, Alice. The number of graveside attendees had now tripled, and more were coming.

"The Reverend told me there's a problem with the casket lowerer," Cisco said to Mrs. Marks. "I think I can help, but I wanted your permission first." He relayed his idea. She seemed dubious.

"Will there be enough able-bodied men?" she asked.

"Definitely, starting with these two," he said, pointing at his sponsees. Slowly, she nodded her consent. Cisco had Chico and Trevor canvass for help, and it didn't take long to gather four more men and two women. Mr. Arkin, whom Mrs. Marks had correctly pegged as the take-charge type—and not an unhandsome one, either—consulted with Old Charlie, who nodded enthusiastically, sending Young Charlie back to the church's toolshed to retrieve sections of rope.

The day was warming, but not much, and the cold was taking a toll on the "on-time" parishioners. No one wanted to leave, however. Markie Marks's funeral was generating unexpected social energy, so no congregant was going to leave before witnessing how this out-of-the-ordinary burial, with its broken lowering machine and late-arriving strangers, would conclude.

The ropes were given to the volunteers who paired up, snaking them underneath the coffin. The machine had a catch allowing the webbing to drop. With crossed fingers, Old Charlie pulled it. To his relief, the webbing dropped away. He and his grandson then moved the machine out of the way. With that, the four pairs, including Trevor and Chico, lowered Mark Marks's casket slowly into place.

After the ropes were retrieved, Reverend Kristee, keenly aware of the crowd now assembled—thirty-five people—melodiously read two more Psalms. Local and visiting guests then lined up to use a pewter scoop inscribed with the church's founding year, 1792, to sprinkle dirt onto the grave. Someone began singing "Amazing Grace." Others joined in, including Old Charlie, wiping his eyes as he did—these out-of-towners, whoever they were, had rescued him. Others teared up as well, feeling much more comfortable doing this because Mrs. Wilhelmina Marks, despite real or imagined vicious tongues, was openly sobbing.

After the last person threw dirt, the event, for that was what it was turning out to be, moved to the church's basement. *Food!* Mrs. Marks panicked. There were only the limited hors d'oeuvres laid out from last night's wake. Whatever remained was to have been loaded into the church's meals-on-wheels van, to be parked under the I-68 overpass that soullessly straddled downtown Cumberland. *To feed your son's friends,* a voice inside Winnie spoke. *You know, the* other *bums under the freeway.*

"There won't be enough food!" she exclaimed to her hens.

"Not to worry, Winnie," Mrs. Ripple and Mrs. Beacon told her. "We're on it, sweetie."

The hens swung into action. The basement refrigerator, a large commercial job, was quickly emptied. Its contents, the remains of recent nuptials, were brought out, including the bottom layer of a wedding cake. Last night's hors d'oeuvres and the reception remnants kept hunger (and embarrassment) at bay long enough for the hens to make SOS calls. Within the hour, hot casseroles began arriving, carried by kitchen-mitted women who Winnie knew would never have attended her son's service unless crisis called. Now they came, arriving in the nick of time to keep the funeral lunch going. The "casserole women" gave curt but respectful condolences to Winnie, usually looking away while they did it, but she no longer felt judgmental. These women had dropped everything to help her in the way small communities will do, in this case, shoving casseroles into ovens like artillery shells, then dashing down the street with them.

Mrs. Marks was now the center of attention. The out-of-towners greeted her pleasantly, sharing stories about her son, many of them funny. They knew Mark well, or at least the big city version of him. It was bewildering; how could so many people know *this much* about her Markie and not she? Discussion in the basement started softly, but as the casseroles arrived, grew louder. As odd as it was, Mark Marks's funeral rite, a rite of the dead, was becoming quite lively, and with stomachs filling, the townspeople and the AAs began mingling. The Cumberlanders got the skinny on their hometown pariah—per the AAs, Markie Marks, at least when he was sober, wasn't a bad sort. The Christ the Redeemer congregants were also fascinated to learn that their banished boy had a mystery nickname, "Prophet," who'd put together several intervals of sobriety, the longest being two years. Prophet had even owned a car, which he sometimes lived out of, but otherwise used to take newcomers to meetings. He did odd jobs: painting, landscaping, even becoming a self-taught piano tuner. He'd also worked two years for a distributor in Silver Spring called Nelson's Paper Supplies.

Mrs. Marks found the AAs fascinating. First, they didn't look or sound like drunks. She'd seen her Markie between binges long enough to know that even when sober, something was off-looking about a drunk. Second, for an anonymous program, they made no effort to disguise their identities other than not using their friends' last names, which apparently most of them didn't know anyway. Third, one did not speak ill of the dead, at least on the day of his funeral, so perhaps these fine folks were ginning their stories as people at funerals sometimes did, but even so, they talked *well* of her son, who by now was sounding like a stranger, a nice one.

Congregants learned that their Markie, a high school dropout and the town's designated bad example, had gotten his GED. Their Markie, an angry, cursing drunk, had morphed into a decent human being—when he wasn't drinking, of course. Even the AAs agreed Markie was no picnic when plastered; they didn't shy away from describing the drunkenness, so for the locals, there was satisfaction knowing that even in the big city, *their* Markie, at least some of the time, met hometown expectations: a man reduced to shameful panhandling in the guise of "fortune-telling," meeting a bad end. But the boy—they still considered the forty-two-year-old Markie a boy—was genuinely liked by these AA people.

There was more. Markie had a long-term girlfriend—a member of this alcoholics' community, a poor thing who'd succumbed to liver failure three years ago, which had hit Markie hard. This knowledge, *a girlfriend*, came as complete news to Mrs. Marks. It, and the presence of these well-meaning strangers, brought her to tears again. Her son's successes, no matter how small, were something her neighbors would now have to associate with his name, for surely all these out-of-towners wouldn't lie. The sight of the AAs, their hugs, stories, and good cheer, was priceless to her, and this second wake, one for the son she wished she'd had (and actually *did* have), put her over the moon.

Chapter 26: The Inner Circle

Saturday, 9 January 1999
Enroute to Wheaton, MD

TREVOR AGAIN. BEFORE the service, I'd barely said two words to anyone, but on the ride home, all the funeral discussion about Prophet's good "AA" character brought back seeing, well, really *hearing*, the poor guy die. I feel terrible for him and terrible for not calling 911. I could have done so. The church had a phone, plus there was a payphone right next to where I'd parked my car. *The Alley Killer could have seen you making a call!* my sniveling sense of self-survival says by way of excuse. But as selfish as I am, I'm not buying that.

And why was I even worrying about the killer anymore? The funeral marked almost two months since the murder. Until Prophet's service, I'd been avoiding thinking about Mark Marks' killer, and when I couldn't, I told myself: *It was dark as hell, I saw nothing but his boots, so no way he got a good look at me.*

But I also remember half the people at that AA meeting were wearing boots. The killer could have been anybody, so initially, I'd really sweated, fearing some boot-wearing man would kill me right on the street. But after two weeks, I'd started believing the Alley Killer couldn't ID me or he would have done so already. *And truth be told, Trev ol' pal, since you haven't said anything yet, the Alley Killer likely assumes you never will.* Also, he probably suspects, as I do, that attention to the death of a troubled street drunk would quickly flag, and thus the murder would likely never be solved. The more the murder fades into ambiguity, the safer I feel, and I'm sure the killer feels the same way. But I'm not proud of that. I'm not proud of any of it.

I don't discuss any of this with Cisco and Chico on the ride home, however. Instead, I talk about my older brother, Willie, dead by suicide a year ago. Why? Perhaps he's just a safer subject and talking about him keeps my mind off my own troubles.

I describe my brother, the basics of the club, and how Willie got into trouble.

With his Puerto Rican burr, Chico astutely asks, "So why didn't Willie like the Old Line, *mi broki*?"

"He was tired of selling guns, Chico. Or more accurately, tired of transporting them. He was the club's bookkeeper, but he wasn't exempt from contraband runs. A run could take Willie anywhere, but usually to Baltimore, Jersey, New York, and back. There was an incident on one of the runs. He wouldn't talk about it, but whatever happened, it was why he wanted to leave. But you can't just leave the club—once an Old Liner, always an Old Liner. To leave, you need the unanimous support of every member. Willie was the best bookkeeper they ever had. No *way* were they gonna lose 'Big Brain Willie.' Besides, 'vote-outs' were usually reserved for bad actors—bad by club standards, which is saying something. Anyone who ratted on the club lost his colors, of course, though losing colors isn't the first thing a rat should worry about. Anyway, theoretically, there's no 'good' reason to leave."

"Bad actors?" asks Chico. "Trevor, mi broki, we're talking *bikers*. They're all bad. *Muy malo*."

"It's more complicated than that, isn't it, Trevor?" asks Cisco.

I'm surprised Cisco has something to say. What does a granddad know about gangs?

"No, Chico," I say, "they're not all bad actors. For sure, some are, and they're all rough around the edges, and very dangerous as a group. Hell, they're dangerous individually"—Mullet Man, now debt collector, enters my head—"but most are okay. The Circle, however—all bad actors."

"The Circle?" asks Chico.

"Yeah," I say, "the club within the club, that's the Circle. They call the shots. Those outside the Circle are foot soldiers, grunts. Grunts are in it for the B's—beer, bikes, babes—and that's pretty much it. Most aren't full-time. They got jobs, just show up on weekends at their clubhouse. But it's a full-time gig for anyone in the Circle. Now don't get me wrong: full-time, part-time, you never wanna cross a biker unless you want complicated dental work, but the big decisions—"

"Like killing someone?" prompts Chico.

"Uh, sure. The Circle makes those decisions. If members outside the Circle do unsanctioned big-time shit—"

"Stuff," corrects Cisco.

"Yeah, unsanctioned *stuff*, well, they're made to feel sorry."

"*Caray!*" proclaims Chico. He's thrilled with the topic.

"Anyway," I continue, "in high school, my brother Willie was, let's just say, impressionable. One day, the Pugs are motoring up I-270 to visit relatives in Frederick. A double column of Old Liners roars past us, wheel to wheel, no gaps. It was love at first sight for Willie. He immediately wanted a motorcycle. Naturally, Dad said no. Said Willie could do whatever he wanted *after* he got a degree. Guess he figured if Willie went to college, the biker itch would pass. Willie did okay at University of Maryland at first, liking philosophy courses the best, but could never commit to a major. There was just too much out there."

"Philosophy?" asks Cisco.

"Yep. And biology, cartography, even Roman history. Plus, he went through a math phase, almost cobbled enough credits for a Bachelor's. He understood calculus, non-Euclidian geometry, shit I don't—"

A disapproving look from Cisco.

"*Stuff* I don't understand."

"I thought you said you was a good coder," Chico says. "You gotta be good in math to code, right?"

"I am," I say a little defensively. "I like coding because I *understand* coding. It's just logic loops and basic math. Honestly, anyone can do it. But the killer math Willie could do—jeepers. You okay with 'jeepers,' Jefe?" I ask.

"Pray continue," Cisco says indulgently.

"Anyway," I resume, "the accounting stuff Old Line had Big Brain Willie doing was so beneath him. My brother was smart, *wicked* smart. The tax dodging stuff he did for them was harder, but still not challenging. Honestly, he just did the books so he could be in the club. But you gotta understand how impressionable Willie could be. He wasn't an idiot or seriously gullible or anything—not with day-to-day stuff—it's just that the right guy using the right approach at the right time could get Willie to believe just about anything. Even though my brother could go off the conversational deep end—no biker wants to debate the philosophic differences between Kant and Heidegger because *no biker knows who Kant and Heidegger are*—they kept being chummy with him, telling him he was Circle material, I don't know—maybe as a joke. Old Line's leader, a guy named Christian Luntz—well, Willie adored him, so he wanted to be in the Circle just to please Luntz."

"Luntz, huh?" asks Cisco.

"You know him?" I ask.

"I've heard the name," says Cisco. He doesn't elaborate.

Chico asks about getting into Old Line.

"Not a lot of initiation stuff," I say. "Usually, the Circle just announces that a prospect's a full member, then everyone parties at their clubhouse, this rundown farm in southern Maryland outside Waldorf. At the party, sometimes they make the prospects do stupid shit—*stuff*—like clocks and centuries."

"What are they, mi broki?" asks Chico, sounding fascinated.

"A clock's drinking a case, twenty-four beers, in one day. A century is a hundred beers in a weekend, five o'clock on Friday to midnight Sunday."

"That sounds horrible," says Cisco.

Chico nods gravely. "Agree with you there, Jefe." He's not disgusted; he thinks it's physiologically impossible.

"I know you're thinking, it can't be done," I say. "But the guys are tough, plus the rules on barfing are loose."

"What do you have to do to join the Circle?" asks Chico.

"Willie never said what he'd done to get in, but I could tell it was illegal and he didn't like it. But inside he got, the youngest Circle member ever. Luntz really loved him after that."

"So what made him leave?" Chico asks.

"The Pagans," I answer.

"The who?"

I explain: "The Pagans, a major biker gang. Think Hell's Angels, except the Angels are sworn enemies of the Pagans, but that's another story. At the national level, the Pagans try keeping their rep as clean as they can, so when there's dirty work to be done, the majors get the minor clubs like Old Line to do it. Never tell an Old Liner that his club is minor, but it's true. Most of the time, the majors don't ask too much—torch a car, hassle some guy until he starts paying protection."

"That'd be asking too much of *me*," says Cisco.

"That goes double for murder, Jefe, right?" I ask. Cisco gives me an odd glance.

"They're all murderers?" Chico asks.

"Those outside the Inner Circle, no," I say, hesitating. "But some inside the circle, yes."

"How do you know that?" Chico wants to know.

I'm ready to launch into a long story now. "Willie told me. So things like killing somebody when a major club needs it done is the price of Circle admission. He never told me what *he* did to get in, but he swore up and down it wasn't murder. I believed him. Anyway, he got in and stayed for a year. Then on a gun run, something happened in Atlantic and they wanted Willie to take care of it. Whatever it was, he wouldn't do it, so they gave him a beatdown. After that, Willie went downhill. Luntz started worrying 'cause my brother didn't just keep the lights on, he knew *everything* about the club's finances, which meant he knew about the skeletons.

"Even after Atlantic City, Willie kept his mouth shut about club business. He was no rat. But he couldn't keep quiet about his pet topics, things most bikers, most *people*, don't give a crap about, like man's position in the Universe. Anyway, he was always jabbering about this stuff, but after

Atlantic City, he went nuclear. It wasn't just annoying anymore. Even to me, Willie sounded unstable. Eventually, the club voted him out to save his mental health—and theirs. They stripped his colors, inked an 'X' over his Minuteman tattoo.

"Normally with the Old Line, when you're out, you're out, but in Willie's case, there were practicalities to consider. They encouraged him, forcefully I'm sure, to keep their books going, but no rides, no parties, no clubhouse hangs. Just the ledgers. That kinda crushed him, but even Willie realized how lucky he was for landing the way he did. So once a month, he showed up at their Waldorf clubhouse to write checks. But the new arrangement didn't do the club much good. See, Willie was always searching for 'meaning,' for 'direction.' That hadn't changed. But without regular club interaction and particularly without Luntz's pep talks, Willie *really* started wandering mentally, kinda losing it. The bookkeeping suffered, checks bounced. They reprimanded him again, but all that did was make him flakier.

"Soon after, my brother disappeared. Luntz was beside himself and put the word out: *Find him*. In the meantime, Willie fled to the West Coast, on the run and vulnerable, and that's when the Heaven's Gate wackos got him. They hid him from the bikers, giving him their particular 'meaning of life' spiel while doing so. Applewhite, their head honcho, that guy with the crazy wide eyes and the eyebrows, welcomed my brother with open arms. If Willie liked Luntz, he worshipped Applewhite!

"Willie sometimes called me from San Diego, see? That's how I knew it was bad. Jesus, he was miserable. Spies for Old Line eventually found him. The Circle was gonna take a road trip to deal with him, but Applewhite intervened. Not sure exactly what happened, but I think assurances were made and money changed hands. Luntz reached out to the Pagans to keep an eye on him, but as Heaven's Gate promised, Willie never interacted with the club again.

"You'd think that'd be good news, but it wasn't. Those cult jerks stripped Willie down, taking everything they could. Mom and Dad got calls for money, I got calls, his friends got calls, *everyone* got calls—except the Old Line. Willie's keeping his mouth shut about the club was the only good decision he made in California, but it wasn't long after that he killed himself."

"Heaven's Gate?" Chico asks, now looking solemn. "Those guys that mass-suicided because of that asteroid?"

"Comet. But yeah, those guys."

"Your brother died with them?"

"No, he died later."

With that, I stop talking. I'm exhausted and I nod off. I dream that Carol is locked in a cage, and it's being lowered into a pool. Reesie is screaming at me to find the correct key to let Mom out before she drowns. It's unpleasant.

Cisco is dropping me off at home when I wake.

Chapter 27: Danny Trax

Monday, 14 February 1999—Valentine's Day
Fairfax, VA

IT WAS VALENTINE'S Day and Darius felt surreal, watching on as his team leader, Danny Trax, thumbed through his personnel file. Danny had finally finished, putting a finger dramatically on its top sheet.

"Well, Darius," Danny said, "as you know, your arrest is problematic."

"Problematic" was boss-speak for *You have screwed up to the point that I have to do something about it and I resent it.*

And you do resent it, don't you, Danny?

Before August, Trax had been chill to work for—not too lazy, not too stupid, not too petty, not too pompous. *And unlike now,* D-Kay thought, *not too strange to look at.* "Pre-August" Danny could suds it up with his coworkers, exhibiting that stellar boss trait, level-headed mediocrity, even when drunk. Since August, however, D-Kay now had to deal with the unpredictable *new* Danny, an impish cousin to Dilbert's Bozo-haired boss.

To understand Darius Kay's bind, it helped to understand his profession. D-Kay graduated in 1987 from Virginia Tech with a mechanical engineering degree, and DC-based Def Systems, a major military equipment contractor, scooped him up two weeks after graduation. Def Systems supplied twelve percent of the Air Force's annual equipment needs, including PX chow and flight jackets, but mostly they manufactured large metal objects that flew supersonically before blowing up. Said objects usually did so at high altitudes—satellite level—and Def Systems engineers like D-Kay provided all aspects of their design, testing, production, and maintenance.

On the job, Darius Kay wasn't known as *D-Kay*. His division was formal, full of ex-Air Force officers who disliked nickname chumminess, preferring to be called *sir*. Darius designed guidance hardware for Def Systems' flying bombs and was good at it. Even though the Cold War was officially over, times for military contractors were still good because inside the Beltway, military hawks still really liked missiles, so Darius had intended to ride his good-paying, patriotic job all the way to retirement, something totally doable provided he didn't flame out on booze, drugs, gambling, prostitutes, or get arrested.

"Darius, you wool-gathering? We've got a problem here."

"Yeah. Sorry, Danny."

"That's okay," Danny said coquettishly, which made Darius uncomfortable. "So, how do you propose to solve it?"

Yeah, yeah, thought Darius, *we've got a problem, but I'm supposed to fix it. So much for teamwork.* But the boss was right. It was much more Darius's problem than Def Systems'. The difficulty was this: Darius's security clearance had been suspended, company policy after an arrest or legal action. Popping Kent Ruger in the jaw on live television had certainly qualified.

Oddly enough, Kay had been lionized by a strange cohort of Christians, environmentalists, atheists, and many average joes who swore by the motto *there's only so much crap I'm willing to take.* These people started sentences about the incident with, "I don't condone violence, but in this case . . ." And as with many public spectacles, parents were left holding the bag. "Mommy, that man hit that other man bad. Why is Daddy cheering?"

The weird wave of select public sentiment aside, Darius was in serious legal trouble. To "rescue" him from this, good ol' Kent Ruger had offered a bitter olive branch: if Darius made a public apology, he'd drop all charges and not sue. Otherwise, he'd see him in court. Legal action was a threat to Darius's very necessary security clearance, as a guilty verdict meant saying sayonara to ever working in the defense industry again, and any follow-up civil suit would bankrupt him. His wife, Sandy, who didn't work outside the home and didn't want to, would be forced to.

The effect of the assault charge had been immediate; he'd been pulled off his own project, one he'd managed for two years, replaced by his douche of an assistant, Donald Peabody. If you watched Peabody like a cat watched an aquarium, the guy could be trusted with scut work. But if Darius was sidelined for another two weeks, the project, and possibly his career, would be toast, since Peabody couldn't be trusted to take a dump without being watched, let alone manage a multi-million-dollar missile project. Pentagon money was plentiful, but it wasn't *that* plentiful.

A fine kettle of fish you've got me in, Ruger, you asshat.

The safest course of action was also the most expedient. D-Kay could simply swallow his pride and apologize to the bastard. An apology, however, would require forevermore supporting the Coventry Christmas Carnival (Ruger had gone so far as spelling this out in writing). Considering jail time and a potential lawsuit—*and don't forget that weird dream where he drops a tree on you*—was there any other option?

There was one, but it was a long shot. Unknown to everyone except the Kays, various religious groups had offered assurances of financial support as the incident could potentially serve as a shot across the consumeristic bow. The sums weren't substantial but might increase if the spectacle gathered national, or better yet, international, attention. The American Atheists also smelled blood in the water of public opinion, but their pockets weren't as deep as the Christians', plus Sandy pointed out the hypocrisy of accepting money from both the Jesus and the non-Jesus people. Regardless, would Darius serve the interests of those who had the most to gain from an OJ-esque, *Miracle on 34th Street*-like trial?

Either way, becoming famous (or infamous) would doom his security clearance. Print reporters were already sniffing around. What exactly did this thirty-two-year-old engineer do at Def Systems? Said sniffing made the upper-ups unhappy. Def Systems wasn't exactly the NSA, but it understandably wanted to avoid attention not related to winning contracts or successfully launching missiles.

And don't forget the media hacks. The worst was Channel 4 News. Since the incident had happened live in front of their cameras, Ruger insisted any apology should occur under the same conditions. But Darius didn't want to be a chump. He didn't want to be *that* guy, an organ-grinding monkey Ruger could point to and say, "Darius Kay? I own him." The shame of that alone would force the Kays to move far from DC, putting him out of a job, out of a great house, and out of favor with his wife. (Prophet's prophesy—*And your women's gonna go bad!*—was coming true in Darius's case. Sandy hadn't been in the mood since Christmas; even tonight, St. Valentine's Day, wasn't looking good.)

This was no way to live, but at least it would soon be over. Kent Ruger had given him a deadline, Monday, seven days from now, to decide. On the twenty-first of February, he was to walk over to Kent's front lawn, and with cameras rolling, apologize. It was that or legal action. *Can I depend on twelve random jurists to bail me out?* He didn't think so, plus yes, Kent Ruger had crossed a line decorating his home without his permission, but *boy* did he know how to put on a light show, and now was willing to turn the other cheek so long as he got a big-ass, light show-promoting apology for doing so. (Plus, the assault had gotten him attention, and now this gesture to Kay was getting him even more, something he'd likely use to keep potential troublemakers, like the Horowitzes, in check.

Danny, your mascara is smeared. This observation briefly brought Darius present.

Since August, D-Kay had begun dreading looking at his boss. Old Danny—poker-playing Danny, *male* Danny, the boss he'd had over for grilled mahi-mahi, a guy he'd taken to strip clubs—would never wear mascara. But Old Danny had been replaced by this *doppelgänger*, one implying that if D-Kay couldn't make this Christmas parade happy crappy go away, then Peabody's promotion would be permanent.

Who exactly was New Danny? The new Danny emerged after the old Danny had taken six weeks' medical leave that summer. Since Danny wasn't the most healthy-looking guy at Def Systems to begin with, everyone assumed it was that common middle-management killer, heart disease. Danny had told no one about his leave ahead of time, so rumors ran rampant.

Depending on your orientation on the issue of orientation, this general anxiety was justified. Daniel Trax, age forty-two, a short, overweight bachelor with graying hair, returned to work in September as *Danielle* Trax, a trans bachelorette. No one, least of all Darius, saw this coming. In the five months since Danielle had arrived, Darius and his coworkers had been searching their memories for clues: how could Danny Trax's masculine "lie" have flown under their radar for so long?

Not everyone was in the dark, however. Since June, Danny had kept upper management in the loop, something the brass appreciated. At the Federal level, sexual discrimination was illegal, and since Def Systems' contract language kept them in lockstep with the government, firing, demoting, or otherwise sidelining Danielle wasn't considered. Another reason: he, ahem, *she*, was one of their best managers, and only an idiot would force her to seek out the competition or, Lord forbid, strike out on her own. The word from on high: "Dan is now Danielle. Roll with it."

Everyone was still adjusting. It didn't help that when she'd been out on medical leave, surgically speaking, Danielle hadn't gone "all the way." In fact, all she'd done was start hormone therapy, change her wardrobe, and apply makeup.

And the frickin' hair, thought Darius. Danielle wore colorful wigs to hide a Caesar's crown of limp hair. She'd been wearing a different wig each week since Labor Day, and though some looked better than others, none looked great because, before the conversion, Danny had been a squat Caucasian manager. Now she looked like a dress-wearing, pub-crawling Ed Asner. D-Kay was honestly concerned: Danielle would never have the trans good looks of Jaye Davidson in *The Crying Game*, but without something, a helpful girlfriend perhaps, she'd never succeed.

None of this phased Danielle, however. She believed she'd successfully transitioned into a real-life Cinderella, one currently wearing a Valentine's Day brooch declaring her A CUPID IN TRAINING. Coworkers had picked up on this. Some of the guys had started responding to her coquettish flirtations, particularly that suck-up, Peabody. It disgusted D-Kay how easily Peabody chatted up the new Danielle.

Sandy told him he was being far too judgmental; transitions like this took time. Five years, let alone five months, might not be long enough. The important thing, according to her, was that the woman trapped in Danny Trax's body had finally been released. "Isn't that wonderful?" she'd said. *No,* he mentally responded, finding himself wishing, of all things, for Danny to have had a complete surgical reassignment which would be easier visually. *But that meant a lot of time on the table, and let's face it, woman or no, ol' Danny's probably still attached to his*—her—*penis.*

"Earth to Darius," said Danielle, absently twirling the hair of this week's wig, a Jackie O special.

"Sorry, boss," said Darius. He was still using the term *boss,* working up the nerve to call her "Danielle."

"That's okay," she said. "But really, a hint on which way you're leaning with this Ruger guy, please? Rest assured, I'm rooting for you. No one deserves to come home to an unanticipated house makeover."

Did she understand the irony of what she'd just said?

"Fantastic that you're standing up for the Son of God, really, but practicalities, Darius. This Ruger guy gave you a week to decide. Provided you choose to make nice with him, I still need time to push the next launch back if it's to be under your control again. You need him to drop the charges. Otherwise . . ."

D-Kay told Danielle that he appreciated her advocacy, but he still needed time to decide, even though he knew in his heart he would kiss Ruger's ass on live TV—*smack, smack*—but he didn't want to publicly admit this until he absolutely had to.

Danielle didn't seem too upset. "Well, since you're going down to the wire," she said, fluffing her wig, "I'll be tuning into Channel 4 to see what divine outfit Trixie McPhane will be wearing, and of course, to see what happens."

Chapter 28: The Pitch and the Party Hat

Thursday, 17 February 1999
Washington, DC

"WELL SIRS," PHILLIPE said, "that's my pitch."

He settled back into the leather padding of his high-backed chair, trying to look calm. He'd just asked two of the most powerful men in DC, Adam and David Winsor, old-money hotel multi-millionaires, to reverse a favor they'd granted Councilman Washington based solely on his word. The elderly men, who on Thursday nights at the Men's Lounge went by the nicknames Statler and Waldorf, sat across from him, dressed in matching, smart-looking geisha outfits. Despite his own ensemble, a belle-of-the-ball Havana floorshow special, Phillipe couldn't relax.

"Johnny, that's a lot to ask," said Adam Winsor, aka Statler, the older and grumpier of the two brothers. "We'd like to help you, but your friend's committed a serious crime."

"Allegedly committed," corrected "Johnny Pilot."

"Young Johnny's right," said David Winsor, aka Waldorf, the seventy-six-year-old younger brother, the man who originally invited Phillipe to join the Lounge.

"Yes, yes, dear Brother," said Adam. "*Allegedly*. But that's not the real issue. We called in a favor, Johnny. The fact that this Japanese fellow . . ." He looked at a loss for a name.

"Henry Takahashi," said Phillipe. "And he's American."

"Yes, yes," Adam demurred. "Your vouching for his character is admirable, but Councilman Washington's convinced that Takahashi was caught with a smoking gun, and the police report backs that up. Asking us to reverse course at this point for a guilty man—"

"But he's not guilty, sir."

"Don't interrupt me," Adam said peevishly. "Guilt's for a jury to decide, but to me, the video evidence is compelling. Your buddy Takahashi was filmed holding a gun on the Councilman's son. They were arguing, then the Washington boy, oh what's his name again?"

"'Spencer Junior,'" said David Winsor.

"Right," said Adam. "From the video, it looks like Junior's surrendering, see, then your pal shoots him. You could argue that Takahashi had to have a gun, even an illegal one, to protect his business, but serving as judge, jury, and executioner? The Councilman's got a point. The Jap shouldn't get off scot-free."

Phillipe gripped his cabana dress tightly, bridling at the term "Jap." *Keep your mouth shut, Phillipe, and stay in the game!*

Steve, the attractive female cloakroom attendant he'd met during his initial visit, was serving in the Iroquois Room tonight. A minute before, without prompting, she'd brought him his favorite brand of beer, smiling as she set it down. "It's always a pleasure to serve you, Mr. Pilot," she'd said. *She's keen on me, no question,* he thought, *but I'm too tense to be flattered.* Serving as proof, the beer had sat untouched while he'd laid a case out for Splashdown's innocence.

"I'm sure the DA will offer something reasonable," said Adam. "What was the charge, again?"

"Second-degree murder," answered Phillipe, rubbing the fabric of his dress into his thighs. The image of him falling toward Hanger 18's floor suddenly came to him. *Goddamn it, I hate that dream.*

"Well, that's not exactly murder one, is it? I'm sure the plea deal will be reasonable, perhaps manslaughter."

"But he's innocent!" Phillipe declared, unable to control himself. Per Mr. Kamira, Henry's lawyer who'd deposed Phillipe as a character witness, Henry was planning to fight the murder charge tooth and nail. The illegal gun charge aside, which he'd already copped to, Henry believed himself one hundred percent innocent. So did all the EMBCers. *Apart from Rey,* thought Phillipe. To give him limited credit, Rey did support Henry for "solving matters with his own hands."

"That may be so," David said, "but my elder brother has a point."

Phillipe had dared to hope that the younger David, the more approachable Winsor who did, in fact, resemble the Muppet puppet called Waldorf, might break his way, but he hadn't. "Not to put too fine a point on it, Johnny," continued David, "once we've thrown in on something, reversing ourselves looks bad."

"And costs money," reinforced Adam. "Perhaps we never should have gotten involved with the Jap in the first place, but at this stage, we'd be throwing good money after bad."

"He's an *American*, sir," Phillipe said. *You damn fossil.*

Adam Winsor said nothing.

"Sirs," continued Phillipe, "if you had to spend money on the Councilman's behalf, I'm sorry about that."

"Well, we didn't spend actual money," David conceded. "We spent power. Anyway, we saw his evidence."

Saw his evidence? thought Phillipe. *Did these guys just waltz into the DA's Rockville office for a brief?*

"Didn't Shrimpton seem preoccupied, Statler?" David asked his brother. "Bruce Shrimpton, the DA," he said by way of explanation to Phillipe, "is a frequent hotel guest."

"He sure did," said Adam. "It's that Deerslayer fellow. There's a lot of pressure on Shrimpton from the namby-pambies to stop him, though I don't know why. I swear, the communists could invade—Soviet, Chinese, Cuban, hell, *all* of them—and those bleeding hearts would hand them cookies." David nodded, agreeing.

Despite their racism and misogyny, Phillipe still liked the Winsors. However, he now regretted letting them "sponsor" him, even though that was the only way a guy like him could afford the Lounge. *So, buddy,* he thought to himself, *you ready to quit the only place in the world that unquestionably accepts the real you?* Quitting now would save the monthly fifty-buck "junior membership" fee (four hundred dollars less than the normal rate), but it wasn't only the money. The truth was the Lounge was to Phillipe as a lifeboat was to a drowning man—something you didn't give up.

"We now owe Shrimpton a favor," said Adam, revisiting their earlier topic. Phillipe looked at David, still hoping for support but getting none. In fact, he nodded as if Statler had pronounced a commandment worthy of tablet inscription: *Once asked for, thou shall not recall a favor.*

"Look, Phillipe," said David congenially, violating the Lounge's number one rule by using his actual name, "we understand you wanting to defend your friend. Quite admirable."

"But this is murder," Adam continued. "Someone, even if it was that twit councilman's son, is dead, and all we did was prompt the District Attorney to take a closer look at the evidence, not fabricate anything. The charge against your friend . . ."

"Henry," Phillipe said, gripping his thighs again. "His name is Henry."

"The charge *Henry's* incurred seems legitimate," responded Adam.

David nodded. "I originally gave him the benefit of the doubt, but having seen the tape, it's clear he shot an unarmed man."

Phillipe himself had seen it. Mr. Kamira showed the video at the deposition, asking his opinion. The recording had that gritty feel that continuously taped-over security tapes get. Splashdown and the Washington boy weren't in sharp focus, but there was enough light to tell what went on.

Henry stood next to his car, having just closed its trunk. Washington Jr. magically appeared then, the previously opened trunk door having blocked him from view. There was a short, inaudible discussion—the tile distributor's security camera had no audio—but it was obvious there was a confrontation. A non-viewable static burst came next, then Henry reappeared, pulling an object, pointing it at Washington. It took little imagination for Phillipe to recognize what the object was—Splashdown's gun, Make My Day. Spencer immediately raised his hands. More soundless dialogue, then Spencer flicked his head quickly to his right, looking over his shoulder. There was another visual blip, then the image returned, the gun flashed, and Spencer Jr. dropped out of sight.

The tape wasn't totally damning, but it made Splashdown look like the aggressor—something Washington Sr. had stressed at the hearing, and perhaps that was the logical conclusion—*if* the tape was the only evidence. But factoring in everything, the time of day (nearly midnight), Henry Takahashi having a reason to be in the parking lot and Spencer Jr., a junkie and wannabe thug, not having one, plus the police agreeing that someone might have been in the woods just off camera (based on footprints which unfortunately weren't castable), then there was room for interpretation, which was why Splash had originally been given latitude.

What changed? Phillipe thought. *Councilman Washington running to his codger buddies the Winsors, that's what. The hoteliers then asked the DA to put his thumb on the scale, and that's what he did.*

Had someone else been there that night? From police photos of the area, all that could be firmly concluded was that an unknown person or persons had tromped through the little copse of woods recently. They questioned Junior's known associates (also thug wannabes) about the incident, but all had alibis. *No, no, they'd not been at Henry's business the night of 14 November 1998 when their dearly misunderstood friend, Spencer Jr., was killed during the act of putting his hands up.* "He was unarmed, right?" Andrew Litton, one of Junior's associates, had asked the police. When informed that a six-inch brass knuckle-knife combo had been found on Junior's body, Litton replied, "Proves my point. No gun. Junior wasn't armed." Not perfect logic, but still logic.

The crux of Henry's argument was self-defense, predicated on Washington having reached for a gun. According to Splash, some guy in the woods had prompted him: *Pull yours, Spencer*. The Rambo-worthy knuckle-knife found on Junior's body proved Washington wasn't a choirboy, but the Litton character had a point: a knife wasn't a gun and Junior hadn't been holding it when he'd been shot. All the facts were circumstantial. *En masse,* would they convict or exonerate Henry?

Back in the present, Adam said, "It would be pulling teeth to get the District Attorney to drop the charges now. What would you have us do? Ask him to ignore the evidence?"

To Phillipe, the answer wasn't for the DA to ignore anything. It was for him to have the police look for *more and better* evidence, but he bit his tongue. The Muppet Men had parked their luxury car on an Our Hands Are Tied space with no plans to move it. All their war bragging, all their adulterous adventures, all their power brokering—it was just for show. They were equivocating now, hiding behind the DA's skirts like children.

I thought you guys were cool, but you're pathetic.

Phillipe had been to several Lounge events now, including the pricey New Year's Eve Bash. Though the Bash was the only event allowing outside guests—e.g., girlfriends and wives—to attend, the still deeply closeted Phillipe Gallois hadn't brought Estelle. *Not that I could've afforded to, even if I wanted.* At the Bash, most of the plus-ones had been older women well above Phillipe's social station. Yet he'd had fun, everyone recognizing him as the Winsors' new darling.

Still, Steve, the pencil-mustachioed cloakroom clerk, had given him the skinny that night in the locker room: the old men adopted a young member every few years in an attempt to live vicariously through him—Phillipe was just the latest. She warned him about getting too cocky; the last guy had gotten annoyingly smug. Phillipe assured her he'd be okay. "I'm just a regular guy, Stevie, not a climber." She'd looked relieved, planting a quick "good boy" kiss on his cheek after helping him don shoes that, despite their large size, matched his outfit perfectly.

Phillipe had since thought a lot about that night. Yes, he was happily dating Estelle, and with good reason: she was runway beautiful, fantastic in bed, loyal (perhaps to a fault, a Stand-by-your-man-istan woman if there ever was one), reasonably intelligent, and above all, totally feminine. Nothing in Estelle hinted at girlishness. She was a full-fledged woman and, as such, sought a fully-fledged man.

Societally, Estelle would take Phillipe as high as he wanted to climb, and that prospect both thrilled and frightened him. She could have any man she wanted, but behind her protective pretentiousness, she'd been yearning for a rugged, square-jawed Heathcliff, and *he* was him. That Gallois found "Steve" attractive wasn't surprising—she was good-looking—but Estelle was beautiful. Steve was obviously smart, too, quite capable of clobbering Estelle in *Clue* or *Connect Four*, but what Estelle lacked in intelligence she made up for in shrewdness—the "dumb" things she said publicly were said for effect. Steve was an empathetic woman who read individual people well, but Estelle read the room. *So don't lead Stevie on,* Phillipe thought. *Plus, surely there's a real-life guy just perfect for her, perhaps named 'Steve.' Who am I to come between Steve and Steve?*

It's because Stevie knows your secret and Estelle doesn't, an internal voice said. The statement hurt him because, even in her vainglorious, backbiting way, Estelle played square. As far as she was concerned, there was only one unforgivable sin: betrayal. *Never humiliate me by being that which you are not.* The cross-dressing: how could she live down the shame of not knowing? How could such a worldly woman so thoroughly miss *that* boat? She would never suffer such disgrace lightly. Phillipe could only imagine the consequences if she learned her manly man knew the difference between silk, cashmere, and taffeta *by feel.*

Vengeance would be swift—everyone would learn his secret: his friends, his family, his Skoal-chewing coworkers, *everybody,* and in spectacular fashion. *Attention! Attention! We interrupt this broadcast to relay shocking news. Phillipe Gallois is a dress-wearing fraud! Find him! Confiscate his man card immediately!*

No, she would never find out.

Somehow, cute, mustachioed Steve knew this and had taken on the role of king's confessor: *Your sins are for my ears only*. The problem was that Stevie was no doughy friar; she was *hot,* and if Estelle knew that he was both a cross-dresser and—sex or no sex—trading intimacies with a cloakroom clerk, she would hunt him down and string him up—Phillipe, six feet tall, one-hundred eighty-five pounds of work-toned muscle, was terrified by this prospect. Unfortunately, the Lounge, meant to vent cross-dressing steam on Thursday nights when Estelle thought he was playing poker, had turned into just another thing to worry about.

Hey Gallois! his internal voice yelled. *Stay focused. Save Splashdown!*

His earlier pitch, appealing to the Winsors' magnanimity, hadn't worked, so . . . *Time for the last bolt in my quiver.* If the Winsors were worried about losing figurative money in the zero-sum game of political backscratching, perhaps Phillipe could save Splashdown with *real* money. Though it would certainly be a stretch, since he carried a fair amount of debt, he offered to pay the Lounge's full monthly fee: $450. Who needed to do anything but eat, sleep, and go to work anyway?

The Muppet Men regarded his offer almost distastefully—his small money meant nothing to them.

Oh crap, now what do I do?

A few moments passed. Waldorf looked at his older brother, then whispered into his ear. Statler smiled. "Put your money away, Pilot," he told Phillipe. "We have a better idea."

Earlier that day, Original Ken had gone to Mrs. Nigel's for his normal appointment. He sat in Nigel's subduedly lit reception room fingering his colorful bowtie, another gift from his sister as delivered through the hellions. Ken had been wearing bowties for two years after having worn one to work at *The Post* as a sort of bygone gag—*Hold the presses! Jimmy Olsen's on the blower with a hot lead!* The newsroom ate it up and now bowties were his wardrobe standard.

He was reading again, but this time it wasn't *Highlights*, or the copy of *Deliverance*, February's EMBC selection he had brought with him—it was *Go Dog Go*. For a kid's book, the illustrations were amazing: lots of dogs, lots of cars, lots of dogs *in* cars, all obsessed with an automobile race and the huge canine party at its finish line. He now knew why Tori had asked if he'd liked her handbag. In the story, a female dog kept running into a male dog. She wore a different hat for each encounter and asked him if he liked it. He always said, "No, I do not like your hat." Each time this happened, she walked away huffily, saying, "Good day." The boy dog responded in kind. At the end of the book, at the big dog party, the female wore a truly outrageous party hat, a Mardi Gras float for the head, and finally, the male dog approved.

I am such a pathetic spy, Ken suddenly told himself.

Unknown to Tori and Mrs. Nigel, Ken had been listening in on their sessions. This was, of course, a privacy no-no on several levels, but Ken, hell-bent on making a "lesbian" confidant, couldn't help himself. He'd begun sitting next to the radio, the one set to Mrs. Nigel's favorite classical station, turning it down to better hear through the door. He was also moving the table away from the vent to Nigel's office. When the building's HVAC wasn't rumbling, he could hear bits of what Tori said:

"Things aren't working out with Patty. Same old story. I'm doing the work, she's not."

"Feels like there's no one out there for me."

"Girls! Girls! Girls!" (He'd heard this before, along with Tori's and Mrs. Nigel's cackling.)

Finally: "That guy Ken you see after me? Probably sitting out there right now. It's the same stupid thing. And that bowtie? Really?"

Interesting! thought Ken. Hearing movement, he turned the radio back up and sat up straight.

Mrs. Nigel's door opened. After hugging her counselor, Tori spied *Go Dog Go* on Original's lap.

Ken felt nervous, like a kid before his first recital, and messed with his bowtie.

She approached him, asking, "Well, Ken, do you like my bag today?"

Original was torn. In the story, the boy dog rejected the girl dog's *chapeau* several times before accepting it. Was Tori wanting to continue their repartee like that or did she expect him to jump straight to the happy ending? *I haven't thought this through,* thought Ken, panicking. Tori looked at him expectantly. His best, on-the-fly logic: since she was carrying the same handbag with the same straps, the same lesbian pink triangle, and the same rainbow, he would once again claim not liking it. This he did.

Tori began looking upset. "Seriously . . . you don't like my bag?"

Uh oh, thought Ken. Hurt feelings weren't part of the script! Was this really the best way to make a gay friend? (Or any friend?) *You've committed,* he told himself, *so stick to your guns.* "Um, no, I don't like it."

"Well, good day then," said Tori. "And good day to that stupid bowtie!"

She stormed out looking very angry.

In the hallway, however, Tori could barely contain her laughter.

Chapter 29: Big Stew

Friday, 18 February 1999
Wheaton, MD

FOUR DAYS AFTER Valentine's Day, the Deerslayer's luck turned. Having thoroughly cleared out his own "backyard," the Deerslayer now had to push deeper into the park to find game; his current "stand" was more than a mile from home. The nighttime travel getting there had him worried, as did the Park and Rec police, who were looking for him. If caught, the man had much to lose.

Given the increased range, the hunter had swapped out walking for jogging, congratulating himself on the shrewd combination of camouflage and speed. His running outfit, a dark tracksuit and a Nike hat, screamed fitness nut, not deer killer. The disguise was necessary. Alert citizens had eyes out for a suspicious-looking man carrying anything resembling archery equipment. As a jogger, he carried nothing and didn't need to—he kept his crossbow and all his hunting gear buried near his stand.

As he trotted down the greenway that evening, the Deerslayer amicably waved to a pair of late-night runners. They waved back. After passing them, his thoughts returned to how pleasant it would be to bag one particular animal, a Hartford-worthy stag he'd nicknamed Big Stew. Big Stew and the herd he led had shown up around Christmas. So far, Big Stew's wide-roaming crew was proving smart, remaining outside crossbow range. If they were no-shows tonight, the Deerslayer would try picking off a stray from some other herd, something becoming harder and harder to do. If he was lucky, however, either Big Stew or one of his environment-killing cousins would be the Deerslayer's ninetieth kill. *Assuming the clock doesn't run out on you,* he thought. *You need to be back for your Law & Order wifey date.*

After ensuring he was alone, he stepped off the greenway's asphalt into the woods, down a dirt trail. He retrieved his gear, then climbed up ten feet into an oak tree, scratching an itchy nose. Tonight's "blind" consisted of the trusty two-by-twelve which he'd wedged between three of the oak's largest branches. Once laid across it, he pulled a shredded blanket over himself. It served to break up his outline and marginally protect against the cold night air. It was 7:15 p.m. Except for the low drone of the surrounding city, there was no noise—he could almost hear his breath fogging. To be home by 9:00

for his TV date, he needed to kill by 8:00, 8:15 tops. Forty-five minutes to an hour wasn't much time, but these days he took what he could get.

By 8:00, no deer had come. His nose itched. Some nights were like this—the further into the evening it went, the more likely the herds had chosen to bed down elsewhere. He gave it a few more luckless minutes before deciding to pack up. The Deerslayer dropped the blanket to the ground and was beginning to climb down from the oak when he heard something and lay prone again. Beyond him in the dark came the soft sound of cautiously approaching hooves. Though they were still essentially tame during the day, the deer moved warily at night now. *Thanks to my productive hunting.*

He smiled. *It's Big Stew!*

Big Stew stopped a hundred feet short of the crossbowman. The stag stood still, sniffing the air, rotating his ears slowly. *Trying to suss me out, Stewie?* the Deerslayer thought. He could take the thirty-yard shot now but that distance was the limit of his range, particularly on moonless nights like tonight. *So keep coming, Stewie, you and your ten-point rack.*

But Big Stew did not come. *C'mon, dude, I'm fighting the clock here.* Stew and his herd, however, moved no closer. The Deerslayer's anxiety mounted. He pinched the light for his digital watch—8:19—and continued waiting.

To distract himself, the Deerslayer scoped the rest of the herd, about ten heads. Though it was February, these deer carried more weight than last spring's anorexic animals. His summer's hunting had allowed the previously annihilated scrub-shrub layer to recover, which in turn provided more food for the remaining deer. *You're closer to what you're supposed to be: sleek, beautiful herbivores. Damn careful ones, too, not last year's stupid, lazy beasts. Again, you can thank me for that.* His nose itched again but now wasn't the time to scratch it. Under his breath: "Come on, Mr. Nine-Zero, I don't have all night."

The stag continued standing still. *Why's he taking so long?* Though the Deerslayer had been (illegally) hunting for eight months now, that hadn't made him a deer whisperer. Still, he knew Big Stew wouldn't take so much time if he really didn't want to move in the man's direction. The pungent odor of Antler Advantage deer chow sprinkled around the base of the oak was surely the reason for this. Big Stew looked back at his herd for a moment, turned again in the man's direction, hesitated, then finally made up his mind.

He turned his herd around, away from the hunter.

Oh damn, it's now or never! But the Deerslayer hesitated. *What am I afraid of? I've never missed.*

This was almost true. He'd winged two deer his first month; both had run off. Luckily, each bled out quickly, away from residences and roads. Still, eighty-nine total kills later with no survivors was certainly confidence-building. *And I've shot longer than this,* which was mostly true as well.

The man's itchy nose flared.

Goddamn it, shoot him now! But despite this hyper insistence, rationality spoke: *Let him go. Get number ninety tomorrow night. Or the next night. Better safe than sorry.*

But he wanted ninety now.

He depressed the crossbow's trigger. Unfortunately, his nose also spasmed.

The bolt went straight but not true, hitting Big Stew on his torso above his leg, a glancing, non-fatal blow skewering the fat beneath the animal's coat. The magnificent stag now looked like it had been pierced by an obscenely large safety pin. Big Stew, startled, let out an almost human cry. The herd stampeded. The buck reared, then did the same.

Oh no-no-no!

The animals crashed through a large grove of tulip poplars in the general direction of Georgia Ave, a quarter mile away. This was potentially a worst-case scenario: a buck pierced by a highly visible crossbow bolt, running for miles, advertising *I've been illegally shot on protected land by some pathological human asshole—not for food, not even for sport, but just to see me die!* The Deerslayer jumped to the ground, landing roughly on his side, driving his hunting knife into his thigh. The scabbard protected his leg, but it still hurt.

Big Stew's herd was gone. *What am I gonna do, chase 'em? Even if I had time, which I don't, how am I gonna follow a blood trail I can't even see? Dammit!*

But he did chase them. He ran, dodging poplars, hopping over logs, scrambling madly after the fading sound of hooves. After a half-minute's run, he slowed to a jog because his rational voice had resumed: *Look, pal, the game's over. You've had your fun. Now it's time to wipe your equipment down and get rid of it, 'cause sooner or later Big Stew's gonna be found dead with your expensive bolt stuck in his shoulder. You're the freaking Park and Rec arborist, for Christ's sake! Who would ever suspect you? Go to work tomorrow, talk up Stephen at the Park Police barracks, see what he knows.*

Reason convinced him. It was stupid (and dangerous) chasing quicksilver deer through broken terrain at night, so he stopped jogging. *Pitch your gear,* he thought. *Head home.*

But just then, he heard the screech of locking brakes, then a fleshy crack, then a second much louder impact. *Georgia Avenue!* An idea: if Big Stew had been hit by traffic, the Deerslayer could be a "helpful" bystander, removing the bolt when preoccupied people looked elsewhere. *The hunt needn't be mothballed. Small risk, big reward!*

No! demanded Reason. *Not enough time!*

But he ignored Reason, running toward the lights of Georgia Ave visible through the woods a hundred yards away. The Deerslayer moved quickly, mindless of the branches switching his face. He arrived with the crossbow still in his hands, barely remembering to jettison it before emerging from the tree line onto the shoulder of the southbound lanes. Georgia Ave was a well-lit north-south arterial, three lanes each way. What greeted him there shocked the Deerslayer: an ugly-looking, traffic-stopping wreck in the northbound lanes. The first impact had been between a fifteen-passenger van and a deer. The animal now lay in a grotesque heap of unnatural angles, which for some reason reminded him of a woodchipper. A second vehicle, a Buick sedan, had been the source of the louder impact. To avoid the van, it had swerved into a wall of Jersey barriers protecting an open utility trench. The barriers had held; the sedan was totaled. Currently, its stunned occupants were sluggishly pushing away flaccid airbags. However, other than a mangled grill and one broken headlight, the van, an empty BWI passenger shuttle, appeared unaffected. The northbound DC commuters had already begun snaking around the wreck while the southbound lanes rubbernecked.

The Deerslayer ignored the vehicles, running instead to the animal carcass, turning it over to expose the shoulder with the bolt. But there was no bolt. Had the force of impact sheared it off? He looked around: blood and broken headlamp plastic, but still no bolt. "Hey buddy!" yelled a passenger from one of the vehicles snaking around the crash. "That thing's dead. How are the people?"

Right, thought the Deerslayer, *I better look like I give a shit.* And he did, but the people weren't his priority—hiding his crime was. *Big Stew's got no bolt. Wait. He's got no antlers, either.* The unfortunate creature was a doe, not Big Stew! Relief washed over him. His knees popped as he got up to help the accident victims, heading first to the passenger van. The man was talking excitedly to someone on his dispatch radio in a language the Deerslayer neither understood nor recognized.

"You okay?" he asked him through a half-open window. The driver said in clipped English that he was. Somewhere to the south, two sirens wailed.

The Deerslayer turned his attention to the Buick. The sedan's occupants, an older, well-dressed couple, had emerged from their car. The husband was holding his wife; both looked shaken. "Never saw them coming," he said. "They're just everywhere now, aren't they? I wonder what made them cross all that traffic."

"Them?" asked the Deerslayer.

"Yeah, it was several deer, maybe a dozen," the husband said, caressing his wife's shoulders.

"Is she hurt?" asked the Deerslayer.

"No," said the wife, answering for herself. "It was so awful. One minute we're leaving downtown, the next these poor creatures leap out of nowhere. And that *sound!* It was dreadful!" A tear began rolling down her cheek.

"They came from over there," said the husband.

Everyone looked to their left, across all six lanes toward the parkland where the Deerslayer had earlier emerged. Then they looked back at a spot on their side of the road toward a thin wedge of woodland beyond the utility trench. The scrub was bordered by a Church's Chicken to one side and a Jiffy Lube on the other. To flee the Deerslayer, the herd had crossed a half-dozen traffic lanes, then jumped a wide trench bracketed by the Jersey barriers. *It's a wonder there weren't more wrecks,* thought the Deerslayer.

A Montgomery County Police cruiser and an ambulance arrived behind them, having driven up the northbound shoulder. Two officers emerged from the cruiser, two EMTs from the ambulance. One officer and one EMT came toward their little group, the other pair went toward the shuttle van. The Deerslayer peered closely at the small woods between the fast food restaurant and the lube shop. The strip wasn't very wide, no more than thirty feet. It would be hard to fit ten deer into such a confined patch but not impossible. Peeling his eyes, he thought he could make out Big Stew crouching low, the rest of his herd behind him.

"Are you okay?" the first officer asked everyone. Heads nodded. The other EMT could be seen talking to the shuttle driver while the second officer began laying down road flares. The couple from the Buick introduced themselves as the Shermans of Olney, Maryland. The Deerslayer felt nervous and out of place. *How am I gonna cross back over six lanes of traffic without looking funny? And my bow. I need to get rid of it.* His watch read 9:05. *Law & Order* had already started. *Cindy's gonna be pissed.*

"Sir."

The Deerslayer realized the first officer was talking to him.

"Yes, officer?"

"What's your story?" the policeman asked. The Deerslayer gave him his full name—he was too rattled to do otherwise. "Was just walking by, thought I'd try to help."

"So you saw it happen, Mr. Spicotti?"

"I was on the other side of the road," said the Deerslayer. "I didn't see it, I heard it."

"Mighty tight walking, that side of Georgia," said the officer. "No sidewalk. Why weren't you over here?" the officer asked congenially. He nodded toward the well-lit northbound sidewalk that any sensible pedestrian would choose over the poorly-lit south breakdown lane. The

Deerslayer shrugged: Georgia Avenue was notoriously pedestrian-unfriendly, so it wasn't unheard of for people, usually young, perhaps foolish, to walk along the southbound shoulder.

The second officer finished laying out flares and approached the group, looking the Deerslayer up and down. He introduced himself quickly—Officer Ratello—asking the Deerslayer his name as the first officer had done, then said, "Sir, the shuttle driver,"—here Ratello pointed back to the van—"said you came out of the woods over there." The officer pointed west across the crawling traffic. "That the case?"

Wow, thought the Deerslayer, *that driver can speak English better than I thought.* "Yeah, um, that's true. And a bit embarrassing. I was on my way home and needed to use the bathroom. I, ah, couldn't wait."

"Which way were you originally heading, sir?" Officer Ratello asked.

"North." For emphasis, the Deerslayer head-nodded in that direction.

Ratello seemed skeptical. "You couldn't go another block and use a business restroom?" He pointed further north—Ratello seemed to enjoy pointing—where strip stores lay as far as the eye could see. "Or behind you?" He pointed to several businesses the Deerslayer could have stopped at.

"Like I said, I had to go."

"Sir, have you been drinking?" Officer Ratello asked.

"What? No," said the Deerslayer, "Just poor planning on my part. Anyway, I popped out of the woods after doing my business. This was just after it happened."

Both officers, as well as the Shermans, were now looking at his hands and the knife sheath hanging from his belt. "Is that blood, sir?" Ratello asked.

"Yes, from the deer."

"From the deer?"

"Yes," the Deerslayer confirmed.

"You were worried about the deer, sir? Really?" Ratello asked incredulously. "You some sort of vet?"

Luigi "Loo" Spicotti, whose alter ego, the Deerslayer, kept the hiker-biker trails free from the eco-destroying rats with antlers asked himself, *Are these guys* programmed *to assume I'm lying?* The answer seemed to be yes. "No, I'm not a veterinarian. The people seemed okay. The BWI guy was already calling 911, so I went over to the deer to see if it was still alive."

"Is it?" Everyone looked at the mangled pile of remains.

"No."

"What would you have done if it was still alive, sir?" Ratello asked.

"Officer, I don't know," said the Loo defensively. "It's all so freaky. Anyway, I thought you guys wanted the public to stay involved, right? That's all I was doing."

Ratello, who did not appreciate the cheek, regarded Loo like a three-dollar bill. He put his hand on the butt of his gun.

It was then that Luigi Spicotti, co-creator of the Evil Men's Book Club, head arborist for the Park and Rec Department, vegetarian, and anti-gun political peacenik, fully understood the trouble he was in. What was it that Prophet had predicted? *You're gonna get arrested, all a' you.*

"Sir, you came out of the woods dressed like a ninja just after a bunch of deer ran across a six-lane highway. I'm gonna need to see ID. And keep your hands away from that knife."

Chapter 30: El Conde's Wallet

Sunday, 17 April 1977—Day 46
Colombia, South America

DINNER THE NIGHT of the shirts and skins fútbol game where Gustavo Ruiz punched Jack Sparks in the face was a typical carb-heavy affair: fried cornmeal *arepa,* beans, and a rice-yucca combination covered in some mystery gravy, plus panela-laced Frutino. The gravy meat could be anything hustled up from the forest—armadillos, caimans, javelinas—and that night it was mostly caiman.

Normally after dinner, the boys and the captured Colombian soldiers were allowed, under guard, to kibitz with the FARC. Card playing was popular, as were boardgames: Backgammon, Battleship, Operation, even Monopoly, which the Marxist guerillas were oddly adept at. But nothing beat Risk. Money and candy bars were wagered on the outcomes of Risk campaigns, some taking multiple nights to complete. To the Caucasians, 6 p.m. meant a reprieve, a reminder that the FARC soldiers were people who would eventually let the boys go. At 8 p.m., nationalist songs were sung in low voices by the FARC and captured Colombian soldiers alike. The boys dreaded what came next—being led back to their coleta to be chained for the night. By 8:30, it was lights out until 6 a.m. On Night 46 of their kidnapping, however, the boys neither ate dinner nor played games—the savagery of the fútbol match had ruined their appetites. Jack spent the evening breathing through his mouth as best he could, eventually falling asleep clutched in Walter's arms.

18 April 1977—Day 47

The next day dawned. Walter was still angry about the fútbol match.

"I hate these little brown bastards, Jack, I hate them!" he said, spitting nails with his eyes at their guard.

"Give it a rest, Bruce," Jack replied irritably, finding it difficult to talk through broken cartilage. Walter continued glaring at the guard. Just then, Camarada Sebastian walked by on his way to a briefing, and Walter began eyeballing him instead. Camarada saw this and approached their coleta.

"I'm not kidding, Yank," Jack growled. "Stop it!"

From his face, Walter could tell Jack really meant it, but he didn't stop. Comrade Sebastian Ruiz looked down at him, amused. After a contest of wills, Walter very bitterly dropped his eyes. The Camarada moved on.

"Here, come help me," said Jack.

"With what?" asked Walter.

"My face, that's what." With Walter's unenthusiastic support, Jack reset his own nose. Painfully but more clearly now, he said, "We must make the best of things, Bruce. Remember that."

Well before Day 47, Jack had become popular with the FARC, saying the right thing at the right time, laughing at punchlines no matter how stupid. It helped that he was entrepreneurial. The FARC soldiers, the Colombian prisoners, the two boys—everyone—were given cigarettes to combat boredom. Walter gave his to Jack who in turn traded the "ciggies" for things they wanted, like candy bars and extra socks. To watch Jack operate, Walter would swear the boy was suffering from Stockholm syndrome. The Aussie laughed at everything, even unkind jokes about Australia. But each night after being chained, Jack assured him:

"When in Rome, Bruce, I act like a Roman. I follow the boots. But in my heart, we're the good guys, they are not."

His attitude worked well for most of the FARC soldiers, but not for Camarada Sebastian or his nose-breaking younger brother, Gustavo. Despite warnings from La Madre and Lt. Buscar, the brothers continued making life hard for *los reyes gringos*.

Despite the bullying, the boys' stay at Camp Mimada was otherwise tolerable. The food was okay once they got used to it; the only real problem was quantity. La Madre, the camp's head cook, had over a hundred twenty mouths to feed. This often meant there was just "enough" chow, leaving the boys disappointed if their portions were shorted, even sad if the protein-rich fish heads' eyes were missing from their fish head soup.

The days were sweaty and humid and the nights surprisingly cool. The FARC provided each guerilla with a uniform, a weapon, ammo, a pack, and a few essentials like soap. Beyond that, they were on their own. Since they weren't issued sleeping bags, the soldiers provided their own homespun wool blankets. The chained boys were given one each, which was sufficient most nights. Even so, Walter hated the camp's humidity and gloominess. He hated the acned, crotch-scratching teen guards and the fact that for miles in every direction, there was only jungle, a surprisingly *loud* one. By day, flies buzzed, birds cawed, and tiny primates screeched. By night, carnivores bayed, rodents chittered, and thousands of bats flapped after millions of insects. Even the ants made noise.

This racket wasn't loud enough for Lt. Buscar's liking, however. Despite strict noise discipline, he constantly worried his soldiers would be discovered. To counter this, he sent out patrols to probe for trouble and he stayed in radio contact with other FARC groups, constantly updating his threat map. There was good news: the Jaguars hadn't seen government troops in months. Buscar knew the military was looking for his two little cash cows but wasn't that concerned; through the FARC's network of spies, he knew that the thinly stretched, resource-weak army had no idea where to look. No, it was the paramilitaries Buscar feared—the *escuadrones de la Muerte,* the death squads—private armies of plantation owners, politicians, and drug lords.

Three paramilitary forces operated in the area—all dangerous. First were the coca growers whose crops would be converted to cocaine. Their chain of command ended with Pablo Escobar, a swiftly rising drug lord. Relations with Escobar's coca men were beginning to deteriorate—some growers who normally paid extortion to the FARC were increasingly unwilling to do so, but Escobar's thugs numbered few in the north. The situation for now was stable.

Second was the *Ejército Popular de Liberación*, better known by their initials, the EPL. The EPL were Maoist revolutionaries who competed with the FARC for the same pool of "rural" conscripts. But Buscar didn't worry too much about them, either; an informal truce between the factions, based on their mutual goal (overthrowing the government), was currently holding.

It was the third force, El Conde's men, that concerned Buscar. El Conde (the Earl) was a wealthy landowner instrumental in the government's procurement of land around Cerrejón for the new mine. To the outside world, the Earl was an elderly gentleman-statesman, a remnant from the country's colonial past. In reality, he was an uncompromising man with a large stake in the success of the mine. To protect his investment, El Conde employed a private militia, the province's largest. Because he was a businessman and not a general, the Earl left its day-to-day operations to his right-hand man, known as *El Fantasma* (the Ghost). El Fantasma was the Earl's long-leashed dog of war in command of eighty highly-trained men. The FARC feared *Los Fantasmas* (the Ghosts) because it made sense to do so—they were well-paid, well-equipped, and the government cast them a blind eye.

They also feared the Ghosts' calling card: collecting the severed fingers of their victims.

Buscar was also worried about Los Fantasmas for another reason. During the bus hijacking, La Madre's soldiers had unknowingly killed three of El Fantasma's men; though the Jaguars knew the guards in the lead Rover were from Bogota and thus okay to attack, El Conde's men had been driving the rear Rover. Given the Earl's large investment in Cerrejon's future, he'd begun loaning mercenaries to Intercor now that mine prep had begun in earnest. The FARC spies had missed this important detail, along with the correct identities of the bus passengers.

Unsurprisingly, the loss of his men angered El Conde. Few, however, knew what a black eye the kidnapping (of children, no less) meant for his under-the-radar mining interests. Overnight, the coal project had garnered unwanted international press. To minimize the damage, the Earl assigned El Fantasma to scour the countryside for the FARC guerillas responsible—Lt. Buscar's Jaguars. The Earl wanted the Lieutenant, as the cliché goes, dead or alive, and had set his finger-collecting Fantasma loose, this time with no leash at all.

Buscar had lost men as well. In addition to Gomez, who'd died of the leg injury received during the bus attack, he'd lost two others to Los Fantasmas, one killed outright, one captured. The captured man had surely been tortured to reveal the positions of Buscar's field camps (or give the information willingly in the hope that El Fantasma might spare his life, if not his fingers). Buscar had been moving his existing camps, but El Fantasma's men had already burned two of them to the ground with homemade napalm. So far, the location of La Finca Mimada, Buscar's base camp, remained undetected and, according to his secondaries, the captured man, a recent recruit brought from the south, hadn't known its location. He hoped this was true.

If found, Buscar had two options. The first was fighting it out, something he couldn't afford to do because he didn't have enough men. El Conde was sure to have opened up his wallet, swelling his militia, and since the FARC leadership didn't want an all-out war with a well-trained, well-equipped death squad, getting FARC reinforcements from the south was unlikely.

His second option was border-hopping to a hideaway in Venezuela, an illegal camp made available by socialist elements of Venezuelan President Pérez's government. The international border was the key—El Fantasma's paramilitaries wouldn't cross it, and Colombian troops couldn't. But the optics of a border jump were poor. The Venezuelans allowed it only under dire circumstances, and even then, for brief stayovers, measured in days, without supplies that could be construed as "aid." The camp, which the FARC loathingly referred to as *el culo del mundo* (the asshole of the world), was in an exposed coca clearing perched on a south-facing hillslope—no place for an extended layover. Buscar likened the waterless hidey-hole to a shoddy parachute: it would get you down from the sky, but not without breaking your legs.

Chapter 31: Happy Crappy

Monday, 21 February 1999
Reston, VA

FEBRUARY 21 ARRIVED, the day the Christmas Carnival apology was due, and D-Kay was miserable. Work dragged like a slow execution. Danielle, his trans boss, had pestered him all morning—"What do I tell corporate about that Ruger guy?" Finally, D-Kay admitted, "Danny, I'm gonna have to apologize to that rat bastard."

On one hand, Danielle was pleased. Darius would get the missile program back on track, rescuing it from that ham-handed suck-up, Peabody. On the other, she was disappointed. After forty-two years of waiting to play the "distressed damsel," she'd hoped her favorite project manager, Darius, would have championed protecting the true spirit of Christmas so she could root for him. Alas, her wait would continue—Darius Kay was taking the sensible, career-saving way out of his mess, which was, admittedly, what she would have done. *Still, wouldn't it have been something to see him stand up to that Ruger idiot, mano-a-mano, cameras rolling, telling him to lump it?* With the outcome now known, she wouldn't have to watch it on TV. *But I'll still be tuning in, boys and girls, because with Darius Kay, you just never know.*

The official end of Darius's workday, 4 p.m., finally arrived, so he grabbed his attaché case and waved his lariat badge to security on his way out. A guard asked him which way he'd go (everyone had been asking this all day) but except for Danny, D-Kay told everyone he was still making up his mind.

"Odds are three to one says you don't apologize," the guard said. "Got twenty on a non-apology. Am I throwing my money away?"

"Tune in at five for the happy crappy to find out," D-Kay said enigmatically.

He arrived home at 4:30. Channel 4 was already set up on Ruger's lawn with cameras and a mic stand that looked like a burdened radio tower; pickups from a half dozen news outlets were attached to it. Ruger stood in front of everything, all smiles, giving some sort of pre-apology interview to Trixie McPhane.

Chatting up the McPhane twit, Ruger? thought D-Kay. *Really?*

Sandy hugged D-Kay when he came through the door, knowing tonight would be tough for him. *Tough for us,* she corrected herself. If D-Kay had decided not to apologize to Ruger, she would have supported him. After all, various groups (albeit somewhat fringe) were willing to finance a fight. But that would put them squarely in the middle of a years-long media circus. *And Darius's job would still be toast,* she reminded herself, *along with this house. And don't forget a lawsuit . . . or worse, jail.* Sandy was relieved her shoot-from-the-hip husband was choosing discretion over valor.

She was amazed that Ruger had given Darius two months to make up his mind, but it made sense now: Ruger was milking the situation for all he could get. Today, however, was apology day, which meant suffering the indignity of becoming carnival light show rah-rahs for as long as they lived in Reston. *We'll have to move,* she thought. *No way am I gonna wave to these carnival crazies for the next twenty years like a Stepford Wife.*

Ben and Halle Horowitz came over to let them know not everyone in the neighborhood was on board with Ruger's stunt. Ben, a retired lawyer, had previously reviewed the agreement Ruger had given the Kays, the one Darius would need to sign at the time of the televised apology. Ben had told them it wasn't professionally written and there were onerous "grovel" stipulations; for example, requiring the Kays not to park on the street for the entire month of December to facilitate carnival traffic. "Just shake that idiot's hand in front of the cameras," he said. "No one will think less of you."

"Thanks for your support, Ben," said Sandy. "You guys are great. We have angels on one side and an anal-retentive devil on the other."

Both Horowitzes chuckled. "We're pulling for you either way," Halle said.

D-Kay had told no one but Sandy and Danny that he would apologize. The Horowitzes and the rest of their neighbors, along with the entire DC TV market, would learn soon enough—though from the looks on the Kays' faces, it was obvious which way the wind blew.

Halle continued. "Of course, you never know what might happen." Ben shook D-Kay's hand, Halle hugged Sandy, then the Horowitzes went home.

At five minutes to 5:00, D-Kay and Sandy headed to their door, both thinking, *Let's get this over with.* The Horowitzes emerged from their house dressed as for a funeral. Other neighbors, a dozen or so, had stepped out with them; apparently some sort of pre-apola-geddon support meeting. Sandy almost cried seeing this.

What started as a small crowd on Ruger's front yard at half past four had, by five, swollen to a hundred, not including the press. The small pro-Kay crowd, led by the Horowitzes, was there, along with a larger troop of pro-Carnival neighbors—Kent Ruger toadies who D-Kay assumed expected a crotch-rubber of a mea culpa. Most did, but some in the crowd were just curious neighbors: mothers holding snowsuited babies, fathers with dogs.

D-Kay wondered whether in the future these people would ask, *Never mind Kennedy, where were you when Darius Kay had to suck it on live TV?*

He walked over to Ruger. An idiot ring had been spraypainted on the snow in front of the mic by the TV people: STAND HERE. Ruger, in an overcoat, dark green suit, and a red tie, was dressed for a holiday already two months in the rearview mirror. The moment D-Kay stepped in front of the TV lights, the "realness" of the situation hit him: *This is going to totally suck, now, and for the rest of my life.*

Ruger, beaming, asked, "You ready, neighbor?"

"Sure," said D-Kay. "You got a copy of that agreement for me to sign?"

"Right here." Ruger pulled it partially out of his suit pocket.

"It's the same version you already gave us?" D-Kay asked under his breath. "Because I'll sing like a canary if it isn't."

"It's the exact same," Ruger said, turning down his smile to a more believable level.

Afterward, Darius would read it again. *As Reagan said, 'Trust but verify.'* Plus, it was only two pages long.

"Say, before we get started," said Ruger, "Trixie McPhane at Channel 4 wants to say a few words."

Good God, thought Darius miserably. *That tree I keep dreaming about, the one about to fall on me? Now would be a good time.*

McPhane stepped forward wearing a thin coat and a snug dress inappropriate for the weather, reinforcing Sandy's opinion that she dressed like a call girl.

Into the happy crappy we go, thought D-Kay. She shook his hand.

"And we're live in three," said the cameraman. After shaking her blonde hair once to fluff it, she introduced herself to the camera and began summarizing the history behind the night's event. D-Kay looked pained, like a man forced to eat a turd sandwich, while Ruger looked elated. As Trixie wrapped up her summary (timed to allow the boys in the studio to roll Darius punching Ruger's lights out), Ben Horowitz unexpectedly stepped into shot.

"What's up, neighbor?" asked Ruger, surprised.

Ben ignored him, whispering something to D-Kay.

What the hell is this? thought McPhane. "No secrets, sir," she gently chided. Ben ignored her, instead handing Ruger a folded paper before walking back out of shot.

"Well, this is a little irregular, don't you think?" Ruger asked Trixie, his eyes following Ben's retreating boots.

"I think it's exciting!" declared McPhane. "What does it *say*, Mr. Ruger? Is it a reprieve from the governor?" Light laughter from the crowd. They, like

Trixie, now waited with bated breath. Ruger stood dumbfounded, so Trixie prompted, "Any idea what it says, Mr. Kay?"

D-Kay, having no idea, shrugged his shoulders. He only knew what Ben had whispered, "Say you're sorry, shake his hand, but don't sign *anything*."

Kent stood uncertain for a moment longer, then joked to Trixie: "This just in, folks," then began reading to himself:

> *Kent:*
> *You will accept Darius's apology, then you will say words to this effect: "Thank you. All is forgiven and Mr. Kay won't have to agree to any conditions." You will not grandstand afterward.*
> *If you do not comply, the following will happen:*
> 1. *The undersigned will no longer support the carnival.*
> 2. *I will serve as the Kays' pro bono legal representative.*
> 3. *I will use the funds provided by the entities below to defend the Kays in court.*
>
> *Sincerely, Ben Horowitz*

The organizations, eleven total, were listed at the bottom of the page, along with the amount of money each group promised—totaling nearly thirty-thousand dollars. The groups were diverse, from the 700 Club to the American Atheists, plus Greenpeace, who Ben noted as being eager to draw attention to the carnival's whopping power bill. Along with Ben's signature were several other neighbors, including, to Kent's horror, two of his staunchest carnival supporters.

"*Well, Mr. Ruger?*" cooed Trixie. "Are you going to share with the rest of us?"

The crowd murmured, just as anxious to know what was making Ruger blanch. "Just a minute," Kent responded irritably as he re-read the letter, including the signatories. If all these people pulled out, next year's carnival would have the charm of a black-toothed hobo.

"Any idea at all, Mr. Kay?" Trixie Malone asked D-Kay again.

"None," D-Kay answered.

She knew Darius spoke truthfully. Though Ken Ruger's delay might affect Channel 4's commercial cycle, the building tension was priceless. *This is twenty-four-carat gold!* she thought. *National material! Something Americans will actually remember, along with who I am!*

Ruger gave Ben Horowitz a glare of fortified death. Ben looked back innocently. (After the interview, a media stampede would almost bowl Ben over.)

D-Kay, still confused, assumed it was time to say something. He extended his hand, saying, "Mr. Ruger, I'm sorry for what . . . uh . . . transpired to bring us together tonight."

Ruger looked at him pointedly. *And?*

"Oh, and I forgive you for illegally trespassing on my property."

Trixie clucked. *This is just getting better and better.*

Ruger's eye ticked; he looked flustered. Gathering himself, he shook D-Kay's hand, three manly pumps, all the while fantasizing about killing him.

"I accept your . . . apology, Mr. Kay, which I assume was meant to cover almost breaking my jaw, but I want you to know that . . . in the true spirit of Christmas, I harbor no ill will." His eye ticked twice. "I look forward to your permanent, enthusiastic support of the Coventry Lane Christmas Carnival of Lights, which this year"—Kent faced the cameras, smiling forcefully—"was three blocks long!"

Ruger's response, more involved than the directions Ben had given him, was met with polite applause. Kent and Darius still held each other's hand.

Ben nodded from outside the TV circle, saying loudly, "You're not going to require Mr. Kay to *sign* anything, are you, Mr. Ruger?"

Oh Horowitz, you bastard, thought Ruger. *Never mind Kay, I should kill you!*

"No, of course not," Kent said. The crowd cheered more generously this time.

But it wasn't over. Kay's apology was middling at best, and Ruger's pharisaical response wasn't much better. Ruger waited for Kay to release his grip so he could at least claim a dominant hand victory. Darius, however, wasn't letting go. They continued gripping each other's hands like awkward gladiators, and the crowd grew uncomfortable. *Time for you clowns to knock it off.*

Trixie McPhane, however, wasn't uncomfortable at all—she was jubilant. *These guys hate each other!*

Kent's eyes: *Don't push it, Darius.*

D-Kay's body language: *I can stand here all night, pal. How do you like* that *happy crappy?*

The crowd began murmuring and someone exclaimed, "Oh, just get on with it."

Slowly, Kent's eyes changed from steel to pleading. *Darius, buddy, throw me a bone here!*

But D-Kay had no intention of doing so. With a brief but intense look of hatred, Ruger finally let go. Another cheer went up, more from relief than approval. D-Kay stepped next to Ruger, putting his arm companionably around his shoulders. After a pause, Ruger did the same, gripping Darius's shoulder to the point of pain. Trixie McPhane, who believed fortune favored the bold, invited herself into their embrace. They unclasped, accepting her—Ruger miserable, Kay smug.

Yep, twenty-four-carat gold, thought Trixie, giving the camera her best smile.

Chapter 32: Loo's Reputation Wake

Friday Night, 25 February 1999
Wheaton, MD

EVEN THOUGH LOO was released the night of his arrest, the EMBC took the accusation hard, the net sentiment being *Spicotti's the Deerslayer? Are you kidding?*

They and their significant others had been supporting the Spicottis, but getting through the media ring surrounding their household that week had proved difficult. If Loo so much as poked his head outside, reporters shouted:

"The deer slayings surround your neighborhood, Mr. Spicotti. Your house, in fact. Care to comment?"

"A runner carrying a hunting knife—care to explain?"

Visitors got hassled, too:

"Did you ever suspect your friend was the Deerslayer?"

"Why do you think he did it?"

Ken, Phillipe, and D-Kay had assembled the Friday evening following Loo's arrest to grumble about it. The guys met at a Wheaton bar, the Quarry House, for an "emergency meeting" to discuss what they could do besides blowing off the press. They believed Loo innocent but acknowledged that the public, based on circumstantial evidence—his railing against deer overpopulation, his jogging with a hunting knife, the fact that no deer had died since his arrest— considered him guilty. The three talked and drank but had no brainstorms.

The scoring for January's book came up (*Last Exit to Brooklyn*: six thumbs up, one thumb down, and a very evil score of 8). That meeting had gone well, as had February's (*Deliverance*). But given the recent arrests, should they hold the March meeting? (Was Prophet's curse coming true?) It was a fair question. Splash had been arrest #1, D-Kay #2, and now both founding fathers, Trevor and Loo, had also been detained. Trevor (arrest #3), was still laying low after destroying three Crown Vic Police Interceptors (twenty thousand a pop, thank you very much) and now Loo (#4) found himself besieged by the media. Confounding things, Ken had gotten a call from a fellow *Washington Post* correspondent asking if Loo and Ken were members of a satanic book club.

"No way, Ken," said Phillipe. "That hits too close to home."

"'Satanic book club? Don't know what you're talking about,' is what I told him. What else could I say?"

The three sat silently, as if observing a wake for the death of their friend's reputation. Spirits rose briefly when D-Kay, for the umpteenth time, relayed the highlights of his Christmas Carnival non-apology apology, and how thoroughly it had gotten under his neighbor's skin.

But then conversation went quiet again, leaving D-Kay time to think. *If people knew I was a member of some 'demonic' book club that the Deerslayer belonged to—alleged Deerslayer, that is—Ruger'll have a field day.* This scared him. For diversion, he asked Phillipe, "Trevor says you've made a dress big enough for a sasquatch. That true?"

Phillipe, startled, replied, "My dad's a tailor, my mom's a seamstress. Runs in the family. And it's for Estelle, not Bigfoot. The Triple Play's messed with his head." The Triple Play was what the guys were calling Trevor's three-cruiser pile-up. "And seriously, what does a dumbass like Trevor know about dress sizes anyway?"

"Good point," said Darius.

Phillipe relaxed. D-Kay's jibe was nothing new—his clothier roots were a constant source of club fodder. Admittedly, today's assault had come from left field, but why worry? No one knew about the Men's Lounge. He did worry about Trevor, however; not because his ex-houseguest had seen his oversized dress, but for what he *might have seen* if he was the snooping type. Was he? Phillipe wouldn't have thought so before, but now that Trevor had racked up ridiculous bar debt, tanked his job, and triple-played his license away, he wasn't so sure.

Phillipe's fear was, in fact, justified.

Back in January, Trevor had arrived at his friend's apartment with the three changes of underwear his furious wife had packed for him under the assumption that her husband would do his own laundry. Once out of boxers, Trevor instead plundered his host's dresser to search for skivvies while Phillipe was at work ensuring no one at Southwest's Hanger 18 was doing anything remotely like screwing up. After going through the dresser, curiosity got the better of Trevor, so he reconnoitered his friend's closet: one well-tailored suit, khakis, Oxfords, a bathrobe, a belt rack, what seemed like an excessive number of silk ties, and a dozen Southwest work shirts. Nothing surprising unless you counted a large garment bag labeled *Flight Suits* and what seemed like an excessive number of shoe boxes along the closet's back wall.

In for a penny, in for a pound, thought Trevor, crouching to examine three random shoe boxes—Nikes, Brooks, and some expensive loafers. All seemed in order . . . except a pair of work boots in the corner. *Just like the Alley Killer's.* Trevor shuddered but continued spying until only the two-section garment bag remained. The front section contained flight suits as advertised. He rotated the heavy bag with difficulty, then opened the second section expecting more of the same. Instead, he found dresses—*Phillipe-sized* dresses. He stared disbelievingly.

Oh my God! Phillipe, you sly transvestite!

He closed the bag, rotating it back. *I have to know,* he told himself, opening the remaining shoeboxes. To his relief (he assumed), they contained the brands their cartons described. It was weird that a guy kept his shoes in their original boxes, but that was small potatoes compared to the dresses. As he closed the last shoebox, he accidentally bumped the back wall of the closet, producing an unexpected *reet* sound.

A spring-loaded trim board?

Behind it was a double row of stylish women's shoes, each pair large enough to fit a troll. At last, he closed the cubby and left the bedroom, disappointed not to find panties or, better yet, a Madonna cone bra. But he was still pleased that for the first time in weeks, someone else's problems rivalled his own. *Based on the number of dresses, my friend, you've been doing this for some time.* He couldn't fathom why, but he understood that "outing" Phillipe would destroy a man whom, even in the light of this revelation, he still respected. *I will keep your secret, even from you, Phillipe.* And he did.

Or so he thought.

Back at the Quarry House, Henry Takahashi arrived, declaring, "I'm so happy to see you guys!" And indeed, Splash looked happy. In fact, he looked elated.

"Splashdown in the house!" shouted D-Kay, pleased to see his mate who had been laying low while awaiting trial.

"Surprise, guys, I'm free!" Splash announced loudly.

"Cool!" said D-Kay, smiling, "but what does that mean?"

"The charge was dropped."

"Fantastic!" said D-Kay, bear-hugging him. Phillipe joined, too, and once they let go, Ken clasped his arm around Splash, saying, "Well, *do* tell."

And tell he did, at least the parts he knew.

For reasons unknown to him, the police had re-canvassed Spencer Washington Junior's accomplices. The story from Andrew Litton, Junior's best friend, no longer checked out.

During his first interview, Andrew had held his own with the detective, lying to establish his alibi (being with a friend far from the business park where Junior had been shot) but otherwise answering questions truthfully. "We found a brass knuckle/knife combo on him as illegal as Jesus is holy," the detective told him. Litton confirmed that Spencer always carried the WWI relic. Andrew was a good liar and knew when not to push it. He didn't need to—the detective had bought his alibi and understood his implication: even if Junior had pulled his blade, which Litton knew he hadn't, bringing a gun to a knife fight made Takahashi look bad.

But during his second interview, the police came at Andrew with a full court press: not one but three detectives, grilling him for two hours. During the first hour and a half, Litton couldn't be shaken from his alibi, so the detectives tried a different tact, asking him detailed questions about what he'd learned about the murder from TV news. The questions came quickly and relentlessly. Litton rolled with them well enough until asked, "According to the TV, what did the guy in the woods say to Junior before he got shot?"

"Pull yours, Spencer," replied Andrew. This was the correct answer, so Litton smiled confidently, but then the detectives informed him that this bit of dialogue had never been made public. Litton's smile died. He'd claimed all along he'd never been there, so how could he know this? He spun gears for another twenty minutes before finally accepting his fate: in exchange for rolling on Spencer's intention to rob Henry, plus pleading to a lesser charge—abetting assault—he was promised leniency.

Later that day, the DA's office notified Mr. Kamira, Henry's lawyer, of the good news. Kamira insisted on driving Henry to the Rockville courthouse steps where he announced the charge had been dropped. (The illegal gun possession, pled down to a year's probation, wasn't mentioned.)

"Seriously," Splash continued, "you cannot *believe* how good I feel." Gone was his second-guessing, and gone, at least temporarily, was his sadness for taking a life. After all, it had been verified: self-defense, plain and simple, and as dark as the Deerslayer business was proving for Loo, all agreed that Splashdown's good news deserved celebrating.

Two hours later, everyone left for home. Splash jogged through the cold to catch up with Phillipe before he reached his aged but meticulously kept Grand Cherokee. "Hey Gallois, hold up a sec."

"What's up?" asked Phillipe.

"Wanted to say thanks," said Splash.

"For what?"

"My lawyer said you got a couple of high rollers to pull strings and get my case reopened. Don't know how you did it, but *wow*, you did! I didn't want to make a big deal about it in front of D-Kay and Original."

I'm glad you didn't, Phillipe thought.

"Anyway, I owe you everything."

"No big deal," said Phillipe.

"Enough with the modesty, Frenchman, take a bow already. And tell me about your patrons—Mr. Kamira said they were old fuddies in the hospital business?"

"Hotel business," corrected Phillipe.

"Which hotel?"

"The Winsor, downtown. You know it?"

"Of course I know it! Holy crap, you know the Winsor Brothers? *Personally*?"

"Um, yeah, I do," said Phillipe. *Unfortunately*.

"Who did you have to blow to talk with them?" asked Henry excitedly.

"I didn't blow anyone," replied Phillipe.

"Sure, sure—sorry. I mean, how did you meet them?"

"Heard about an opportunity," said Phillipe. "The Winsors were looking for a full-time jet pilot."

"Cool!" said Henry. "Very cool! Frickin' great, in fact. Curious though—how'd you do it? Call their butler or something?"

Well, if you must know, thought Phillipe, *first I joined an expensive club of fellow cross-dressers—a total state secret, I might add—then I asked two septuagenarian Muppets named Statler and Waldorf to cancel a valuable 'marker.' I must look good in a dress, 'cause they did it, but not without committing me to night school to become a glorified sky hack.*

"No butler," Phillipe said, imagining Stu Pendous in some *Upstairs, Downstairs* outfit. Phillipe hated to lie, but he did: "A buddy of mine recommended me for the job."

"What's Estelle think?" asked Splash.

"She's supportive. Always wants me to better myself. I'm not jumping ship right away, though. I need to get certified—night school—gotta pay for it, but they'll reimburse me when I get my license. But you know, Splash, I'm a little worried," Phillipe continued. "Estelle's shrewd. Between fifty hours at Southwest *and* night classes, how much time's left for her?"

"Not much," acknowledged Splashdown.

"It's worse," continued Gallois. "Night classes are Monday-Wednesday-Friday. I need Tuesday night and Saturday for studying and all day Sunday for flight time."

"That leaves Thursday," said Splash.

"Yeah, and I play poker Thursdays with my Hanger 18 buddies." A whopping lie.

"Maybe you should ax poker night," Splash advised.

"Can't do that. It's sacred," Phillipe said firmly.

"Really?" asked Splash, surprised. "Anyway, I'm just so glad that frickin' murder charge isn't hanging over my head anymore. I owe you. Seriously, I *owe* you."

"You gonna open up the studio again?" asked Phillipe.

"Not sure. After the murder, I mean the justified self-defense—still getting used to saying that again—I'm not sure anyone, even someone edgy, would want to show their work in a space whose owner has, you know, killed somebody."

"Oh contraire," said Phillipe, "that's *exactly* where edgy artists would want to."

"Plus, the price, which is next to nothing, is right," Splashdown admitted.

They both laughed. "Hey, it's cold," said Phillipe. "I'm heading home."

"Me too," said Henry.

A lot transpired to clear Henry Takahashi, much of which Phillipe didn't know.

David Winsor, the younger and more approachable brother, had called Bruce Shrimpton, the DA. Shrimpton wasn't receptive to asking the police to re-review the evidence. After all, he didn't direct the county's police force. But he could ask Wacoby, the County Sheriff, for help. Wacoby was also adverse; budgets were tight, plus didn't Shrimpton already have his man? But Winsor pushed, so Shrimpton pushed. Sheriff Wacoby gave his detectives another week to turn up new leads. Nothing was found, so Wacoby kicked it back to the DA: *If you want to drop the charge, drop it. Don't put it on us.*

Shrimpton was about to contact David Winsor with the bad news when his secretary informed him the State Department was holding on Line One. It was a Mr. Phillip Rammers, the assistant to the Undersecretary for Public Diplomacy and Affairs, apologizing for the need to take up Mr. Shrimpton's time, but could Mr. Shrimpton, on behalf of the Undersecretary, kindly bring Rammers up to speed on the Spencer Washington Jr. investigation? It seemed that the Japanese Ambassador had taken a personal interest in the case, concerned about public perception surrounding how American law enforcement treated young Japanese-Americans. The ambassador had questioned the oddness of filing a second-degree murder charge after the

DA initially heralded Henry Takahashi's Second Amendment right to protect himself. The ambassador wanted to know: Was everything done by the book? Bruce Shrimpton assured Mr. Rammers that the investigation, conducted twice now, had been diligent.

He relayed this politely, but the truth was Bruce wasn't intimidated by some stooge from the State Department. If the Undersecretary for Public Diplomacy and Affairs really had a concern, then said Undersecretary could call himself. When Rammers began turning up the heat—"Surely, Mr. Shrimpton, you want to help the government maintain good relations with Japan?"—he didn't feel it. The only thing Bruce feared about diplomats was being run over by one. Rammers did offer him people to help, or at least a person, anyway—a "resource officer" named Dr. Graft.

Rammers and Graft, thought Shrimpton. *There's a pair of names for you.*

"You can have him for a week," said Rammers. "He's quite effective."

"Great, Mr. Rammers, but what does Dr. Graft bring to the table that our sheriff doesn't?"

"Let's just say Dr. Graft thinks outside the box."

I've heard that before, thought Shrimpton. But what could it hurt? If the State Department wanted to keep an ambassador happy on their own dime, why not? "Okay, Mr. Rammers, one week. You got yourself a deal." Shrimpton relayed the details to Sheriff Wacoby.

Whatever mental picture Wacoby had of a resource officer, he got it wrong. Dr. Graft was no tall, square-jawed "agent." Wacoby was underwhelmed, but Graft had shown up early and was energetically serious, so he spent an hour walking him through their case. Except for a few targeted questions, Graft sat silently the whole time, absorbing everything presented. Wacoby found it a bit creepy.

When he was done, Graft spoke. "Sheriff, please bring Andrew Litton back in. I have an idea." Wacoby didn't think it would work but agreed to try.

Graft was present for Litton's questioning. After a few last-minute instructions to Wacoby's detectives, Dr. Graft stood unmoving on his side of the one-way glass for one-and-a-half hours. When the Litton punk finally perjured himself, he grinned.

Phillipe didn't know what happened behind the scenes after David "Waldorf" Winsor called Bruce Shrimpton, but he remembered what the Muppet Puppets had required of him:

"Johnny," Adam Winsor, the older brother, had said with an overly large smile, "in exchange for helping your friend, you can fly us around. Be our pilot, you understand. Palm Springs is a slice of heaven this time of year." Phillipe had been stunned, realizing for the first time that his friendship with Henry might have limits. Even if he was a licensed jet pilot, which he wasn't (he was certified for prop planes only), and even if he had a jet, which he most certainly didn't, how could he afford it? Jet fuel alone was running forty cents a gallon. He couldn't afford to fly these mossbacks to Pittsburgh, let alone Palm Springs. What were they thinking?

"Uh, I don't have the resources to do that," said Phillipe. "You know I don't."

Mr. Pendous, who stood behind David Winsor's chair, flagged their waitress down. "Steve, be a dear and bring Mr. Pilot another drink."

"Certainly, sir," Steve said, briefly glancing at the crestfallen but still quite handsome Johnny Pilot.

"I think you don't understand what Mr. Statler is asking," continued Pendous. He explained the proposition in more detail. After hearing it, Phillipe felt better, but only some: to save his buddy, he'd have to turn his life upside down and surrender all his free time. And Estelle, oh she'd *love* the plan; every woman wants to be ignored.

Pendous spoke up again. "Gentlemen," by which he meant the Winsors, "perhaps we should let Johnny think on it." No dissent from the Muppet Men, who looked pleased with themselves, particularly Adam. "Take all the time you need," Pendous said. "Sleep on it." Steve arrived, handing Phillipe another beer. He absently accepted it, then stared into the fire crackling in the ballroom's hearth. The old men smoked their stogies, pleased as punch to watch young Pilot wrestle his morals.

Phillipe drew a breath, then said, "I don't have to sleep on it. The answer's yes." He pulled heavily on his beer, adding, "Have Pendous contact me with the particulars." He stood, brushed out wrinkles from his dress, then walked away authoritatively. Phillipe's dismissive tone had raised Pendous's eyebrows, which sent David cackling.

Adam joined in, crying, "Well done, Johnny! You're a man's man, Pilot. A man's man!"

When Gallois got home, he felt like the wind had blown around the leaves of his mind. He collapsed into bed—his sleep fitful, full of anxious dreams, including the one where he fell off a ladder from three stories up onto a half-dozen cartons which might save his life. A familiar-looking person resembling the dead homeless man, Prophet, stood by cartons. As he fell, Phillipe, to his horror, realized the bearded crazy man had begun pushing them away.

Chapter 33: The Close Call Wall

Saturday, 13 March 1999
Silver Spring, MD

A TIPSY WOMAN at the bar was asking Poland Manchester what the glass case labeled SHORT ROUNDS was about.

"Short rounds is shells not reachin' their targets," answered Manchester. Behind the bar, where normal owners stocked shelves with colorful liquor bottles to encourage business, Manchester had mounted a museum-style glass cabinet with a collection of things that normally went "boom": a German WW2 potato masher and a US Army "pineapple" grenade—three mortar rounds, including a Vietnam-era 81 mm, and a claymore mine with FRONT TOWARD ENEMY facing the customers. "They're all UXOs—unexploded ordinance," he said, delivering the line like he had a hundred times before.

The lady gulped. "You mean that stuff's real? As in *boom* real?"

"Yes," said Manchester, nonchalantly setting beers on a tray for his nephew, Brian, to serve.

The woman paled. "Isn't that dangerous?"

"Nah, it's all deactivated," Manchester said, deciding not to drag it out too much.

Attached to the outside of the glass were photos of other war artifacts that apparently had not gone boom either: a V-2 rocket wedged in the muck of the Thames, a US 155 mm round half buried in a Korean mountainside. There were a dozen similar pictures. "People give me this stuff," said Manchester after noticing her looking the photos over.

"Were those all duds too?"

"No one survives successful booms."

"Good point," she said, polishing off her drink and ordering another.

As she looked to be settling in, Poland added, "People call it the Close Call Wall."

"In that case, can I mail you my ex-husband?" she asked.

"I don't know," said Manchester with a cheeky grin, "has he been deactivated?" The woman laughed. Poland turned up the TV. Per Channel 4 News: apart from one buck, no deer had been slain in the four weeks since Luigi Spicotti's arrest. Loo's arrest photo was recycled on-screen. *Nah,* thought Poland, *Spicotti's not the Slayer. Don't have the nerve. None ah those punks do.*

In the back room, the March 1999 EMBC meeting was in full swing. Except for the home-bound, besieged Loo Spicotti, it was a full house: Original Ken, Death Rey, Trevor, Phillipe, D-Kay, Gary the New Guy, and the recently exonerated Splashdown. They had already recited the club motto and read the "rules."

Trevor had violated his home detention "order" to attend that night, lying to his wife ("Honey, I'm meeting with Cisco") and his sponsor ("Cisco, I'm staying home with Carol"). He'd been absent from the club for five months, and the guys were initially wary: was it wise having their newly sober friend back in a bar? Since Trevor never mentioned his pending court date or the money he owed Old Line, everyone assumed he had his act together—enough, anyway. Besides, it was a free country.

Dr. Pepper took him to task early, sending Pug to the Gents where he read the graffiti added during his absence.

Barbara's a slut! (Phone number listed.) Underneath was written *No Slut Shaming!* and under that, *Except for Barbara. She's a whore.*

Everyone hates racists, but racists only hate some people, so who's really racist? Next to it, a sad-faced Hitler.

Bis get it both ways. Underneath that, *I don't want it both ways,* and underneath that, *But you do want it always.*

Lastly: *If you ever feel powerless, know that a single one of your pubes will shut this place down.*

He returned to find his compatriots rehashing the previous month's book, *Deliverance.* Sodomy notwithstanding, it had only pegged "5" on the evil meter but had been thumbs up across the board, with the bonus of allowing club members to sing the first nine notes of "Dueling Banjos."

After stopping Gary from going on a tangent on how to best tune stringed instruments, they began discussing March's book, *In Cold Blood,* Capote's recounting of events surrounding the 1959 murder of four members of the Clutter family of Holcomb, Kansas. The guys gave their opinions and quoted select lines, having found the subject matter and the author's obvious crush on one of the two incarcerated killers fascinating (evil score: 7).

Not all opinions were positive. "It was okay," said D-Kay, "but it wasn't *Lolita.* 'One man's journey across the country with a twelve-year-old.' That's eviler."

"First," said Rey, "you're a pedophile. Second, *Lolita* was seven books ago—try to keep up. Third, empty your Internet cache."

"Sir Reymond of Death," D-Kay responded, "don't be so sensitive—this is the *Evil* Men's Book Club after all."

"D-Kay, you're a waste of flesh."

"'Waste of flesh?' Rey, you really know how to hurt a guy." D-Kay was laughing, looking far from hurt.

"'*The wastrel's life is the shortest path to sainthood,*'" quoted Gary suddenly. "Hermann Hesse."

"What does *that* mean?" asked Splash.

"It means even a pair of assholes like Rey and D-Kay can get halos," said Phillipe. "Not that they will."

"Despise me if you want, mechanic," Rey told Phillipe smugly, "but remember what Caligula said: *Let them hate, so long as they fear.*"

"Point, Reymond," D-Kay said, impressed.

"A point for Rey?" asked Trevor. "Are you serious?"

"How was I to know he'd pull something like that out of his ass?" D-Kay answered. "I'm tough, but I'm fair."

"Actually," said Gary, "Lucius Accius, a Roman scholar, said it some time prior to 86 B.C. Caligula wasn't even born yet."

"Jesus, New Guy!" said D-Kay. "How can you possibly know that?"

"My job affords me reading time," Gary responded. "Do you want to know more?"

The entire table: "No."

"Okay, but can I have Rey's point?"

"Sure," said D-Kay.

"Awesome," Gary said, happily marking it down.

"If Jesse Ventura can get elected governor of Minnesota," D-Kay said randomly, "then I'm running for office because I like ribbon cutting." In addition to distributing nicknames and conversational "points," D-Kay took his non-sequitur insertion duties seriously.

"Duly noted," Gary said, scribbling. "If the club ever opens up some Bruce Wayne-like Home for Wayward Girls, we'll pitch in for a giant pair of scissors." The guys laughed; Gary's brand of humor was growing on them.

Conversation lulled. For no conscious reason, each man suddenly recalled their recent visions. The bearded truck driver in Splash's last dream had passed so close to Henry that he'd ground his Challenger's blue paint all along the guardrail. For longer and longer periods, a similar man continued waterboarding Gary and was getting good at it. Rey's Gun Girl now had a beard and seemed ever less willing to spare his life. The bearded man in Phillipe's dream had already moved two cartons away from the 737 Phillipe was inspecting, leaving only four to break Gallois's three-story fall. A similar man now pushed the ref into Original so quickly that Ken had only time to throw up one protective hand, not two, before hitting the bleacher headfirst. A bearded, wood-chopping Kent Ruger was getting a better bead on D-Kay.

A similar man sat poolside as Trevor struggled to find the correct key to free his wife from her submerging cage. Unknown to the table, Loo at home was recalling the bearded man in his own dream (one wearing a Park and Rec uniform) and how he'd been forcibly pushing Loo closer and closer toward an infeasibly large woodchipper.

Feeling tense, Trevor spoke for the group. "So how's the club faring curse-wise? And what was the exact deal again? I wasn't there that night."

The guys filled him in—lost jobs, lost loves, arrests, deaths. "Well," he continued, "four of us got arrested: me, D-Kay, Loo, and Splash." He paused, reflective. "Curious—anyone been arrested before last November, say in the last ten years?" No one had. "And now four in five months . . ."

But is it really curious, Trevor? thought Phillipe. *Splash was mistakenly arrested. Loo too. D-Kay got a pass on live TV. It's only your drunk triple play that really deserved honest-to-God handcuffs.*

"Next, jobs," Trevor continued. "Loo's been put on leave at Park and Rec, so I think that counts. Splash, you had to shut down your studio for a while. Count that?"

"Yeah," said Splash, "but I'm back open now, baby!" The table cheered.

"And I, ah, lost my job," admitted Trevor. The guys had assumed it was Trevor's DUI arrest that made Frank Deguzman fire Trevor. The fact that he lost his position *before* the now infamous triple play was something only he knew. "Anyone else lost a job in the last ten years?" Pug asked. "Layoffs count, quitting doesn't." Two had. "So two in ten years versus three in five months. Not great. Okay, let's move on to hopefully better news. So . . . anyone's woman go south on them?" Chuckling, but no laughter. "Roll call," Trevor announced.

D-Kay reported no problems. Given the reversal of fortune vis-à-vis the Christmas Carnival Apology, Sandy was treating him like a king. Regarding Loo, it was clear that Cindy Spicotti was in full stand-by-her-man-istan mode.

"What about you, Rey?" Trevor asked.

"Come to think of it, no dates since Prophet died."

"So it's Prophet's fault you can't get a date?" asked D-Kay. "Not your general asshattery?"

"Sure," said Rey, "let's blame him." Normally he'd have responded with something more biting, but an unusual gust of wind had just hit Shortie's front door, rattling it loudly. Rey shivered unconsciously.

"Moving along," said D-Kay, jumping in, "how's that lesbian jinx, Original?"

"No dates, which means no change," Ken answered coolly.

"D-Kay, stop riding him," said Trevor.

"Sorry, being an asshole's part of my job description," D-Kay replied. Moderate laughter.

Phillipe reported that "relations" with Estelle were never better. Gary the New Guy relayed no problems on the home front, but the normally talkative man's answer was brief and flat, which was unusual. When asked, Splash rolled his eyes. For weeks, Juri, the Ambassador's daughter had been blowing up his phone. He planned to buy a new Nokia the minute the ambassador paid him. "I'm not dating anyone, particularly anyone underage," he emphasized.

Trevor reported no problems with Carol, but couldn't help thinking, *The streak's still intact, so I think we're alright, but with all the "mandatory" AA meetings, I'm too tired most nights to put the moves on anyway.* On top of that, Carol was balancing housework with a full forty hours at Hallmark and weekends watching Sunny so David Chin could work on his dissertation. *If I'm tired, then she's exhausted.*

Trevor went on. "So in the last five months, no one's lost a love, or . . ."—here he eyed Rey, Splash, and Original—"had the opportunity to, so I'd argue that we're holding steady in the kiss-kiss department."

"Sounds like the green zone to me," said Phillipe.

"Yes, and everyone's alive, so we're green there too," Trevor continued. "So Prophet's batting 0.500 for arrests, which is high, and 0.375 for lost jobs. Not bad at all. He should be in the majors. But death and love? Zero point zero. It's weird about the arrests, but overall, I think we're doing okay."

"It's all just coincidence anyway," said Rey, and everyone concurred.

Yet no one felt particularly inclined to discuss their dreams.

They began discussing more fictional "stan" countries. Everyone agreed that United-we-stan was a democracy and that the relations between Stand-off-istan and its neighbor to the south, Mexican Stand-off-istan, were piano-wire tight. Everyone also agreed that Up-against-the-wall-istan was governed by some brutal regime but disagreed as to what type: Religious zealots? Fascists? They debated this while motioning Brian to bring more beer.

Dr. Pepper once again overwhelmed Trevor's bladder. This time, however, the Gents was mobbed. *Fortune favors the bold,* he thought, unknowingly echoing Trixie McPhane, then popped unnoticed into the Ladies, relieved to find it empty. After locking himself in a stall, he urinated for what seemed the length of an Inaugural Address, giving him time to look about. The Ladies had less graffiti and what it had was neater. On the right wall, a woman with an eye for scale had drawn two rulers, one larger than the other, captioning both as *7 boy inches equals 4 real inches*. Above this illustration and possibly in no relation, *Go home, you're drunk*. On the lower portion of the stall door, someone had drawn a downward arrow warning *BEWARE OF LIMBO DANCERS*. On the left wall, someone else had written, *The girl in the other stall just gave birth.*

He zipped and flushed. Still alone, he risked examining the past "maternity" stall. Within: *If we can send one man to the moon, why can't we send them all?* Underneath this was parenthetically added, *And their tiny dicks*. On the opposite wall: *If I had a dollar for every guy I blew, I'd no longer have to blow guys*. Underneath, in very large, declarative letters, a disapproving sister had written *YOU'RE A SLUT!* Underneath that, another sister had written *Yes, but she has a point.* Chuckling, Trevor, washed up. On the intact mirror above the washstand—the Men's mirror had been missing for months—was written in lipstick: *No boys noticed me until I sprouted tits, now that's all they notice.* Trevor's favorite message, however, was written above the coin return on the wall-mounted condom dispenser: *For refund, insert baby.*

Dark, ladies. Very dark.

"Alright guys, now that Pug's back from the can," Original said, "a challenge: What are the advantages to having a lesbian friend?"

"Well, you should know, Jinx Boy," said D-Kay.

"For some insane reason, I'm asking you idiots," said Original, "so humor me."

"Okay," D-Kay said. "How about watching her make out with her girlfriend?"

"Not some porn lesbian, you dumbass," Original clarified, "a real lesbian."

"Oh," said D-Kay, concerned, "you mean one of the angry ones?"

"Hey numb nuts," said Original, "there's more than two types."

"There are?" asked D-Kay.

Scattered laughter, but Phillipe confronted Darius, saying, "Of course there are. Don't insult my aunt." Other guys acknowledged knowing lesbians: family members and cousins, workmates, even an ex-sister-in-law. D-Kay had stuck his foot in his mouth, something he often did, but rarely did he feel bad about it. "Sorry, guys."

"So again, *not* a porn lesbian," Original stressed. "And not D-Kay's angry 'bra burner.' Just a garden variety gay woman."

"So no possibility of sleeping with her?" Splashdown asked.

"None."

"And no watching her make out with her girlfriend?" asked D-Kay again.

"No!" Original barked. "Jesus, D-Kay, it's not a hard concept to grasp. You have a gay female friend—*who is single*—and who, for some strange reason, has befriended your cretin ass. Okay? Got it?"

"Yes," said Darius.

"So, advantages?" Ken asked again.

"Does she have good legs?" D-Kay now wanted to know. Ken looked at him contemptuously. "Hey, I'm a leg man," insisted Darius. "They were the first things I saw coming out." Laughter.

Testily, Original spelled out: "What. Are. The. Advantages. Of. Having. A. Lesbian. Friend."

"Watching her make out with her girlfriend?" asked D-Kay, obeying his instinct to always overdo things. In a let's-clear-this-up tone, Kay added: "I don't need to be there *in person.* They can video it. I'll watch later." More laughter.

"Damn it!" exclaimed Ken, losing grip. "It's a fucking *platonic* relationship with *one* lesbian. Okay, *Dari-ass?"*

"Okay, okay," said D-Kay, "don't get your panties in a wad. So we all have a lesbian friend. *Just* a friend. Got it. What's the question again?" More laughter.

"Kay, you really are an agent of chaos," Ken muttered testily.

"A really *dumb* one," added Rey.

"Ken, you'd have more luck stopping an ocean wave," Phillipe said sympathetically.

"Relax, Original," said Splashdown, "I'll give it a go. Well, why not ask her for dating tips?"

Original looked at Splash with an expression bordering love. *Finally,* someone was taking him seriously.

"I agree," said Brian, dropping off two more pitchers. "If you have a friendship with a woman, it helps to demystify women in general."

"Holy crap," said Original, "that's beautiful, Eeyore, really! Gary, give that man a point!"

"Look guys," said Brian, oblivious to the club's inscrutable point system, "if you turn down having a female friend, gay or not, then you're turning down someone willing to tell you when you're dressing badly, someone willing to warn you against undesirable women—"

"Undesirable women?" asked Splash.

"I think he means skanks," D-Kay clarified.

"Oh."

Brian looked annoyed, but bravely continued. "A friend that's concerned about what you eat, remembers your birthday, hugs you when your life's falling apart. That's what a friend's for, right?"

"That really is beautiful, Brian," said Gary, genuinely impressed.

Rey wasn't. "Eeyore, do you even *have* a girlfriend?"

"What's that got to do with it?"

"Let me interpret for you guys," said Rey. "That means *no*."

It was cruel to laugh at Brian after he'd offered such vulnerable advice, but Splash, Rey, and D-Kay did, Darius laughing the loudest. Brian gave them a look of boiling vinegar, then left.

The exchange got Trevor thinking. *Is that the way the guys made Prophet feel?* Not only did he feel badly that Mark Marks died violently (and that he'd not reported it), but he also felt sad picturing Mark's final hours. *You were in AA, Mark. You tried hard. Who knows, you might have made it eventually. Being harassed by a table of asses? You deserved better than that.*

"I went to Mark Mark's funeral the first week of January," Pug said suddenly.

"Who?" Phillipe asked.

"Prophet," he clarified. "The guy who died behind Shorties."

"Why?" asked D-Kay.

"I didn't have a choice," said Trevor. "My AA sponsor made me."

Original's brow wrinkled. "Didn't Prophet die in November? He would have been buried well before you did the triple . . . before you joined AA."

Trevor explained the circumstances surrounding Mark's delayed service.

"Wow, that must have been awful for his mom," said Original. Everyone agreed, even Rey.

At that moment, eight Latino men entered Shorties, interrupting their introspection. *What the hell?*

Hispanics patronizing The Short Round, Silver Spring's yuppie oasis, wasn't unheard of, but it was unusual, especially because these gentlemen were making a point to stand in the middle of the bar for attention. The pub went quiet, many people looking uncomfortable. From behind the bar, Manchester gave them a measured look. Had Loo been at the meeting, he would have recognized their leader as Storyteller, the "wetback" Rey Perkins had berated in December. The man looked directly at Rey, then slowly lifted his hat an inch. Rey stared back, trying not to show his fear.

Under Manchester's cool gaze, Storyteller and his amigos then left, saying nothing.

"Who're your friends?" Poland yelled to Rey.

"They're not my friends," he responded, looking ghostly pale.

"You don't approve of all the squares in our multicultural American quilt, do you, Rey?" Gary asked him, looking waggish.

"Not the illegal squares," Rey replied. "And fuck off, Gary. You talk too much."

Gary chuckled. Bar conversation resumed around them.

"Got a story, Rey?" asked D-Kay. "Knock up a chica?" Nervous laughter.

"Owe money to the Spanish mafia?" Phillipe asked. More nervous laughter.

"I don't owe those brown bastards anything!" screamed Rey suddenly. "Not a damn thing!"

The bar went silent again.

After an angry huff, Rey threw money on the table and left.

"Should we be concerned, Gary?" Phillipe asked. "You seem to know something we don't."

"How should I know?" Gary asked. He paid his share, then left as well.

Chapter 34: The Compound

Saturday, 20 March 1999
Waldorf, MD

CHRISTIAN LUNTZ STOOD behind the bar smoking a Winston. Various papers and envelopes were spread out in front of him, along with a ledger, a book of stamps, a worn Texas Instruments calculator, two pens, a sweating Falstaff beer, and a Redskins ashtray. Luntz carefully tapped his ashes into the tray, remembering Willie Pug always saying, "No ash on the bills!" After a final drag, Luntz neatly butted his cigarette. *See Willie, no ashes.*

The structure Luntz stood in was a rustic outbuilding, a large, decades-old tobacco drying shed called the "barn." It had been a generation since the Southern Maryland farm hosting it was a going concern, but despite years of hard partying, the barn still smelled of the shag leaves once hanging from its beams. It and a modest farmhouse sat on sixty-four acres of land owned by the Old Line Motorcycle Club. Fifteen of those acres fronted County Road 4 and were farmed by an adjacent neighbor who grew winter wheat and summer melons. Except for those acres, the approach drive, and the buildings, however, the entire remainder of the property had reverted to forest.

The bar beneath Luntz's bills and half-full ashtray ran the length of the barn's longer side. Besides Luntz, the Old Line president, three muttering beer refrigerators also stood behind it, their dead brothers and sisters rusting out back. One end of the barn held a primitive stage while the other had a billiard table and three pinball machines. In between everything stood several tables—seating for thirty, a typical weekday—but tonight it might easily be twice that.

It was 10 a.m. and the barn was empty. Luntz lit another cigarette. Earlier, he'd discovered one of his lieutenants, Mullet, asleep on the pool table. If left there, Mullet's boots were sure to gouge the felt, so Luntz had made his other lieutenant, Rocker, drag him out onto the lawn. Once outside, the thirty-degree weather would either sober him up or freeze him to death. The choice was his—Old Line believed strongly in personal liberty. Fealty was Rule Number 1, of course, but freedom came second, and when the club said freedom, they meant it: freedom from government, freedom from convention, freedom from the law, freedom of the open road, and freedom to party—anytime, anywhere. Luntz's pitch was, *Only outlaws are truly free of everything, even death. Swear allegiance to the club, buddy, then do whatever the hell you want.* It was a great deal, and Luntz wondered why more men didn't take him up on it.

Part of the problem, he knew, was Polite Society, meaning outsiders. Polite Society disdained the Old Liners, thinking them losers. "We're not losers, Willie," Luntz once told Trevor's older brother. "Losers and outlaws is always gettin' shit on, but losers take it lyin' down. Outlaws fight back. Winnin' ain't even the point. It's makin' a scene. *That's* the point."

We're not losers, Willie. Sure, the club had some marginal members, but once on their Harleys, Luntz thought even the fuckups looked like royalty. Why? Because their hogs were intimate beasts that each man had customized into his own personal monument, a purring idol to be kept impeccably clean. *"A Harley at rest is a siren in the sun; a Harley in motion is a chrome chariot"*—another Big Brain Willie Pug saying.

Luntz wasn't just the Old Line club president, he was also the founder. When he came of age in Sumter, South Carolina, he'd had little going for him—a ninth grade education, afternoons pumping gas, a mom on dialysis, and a shooting war in Vietnam. In '68, courtesy of the family's second-hand Zenith TV, he watched unruly students protest outside Chicago's Democratic Convention. That year, the black and white brought the Luntzes a lot of bad news: social unrest, riots in over a hundred cities, nightly Viet Cong body counts. His parents were appalled by what they saw—the student protests, not the war, which they thought was going along swimmingly. For his part, Christian found himself ambivalent about everything. *World's goin' to hell—what can I do about it?*

In '69, his buddy Doug returned from Woodstock, raving, "Man, it was so beautiful, Christian! One giant groovy family!"

When Doug heard there'd be a west coast festival as well, he and Christian hitched their way to Altamont, California. There, Luntz watched a different sort of unrest unfold, but this time he was smack in the middle of it.

From a last-minute venue change to poor stage set-up, the Altamont Speedway Free Festival went poorly at every turn, and the crowd's mood reflected this, taking little time to change from loving to loathing. They directed their anger at the Hells Angels providing stage security—a few dozen men, paid with beer, standing between the platform and three hundred thousand people.

The concert goers viewed the Angels, who threatened violence against anyone venturing too close, as thugs. Christian Luntz, however, felt no contempt for them. What he saw was a small group of ridiculously outnumbered men managing to keep the crowd from tearing the stage to pieces. The performers, the promoters, the stage grips, the press, the public—in short, everyone—maligned the Angels, but not Christian, who saw them as *The Magnificent Seven*, holy brothers living a vandal's version of Camelot. There and then, he decided to form a club back East, and except for a '71 tour of the Mekong Delta courtesy of Uncle Sam, he'd been an Old Liner ever since, never questioning his choice. Those students wanted their freedom but weren't willing to pay for it. The Angels, the Old Line, all the *real* clubs, on the other hand, would pay for freedom with their lives if they had to. *Everyone believes in something*, he thought. *Some people believe in God. I believe in the Old Line.*

But Altamont was thirty years ago and now Christian was pushing sixty, having to knock back arthritis with Advil.

He examined his bills—the weekend blowouts, the two-week pilgrimages to Sturgis. All of it cost money. Money for beer, money for electricity bills, money for bribes, money for plumbing repairs, money for their mole at the Charles County Sheriff's Office—in short, money to keep a club with thirty-five active members solvent. *That's why you were so damn handy, Willie. You knew money.* Old Line tithed its members quarterly, but that just kept the lights on. The farm rental money helped, as did free labor from the prospects. They also extorted a few local businesses. Still, the club always needed more money. *Which is why we have to traffic guns*, he thought.

But God, the paperwork. He stubbed his Winston out.

There was one more source of revenue, a high-risk one. Whenever the nationals like the Mongols or the Angels needed dirt done in the Mid-Atlantic, particularly along the Baltimore-Washington corridor, the clubhouse phone rang. The money was good, though even when it wasn't, Luntz never complained. Best to keep the nationals happy.

Of all the major clubs, the Pagans mattered most. They were expanding, which meant every so often they threatened to move into Southern Maryland and patch over the Old Line. To maintain their independence, Luntz's Inner Circle did whatever was asked: beatings, shakedowns, theft, arson, or in rare cases, murder. It was the last club killing that had sent Willie Pug over the edge. Luntz knew now what a mistake it had been to bring Big Brain along on that Atlantic City run.

Can't change the past, though, can I? he mused.

Luntz lived Old Line a day at a time, a catchphrase eerily matching AA's. But whereas AA counseled living in the present so the future could take care of itself, Old Liners lived in the moment *to live in the moment*.

Club life wasn't twenty-four-hour chaos, however. Old Line had rules, many codified. A significant one was "fight one, fight all," expressed more formally as the bylaw, *When one Old Liner throws a punch, all Old Liners will participate—no exceptions.* The bylaw following it, however, was more ominous: *An Old Liner shall surrender his colors only upon death.*

Luntz drained his beer, lit another Winston, then lapped the pool table to stretch his legs. After spending an hour punching the smudged keys of his calculator, scribbling numbers, and writing checks, he needed the diversion. Keeping the books wasn't rocket science; Christian's math could keep up, but he still hated it. *But don't really got another choice right now.* He'd had others try their hand, but either they weren't good enough or they weren't trustworthy. *Good ol' Big Brain Willie I could trust. Damn do I miss that sonofabitch.*

Willie had been to-the-penny accurate, completely dependable, and efficient. He'd rooted out wasteful spending (and thieving), paying everything on time, even putting club money in the markets. *You were as smart as Mullet is dumb.* But being wicked smart had been Willie's downfall. Willie Pug's brain was full of egghead stuff no one, least of all bikers, cared about. Willie had spouted arcane facts all the time. When the ridiculously bright Willie attended Compound festivities, the guys ran a cash lottery for the young "sweet butts." *Good news, hon! You won the lottery. Bad news is you have to screw Willie quiet to collect.*

All those eggheaded quotations, thought Luntz, *like "Whom the gods wish to destroy they first call promising."*

"That was Cyril Connolly, whoever the hell *he* was," Luntz told the empty barn.

Willie drove the guys nutzo with his quotes, but not Christian. Luntz loved them, memorizing dozens, dropping them into conversation when one seemed a good fit. Sure, Big Brain Willie talked some crazy shit, but as Christian reminded his brothers, no other club in the world had a guy who could quote Shakespeare, Che Guevara, and Mister Rogers in the same breath.

Wicked smart you were, Willie, thought Luntz, *but you're gone.* The only man left to teach him any new quotes now was Mr. Arkin, and Arkin wasn't what you'd call a fan of the club.

After retrieving another beer from a wheezing fridge, Luntz wrote a final check—Baltimore Gas and Electric. As he put it in its envelope, he thought how sad it had been watching Willie fall apart after Atlantic City. Willie had refused to pull the trigger, and the Inner Circle had been so furious they made him stand next to the victim as Mullet shot him. Willie had shrieked, pawing gore off his face. *Yeah,* thought Luntz, *that was the beginning of the end.*

Refusing a direct "order" was a serious club offense, and retribution ranged from a beating to expulsion to a shallow grave. The Circle gave Willie a beatdown, costing him a bicuspid. After that, Willie began fading away, finally skipping out to the West Coast to hook up with those crazy Hale Bopp whack jobs. *Hope my boy annoyed you a-holes as much as he annoyed us.* Christian picked up his beer, pulled, then smoked his cigarette to the filter, butting it neatly in the Redskins ashtray next to the others. (Christian Luntz may have been a multi-felon, but he was no slob.)

A young woman came in to start sweeping up the floor from the previous night's revelry. He motioned her over.

"Wanda, right?" asked Luntz. She nodded yes. "Go check on Mullet." Since Mullet had been unconscious when Rocker pulled him outside, Luntz figured it wasn't exactly fair applying the club's freedom-to-die credo. "It's on you if he freezes to death." He handed her several stamped envelopes. "And then mail these."

"Yes, Christian," Wanda said, looking pleased. Luntz had remembered her name! For Wanda, a twenty-something looking to establish a reputation, this was big.

Luntz packed his paperwork into a battered valise, then headed toward the farmhouse, only to see the one-hundred-pound Wanda struggling to drag Mullet back into the clubhouse. "Let me help you, hon." With his assistance, they made quick work of it, and she thanked him profusely. "It's nothin', girl. Now go put those in the mailbox."

Luntz was at the farmhouse door when he heard Wanda shout from the barn, "Christian, phone for you!"

In 1999, cell coverage hadn't yet reached the compound. The clubhouse phone was the only way to reliably reach Luntz. Answering the phone had been another Willie job. Luntz remembered the crazy way he did it: "Old Line clubhouse. Willie, head myrmidon, speaking." Knowing Willie like he did, Luntz knew that whatever the fuck a myrmidon was, it was cool. "Take a message," Luntz yelled back.

"That's what he'd said you'd say, Christian!"

Luntz, whose curiosity these days, like his libido, needed encouragement, didn't care. "Take one anyway."

"His name's Cisco something. Maybe Akron? Says it's important. Said to say it's about some guy named Pug."

That did encourage his curiosity. *So the old goat's calling 'bout Pug, huh? Which one, Willie or Trevor?* He figured it was the latter. Men like Cisco Arkin didn't cry over spilt milk. Or dead men.

Chapter 35: The Fourth Column

Saturday, 10 April 1999
Wheaton, MD

CISCO AWOKE WITH a start. He'd had the Korean dream again and this time the bullet had grazed his temple. He touched the side of his head—a wound! Cisco stumbled to his bath, flicking on the light. In the mirror stood a man with an angry crease across his forehead. He gently touched it again—it was dry. "Hold the Purple Heart, Maggie," he told his dead wife, "I'm not bleeding. Just got bunched up in the sheets." He rubbed the indentation, but even as it disappeared, it still hurt.

It was 5 a.m.

After Cisco recovered, he made coffee, got his paper, then cooked pancakes for himself and Roger, a sponsee who had "gone back out" and was now sleeping it off downstairs. After descending the cellar steps to leave Roger a plate, Cisco returned to the main floor to eat, peruse his paper, and receive sponsee check-in calls (unless other arrangements had been made, they phoned each morning). After the last call, Cisco listened at the cellar door. Hearing nothing, he locked it and went to pick up Trevor Pug.

It's Trevor again, guys.

"Did you complete your Fourth Step list?" Cisco asks me, sipping his diesel-strength coffee. I've drowned mine in milk, the only way I can stomach it without gagging. We're currently sitting on the couch in the cellar "drunk tank." I'm here for the Fifth Step, which means reviewing my Fourth Step list with another human being.

It's 11 a.m. and Roger, the guy who'd been dropped off the night before, has just stepped out. From outside comes the sound of gagging. *There go Roger's pancakes.* According to Cisco, this is Roger's second stay at chez Arkin. During his first, he'd vomited in bed, so puking on the lawn represents progress.

"Yes, I finished it," I say. Two days ago, Cisco instructed me to create an inventory of "fears and resentments." I'd done so the night before while watching *101 Dalmatians* with Reesie—Carol was out with the ladies, getting desperately needed girl time.

"Hand it over, please," Cisco says.

"You gonna read it?"

"What did you think would happen?"

I hesitate, then give the two folded papers to him, each divided into four columns per his instructions. The first column is for the people, places, and things I resent or fear, like my mother-in-law, Gladys Edock. The next is for listing whatever the issue is. I'd written several things for Gladys, including *Constantly reminds me Carol married beneath herself.* The third column is for recording what the resentment or fear affects. For Gladys, I'd made multiple entries, like "financial insecurity." *When Gladys dies, all her money's going to Carol's sister,* I think. *She hates me that much.* Cisco had given no instructions for the fourth column, so I'd left it blank.

"The list was hard to start," I say, "but once I did, it just sort of came."

Cisco nods and begins reading.

"At first, I scratched a lot of stuff out," I say to fill the silence. "Not misspelled or anything—just didn't like what I wrote. Did better on the second sheet: more organized, less scratch outs. 'Cooking with gas' as my mother says." *I wrote down everything I could think of, except the Alley Killer. Sure, I'm afraid of him, but I'm not explaining witnessing a murder to Cisco. Who knows what he'd have me do.*

Arkin mutters to himself as he reads. In the cellar's subdued lighting, I realize he looks very tired. Or sick. "You sleeping okay, Jefe?"

"Some bad dreams," admits Arkin. "That's all."

A lot of those going 'round, I think, recalling Carol in a cage and that jangled mess of keys.

Oh folks, by the way, there's some pretty personal shit on my list. Cisco isn't a stranger by this point, but how much can I really trust him? *And the muttering . . . It's a little creepy.*

Cisco continues reading. And muttering.

Why do I have to share this list with him, anyway? It should be enough that the all-important higher power Cisco keeps talking about "sees" it, right? Hey Upstairs Man, if you really want to help me, how about knocking the pins out from under those Old Line buzzards? And while You're at it, explain why three cops had to park nose-to-butt like that.

Cisco finishes reading. "Your wife's on the list," he says, nodding. "Your mother-in-law is too. Good. Your dad, your former boss. Your high school football coach. The Old Line, of course. Your brother and Heaven's Gate, that makes sense, as does the IRS—everybody hates them. Who is Rey?"

"A fellow coder," I answer. Cisco isn't following. "Computer coding," I explain. "You know, what I do for a living."

"Ah, a professional peer," says Cisco.

I can think of many ways to describe Rey—shining asshole, for one—but *professional peer* isn't one of them.

"This is a good start, Trevor," says Cisco.

Just *a good start?*

"Let's tackle that fourth column."

At the tiny kitchenette table, Cisco reveals its purpose: listing my "part" in each issue. One by one, we go down the list. I find the process deeply revealing, and not in a good way. I'd always thought myself a solid guy—maybe a little complicated—but solid. *Everybody's got their angels and devils, okay? And maybe my life's not the greatest story ever told, I'm not Leonardo da Vinci or anything, but at least I have interesting motives, right?*

Alas, no.

We're barely halfway done before I realize the brutal truth—every motivation I'd ever had in my life falls into one of two categories: either avoiding something I didn't want, like jail time, or not getting what I thought I deserved, like a decent job now that I'm a teetotaler. *And even those two can be boiled down to something simpler: fear.* Titanic intrapersonal struggles between right and wrong? Apparently, not so much.

I'm a schmuck totally controlled by fear—what a letdown.

Despite this depressing realization, I feel justifiably angry about most of the items on my list. I resent paying taxes and *really* resent when other people don't pay taxes. I resent The Police for breaking up. I resent Bill Clinton—I'm *not* looking forward to explaining to Teen Reesie that oral sex is still sex. And on that note, I also resent cheaters.

I've never cheated on Carol.

"What is your biggest fear, Trevor?" Cisco asks, bringing me back. "Doesn't have to be something from your list."

"Death," I say quickly. "And humiliation. I watched my brother get humiliated in high school, then by the Old Line, then by those Gate of Heaven wingnuts. It was awful. Humiliation's a lot like death."

Cisco nods. "It is."

I continue: "I fear the Y2K mess. Seriously, I don't care if your microwave works on New Year's Day, but I do care if ICBM launch code written by some low-bid government contractor doesn't work. America's probably gonna be okay, but we're not the only ones with missiles, are we? There's over ten thousand worldwide." *Including those Soviet 'stan' countries,* I add mentally, *Stand-off-istan and Mexican Stand-off-istan or whatever the hell their real names are.* "Some of that Russian stuff's not gonna get fixed in time. And the breath of old people," I say, but then add apologetically, "Not *you*, Jefe. I mean *really* old people."

Cisco smiles blandly: *Of course that's what you meant.*

"I hate flying. I'm terrified of snakes. I fear clowns. That's a real thing, by the way. 'Coulrophobia.' Look it up if you don't believe me."

Cisco's smile remains but without much warmth. *I realize he asked about my biggest fears, not my phobic greatest hits.*

"Okay," I admit, after the lack of an amused response from Cisco, "maybe some of those sound stupid. Here's some that aren't: I fear prison. I fear Old Line foreclosing on my debt by shivving me while *in* prison. I fear never getting another decent job again. I fear Carol—" I pause. "I fear Carol leaving me." My mind brings the unwelcome image of the thin smile she'd given me a few nights ago after a particularly long shift at Hallmark.

"What's the point of dredging this up again, anyway?" I ask Cisco. "I drank to forget this stuff!"

Cisco stops smiling altogether, and I'm glad.

"Let's take a break from your list, Trevor," Cisco says. "How goes trial prep?"

I bring my sponsor up to speed. I'm focused on one goal—staying out of Seven Locks, Montgomery County's house of detention. I relay what Janice Bees, my lawyer, told me: "'If you show up to court looking respectable, with your signature sheets, Judge Freese will be reasonable.' Per her advice, I'm pleading guilty and throwing myself at the mercy of the court. Why not? I got no priors and I look good in a suit. There'll be probation and fines, of course, but I shouldn't serve a day in jail . . . right?" Cisco's bland smile returns. *I didn't like it before, but now I hate it.* "But just in case, Carol's teaching me to fold shirts if I end up doing prison laundry—haha."

As terrible as the man's smile is, it's the pity in his eyes that truly bothers me. "She's home now watching Reesie and the Chin boy, Sunny." (By the way, I can't multitask—watch Reesie and write code at the same time.)

David Chin, house appraiser by day, fire ant thesis guy on nights and weekends. And marriage-wise . . . something's rotten there. Angie's appearance has had me suspicious since the beginning. The guys salivate over Estelle, who's certainly glamorous, but Angie Chin, a size 0 dress-wearing divorce lawyer, looks, well . . . dangerous. *Opposites can attract, but Angie's a nine, good ol' Fire Ant Chin's a four. They don't talk—I hardly ever see them together. Maybe I'm an asshat for saying so, but even Carol agrees—one day, the Chin's marriage is gonna jump track. Hell, she's a* divorce *lawyer for God's sake!*

Despite my recent eff-ups, Carol and I are solid. Yesterday she'd said, "I've been hard on you, Trev, but I want you to know how proud I am that you're sober. I love you." *Real mushy stuff.* "You're so lucky to have a man like Cisco Arkin showing you the ropes. He's wonderful! Janice says stick with him and you'll be home free. Keep going to your AA meetings, hon, and keep up the side gigs 'cause every penny counts. Better times ahead, Trev!"

Yes, Carol, better times ahead. The whole thing, even the part about how necessary Cisco is, had me feeling good. *But there still could be jail time.* "Carol worries about prison," I tell Cisco. "Hell, *I'm* worried about it. Five years is a long time." *Five years.* It feels like a cloud passed over me just saying it. She'd visit, at least at first, but the marriage? Five years . . . Would she eventually check out of Motel Wedding Vow? I figure if it happened, it would happen in Year Three: Carol would meet Brad in the ten-items-or-less lane at Safeway. He'd wink when she scolded Reesie for reaching for those candy bars they keep at kid level. One thing would lead to another, and six months later: "Trev, I've met someone. Sign these papers." *That might not kill me, but Brad's promotion to stepdad surely would.*

"Trevor," Cisco says, bringing me back again, "just do what Janice tells you and you'll be fine."

You sound just like Carol.

We talk through my final entries. He helps me find all sorts of "harm" Easter eggs, acts of self-sabotage that for the life of me I'd never have recognized without the old man's help. It's like being morally X-rayed.

"Willie" is my last entry. Did I harm my brother, ex-Old Liner, and cult member? Willie made the resentment list for abandoning the family and then for dying, so I resent the hell out of him, but I also feel guilty about that resentment.

"I should've gotten more involved at the end," I tell Cisco. "Should have jumped on a plane and brought him home from California—that's what Mom wanted me to do—but no, I told myself, 'Big brothers look after little brothers, not the other way around.' God, that sounds so lame now. Mom won't admit it, but she blames me at least some, and she probably should. After all, I was the sane one."

"No one's sane," Cisco says. He folds up my list and sticks it in my cubby. "Congratulations, kid, lunch break."

Cisco goes upstairs, returning with sandwiches and ice cream. The step work was fatiguing for both of us, so we eat silently at first. Once we get to the ice cream, Cisco speaks again. "It was always the first thought that got me in trouble."

"First thought?"

"My first instinctual reaction to anything." I look at him, not understanding. "An example," says Cisco. "Let's say someone asks you to be kinder to Carol. What's your first thought?"

"She deserves it," I say.

"No, kid, that's your second thought. I mean your first thought."

"'She deserves it' *was* my first thought."

"No, it wasn't."

"Seriously, Cisco, it was."

"No, Trevor. 'She deserves it' was your *second* thought."

"*No, it wasn't,* okay?" I insist, frustrated. "What is this, second grade? 'I am rubber, you are glue?'" I feel pissed, but also concerned. Since I met Cisco last November, the man looks like he's aged ten years. Is he getting senile?

"Trevor," he says, "Think back. When I brought up being kinder to Carol, wasn't your first reaction something like, *Oh no, more work for me*?"

I realize immediately that Cisco is right, but instead I respond, "It wouldn't *be* work."

"It'd at least be a burden, Trevor, otherwise you'd already be doing it."

"No," I insist. I feel guilty as hell about what I've done to my family, but thanks to AA, I've been better. A *lot* better. I confidently say this, but Arkin sighs.

"Trevor, I don't believe you."

Stunned silence.

I finally speak up. "Believe me or don't believe me, Cisco, I don't care." I know I sound sulky. *It's cold outside,* I think, *but maybe it's time I walk home anyway.*

"Relax, kid," Cisco responds, his voice softer. "Let me ask you this: why *wouldn't* you feel burdened having to be more kind? Look at everything on your plate. You're working dozens of those 'crappy coding assignments'—your words, not mine—to pay off a biker gang. When you're not doing that, you're going to AA meetings, and when you're not doing *that,* you're providing childcare for your daughter. I'll mention AA again: you're trying to stay sober—early sobriety is a full-time job. Don't forget the trial and the potential jail time hanging over your head. Honestly, Trevor, when *could* you be kind?"

If Cisco is trying to calm me down, he's failing. "I just watched Reesie last night so Carol could hang with her friends," I say, "wasn't *that* kind?"

"Kid, all I'm suggesting, and it's a program of suggestions, by the way—"

Suggestions, my ass, I think. *Your reputation precedes you, old man. If I don't do what you say, you'll fire me.*

"—is for the next week, listen to all your first thoughts. A hundred bucks says they'll be self-centered. Second thought's usually better, but that's not guaranteed. With practice, however—"

"Practice?" I interrupt unhappily.

"Yes, practice. Every day, think, 'Let my second thought be the opposite of my first.'"

"Isn't that lying?" I ask. "Because you're right. With Carol, I . . . don't have the time. Or energy. Definitely not the money. I have nothing." I no longer feel angry, I just feel ashamed.

"Changing your perception isn't the same thing as lying," Cisco says. "At its core, alcoholism is a disease of perception."

"Look, Jefe, I know you mean well, but I'm just trying to stay sober here. I don't need marital advice," I say, having no idea how much saying that would later haunt me.

It's past 2 p.m., and even accounting for lunch, we'd been at it three hours. We're both tired, but Cisco looks *spent.*

I look at him, finding the energy to smile. "It's alright, Jefe. Poking 'round my marriage at least shows you care." Cisco smiles back. To my relief, it's a full, warm smile, one making him look younger, or at least healthier.

Arkin stands up from the table and gathers the dishes. "Before you go, kid, I need a hand with some things upstairs. Do you mind?"

I'd never been upstairs, and am curious, so I don't mind at all.

After getting Trevor to move some heavy boxes, Cisco drove him home. Returning to his own home, Cisco assessed Trevor's recovery. The truth, which the Pug kid couldn't see for himself, was as plain as day to him. Despite appearances, Trevor was unconsciously biding his time, waiting for the "all clear" to sound so he could return to the bars a chastened hero, one taught by AA how to once again drink like a gentleman.

Which is a total pile, of course. Within months—weeks, perhaps, Trevor would be sitting at a bar spinning up another alcoholic twister, one making servitude to the Old Line look good by comparison. Cisco saw the kid as squarely among his peers, a newly-minted "recovered" alcoholic who thought he was too special to fail. Trevor believed himself the victim of forces, forces taking away his "right" to drink. At least the kid's legal troubles had sunk in—he was scared. *Good.*

And you're doing some things right. For now at least, Trevor was adhering to Step One, putting the drink down. Trevor believed in the Upstairs Man—

Step Two—which was great. However, he either didn't trust Him or thought he didn't need Him. Belief in a Higher Power was critical for restoring the alcoholic's sanity, but Trevor didn't really think he'd lost his life-management marbles in the first place, not long-term, anyway, and with more effort on his part, he'd once again control his own life.

Self will run riot, thought Cisco.

To Arkin and millions of other alcoholics, recovery meant more than just believing in God, it meant turning the reins over to Him—Step Three. Trevor, listening to AA with one ear and to his disease with the other, wasn't ready to relinquish the reins.

You think you're done with rioting, my young friend, but the rioting's not done with you.

Chapter 36: The Liar's Club

Saturday, 17 April 1999
Kensington, MD

AFTER THE NIGHT he'd tragically spooked Big Stew's herd and gotten arrested, Loo Spicotti had been released on his own recognizance. As large as his alleged crimes loomed in the minds of many, the County police could only charge him with poaching, a misdemeanor. Park and Rec law enforcement wanted to file more serious charges, like criminal trespass and reckless endangerment, but Loo hadn't been arrested on parkland, and the two litigiously sensitive departments were still sorting out jurisdiction.

Another reason was evidence. The County officers had found a crossbow with no usable prints (cold weather equaled gloves). Unsurprisingly, his knife did have his prints, but no blood (Loo kept his gear clean). Search dogs had located his blanket, but two days of rain and likely use by itinerants made its discovery unremarkable (the discoverers believed the board in the tree had been used by vagrants for sleeping on). The dogs missed his buried stash of bolts.

Loo didn't worry about a home search, having kept his alter-ego's equipment off his property. There was no map marking his eighty-nine kills, which was good, because it would show every one being within a mile or two of Spicotti's Kensington home. However, said map would also show how truly populous Kensington was; any citizen could be the slayer. The only thing Loo sweated then was where and when Big Stew, with Loo's bolt stuck through him, would die a presumed wretched death. For this he felt awful.

Loo vehemently denied being the Deerslayer, but this didn't dissuade the media. Accurate or not, the possibility that the Deerslayer's identity had been established—particularly, irony of ironies, the Park and Rec head arborist and assumed Lorax—was just too juicy to ignore, and because of that, Loo's work consequences were swift: unpaid leave, probable job loss. After receiving a letter from Loo's lawyer threatening wrongful termination, however, Park and Rec Legal backed off, switching him to paid leave.

The letter was also an evidence-sinking torpedo: the hunting knife was a legal-length blade carried for self-defense; his outfit on the night of his arrest was all dark colors, sure, but not hunter's camouflage or a genuine ninja outfit; the crossbow had no prints; his appearing after a dozen deer sprinted across busy Georgia Ave was mere coincidence; and his outspokenness about deer overpopulation was one voice out of hundreds of others, including other Park and Rec employees, not to mention that Loo had never advocated violence.

Since taking up his vigilante role months ago, Loo had been publicly circumspect about it, often opining *against* the Deerslayer's methods. In fact, Loo's lawyer made clear that his client's ardent gun control beliefs extended to weapons of all types. Yes, his job provided motive and opportunity, and yes, as a professional he witnessed firsthand the destruction of the forest understory, but that was at best guilt by association. "And they can shove *that* up the ol' yin yang," his colorful lawyer bragged. "Threaten to sue, Mr. Spicotti, always threaten to sue." Loo did. He also released a brief statement: "I'm an honest man. I'm being railroaded and I'm not going to stand for it." He was lying through his teeth, of course, something he wasn't good at, but he was getting better.

The only real worry: now that Loo was in the public eye, folks were bound to notice the slayings had stopped, drawing the same conclusion Channel 4 had. His buried gear wasn't worrisome; if it hadn't been found by now, it wasn't likely to be, and besides, how would he get past the press ring surrounding his house to get rid of it? On that front, Washingtonians witnessed Mrs. Spicotti's stand-by-her-man-istan defensive tactics: shoving microphones back in the faces of officious reporters, declaring, "My husband's *not* the Deerslayer. He wouldn't hurt a fly. You print otherwise and I'll sue your ass off!"

Still, Loo worried about what his wife really might be thinking: *He says he's innocent, but the slaughter's stopped now, hasn't it?*

On this front, Big Stew really came through for him. The stag's wound had gotten infected. It took six days, but the poor animal finally died, his bolt-shot body found by a dog walker far from Loo's house. Did this kill, a week after Loo Spicotti's arrest, prove it wasn't him? The head of Park and Rec Police wasn't buying that—she'd assumed (correctly) that Big Stew had really been shot the night of Loo's arrest; she wanted to establish exactly when the animal was injured, but by then the carcass had already been disposed of. So to the public, the Deerslayer was "active" again. They'd been entertained by some patsy (Loo) being blamed, but now the real killer's compulsion had finally returned, which is what many wanted.

But as February turned to March and March turned to April, there were no new kills. This was a problem for Loo.

The core of the book club met with him the day after his arrest to support their anxious brother caught up in a case of mistaken identity. Loo adamantly denied all allegations and his buddies backed him, but the guys had their doubts. A guilty but otherwise honest man cannot deceive smoothly, at least at first. But were Loo's "subliminal tells" worth challenging a friend's word? The guys thought not, plus, if he was guilty, then weren't they guilty too? Not of the actual crimes, but of not putting two and two together? No one wanted to have to answer the question *How come you guys didn't know*?

As they wrapped up dinner at home, Trevor said, "Ladies, time for dessert. How about ice cream?"

"We don't have any," answered Carol, who'd planned on serving budget-friendly graham crackers instead.

"No?" asked Trevor innocently. "Can you check?"

Carol made her way to the fridge, eyeing the twinkle in her husband's eye. She opened the freezer, declaring, "Butter brickle! Thanks for thinking of us, hon, but where'd you get the money?"

Reesie shouted in excitement and jumped up to get bowls. When she wasn't looking, Carol mouthed, *Did you steal it from my purse?*

"I earned it," said Trevor, "thank you very much."

"Trev, didn't we agree that for now, *I* dispense the money? That includes ice cream money."

"Relax, babe. I helped Cisco. Carried some heavy boxes to the curb for him. Got paid in ice cream."

"He likes butter brickle?" she asked, smiling at the mention of Arkin's name.

"The man loves ice cream. Any flavor."

"There's a note on it," Carol said, looking at the carton top.

"Well, babe, what does it say?" asked Trevor, helping Reesie, whose hair smelled like shampoo, into his lap.

Carol read the note: "'Guilt-free ice cream, no Breyer's remorse.' Trev, that's a terrible pun," she said, laughing.

"I don't get it," said Reesie.

Carol explained the concept of buyer's remorse as best she could to her daughter, who nodded half-understandingly. Carol simplified: "Daddy's puns stink, Reesie. That's all you need to know."

"But they make you laugh," said Trevor.

"That's true," she said, kissing him, then Reesie. All three enjoyed the moment.

"Let's get this served up," said Carol. "Chico's gonna be here any minute."

As if summoned, Chico's Honda beeped twice from the curb. "None for me," Trevor said sadly. Chico was taking him to a meeting.

"Don't worry, we'll save you some," Carol said. Reesie nodded affirmatively: good daddies deserved ice cream.

"Thanks, ladies," said Trevor, grabbing a jacket.

"And ice cream's not the only thing waiting at home," Carol whispered in his ear. "Now get going."

When Trevor and Chico arrived at the St. Paul's Liar's Club meeting, the one held in the large basement where Trevor had first "discovered" Alcoholics Anonymous in November, the six-foot-two Thumper, Wheaton AA community's mountain-man preacher, headed straight for them. "Hello, Chico," he said congenially. Then to Trevor: "Bud, you're back." The implication: between the last time Thumper had seen him (two weeks ago) and now, Trevor had "gone back out."

"Still sober, Thump," responded Trevor, adding, "since Christmas."

Thumper looked unconvinced. "It asks in the *Twelve & Twelve*, page 51: 'Did I try to cover up those feelings of inadequacy by bluffing, cheating, *lying*, or evading responsibility?' What's your answer, Bud?" (Thumper pointedly still called Trevor "Bud.")

"No," replied Trevor.

"Huh," said Thumper, scratching his beard. "Bud, lying's killed better men than you."

"Good to know," Pug said dismissively, then walked away.

"He's an asshole," Thumper told Chico.

"Yeah, but we work with what we got, right?" Chico responded.

"You said it, friend."

Trevor couldn't imagine now why Thumper had so terrified him the night of Prophet's murder. The large man *had* cornered him in the bathroom, that was true, and back then Trevor had been sure the boot-wearing man was the Alley Killer. Now, however, it was wholly apparent that despite Thump's size and demeanor, he stuck to harmless sermonizing.

Cisco told Trevor to treat Thumper respectfully because the man's intentions were good. All recovering alcoholics were supposed to reach out to newcomers, but this was supposed to be done through attraction, not promotion; proselytizing was strongly discouraged. The Thumpers of recovery ignored this advice, however, telling newcomers they had two choices: AA or Hell. Some wanted Thump to tone it down as his message scared people off, but since the only requirement for AA membership was a desire to stop drinking, something Thumper surely had, there was no voting him out; AA didn't work like that.

"Yes, he's loud and opinionated," Cisco had told him, "but he serves an important purpose. There are drunks, perhaps one in two hundred, that only Thumper can reach. They *need* doomsday AA. Laugh if you want, but Thumper's Army is bigger than you think." By Thumper's Army, Cisco meant Thumper's sponsees.

"I don't need doomsday AA," Trevor had responded.

"Not to put too fine a point on it, kid, but right now, you're not the best judge of what you need."

Trevor hadn't liked hearing that.

Presently, he took his seat next to Chico for the night's open discussion meeting. He liked Chico Rodrigez, who was in his late twenties and nearly shared Trevor's sobriety date. (They thought themselves members of the 1999 Class of Jefe High.) Both men had been attending meetings daily for fifteen weeks now but had yet to speak during them. Cisco banned his sponsees from sharing at meetings until they had at least six months. "You don't know anything yet," he'd told them. "And when you *do* start sharing, fellas, stay on topic, which is always recovery from alcoholism. Always."

Tonight, Wynona W, a middle-aged woman known for wearing colorful hats, was the meeting chair. For discussion, she'd selected an AA standard, *gratitude.* Trevor settled in to listen to what others would say, likely in the form of *how it was, what happened, and what it's like today*. He knew most people would share Cisco-style—pithy, topical, upbeat—but despite the softball subject, some would end up damning gratitude with faint praise: "Got a shit job with a shit boss doing shit work for shit pay, but yeah, I guess I'm lucky to have it." (Bravo, friend, bravo.) Trevor listened, but it was mostly Wynona's robin-egg-blue hat holding his attention.

The first two sharers kept on topic, but the next three didn't. The first of these vented about his "evil" ex-wife. Wynona drummed her fingers, staring at him until he took the hint. The next sharer, a woman, droned on about the importance of saving AA from the addicts, fatties, and sexaholics. After two minutes, Wynona politely but firmly cut her off. The next share, a diatribe about how the ills of the current administration were "forcing" the sharer to drink, blew Wynona's cool.

"Look, people," she said, "I don't want to die from this disease, okay? Share the solution, not the sickness."

The last three clunkers got Trevor thinking about sharing styles. There were the jokesters: *Why did the chicken cross the road? (To get to the bar.)* There were self-reporters: *I slipped last week and woke up in my prom dress. Folks, I'm thirty-eight years old, and I'm here to tell ya, it don't fit no more.* There were the virgins, those who'd never shared before. Tonight, there would be one, a guy named Mustafa who, despite Sharia law, fermented fig jack back in Iran through sheer alcoholic desperation.

There were less pleasant sharing styles, like cross-talking—AA, by its very name, was supposed to be anonymous to those outside the Fellowship, but also to those within. Cross-talking, the proffering of unsolicited critique—*Well, Phyllis, some women just aren't meant to be mothers*—was strongly discouraged. There were the *you-gottas*, as in *You gotta do exactly what the Book says, page 69, or the last thing you'll ever drink will be embalming fluid.* Thumper was a you-gotta, but he at least practiced what he preached. Most you-gottas didn't.

Trevor thought about what long-term sobriety really meant to him because he was learning that in AA there was no finish line, no stage to walk across for a diploma. *The AAs say you don't have to quit forever,* he thought, *just today, but those people are lying. If you add today to tomorrow and keep adding tomorrows, you'll get to forever pretty damn quick, so don't tell me AA's not a program of abstinence, because it is. Plus,* come on, *all these guys must be secretly drinking. There's no way they're staying off the sauce for decades. Well, Cisco, maybe, but look how happy* he *is.*

At the halfway point, the donation "hat," an old Eight O'clock Coffee can, was passed around. When it came to Trevor, he put a dollar in, as did Chico. Chico passed the can down the row and two more men put in their dollars.

Then it came to Charlie. Trevor had never seen the impeccably dressed man put anything in, and tonight was no exception. *That's just rude,* he thought. He snorted condescendingly, ensuring Charlie heard. *I owe a biker gang, but I can come up with a dollar. What's your problem?*

"You okay, mi broki?" Chico inquired.

Trevor took a breath. "Yeah. I'm fine."

But he wasn't fine, and it was Charlie's fault. *All that free coffee you're sucking down's gonna bankrupt this meeting! . . . Okay, maybe your missing buck's not exactly gonna tank AA, but still, it's the principle of the thing. You dress like a million bucks—cough up a freakin' dollar.*

"Really, you okay?" Chico asked again.

"Yup, smooth sailing, amigo."

Cisco sat in the row behind the young men. Sitting behind new sponsees was something he did on the off chance he needed to smack them to keep them from sharing. Before and after the meeting, however, that was a different story. Then, he encouraged all his sponsees to talk to as many alcoholics as possible.

As was his habit, Cisco tried focusing on the current sharer. However, he, like Trevor, was having trouble concentrating. The sharer was discussing her sister-in-law's drinking and not her own, which Cisco found disingenuous, and his mind wandered.

Arkin thought about a phone call he'd made to Christian Luntz three weeks ago, asking him to drop the interest on Trevor Pug's "loan" to something more reasonable than twenty percent monthly. Christian had refused. Out of respect for the program, however, he'd been polite about it, knowing that over the years, he'd sent more than one Old Liner Arkin's way to get their drinking under control. Considering how much Old Line worshipped alcohol, this was really saying something. Cisco would channel the man to the right AA sponsor, usually Thumper, a fellow biker. But despite all that Cisco and Thumper had done for Old Line, Luntz had said, "Sorry, Mr. Arkin, a deal's a deal." Christian had no qualms about refusing Arkin because he knew his AA fundamentals. Twelfth Step work was to be selfless as well as anonymous, so when working with Luntz's bikers, Cisco wasn't supposed to ask for anything (like lowering an interest rate for his sponsee). Luntz reminded him of this.

Didn't think that would work, Cisco thought at the time. *But . . .* "What if a friend paid Trevor's debt off?"

Luntz said no to that too. He then began reminiscing about Willie's salad days as the club's treasurer, going on about Trevor's older brother's math skills, which told Arkin what he needed to know: this was all about Luntz getting younger brother Trevor in the club, or at least associated with it.

That would be a terrible idea.

Arkin's next thought was *I need a fifth*—normally a disastrous wish for an alcoholic, but not in Cisco's case. He kept whiskey in his truck (and often in his pocket) to keep deathly ill drunks from shaking to pieces. This was prudence, not indulgence; tapering off was sometimes necessary, and Cisco had distributed his last bit of "medicinal" alcohol two days before. He made a mental note to buy more.

Back in the meeting, his friend, Reggie, began sharing. *A reprieve from my sponsee worries,* Cisco thought. Even though Arkin had heard his friend's story dozens of times, he never tired of it, or of how Reggie expressed gratitude for circumstance: "Don't knock livin' under a bridge, people. Beats sleepin' in the rain every time!" As usual, Reggie earned chuckles.

The hour was almost up. Wynona recognized one last sharer, a sincere woman who unfortunately mumbled, sending Cisco's mind wandering again. *I'm rested,* he thought. *Why can't I pay attention?* Indeed, he was rested, not having had the Korean nightmare since the day of Trevor's Fifth Step. But boy, he'd been tired *that* day, exhausted after waking up wrapped in his sheets.

He recalled letting Trevor upstairs. He rarely let sponsees into the main level of his home, his logic being the basement held cast-off items he didn't mind having stolen, broken, or vomited on—upstairs held what he materially valued and was hence off limits. Trevor had moved six heavy boxes marked GOODWILL to the curb for Cisco. After taking the last one, his eye had gone to a stack of Arkin's mail, particularly to the return address of the unopened top envelope.

"A letter from Prophet's mom?" he'd asked. "You haven't read it?"

"Nope."

"Why not?"

"I'm not sure." This wasn't true. Cisco knew exactly why he hadn't read it.

"What is it, a love letter?" Trevor had asked with a cheeky grin.

Cisco had paused, then gone against his better judgment and explained. "No, it's not a love letter, but still, I don't want to encourage her."

"Encourage her?"

"Yes. I signed the register at Mark Mark's funeral, so she sent me a thank you note for attending."

"She sent me one too," Trevor had said, "but mine wasn't a big fat envelope like this baby." He'd twirled it by its corners. "This is no 'thank you' note, Jefe, it's God-honest *correspondence.*"

"Trevor, unless you're now the Postmaster General, put my mail down."

"Sorry, Jefe." He remembered Trevor putting it back. "But really, how'd you go from a thank-you note to whatever that is?"

"Well, in her first letter, she asked if I could tell her more about her son," Arkin had said. "I'm not John Updike or anything, but I sent her a few pages."

"That's cool."

"I figured it was 'cool,' too. And the end of it. But she wrote back again."

"Okay," said Trevor.

"No, not okay. More questions. I sent her another two pages, but really couldn't see the point in going on about Mark Marks. He was a sponsee, and as such, there was his anonymity to consider."

"Well, she *is* his mother. Maybe she needs, you know, closure."

"Maybe," Cisco had said, then crossed the room to another table, retrieving two more envelopes, both open, both bearing Mrs. Mark's return address.

"My God, Jefe, you've got an admirer! A sweetie in Cumberland!"

"Oh shut it," Cisco had growled. Trevor shut it but grinned in a way that made average men handsome and handsome men irresistible. *I'll give it to you, kid, you got charm.*

"That letter," Cisco had continued, pointing to the unopened envelope, "makes three. Based on various invitations back to Cumberland she's made so far, I'm afraid to open it."

"Arkin, you old Romeo! You're blushing!"

"I'm not blushing," said Cisco, his face red.

"Oh yes you are," Trevor had taunted. Then, more seriously, "So, Jefe, whatcha gonna do?"

"I don't know," Cisco had answered honestly.

"How about reading the latest letter for starts," Trevor had advised. "I mean *three* letters—at this point, not responding would be rude."

"But, son," Cisco had begun, flustered, "I don't want to . . . lead her on."

"Then don't," Trevor had said.

"Don't?" He remembered the kid's annoyingly smug look. "I'm out of things to say about Mark." He knew he'd sounded forlorn, showing some of the pain he felt for Prophet. How painful, though, the kid hadn't known, and Cisco meant to keep it that way.

"It's like you told me, 'Why lie when the truth will do,'" Trevor then said. "How about this? 'Dear Mrs. Marks, I'm sorry for the delay in responding. I've been preoccupied with my AA work, helping others like your son. Thank you for your kind invitation to visit, but my work keeps me busy here in Wheaton. Feel free to continue writing. Yours sincerely, Cisco 'Jefe' Arkin, Esquire.'"

"Young man, you make brushing someone off sound easy."

"It is easy. You redlight 'face-to-face' but greenlight more letters."

The kid has a point, Cisco had thought. "But pen pals, Trevor? What do I write about?"

"I'm sure seniors like yourselves have plenty in common," Trevor had suggested. "Macular degeneration. Coffee discounts. The importance of roughage."

"Can the elder abuse," Cisco had ordered. "And while you're at it, can that annoying smirk."

"Sure," Trevor had said, sniggering.

Hearing him, Cisco couldn't help but laugh too. The kid's charm was simply irresistible.

Later, Cisco would read Mrs. Mark's letter, which began "Please call me Winnie." He would never admit to taking his sponsee's advice, but he wrote Winnie back that night. He was respectful but forthright, nixing future invitations but allowing further correspondence if she so desired, which, given the several-page, beautifully handwritten letters he'd been receiving, she did. "If you're looking over me, Maggie," he told his dead wife, "please keep this Winnie woman two hours away."

Back in his chair behind Trevor and Chico, Cisco thought about Mark Marks' many attempts to stay sober. The truth was AAs who attended meetings and worked with their sponsors usually achieved long-lasting sobriety. For those like Prophet who stopped attending meetings or calling their sponsors, however, the opposite was true.

Even so, Cisco's success percentage was impressive considering he worked almost exclusively with low-bottom drunks (Trevor was an exception: despite his recent behavior, Cisco didn't consider him low-bottom, not yet at least). High or low, Arkin worked hard with his sponsees, or more accurately, worked as hard as they were willing to work themselves, having learned to not want a sponsee's sobriety more than he did. Mark Marks—"Prophet" to the EMBC and most of downtown Silver Spring—had sadly drifted away from the program one last time, dying tragically after a three-month bender. Cisco knew it wasn't her son's pain Winnie wanted to hear about, but the hope and happiness AA had provided for him. She wanted to know who her son might have matured into. (She also, in thinly disguised fashion, wanted a date with a certain gentleman from the big city, but that was another matter.)

"Maggie, please forgive me, but I'm going to continue writing Mrs. Marks. Don't ask me why, but it's helping somehow with Jamie Took."

There was no rational reason to link Winnie Marks to his Korean nightmare, but he did. Two months ago, he'd tied Trevor's step work to keeping the bullet nightmare at bay because the dreams had stopped then. But the effect hadn't lasted, and soon the dream returned with an even more terrifying ending. But the night he'd written again to Mrs. Marks, as Trevor had suggested, he'd slept like a baby. So, despite logic (and if he was honest, the *other thing*), he'd continued corresponding with the widow to keep the dreams arrested.

The Alley Killer still attended the 10 p.m. Friday night "Last Call" meeting at St. Paul's in Silver Spring where he'd chased the witness into back in November, but he was now expanding his search, branching out to other meetings. In fact, he'd attended The Liar's Club meeting that very night, sitting not far from Trevor, who he deemed a likely candidate. Now it was possible that the man he'd chased wasn't one of these drunks and would never return to Last Call or The Liar's Club or any other AA meeting ever again, but he believed the witness was a "regular," and though the man hadn't gone to the police, his conscience might prompt him to do so at some point, and that wouldn't do.

Since November, the Alley Killer's memory of the man hadn't improved, but it did clarify. He'd not seen him clearly but believed he was between twenty and forty. He could picture the man's build. When the man ran away that night, his long, unbuttoned coat had flapped as he'd fled, its large metal buttons catching the limited light. The coat was the key, allowing the killer to narrow down his pool of "suspects" from three dozen to six. It was April and DC-area coats were all hanging in their closets now, but tonight he'd been checking out Trevor's and another man's frames, deciding after long examination that the other man's build wasn't a match. That now left Trevor and four others. Trevor was the most promising candidate so far, but the killer would be thorough, eliminating the other four first.

Chapter 37: The Handbag Date

Thursday, 22 April 1999
Silver Spring, MD

MRS. NIGEL EVALUATED Ken Ert over the top of her reading glasses, ones secured with a rhinestone neck-strap that professional women above a certain age preferred. "Mr. Ert," she said, "we need to talk."

"Sure, Mrs. Nigel. Isn't that what we do every week?" Ken had responded for form's sake—from her authoritative tenor, he knew she meant *You need to listen.* "And do I really deserve the 'principal' tone?" he asked.

"Yes, you do."

"I do?" he said innocently but knew what was coming.

"Ken, in order to keep seeing me," Nigel said, her rhinestones twinkling, "you must stop listening in on other clients' conversations."

Wow, thought Ken, *no benefit of the doubt. Of course, I* am *guilty as hell.* "What do you mean, Mrs. Nigel?"

"After our last session, the last one of the day, I'll add, I straighten up. I've noticed that someone's been turning the waiting room radio down, which sits next to my office vent. Someone's also been moving the table it sits on away from that vent. I suspect it's been going on a while, but last week, someone forgot to move the table back."

"Oh, *that's* what you mean," Ken said. "Yeah, okay, Mrs. Nigel, that was me."

"Do you have an explanation?" she asked, pleased that Ken hadn't lied.

Ken paused. "Weeks ago, Tori was so loud, I could hear everything she said. She's obviously a lesbian, so I figured since I wanted a lesbian friend—"

Mrs. Nigel interrupted: "So you thought spying on Tori, betraying her trust, and mine, would be the best way to start that friendship?"

"Sounds bad when you put it that way," he admitted.

"The two of you were talking before you came in," she said. "May I ask what about?"

"We have a little ritual, Mrs. Nigel. I insult her handbag, she insults my bowtie."

Putting Ken's espionage aside for the moment, she asked, "How's that working out?"

"Great, actually. We're meeting for a drink later tonight. Sort of a lark. 'Go on a date with anyone.' That's what you said."

"We talked about that in February," said Mrs. Nigel, surprised. "It's almost May. I'd assumed you ignored my request."

"Well, I didn't want to rush into anything," continued Ken, "and besides, it's not a real date since she's gay, but hey, you said 'single and available,' so she counts."

"Well, Ken," Mrs. Nigel said formally, "as to what you do outside our sessions, and with whom, that is your business, but eavesdropping on another client *is my* business and it isn't acceptable."

"Are you firing me?" Ken asked, concerned.

"No, but you can understand why I cannot have you and Tori as back-to-back clients anymore. Too much temptation. Since you are the transgressor, I'll need to move your appointment time. My schedule is full, but I'll call you tomorrow and we will reschedule. Agreed?"

"Agreed," said Ken, relieved. *It's funny how the British say 'schedule.'* "And sorry to have put you out."

"It's settled now," said Mrs. Nigel perfunctorily. "Okay, what would you like to talk about? Still feeling jinxed?"

"Since I'm meeting a no-surprise lesbian tonight for advice, I feel less jinxed than usual."

"Interesting," Mrs. Nigel said, smiling. *But surprises?* she thought. *Young man, you're in for one.*

Tori Bora and Ken Ert met downtown at 9:00 that night at The Irish Times. After complimenting each other on punctuality, a shared value, they were shown a table. He ordered a stout, she a pilsner.

Tori wore a black dress. Ken found it surprising—two solid steps up from her normal blouse and jeans. She was also lightly made up.

Tori wasn't surprised seeing Ken's bowtie, but she'd never seen him wear a pink one. *Good Lord.* She didn't care for it, but she did admire his well-fitted sports coat. *And the slicked hair and high cheekbones,* she thought. *An impressive WASP. But God that bowtie's mercilessly pink!*

The pair chatted, mostly about how wonderful Mrs. Nigel was as a therapist. They traded minor personal information—Ken talked about his crazy cousin, also named Ken Ert, who juggled chainsaws, and Tori had an older sister and a brother fourteen years younger whom she called the Date Night Surprise. This cracked Ken up. The energy between them, subtle, yet noticeable, started then, and one could be forgiven for thinking them first daters.

When they ran out of small talk, they became uncomfortable. *Was now the time to discuss the white elephant?*

"Another beer?" Ken asked.

Tori considered. "Maybe, but first, Ken, is there something you want to tell me? Something you need to get off your chest? I promise I won't judge. I respect people like you, I really do."

"People like me?" asked Ken, puzzled. "I'm not sure what you mean."

Really? Tori thought. *The bowties and everything else?* She sighed. *Okay, fine, we'll play it your way.* She began speaking but stopped, confused by his gaze.

Since being seated, Ken had been looking at Tori, very politely, but still *looking*. Her understated makeup and not overly slinky (but still somewhat slinky) dress was hard for him to ignore, making it difficult to reconcile tonight's version of Tori Bora with the one from Mrs. Nigel's waiting room. *And those calves,* he thought. *Wow.*

"Why are you looking at my legs?" Tori asked nervously, scooting her ankles beneath her chair.

"I'm not," said Ken awkwardly, pivoting his gaze. "I'm looking at your handbag."

"Oh, do you like it?" Tori asked, relieved. She picked it up off the floor to show him. "It's new."

It was a different bag, yes, but to Ken it still looked atrocious, much uglier, in fact, than her "knitting hauler." She'd even transferred over her gay pride buttons, which wasn't helping. "New?" he asked.

"Well, new to me, anyway," she answered. "See, I only shop at thrift stores." She paused. "Ken, you're turning red. Why?"

"I'd rather not say," he answered.

"You don't like my new bag?" Tori asked. "Tell the truth."

She sounds so vulnerable, thought Ken. "Well, um," he started. He didn't want to hurt her feelings, but like a swimmer gasping for air, the more he suppressed his real opinion, the more desperate it needed to surface. "It's ugly," he finally blurted.

Tori looked crestfallen and began crying.

Oh shit! I feel awful!

But something didn't seem right. Tori wasn't so much crying as sniggering, eyes shut, teeth clenched in an unsuccessful attempt to suppress laughter. "What's so funny?" Ken asked.

"You are," she said.

"Why?"

"Ken, this is the ugliest bag the Salvation Army had." She began laughing so hard she snorted. "Believe me, I spent a whole afternoon looking." Another snort.

"This was some sort of test, wasn't it?" Ken asked as stiffly as he could, but Tori's snorting made that difficult.

"Yes," she said, laughing even harder.

"Hilarious. Did I pass?"

"I'm not sure."

"Well that makes two of us." Tori Bora continued snorting. "Hey, Tori, you okay? I mean, do you need oxygen or something?"

"I'll be f-fine," Tori gasped. After letting her laughter subside, which took a while, she became serious again. Discreetly, she asked, "So let's get down to business, Ken. Are you gonna admit you're gay?"

Ken miss-swallowed his beer. After a coughing fit, he croaked, "What?"

Tori stared. In a louder, displeased voice: "Ken, I really don't have the energy to drag another one of you out of the closet."

"Out of the closet?" asked Ken, confused. "What do you mean?"

The way you express yourself, Ken, she thought, *your appearance. Honestly, what straight man proudly wears pink bowties? Now admittedly, you may be in the closet so deep you don't even . . .*

"I'm not gay," said Ken defensively. "You're the one who . . ."

A moment's silence. "I'm the what?" Tori prompted.

"If anyone's gay here," Ken declared, "it's you. Hell, I'm here tonight *because* you're gay."

"What?" responded Tori, looking as confused as Ken now. Tersely: "I'm not a lesbian."

"Really?" said Ken, pointing. "What's with those buttons on that . . . truly *ugly* handbag?"

Tori had acquired the bag solely to offend Ken. *And apparently, I succeeded,* she thought. She examined the buttons—pink triangles, rainbows—realizing what Ken, assuming he actually *was* straight, might be thinking. *The buttons are for solidarity, mister, but I could see where that could be . . . Okay, okay, let's straighten this out.*

"My sister's gay, Ken, something it took Patty forever to admit. It's the bravest thing she's ever done. Now that she's out, she's fighting stereotypes—hence, the buttons. The way you looked at them at Mrs. Nigel's, I thought you *liked* them. Don't tell me you're gay *and* conservative."

As reasonable as Tori's explanation sounded, Ken challenged it. "Your haircut?" he asked.

"Patty's a stylist," Tori said. "I like it, though yeah, it's shorter on the one side . . . okay, way shorter. But she does a great job, plus, being my sister, it's free. And she's a seamstress. She made this dress."

And it's a pretty one, Ken thought. He said so. Tori quietly thanked him. "You're really not gay, Tori?"

"No, Ken, I'm not," she answered. "And really, based on some buttons and a haircut, you went *there*?"

Anyone would have, thought Ken.

The conversation caused Tori to dust off a long-held anxiety: as much as she loved Patty, she worried that her haircuts did, in fact, make Tori look butch, at least a little. *And her homespun clothes, a bit too granola—this black dress excepted, of course.* Still, Tori wondered why she was on the defensive. She'd not dated extensively but knew the difference between gay and straight men. *At least I do now.* Yes, it was possible that Mr. Bowtie wasn't queer, but her mean-spirited luck said otherwise. *Tori, he's on the hunt for a fag-hag and* boy *do you look the part.* Tori suddenly felt crushed.

"Well," said Ken, choosing his words carefully, "the hair, the buttons, some of the things I've overheard from your sessions—sorry, but you're kind of loud, and the way you, um . . . conduct yourself, you don't come across as, well . . ."

A silence tense enough to attract the attention of surrounding patrons enveloped them.

Ken knew before seeing her wet eyes—real distress this time—that he'd messed up. *Good Lord, what did I just do?* "Don't get me wrong, Tori, you're a beautiful woman," he offered. Then he collected himself and spoke again, forthrightly, "Tori, I'm not sure if this is a date or what, but I really do find you attractive, very much so."

I've heard that *before,* thought Tori. Which was true—the last time as part of an ill-advised romp with a married dentist. Tori was ashamed now of the adultery, but what truly sickened her was the way Dr. Weeks had used her, then dumped her for someone else—a hairy *man* named Oscar.

She wiped a tear away. "You're just saying that."

"No, I'm not just saying that," Ken said. "Seriously, are you kidding? And why would I lie?"

Tori took a moment to compose herself. Formally: "This is not the first time I've heard that."

"Well of course not," said Ken, confused. *Why would you be upset about a compliment like that?* The stares from the surrounding tables added to his confusion.

Tori clarified, "Okay, my past two boyfriends, the only long-term ones I've had, by the way, both turned out to be gay."

"No way!" Ken said, genuinely shocked. And intrigued. "*Both* of them? Are you sure?"

"*Yes, Ken, I'm sure,* you bowtie-wearing idiot." At the next table, a woman mouthed to her friend, *That date's not going well.*

Another pause.

"Yeah, okay, Tori, of course you would know," said Ken. "Stupid of me. It's just that, well, honestly, you're not gonna believe this, but my past girlfriends were also—"

Ken's phone rang.

He looked at the number, grimacing. "I'm so sorry Tori, it's my sister. She wouldn't have called if it wasn't an . . . I have to take this." He excused himself, stepping away from the table.

Who is Mr. Pink Bowtie to take a call during our date, she thought. *Wait, did I just call this a "date"? Uh oh . . .*

Despite the background noise, Tori could hear his end of the conversation, which had no preamble:

"Which one? Both? Figures. Okay, put one on. Doesn't matter which."

"Georgie? This is Uncle Ken. Not interested in your side of the story. Pipe down and listen up. First, grab the yellow bucket and fill it with water from the blue jug. DO NOT use tap water. Let your mom pick through the glass for the ones still alive. What? You've already got the bucket? Great! After you help her rescue the fish, put my hockey stick back in the basement where it belongs, then you and your brother brush your teeth and go to bed. Do all that and I won't box your ears when I get home. Got it? Tell Gregory."

There was a short pause while Georgie, who didn't suffer from conversational circumspection, loudly relayed his uncle's message.

"What?" asked Ken. "Why am I not home? Didn't your mother tell you?" Here Ken looked at Tori, four yards away. "Because I'm on a *date,* Georgie, that's why. Yes, I said I don't date, but—" He looked at Tori again. "I've changed my mind," he said curtly. The briefest of pauses, then: "Yes, very much so. Now put your mother back on."

"Really, Sylvia?" said Ken. "Just one dead fish? Caught a break there."

Tori heard Sylvia ask Ken something.

"Um, yeah, sure, it's going well," he said, looking guiltily at Tori. "Is that Gree crying? Tell him I will never leave him. Or his brother. Or you." Ken gave Tori an I'm-wrapping-up twirl. "Sis, I gotta go. See you tonight. Love you. Bye."

He returned to their table. "Jesus, I'm so sorry. This"—he waved around the bar, then back and forth between he and her—"maybe wasn't the best idea."

Tori, more composed now, asked, "You live with your sister?"

"Yes," said Ken with another grimace, realizing she'd been able to hear his conversation.

"How long?"

After a pause, Ken answered, "Seven years."

"Is she divorced?" asked Tori.

"No, not officially. Her husband, uh, ran out on her. Ran pretty far, actually. No one knows where."

"Oh." Tori looked thoughtful. "Your nephews sound like a handful."

"You could say that," answered Ken.

Unbidden words now flashed across Tori's mind: RESPONSIBLE, then FAMILY MAN, then GOOD LOOKING, which, if she were honest, had read SEXY. There was one last but very important word: STRAIGHT? Alarm bells blared. *Oh no, not again!*

Tori believed that she exercised good judgment in all things—except dating. She'd spent countless days dissecting her failed love life, and now did so again. To be fair to her, she'd honestly missed the clues that her first boyfriend, Darren, was gay; being in love had blinded her. Her last lover, however, Richard the Dentist, who'd ended up cheating on his wife *and* his mistress (Tori) with Oscar the hirsute sports memorabilia dealer, really had been a mystery. Richard seemed straight as an arrow, an apex male with an unnecessarily large riding mower, a German Shepherd, two kids, and a wife (who he'd promised to leave, and finally did, but not for Tori). His hooking up with Oscar the Ape Man had been an unfathomable left turn, shocking Tori, not to mention his now ex-wife. After Richard, Tori Bora no longer trusted her intuition.

"Earth to Tori."

Bowtie Man wants your attention, her intuition announced. "Sorry, Ken, what did you say?"

"I said I'm glad you're no longer upset. You're not . . . right?"

"Yes, yes, never mind that," Tori responded almost dismissively. "Tell me about your nephews."

"George and Gregory?"

Ken described moving in with his sister and her boys a year after her husband had abandoned them. He relayed how lovable the twins were, deep down inside, anyway. And yes, how destructive: armed with a single screwdriver, the pair of determined nine-year-olds recently disassembled their neighbor's AC unit.

"Do they act out because their father's not in the picture?" Tori asked carefully.

"Maybe," said Ken, "but the truth is they were always a handful. A hundred-ten percent boy." He paused. "They'll turn out all right in a few years. Okay, maybe more than a few, but even though they fight constantly—recent AC disassembly cooperation excepted—they're not mean-spirited. I don't know if that makes any sense."

Tori nodded, thinking of Date Night Surprise, her kid brother who she loved dearly when she didn't want to strangle him.

"It's good I wasn't talking to Gregory," Ken added.

"Why's that?"

"The dead fish was Gregory's favorite."

"Did it—the fish—have a name?" asked Tori, intrigued by the names people gave their pets.

"Ah," said Ken, hesitating, "it sure did."

"Well," said Tori, "what was it?"

More hesitation, then: "Mr. Fish Farts."

Tori slapped her hands to her mouth, but it was too late. What came out was a combination of gaspy, snorty inhalations, inflaming every capillary in her face. "I'm so"—*snort!*—"sorry to be"—*snort!*—"laughing at the name"—*snort!*—"Mr. Fish Farts." *Snort-snort!* She began cackling.

"Haha," said Ken, trying to remain deadpan. "He's nine. What did you expect? Beowulf? And stop snorting. It's not that funny." She snorted even harder. "You know he's quite upset over Mr. Fish Farts' death, totally broken up in fact, so you're a terrible person for laughing."

"I want you to know that"—*snort!*—"I'm taking the passing of Gregory's"—*snort!*—"favorite fish"—*snort!*—"very seriously." *Snort-gasp.*

"You're heartless," Ken replied. He tried sounding judgmental, but ended up laughing too. Yes, a living thing had died, which was sad, but *Mr. Fish Farts* really was the perfect name for a nine-year-old boy's pet fish.

It took a minute before they settled down again. There was still cheer in Tori's eyes, but internally, she weighed something, telling herself, *Okay, girl, out with it already.*

She gave Ken the rundown on her two gay boyfriends, leaving out the dentist's marital status, but oddly enough mentioning losing her virginity to her first boyfriend Darren in a laundromat utility closet, something she thought forever marking her as a slut. "Pathetic, huh?" she asked, meaning the utility closet.

Ken, who'd been listening intently, said, "At least you lost your virginity *indoors* to someone you cared about. I lost mine in a parking lot to a Slayer groupie."

"Really?" said Tori, choking a baby snort before it could mature.

"Yes, really," Ken said. "Well, I'm happy that bit of personal trivia amused *somebody.*"

"And you're *sure* you're not gay?" Tori asked.

"I'm sure," Ken said, smiling broadly now. "Say, Tori, I've got some stories I think only you could appreciate. Can I order that beer now?"

"Yes please."

Chapter 38: A Wad of Twenties

Saturday, 24 April 1999
Wheaton, MD

"SPLASH, IT'S LOO."

"What's up, Luigi?" Henry asked, having managed to grab his phone before it vibrated off his stepladder's tray into a can of Eggshell White. Loo had called while he was arranging an exhibit wall, one of four showcasing the Japanese ambassador's daughter's anime sketches. He carefully held the frame of one—shapely Amazons atop winged tigers—in his hand while cradling the phone.

"The usual," said Loo. "Consuming and excreting in proportional amounts. Usually, anyway. You?"

"TMI, Spicotti, but since you asked, I'm great. A little tired, but great. Putting up the last of Juri's artwork. After the shooting, thought I'd never hear from her again, but after three months' delay, the show's tonight, catered and everything. And the best part? Her work's really good."

"So, no EMBC meeting for you?" asked Loo.

"Sorry, duty calls," Splash said, thinking, *It was my missing November's meeting that led to the faceoff with Washington Jr. in the first place. And now the dude will never draw another breath.*

"Well, of *course* duty calls," said Loo, unaware of Henry's painful memory. "Juri's hot for her Henry-san.'"

"She's sixteen," Splash said flatly. "A minor."

"Oh yeah," Loo said, chastened more by his friend's tone than his words. "Sorry."

"She's also psycho," Splash added.

"Really?"

"Yeah, daddy issues for starters, plus she talks a mile a minute. I can't understand half of what she says, and what I can understand is *way* out there." Henry paused, looking at Juri's sketch. "But she draws beautifully, like Akira Toriyama."

"No kidding?" asked Loo.

"Yes, she's that good."

"Sounds like a match made in heaven, Splash. You, the gallery owner, she, the ambassador's artsy daughter."

"Get stuffed, Loo," Splash replied.

"God, Henry, don't be so sensitive."

"Did I mention her *age,* Luigi?"

"Okay, okay," responded Loo, "You did. Poor taste. Ten yards."

"Sorry, man," Henry said. "I'm just busy getting ready for the showing. Little on edge. What can I do for you?"

"Um, I'm actually outside your gallery. Mind if I come in?"

Henry hadn't expected this. He didn't know why his friend had come calling but figured it might be serious. "Sure. Get your ass in here. You can help me."

The studio's front door squawked noisily as Loo came in.

The reason for Loo's visit turned out to be very serious.

"Jesus, Loo," said Henry from his stepladder, "you want me to do *what*?"

They were alone, but Loo whispered anyway: "Kill some deer . . ."

"Seriously?" responded Henry. "What, you want me to whip out Make My Day, a gun I don't have any more, by the way, and start blasting?"

"A handgun?" replied Loo, shocked. "God no."

"Well that's good, Tree Boy," Henry said angrily, "because if you think I'm a gun for hire just 'cause I killed someone—in *self-defense,* remember that?—then you can kiss my ass. I mean *really,* Loo, why would you ask me to do something so messed up?"

"Because I'm in serious trouble, Splash," Loo said. "That's why."

"So, you really *are* the Deerslayer?"

A moment's silence, in which Loo uncomfortably recalled the woodchipper from last night's nightmare, then, "Yes."

Henry looked at him as if he had two heads, demanding, "Explain yourself."

Loo cleared his throat, then began explaining, starting from his first kill up to being arrested after chasing Big Stew's herd.

Loo's confession didn't totally shock Splashdown—he, like the other guys, had had his doubts about Loo's story, but it was still unsettling to hear. "So this big deer," said Henry, "the one the Bambi Killer supposedly shot a week after your arrest, the one 'proving' you aren't the Deerslayer, proves that you are? And now you want me to hunt deer on parkland—something I've never done, by the way—to what, firm up your alibi? That right?"

"Yeah," said Loo sheepishly. "Pretty much sums it up."

Splash mounted another sketch, then pointed at the next drawing, impatiently motioning Loo to hand it up. "So you straight up lied? To everyone?"

Loo handed Splash the sketch—chiseled male warriors astride dragons—which Henry mounted adjacent to the Amazons-on-tigers. "Yes, I *lied,* okay?

Look, Splash, there's gonna be a cloud over the rest of my life unless the deer start dying again."

Henry looked down, his gaze penetrating. "Maybe you *deserve* a cloud, Loo. Thought about that? Thought about how lucky you were *not* getting caught the first eighty-nine times?"

Loo looked up, noting the dark rings around Henry's eyes, ones making him look owlish. "Yeah, okay," he said, "I went crazy, took things into my own hands, tied my own rope, et cetera, et cetera. I deserve a shit-ton of grief for that. But now it's about protecting Cindy, protecting the kids. They don't deserve a cloud over them for the rest of *their* lives, do they?"

This isn't about them, thought Splash. *This is about saving your own ass.* "So, since I have 'experience,' I'm your best bet to save your family from infamy?"

Quietly, Loo said, "Yes."

Henry had to hand it to him—though his friend was embarrassed about what he wanted, he wasn't looking away. Splash stepped down to face him. "Putting aside how wrong what you did was, and how wrong it is hiding behind Cindy, Hanna, and baby Joshua"—here Loo flinched—"you think it's a-okay to ask a guy who's just barely avoided prison to illegally hunt in broad freakin' daylight?"

"Daylight? No, Splash, bad idea. At *night*. And no gun. You'll need a crossbow. I got money for that." Loo offered him a wad of rubber-banded twenties. "And there's a half-quarrel of bolts still stashed in the woods."

Henry stepped closer to Loo, nearly toe to toe, and an image of the bearded Peterbilt man flashed through his mind. As idiotic as it was, he could get his head around Loo's request, sort of, because Spicotti was obviously desperate, but he didn't understand how cut and dried Tree Boy was being about it, as if he'd already taken "yes" for granted. They stared at each other—Henry, mad, Loo, hopeful—the money between them.

Henry reached forward. At first, Loo thought he would take the cash, but he'd badly misjudged his friend. Henry took Loo's wrist instead, squeezing it, sending the money flying. The wad slid across the studio's parquet, coming to rest against the open paint can. Henry let go. "Pick up your money and leave."

Loo, shocked, retrieved his roll, but didn't pocket it. Instead, he placed it on the stepladder's foldout shelf. "I'm going, but I'm leaving this," he said. "If you don't want to help me, Splash, fine, don't, but keep the money." Loo looked around at the walls of Henry Takahashi's fledgling studio. "Consider it . . . an investment." He walked toward the door.

"Come back and get your money, Spicotti!" Henry yelled. "You're burning a bridge if you don't!"

Loo opened the studio door—*squawk*. "Splash," he said, trying to sound helpful, "you should really oil this thing."

Henry bolted to the door after him, tearing it open so suddenly it had no time to complain. He wanted to yell obscenities at Loo but instead watched him—one of his best friends just twenty minutes earlier—get in his sedan and drive away. As the door screeched on his way back inside, Splash kicked it to teach it a lesson, then marched to his supply closet, retrieving a can of WD-40. He paused by the stepladder, whose foldout shelf held Loo's money out to him like a lozenge on a tongue.

He felt like burning it.

But face facts, he told himself. *I'm carrying a steep loan on this place . . . but no, not taking Tree Boy's money.*

Tired as he was, Henry had an idea. He grabbed the money and threw it in his desk drawer where it landed next to his copy of EMBC's April selection, *Geek Love,* a book that studio prep had kept him from finishing. He made a call. After a discussion, he hung up to thumb through the Yellow Pages, calling a local sporting goods store, inquiring about crossbows. Once done, he sprayed the front door hinge generously with WD-40 and returned to work.

The phone rang five minutes later. "Gate of Heaven Studio, Henry speaking."

"Koneko!" Juri Ito exclaimed. "Everything's perfect for my exhibition tonight, right?"

"Yes, Miss Ito. Mounting the last of your sketches as we speak. And my name's Haru or Henry, not Koneko."

"I'm your client, so I'll call you whatever I want. And I like all this 'mounting' talk! Keep it up, Koneko. And call me Juri."

Henry, who'd been hearing from the tenacious sixteen-year-old for weeks, was no longer shocked by her directness. "Yes, Miss Ito," he said. "Call you 'Juri,' got it."

"Seriously, call me Juri or no paycheck, Kitty," she said.

"Your dad's the signatory, Miss Ito, not you, so see you tonight. Be here no earlier than five."

"I'll come at four, so we have time to fool around."

Good God, thought Henry. "The building will be locked then, Miss Ito, and I won't be here. You're welcome to hang out in the parking lot if you want." *Where I killed someone.*

To Juri's annoyance, Henry rushed her off the phone—there were caterers, embassy security, even the press, to prepare for. So much to do—7 p.m. seemed right around the corner. Loo's problems, or more correctly, the Deerslayer's problems, would have to wait.

Chapter 39: Who the Hell's Walter?

Saturday, 24 April 1999
Silver Spring, MD

"NINE: A STAN where you get stuck," declared Original.

"Quick-istan," D-Kay answered. "Or Trap-istan. Take your pick."

"Damn, thought I had you there," Original said, looking at his list. "Okay, last one. Ten: a 'situational' stan."

D-Kay, once again defending his Babble King title, struggled for a half minute before coming up with, "Where-do-things-istan." The EMBC members cheered.

"You pulled that last one out of your ass, Tooth D-Kay," groused Original. He'd spent his entire Saturday morning developing new "stan" countries with which to stump Darius, only to have the bastard muscle his way through nine out of ten, including giving three answers cleverer than his own.

The men had once again mustered at Shorties, this time for their April 1999 club meeting to discuss *Geek Love* by Katherine Dunn. In attendance: a subdued Loo, Trevor, Gary the New Guy, Death Rey, Original Ken, Phillipe, D-Kay—everyone except Henry, who the guys hoped was wowing art critics.

Trevor, still abstaining from alcohol, was again riding a Dr. Pepper rush, making him chatty and a little nervous—he technically wasn't supposed to be there. How many times could he play the I'm-going-to-a-meeting card before Carol or Cisco found out? He experienced a moment of clarity: *I should go home. Now.*

But not before razzing Phillipe one more time, he thought, something he'd been doing sporadically all evening. "I think I'd look good in a dress," Trevor declared.

Heads turned. "I'll bite," said Gary. "Why?"

"Just a feeling," he answered. "I could borrow something strapless from Phillipe." Scattered laughter. "Whatcha say, pilot?"

"Trevor, no one wants to see your hairy back," Phillipe quipped. His parry got laughs, but only Trevor understood it fully: *Stop going to the well.*

"The pilot has a point," Loo said.

"Trev's a fucking sasquatch is the point," said D-Kay.

"So, the curse?" Trevor asked. "How are Prophet's powers of prediction this month?"

Six months after Prophet's prophetic warning, it was still four arrests, three lost jobs, no lost loves, no deaths: 4, 3, 0, and 0, and if one factored in only the charges that stuck (Trevor) and permanent job losses (again, Trevor; Henry was back in his studio and Loo had been reinstated) it was more like 1, 1, 0, and 0.

Not much of a curse.

The dead man was eight for eight for unsettling dreams, however. Last night, Carol's head barely stayed above water by the time Trevor found the cage key. D-Kay had to really sprint to clear the falling tree that the half-Ruger, half-Prophet character was trying to kill him with. Gary's lungs burned as the bearded man held him under for so long that Dream Gary blacked out. Phillipe now fell thirty feet toward three boxes instead of six, and in Loo's case, the bearded semi-Prophet was pushing him even closer to an angry-looking woodchipper. Ken barely got one hand up to protect his head. Rey was waking up moments before the ugly, bearded Gun Girl finally made up her mind to shoot him this time.

But the worst dreams were the absent Henry's. The bearded trucker who'd forced him against the guardrail had passed so close last night that Henry's driver's side mirror had disintegrated.

But no one brought up the subject of dreams that night. Why? Each man felt an intense, perhaps unnatural privateness about his nightmare and therefore kept his own counsel. Later, after men started dying, the survivors would talk, wondering if their initial hesitancy to voice their dreams was by karmic design.

Trevor again, guys.

Dr. Pepper has once again taken its toll, so off to the Gents I go.

After relieving myself, I read the latest graffiti: *Napoleon yanked his Bonaparte,* accompanied by a poorly drawn, furiously masturbating French emperor. Another: *If you take a shit, be courteous and leave one.*

Not bad, I think, making my way to the sink.

Unbeknownst to me in that moment, Phillipe has entered the Gents. Had Poland Manchester replaced the bathroom's missing mirror, I would have seen his reflection, since he's standing right behind me. After toweling up, I turn to leave—you guessed it—right into him. I involuntarily step back and nearly sit in the sink.

"Christ, dude! What the hell!"

Phillipe doesn't look apologetic. "Trevor, whatever you're driving at with all this cross-dressing talk, you need to stop."

"Come on, Phillipe, they're just jokes."

"Well I don't think they're funny," Phillipe snaps.

"Why's that?" I ask sarcastically.

"You know why," Phillipe replies, staring me down. There is no mistaking the anger in his eyes.

"Well, I suppose I can cut back—"

"Let me explain things clearly," interrupts Phillipe, putting his hands on my shoulders. "The dresses? I don't know what you know or how you know it and I don't care, because, like usual, your drunk ass doesn't understand a damn thing correctly, so listen up: if certain knowledge, from *any* source, gets back to people I care about, I'm holding you personally responsible."

"Listen, I can stop the jokes, but I can't be held responsible if other—"

"Yes, you can," Phillipe says, cutting me off again. "And I will."

Phillipe removes his hands distastefully. "Why are you even here? Shouldn't you be with the other drunks at one of those AA meetings? Honestly, I always knew you were a bit of a fuckup, but you're really going downhill, aren't you? The other guys may not see it, but I do. And you're taking your *family* with you, and you don't seem to care."

"Look, asshole," I say indignantly, "I haven't had a drink since Christmas, and personally, I don't care if wearing a prom dress gets you off—"

Slap!

He strikes me with an open hand, but my ear still rings. "Anything gets out, you stupid lush, anything at all, and I'm coming for you."

With that, Phillipe leaves.

I turn to stare into the nonexistent mirror above the wash basin. The graffiti in its place—*Just assume you look like shit*—stares back at me judgmentally.

On his way back to the table, Phillipe stopped at the bar to ask Vicky, their server, for another pitcher, offering to take it back with him. She thanked him for his kindness. He waited while she filled it, watching another Channel 4 News promo: teasers about Y2K gloom and doom plus another Deerslayer re-hash. The slayings, including their cessation, were old news by this point, but Channel 4 still showed Loo Spicotti's mugshot, implying that the killer had already been caught.

He reached the table in time to hear D-Kay promote his latest opera concept: four Russian brothers, all military officers: Lt. Jerkov, Colonel

Fuckov, General Pissov, and Admiral Whackov. The guys groaned. "What, you liked the Italian theme better?" D-Kay asked.

"You should've stuck to the Stans," said Loo.

"Yeah, I can't-istan your childish sense of humor," said Original.

"Point, Ert," said Gary.

"Hey, New Guy," said D-Kay, "I give out the points."

"And *I* control club history," said Gary, patting his notepad officiously. 'Those who control the past control the future.'—George Orwell."

"Okay," D-Kay agreed, "so long as you lay off the Phoenician dietary lectures."

"Hey, where'd Trev go?" asked Loo.

"Home," said Phillipe.

"He didn't pay for his sodas," said Rey.

"Don't get your panties in a bunch," said Phillipe. "I'm sure cheapskate here will pick it up." He pointed at D-Kay, notorious for not pulling his financial weight.

D-Kay flipped him off, then turned to Rey, saying, "Really, don't worry about the bill, Perkins, worry about those illegals looking for you."

"What's that supposed to mean?" asked Rey, sounding protective. "I'm not afraid of them."

"Yes, you are," said D-Kay.

"Bite me, Kay."

"Rey, care to tell us why those El Salvadorians have you so concerned?" Gary asked innocently.

Around them, the bar continued humming, but the guys were in their own world now.

How did Gary know they were El Salvadorians? Rey asked himself, feeling cornered. Aloud: "I can't help it if their presence sickens me."

"So if they come in again, you gonna give them a piece of your mind, like you did at the bodega?" asked Loo. By now, everyone knew about Rey yelling at the Latino painters.

"Sure," said Rey. But he didn't sound sure.

"I think you're full of shit," said Loo, remembering how uncomfortable Rey had made him feel the night he'd gone off on the Latinos.

"Maybe I am, but at least I'm not getting *my* jollies off snuffing Bambi," Rey replied coolly.

The table went silent.

"That's hitting below the belt," declared Original.

Rey didn't back down. "Sorry," he said facetiously, "*alleged* Bambi snuffer. That better?"

"He's our friend, Perkins," Original said stiffly. "He said he didn't do it, so he didn't do it. That's good enough for us, which means it's damn well good enough for you."

"It's okay," said Loo. "I don't care what Rey thinks."

"No, it's not okay," insisted Original. "And why do we have to put up with Trevor's asshole work friend, anyway? He's just another stupid 'new' guy. 'Last hired, first fired' is what I say."

"So what, we're having a literary layoff now?" Rey asked snidely. "Might as well since we haven't spent one second talking about the book." He knew this wasn't the right approach but couldn't help himself.

"Hey guys," said Gary, trying to lighten the mood, "I'm technically the new guy, so Rey's—"

"Shut up, Gary," Ken said.

"Yeah, shut up," agreed Rey.

"Enough," intoned Phillipe. He had not shouted, but he may as well have. Just as quickly, Phillipe pivoted to humor: "You two crankie-pots obviously need naps." He didn't normally clown like that, so the guys paid attention—with that, the tension had been broken.

Loo looked at his watch: "Paying the check, what a good idea." He waved at Vicky, who brought their bill over. Gary, the club's de facto accountant, took it, announcing totals for each member. After some groaning, everyone handed Gary money or cards. Rey began counting out bills but looked to be coming up short. "I'm good for it guys, just need a minute." (Though he was unpopular at the moment, no one doubted him—Rey could be prickly, but he wasn't cheap.)

Gary totaled everything up. "Boys, even accounting for what Difficult Rey's good for, we're light."

"I covered Pug's sodas, but here's a few more dollars," said Phillipe. Others put in. Everyone except Darius.

"We're still short," said Gary. Everyone looked at D-Kay.

"Don't look at me," he said; "I paid for what I ordered."

"Plus tip, right?" asked Phillipe. D-Kay nodded. "So how much did you tip?"

"Well, I don't remember offhand," D-Kay said evasively.

"What was his total?" Original asked Gary.

"Gary said eighteen," D-Kay answered for him.

"No," said Loo. "Gary said eighteen *fifty*. How much did you put in?"

"Enough, I'm sure," said D-Kay.

"You put in twenty," said Gary. "You must think that covers it?"

"Yes," replied D-Kay warily.

"Don't think so," said Phillipe. "That's only eight percent. Fifteen to twenty's customary. So, Darius, what didn't you like about Vicky's service?"

"Well, nothing really—"

"Well there *must* be," insisted Phillipe. "*Eight percent* says so. Hey Vicky," he yelled. "Could you please come over here? Urban D-Kay's gotta service gripe."

Vicky approached, looking down at D-Kay. Perfunctorily: "Problem with my service, sir?"

"No, no, Vicky—" began Darius.

"Yes, yes, Vicky," said Phillipe, "there most certainly is. He's only leaving eight percent."

"Eight percent?" said Vicky, sounding shocked.

"Well, I can explain—" began D-Kay.

"No need for that, sir," Vicky said, winking at Phillipe. "The customer's always right. Eight percent, huh? I'll need to step up my game." She leaned in toward D-Kay, an act accentuating her cleavage. "Tell me, Darius, or do you prefer Mr. Kay? Perhaps that's the problem? I'm being too, oh, what's the word I'm looking for, Randy?"

"'Familiar,'" her twin said as she passed the table carrying food.

"Thanks, Sis."

"Don't mention it."

"Was I being too *familiar*, Mr. Kay?" Vicky asked.

"No, no—" D-Kay began again.

"No?" she interrupted, coming eye level with him. "Okay, tell me, Mr. Kay, what gets me to fifteen percent?" She leaned closer. "I know the other guys," Vicky waved expansively around the table, "tip good because the table always tips twenty, so I feel terrible they're covering up for the poor service you're getting. Unfair, right?"

This is unfair to me, D-Kay thought. He tried maintaining eye contact, but Victoria's cleavage was proving distracting.

"Earth to Mr. Kay, come in, Mr. Kay," said Vicky. "Maybe I should bring your food out on a nice warm plate, huh? Oh wait, I already *do* that. But to get to fifteen percent, Mr. Kay—I don't need twenty, I'm not greedy—perhaps I should bring it out under a fancy dish cover."

"To retain moistness," Randy added, passing the table again.

"Exactly, Sis!" agreed Vicky. "I want you to know that I'll buy a silver dish cover just for you this week, Mr. Kay. 'Course, I won't be able to pay next month's rent, but that's a small sacrifice, right?"

The EMBCers were lapping everything up.

"Really," said D-Kay, "that's not necess—"

"I got an idea!" interjected Randy from two tables over. "We can bring his food out clapping like they do at Chili's. Maybe Daddy can join in. Daddy!" she yelled. "We still got that mini gong under the bar?" Poland grunted. It was unclear if this meant yes or no.

"A parade! Fantastic idea, Randy," said Vicky. "Darius—it's okay calling you Darius, isn't it?"

"Now look here," D-Kay said, "I really don't think—"

"Next time, can you bring out my nachos with sparklers?" asked Rey, getting into the act.

"Maybe on Independence Day, handsome," Vicky said.

"Actually, sparklers are illegal in Maryland," Gary added, but no one minded him.

"So really, Darius, what gets me to fifteen percent? Do you need to see more cleavage?" She moved her chest comically close to D-Kay's face. The table howled.

"I'm good for thirty percent!" Loo declared.

"Settle down, Mr. Spicotti," Vicky said assuredly. "Now's not the time to get excited."

"Oh yes it is!" he shouted, laughing. Everyone was roaring now—across the bar, even Poland smirked.

Darius retrieved a ten from his wallet and handed it to Gary. Vicky stood back, grinning like the champion she was. "Thank you for not suffocating me," D-Kay said.

"Wouldn't be the worst way to go," quipped Loo. Vicky playfully pinched his cheek.

"Reymond," said Gary, "we just need yours."

"Yeah, yeah, I know," Rey said, once again annoyed. Always a cash customer, he realized he didn't have enough, and given the way he'd been antagonizing the table, he knew no one would cover for him. Reluctantly, he took a card out, handing it over.

"We're good, Vicky," Gary said. "Twenty-one point five percent tip. Death Rey and Urban D-Kay here put us over the top." Everyone but a preoccupied Rey cheered. Vicky took everything to the register, returning with their cards and handing signature slips out.

"Phillipe, here you go, hon. Ken, here's yours. And last but not least, this card belongs to Walter, whoever he is."

"Walter?" exclaimed D-Kay. "Who the hell's Walter?"

Reluctantly, Rey reached for his card.

Chapter 40: Los Fantasmas

Wednesday, 11 May 1977—Day 70
Colombia, South America

DAY 70 OF the boys' capture and the sixty-second day spent at Camp Mimada arrived like other days: pre-dawn jungle noises, a 6 a.m. wakeup, then standing in line for Big Stinky. But today would end differently. The previous evening, the camp's most olfactive *perro,* a dog who'd saved the FARC from past ambushes, had gone missing. There was no worry—sometimes male dogs took off to pursue females in heat. The missing dog would return within a day or so, and if not, though the pooch was good at his job, there was no shortage of dogs. Besides, it had been two months since the FARC had mistakenly killed El Conde's men, and since Buscar's patrols turned up no more signs of El Fantasma's paramilitaries, the Jaguars were breathing easier.

At 7:00 a.m., while the camp was still dark due to the overhead canopy, one of the Lieutenant's patrols returned early, running straight to Buscar's coleta. The dog had been found two kilometers away, dead, its digits cut—El Fantasma's calling card. There was terse discussion, then Buscar growled an order. Camp was to be abandoned, and everyone was given ten minutes to gather their belongings and the crucial common gear (the radio, ammunition, medical supplies, food). Walter noted that by seven-thirty, the prisoners and over a hundred FARC guerillas began marching into the jungle. He asked their guards in his best pidgin Spanish: Where are we going? *"El culo del mundo,"* one responded unhappily.

"This won't be a pleasant walkabout," Jack said to Walter.

And it wasn't. The guards tethered the boys' wrists together to the POWs, then began leading them, sporadically tugging them to keep up the pace. "Whatever's going on," Walter said under his breath, "they're not fooling around. And they're scared." Throughout the day, the pace didn't slacken: *Follow the boots! Follow the boots! March, gringos, like your lives depend on it!* Which was true: if the FARC were attacked, as the Lieutenant had explained on their first day at Mimada, the boys would be killed.

Everyone, the captured included, moved quickly. No breaks. No food. They trudged through thick brush all day along a poorly maintained dirt road toward the border. A handful of Venezuelan "agents" met them on their side of the nominally marked international boundary, a steel gate between two opposing guard shacks, one on each side of a wire fence running along the border. The Colombian guard shack looked abandoned. Two chain-smoking uniformed soldiers sat on chairs in front of the Venezuelan guardhouse, however, looking bored and vaguely dissatisfied. The other Venezuelans present, the shadow government agents, opened the gate, motioning the caravan through. The Jaguars didn't go far, perhaps three hundred meters, before the agents shunted them down a steep hillside to an abandoned coca field with a few primitive coletas but no water and no overhead trees. The site was completely exposed. The agents had a brief, heated discussion with Lt. Buscar. The boys' grasp of Spanish had significantly improved, but the agents' dialect was too new to understand completely. However, the message seemed obvious: *No supplies. Don't stay long.* The agents returned upslope. Once gone, Buscar could still see other agents watching down over them from well-chosen vantages.

Buscar recovered quickly, directing La Madre to organize camp. It would be dark in a few hours, and no one had eaten. A meal of odds and ends, including a weak stew of beef and beans hopped up with panela sugar was prepared, the largest meal the boys or anyone else would eat for the next fifteen days. "Clacker Camp," as the young Caucasians soon referred to the place—they'd voted between *Camp Butthole, Ass Camp, Camp Browneye,* and several other possibilities before settling on *Clacker,* Aussie for anus—was an open area less than a quarter of a fútbol field in size. It was meant to hold perhaps three dozen; Buscar had nearly four times that number. The abandoned coca field was hemmed in by steep hillsides to the north, west, and south, but open to the east via a rough cliff face with a substantial drop. The nearest stream was two kilometers away, downhill, and there were no trees to build shelters with. Though the agents were sympathetic to the FARC's cause, they had made "the Clack" inhospitable on purpose. Though they were keen on destabilizing Colombia, they weren't keen on having FARC soldiers on their own soil, something internationally volatile. The Clack was meant for temporary use, like an air raid shelter. The contempt on the departing agents' faces—*you should be fighting your enemies, not hiding from them*—said as much.

Buscar's young soldiers were used to quick movements, but the full-on, immediate retreat from Los Fantasmas had panicked them. In the rush to avoid losing their fingers, not to mention their lives, Los Jaguares arrived at the Clack with little to show for it. The dogs had followed the FARC soldiers out of loyalty, but the pigs and goats, as if sensing what fate might have in store for them, had not. There'd be no help of any kind; the agents had made that clear. The Six Jaguars, one-hundred-twenty soldiers plus six POWs and two ransomees, would have to subsist on the contents of their pockets. Some food, including half a stringy cow carcass, had been brought with the cooking gear, but 128 mouths were 128 mouths. What would they eat?

Water was a two-klick hike at the end of an otherwise inaccessible canyon, so returning to Colombia was the only way Buscar's men could leave. Agents continued watching from on high.

"Are you scared?" Walter asked Jack that night.

"Yeah, Bruce," he answered. "I'm scared because *they're* scared. But hey, let's count our blessings. At least we're not following the boots anymore." Walter nodded but felt somehow that following the boots might be better.

11-26 May 1977—Days 70-85

The next two weeks slowly descended into anger, sunstroke, and starvation. The clearing was small, the FARC's numbers large. Shelters of tarps and sheets were erected where space could be found. Combined with blankets and ponchos stretched between flimsy sticks, about half the soldiers could be protected from the sun at any one time. The glare hurt the boys' eyes, but the tarp Jack and Walter had been given at least kept them from getting sunstroke. For the unsheltered guerillas accustomed to jungle twilight, the sunlight was murder.

A shallow latrine had been dug into the camp's hardpacked clay but was filled by the third day. Despite a layer of capping dirt, its pungent stench gagged, so with real estate at a premium, a new one wasn't dug. Instead, everyone, girls included, began relieving themselves at the end of a spit of rock jutting out over the eastern drop. Excreta fell several meters onto treetops where a lower thermal mostly kept the smell at bay, a blessing very much appreciated after diarrhea gripped the camp. The FARC named the irregular, four-meter-long prominence *Salto del Amante*, "Lover's Leap." A strung-up blanket initially provided privacy, but within a day, the blanket was commandeered as a sun shield, leaving the Leap bare. After two days without the blanket, decorum vanished and no one, women included, cared if someone watched them squat.

For the first week, Walter and Jack counted themselves lucky: as prized prisoners, they were fed something once a day. Because of this, they were eyed sullenly by the guerillas and captured government soldiers alike. Lack of food gnawed at everyone. The prevailing gallows humor? Jumping off Lover's Leap was the best cure for hunger pain. Fortunately, the young soldiers had something else to obsess about besides the provisions wasted on the tall Rafa and the kangaroo boy, Guro. Each day, with the agents' permission, Buscar sent a five-man patrol back across the border to scavenge. It was a tough but popular assignment. The scavengers were given extra rations, and though reentering Colombia was dangerous—El Fantasma was searching for the fingers denied him earlier—patrolling meant raiding farmers' fields and, when those were picked dry, hunting small game: monkeys, toucans, and ever-present, somewhat dim armadillos. Each night, the patrol's return was eagerly awaited: what food did they find, and how much? The first week was promising, but then the farmers began hiding their stores and the wildlife started disappearing. Even the dim armadillos wised up. La Madre stewed whatever she was given, including, unfortunately, their loyal dogs, but with so many mouths to feed, the food gathered by the patrol was never enough.

Parasitic *chuchorros* took advantage of the weak, of which there were many. Worse were wormlike *nunches,* which emerged after a certain fly species inserted eggs beneath the skin. Then leishmaniasis took hold, a gruesome skin disease requiring a month's worth of unavailable medical treatment. As awful as the parasites and skin maladies were, La Madre, the company's de facto doctor, really feared cholera. Hunger and parasites were one thing, and even the arrival of dysentery during the second week could be weathered—it didn't take long for the Leap to be renamed *Roca de Sangra* (Blood Rock)—but cholera killed.

In addition to the extravagance of the giraffe and kangaroo boys' more generous rations, the FARC began to hate the well-fed agents surrounding their camp. The Venezuelans sensed this, fighting fire with fire. They began demanding money from the FARC for staying too long, and each day they brought in more agents, their numbers growing relative to the potential bad decisions starving soldiers might make. Soon, the FARC's money ran out, and everyone except the hardcore politicos and Buscar's loyal lieutenants discussed rushing uphill to steal from the agents. A machine gun emplacement installed on Day 76, however, as well as a second on Day 78, checked this desire.

Late in the second week, fights broke out over food hoarding and the shirking of water-hauling duty. Buscar whipped two men publicly with his belt as a warning, but it did little good; hardy as the rural FARC guerrillas were, the Six Jaguars had now run out of food. The specter of starvation arose. Three were dead already from illness—one guerilla and two of the Colombian captives. Buscar knew that in another week the bodies would drop faster. Then it would be low-grade mutiny because, despite the finger-collecting "ghosts," his soldiers would start slipping away by ones and twos back into Colombia, to first renounce, then sell out, the remaining FARC guerillas.

The lieutenant was at his wit's end. The few times he could establish contact with the FARC's southeastern leadership (the intervening ridge separating the countries made radio communication difficult), he received little encouragement and no promise of aid. Jojoy's message was clear: *return and fight the paramilitary pigs,* and for the first time since joining the FARC, the lieutenant understood that he was truly alone.

At the end of the second week, Day 85 of the kidnapping, Buscar caught a break. For the past two days, his Colombian patrol had been going further and further in-country, luckily finding no sign of Los Fantasmas. Locals relayed that El Conde's death squad had finally moved south, away from Camp Mimada, which the paramilitaries had unfortunately burned to the ground. Multiple sources, including radio contact with one of the lieutenant's spies, confirmed the news: it was safe to return.

"*Companaras,* pack up!" Buscar shouted. "Today we return to the motherland!" A muted cheer went up from his men. The agents behind their machine guns (there were now three emplacements) didn't cheer but did look relieved.

The march to the Clack had taken twelve hours, but despite their enthusiasm and lighter loads, the weakened guerillas took over twenty hours to return to Mimada. Hunger-induced exhaustion slowed the caravan's progress, but discipline held. As day turned to night, the silent soldiers held onto the belt or pack strap of the guerrilla in front of them lest they lose their way in the dark. Walter, Jack, and the surviving Colombian prisoners, including Jacinto and Hernandez, were again strung together for the march. They didn't much mind their ropes—ropes weren't chains.

The company marched through the night, straggling back into the remains of their base camp the following afternoon. The coletas, the camp improvements, every single bit of gear, had been burned. The jungle was reclaiming its own, however; vines were already working their way up the blackened trees. Even so, the overhead canopy was gone. Camp Mimada could now be seen from the air.

Buscar sent half of his men to forage and search for signs of Fantasma's men. The other half began hacking burnt forest saplings into tablas to create new shelters. The foragers returned hours later with a veritable feast: fruit and vegetables begged from farmers they'd had previous rapport with, plus a half dozen assorted birds and monkeys, a young cow, and a herd of nervous-looking goats. No sign of the paramilitaries, government troops, or the rival EPL revolutionaries. La Madre gathered exhausted but cheery girls to help prepare a meal of fruits, starchy palm tree centers, and a delicious stew made with everything that had been brought to them. For the first time since fleeing base camp, there was enough to go around.

That night, a contented sense of gratitude overtook the camp. Extra guards had been posted, but even plied with strong coffee and threats from Buscar, they could not stay awake. No one could, not La Madre, not Buscar, not even the most ardent Jaguar, Camarada Sebastian Ruiz, so total was their enervation.

The next morning at dawn, Los Fantasmas attacked. This time there was no warning—there had been no patrols to intercept them, no dogs to smell intruders, no alert watchmen. The Jaguars had been set up; El Conde had bribed the local farmers handsomely to tell Buscar's foragers that Los Fantasmas were many kilometers away. The ploy had been masterminded by El Fantasma, the Ghosts' leader, who knew the half-starved guerillas would sleep deeply after feasting.

Like the closing jaws of a Pac-Man, El Fantasma had his forces attack in a vise formation, starting at the edge of camp without the prisoners. They heralded their assault with a rocket-propelled grenade attack. Noise, shrapnel, blinding flashes, and human cries erupted at once. Jack, Walter, and the four remaining Colombian prisoners had been sleeping collectively in a pile to keep warm, their hands still roped together. They awoke, startled. Their guard had also been sleeping but was wide awake now. Hernandez asked her what was happening, but the young woman sprinted away.

"This is our chance!" Hernandez cried, crawling toward the woman's abandoned machete. He couldn't reach it. "Get your thumbs out of your asses! Help me before we're executed!"

The others tried assisting but were hampered by their ropes—Hernandez got closer but still couldn't reach the weapon. "Everyone! Move in one direction!" Loud booms, more flashes, flying debris. Staccato rifle fire began. Who was shooting? The FARC? The attackers? Both?

Blurry figures ran in all directions. In the scrum for the guard's dropped blade, Jack ended up closest. Hernandez shoved him further, yelling, "Guro, get the machete!" Jack couldn't use his hands but could stretch out his neck to bite the pommel, spitting the weapon back to Hernandez who began cutting his knots. Once freed, he started liberating the others, cutting the ropes between them so they could at least run, but with the surrounding firefight, it was unclear where to run to, so no one did.

Instead, everyone begged Hernandez to cut the knots still tying each one's hands together. He started with his fellow soldier, Jacinto. Jack the Guro was next. Before he could completely free him, however, Hernandez's and Jacinto's bodies bucked unnaturally, and they fell to the ground. Behind him were three men holding smoking rifles: Camaradas Sebastian Ruiz, Jaws, and Gustavo.

"Stay where you are, or you'll be shot!" For the brief second that the guerillas took to reload their Galils, no one moved. Then, per the mutual understanding that they would be killed next, everyone scattered.

Jack grabbed Walter, dragging him several yards before both boys tripped over a root, sprawling. Undaunted, the Aussie began bellycrawling, working his way out of the guerillas' line of sight, pulling a stunned Walter behind him.

With the gringos down, once reloaded, the revolutionaries began shooting at the other fleeing prisoners. Just then, one of yesterday's quickly assembled coletas disappeared in a flash of light. Next, a deafening explosion caused the ground beneath the boys to swell, tossing them as if on a trampoline.

Walter looked back toward the three guerillas. Jaws was rolling around on the ground, screaming. Gustavo lay still in the sooty mud. The Camarada had been knocked down but was, with difficulty, regaining his feet. He spied the boys and lurched toward them, swaying at half equilibrium. There was a tugging on Walter's neck. He heard the voice of someone screaming in English as if from a great distance. Despite the insistent tugging and yelling, Walter refused to move—if he'd been stunned before the last explosion, he was in shock now. Camarada Sebastian approached the boys, stopping five meters away, pointing his Galil at them. Jack, who was struggling to pull Walter behind the roots of a burnt ceiba tree, yelled, "Get going, ya Yank wanker!"

Sebastian fired a burst of rounds, pitching bits of bark into Walter's eyes. Suddenly, Walter understood. He swiftly scrambled to shelter behind the wall-like roots of the blackened ceiba, just as he'd hidden weeks ago from the dung-throwing monkeys. Sebastian staggered forward until he stood over the boys. Half equilibrium or not, he had them now. The Camarada smiled crookedly. He raised his rifle, relishing the fear in their eyes, happy at last to kill the stupid gringo "kings."

Just then, La Madre and several guerillas ran past. She recognized her sons and stopped, yelling to those with her to grab Gustavo. But they were exhausted, and Gustavo was obviously dead; no one would pick him up. So focused was La Madre on her dead son and the live one swaying in front of her that she didn't see the cowering Caucasians. She took Sebastian's Galil and began shouting at him, demanding that he flee with them through the still-open portion of El Fantasma's closing "vise." Sebastian pointed out the boys, pleading for his mother to kill them.

"Never mind the gringos, *mi hijo,*" she said quickly. "Leave them—they're who *Los Fantasmas* came for!" Sebastian's face clouded unhappily but, before he could argue further, La Madre shouted, "*Mi Dios!* The back of your head! Tatiana, your brother's been shot! Staunch it. Bruna, come. Help me take him." She and Bruna supported Sebastian, one on each side, while Tatiana, with no other resource, pulled her shirt off, wrapping it around his head.

In that moment, Tatiana, backlit by the burning coleta and nude now from the waist up, looked goddess-like to Walter. Her ribs were prominent from two weeks of hunger, yet she was beautiful and very sure of herself. She turned to her sister, saying, "*Vamos!*" before pushing Bruna, her brother, and her mother in the direction the remaining Jaguars had fled. As Sebastian was dragged away, he yelled at Tatiana to shoot the gringos. Her mother screamed at her to run.

She did not run. Instead, she crouched over the boys as they huddled together between the charred ceiba roots. Her naked torso, slick with sweat and heaving from running so hard, glowed in the firelight. A pistol materialized in her hand. Walter flinched: surely they would die now. He felt unexpectedly warm. Tatiana stared at Walter for a moment, then leaned into the boys' faces, first kissing Jack's cheek, then kissing Walter passionately on the lips. "*Adiós*, Guro, *adiós*, Rafa," she said. "Rafa, maybe I come to America."

She then ran to catch up with her family.

Jack looked at Walter. "You gotta lip-lock . . . all I goss a lousy peck oh cheek," he slurred. "It's cuz yer-so-tall . . . ya wanker." Walter realized why he felt warm: Jack had been hurt somehow and was bleeding. The battle, Tatiana's passionate kiss, Jack's blood—it all confused him.

The firefight petered out. Except for the cries of the wounded—including Jaws, who lay near the boys, moaning—and the crackling of dying flames, the jungle had returned to its normal noises. True dawn began filtering through the leafless canopy.

A pair of unfamiliar men approached. They were large, even by North American standards, well-fed, wearing black fatigues and bandanas wrapped robber-style around their faces.

"*Eres Americano*?" one of the men asked. "*Si, soy Americano,*" Walter answered. He thumbed to Jack who he'd been holding in his arms, adding, "*El es Australiano.*" Jaws, who had momentarily gone quiet, started moaning again. The second man swung his rifle off his shoulder, then queried: "*Australiano?*"

Walter was terrified again. After all they'd been through, were these black-clad men going to shoot them? But the rifleman shot Jaws instead, silencing him. He re-shouldered his weapon and lit a cigarette, looking as if he'd completed some annoying task. "Looks like we found the lost chicks," said the other man, who then squatted next to Jaws to begin removing his fingers.

5 June 1977

Hospital in Bogota

Jack had just awoken from a nap. Walter stood next to his hospital bed.

"G'day, Bruce," Jack said, his voice muffled by the bandage across his face. He looked around. "And g'day to you, Mr. and Mrs. Perkins."

"Good day, Jack," Walter's father and mother responded. "Your mom stepped out for some coffee," Walter's father said. "She'll be back soon."

"So, this is goodbye, then?" Jack asked.

"Yes," said Walter's mom. "I'm sorry for the circumstances, but it's been great meeting you. Thank you so much for everything you did for Walter." She began choking up. "He . . . he said you were a rock, someone he could really depend on. We're gonna miss you." She hugged him, then Walter's dad shook his hand. In the three days Walter's parents had been at the hospital, they had gotten to know Jack, highly approving of him.

"Let's give the boys a few minutes alone," Mr. Perkins said, guiding his damp-eyed wife toward the door.

"Goodbye Jack!" she said. "Careful with those stitches!"

"No worries," Jack said, patting his own shoulder lightly to show he was being careful.

During the dawn firefight, Jack's shoulder had been clipped by shrapnel, the wound bleeding profusely. It had been touch-and-go, Jack had gone cold with shock, but after staunching his wound with a field dressing, the black-clad mercs wrapped him in a blanket, then carried both boys three kilometers to a road large enough to accommodate an ambulance. From there, they were driven several hours to a Bogota hospital to be treated for wounds, parasites, and malnutrition. In addition to Jack's flesh wound, the doctors also treated him for dysentery. The American ambassador arrived within an hour of their admittance, presenting them with a large wreath of flowers (though not as large as the one that would arrive from Intercor Oil). He shook the boys' hands, telling them how brave they were, all while being photographed with them.

Both boys spent eight days recovering from their ordeal. Walter, who'd shared a room with Jack until yesterday, was leaving today. Jack, whose nose had been re-broken and re-set by the doctors the day before, needed more time. During their hospital stay, the boys slept and ate, but also sat through a series of debriefings with various men wearing suits and uniforms. For the initial interviews, Sr. Campeón, Intercor's representative, was present—unnecessarily, it turned out—but he wouldn't hear of leaving.

"These boys were my responsibility," he said in Spanish, then in English, though the boys no longer needed translation. He mentioned more than once that the valiant bus driver had been given a promotion, and that the cowardly Barro had been fired on the spot. "You weren't there like I was," Campeón said stoically to the government officials. Walter appreciated the Señor's fatherly attention, but the attack took two minutes, nothing compared to the eighty-seven days the boys had spent as kidnap victims. Plus, everyone knew Campeón was exaggerating wherever possible to protect Intercor. After the first day, he was asked to leave.

"Well, just us blokes now," Jack said to Walter. Except for an unidentified member of the Colombian army (or maybe a policeman—the uniforms were similar) standing outside the door, they were alone and feeling awkward. Jack pointed to his sewn-up shoulder wound and said, "The ladies are gonna love it." Jack was very proud that despite good suturing, the shrapnel, likely an RPG frag from the exploding coleta, would leave an impressive scar. Walter nodded, agreeing. "Not gonna miss those debriefings, will we, mate?" Walter again nodded, thinking, *But they were helpful*. During them, they'd learned of the tremendous effort undertaken by Exxon and the Colombian government to rescue them, backed quietly but powerfully by the governments of the United States and Australia. He had a lot to be grateful for.

What wasn't explained to them clearly, or at all, was why they had been rescued by mercenaries, ones that were not on especially good terms with Bogota, instead of actual soldiers. The American and Australian ambassadors told them a coordinated effort had been needed on the part of many different parties due to political "sensitivities," and that since all had turned out well, they needn't worry about the details.

"You notice they asked us a lot of questions, but dodged most of ours?" Walter asked. Jack nodded, finding talking through his bandage difficult. "At least they called me 'Mr. Sparks' the entire time. No kangaroo references—won't miss being called 'Guro.' And speaking of mantles," he continued, "will you miss all yours? Rafa the Giraffe Boy? King Gringo? El Niño Americano? Tatiana's love slave?"

Walter laughed at the last one. "Don't forget 'Bruce' and 'mate,'" he said. He thought again of how eerily beautiful Tatiana was in that final moment. "Are you still jealous?"

"Of course I am, you Yankee idiot," Jack said, knowing what Walter meant. They both laughed genuinely, but not loudly; three months of imposed silence was hard to shake. "Maybe I'll drop Rosa from Madrid a line. Now *she* had taste."

"Good, 'cause you're not getting a goodbye kiss from me," Walter said.

"Don't make me laugh, ya wanker. Makes my nose hurt."

Despite Jack's entreaty, they continued chuckling, even though Jack's bandages made his laughs sound more like brays. When they settled into silence again, Walter said, "You know, Jack, I never minded being called 'Bruce.' Kinda sounds powerful. Not like anything those little brown bastards called me."

"Well, what we went through sorta changes you," said Jack, averting his eyes. "Say, Bruce, why not change your name? Not legally, ya know, just a nickname. Go by 'Bruce.' I agree, it's very manly. You could do a lot worse—like 'Walter.'"

"Haha," Walter said, punching Jack's non-injured arm lightly. "But, you know, not a bad idea. I might just do that." Walter didn't mention that he'd already picked a new nickname for himself, and it wasn't "Bruce." "Well, this is it, Kangaroo," said Walter. "Maybe I'll write."

"Maybe me too," said Jack.

They stared at each other, knowing they had formed an intense friendship under high stakes. But Walter had sensed things were already changing during the ride in the Bogota-bound ambulance. He wondered: *Can we still be friends after this? What kind of friendship's gonna survive something we want to forget?* He'd more than once cradled Jack in his arms, but now could only rest his hand uncomfortably on Jack's uninjured shoulder.

"Get going, Yank," said Jack.

"Goodbye, Jack." Walter turned to the door.

"Walter," Jack said, calling him back. "Truth-sees, I was just thinking . . . You know that anger we got? I've seen it in your eyes—I know you have it too. Well, my dad says we need to let it go or it'll burn us up. You know, from the inside."

Walter realized this was the first time Jack had ever used his given name, which meant his statement had been important.

"It'll be fine, Kangaroo," Walter said, looking away. "Don't be so dramatic."

"It's over," Jack said. "Let it *be* over."

No, it'll never be over, Walter thought, but he said, "Okay, mate," then left the room.

After a few unanswered letters from Jack, they would not communicate for another twenty-three years.

On the flight home, Walter announced to his parents that he wanted to be called "Rey" from now on. The Perkinses, who were prepared to do anything for their traumatized son, nodded in puzzled agreement.

"Sure, Walter," his mother said. "I mean 'Ray.' Anything you want.

His father asked, "Why 'Ray?'"

"I just like it. And it's 'Rey' with an *e,* not an *a*. It's Spanish." But he didn't just like it, he loved it. As the brown bastard FARC soldiers had taught him, *"rey"* meant *king*. During the forced marches, he hadn't just been reciting the mantra of *follow the boots,* he'd also been swearing an oath to himself. If he survived, *he* would be king.

Specifically, a king of vengeance.

Chapter 41: The Hunting Club

Saturday, 24 April 1999
Twinbrook, MD

ON THE SATURDAY morning before the April EMBC meeting, about the time Henry was sending Loo packing from his Gate of Heaven art gallery, Christian Luntz had Rocker and a prospect drop off three crates to Mullet's house in Twinbrook, Maryland. Each crate was labeled differently: Bellec Auto in Dundalk, P & L Cold Storage in Capitol Heights, and First Baptist Church in La Plata—all Maryland addresses. Each crate contained different items—distributor belts, bags of coffee, hymnals—and all contained illegal guns hidden in false bottoms.

Two of the three crates, the coffee for Capitol Heights and the belts for Dundalk, made it safely to their destinations; the third did not. Mullet and the prospect would transport the first two crates later that day, but not the hymnals. Sammy Smith had called requesting that he, Sammy, drop by Mullet's to pick up the last crate, transporting the songbooks himself. This was highly unusual, but Sammy was a longtime customer, and if it saved a trip for Darin "Mullet" Holmes, currently on probation, then he didn't mind. However, he did mind waiting. Mullet impatiently smoked on his porch, watching his street, looking for Sammy's Lincoln Continental. Finally, the Continental began creeping up his road. (Smith, with several annoyed drivers behind him, was closely examining house numbers.) *Jesus, Sammy,* thought Mullet, *you leadin' a parade?*

Sammy hated big cities—the graffiti, the crime, the undeserving minorities, half of whom couldn't speak a word of English. Though Twinbrook was technically a suburb, the xenophobic Sammy Smith believed it counted.

As Smith finally turned in, Mullet heeled his cigarette, signaling him to pull into the driveway so the Continental would be less visible from the street. "You're late," he told him. Sammy nodded apologetically, showing no inclination to get out. "Pop the back."

Sammy did, saying, "Sorry, Mr. Holmes, right away."

Mullet loaded the crate, closing the trunk. "Tell Jacobsen's boys no more last-minute changes."

"I'll sure tell 'em," said Smith, looking like leaving Twinbrook was the best idea he'd had in weeks. "Again—sorry."

"Remember, Sammy," replied Mullet, "from this point, you're responsible for the delivery." Sammy nodded gravely, saying, "Understood, Mr. Holmes. Have a great day."

Luntz was a successful businessman in part because he ran background checks on all his gun trade customers—property tax payments, credit scores, arrests, etc. The checks were originally Willie Pug's idea, back when he was still around to do them himself. Now, Christian paid a private investigator to run them twice a year on every customer, even long-timers like Miles Jacobsen's race war preppers. Luntz's guy was good; it paid to have a pro do it. But like Darius Kay, Luntz was also frugal, and since things seemed to be coming along with this whole worldwide internet thing (provided it didn't implode on New Year's Eve, 1999), he wanted someone tech-savvy, like Trevor Pug, to take over.

The club's gun trade was triangular. Leg one: Old Line fronted straw purchasers money to buy specific models from Maryland, Virginia, and West Virginia gun shops. Leg two: upon delivery of the weapons, the strawmen were paid off, usually at bars like Mullet's favorite, Hell. Nothing ever exchanged hands on club property. Leg three: After purchasers paid in advance, Old Line delivered their guns, generally twice a month in innocent-looking containers. Usually, they shipped one or two gun orders at a time. Today it was three, including Sammy's order. Unusual, but not unheard of.

The club had solid domestic markets (Baltimore being good, and DC, where guns were illegal, being better), but the real money was international. This year, 1999, wasn't a banner year for American gun manufacturing, but it wasn't shabby, either: four million made, nearly all of excellent quality. The Central and South American markets, fueled by drug production, coups, and cartels, were booming. Intermediaries received the Old Line gun deliveries, hiding them in transit containers, taking advantage of NAFTA to drive them across the southern border, or ship them overseas from Baltimore, Wilmington, Norfolk, or the Port of New York. The southbound weapons paid for the northbound drugs.

As he drove home that night from Shorties, Rey realized how much he'd enjoyed *Geek Love*, and how little the guys had talked about it. *I mean, it's a*

fucking book *club. Spend at least ten goddamn minutes discussing the book!* Between that glaring oversight, the jabs about the illegals, and the unkind comments from some about his real name, Rey wouldn't be returning. He'd initially joined at his therapist's urging as part of trauma recovery counseling—the jungle ordeal had long ago stopped impacting his days, but still affected his nights, especially recently.

It began last August when he'd overheard Trevor Pug talking up his Evil Men's Book Club to a coworker. They were standing in Sim 2K's sorry excuse for a lunchroom, a glorified closet with a coffee maker, fridge, microwave, and a curling *Your Work Rights Explained* poster.

"Yeah, we get together at a bar," Trevor had said then. "We read things guys want to read: war, sex, death. *Not* Oprah's Book of the Month. For instance, this month, we're reading *Lolita*."

Rey had to admit it had sounded appealing, since the rules, such as they were—meet at a bar, reading is optional—were very straightforward. He wasn't sure about *Lolita*; Rey read extensively but generally avoided novels, but perhaps this "Evil Men's Book Club" might change this.

So though Trevor was a blowhard who drank too much, Rey jumped in feet first. He read each month's selection immediately because he loved reading. During his months in the jungle, Mimada's tattered book collection had sustained him; he'd controlled little else but could read at will. Rey was polite the first few club meetings, getting the lay of the land, but it soon became obvious that Trevor and his friends were idiots, bozos with budget degrees, nothing to compete with his master's from Brown. *And I would have gotten a doctorate if the Exxon money hadn't stopped on my twenty-first birthday.* He still had a good pillow, enough to live on modestly, but five or ten more years at Sim Systems would secure real financial freedom.

Perkins held opinions about each club member. Phillipe seemed capable and logical—a natural leader. Rey respected Henry Takahashi if for no other reason than the man had put his money where his mouth was when it came to personal defense.

That's where the positive opinions stopped.

Urban D-Kay was just another Jersey asswipe who thought he was funnier than he was. Rey didn't care for Original Ken Ert, the sportswriter with the stupidest nickname, but Rey acknowledged that he wasn't much of a sports guy. Trevor was a drunk who peaked in high school, screwing up so badly that Rey now had his job responsibilities. Gary the New Guy? Based on his suspicion that the FNG may have stolen his battery, Gary wasn't on his Christmas list.

Which left Loo.

At first, he didn't care for the bookish Spicotti, who'd given Rey no support the night he challenged the bodega wetbacks, but boy had he been wrong about the mild-mannered man, who was obviously the Deerslayer. *Sorry. "Alleged" Deerslayer.*

Rey felt the club, like most people, misunderstood him. He hadn't insulted Loo because the man was killing Bambis, but because Spicotti had spent so long *denying* it. When Rey first heard about the arrest, he'd been pleasantly surprised. *Holy shit, Spicotti, you got a secret life! And balls big enough to put your "save the Earth convictions," not to mention your personal freedom, on the line!* Rey respected that.

Loo had also hidden his alter ego in plain sight, fooling everyone, but as cool as that was, it somehow hurt Rey's pride. *How did I not figure out his identity?* In this respect, Rey was being too hard on himself. Everyone, Rey included, had expected the killer to be Hollywood's version of a sociopath—unshaven, underweight, some urban version of the hillbilly inbreeds from James Dickey's *Deliverance* (February's EMBC reading selection). No one suspected Larry Lorax.

Still, Rey felt misled. At least in the jungle, all the players were clear—the Army, the militias, the captives, the POWs, and, of course, the FARC fucknuts—as well as their agendas. There was no pretention, let alone deceit in the rainforest; its relentless heat and nighttime clamminess wouldn't allow it. So discovering that nature boy was really a killer too afraid to own it disgusted Rey.

Never mind, he thought. *Tomorrow's Sunday—relief!*

In the morning, he would attend church for the first time since childhood, but that wasn't what made Sunday great—it was Sammy's Club.

Rey had met Miles Jacobsen, Sammy's Club's elderly leader, in an internet chat room the previous year. Perkins had posted regarding Bill Clinton's 1996 Illegal Immigration Act, complaining that despite a border wall to be built in San Diego, it was an otherwise token effort not addressing the real problem. A "Mister J" had chimed in, agreeing with Rey. Chat dialog ensued, continuing for weeks. Then a phone call with Miles Jacobsen occurred, and shortly after that, Rey was invited to join Sammy's Club.

The first thing a smiling Miles Jacobsen told Rey after meeting him personally was, "Young man, consider yourself at home." Others surrounding Jacobsen agreed. Age-wise, Jacobsen was a contemporary of the Winsor Brothers, but taller and in better health, with a silver tonsure and a sun-worn but cleanshaven face. He spoke with a Carolina accent and laughed warmly, brown irises behind his horn-rimmed glasses shimmering when he did. Looking ever the part of an ideal dinner guest and a well-intentioned tousler of children's hair, he oozed Southern hospitality.

He was utterly charming. And completely racist.

To his credit, the erudite Jacobsen didn't rant about his racial views. He was a gentleman, and as one, purveyed his opinions on race relations, as convoluted as they were, professorially, leaving the job of bull-horning to his less polished aide-de-camp, Sammy Smith, owner of Sammy's Hunting Club.

"Rey," continued Mr. Jacobsen, "I commend your stance on immigration."

"Yeah," agreed Sammy. "We *got* to keep 'em out of our country. White folks is getting way too thin." He spat tobacco juice expertly into the center of a Pennzoil can before continuing. "But I'm tellin' ya, friend, immigration, desegregation, it all leads back to the Heebs."

"Heebs?" asked Rey.

"The Jews!" said Sammy. "Who else would I mean?"

Rey learned quickly that in Sammy's considered opinion, behind every societal ill, no matter how small, lurked the Jews. The Jews, as Sammy was sure everyone knew, owned most of the world's levers of power and were buying the rest. This was common knowledge, and if you denied it, you were simple, and he had no problem telling you so in Southern Delmarva: *"Yur-in id-ee-it."*

"Yes," Mr. Jacobsen said, looking at Sammy irritably. "As I was saying, Rey—a young man of your caliber, one so well-versed on immigration issues, *that* man should be in front of people promoting patriotic ideals, yes?"

It was hard to say no to Miles Jacobsen, especially when Rey completely agreed with him. "Yes, Mr. Jacobsen," he said, smiling.

"And there you have it, gentlemen," Jacobsen said, laughing, putting a friendly arm around Reymond.

Out of the chatroom gate, Rey Perkins and Miles Jacobsen were in immigration lockstep, not minding it from Western Europe but minding it a hell of a lot from everywhere else, particularly from the south where hordes of Cuban, Haitian, Mexican, and El Salvadorian criminals were marching unimpeded across the shallow Rio Grande. Because of this, Rey's Spanish fluency thrilled Jacobsen, as did his grasp of Central and South American politics, a byproduct of the young man's job contacts and extensive political reading. (Rey readily absorbed his Madrid clients' prejudices as few of them hid their disdain for the politics and temperament of those hailing from their former South American colonies.) In this regard, Miles could not believe his luck. Rey, who hated the "little brown bastards" (Rey's words, not Miles's, though he quite agreed), would be the perfect banner carrier who, hallelujah, could stick it to the illegals in their own language!

With Sammy at their heels, Jacobsen began introducing Rey to other club members, mostly Charles County buddies of Sammy Smith, but a handful of urbanites as well, men whom Miles saw increasingly as the future of the movement. Jacobsen's emphasis on city boys hurt Sammy's pride, but even Sammy knew if he wanted his "megaphone" to reach farther than Charles County, city folks were needed. Sammy never questioned Mr. Jacobsen about his decisions, so if "suburban warriors," as Mr. Jacobsen called them, were needed, then they were needed, and if "Handsome Rey" (Jacobsen's words, not Sammy's) was specifically what the club needed, then Reymond Perkins, bless his snide little heart, was in.

But Perkins was too good to be true, and Sammy knew it. Rey's stool only had one leg: anti-immigration. He was missing the other two: a robust belief in racial purity and a commitment to major anti-Semitism (a good dose of homophobia also helped). Perkins was unacceptably ambivalent about the Jewish question and seemed okay with having black friends. Part of Rey's problem, Smith knew, was the club's careful, almost surgical avoidance of publicly denigrating any one group or creed—Blacks, Jews, gays, etc. Everyone, even the Quiet Right, as the club called mainline conservatives, denounced men like Jacobsen if they openly espoused racism. Unfortunately, everyone, including the Quiet Right, was hamstrung by the leftwing political correctness strangling the nation. In the future, Miles planned to be more open, but for now, movements like his, especially ones stockpiling arms and ammunition, had to be careful.

There was good news. Where many like the fifth-generation tobacco grower Sammy Smith saw America sinking into multiculturalism, Jacobsen saw opportunity. He knew Sammy was right in many respects, including the lack of Whites (and less of the right type of White person) to shoulder the responsibility of maintaining racial purity.

But Rey's not right for us, Mr. Jacobsen, thought Sammy. It was fifty-seven-year-old Smith's considered opinion that Mr. Jacobsen, as wise as he was, was wrong about Rey.

As he left Twinbrook, Sammy thought, *Might have to do somethin' 'bout that.*

Arriving home after his now ex-book club, Rey parked, leaving the crate Sammy had asked him to take to La Plata in his trunk. He was tired, seeing no purpose in lugging a box of hymnals up the steps to his condo, only to put it back in the car in the morning. Tomorrow, Sunday, he'd spend the morning driving an hour south to La Plata to drop off the songbooks and attend church, then the afternoon at Sammy's Hunting Club, a breath of fresh air compared to the left-skewing EMBC. Sammy's Club did have one thing in common with the EMBC, however—apart from the visionary Mr. Jacobsen, the other hunting club members, particularly Sammy, weren't intellectual giants, either.

Sammy's Club was a private hunting lodge located at the end of a long gravel road, one lying east of La Plata and south of Waldorf, not far from the Old Line Motorcycle Club compound. Sammy's Sunday barbeques attracted few Republicans—whom Smith and Jacobsen considered tame—no moderates, and absolutely no liberals. "Patriots only," said Sammy. The men Miles and Sammy courted were those who, though seriously dissatisfied with the system, were placed (or willing to be placed) within it to create systemic change when the time came. These patriots believed their future revolution to be about as American as you could get, but also believed there was no reason to train arduously, so other than target practice, the typical Sunday included beer drinking, bass fishing, steak grilling, crab steaming, and four-wheeling.

The lodge itself was a simple but well-kept, one-level hardwood structure with a wraparound porch. It slept ten but went unused six out of seven days. On Sunday afternoons, however, it was busy, much like Old Line's converted tobacco barn on Saturday nights. A detached shed housed the club generator, several ATVs, and a riding mower to keep the weeds from obscuring the practice targets. By design, the lodge was a getaway—no phone, no cell service. On Sundays, Sammy, who after years behind a survey level had skin as dark as a Black man's, was always in his element, handing out beers, slapping backs, grilling, relishing his role as master of ceremonies, second in importance only to Mr. Jacobsen himself.

At first blush, Sammy Smith, with his small-eyed xenophobia, could be written off as just another racist redneck. While he, in fact, *was* one, there were several things he wasn't. He wasn't stupid. He wasn't illiterate (among other genres, he read mysteries, college-level agronomy textbooks, and hate literature). Though he was known to tip a few, he wasn't a drunk. Sammy drove an aging but well-maintained Lincoln Continental, not a pickup. He attended church regularly, singing with an agreeable voice. The Lord had also blessed him with people skills and a keen understanding of business. Unless agitated, he was a pleasant, almost painfully courteous man, never having insulted a woman, even one of color.

His family lived in a sturdy brick farmhouse, a shiny GM Scenicruiser with stickers from forty-nine states parked behind it. There was an

American flag proudly hanging next to his door and two relatively non-offensive sun-bleached lawn jockeys in front of it. Behind his home, at the end of a gravel road snaking through forest owned by the Smiths, lay the hunting club itself. Unlike his road-facing house, however, the lodge flew a Confederate Flag, and its lawn jockey's black paint was kept fresh.

Sunday, 25 April 1999

The earliest you could arrive at Sammy's was 11 a.m.—Mr. Jacobsen encouraged all members to attend morning services before going to the club. Rey wasn't the church-going type, but Mr. Jacobsen was working on that, enticing him to join First Baptist, talking up the single women Rey's age who attended.

Rey drove to La Plata that Sunday morning thinking, *I'm not sure getting up for 9 a.m. services at a church an hour away to meet women who won't have premarital sex is a winning strategy . . . But I did promise Sammy I'd drop off these hymnals.*

Despite waking after having the damn Gun Girl dream again, Rey appreciated that April morning's sunshine. He was driving on I-95, about to take Route 5 south toward La Plata and the First Baptist Church, when he was passed by a Prince George's County police cruiser. It popped its lights, blocking him from taking the exit. In his mirror, two more flashing cruisers fell in behind him. The quartet, including Rey's Acura, moved toward the breakdown lane. Rey assumed he'd blown through a speed trap, but why on Earth did they need three cars to pull him over? His stomach clenched, partly from the I'm-being-pulled-over jitters all honest citizens get, and partly from the points he carried—traffic school was a real possibility.

It's my own damn fault—I drive too fast. After the forced marches through the jungles of Colombia, the open highway enthralled Rey. He always drove fast, an imaginary one-fingered salute toward South America as he did.

Nah, I was only doing seventy-five. And I got money for traffic school. Regardless, I'll take American law enforcement over those FARC bastards any day of the week.

He slowed to a stop on the debris-strewn shoulder. An officer approached his window quickly, which didn't feel right; usually they dawdled, calling in tag numbers or whatever they did before getting out. He wasn't scared, though—unlike those brown bandits who kidnapped him on the way back from Cerrejón, American police weren't going to abduct him. Rey had his license and registration ready, but the officer ignored them, instead ordering him to step out of the car.

Rey complied, noticing the officer's hand resting on the strap of his holster. A second officer appeared next to the first, saying, "Hands on the hood of your car, sir."

This doesn't bode well.

A third officer materialized—they were materializing quickly—asking, "Sir, may I inspect your trunk?"

It sounded more like a command than a request. "Sure," said Rey, unperturbed. He kept nothing suspicious in his trunk, or anywhere in his car for that matter, except—

The officer reached through the open driver's window and popped the trunk. A fourth officer then opened it. With some effort, Officer Four picked up the heavy wooden box of hymnals Sammy had given Rey to deliver to Mr. Jacobsen's pastor, placing it gently on the pavement. She opened the crate top, revealing brand-new hymnals with gold-leafed covers that glittered in the sun. The books came as no surprise to Rey, who'd previously checked them out. Officer Four then began removing the top layer of hymnals, placing them on a tarp laid by a new officer, Officer Five. Five then assisted Four as she unloaded all the hymnals, carefully placing them in piles on the tarp. Per the crate's label, it contained fifty songbooks, now in five orderly stacks. Officer Four flipped through a hymnal perfunctorily, fluttering its gold-edged pages, then returned it to its stack.

Then things went seriously south for Rey Perkins. Officer Five used a pry bar to remove a false bottom from the crate. There for all to see in the glorious sunshine: a collection of pistols and revolvers.

"You're Mr. Walter Perkins, correct?" asked Officer One, who had never left Rey's side.

"Yes," said Rey.

"Can you explain these?"

Walter "Rey" Perkins could not.

In hindsight, it was obvious that Sammy had set him up, but with the panic of the traffic stop and subsequent search, Rey hadn't immediately perceived *why* Sammy had done it. He knew Smith didn't like him, but most people didn't like him. As he sat handcuffed in the back of one of the cruisers, it finally clicked: Sammy feared Rey would replace him as Miles Jacobsen's Number Two. That was why.

Rey was very close to right. Sammy knew that once Mr. Jacobsen settled on a successor, his days as Jacobsen's right-hand man were over. Jacobsen had been looking for a new number two for the last two years, coming close once with a salt-of-the-earth cousin Sammy personally recommended. Jacobsen had been bullish on Sammy's man initially, as "Cousin Richie" was quite the believer, but ultimately, Richie wasn't polished enough—true belief was a requirement, but not the only one. Miles's protégé would also need to be a talented communicator. When he ditched the snark, the multilingual Rey Perkins was well-spoken, plus it didn't hurt that he was tall and handsome.

But Sammy knew better than anyone that Rey only checked one of the three believer boxes: anti-immigration. (Obviously, the young man hated wetbacks. He'd heard Rey had been kidnapped and held for ransom in some banana republic in the seventies—bully for him.) But that still left two boxes to check: a Black one and a Jewish one. Rey's opinion of Jews wasn't particularly positive, Sammy knew, but it wasn't particularly negative, either. Initially, Sammy thought he'd be able to straighten Rey out on the Jewish question because his collection of hate literature made him an authority on the subject. Sammy had studied up, knowing Jacobsen wanted him to remove the secular scales from Perkins's eyes. He was proud of this assignment, a chance to shine in front of Mr. Jacobsen.

But Sammy's froth-at-the-mouth fervor regarding the evils of the Jewish Conspiracy did little for Rey. And no matter how often Sammy explained that in seven generations since the Civil War, the former slaves hadn't done *jack* to elevate themselves, his anti-Black rhetoric fell even flatter. Rey had Black *friends* for Christ's sake!

Sammy became frustrated. Not only was his bullhorn approach not working, but the punk was also making fun of him—everything from Sammy's accent to his hobnail boots. He laughed off the jabs but mentally filed each one away because Rey (and what was this business about spelling Raymond with an E?) was an arrogant ass. The boy was no churchgoer—Sammy suspected he was an atheist—and for a college boy, none too practical. The bottom line was that Sammy could see what Mr. Jacobsen couldn't; Rey would never believe, not completely.

Sammy practically worshiped Miles Jacobsen, but sometimes heroes needed to be protected from themselves.

Chapter 42: Getting Marco's Help

Sunday, 24 April 1999
Wheaton, MD

ON THE AFTERNOON of Rey's arrest, Estelle Largo went to Phillipe's apartment to retrieve a change of clothes for her boyfriend. They were meeting for dinner later that night, a date they'd shoehorned into his busy training schedule. She would pick him up from the Montgomery County Airpark after he completed that afternoon's jet flight instruction time.

She arrived, letting herself in with a key he'd given her on their first dating anniversary. After using Phillipe's reasonably clean bathroom—the man did try—she went to his closet, retrieving a collared shirt, dark pants, and a sports coat. She chose a pair of Allen Edmond shoes she'd given him as a gift and also selected dress socks, a tie, a t-shirt, and underwear (just in case), taking a moment to confirm that the tie matched the coat. *Yes,* she thought, modeling it in Phillipe's dresser mirror.

On the bureau was a mason jar with change, Phillipe's Redskins stress ball squeezie, his spare pair of Aviators, a stack of business cards, and a pile of receipts. One business card, a bright yellow one, caught her eye. It had an outline of a man wearing a cocktail dress on one side, and *Men's Lounge: Thursdays* printed on the other, plus a local phone number. No business hours, no address.

Perhaps it was some souvenir from travel? After all, every year Phillipe went to New Orleans for Mardi Gras. Or maybe it was his maman's? She'd ask him about it at dinner. Estelle didn't take the card—it wasn't hers, plus she had an excellent memory for numbers. After putting Phillipe's clothes neatly on a hanger and placing the other items in a travel bag, she checked her makeup, turned out the lights, and left for the Airpark.

Estelle pulled out into traffic, nearly colliding with a man in a Mazda. She tsk-tsked his bleating horn and one-finger salute, thinking, *Some people just wake up angry*. Traffic made the trip tedious, so for fun she called the number on the card. The phone rang four times before a gruff voice answered.

"Men's Lounge."

"Sir," Estelle asked using her best door-opening voice, "can you please tell me what type of . . . *lounge* your lounge is?"

"Lady, it's a lounge for *men*," the gruff voice replied. "Hence the name 'Men's Lounge.'"

"Yes, but what *type* of men?" she asked quickly, fearing he'd hang up. "My name's Estelle, by the way. Estelle *Largo*. May I have yours?"

"No you may not," the voice said.

She was put off. Normally men didn't stonewall her. She took her anxiety out on the traffic behind her, swerving suddenly to make a left turn, cutting someone off. She heard the gruff man jostling his receiver. "Don't hang up," said Estelle. "Perhaps you know my boyfriend, Phillipe Gallois? He's a pilot."

A slight pause before Mr. Gruff said, "I don't know him. How'd you get this number?"

"I found it on a business card."

"Then, ma'am, I can assure you the card wasn't meant for you." This time Mr. Gruff did hang up.

"It's 'Miss,' not 'ma'am,'" she fumed. Estelle accelerated through a yellow light, earning more honks. *That pause*, she thought, *the one before 'I don't know him.'* It had been brief, but she'd caught it. It told her he *knew* her boyfriend and was lying about it. And that condescending *Ma'am, I can assure you the card wasn't meant for you*—there was a definite message there. As she cut in front of someone less deserving of the left lane, she asked herself what it all meant. *Well, if it truly is some sort of "men's" lounge, then perhaps Mr. Gruff's attitude makes sense,* she thought. *Still, no one worth less than five million stonewalls a Largo. I need to enlist help.*

Estelle abruptly pulled over to the shoulder to call Information, but the number was unlisted. She then called a dear friend she could always count on. Marco was gay, which was what she needed at the moment, but more importantly, Marco was discreet. After painting the situation in broad strokes (leaving out Phillipe's possible involvement), she asked him to call Mr. Gruff. It was a maddening four minutes before he called back.

"Marco!" declared Estelle.

"Hello again, doll," he said.

"Spill it, dear."

"The first thing he asked me was who I was and how I'd gotten his number. I lied on the fly, telling him someone gave me that card you described. Pretty clever, huh? But *then* Mr. Gruff asks me my name . . . *and I gave it to him!* My real name, Estelle. What was I thinking?"

"You didn't, Marco!" she exclaimed.

"Oh yes, doll, I did! Then he tells me I'm not on the list. 'What list?' I ask. '*The* list,' he says." Marco tittered. "A list, Estelle, a list! Sounds so mysterious, so *exciting*, doesn't it? You know, my friend Enrique is *always* having these invitation-only dinner parties—maybe it's something like that. By the way, this Mr. Gruff guy doesn't sound gay. But here's the scary part. *Then* he asks me if I'm a friend of yours, doll! Can you believe that? I panicked and hung up. *Terribly* sorry, dear."

"Not to worry, Marco," she said. "Thanks for indulging me." They chatted a bit more, then Estelle hung up, swearing him to secrecy. She pondered what Marco had shared, thinking, *I have time,* then jumped back into traffic, executing an abrupt U-turn.

Once back at Phillipe's, she began searching, though she wasn't sure what she was looking for. It didn't help that she was short on time—dinner was in an hour. She returned to his dresser, sorting more carefully through the pile of cards and receipts where she'd originally discovered the yellow card, starting with a sporting goods receipt for three hundred and eighty-seven dollars. Despite the irrational fear driving her to ransack her beau's apartment, the figure didn't shock her. Everyone knew real men required real (and expensive) toys, in this case, a crossbow. She examined the Men's Lounge card again. It *had* to be a gag. What was she afraid of? Phillipe was a testosterone-fueled love machine. The big, strong, sexy man was the best lay she'd ever had—Adam and Eve good. There was simply no way she'd misread his machismo.

A voice inside: *Just ask him at dinner, which, if you don't get going, honey, you'll be late for, and Phillipe will have to sit in a three-star restaurant in his flight suit, and although he looks fabulous in it, it's not eveningwear.*

Flight suit. The thought directed her gaze toward Phillipe's closet, and the garment bag labeled *Flight Suits*. On a whim—intuition, she later deemed—she opened it. Unsurprisingly, the bag contained what it advertised. At least its front half did; it had two compartments. There was no way to easily reach around to the bag's other side, because the container was large, eighteen by eighteen inches, and hung heavily against the wall.

Estelle oozed femininity, but she was also physically fit. Grunting—flight suits, the thick cotton/polyester ones Phillipe preferred, were heavy—she turned the bag around. *Should I open this?* she asked herself. *Sure, what's to find, anyway?* She unzipped the bag six inches, putting her hand inside. Whatever this half of the bag contained, it was sheer, not the stiff material she'd been expecting. Nervously, she pulled down the zipper completely, revealing a dozen beautiful, handmade dresses, each sized for a giant.

Oh, Phillipe! No!

Rarely was Estelle's world rocked. This was one of those times.

A thorough inspection of the closet yielded a sizable number of women's shoes and a box of costume jewelry behind a false baseboard. *At least no makeup*, she thought. *Or gay porno*. She also found a thick sketchbook of dress ideas, some of the earlier drawings being mockups for the ones currently in the garment bag. The faceless mannequin in each sketch bore a striking resemblance to her square-jawed boyfriend. She thumbed through the pad, each new sheet making her sicker. At the last rendering, she thought *Oh God,* then bolted to the bathroom to vomit.

Getting ill was unpleasant but did her good. After cleaning herself up, she returned everything to where she'd found it, forcing herself to focus on her *non-shocking* discoveries. A mini shop-vac. A handgun lock box. Several books, including a pair of tomes entitled *Hitler's U-Boat War, Volumes 1 and 2*. On the flyleaf of the first volume, Phillipe had sketched an exploded view of a U-boat and had labeled its compartments. Even amid her meltdown, she marveled at the depth of his reading. When Phillipe read something, he *read* it.

But did that matter anymore? Her perfect, manly-man beau was secretly a cross-dressing freak, one partial to bad jewelry and giant high-heels. Phillipe, the sexy pilot. Phillipe, the natural leader. Phillipe, who balled like a prize bull—all for show, all window dressing to cover his true nature. Phillipe was a man so ashamed of his identity, she believed, that he'd built a complex masculine shell to protect it, one so thorough, so well-made, that even the worldly Estelle Largo had been fooled.

Fooled for two years, she thought scornfully.

Maybe it's not that bad. Maybe he's just exploring his options—cross-dress curious, so to speak. But no, that was somehow worse, because Estelle Largo, a pulse-quickening maven, a star of men's dreams, *not* able to keep the sexual attention of one man? *Perish the thought.*

Seriously, perish it.

Dinner was a short affair. Parking by the Airpark's small tower, she apologized for being late and gave Phillipe a perfunctory kiss along with his clothes. He changed quickly, emerging from the tower's cramped bathroom to say, "How do I look?" Though he looked good, *great,* in fact, she, again on the verge of nausea, could only nod.

The chaste kiss, the minimal nod—Phillipe knew something was wrong. "Are you feeling all right?" he asked. "Fine," she said, nodding again.

They drove to Leomonde's, an upscale eatery in the "old town" portion of Gaithersburg, fifteen minutes away. Though quite late, they were seated quickly; Largo money—nothing on the scale of the Winsor Brothers' fortune, but substantial nonetheless—bought that sort of thing.

"Shall I order us some vino?" Phillipe asked, opening the wine list. In his two years dating Estelle, he'd studied his wines and, though no sommelier, was getting good at it.

No longer able to contain herself, Estelle blurted, "Phillipe, I found your dresses."

Phillipe gaped, dropping the wine list. One moment, he was anticipating an evening of fine dining and amorousness, the next, he was some Heston-esque character watching Earth's last rocket blast off without him. A pit in his stomach opened, trying to swallow him.

Then the anger came. "Did Trevor tell you?" he asked.

"Does it matter?" Estelle responded. She began crying.

"I guess not," answered Phillipe. But it *did* matter. It mattered hugely. Without another word, he rose from his seat, put money on the table, then left to call a cab.

Chapter 43: Agent Feldman

Sunday, 25 April 1999
Prince George's County, Maryland

TWENTY-TWO YEARS AGO, at the end of his Colombian ordeal, Walter Perkins had declared himself a king. He was currently riding in the back of a Prince George's County Sheriff's police cruiser, however, which didn't feel regal. Neither did wearing handcuffs.

At the stationhouse, he was booked and brought into a conference room for questioning. The space had a table and chairs, plus a window overlooking the precinct floor and a mirror on the opposite wall. He sat facing a very large Black member of the P.G. County Sheriff's Department, a man named Tate, in a well-starched uniform. Sheriff Tate was in his mid-fifties. An outsized hat sat on the table in front of him. Another Black man, a detective by the name of Roberts, sat next to him.

It was 3 p.m. The pair had been interviewing Rey for an hour, laying out just how bad his situation was. Tate was speaking. "You don't like Black people, Mr. Perkins, do you?"

"I like them just fine," Rey answered carefully.

"Really, Mr. Perkins?" the sheriff asked. "Seems odd, you bein' a member of Sammy's Club and all."

"Sammy's Club?" asked Rey. The club hadn't yet come up.

"Yeah, Sammy Smith's Hunting Club in La Plata, where you was headed—after the church service, that is. You know, those tasty Sunday barbecues, with Jacobsen's . . . acolytes."

It didn't bother Rey that they knew about Sammy and Mr. Jacobsen. It was a free country, after all, and like-minded individuals were allowed to assemble; it said so right in the Constitution. Sammy's Club—the porch politics, the smell of steaks and steaming crabs, the *pfft* of bullets striking paper targets—none of that was illegal. What bothered Rey was how purposefully Sheriff Tate had said "acolytes," as if baiting him. *Who gives a shit about vocabulary, Rey? Keep focused. What should bother you is how that bastard Sammy completely screwed you.*

He couldn't believe his naivete. Smith had called him Saturday afternoon, letting him know he'd picked up some new hymnals from a print shop in Silver Spring for the First Baptist Church, where Smith, Jacobsen, and the other local club members worshiped. Sammy meant to return to La Plata that night to drop them off before Sunday services, but there'd been a problem.

Reymond, so glad you're home, son, because that's where you come in, see, as I'm in Silver Spring right now with a crate of hymnals and, so sorry to ask, but wouldn't you know it my wife called to say Cousin Rufus, my cousin from coal country, by which I mean West Virginia, has gone ill all sudden, so's I'm on my way west to see him right now, as it might be Rufus's last night on Earth and could I ask that you, Rey, take the hymnals yourself to First Baptist, 'cause Mr. Jacobsen told me that you—the fine young man that you are, and I couldn't agree more—is goin' to the 9 a.m. yourself and though it's not like they need *the hymnals—sharin' is right Christian, after all—but I was sure hopin' I could prevail upon you, son, to take the hymnals and deliver 'em anyway, and it's* awful *that I have to ask you spur-of-the-moment-like, but is there someplace in town we could meet?*

Someone was dying—who was Rey to say no? And after all, he rode Sammy pretty hard, and since cutting back on being a dick was a personal goal, ferrying the hymnals seemed logical. They agreed to meet in front of Shorties at 6 p.m. and did so. Rey opened the crate in front of Sammy, picking through a few hymnals, demonstrating that he was no fool. This piqued Sammy, but whether he was annoyed with Rey's wariness or just anxious to get going, Rey couldn't tell. Now, of course, he knew.

Why don't I have a lawyer yet? Rey asked himself.

Three reasons. First, the post-kidnapping legal representation his father could afford in 1977 had been no match for Exxon's sharks. The entire experience killed any respect Rey, then a teen, had for the profession. Second, the money. Getting out from under a federal gun-running charge would be very expensive, and even if he were uber-wealthy, which he wasn't, success wasn't guaranteed. Conversely, he wasn't about to turn his fate over to some overwhelmed public defender ready to stampede him over Plead Deal Cliff. But the third reason mattered most: the detective had hinted at some sort of deal if Rey didn't lawyer up.

"Did you hear the sheriff's question, Mr. Perkins?" asked Detective Roberts. "You a member of Sammy's Club?"

"There's no club," said Rey, "and if there was, I'm not a member."

"Our sources say otherwise."

Walter "Rey" Perkins sat with his six-foot-plus frame as upright as possible to avoid looking nervous. The guns the hunting club used for target practice were legal—each man brought his own—and until this morning, Rey had no reason to suspect the club was stockpiling weapons, legal or otherwise, as it didn't feel right—where would they keep them? (There was no below-grade bunker on the property, no door anywhere protected by a padlock.) Still, the boys did like talking a good race war. Should he have foreseen this?

Our sources say otherwise sounded ominous. Did they have a mole in the club? Rey now regretted ever having met Jacobsen's goober army, and especially the double-crossing inbred Sammy Smith. *Relax,* he told himself. *You speak English, Spanish, and you're learning Portuguese. You're the best coder at Sim 2K. You're smart, cleverer than these guys.*

"Are you *sure* you like Black people, Mr. Perkins?" Detective Roberts asked, "You being Miles Jacobsen's rising star?"

"Dude," said Rey defensively, "I've got Black friends."

He had two, so this was technically true. There was his pal, Rick, a fellow coder and occasional after-work beer buddy even haughtier than Rey was. However, though it'd been more than a decade since they'd last met, the closer friend was his elementary school chum, Derek Crown. Derek and Rey, then known as Walter, were responsible for raising the American flag in front of North Springs Elementary each morning and lowering it every afternoon, something they both took pride in.

"We're Uncle Sam's boys," Derek had often said. *Yes, Derek, we were.* Perkins admired Crown, who was principled, funny, and never had a bad word for anyone. They were friends through all their school years, and after Colombia, Derek was the only one who didn't mishandle Walter's return to junior high, giving him the space he needed, because re-immersion had been sketchy—given Rey's missed lessons, PTSD-fueled panic attacks, and scrapes with other hotheads, his parents decided to pull "Wally" from public high, and—thanks to the big oil apology money—enroll "Rey" at a mid-tier private institution. With an anonymous start, Rey did better, no more fighting. Derek continued to flourish at Woodard Heights, and they managed to stay connected through college.

"My name's Detective Roberts, Mr. Perkins, not 'dude.'"

Rey's snark had been intentional, meant to probe his limits. "Sorry, Detective, but really, it's true. I've got Black friends."

"Great," said Roberts brightly. "And what would your Black friends think about Sammy Smith?"

"Not much," admitted Rey.

"Or of you hanging out with his . . . acolytes?"

"Again, not much. So what's this got to do with my arrest?"

"Not much *good*, right?" asked Roberts, ignoring his question. "Your Black friends wouldn't think much good about your hunting buddies."

"Yeah," said Rey uncomfortably. "Not much good."

Sheriff Tate joined in: "Then why are you a club member?"

"Because they're right about immigration," said Rey. "But I'm not a member of anything. I show up every so often to eat barbecue and shoot guns. That's it."

"So, you like guns?" asked Detective Roberts.

"Yes, I do," said Rey, defensively. "And it's my constitutional right to bear them."

"Within limits imposed by law, it *is* your right," conceded Sheriff Tate. "So, you're an immigration hawk, Mr. Perkins?" he continued.

"Yes, Sheriff. America's full."

"No more wide-open spaces, huh?" Tate asked.

"No, none," said Rey. "So what about this deal?"

"We're almost there," said Roberts.

"I'm getting impatient," said Rey, stifling a yawn. "I might want that lawyer after all."

"Your choice," said Detective Roberts, "but then no deal. Instead, we will formally charge you, and if you can't make bail, you get a comfy jail cot. That what you want, Mr. Perkins?"

Rey said nothing.

"Looks like that's what he wants," said Tate sunnily, getting up. When seated, Sheriff Tate was large. When standing, the sheriff was, well, the word *ginormous* came to Rey's mind. "Okay, okay," he said. "Point taken."

Sheriff Tate sat again, then glanced at the room's mirror.

"It's just that it's taking a long time," Rey said, looking at the mirror as well. "Hey, are we waiting on someone?"

"You're insightful, Mr. Perkins," said Detective Roberts. "We've been waiting on some folks, in fact, but in full disclosure, they've been listening in already." Roberts pointed toward the mirror, implying it was one-way. "I understand you know one of them."

In came two visitors. The first was a diminutive woman in her fifties with prematurely gray hair, but Rey paid her scant attention because behind her stood Gary the New Guy Graft! *Evil Men's Book Club* Gary! The entrants nodded to the sheriff and detective, then the woman presented Rey with her ID, shaking his hand authoritatively.

"I'm Special Agent Rose Feldman from the Bureau of Alcohol, Tobacco, and Firearms," she said. "And this is Dr. Gary Graft, who I believe you know." Gary shook Rey's hand as well but stayed silent.

"Good to see the cavalry," said the sheriff. "You don't need us locals anymore." Tate and Roberts got up to leave.

"Thanks, gentlemen," said Agent Feldman. Rey watched as Sheriff Tate ducked through the conference room door so as not to lose his hat.

Agent Feldman and Graft sat down. "Mr. Perkins," began Feldman, "it's the Bureau's understanding that you haven't been charged for felony gun trafficking yet. Is that correct?" Feldman delivered this question evenly, perhaps a little louder and slower than was necessary.

I'm not a simpleton, thought Rey, *or deaf.* He said a curt "Yes" to Feldman, then, "Gary, buddy, what's going on?"

"During this interview, you'll refer to Dr. Graft as 'Dr. Graft,'" said Agent Feldman.

"Sure," said Rey, looking at Gary for some explanation or sign—anything—but getting none; Gary might as well have been a lamp. "So it's 'Agent Graft?'" Rey asked.

Feldman answered, "No—*Dr.* Graft."

This was all so odd. Why wasn't Gary, a known chatterbox, saying anything? "Gary, I mean, Dr. Graft," Rey asked, "what do you do?"

Without hesitation, Feldman said, "He works for the government." For clarity, she added, "Our government."

"Any particular part of 'our government,' Dr. Graft?" Rey inquired.

Gary remained silent.

"Dr. Graft is more of a listener," Feldman explained.

"Oh," said Rey, intrigued. "It's just that at our book club, we . . . uh . . . can't seem to shut him up."

Now it was Agent Feldman's turn to look intrigued—*Graft was in a book club? Graft actually talked?*—but she said nothing. Instead, she opened a half-inch-thick Duo-Tang labeled WALTER PERKINS. Underneath it were two thicker folders. The second was titled ATF 1999 #63: LA PLATA PATRIOTS (AKA SAMMY'S CLUB). The title of the third folder wasn't visible. It concerned Rey that the ATF not only considered Sammy's Club some sort of terrorist organization but that there might be sixty-two others.

"So, Mr. Perkins," Agent Feldman continued, "you've been informed that the gun trafficking felony carries a mandatory minimum sentence of one-hundred-twenty months—ten years—yes?"

"Yes," said Rey.

"Unless, of course, twelve of your peers deem you innocent," she said dryly.

"Look, Agent Feldman, like I told those guys earlier—first, I'm not a racist, and second, I had no idea there were guns at the bottom of the—"

"We heard," Feldman said, holding her hand up. "But the guns were found in your possession, Mr. Perkins, so it's like musical chairs—you're the one left standing." She looked at Gary, who nodded tacitly. "And Mr. Perkins, your racism isn't my problem. Fourteen straw-purchased guns, *that's* my problem."

Rey paled.

Second to getting convictions, watching guys like Perkins sweat was the most enjoyable part of Feldman's job. Today, however, time wasn't on her side. "Let's cut to the chase, Mr. Perkins. Would you like the trafficking charge to go away?"

"I *would* like that," said Rey, earnestly. "Do you need me to give you Sammy? Or someone higher up?" It appalled him how quickly he was willing to roll on the club. Rat on Sammy? Sure, Sammy had it coming, but Miles Jacobsen, someone he respected? He'd feel bad about that.

But what did he have on the club, anyway? Despite all the bitchy beer talk about white genocide while they cleaned weapons, he'd observed them doing nothing innately illegal. He had no dirt on anyone, least of all Jacobsen. He could volunteer to wear a wire like he'd seen on TV, but that sounded dangerous. Still, he'd do it—no *way* was he going to prison. That would be Colombia all over again.

"As much as we appreciate your willingness to share about the La Plata Patriots," said Agent Feldman, "this isn't about a domestic threat."

"It's not?" asked Rey, puzzled. He looked at Gary, who remained expressionless.

"No, this is about *international* terrorism," Feldman continued. "Specifically, the FARC."

Rey turned cold. "The FARC? I don't understand. It's been years since I was kidnapped."

"Yes," said Feldman, "but something's happened regarding the FARC terrorists that held you from, let's see"—she opened the third file with the mysterious title ENZO8—"from March 2 to May 28, 1977. Three months."

"Eighty-seven days," said Rey, correcting her.

"Right, eighty-seven days," said Feldman. "During that time, do you remember one of your FARC captors, Sebastian Ruiz? He would have been in his mid-twenties."

At the mention of El Camarada, the man who'd terrorized Walter Perkins and Jack Sparks and had come within inches of killing them, Rey's stomach flipped. Like a pack of cards at the ready, his brain immediately started flipping through all his jungle captors. The final card? Tatiana. The memory of the breathy kiss she'd given him before disappearing into the brush returned. Never before nor since had a girl looked so alluring to him. What had she said at the end? *"Adiós, Rafa,"* and then in English, *"Maybe I come to America."*

For years now, Tatiana had been the Gun Girl of his nightmares, counting down his fate. This "normal" dream was bad enough, but in the last half-year, as she began resembling the homeless Prophet character more and more, it had gotten much worse.

"Mr. Perkins, you look pale. Do you need a minute?" Rey said no. "I was asking if you remembered Sebastian Ruiz."

"El Camarada. Yes, I remember him. He was injured badly, a headwound, when I was rescued." Rey remembered Sebastian, El Camarada, lurching and bleeding, trying to shoot him before being assisted into the jungle by his mother and sisters. He remembered Gustavo the younger brother—"Sadism in a Can" as Jack had liked to call him—dying in an explosion. *Good riddance.* "I doubt Sebastian lived."

"He's alive all right," said Agent Feldman. "He, his mother, his sister, and at least a dozen others escaped the firefight that night."

"You're sure he's alive?"

"Yes."

"What about the others?" asked Rey.

"The Colombian government suspects that the mother, Annabel, is dead. The sister—"

"Tatiana?" prompted Rey.

"Yes," said Feldman, "we know she's alive, working with her brother."

Terrorist pendejos, thought Rey. "Working? What's that mean?"

"The short of it's this: these terrorists, each with a Bogota police file—Sebastian's being much thicker than Tatiana's—want to enter our country." He frowned, which she took as confusion. "*Illegally* enter," she clarified.

Rey wasn't confused—he was afraid. Afraid of the 1977 ordeal and the outsized part Sebastian had played in it. Afraid that El Camarada was on his way to America, *right now,* to complete the unfinished job: killing Walter Perkins. "They're coming here?" he asked. "To do what?"

"We're not sure," answered Feldman.

"So where do I come in?" asked Rey.

Agent Feldman looked at Gary, getting the nod. For whatever reason, she was deferring to him. "We've picked up chatter," continued Feldman. "The Ruiz's are working with *coyotes*—"

"Human smugglers?"

"Yes," said Feldman. "We think they'll be brought in by boat somewhere along the West Florida coast."

Maybe my dream's prophetic, Rey thought. Was Gun Girl turning into what Sebastian looked like now? Fear made him ask: "Are they coming after me?"

"In a sense," Agent Feldman said. "Tatiana Ruiz has been doing the legwork, communicating with their stateside coyote, arranging payment, etc. We haven't heard anything directly from Sebastian, but she's made it clear he's traveling with her."

"Oh, okay," said Rey. "So . . . what do you need me for?"

"Your name keeps being repeated in the chatter."

"Why?"

"That's what we're hoping you can help with," she said. "Why *would* she specifically seek you out? It's been two decades since you were the FARC's prisoner, right? Why would Tatiana Ruiz, an old foot soldier at this point, be trying to contact you? Big Brother Sebastian, makes sense he's coming to the States to make trouble, but her? Does it have something to do with the prizes at the bottom of your hymnal box?"

"What?" said Rey. "No way. I don't know anything about those guns, and I don't care about them. El Camarada was trying to kill me the last time I saw him. *That* I care about."

"What about Tatiana?" asked Feldman. "What was she doing the last time you saw her?"

She was looking beautiful, Agent, and she was kissing me. For a moment, Rey was lost in the memory again: the dying light of the burning jungle and the coming light of dawn, Tatiana standing in front of him, midriff bare. *Maybe I come to America* is what she'd told him, and now she was, her murderous brother in tow. *Why after all these years, Tatiana?*

Certainly not for love.

Rey was a tall, bright, good-looking thirty-five-year-old man with a good job. He'd dated sporadically, nothing recent, but he liked women as much as the next guy, so it certainly wasn't his Colombian teen crush, Tatiana, holding him back. Seeing her thin fire-lit body, her face shocked by the turn of events, yet still somehow confident, had certainly been a "moment." But how much could a twenty-year-old moment be worth? *Perhaps it was the kiss?* Since that night, he'd slept with a half dozen women, most more striking than Tatiana's poor, half-starved frame could have ever matured into. Sure, during three intense months of captivity, he'd become smitten by a girl on the cusp of womanhood, one desperate to free herself from her mother's cloying protection.

Years of hindsight, however, told Rey otherwise: Tatiana was just a teenage guerilla in heat, ready to shack up with the first available freedom fighter. And how old was she now, anyway? Thirty-four, thirty-five? In the jungle, that was a lifetime.

Still . . .

Still nothing, Rey! What a monstrous ego you have. Twenty-two years is a ridiculous amount of time for a girl to forgo all others. Do you really think your teen hottie could escape the FARC, the drug lords, the Colombian Army, the police, then hop multiple international borders and cross a very large ocean to find one Walter Reymond Perkins, address USA? Jesus, you're an idiot.

"You seem upset, Mr. Perkins," said Feldman. "Getting arrested can throw you off your game, we certainly recognize that, but time's of the essence. What else can you tell us about Tatiana?"

"I taught her a little English. And maybe she had a crush on me. I don't know." Rey collected himself, explaining what he remembered in more detail, answering the agent's remaining questions as forthrightly as he could.

Feldman also doubted the unrequited love angle, but Rey was at least one American Tatiana knew. "Imagine her face when she discovers how much you hate immigrants," Feldman said. "Not going to be the reunion she's hoping for, is it?"

"You tell me, Agent Feldman," said Rey. "I still don't know why I'm here."

"You made an impression on her. You even have your own code name—*Rafa*. What's 'Rafa' mean?"

"'Giraffe,'" said Gary, "but that's not important right now." This was the first time he had spoken since entering the room. Rey looked at him: *Thanks, Gary, I think.* "Please describe our offer," Gary continued.

Agent Feldman looked askance at "Doctor" Graft. Rey suspected a marriage of professional convenience. "Mr. Perkins," she said, "we think you can help us help you. Tatiana does all the communicating with their coyote's stateside people. It's done over shortwave using FARC code."

"So, you want me to, uh, help interpret?"

"Yes. We already have an agent in the communication chain," said Feldman. "Her Spanish is good, but she doesn't understand Tatiana's dialect well. We need someone like yourself advising her, someone fluent, *East Colombian fluent,* with firsthand knowledge of the Ruizes."

"Nothing face-to-face?" asked Rey.

"Of course not," she answered, amused. "But we're having to pull in shortwave from somewhere in the Gulf of Mexico. The signal's weak, so you'll need to travel to Florida where we're set up."

"For how long?"

"For as long as it takes the United States Government to be convinced you've fulfilled your agreement, Mr. Perkins," said Feldman. "We'll need you sometime in the next few months."

"I don't know, I'll need to take time off from work—"

"Look, Mr. Perkins," Agent Feldman said stiffly, "a few days' vacation or ten years in federal prison—your choice."

"Yeah, yeah, okay," said Rey deliberately. "Where do I sign?"

After the paperwork was finalized, Feldman shook Rey's hand again before leaving and said, "The Bureau will be in touch." This left Perkins and Graft alone.

"Gary," said Rey, "can you explain what's going on?"

"What do you mean?" asked Gary.

"Well, first, what in Christ do you do for the government?"

"I can't say."

"Okay," said Rey. "Second, I don't understand—at book club, you have an opinion on everything, but with my future on the line, you don't say *anything*? What the hell, man!"

"Walter," Gary said patiently, "our new relationship"—he waved around the room—"needs to remain confidential, including the book club, which you need to return to, or the agreement's void. No one must know. Understand?"

Rey hesitated, then nodded. Understanding really was dawning on him. "Is this"—here Rey waved around the room as well—"the reason you joined the book club? And did you steal my battery?"

"Yes, that's why, and yes, I stole your battery. Your distributor too." Gary smiled. It was what Rey now called Graft's Goofy Smile, one he put on as some sort of act since apparently the real Graft didn't smile much. "For now, you're free to go," said Gary. "See the desk sergeant about your car."

"What about the guns?" asked Rey nervously. "And what about Sammy? Won't the club be suspicious?"

"You're in the clear with the club," said Gary. "They got their guns. Drove them to First Baptist myself. Claimed to be your buddy. Not too far from the truth, right, Rafa?"

Chapter 44: Chicken

Friday, 7 May 1999
Fairfax, VA

HENRY HAD BEEN the second man to dream, but he was the first man to die.

Splash had been driving in Fairfax, Virginia on Braddock Road, returning from an outlet that gave him a great deal on framing—his Ford's back seat was crammed with exhibition frames. Visibility was poor: thick rain fell as if being poured from a ladle in the sky. He was speeding, which wasn't new—the only club member who drove faster was Rey—and Splash had a reason. He needed to return to his gallery in time to complete the setup for his third exhibition!

It had been raining on and off all week and every DC area waterway was flooded. So was Accotink Creek, high enough, in fact, to get the attention of curious commuters who gawked at the trash and tree limbs the churning stormflow carried. Though it was 3 p.m., it was dark enough already that most headlights were on.

Henry was not at his best. Like the other club members, he'd been sleeping poorly. He was smoking to combat this. As evidence, a tendril from a cigarette now propped on his ashtray lazily wrapped its way over his dash. Henry was talking on this phone.

"Ken," he said, "I hear ya, I've been sleeping like crap too."

The two of them had been discussing their unusual fatigue. Ken had broached the subject, but it was Henry who did most of the talking, explaining how difficult it was balancing his normal studio demands, Domino's deliveries (still very much part of his financial plan), and time with his parents. As well, the tenacious Juri was preparing more drawings for a second show, many sketches featuring an over-muscled version of himself. Mostly these were good problems. The Ambassador was going to pay for another show later in the summer since he and Juri were returning to Japan at the end of the year.

"Yeah, I keep having these dreams, Ken."

"Like what?" Ken asked.

"I'm driving like I am now, but in a muscle car, flying through the desert on a highway, playing chicken with a semi."

"Sounds intense," Ken said, recalling his parent/ref dream.

"Yeah," said Henry, "first, this guy driving a Peterbilt forces me toward the guardrail on my side of the highway. Each dream, he's closer. Two weeks ago, he took off my mirror. Two nights ago, he scraped the paint off the driver's side of my dream car—a 1970 Challenger."

"Yikes."

"Last night he peeled off the front corner panel *and* my door. When I woke up, my left arm was killing me. Tonight," Henry laughed nervously, "I think he's going to get me."

"Maybe . . . but then you'll wake up," Ken said supportively.

"Yeah, sure. Just a dream. Sorry to be so dark. Traffic sucks. Let me call you later."

"No problem," said Ken, who was looking at himself in the reflection of a laid-off colleague's powered-down monitor. Ken's reflection didn't look great, in part due to his job. The combination of a recent downsizing at *The Post*, along with a couple of bungled sports articles (one where he'd reported the wrong score, the other where he'd completely goofed the star pitcher's stats), had him worried. But it was his dreams about flying headfirst into a metal bleacher that concerned him the most. They led to focus problems, which led to the article screwups. *Hell, I didn't even leave the announcer box last game. No way was I going to be anywhere in the stands.*

He knew another round of layoffs was likely. Would his recent poor work be used against him? *If I was making the calls, I might let me go.*

What a depressing thought.

Of the two men talking on the phone, however, it turned out Ken fared far better than Splash. The club would quickly learn that Haru "Henry" Takahashi had hydroplaned off Accotink Road into an immersed bridge abutment that Friday night after which his vehicle submerged in the flood waters. It wasn't immediately known if he died during the initial impact or drowned, as his body couldn't be retrieved until the next morning when the flooding subsided. A copy of that month's EMBC selection, *A Perfect Storm* by Wolfgang Petersen, was found in his coat pocket.

"Look, Gary, I didn't sign up for this," said Heather Graft, Gary Graft's wife. "The kids never see you. *I* never see you."

Gary, who felt overwhelmed, gathered his thoughts as best he could, but what came out wasn't helpful: "Heather, you knew the deal when we got married. Long periods away."

"I know, but that was supposed to change when you got back stateside, you know, *home*. But it's worse now than your foreign posts . . . wherever they were, which you could never tell me."

"I'm back, hon," he said defensively, "but it's still a demanding job."

"Yes, but you've made promises—birthday parties, sports events—and you're not keeping them. At least when you were doing whatever it was you do for Uncle Sam overseas, I didn't expect you to make promises."

"So you want me to stop making promises? Because that's something I can do," Gary said crossly.

Domestic Gary was a hybrid of the garrulous EMBC Gary and serious Dr. Gary who rarely said anything. Three roles, three personalities, *Which used to be easier to juggle before taking on the La Plata Patriots case,* he thought. *More accurately,* he told himself, *since joining that book club. God, I'm tired.*

Gary realized Heather was still talking and he'd no idea what she'd said. Heather was a good woman, an intelligent, observant one who, despite her anger, was calmly asking an increasingly repeated question: "Where did you just go, Gary?"

He'd been watching a man get waterboarded, someone he'd helped interrogate. He also recalled his bathtub dream. He said nothing.

Heather said nothing as well. She knew better than to ask again. Anything job-related was a black hole, a void to shout into with no response. She resented this, the cost protecting the nation had taken on her marriage, but over the years had accepted it. What she truly hated? Gary using his job to avoid talking about the hard parts of marriage. *How much longer am I willing to put up with this?*

Chapter 45: Blackout

Tuesday, 11 May 1999
Rockville, MD

HEY, IT'S ME again, Trevor Pug. I'm back, having really shat the bed this time. It started in Hell—the bar, not the afterlife. Picture Sunday evening, May 2, about a week ago—I went to Hell to drop off this month's "payment." I gave the envelope to Darin, better known as Mullet. These days, he's always glad to see me. Carol included a receipt with it—she tracks the math because though I can code like a bandit, monthly compound interest confuses me. We'd been doing okay, chipping away at the principal. Carol figured we'd be out from under by Christmas.

But that's where the bed-shitting came in.

I declined the beer Mullet offered. AA or no AA, it's best to refuse beverages from steroid freaks to whom you owe money. Drinking for me is a terrible idea, anyway. And I wasn't *thirsty*. You know the thirst I'm talking about—the one only alcohol will satisfy, the one that'll stand up your taste buds in anticipation. I swear it wasn't like that. I *know* that thirst, and as God is my witness, I didn't have what the AAs call the craving. I'd just gone to Hell to pay racket money. That's it.

Carol accompanied me, but only to the Gates of Hell. She wouldn't come in and I didn't blame her. She never wanted to see Mullet or any of his lawn-ruining Neanderthals again. I gotta hand it to her—since Mullet wouldn't meet us anywhere but that dump, she was being a trooper. Looking back, however, I should have taken someone else, maybe D-Kay, maybe Loo, but at the time, getting those guys involved for a five-minute in-and-out seemed like overkill.

It was raining and Carol was outside under an umbrella; she's the kind of girl who brings one no matter what the weatherman says. I went in, found Mullet, declined his invitation to a sit-down—"Trevor, pal, c'mon, have one on Old Line!"—and discreetly slipped him the money. Then I left. That's it.

We were still carless, so the next step was for Carol and I to walk two blocks back to the bus stop to wait for our home-bound bus. Like I said, Carol came to keep an eye on me when I dropped the money off, knowing I'd never leave her standing in front of Silver Spring's most infamous dive bar any longer than I had to. Show me a man who does that, and I'll show you an ex-husband.

But our system didn't work that night. I remembered sliding the money under Mullet's greasy basket of fries like I always did—Mullet loves his fries. I walked back toward the Gates of Hell, looking forward to standing with Carol under her umbrella, and then I think someone said, "Hey, Trevor! Heard about Splashdown." I think I helloed back.

I don't remember anything after that.

Not a single thing.

Guess where I end up? The worst place possible: Old Line's Waldorf compound. Passing out at Hell would have been better, a *lot* better. I wake up in their god-awful tobacco barn. I'd seen it once before; Willie took me when I was seventeen. He got a talking-to about that. No one under twenty-one was allowed in the barn unless you had a fake ID at least, which any teen worth his salt did, but I didn't. Anyway, I'm at the foot of the bar, a plywood mess even a ham-handed stooge like me could have built better. I'm told later that I'd been placed *on* the bar but rolled off in my sleep. From that drop, I'd earned a bruised shoulder and a knot on my head. An oaf with a braided beard named Rocker is sitting on a barstool next to me, flicking paper matches at my head, one at a time, out of boredom, I guess. At least they aren't lit.

"Mornin', asshole," he says.

I'm so hungover I wish for death. Seriously, I'm not kidding. I'm ready for some demon to carry me off to the afterworld, so long as he does it quietly. (Might cost me my soul, but I'm currently not using it.) There's bile stains bright as antifreeze on my shirt and there's blood, too. I've had hangovers before, terrible ones in fact, but nothing compared to this. Every part of my body is revolting—Bastille Day at the cellular level. I want to beg Rocker to kill me, but I can't move my lips.

I feel for my wallet. There's not much in it these days besides my ID, but it's missing. So's my phone. I do still have my watch: it's 2 p.m.

Bathroom! I need one urgently. I have to crawl because Rocker won't help me, so it takes three days to get there, pulling myself through spilled beer, crushed butts, and trash that, quite frankly, even a hole-in-the-wall like Old Line's barn should have already swept up.

As I crawl, I think, *There's somewhere important I'm supposed to be . . . Oh my God, my court date! Where's my car? Dumbass, you no longer have one. Or a license. You're at Old Line's biker compound relying on the kindness of strangers, strangers like Rocker the Match Flicker.*

Oh boy.

I reach the bathroom and am sick—more antifreeze vomit. "After you finish barfin', Luntz'll see you at the house," says Rocker from the door. I still can't talk so I just nod. I don't see Luntz for another hour because it takes me that long to get vertical. My brain is broiling, but the thought of drinking water, even a teaspoon, makes me gag. I try my best to ignore my thirst as I finally start stumbling to the farmhouse.

Luntz is waiting for me on the porch. "Trevor," he says.

"Christian," I croak, "I need to get back—"

"Home. Yeah, sure. Normally we don't provide taxi service but given your brother's past work, Rocker'll take ya."

"Don't barf on my bike, asshole," says Rocker from behind me, his beard braids swinging.

"Don't worry," I say. "Got nothing left." This is true—though my stomach feels like twice-ate kimchi, I'm done heaving.

"You'll have to ride bitch, of course," says Luntz, smiling, "but given the shape you're in, I doubt Rocker'll stop to diddle ya."

"I like my meat responsive," agrees Rocker. The Cro-Magnon waggles his eyebrows like he's the height of entertainment.

"What kinda man sits home while wifey sweats the bills?" Luntz asks me. "You should be working." He smiles again like I'd forgotten that I still owe the club twelve grand. Or maybe it's thirteen. "Bein' unemployed makes it tough makin' ends meet," he continues, "but if you want out of debt ricky-tick, gotta good-payin' job for you."

"No," I mutter.

"Okay, Trevor," Christian says, "but since you're good for another thirty days, why not think about it? And by the way, I like your wife's little tally notes. She's got a brain to go along with that good-lookin' handwritin'."

Rocker cackles hearing this. They are both undressing Carol just to mess with me, but I'm too overcome with dread to care. I'd just spent months in AA and a lot of money setting up a "plea" deal. Without it, I'm looking at five years.

"Heard you totaled three cop cars," Luntz says. "Impressive. No Old Liner's done anythin' like that."

"Not that we'd admit to," adds Rocker, again with the Groucho brow-waggling bullshit.

I think, *Someone larger than me please tell him he's not funny.*

"Climb aboard, fucker," Rocker says, mounting his bike.

"No need to speed, Rocker," Christian chides. "Pug's got all the time in the world now that he's unemployed. Every day's Sunday. Ain't that right, Pug? Permanent vacation."

"Sure," I say, not clarifying that I'm working side gigs. Rocker is straddling his bike. I can hardly stand up straight, and I know a ride from him will kill me. "I'll find my way home," I tell him.

"Suit yourself," Rocker responds, dismounting. I start walking; they make no attempt to stop me.

I hear Christian tell Rocker: "'He's the wanderin' outlaw of his own dark mind.'—Byron."

Fuck outlaws and fuck Byron.

The walk down Old Line's half-mile potholed driveway is painful. Plenty of time to think about the five months of sober time I've just blown.

What happened yesterday? I swear I'd just wanted to get home and watch the tube with Carol. The next day's plan: Carol would drop Reesie off at David Chin's house as usual, then take the bus to work like normal. I'd stay home, coding for hours—disturbance free, the only way I can do it.

But none of that happened.

I finally reach the paved road, but the first eight vehicles don't stop. Lucky number nine does pull over, but if you can believe it, it's an unmarked police car. I'm too sick to lie effectively, so I don't bother. I tell the officer who I am, broadly describing my circumstances. She dickers on her dash-mounted laptop, then gets out quickly, telling me to put my hands on top of her cruiser—there's a warrant out for me.

"I won't be trouble, officer," I tell her. She seems to agree and isn't aggressive with the cuffs.

In a sense, I'm glad I'm taken into custody, since I really don't want to face Carol. I do see her the next day, however, along with my lawyer, Janice Bees. Carol informs me she isn't posting bail this time. "We don't have that kind of money, Trev," she says, which is true, but there's more to it. I expected some reaction. Yelling, sobbing—something—but her look is half chastisement and half determination, as in *Trev, for the sake of our family, I'm going to drag your sorry ass across the finish line.*

I don't blame her for feeling that way, but I tell her it *can't* be my fault. Something beyond my control must have happened. Maybe someone drugged me. Carol nods, but it's obvious she doesn't believe me, and that hurts.

Here's the lecture Janice gave me: "You need to prepare yourself for the very real possibility of jail time, Trevor. Judge Freese hates tardiness, but I can't *begin* to describe how she feels about no-shows. If you had just shown up—hungover, loaded even, I don't care—it would've been fine. But you *disappeared,* Trevor. You left me with no defendant to defend. I watched Freese's face twist until she was only too happy to issue a warrant. Hope you have a lamp with a wish-granting genie because you're gonna need it."

Hey, enough with the speechifying. I'm the one paying you, remember?

There is an advantage to remaining in jail—I'm guaranteed to make my new court date the next day. I plead guilty as Bees originally directed me while sitting next to my stack of signed AA meeting attendance sheets, but the damage is done. Though it's my fault, when Judge Freese doles out my sentence, it feels surreal. The whole time I'm thinking, *This can't be happening to me.* I should be thankful, Janice says. I could've gotten the full nickel. Post-trial, I'm put back in the holding cell beneath the courthouse until all the remaining day's cases are heard, then I'm bussed to Seven Locks, Montgomery County's jail, with everyone else.

So currently, I and my five blown months of sobriety are lying on the top bunk of a prison cell. I'm awaiting transfer to a state facility to begin ten months' incarceration, hoping for a low-security deal like Central Maryland Correctional, and not Hagerstown (medium security), or Jessup (max).

County is awful. The food's disgusting and there's little outside time. I'm stuck in this cell, totally depressed. Seven Locks is a multistory facility; at least thirty guys on my floor alone. Some of them are coming off sedation drugs, either for mental illness, violence, or both. My cellmate, Otis, is a first-timer too. By mutual consent, we keep our mouths shut and our heads down. Otis watches TV—that's all he does. I read, sleep, and pick through disgusting lumps on my meal tray. Tomorrow we'll be sorted and sent to state. There's a lot of loose talk about going "state." Apparently, some places are worse than others. The old hands say it's all about the food. At least at state, they say, the food's a step up from county. That's a low bar to clear.

Chapter 46: Cider

Thursday, 20 May 1999
Waldorf, MD

NINE DAYS AFTER the Sunday Trevor Pug woke up in Old Line's barn, and thirteen days after Henry Takahashi died, Cisco paid Christian Luntz a visit.

Luntz watched Arkin get out of his truck. Mr. Arkin was at least seventy now and limped slightly, but the man had always limped, some Korean War wound. *Ya' look tired, Mr. Arkin,* he thought. *And ya' lost weight.*

The phone call from Mr. Arkin in March hadn't surprised Luntz—they occasionally talked on the phone—but today's in-person meeting request did. It had been a year since Cisco last visited the compound. The old man rarely made house calls these days, especially this far from Wheaton. Christian, who always used Cisco's surname, *Arkin,* had to hand it to him: no matter what kind of greeting he received at the compound (for instance, the muscled twenty-something prospect named Archer now standing in his way), Mr. Arkin never looked intimidated.

"Son," he said, "I got things growing on my keister twice as old as you. Now get out of my way." Luntz and Rocker, both witnesses, laughed. Archer, unsure of himself, stepped aside.

Although Luntz respected Arkin's tough-guy demeanor, he really admired the man's AA work. With one phone call, Christian Luntz could turn his worst drunks over to him, no questions asked. Mr. Arkin, usually with that big bastard Thumper's help, would then ferry the man to a treatment center or Arkin's basement, a bottle in his pocket for the man's DTs.

When they'd first met, Mr. Arkin had said, "I'll pick 'em up here"—*here* meaning Old Line's compound—"but if they can't follow suggestions, they're coming right back." Christian learned that Arkin's suggestions were really edicts, since after forgiving one or two false starts, he returned the slackers, but these days, that was rare. "Do what Mr. Arkin says or don't come back" was Luntz's handoff speech. Some club members, like Blister, the man Arkin picked up after six hospitalizations for acute alcohol poisoning, literally owed their lives to Arkin and Thumper. And the AA guys never accepted payment. The successful guys like Blister still worked the "program," as Arkin called it, which always sounded funny to Christian, like AA was some sort of Jenny Craig weight loss deal.

Luntz knew AA wasn't bulletproof, of course, and that it came with strings. Blister still paid dues, still rode with the club, and still did what he was asked, like assuming the club's maintenance duties given he was a talented Harley mechanic, but he no longer partied and always left the compound before dark.

"Sorry 'bout that, sir," said Luntz, referring to Archer's earlier posturing. To the prospect: "Archer, get your sorry ass over here an' apologize to Mr. Arkin."

Archer came up quickly, saying, "Sorry, sir." Cisco shook his hand. *No hard feelings.*

"Now get lost," said Luntz. Turning to Cisco, he asked, "Sir, to what do I owe the pleasure?" Arkin had never *asked* to come before.

"Christian," said Cisco, "I just need a minute." Standing in front of the tobacco barn, they both knew the other was lying—Christian knew exactly why Arkin was there and Cisco would need more than a minute to make his request. "Your time is valuable, so I'll be brief. Since we talked in March, Trevor Pug's situation has changed."

"Meanin' he's in the clink now," Luntz said.

"That's right," said Cisco. "So are you going to suspend payments on Trevor's loan while he's incarcerated?"

"Why would I do that, Mr. Arkin?"

"Because it's the moral thing to do," replied Cisco.

"Ah," said Luntz, "'Morality is the herd instinct of the individual.'—Friedrich Nietzsche."

"Very good, Christian," said Cisco, impressed. "You remembered that one."

Hearing this, Christian did something rare—he blushed. "I dropped Byron recently too."

"No kidding," said Arkin.

Mullet emerged from the barn asking, "Who the fuck is Friedrich Neese?"

"*Nietzsche*, not Neese, asshat," said Luntz.

"Okay, 'Nietzsche,'" said Mullet carefully. "Who is he?" Christian's blush darkened—he didn't know the answer.

"He was a German philosopher," said Cisco, covering for him.

In a rare moment resembling insightfulness, Mullet asked, "Was he a Nazi?"

"No," said Arkin. "He predated that."

"Oh," said Mullet, disappointed.

"Mr. Arkin," said Christian, motioning toward the barn, "come inside." Mullet trailed in like a loose end behind them. Once there, Luntz kept with tradition, engaging in their private joke, offering Cisco an on-the-house beer. As usual, Cisco politely refused.

"Sorry, Mr. Arkin, but nothin's changed since March," said Luntz, getting down to business, "includin' the terms of the debt. What Pug does on his own time—in this case, havin' to *do* time—that's on him."

"Heard you offered him a job," said Cisco. He had spoken with Trevor about this during his first prison visit.

"Yup. Even offered to re-work the payment plan, but he didn't go for it. Foolish of him."

Cisco looked around at the cheap tables and chairs, the plywood bar and pin-up posters, thinking the only non-foolish thing Trevor had done recently was refusing Luntz's employment. "You gonna hold that against him?" he asked.

"Not 'less he misses a payment," Luntz answered, flexing his hand.

"For discussion's sake, Christian—say his wife continues making the payments. Does it make sense to protect Trevor while he's inside?"

"Where'd he end up again?" asked Luntz.

"Maryland Central."

"Central's minimum security, Mr. Arkin. If he keeps his head down, he'll do all right."

"Do you have anyone at Central now?" Cisco asked.

"No. My boys usually go straight to Jessup."

This didn't surprise Cisco. "Could you call in a favor?"

"I could," said Luntz, "but it'd cost me. Ya don't mind me askin', why ya so keen on keepin' Trevor out of trouble, sir?"

"It's not just Trevor I'm concerned about, Christian. Alcoholism, you understand, is a family disease."

"Imagine so," Christian said agreeably, thinking, *If you want Trevor's little wife taken care of, ask for it. Tell me I owe you for all the guys you helped, like Blister, who, yeah, I'll admit, should be dead.*

Cisco knew Luntz wouldn't budge; Trevor had gotten himself into this mess, Trevor had to get himself out. He knew Christian respected him, but he also knew Luntz never passed up opportunity. Christian wanted Cisco to beg. If Cisco begged, then Luntz would own a piece of him. They stared at each other, Arkin's silence rebuking Luntz's wish to have him under his thumb.

Finally, Luntz asked, "So, sir, do ya want Old Line protectin' him or not?"

Cisco considered, answering, "Not if it costs."

"Okay," said Luntz, disappointed.

Just then, Rocker came in, a large jar of brown liquid under his arm. "Mr. Arkin, I'm puttin' this in your truck. You know, for what ya done for Blister."

Cisco nodded. In season, Rocker harvested apples from a scrubby orchard behind the farmhouse; out of season, he made cider. When it came to farm produce, Arkin wasn't a stickler about his no-fee policy, but free cider didn't make him a fan of the club. "You know, Christian," said Cisco, "Trevor's not the financial genius his brother was."

"That may be true, but runnin' books ain't rocket science, either. It's a square job somebody needs to do."

Square job, my ass, thought Cisco. "Then you'll need 'somebody' to do it. Trevor won't even be out until next year."

"That's okay," said Christian, "I can wait."

"All right then, Christian," said Cisco. "Thanks for your time."

"Before ya go, sir, do ya have somethin' for me?" asked Christian expectantly. Each time they talked, Arkin gave Christian a semi-famous quotation to memorize like Willie used to. Christian relished this, working hard to commit it to memory.

"Yes, I almost forgot," said Arkin. "Here goes: 'Freedom for the pike is death for the minnows.'—R H Tawney."

"Oh yeah," said Christian approvingly, "I like it."

"Pike, like an axe?" asked Mullet, who'd been eavesdropping. "I don't get it."

"No," chided Rocker, returning from his task. "A pike's a fish, you moron."

Luntz laughed out loud. Cisco smiled discreetly.

Mullet, embarrassed, huffed, "How the fuck was I supposed to know that?"

Returning to Wheaton, Cisco dropped off a bag of roadside vegetables at Carol Pug's house. Before retiring that night, he drank some of Rocker's cider, which was delicious, then hit his knees, praying earnestly for all three Pugs.

Chapter 47: Sick Statistics

Wednesday, 7 July 1999
Wheaton, MD

"OUR BOOK CLUB boys are tracking some really sick statistics," said Cindy.

"Statistics?" asked Carol distractedly. She spoke, phone in hand, while cooking dinner and discouraging her daughter from trying to capture their cat in a cardboard box. "*Reesie! Leave Kitty Batman alone!*" she barked, wiping sweat from her forehead. It was July and the kitchen was hot because her AC wasn't keeping up. "Sorry, Cin. You were saying?"

"Do you remember back in November, a street person got killed behind Shorties?" Cindy asked.

"Maybe," Carol said.

Cindy coughed, then relayed, "It happened on book club night."

"Oh, yes, now I remember," said Carol. "Sandy told me about it. How sad. I remember Trevor came home early from the meeting."

Trevor didn't even attend that night, which really torqued Loo, Cindy thought, *but with all you got going on . . . I won't correct you.* "He had a name," she resumed, "a street name anyway: 'Prophet.' He predicted people's fortunes for drink money. You know the type." Carol, a lifelong Washingtonian, said she did. "He went into Shorties that night to panhandle."

"I bet *that* went over well," said Carol, stabbing apart some ground beef as it sizzled in a pan.

"Yeah," said Cindy. "So Prophet hit our boys up for change, then the owner, that guy Manchester, threw him out."

"I'm sure he deserved it."

"Guess so," said Cindy. "But Loo told me they made fun of him, were a bit cruel about it. Maybe not our boys' best moment, but still, what'd he expect barging into a bar like that? Anyway, Loo said the guy 'cursed' them."

"Cursed them how?" asked Carol.

"Something about them losing jobs, et cetera."

"Really, how *dramatic,*" Carol remarked dryly.

After a pause, Cindy added, "He also said something about them getting killed."

"Okay, that *is* dramatic," said Carol. "And given Henry's death . . . that really *is* sick." She poured the contents of a Hamburger Helper box into the pan with the beef.

"Yes, not exactly something to laugh off," Cindy agreed. They gave Henry a moment of silence, each remembering the beautiful but very sad funeral service six weeks previous. Haru Takahashi had been a talented man cut down in his prime, dying in a way anyone could have: a traffic accident—he'd even been wearing his seatbelt. It was well attended and—except for Trevor, who was incarcerated, and Rey, who wasn't missed—everyone in or related to the book club had showed. It was the first time Cindy had worn a funeral outfit for someone she wasn't related to. She coughed again and took a sip of hot tea, thinking, *I still can't believe that wonderful guy is dead. Thank God he died right away. Drowning would've been horrible!*

"Are you ill, Cin?" asked Carol, concerned. "Are you feeling up for Ladies Night on Friday?"

"No, just allergies," said Cindy, sniffing. "I'll be there. So, it's been Darius's idea to keep stats on the curse, you know, to see if it's real, even if it's in poor taste."

"No surprise there," said Carol. Everyone knew D-Kay was the club's designated cad. "What exactly are they tracking?"

"Lost jobs, arrests, wives and girlfriends bailing on them, and . . . deaths."

"Are things actually bad enough to track?" asked Carol.

"Three jobs lost, four arrests, one tanked relationship, and . . . Henry," Cindy said, her voice getting quiet as a lump formed in her throat—Splashdown's death still felt raw.

"Oh Cindy, I know. Splash was such a good guy."

"Yeah . . ." Cindy said, taking a breath. "With an *actual* death, it makes the boys' curse seem very real and very unfunny."

Carol steered the conversation toward Cindy's husband. "How long's Loo been back at work now?"

"Two months."

"Reesie, I told you to leave Kitty Batman be!" Carol shouted as the feline bolted past, a box-carrying girl in hot pursuit. "Sorry, Cin. Loo must be thrilled now that his name's cleared."

"Yes," Cindy said, "what a nightmare! Those pathetic reporters! Camping out every night, shouting questions. This will sound bad, but I'm glad the real Deerslayer's killing again. It finally forced those press buzzards to move on. Thanks for being our lifeline to Safeway back then. *Huge* help."

"Was glad to," said Carol, popping a bag of frozen broccoli into the microwave. "How's Hanna holding up?"

"For a five-year-old, she's surprisingly resilient," said Cindy. "I told her early on it was all a mistake, that Daddy would put it right. She was scared sometimes, worried about other kids at school. I spoke to her teachers, got assurances she wasn't being ridiculed . . . Actually, I may have gone a little *too* mama bear on that front. But the worst thing, Carol? Our neighbors—the looks of judgment. And the other people *congratulating* me on my husband's 'initiative.' I couldn't agree with them, of course. Loo wasn't who they thought he was, but when I told them that, they got pissed off, like I was stabbing him in the back. Awful, I tell you."

Cindy went on, and Carol listened supportively. It was good hearing her friend vent because by the time the cameras had finally left, Cindy's normally thick skin—"Hey! Get your mic outta my face!"—had been worn thin fending off questions and photos and God knew what else.

But Carol didn't believe Loo was innocent because Trev didn't.

Loo and Trev, two peas in a pod, she thought. *Best buds.* Trev was sure about this, telling her the normally mild-mannered Loo was a forest sleeper agent, the kind of patient outdoorsman willing to lay in wait for his four-footed enemies. And his Lorax politics? Sure, they made Luigi a target for good-natured ribbing, but that was Trev's point: Loo had strong opinions and though he didn't seek out political fights, he didn't back down from them, either. Loo believed heart, soul, and sinker that the forests were dying, and he could show you the going-to-hell statistics to prove it. Loo would impress upon anyone who would listen that the Earth was mankind's mother, and therefore shouldn't he, shouldn't *everyone,* protect her? If that meant going "ninja" to suppress an exploding deer population, then that's what it meant.

And you never really know someone, do you?

Did she suspect Trev would run up bar tabs with credit cards she didn't know he had? Did she think he'd drink on the job? Did she guess her man would drive blotto, wrecking three police cars? If Trev could have a secret drinking life, then surely Loo, apparently Park and Rec's answer to Rambo, could kill some deer.

Carol had lost the thread of the conversation. As a restart, she asked the first thing coming to mind. "Cindy, can you believe what my mother did?"

"What's it this time?"

"She found out about Old Line. Told me she'd pay off those creeps. *And then,* drumroll please, pay off our mortgage."

"*Iiiiif,*" said Cindy, dramatically.

"*If* I divorced Trev."

"She didn't!" Cindy exclaimed.

"Oh yes, she did. *And* she'd also pay for that too."

"She hates him that much?"

"Uh-huh."

"So, you gonna take her up on it?" Cindy enquired, pausing to cough again.

"No, of course not."

"You sure?" asked Cindy curiously. "Makes sense she'd offer, her being loaded."

This was true. Carol's parents, reasonably well off to begin with, benefited from the sale of two patents her father had filed shortly before his unexpected death. Carol's mother, Gladys Edock, was indeed loaded.

"Am I sure the answer's *no*? Yes, I am. I love my husband, and despite"—Carol quickly confirmed that her daughter was out of earshot—"his recent fuck ups, he's my man, the father of my child."

She did genuinely believe this, but she also believed that considering recent events, putting her love of Trev aside, it wasn't out of the realm of possibility to consider financial "salvation" so long as it came from someone besides her mother. "She's willing to pay to be 'right' about Trev, that's all," continued Carol. "Can you believe it?"

"Yup," said Cindy, knowing Carol's long-running conflict with her mother.

Mother and daughter weren't always at odds. They shared a motivation for fiscal responsibility, swapped recipes, had a love of cute cat videos, could talk books to no end, and Gladys anxiously awaited Carol's debut novel, assuming she ever completed it, but there were several minefields: politics, religion, child-rearing philosophies, and, of course, Gladys's currently incarcerated son-in-law.

Cindy asked, "So how's Reesie holding up with her father, you know . . . not being home?"

Carol embraced the subject head-on. "She's sad, of course, but I think she understands that Daddy has to be 'where he can get help' to get better. That's what I've been telling her, anyway. And just like you, I talked to her teachers. No one's been mean to her, so far, anyway."

You poor thing, Cindy thought. To change the subject, she asked what else was new.

"Well, it's hot in my kitchen," said Carol. "My AC's not keeping up, and I can't afford to fix it, but that's not new. What are you cooking for dinner tonight?"

"Nothing," said Cindy. "Loo's picking up tapas on the way home. That is, once I remind him to. What's up with the Chins?" she asked, knowing the subject might cheer Carol up.

"The usual," said Carol, "I still don't see what David sees in her. She hasn't changed."

True, mostly anyway, agreed Cindy, meaning Angie's bearing. Angie certainly wasn't a magazine model beauty like Estelle, but she had the same pouty look, though in more of a scolding way. *But some men like that.*

"Sandy thinks he's just a puppy dog," Carol continued. "Angie's *so* not his type."

"What *is* David's type?" asked Cindy.

"Not bitchy."

Cindy decided to go out on a conversational limb. "Angie's bitchy, yes, but overall, I have to say . . . She's not a bad looker. Not the kind who'd have to, you know, *settle.*"

Carol responded defensively, "If anyone's settling, it's him. And maybe she looks okay now, but in ten years, you can put her fat ass out to pasture." Her tone was much nastier than Cindy felt reasonable.

"David's probably not thinking that far ahead right now," said Cindy. "Besides, love's blind, Carol, right? And why do you care?"

"David seems . . . unhappy."

"Duh, he's married to a shrew."

"Well, I'm thinking selfishly, I guess," conceded Carol, "I just don't want an *unhappy* man watching my child."

Makes sense, thought Cindy. "Surely you don't think that makes him a bad sitter?"

"No, no," Carol said, "but you wouldn't want Hanna's daycare provider being distracted, would you?"

"No, I guess not," admitted Cindy.

"And I worry about Sunny. If it's Splitsville, he'll be shuttled back and forth between Mommy's house and Daddy's new apartment. That's no way to grow up."

"Being the super divorce lawyer, won't she get full custody?"

"If she wanted it," said Carol, "but honestly, I don't think she would. As it is, she's hardly ever home. It's like David's a single dad."

Carol continued grousing about the Chins, and Cindy listened politely. Lately, Carol seemed to be analyzing the Chins more and more, and Cindy thought she knew why. *Worry not about the mote in your neighbor's eye, tend to the log in your own.* Carol's life had taken a huge left turn—a drunken husband serving ten months for a felony DUI, leaving her to pick up the pieces. Who wouldn't want to dissect a neighbor's life rather than deal with their own?

Plus, interestingly, Angie herself was sending David mixed signals. On one hand, she was encouraging him to hurry the hell up and complete his dissertation so he could get a high-paying job killing ants. That made sense: according to Carol, the Chins were carrying a business loan on top of a frighteningly large mortgage, plus student debt, so her husband "slow walking" his Ph.D. by providing childcare was probably killing Angie. But on the other hand, having a house hubby made financial sense. Instead of paying for outrageously expensive DC-area childcare, David watched Sunny, getting under-the-table cash from the Pugs. Plus, who handled Sunny's colds? Who cooked for him? Who defused his tantrums, and took him to T-ball? David, of course. And best of all, David had dinner on the table for Angie when she came home. Who wouldn't want that?

"Hey, I still can't believe the prom king and queen are no more," Cindy said.

Carol didn't need clarification; the reference meant Phillipe Gallois and Estelle Largo. "I still can't believe it, either," she said, "but isn't it great?" After a pause, Carol added, "Was that a bad thing to say?"

"No, it's not," said Cindy. "At last, our man has come to his senses."

Two years previous, Estelle had flown into their flock like a falcon, swooping up Phillipe Gallois, the girls' favorite single male friend, totally upsetting the apple cart. The pompous debutante's first mistake was claiming him without their blessing, which was bad enough, but worse, she implied that in doing so, Estelle was saving Phillipe from the clutches of lower-class harpies. Not in those exact words, of course, but one would be an idiot to miss her disdain. Anyone that is, except their stupid husbands, besotted by her perfect skin and a chest that kept on giving.

So, it was with delight that the EMBC wifely triumvirate—Cindy Spicotti, Carol Pug, and Sandy Kay—witnessed the overnight fall from grace of their estrogen nemesis, Estelle Largo. Still, Cindy begrudgingly gave the woman credit—no matter how much they hated her, Phillipe now dressed better, knew his way around a wine menu, and had acquired a few Washingtonian friends the women could actually stomach. *And soon,* thought Cindy, *you'll be a highly paid jet pilot, Phillipe. Oh how fun it will be to once again play matchmaker for you!*

Cindy had pressed him on why the happy couple had split, but Phillipe would only say it hadn't worked out, and seemed genuinely glum, which was understandable. No man, *no one,* wants to be seen as a failed lover.

But there's more to their breakup, she thought, *I just know it*. Phillipe wasn't just sad, he seemed scared. Was there a possibility that Phillipe had done something wrong, something awful? *No,* Cindy thought. Part of his charm was his character. Phillipe Gallois would rather be eaten by wolves than violate his principles. If Phillipe had strayed (even the great Phillipe was not above temptation), he would have shamefacedly fallen on his sword so many times that even Estelle would tell him to knock it off.

So if you didn't screw up, what makes you so afraid, Phillipe? Is Cruella de Vil holding something over your head? Could she tank your job? No, Southwest was union. *Take your money?* She thought not. They weren't married and, more importantly, he'd no assets to plunder. Could it have been that classic villainess move, trapping him by getting pregnant? Though Cindy wouldn't put it past Estelle, there was no way she would carry a fetus to term and endure the pre-marital embarrassment accompanying that.

And to your credit, Estelle, you don't seem the two-timing type. Estelle's code was shallow—*He's mine and you can't have him*—but a code was still a code.

At last, a sweaty Carol pronounced her dinner cooked and the two friends hung up. Carol yelled for her daughter to come free Kitty Batman from cardboard prison and eat. Cindy called Loo to remind him to pick up tapas.

Chapter 48: Pavilion 4

Thursday, 8 July 1999
Glenmont, MD

LOO SPICOTTI, THE former Deerslayer, watched his crew trim dead limbs from the trees surrounding Pavilion 4, grateful to have his arborist/head groundskeeper job back. At first, Park and Rec Legal fought his reinstatement, believing him a fox among chickens, but between the circumstantial evidence, the still unresolved issue of jurisdiction, and most importantly, the deer being slaughtered again by someone not named Spicotti, they backpedaled fast enough to create a wake. Everyone in Legal, initially so eager to hang Loo by the balls, was now bending over backward to kiss his ass, saying how sorry they were for his ordeal and how lucky *everyone* was to avoid such a miscarriage of justice. A healthy salary bump helped Loo agree with them.

The public now assumed the real Deerslayer was back in business. Loo of course knew the new guy was a poser, someone getting off on copycatting. Who the guy was, Loo didn't know, but he knew it wasn't Henry, because poor Henry was dead, yet the deer were still dropping, though not nearly as quickly as before.

Professionally, Loo was back where he should be, directing staff to re-shingle roofs, mow fields, and mulch beds. And of course, protect the trees. Despite the park system's relatively large swaths of forest, nearly every tree present was four, five, sometimes six generations removed from the discovery of the New World—there were few large trees left. There were, however, a few older trees that by virtue of being tucked away in places too difficult to log, had escaped America's hunger for cabinets and toilet paper. For instance, some trees planted as seedlings along the driveways of former estates were now quite large. Few of these properties' buildings remained, so these sentinels were the last evidence that parcels now owned by Park and Rec were once farms, manors, and unfortunately, plantations. Some of these trees were what arborists called specimens—particularly large, old, or otherwise impressive examples—and Loo knew the location of each one.

Loo also knew that people, though generally cognizant of what woodlands were, unfortunately took them for granted. "How old's that tree? Let's cut it down and count the rings!" *The public can be stupid,* he thought. *Urban saplings aren't the same thing as old growth, plus, young or old, pollution's tough on all trees.* Where the public saw squirrel nests, he saw heat stress; where people saw leaves, he saw mold; where a jogger saw a tree leaning over a stream, Loo saw an eroded root mat whose failure during the next storm would doom it.

"Hey Ricky!" yelled Loo. "Careful trimming 'round that black oak! It's the largest one in Montgomery County and older than the cheese in your ass. And for Christ's sake, put *all* the branches in the chipper, even the small ones."

Rick dutifully did as he was told, which pleased Loo. Ever since returning to work, the guys, some of whom probably doubted his innocence, took him more seriously.

Good to have the book club guys back in my corner too, he thought. Loo felt thankful that the tells of his buddies' doubt were gone. The goodwill of his neighbors had returned as well. Couples he and Cindy used to have over for dinner were back again—most of them, anyway, the ones who hadn't burned bridges by actively shunning them.

It seemed half of Washington, including some of his neighbors and most of the EMBC, were celebrating the return of the Deerslayer, or more accurately, the return of his notoriety. Cindy was of course regularly proclaiming "My husband's been cleared of all charges!" Though he'd been arrested, Loo in fact hadn't been charged, but he never corrected his wife, because down deep, he wasn't sure Cindy completely believed him. *Did we just adopt our own white elephant, one with antlers?*

There were conspiracy theories about the slayings. The government was behind it as a trial run for human population control. PETA was doing it for fundraising and a chance to stick it to the NRA. Loo, being the real killer, had cleverly engaged an accomplice (or in some versions, a patsy) to cover his ass. The fact that these last theorists were mostly correct was a tasteful pleasure only Loo and his unknown savior could enjoy.

Loo looked around, noticing that Fernando, the chipper operator, had taken his safety glasses off. This horrified him.

"Jesus, man! Your glasses!"

"Sorry, Loo," Fernando said, putting them back on, chastised. Fernando was also a little puzzled. Feeding the chipper was the fun job, so all the guys wanted to do it. In the past he'd thought Loo voluntarily passed on chipper detail to show what a humble boss he was, but now, Loo seemed genuinely afraid of the chipper and wouldn't go near it.

For his part, Loo *was* very much afraid of it—the woodchipper nightmare was getting worse, but at least Fernando looked nothing like the man in his dream.

To take his mind off this, Loo thought about his baby, the Evil Man's Book Club. It was Trevor's baby, too, but that annoyed him. Pug's months-long felony sentence was just another example of him fumbling his responsibilities. Sure, the man had a drinking problem, but Trevor had never been a "closer," and their shared idea of a book club for dudes exemplified that. After the two of them came up with an idea, the book club for instance, the first step was promotion: Trevor, a likable pitchman, would bombard everyone with enthusiasm. This was A-okay with Luigi. Cheerleading wasn't his strength—doing real work was. In the club's case, he scheduled the meetings, made sure the guys picked next month's book, and had someone scratch down their comical "minutes," though this was a duty Gary the New Guy had since adopted.

But invariably with new things, Trevor's enthusiasm would wane because the man easily bored. Without Trevor's rah-rah, no matter how hard the industrious Loo pushed things, the venture would dry up. *Trevor,* he thought, *you lack follow-through.* All Loo had ever asked of Trevor club-wise was to remember the meeting dates correctly—some potential members had showed up on the wrong night and had been understandably turned off. *How effing hard is it to remember something when I tell you it, leave it in a phone message, and put it in an email? I know you have a drinking problem, but even before the shit hit the prison fan, you missed meetings—surprising considering how much you love beer.*

Enthusiastically, Loo thought, *But your slackness didn't kill the club.*

Loo was thrilled these days—the club was getting real legs now. New guys were joining, and it was becoming something bigger than either of the co-creators imagined, something that, despite Trevor's absence and some creepy curse (that for sure didn't kill Henry because curses *weren't* real), was doing just fine.

"Fernando, shut the chipper down. Ricky, tell the other guys it's lunch break."

"Yes, Loo," they said.

You know, Trevor, it's not your "old" slackness that's pissing me off, Loo thought as he grabbed his lunch cooler, *it's your new neediness.* Since Trevor had been shipped to Sykesville, home of Maryland Central, he'd been calling Loo, begging him to visit. Spicotti had yet to go and felt guilty about it. Despite being the anti-deer vigilante, Loo believed himself a nice guy, but after work and family—*and don't forget all the post-Big Stew legal hoopla*—he'd only so much energy left for anyone else. He was trying, but Phillipe, the club's *outlando d'amour,* had lost his girl and was still messed up about it, plus he now had a demanding combination of training for the new jet-jockey job and working for Southwest, something grinding him down. Loo called when he could to keep his spirits up. He called D-Kay, too, who'd taken Splash's death especially hard. Luigi pestered Darius to stay active in the club, which he was doing.

Sorry Trevor, but I got nothing left for a guy who drank his way to prison.

He carried his cooler over to Pavilion 4 to eat with the guys, sitting near the record-sized black oak and as far from the woodchipper as possible.

For her part, Cindy steadfastly supported her husband, but did have her doubts. After nine years of marriage, she'd suspected something was wrong. Her initial take on the night of Loo's debacle was that it happened so quickly that her innocent but panicked husband had simply said the wrong things. There would have been no time to create some story, and Loo was a lousy liar to begin with, which was one reason why she'd married him in the first place.

But in the ensuing weeks, doubts developed. She could tell he was lying about something—not about being the Deerslayer, of course, but something.

I don't know what it is, she'd thought, *but you're no killer. You'll stop traffic to help a box turtle cross the road. You install PLANT MILKWEED! signs on our lawn for Monarch Butterfly Day. You'll lecture anyone who'll listen (in that adorably liberal way of yours) about the evils of guns. You killing one deer, let alone dozens? Not possible. And with a crossbow? You'd never be able to live with yourself if you shot some poor animal only to have it run off and bleed to death . . . could you?*

Chapter 49: Mrs. McGovern

Thursday, 8 July 1999
Wheaton, MD
THAT NIGHT, AT Mr. Arkin's urging, Carol Pug stood in front of a large suburban home ringing the bell. The door was opened by a woman so matronly she could be a TV grandmother.

"Mrs. McGovern?" Carol asked.

"Hello, Carol. Come in, and please call me Alice."

Alice led her to a front room with leather furniture she'd seen in movies from the 1930s. The pieces were large, solidly built, and spotless. Carol suspected Alice McGovern cleaned them religiously. The tidy house didn't make Carol feel good, however. Her own home, with its unclosed dressers, unemptied dishwasher, and carpet stains hidden by strategically placed chairs, couldn't compare. *Why did people have to have homes this nice?*

"Your home is lovely, Alice."

"Thanks," she said. "It takes work."

I'm sure it does, thought Carol. *At least you didn't say you "hadn't had time to clean" before I came.*

"Please have a seat, Carol," Alice said, pointing to a sofa. Do you want coffee? It's decaf."

Carol sat, finding the furniture more comfortable than it looked. It was 7:30 p.m., and even decaf would keep her up, but she didn't want to appear off-putting, so she accepted a cup brought to her on a tray with cream and sugar. *And now for the taste test.* If Alice's coffee was subpar, Carol, in some childish way, would feel good about that. But the coffee wasn't subpar. It was delicious.

"So Carol," said Alice, "May I ask, are you here because you want to be?" For a sweet-looking old lady, a widow according to Mr. Arkin, she was very direct.

"Mr. Arkin said I should meet you."

"Yes, Cisco mentioned that," Alice said, smiling. "Did he 'suggest' coming here?"

"Now that you mention it," said Carol, "he used that exact word, but it felt more like a nicely asked order."

"A suggestion from Cisco Arkin might as well be one," said Alice, winking. "He's got that kind of personality." She sipped her coffee. "Do you know what Al-Anon is?"

"Mr. Arkin said it's like AA for spouses."

"That's pretty close," said Alice. "It's a program for those affected by the alcoholic's drinking: wives, husbands, children, brothers, aunts, business partners—you name it."

She has wonderful diction, thought Carol. Mr. Arkin said she was a retired teacher and she sure sounded like one. "Like a support group?" Carol asked. She wasn't averse to this—her friends were great, but they knew her too well. She liked the idea of objective strangers, ones she could educate as to just how bad her husband's drinking had become. But on the other hand, a room full of wives and girlfriends crying and patting each other's hands seemed sort of pathetic.

"They're similar, but not the same," said Alice.

"What's the difference?"

"A support group is meant to assist people who've had, or are having, bad things happen to them. Things they have no control over. Al-Anon does some of that, meaning talking about the damaging alcoholics in our lives, but mostly we work on ourselves. 'Our side of the street' as Cisco would say. Our part of the alcoholism."

Carol put her cup down in surprise, rattling her saucer. "*Our* part? I'm working *hard* to dig my family out of a situation my drunken husband put us in. Other than getting suckered, what part did I play?"

Alice reached from her chair, patting Carol's hand lightly.

She didn't just do that, did she?

"Let me explain, if I can, by example," said Alice. "For years, my husband drank like a fish. He wasn't a mean drunk, but . . . well, I'm getting ahead of myself. When we first got married, the drinking wasn't bad. He had a good handyman business. Did it all: carpentry, plumbing, even had an electrician's license. 'People in the 'burbs are too busy to fix their own homes,' he always said. 'They need me, and that's solid gold for us, Alice!' At first, Carol, it *was* solid gold. Business was great. All word of mouth. He never advertised and I stayed home with the kids." Alice paused. "You like the pictures?"

Carol had been examining the framed photos next to her sofa: adults with children, and the same children as adults, with children of their own—lots of smiles. "Yes," said Carol. "How many kids do you have, Alice?"

"Three. And eight grandchildren. Cisco says you have a daughter?"

"Yes," said Carol. "Reesie. She's five. She'll be six next month."

"Wonderful," said Alice, smiling again. "Where was I? Oh, yes. So John had a great work ethic and valued time—his own and other people's. He was always punctual. But five years and three kids later, his drinking started picking up. His work suffered some, but when he stumbled on a project, he'd make it right to keep his reputation. Home life suffered, too, but I knew he loved us, and he still provided, so as the saying goes, I put up with it. But by our tenth anniversary, his drinking had gone sideways. He started losing jobs, which made him drink more, which made him lose *more* jobs—a vicious cycle. In the end I was printing flyers, putting them in people's mailboxes so John could at least rake their leaves or cut their grass. If he was too drunk to do that, then I had a friend watch my children and did it myself."

"Sounds like a nightmare," said Carol, thinking of how often she'd asked Cindy to watch Reesie lately, how she was juggling utility bills, the mortgage, and of course, that damn biker debt. Working for Hallmark, hourly with no benefits, now meant *no* to everything else. No PTA fundraisers, no school pictures, even no to Girl Scout cookies, but most significantly, no to her novel—no time for her "paper baby" anymore thanks to her drunken husband. *Drunken husband.* Trev's new, undignified title.

"John made my life a nightmare," said Alice. "I was so angry. So embarrassed and humiliated." She paused, asking, "Does any of this sound familiar?"

It did. "Yes, a little," said Carol.

"What hurts most?" Alice asked.

"I don't know. Maybe because he's broken his vow to, you know, be a good husband. A provider. A protector."

Alice looked at her kindly, nodding. Carol was relieved. When she said things like this to her "liberated" friends, some of them rolled their eyes. *Well ladies, if I truly thought I could do it on my own, I still wouldn't have. I like old-school marriage.*

By her expression, Alice seemed to share this view. Before last year, Trev was still a great husband. Not perfect, of course, but loving and most of all, *fun*. Fun was something Carol missed. Prison visits weren't fun.

"So, with John's terrible drinking," continued Alice, "it made it easy to ignore my side of the street."

"You enabled him?"

"Yes I did," Alice said matter-of-factly.

"So, it was *your* fault what he did?" said Carol incredulously.

"For my part in it, the enabling, yes," said Alice.

"I think I see." Carol *didn't* see, but admitting that wasn't going to stop the martyr-ville express.

"Great," said Alice. "Carol, do you feel you enabled your husband's drinking?"

Whoa, Alice, that's direct. "Maybe," said Carol, "but not when I first met him. Back then it was just trouble with the basics—the dishes, doing laundry. He faked helplessness to avoid housework, but I wouldn't have it. He learned, even discovered a love of vacuuming. Aces with the Hoover. He was very methodical."

"*Is* very methodical," prompted Alice.

"Yes, that's what I said."

Alice let this slide. "At Al-Anon meetings, it's a safe place to work on ourselves, to stop the enabling, to establish boundaries."

"Is that the 'tough love' I've heard about?" asked Carol.

"Yes," she said. "I did it with John, who eventually saw the light, joined AA, straightened out, which eventually allowed me to begin teaching, and we had a pretty happy ending. He died sober, which was great, but he also died still having the disease. Sounds like your man's got it too. Everyone—possibly even Trevor—can see it, right? As his wife and the mother of his child, you fear the future, which I completely understand, but today, *right now,* take a breath. Trevor's in a cell tonight, safe enough for the next twenty-four hours. That's what they teach in AA—one day at a time. Al-Anon's the same way." A pause to sip coffee. "So how are you tonight?" Alice asked gently. "Right now."

"Okay, I guess. I mean I'm stressed, mostly about money, and keeping Reesie's spirits up. Also, keeping my jailbird husband from worrying about me having to clip coupons."

"Do you think maybe he *should* know about the coupons?"

Jesus, thought Carol, *that's the last thing he needs.* "I'm not adding to Trev's burdens, Alice. That makes no sense at all." She was beginning to regret her visit.

"My point is he's probably not aware of everything that you do for him," said Alice.

Duh, thought Carol. "I know he's not."

"When John was in his cups and customers called, I lied for him," Alice went on. "This was before the leaf-raking flyers. I said, 'John's a little under the weather,' which was true if you count hangovers. It was amazing the number of maladies my John had. Once I said he had Beriberi, which was just ridiculous since the customer was a doctor. Did you ever field calls like that?"

"No," said Carol. Trev had been hungover a lot over the past year, but he always went in. He might look like death, but he went.

"Anyway," said Alice, "that's an example of enabling." She sipped her coffee. "How about this more indelicate topic—I worried John might have been unfaithful. It wasn't out of the question. He was a handsome man who frequented bars. I said to myself, 'Okay, it's not the end of the world, the bars, right?' I figured, hey, I'll just tag along, keep an eye on him. At first, he was tolerant, but I soon realized his stare meant I was holding him back from drinking the way he wanted to drink. When I was ready to go home, he'd hand me the keys, saying, 'Take the car. I'll get a ride.' Hearing that, I'd bite the bullet and stay longer, trying to keep up with him, which I couldn't." *But I sure tried,* thought Alice. *Which is one reason I'm an alcoholic too. But not useful information for you right now, Carol.* "How's your drinking, dear?" she asked.

"It's fine," said Carol. She was ready for Friday Ladies Night at her house tomorrow: Carol, Cindy, and Sandy. Two bottles usually covered it, but she had three. "I don't have an issue."

"Good," said Alice, sounding sincere. "Another way I tried controlling John's drinking was I'd offer to buy it for him. That way I could buy the cheap stuff, which was all we could afford, anyway, and then ration it." She paused. "Rationing didn't work. Anyway, we needed money, and at that point, I was the only adult in the house. I got up super early to deliver newspapers before the kids woke up. And for three years, I traded watching the children with a neighbor so I could sling hash in a school cafeteria." To Carol, this sounded eerily familiar. "All this while John's drinking the cheapest wine you can possibly buy, the 'no grapes involved' kind. He and I fought all the time. Like I said, he wasn't a mean man, but like all men, he had a temper, and when he was drunk, I sometimes saw it.

"I was so afraid of the things I couldn't control. The more I confronted him, the more I worried he'd leave town or rush into the arms of another woman. But Carol, I'm here to tell you that a woman can only take so much. I finally reached that point where you just don't care anymore—not about where he was, or what the neighbors thought, or what my mother thought, or what his mother thought. What *anyone* thought."

"Sounds terrible," said Carol. The childcare trading had really hit home. Alice was throwing ringers, and she didn't like it. During a long pause, her eyes drifted to Alice's photos again, then to the front door.

"Carol," said Alice bluntly, "I don't think we're connecting the way I'd hoped, but please don't let that keep you from attending Al-Anon. Al-Anon is wonderful. Alcoholism's a family disease—it wants everyone ill, not just the alcoholic. We can't fight it on our own. We need 'outside' help, just like the alcoholics do. We even use the same tools, the Twelve Steps."

"Really?" asked Carol. "Why? I mean, we're not the alcoholics, *they* are. Don't we need something different?"

"Same 'family' disease, so the same steps, almost word for word. They work for the drunks, and they work for us too."

If you think for one minute I'm gonna go to some group of handwringers and do the steps my drunken husband should be doing, thought Carol, *then you got another thing coming.* "Well, you've given me a lot to think about, Alice," she said, getting up to return her cup and saucer to the kitchen. "Thanks for the coffee."

"You're welcome," said Alice. "Just leave the cup in the sink—I'll take care of it. I know it's a lot to take in at once, and I probably overwhelmed you. Don't worry, dear. As we say in Al-Anon, 'Take what you can use and leave the rest.' By the way, what are you doing for transportation now?"

"I take a bus," answered Carol. "Trev wrecked our car."

"Can I give you a ride home?"

"No thanks," said Carol. "I borrowed my girlfriend's car tonight."

"If you want to go to an Al-Anon meeting, there's one tomorrow night at eight. I can pick you up at seven-thirty."

"I've got plans with some girlfriends," said Carol. "Perhaps another night."

"Alright," said Alice, walking her to the door. "Nice meeting you, Carol."

"Likewise, Alice."

Carol walked to Cindy's car, relieved to be out of Alice McGovern's house.

Chapter 50: Mandatory Sex

Friday, 9 July 1999
Wheaton, MD

AFTER A LONG Friday at the Hallmark store, Carol had been looking forward to ladies' movie night. Cindy Spicotti, one neighborhood over, and Sandy Kay, who lived across the Potomac in Reston, were coming to drink wine and watch *Shakespeare in Love*. Reesie was at Grandma's, no doubt being spoiled rotten, but the sleepover was well-timed.

But now movie night's cancelled, Carol thought, frustrated.

Cindy had called earlier saying she couldn't make it—her allergies on the phone a few days ago had turned out to be a cold in disguise. Sandy called with regrets as well. She'd been heading out the door when Channel 4 News announced a major wreck on the Beltway, one with fatalities: I-495 was closed in both directions. Carol, having prepared an appetizer plate of shrimp tacos, was disappointed. Canceling movie night meant a wasted opportunity to escape work worries, the recent toxic discussion with her mother, and looks from pitying neighbors: *Poor Carol, will she divorce Trevor?*

No, folks. I'm not a quitter.

Fortitude aside, turning her mother's money down had been harder than it should have been. Without Trev's piecemeal gigs, she was still paying Old Line monthly, but wasn't chipping away at the principal anymore. Due to recent layoffs, she was now the Hallmark store interim manager. This was good; she needed the hours. But when the owner, Mrs. Dills, visited earlier in the week to announce more belt-tightening measures, she felt uneasy. Scuttlebutt was that Mrs. Dills was juicing the numbers so she could sell. Carol, already uninsured and one hospital bill away from financial disaster, would lose her job if that happened, something which frightened her.

On the Old Line front, she'd been bringing Sandy Kay along with her to Hell. Sandy was a good companion as she, like her husband, D-Kay, didn't suffer fools gladly. Mullet, the "gentleman" he was, had offered to swing by Carol's house to make their transaction easier, but she refused outright. *I can't stand the dirty way he looks at me.*

Well, since movie night's not happening, what do I do with these tacos? She pondered, then had an idea and made a call. Satisfied, she put the food in a travel container and walked two houses down to the Chin's, where David met her at the door.

"Huh-huh-hi," said Carol, choking back a laugh. David had a sweat sock comically pulled over his head. "Hi, Carol," he said, self-consciously touching his skull. "I'm playing Sock Heads with Sunny. Thanks for bringing over dinner."

"You're welcome," she said, coming inside. Carol, who after numerous daycare swaps knew her way around the Chin's open floorplan, parked her container and an envelope on the granite-topped central island, then went to the family room where she'd heard giggling.

"Is that you, Sunny?" she asked. Out of view, Sunny giggled more, then popped his head up from behind a couch with a sock on his head, grinning like a goblin.

"Hello, Mrs. Pug!" declared the four-year-old. "We're playing Sock Heads. Wanna join? I can get one from the orphan box." By orphan box, Sunny meant the basket containing the Chin's unmatched socks.

"Maybe later, Sunny. How was your day?" She was genuinely curious—Gladys had picked Reesie up from David's, which meant Carol hadn't seen her daughter yet.

Sunny pointed to something large hanging from a lamp. "We made a dragon!" The six-foot-long creation had a green head with large black eyes, a pink snake-like tongue, and multicolored construction paper scales covering its body. David, great with kid projects, mentioned that even with his help, it took the children all morning to assemble. Carol smiled. Kiddie projects were the only time David was guaranteed to look excited.

Sunny then spouted off, "After the dragon we went outside, and I chased Reesie, and she chased me. But I was faster. Then we had lunch! Then I had to take a nap, but Reesie didn't." Sunny pouted. "She's a big girl. Too old for naps! Then it was story time, then Daddy took us to the grocery store."

"They ran around the backyard again before your mother picked Reesie up," David added.

While in the kitchen, Carol had put a check on the island—payment for David watching Reesie this week. Before Trev had self-destructed, childcare was based on barter. *I watch the kids today, you watch them tomorrow*. But when Carol went full-time and needed more daycare coverage, Angie insisted on payment. Setting the price was one of the rare squabbles Carol overheard the Chins having. She'd imagined Angie, who won most "fights," would win this one, too, but she hadn't. David insisted payment be set at a quarter of the going rate. Since then, Angie had been crisp toward Carol, and she couldn't blame her.

Given the Chin's own money troubles—a whopping mortgage on their Taj Mahal teardown and the business loan they'd taken out to start Angie's firm—she was amazed Angie had given in. And it wasn't just about the money—Angie clearly thought the deal was unfair to David, which it was. He now only had nights and weekends for his thesis. To Angie, David had explained, the thesis equaled a doctorate, which equaled a job, and fire ant control was big business—companies like Bayer CropScience and Monsanto were already making inquiries. It was, in Angie's eyes: *You're keeping my husband from paying off.* The fact that David was saving Angie close to ten grand a year in childcare was likely the only thing keeping her civil.

Sandy had once called David "an ugly puppy," and when David removed the sweat sock from his head, he looked it. The sock had hidden his receding hairline, but not his large ears or weak chin. *Weak Chin-chin,* a thoughtless jibe Trev used behind David's back. *Very mature, dear. Well, 'Chin-chin' watched your daughter for nine hours today, keeping her safe. What did you do, make license plates?*

In less than two months it'll be September, she continued thinking. *Reesie will be in first grade, childcare will be more manageable.* Though this was a great reason to look forward to the beginning of the school year, it also meant barely six weeks of summer separated her from explaining why her husband wouldn't be attending parent-teacher conferences.

Carol crouched next to Sunny as he stacked several red cardboard building bricks. "Why don't you two build something?" said David. "I'll warm up the tacos."

"Mac and cheese for me, please," said Sunny.

"You bet."

She helped the boy set up several walls, which Sunny took great delight in knocking down. As she did, she considered how plain David was compared to her husband. Trev was five-eleven, one-eighty, with a well-proportioned torso and soft, baby-brown hair she loved running her fingers through. Trevor also had a quirky, irresistible grin to go along with his good looks. "Christian Bale's brother," Sandy declared after meeting him. And so charming. Before marriage, girls flocked to him, but despite the current disaster which was his alcoholism, she believed Trevor loyal.

And anyway, you're locked away from temptation for the next eight months, aren't you? But this only reminded her of how much she missed him. Until two months ago, the sex was still good, and just as important, reliable. He wasn't as romantic anymore—no more goofy notes hidden in their bedroom—but he'd brought flowers home occasionally and still nuzzled her neck while she cooked. "God, I miss that," she said.

"Missed what?" asked David.

"Ah, nothing." She surreptitiously eyed him while stacking a new wall for Sunny to run through. What did Angie see in him physically? She was loathe to admit it, but Cindy was right—Angie needn't have "settled" for David. Angie was short, perhaps too much, but decently proportioned, with an endless supply of fashionable dresses and smart-looking pantsuits. *Don't forget the shoes.*

She imagined Angie presenting a case, the *click-click* of her heels keeping the court's attention. She didn't care for the image, but charitably thought, *For all your failings, Angie, at least you're not Estelle.* Estelle was chatty and false; Angie Chin was abrupt but at least genuine. They both treated their men poorly, but at least Phillipe was done with the bitch from Bethesda.

Phillipe . . . Trev was good-looking, confident, and charming. Phillipe, however, was *very* good-looking and *very* confident. Luckily for Trev, however, Phillipe wasn't quite as charming. *Or funny.* Otherwise, a decade ago when their post-college friend-pack sorted itself into couples, things might have turned out differently. *But when you have a love like Trev and I have,* she thought, *good love—physical, emotional—you're set.* But Trev wouldn't be home from Maryland Central for months, and of course she worried about him there. Not about him being abused or anything—Trev said that stuff was really exaggerated—but about whether he was brushing his teeth.

"These tacos are great, Carol," said David, eating one before pouring Sunny's hot macaroni noodles into a colander. "Thanks for bringing them over."

"Sure," said Carol. "Save some for Angie."

"Can't promise—she's in Atlanta for work. Be back tomorrow."

"Oh, okay," said Carol. "Well, I'll be on my way."

"Have you eaten?" David asked.

"Yes."

"Sorry you had to cancel your movie night. What were you guys gonna watch?"

"*Shakespeare in Love.*"

"Oh, I heard it was good," said David. "Oscar material."

"Do you wanna borrow it?" she asked. "I have it for three days."

"No, that's okay."

Carol, who was more upset about movie night's cancellation than she cared to admit, decided suddenly that she really wanted to watch the movie and didn't want to watch it alone. "Hey David, here's a thought. After you and Sunny eat, I could bring it over and we could watch it."

"Is it appropriate for kids?" he asked.

"Probably not."

"Well, Sunny goes down about 7:30," said David. "Can you come back in an hour?"

"Sure, sounds great," she said.

"Okay, see you then. Sunny, say bye-bye to Mrs. Pug, then come eat your mac and cheese."

Carol walked the short distance home, puttering around the house until 7:45, then grabbed the Blockbuster VHS tape and, on a whim, one of her bottles of wine, but then thought better of it. *Bringing wine into a man's house when his wife isn't home doesn't look good, even if it's just David.* It pained her some putting the bottle back—she really wanted a drink.

David let her in. "How's Sunny?" she asked.

"Good. He went down fast, all that running around."

"Here you go," said Carol, handing him the tape. "How were the rest of the tacos?"

"Delicious, thanks."

Carol realized he'd moved the VHS player into the kitchen, replacing the normal chairs with two comfortable ones from the living room. Looking a bit sheepish, David asked, "I hope you don't mind us watching it in here? Don't want to wake Sunny."

"Fantastic," Carol said, thinking it was good that he worried about appearances as well.

"I made some popcorn," David said, pointing to a heaping bowl of it. "Would you like a soda?"

"That sounds great," said Carol gratefully, though a little disappointed it wasn't wine.

They began watching the movie, which lived up to the hype. David didn't laugh much but occasionally talked back to the actors. His comments made Carol laugh, which she then felt guilty about. If Angie came home right now, what would she say? *Sorry for watching a rom-com with your husband while we thought you were out of town.* Well, she, meaning Angie, needn't worry. David was sweet, but David was no Trev. More importantly, Carol wasn't that kind of woman. *Still, best to make a quick exit as soon as the credits roll.*

Carol laughed loudly at a comical moment, but then the scene transitioned to an amorous encounter between the leads, Gwyneth Paltrow and Joseph Fiennes. *Will David be uncomfortable?* So far, the romantic shenanigans had been innocent, even fun, but it was obvious Paltrow and Fiennes were getting serious. Would David have something witty to say then? She didn't think Paltrow, who she considered a class actress, would get naked, but Carol was wrong. Embarrassed, she looked quickly at David, who stared straight ahead, obviously wishing the scene would end.

From the top of the stairs, Sunny quite unexpectedly said, "Daddy, what's wrong?"

"Nothing's wrong, Sunny," David said quickly, jumping up.

"I heard laughing," continued Sunny. "Is that Mommy?"

"No, Sunny," said Carol, watching David fumble for the remote. "It's me, Mrs. Pug. I was the one laughing. Sorry I woke you up."

A sleepy Sunny entered the kitchen just as David managed to pause it mid-frame, Paltrow's naked torso frozen in Fiennes's embrace. Sunny looked at the screen briefly, mumbled the word "kissing," then turned toward the mostly empty popcorn bowl.

"Mrs. Pug didn't have popcorn at her house tonight," David explained, "so I made her some."

This made sense to Sunny, but he wanted clarification. "Where's Reesie?"

"Reesie's with her grandma tonight," said Carol. "A sleepover. Her grandma will be dropping her home tomorrow." Carol, flushed at having to explain herself to a four-year-old, added, "I was just leaving." She stood, taking the soda glasses and the popcorn bowl to the sink, rinsing them quickly. Meanwhile, David, who still couldn't turn the VHS off with the remote, resorted to standing in front of the TV to block it from view.

Tired as Sunny was, the boy sensed opportunity. "Daddy, can you read me another story?"

"Sure, Sunny," said David. "Head upstairs. I'll come up and read to you. Say goodnight to Mrs. Pug."

"Goodnight, Mrs. Pug." Sunny leaned around his father, looking again at the frozen lovers. "Kissing," he repeated, then trundled out of the room. David realized he could manually turn off the VHS and did so. "I . . . think I'll go read to him now," he said.

"Yeah, that sounds good," said Carol. "We can finish watching this . . . another time?"

"No thanks," said David, ejecting the tape, handing it to her. "I think I've seen enough."

"Oh, okay," she said. "I hope I didn't embarrass you."

"No, you didn't."

"You sure?" she asked. It was quite apparent that she had.

"No, it's fine. Goodnight, Carol."

"Goodnight, David."

Carol returned home about 9:00. Her long week, as well as the botched evening with David, had her on the ropes. *I really want a drink.* This was unusual. She often had two or three glasses with the girls on movie night but rarely drank alone.

She opened a bottle of wine. *It's not like I'm gonna swig straight from it. Who would do that?* Trev immediately came to mind. She understood intellectually that he had some sort of "disease," but she'd crawl through broken glass if that's what it took to save her family. Why wouldn't Trev do the same? Before blowing his court date, her husband had, with Mr. Arkin's help, stopped drinking. *So, lovie, why couldn't you stay stopped?* Having no answer, she turned the movie on and snuggled with Kitty Batman and a glass of wine.

As she got ready for bed that night, she thought about how sexy the two movie stars had looked and how much she missed her husband. "Mandatory sex," she explained to Kitty Batman, smiling. The Pugs were quite proud of their track record—in eight years of marriage, they'd not gone longer than a week without intercourse. When Thursday rolled around, if they weren't "current," they made sure to keep the streak alive, a joyful act that also ended many arguments. It was understood: be home Thursday nights, don't break the streak.

Well, Trev, you broke it good.

Kitty Batman hopped on the bed. As she tried to sleep, she wondered what David and Angie's sex life was like. How often did they do it? Were they *still* doing it? If not, that was sad. Surely it must have been good for them, in the beginning, anyway. *Opposites attract, right?* And they were opposites: David, shy, and Angie being what her mom called a fast girl.

I'm lucky, thought Carol. *Trev and I aren't opposites. I'm outgoing, he's outgoing. I'm funny, he's really funny. I'm good-looking, or at least good-looking enough, and he's better-looking now than when I married him.* Contemplating Trev made her feel frisky, reminding her of the particularly good sex they'd had the night before Trev left her standing in the rain in front of Hell. "Well, Kitty," she told the cat, "at least there's you."

She had multiple erotic dreams that night, her lover morphing back and forth between Trevor and Joseph Fiennes. The reveries weren't enjoyable, however. In every dream, Angie and Sunny watched on like judges.

Chapter 51: Visitor's Hour

Sunday, 11 July 1999
Sykesville, MD

OTHER THAN CAROL, who visited weekly, it was Cisco Arkin who saw Trevor at Maryland Correctional the most. He visited the second weekend of the month, continuing to work the program of AA with him, giving Carol every fourth Sunday off. July 11 was that second Sunday. Cisco entered the visitor's lot, parking as far from the entrance as he could. He did this to stretch his legs and work on the twenty-five extra pounds he carried. *Not that walking two hundred more feet's gonna make a difference.*

He went through the main entrance, signed in, then handed over his keys. Arkin, a prison-visit veteran, knew to leave everything else in his truck. An unfamiliar corrections officer wanded him, taking an unnecessarily long time to do so. His companion guard, a man Cisco knew, looked at Arkin charitably. *Yeah, I know. He's new.*

Arkin arrived at the visitor's room, a large space with plastic chairs and bolted-down tables. Fifteen minutes later, a buzzer sounded. A door opened, and inmates entered single file. Trevor came toward Cisco, eyes guarded. He had his institutional stare down now—*I'm looking around you, not at you.* They didn't embrace or shake hands; they weren't supposed to. Pug sat down quickly.

"Hello, Trevor. How are you?"

"Good, Jefe," said Trevor.

"You eating? You look a little thin."

"I am," Trevor said. "Grub's a step up from jail food."

"Sleeping okay?"

"Yeah. Getting along with my cellie. And no problems with the COs."

"Did Carol visit last week?" asked Cisco.

"Yeah, and she brought Reesie. She's a trooper. They both are."

Trevor had said this with conviction, but Cisco knew Pug was worried. Arkin had prior prison experience and understood the effects of correctional officers, bells, and the *tau-ack-ack-ack* of automated gates. The loss of one's freedom, even in a low-security facility meant for non-violent offenders, could still grind a man down. Visits meant everything. "Carol says even without my side gig money, she's got the Old Line payments covered. All the interest, even some principal. She's amazing."

"She is," agreed Cisco. Carol had confided to Arkin that she was no longer able to pay down the principal, but there was no upside to informing her husband of this.

"She told me to stay safe and come home," Trevor said. "Says I'm missed."

"She's right on all counts."

"Oh, and of course, get sober again," Trevor continued. "And stay that way." Trevor knew Carol had faith in Cisco—if he did everything the man told him to, all would eventually be well. But anxiety was a rapacious monkey. All evidence to the contrary, was Carol just going through the motions?

"Okay," said Cisco. "Let's get started."

From memory, they recited the Serenity and Third Step prayers together. "Okay, kid. Who's next on your list?"

"Frank Deguzman, my boss," said Trevor. "Ex-boss, I mean."

For Cisco, reviewing an Eighth Step list (an inventory of all people an alcoholic had harmed) was harder in prison. COs discouraged list-making and forbade the transfer of anything between visitors and inmates. Trevor seemed okay with this, telling him he wanted no records anyway, so memorization, an ability that had returned after two months off the sauce, was fine. Though the first few weeks at MC had overwhelmed him, he was used to it now, and the good news was he didn't want a drink. If he had, he could get it—many of the prisoners worked outside jobs and alcohol was so regularly smuggled in that no one bothered with raisin jack. But Trevor truly had no interest anymore. Prison had given him the "gift of desperation," the push that made him decide to go all in.

He also didn't want to be in Maryland Correctional a minute longer than needed, therefore a clean behavioral record was paramount. MC might be a minimum security facility, one you could just walk away from if you wanted to, but no one did. If you got caught, like a hundred out of a hundred guys did, you were sent immediately to Jessup, where, as the guys joked, they took prison seriously. The way to leave MC was the front door.

So Trevor had committed his list to memory, an inventory including family, friends, acquaintances, colleagues, even a kid from grade school. Creating an Eighth Step "harm" list was straightforward (nothing in AA was complicated): list the people you had harmed, drunk or sober. Cisco had already worked Trevor through the humility and willingness steps, Six and Seven, but Step Eight was the vital step before the Hollywood step, Step Nine, the actual making of face-to-face amends, which would need to wait until Trevor was released. Through phone calls and Sunday visits, the two of them had already reviewed most of Trevor's list, covering twenty-five people and two institutions. Arkin's role was to help Trevor sort through his "catalog," weeding out what didn't belong from what did.

"Deguzman owns that computer company, right?" asked Cisco.

"Yep. 'Sim Systems 2000: Tomorrow's software today.' A great job I drank myself out of."

"True," agreed Cisco without judgment. "What were the specific harms to Frank? Did you take money?"

"No."

"Did you steal equipment?"

"No."

"Not show up for work?"

"I was late sometimes," Trevor admitted. "But hungover or not, I always showed up."

"Late's late," said Cisco. "If you had to quantify the hours you missed, how would you do that?"

"I'm not sure," said Trevor. "Coders are unconventional to begin with: weird hours, weird setups. We got one guy that works from . . . well, we don't know where he works from. In six years, we've never seen him, not once. HR doesn't even have a picture of him. Is that even legal?"

"I have no idea," answered Cisco. "Let's focus on time lost."

They discussed early departures, long lunches, and drinking in the parking lot. After some back and forth, Trevor landed on one full day lost a week over two years. Based on Trevor's past salary, this totaled thirty-two thousand dollars. "Jesus, Jefe, I don't have that kind of money!" he declared. "If I did, I'd pay off Old Line, not Frank."

"If you had thirty-two thousand dollars," said Cisco, "it wouldn't be your money. It would be *Frank's* money. Understand the difference?"

"Yeah, I guess," said Trevor. "Do I need to tell Frank?"

"At this point, that's the last thing you should do. Stay sober, and in time you can figure out a payment plan. Just add Frank to your prayer list." Cisco didn't have to elaborate. Trevor was to pray on Frank's behalf, wishing for him the things Trevor wanted for himself—things like freedom, which probably wasn't in short supply at the Deguzman household, good health, and happiness, and that elusive serenity AAs kept talking about.

"Okay," said Trevor. "Will do."

Next was one of Trevor's old college flames, Suzanne. He had gotten Suzanne pregnant, then stopped seeing her, leaving her to agonize over what to do. She'd eventually chosen abortion. Trevor had never discussed this with anyone before Cisco. Admitting it was a relief, but it was also shameful, and his eyes welled up as he shared. Cisco took the confession in stride. "Okay, you're not the first man to do that. This Suzanne, she's got her own life now, settled down?"

"Yeah, husband, kids," Trevor said, wiping his eyes. "Heard she's happy."

"Good news, kid. This one's a great opportunity to do your first amend."

"What can I do from in here?"

"Easy. Starting now, stay totally out of her life. Never darken her door again."

"But I was *really* shitty to her, Jefe. Doesn't she deserve an apology?"

"Amends aren't about apologizing, Trevor. Apologies mean nothing. I apologized to my wife every day for thirteen years, meant it every time, but until I finally acted, all the 'sorrys' just made her bitter. We make amends *if and only if* doing so won't hurt the person. Or others. Say you cheated on your wife—"

"I swear I haven't," insisted Trevor.

"But supposing you did, and Carol didn't know. Do you think waltzing into the kitchen one morning to apologize for something she never saw coming is a good idea?"

"Heck no," said Trevor.

"The truth is, Suzanne, the one you impregnated, then abandoned—"

Impregnated? Abandoned? "You make it sound so bad."

"The way you handled it *was* bad," said Cisco, his tone neutral, "but that's what alcoholics do. Know your motives, Trevor. What's the real reason you want to dredge up your past with Suzanne? Is it about making amends, or do you just want a pat on the back? How many years has it been?"

"Seventeen."

"After seventeen years, after getting married to that delightful woman, Carol, the love of your life—your words, not mine—after all this time, it's whether Suzanne still wants you, that's really what you want to know, isn't it?"

Trevor stared, amazed at how powerful his sponsor's moral X-ray vision was. Deep down, perhaps not even that deep, this had been exactly what Trevor wanted. "But Jefe, you said I had to make amends so my side of the street would be clean. So if I see Suzanne coming down the sidewalk, I won't have to duck down an alley, remember?"

"Should that unlikely scenario occur, Trevor, you have my permission to hide. For now, it's enough that you, me, and most importantly, your higher power, know that you no longer impregnate women and then abandon them."

"Jesus, Jefe, please stop saying 'impregnate.'" Trevor was practically squirming at this point.

"Time's up," a corrections officer informed the room. "Prisoners stay seated. Visitors move to the exit."

Cisco stood, taking in Trevor's long face. "Why so despondent, champ?"

"Well, Jefe, I can't make amends to my old boss 'cause I don't have any money. I have to wait to make amends to my family and everyone else 'cause I'm in jail. Not much I can do now, is there?"

"Pray. Prayer is something you can do at any time. Pray for Frank. Pray for Suzanne. Pray for all of them. Pray for them what you want for yourself. You know the drill."

With that, Arkin left.

Chapter 52: The Curse Count Update

Monday, 12 July 1999
Wheaton, MD

THE NEXT ARREST occurred earlier that Saturday.

Original Ken had taken his nephews to a neighborhood park to burn off steam and give Sylvia a rest. His new friend, Tori Bora, had gone with him. The remaining guys had yet to reach consensus on Tori. Some believed that Original had finally accepted the terms of his personal jinx, throwing the towel in on straight women by "dating" an obvious lesbian. Tori certainly looked the part, but Spicotti wasn't so sure. Based on chemistry alone, there was something going on. Yes, they looked awkward together, almost as if they were afraid of each other, but they seemed to really enjoy each other's company. If there was genuine attraction on Ken's part, Loo couldn't blame him: straight or not, Tori's intelligence, pert smile, and obnoxious snort-laugh were icing on what he thought was a good-looking cake.

Bravo, Ken.

At the park, the pair had been minding the boys as they ran around a busy playground. With two pairs of eyes, minding should have been easy, but Gee and Gree were called hellions for a reason. Out of sight for just a second, Gregory got into it with another kid, a larger one. George immediately joined. Ken, Tori, and the larger kid's father stepped in quickly, separating the warring parties, but during the melee, a fourth child was accidentally shoved, landing unceremoniously on his keister and began wailing.

Tori handed Gee off to Ken to help the boy. She put him back on his feet, brushed off mulch, and assured him he was okay, which, other than general shock, he was. Forgetting their own boys' fight, Ken and the other father echoed assurances as well, and the child began coming around.

Suddenly, Keister's father arrived, taking it all in. Immediately, he yanked the boy away from Tori, yelling, "Get your hands off my son!" He read everyone the riot act, turning an awkward situation into a stressful one. Mr. Keister's behavior, though certainly not commensurate with the offense, could have been forgiven if he'd then simply stormed off with his son. But instead, he bellied up to Tori, towering over her, shouting, "Your brats, lady," pointing toward the hellions who Ken held in his arms, "attacked my son! Explain!"

Tori stood motionless, too frightened to speak. Keister put a fat finger in her face: "Hey! I'm talking to you! Are you retarded?" Still nothing from Tori. He poked her chest with the same furious finger, enunciating pointedly, "Are. You. Retarded?"

At that, Original released his nephews and tackled the man. Keister, surprised, went down hard. His screams attracted a local Park and Rec police officer, but not in time to avoid a solid punch from Ken.

When she arrived, Keister shouted at her, *"I demand you arrest this asshole!"* The officer spent a minute talking Keister down, then canvassed the playground witnesses. By now, Keister Junior wasn't crying just from pure shock. After calling it in on her shoulder mic, she politely arrested Original for disorderly conduct. He was angry about it but didn't resist.

"Disorderly conduct?" shouted Keister. "That's a goddamn misdemeanor, a complete miscarriage of justice!" With Keister's renewed shouting, his son began crying again.

"Sir," said the officer coolly, "I can make two arrests. You want that?"

Keister grumbled but said no.

Original enjoyed Keister's embarrassment but not the ride to the station. He later plead guilty to the misdemeanor, paid court costs, and spent his next six Saturdays in anger management class.

The Monday evening after Cisco Arkin visited Trevor in prison, Luigi Spicotti talked with D-Kay on the phone. He could hear the sounds of a computer game on Darius's end.

"I don't know, Tooth," said Loo. "Given Henry's death, enthusiasm for next Saturday's EMBC meeting's kinda tanked."

"First, curses aren't real," D-Kay said. "Second, we took May off because Splash died, then another month off for 'mourning.' That was fine, but it's July now, time to get back in the saddle. It's what he would have wanted."

Not sure about that, Loo thought. He originally wanted to talk to Trevor about the state of the club, but his best friend was busy paying his debt to society, so D-Kay, the club's amusing, attention-seeking Babble King was his second choice. Their discussion so far hadn't been amusing, however.

"And while we're on the subject," said Darius, "what are the numbers?"

Loo hadn't known they'd transitioned to discussing the curse, but apparently they had—D-Kay could be like that.

The arrest count was now six. The old total of four—Trevor (DUI), Loo (deer-slaying), Henry (second-degree murder), D-Kay (assault)—had increased after Original's park-date debacle, plus Walter "Rey" Perkins, who, according to his new best friend, Gary, had been arrested for some sort of serious traffic offense weeks ago. New Guy said it was being worked out, whatever that meant. It wasn't important, however—no one expected to see Rey again.

"Six arrests since that Prophet dude cursed us," Loo said. "Out of eight." Nothing but computer game noise on the other end of the phone. "Hey, D-Kay, did you hear me?"

"Yeah," he said slowly. "Sorry, these basilisk bastards are really hard to kill."

"That's just how the higher levels of Doom are," said Loo, commiserating.

"Anybody else get a pink slip?" asked Darius.

"Yes."

"Who?" D-Kay knew about the original three: Sim 2K had let Trevor go, Loo had lost (then regained) his job, and Henry (may he rest in peace) had needed to close his studio for weeks after his murder charge.

"*The Post* laid Original off," Loo told him.

"You're kidding me," said Darius. Arrested *and* he lost his job? Jesus. Know anything more?"

Loo said there wasn't much else. Ken had been out of a job for a few weeks but had only told him yesterday.

"Well, you're on a roll, dude. Keep going," said D-Kay.

"Tanked relationships?" asked Loo. "Still hard to believe that Phillipe and Estelle are done. Thought that four-hundred-person wedding was as good as held."

A series of angry-sounding computer noises on D-Kay's end. "Die, damn you, die!" Darius yelled. Finally having subdued his digital prey, he asked, "Anyone else?"

Loo didn't think so, mentioning how odd—but also cool—Ken and Tori's hooking up was. For the other relationships, Cindy had said that Heather, Gary's wife, seemed a little cold to Gary at Henry's funeral, but that could mean anything. Cindy was adamant that Carol was a solid citizen of Stand-by-your-man-istan, however.

"So just the one relationship going south—Phillipe—which admittedly, no one saw coming, and . . . the death." Here D-Kay recalled the large crowd that had attended Haru Takahashi's funeral, including the remaining book club members and their families.

"One death only," Darius prompted, sounding worried. "Right, Loo?"

"Yes, sorry," he said. "Just Henry."

One dead, thought D-Kay, *which is of course one too many, and creepy as hell.* Though he still didn't believe in it, D-Kay no longer considered the curse humorous. He shut down his game of Doom, giving its hero, Doom Guy, the rest of the night off.

"So eight months in and that's what, 6, 4, 1, and 1 for the curse?" he asked.

"Yeah, in ballpark-speak, that's 0.750, 0.500, 0.125, and 0.125," responded Loo. "'Give that fan a contract.' So you can see why no one wants to meet again, at least right now."

"So you think we should stop meeting because of some 'curse?'" D-Kay asked.

This was exactly what Loo was thinking. "No, just out of respect for—"

"What are you saying?" declared D-Kay. "Look, Splash was my best friend, but we've already mourned him, okay? We need to stop. I think you think Prophet's ghost is haunting us. That's bullshit. If you think that's really happening, why don't we all head to Shorties and sacrifice something on the bar, maybe a chicken or a yak, or, hey, how about a virgin?"

"I'm not saying that—"

"Then what *are* you saying, Loo? If we cancel the meeting, we make this curse real. Screw that noise!"

Eventually, Loo agreed to schedule the next meeting.

Chapter 53: Beer Can Beach

Friday, 30 July 1999
Panama City, FL

THE PANAMA CITY ATF office was housed in an old building called the Isaiah Montrose Center. Working there was normally far from glamorous, but today, when it was 93 in the shade and about a thousand percent humidity, its broken AC made it Sweat Hell. Earlier, the entire task force—ATF, DEA, ICE, the U.S. Marshals, a Coast Guard liaison, a Colombian government consul, and the ever-mysterious Gary Graft—had moved to another building. The shortwave set-up, however, couldn't be moved, so ATF agents Rose Feldman and Gina Guijarro, plus Rey Perkins, remained, perspiring madly.

Feldman fished two Cokes from a bucket of slushy ice water—one for her and one for her co-agent, Guijarro. In doing so, Feldman let her sleeve get wet, relishing the chill.

"You want a Coke, Perkins?" she asked.

"No thanks," Rey replied. "Any waters left?"

"All gone. But there's a fountain down the hall," she said. "Left, then left again."

Rey followed Feldman's directions, locating a tired-looking fountain. The water tasted alkaline but was cool enough. He drank for a long time, then returned to the radio room, a sixteen-by-twenty space with desks, filing cabinets, several "wanted" flyers, Feldman's computer, three overworked fans, and a *Hang in There, Baby!* cat poster. Plus the drink bucket. Agent Gina Guijarro, the team's official interpreter, sat in front of the shortwave solving today's *Panama City News Herald* crossword. Feldman was at her computer, and Rey sat at a desk playing Solitaire with worn cards. The room's windows were open but there was no breeze to let in, only oppressive humidity, so despite the fans, Rey's shirt, Rose's blouse, and Gina's sleeveless dress stuck to their respective skins. It was 3 p.m.

"How's the water?" Feldman asked, eyes glued to her screen.

"Fantastic," said Rey. "Next trip I'm bringing tanning butter and a beach towel."

"Yep," she said, scribbling something on a notepad. It was unclear to him whether she got the joke.

The trio had been communicating with the terrorists since Sunday. Tonight would be the payoff: the Colombians' boat, the *Pollo de Mar* (*The Sea Chicken*), would arrive carrying fanatics, weapons, and drugs. Guijarro, the task force's faux onshore "coyote," had arranged for the targets—the FARC militants, including a mid-level leader named Ramirez, his bodyguard, and Tatiana and Sebastian Ruiz, plus two dozen illegals and their Mexican coyote—to land on a remote portion of coastline ten miles outside Panama City. The area, popular with ATV-riding locals during the day and drug runners at night, was called Beer Can Beach. The heavy lifting, meaning the terrorists' capture, would be managed by the marshals. ICE would scoop up the illegals, ATF would grab the weapons, and DEA the drugs.

Since receiving word that the terrorists were on the move, the task force had spent the last five days rubbing shoulders. This generated camaraderie, but Rey held no illusions as to just how beholden he was to Agent Feldman and New Guy Graft. Each had their role—Agent Feldman was the "bad cop," her stick being Rey's gun-running charge. Her signature would either damn him or set him free. Gary was the "good cop," the cavalry arriving just in time to save Rey from prison. It had been Gary's idea for Rey to cooperate with the ATF. Gary had also delivered the guns to the hunting club so Rey wouldn't get crosswise with Sammy. In short, he was being a textbook pal. This had been Rey's assessment early on, but after five days in Florida, he wasn't so sure. At least Feldman was a member of an official if underrated federal agency. Gary, aka Dr. Graft, on the other hand was some government ghost—no one on the task force knew who he really worked for.

"Feldman," said Rey. (Having spent days together, Feldman no longer insisted on being called *Agent* Feldman.)

"Yep," she replied distractedly.

"You're Jewish, aren't you?"

"Yes, I am, Perkins. That bother you?"

"Well, it depends," said Rey. "Are you part of the worldwide Jewish conspiracy?"

"No," said Feldman.

"Then it doesn't bother me," said Rey. "But why aren't you?"

"Perkins," she said, "my job leaves little time to also secretly run the world. And I already have a hobby—line dancing. It's more difficult than it looks."

Line dancing, thought Rey. *Uh huh.*

Feldman continued staring at her screen as Rey disinterestedly flipped through the cards. Sweaty he was, but bored he wasn't. In Feldman, Rey had found a sort of soulmate, a brilliant cynic with sarcasm as sharp as his. *Agent*

Feldman, he thought, *I am in love with your brain. But that's it.* Feldman was easily pushing fifty, a squat woman whose face had last looked youthful during the Bicentennial. Rey understood that when it came to looks, God doled out unevenly. Not everyone's beauty burned brightly or for long, and in Rose Feldman's case, it was neither.

For her part, despite his racist dickheadedness, Feldman found Rey surprisingly charming. And a looker. In an end-of-the-world scenario, climbing the tall, Morrisey-clone would not be out of the question, but what she enjoyed—guilt-free—was his acerbic wit and stupid ideas. It was fun fencing with the young-ish tyrant, bursting his bigoted bubbles. But she fenced carefully, realizing she was only one of a handful of people with any idea of how badly the boy's Exxon "vacation" twenty-two years ago had damaged him, and how it developed within him a virulent hatred of his captors, one now encompassing anyone south of the border. This was as understandable as it was tragic. Accordingly, Rose never put more into her serve than was necessary because Perkins' hatred was personal. Yes, he could regurgitate Miles Jacobson's anti-immigrant screeds, but the truth was Rey felt little antipathy toward *non*-South American immigrants, even the dark-skinned. To him, skin color wasn't nearly as important as where the skin came from.

Plus there were subtleties. Rey hated South Americans, but not their language, or at least not their mother tongue, Spanish, in which he was very fluent. He hated Colombian culture but could explain it in detail. He had studied his enemy—South Americans—not to destroy them, which was impossible, but to keep them at bay. For Walter Perkins, a specialized xenophobe, exclusion was good enough. *And Perkins,* Feldman thought, *you're otherwise not trying very hard.* His antisemitic, anti-Black jibes may have been enough to convince Agent Gina Guijarro that he was the second coming of a better-looking Himmler—but unless Rey was railing against the Colombians themselves, Feldman knew Rey's heart wasn't in it.

And you've also earned some stripes, Perkins, she thought. From day one, Agent Guijarro struggled to be a believable "coyote"—in 1999, female coyotes were rare. She was fluent, yes, but in the wrong dialect. The confidence to pull off being a no-nonsense *mujer sin tontarias* (a woman to be taken seriously) depended not only on the timbre of her voice but her word choice, and here Rey's FARC nitty-gritty proved invaluable. He fed Gina everything from the perils of maintaining weapons in a tropical environment to the tastiest jungle rodents for spicing up bland meals. He played the fine line between his history with the Ruizes and present circumstances well. It helped that he never spoke directly to Tatiana, who doggedly controlled the radio despite multiple requests by Agent Guijarro to speak directly to Sebastian or their leader, Ramirez. In his abrasive way, Rey counseled patience: "Guys, don't be stupid. Tatiana's a lot smarter than her hothead brother. She's the one we want to talk to." Besides, it was obvious that whenever Tatiana spoke, Sebastian or Ramirez were nearby because she made no decision without consulting them.

Okay," said Gina, motioning to Rey and Feldman. "They're checking in again. Wally, grab your headphones."

Rey didn't care for being called Wally, but one picked one's battles, especially when one was trying to avoid prison. The coyote communication went satisfactorily. There was a moment of touch-and-go where Guijarro slipped on some local lingo, but between Feldman's strong hand on the conversational tiller and Rey's whispered corrections, nothing blew up.

The ne'er-do-wells would be landing sometime after 11:00 that night; Coast Guard triangulation confirmed this. The beach landfall point was technically part of a national wildlife refuge meant for migrating birds and pregnant sea turtles. Most visitors didn't respect this, however, leaving all manner of trash behind, but especially empty cans, hence the name.

Though he tried not to let on, all the "mission" talk was thrilling Rey. He was fulfilling an adolescent dream: being a part of some nerve center where anxious superiors smoked, drank coffee, and sweated into hats. The sweating, of course, needn't be imagined. *Still, this is cool,* thought Rey, *almost cool enough to forget the FARC's on its way to kill me.*

Though Agent Feldman knew the danger risk was nil, she understood near-Morrisey's worry. His life was once in peril for 87 days straight—no one else on the task force had anything remotely like that on their resume.

The operation at Beer Can Beach went smoothly. The humans and the drugs had been shuttled through the surf on a noisy Zodiac in two trips. Once everyone landed—about thirty total, including the terrorists—the marshals pounced. Halogens from hidden vehicles bathed the beach with light, stunning the interlopers and thousands of sand crabs. The coyote high-tailed it back to the boat in the Zodiac, but soon *The Sea Chicken* found itself outlined by the harsh spotlight of a Coast Guard cutter. The coyote, wanted for charges in Miami, was detained, as were all the exhausted and now penniless refugees. Thirty keys of coke were recovered.

The weapons were the disappointing part of the haul. Though the coyote carried a pistol and the captain kept an automatic rifle in a cabinet, none of the FARC members wielded anything more menacing than fixed-handled knives. No gun cache, no explosives. Feldman's after-action report would be a dud.

Everyone was taken to the Isaiah Montrose Center for processing, which at that time of night was at least somewhat cooler. Rey stayed out of the way, trying not to look as nervous as he felt. Several people, including Graft, Feldman, and Guijarro had been in a room with the terrorists for an hour already. Rey hadn't laid eyes on them, and didn't want to, but was told to stick around. At 2 a.m., Gina emerged. "Well, Wally," she said, "time to reunite with the big, bad Sebastian Ruiz. This way."

What the hell? thought Rey. "I don't need to see that lunatic."

"Don't you want positive proof that it's him, Wally?" Guijarro asked, enjoying his discomfort.

"I'll take the ATF's word for it."

"It's actually the marshals' word, but that's neither here nor there. We need you for a positive ID." She held the door open for him the same moment that Gary and Feldman emerged through it. "C'mon, Wally," said Guijarro. "He's in here."

"And he can fucking *stay* in there," Rey blurted. "I don't ever wanna see him again. I fulfilled my part of the bargain, Guijarro. This is unnecessary."

"C'mon, Wally, Tatiana's in there too," said Agent Guijarro. "Don't you want to see your lady love?"

Maybe, but not if El Camarada was with her. "Is Sebastian at least restrained?"

"No," said Guijarro, looking at Graft and Feldman as if all three were in on some joke.

"Well, is there at least a *guard?*"

"Don't worry, Wally," Guijarro said, patting her service weapon, "I'll protect you."

At this, Feldman laughed. Even the serious Graft chuckled. As scared as Rey was, all he could think was *This isn't the best use of my tax dollars.* "Can't I just look through a one-way mirror or something?"

"One-way mirror?" asked Feldman. "Perkins, we're lucky the bathrooms in this building have *regular* mirrors. And Agent Guijarro's right. I can guarantee you Sebastian Ruiz won't lay a finger on you. Come on, let's go."

"How can you guarantee that?" asked Rey, who'd begun shaking. "You bozos never *once* had your rights, let alone your lives threatened. Not once." His twenty-two-year-old terror had returned, paralyzing him.

Feldman realized how truly horrified Walter was and stopped teasing. "Seriously, Rey, don't worry," she said. "Sebastian Ruiz can't hurt you. He can't hurt anyone."

"H-how can you be sure?" Rey demanded, his voice breaking.

"I'll show you," said Agent Feldman, putting a friendly but firm hand on his shoulder, directing him through the interrogation room door. Despite the late hour and two oscillating fans, the room was still uncomfortably warm. Two Colombian men, Ramirez and his bodyguard, sat at a table, along with one woman. All three were handcuffed. In a fourth chair sat an unrestrained blotchy-faced child. Rey wasn't great at judging children's ages but put him somewhere around ten. The kid anxiously held one of the woman's cuffed hands. A solid wall of meat (three marshals) stood guard, and a woman, a rep from the Florida Department of Children and Families with a name badge that read Mrs. Octavio, stood behind the boy.

"Well, Wally," Guijarro mocked, pointing toward the boy, "here's your nemesis, Sebastian Ruiz." The boy moved closer to the cuffed woman, obviously his mother.

"Okay, Agent, you've had your fun," said Feldman. "Now put a lid on it."

The handcuffed woman's attention turned to Rey. After a moment, she exclaimed, "Rafa!"

"Tatiana?" asked Rey.

"Sí, sí! Que bueno verte!"

"Good to see you too," Rey said automatically, then remembered to switch to Spanish. *"No comprendo. Quién es?"*

"Este es mi hijo."

"He's your son?" Rey asked. To Feldman: "I don't understand. Where's Sebastian?"

It was Gary Graft who answered. "The boy's Tatiana's son. His name *is* Sebastian."

"Where's *my* Sebastian?" asked Rey.

"That's the good news," said Feldman. "She swears her brother's dead. In any case, he's certainly not here. Agent Guijarro's gotten as much as we can, but Dr. Graft thought you should try."

"You want *my* help?" Rey asked.

"Yes," said Feldman.

Rey considered awhile. Finally, "Okay, but I got a condition. Agent Guijarro? Get the fuck out." Feldman nodded at Gina, who smiled smugly as she left. Two of the three marshals escorted Ramirez and his bodyguard out. Rey sat down at the table opposite Tatiana.

"So, you're sure she's Tatiana Ruiz?" asked Feldman.

"I'm certain," Rey said, taking her in. Tatiana had aged according to her circumstances, a thirty-five-year-old peasant-born mother living three-quarters of her life in the jungle. In place of a once hauntingly gorgeous girl was now a woman with grey streaks and a collection of what Rey's mother called laugh lines.

Oh my God, how strange is that, thought Rey. Surely Tatiana's life hadn't given her much to laugh about. She was more fleshed out, and bigger through the hips now as well, but given how thin she'd been as a teenager, this didn't look bad. Also, her mesmerizing eyes hadn't aged, and her face still held a trace of that 1977 smugness.

"Rafa, I come to America. I no lie." She paused, adding, *"Eres tan alto."*

"What did she say?" the remaining marshal asked. "And what does *Rafa* mean?"

Before Rey could answer, Gary responded: "She said 'You're so tall.' And 'Rafa' is short for giraffe."

Jesus H, Gary, thought Rey. *You speak Spanish too?* He then asked Tatiana, *"Dónde está* Sebastian?"

"Sebastian?" she replied, confused.

"Sí, Sebastian, *el Camarada!"* Rey said suddenly, startling her. The boy began crying.

"El Camarada esta muerto," Tatiana answered, no longer looking smug.

Rey leaned in toward her, insisting, "He can't be dead. You said you were *bringing him* to America. So where is he?" He repeated himself in Spanish.

"Relax there, killer," said Gary, putting a hand on his shoulder.

Rey shrugged it off, yelling, "Answer me, Tatiana! *Respóndeme!"*

Gary grabbed his shoulder again, this time tightly. "I said relax."

"Seriously, Rey, calm down," said Agent Feldman. "According to Tatiana, her brother Sebastian—El Camarada—died in '77 shortly after you were freed. Tatiana's the only surviving Ruiz. This boy's her son, also named Sebastian. She doesn't know who the father is."

The boy continued crying, and Mrs. Octavio leaned over his shoulder to talk soothingly to him.

Once Rey calmed down, Tatiana gave him more details. El Conde's paramilitary goons had caught up with the fleeing Ruizes and remaining FARC soldiers, killing almost everyone. She escaped death by hiding in an animal burrow for several hours, eventually making it back to the Clack just over the border in Venezuela. To survive there, she became a concubine to one of the Venezuelan camp agents, laying low for several months before returning to rebel-held FARC territory. News of her brother's death hadn't reached the FARC, so seeing opportunity, Tatiana kept quiet, feeding the rumor that El Camarada had survived. She was a concubine for other insurgents over the next ten years, bearing two stillborn children, then young Sebastian.

Tatiana remembered much more.

Being a guerilla with a child meant making tough choices. The officers, particularly the senior ones, wanted younger women, and Tatiana was getting older. She worried about her son's prospects as well. Was there any other future for him besides shouldering an AK-47 once he was big enough to hold one? Tatiana attached herself to an older officer named Ramirez, serving as his cook and maid. Ramirez kept a second, younger woman to sleep with, fathering two children with her. It wasn't a match made in heaven, but the three adults and three children managed.

As useful as Camarada Sebastian Ruiz's reputation was to the FARC, he was only the equivalent of a junior lieutenant in a long-running war. As time went on, his legend waned, but when a foreign press agent interviewed Mono Jojoy, the FARC eastern commander, Tatiana caught a break. As a past favorite of Jojoy's who also spoke some English, Tatiana was interviewed, boasting of her brother's exploits, being vague about his whereabouts. Her side story rekindled Bogota's interest in El Camarada. Meanwhile, her patron Ramirez was accused of stealing money by the FARC. Being thoroughly guilty of this, he'd fled with his brood to Venezuela, where he'd been quietly squirreling money away in the small town of Los Mochos. At Tatiana's urging, Ramirez used his loot to secure passage to Cuba. Rey later learned that Ramirez's Cuban communications had been intercepted by American counter-drug intelligence, starting off the whole operation.

El Camarada's star may have faded within the ranks of the FARC, but he'd never been forgotten by the Colombian Government. Chatter about "Sebastian" having successfully flown the coop with help from Colombia's mistrusted neighbor, Venezuela, didn't sit well with Bogota. As far as the U.S. went, no one cared too much about one FARC officer (Ramirez) and one thug (Sebastian) making their way to Cuba, but their potentially coming to America was a different story. After a month's comfortable stay in Havana, Tatiana's wish was granted. Fidel Castro's government green-lighted (illegal) emigration to the U.S., as it would surely panic the Americans.

It would be a three-stop trip. *The Sea Chicken* would first deliver arms to Haiti in exchange for hard currency. (ATF had misinterpreted this, believing the arms would be smuggled directly to the United States.) Then the boat would make the cross-gulf journey to the Yucatan to buy cocaine (DEA got this part right).

There was a moment of silence in the room after all this information got relayed in two different languages.

"What's gonna happen to Tatiana?" Rey asked Feldman, struggling to take all the information in.

"She'll be extradited to Colombia," Feldman answered.

"Then what?"

"Then I don't know, Rey."

Gary spoke. "A trial, then prison."

"What about her kid?" asked Rey. "He's tiny, for Chrissake." Rey surprised himself here—normally he disliked children.

"Well, at eight years old, he's likely not a terrorist," said Feldman.

Rey didn't appreciate the deadpan. "No kidding. What happens to him while he's still here?"

"He'll be put in foster care while his mother awaits extradition," said Mrs. Octavio.

"After extradition, what then?"

"Then someone like me will claim him when they touch down in Bogota," she answered.

"And then?"

"They'll contact his relatives. Try to place him with family."

"Well lady," said Rey, "don't know if you were listening, but the kid's got no family. Even if he did, he'd just be headed right back to some jungle pisswater." American child welfare was no picnic, but Reymond assumed Colombia would be worse. "Is there any way he can stay in the U.S.?"

"The son of a foreign-born criminal wanted by a government we have extradition agreements with?" asked Feldman. "I don't think so."

"His mother's just a foot soldier in someone else's stupid war," Rey voiced. "Not even a soldier—a camp follower. Her son doesn't deserve this."

"That's for others to decide," said Feldman. "Not someone with a gun trafficking charge hanging over his head."

That again? Thought Rey. "May I talk to her?"

"Sure," said Feldman. "She's right here."

"I meant privately."

Agent Feldman looked at the remaining marshal, who shook his head. "I'm afraid that's not possible."

Gary Graft looked at the marshal as well, speaking definitively, "Mr. Perkins may be an alleged arms smuggler, but I doubt the scales of international terrorism will tip one way or the other if they have a few minutes alone." Outside of book club, this was the longest sentence Rey had ever heard Gary speak.

Agent Feldman raised an eyebrow but nodded. "The marshal stays, everyone else leaves. Perkins, you got five minutes." He was left with Tatiana, her son, and the marshal.

"Do you know Spanish?" Rey asked the marshal.

"What do you think?" the marshal answered, his irritation making it clear he didn't.

Rey moved to mother and son, taking a knee, his back to the marshal. The satisfaction of making it to America, even if only to some stuffy government police room, was still written on Tatiana's face, but so was the fear that she and her son would be extradited, she to rot in some government prison, he to navigate some depressingly crowded orphanage. They began conversing, Tatiana's and young Sebastian's eyes rapt, never leaving Rey's. At the five-minute mark, Feldman and the others returned.

"Gary, I mean, Dr. Graft," said Rey, "what do I have to do to keep her in the U.S.? Or at least her son?"

Feldman answered on Graft's behalf. "There's nothing to be done. You did your part. The charge against you will be dropped and your record expunged. You'll once again be a model citizen."

"But what if there was *more* I could do?"

"Like what?" she asked.

"How bad do you want Sammy's Club? Or their leader, Miles Jacobsen?"

"We've been working the La Plata Patriots case for some time," said Feldman. "We've got it covered."

"How about Old Line? You got them where you want them?" Rey asked.

"Not exactly," Feldman admitted.

"What would I have to do?" asked Rey. "Some sting operation like this?"

"Likely something far more dangerous," Gary answered cryptically. "Still interested?"

No, I'm not, thought Rey. *I'm just stupid.* "I help you get Old Line and in exchange, she stays here, with her kid?"

"Jesus, Wally," said Guijarro, "why don't you ask for a path to citizenship while you're at it."

"Yeah, that too."

Diplomatically, Agent Feldman explained, "Rey, not meaning to pass the buck here, but this is an international deal involving another country's citizens. At a minimum, we're talking signoff from the State Department. And Bogota."

"It's a pipe dream, you idiot," Guijarro said, exasperated. With her sweltering radio mission complete, she no longer had to be civil to Perkins, a condescending jerk who'd constantly hovered over her. It was clear to her that both Graft and Feldman had lost their perspective on this case.

"Dr. Graft," said Rey, "can you come up with something?"

The overworked circulating fans whirred during a short silence.

Finally, Gary said, "Let me talk to the Colombian Consul." Rey smiled with relief. "But Perkins," he continued, "I'll need to stick my neck out. If you screw up, I promise to personally deck you."

"Okay, Dr. Graft." *Way to be dramatic.*

Chapter 54: The Envelope

Wednesday, 15 September 1999
Wheaton, MD

SIX DAYS AGO, Reesie Pug had nearly died.

Initially, she'd come down with a light fever. This hadn't worried Carol too much, nor did one round of vomiting. After all, it was the beginning of flu season. But the confusion worried her—after throwing up, Reesie wasn't fielding questions well. Carol's maternal instinct kicked in; they were at Holy Cross Hospital twenty minutes later.

Once there, Reesie seemed better. "It's probably a virus," the ER diagnostician said. "Lot of it going 'round. We'll prescribe something to manage the symptoms. Follow up with your primary if she doesn't improve."

But Carol, who didn't have health insurance, worried and pushed back. "Look, ma'am, what about the confusion?"

"She's coherent now," said the diagnostician. Carol advocated and the doctor placated, the tense back and forth going for a full minute, until Reesie stood up. Then, to everyone's mutual horror, she collapsed, convulsing. A chaotic medical choreography then began; Carol was told to stay out of the way. When Reesie stopped convulsing, the diagnostician inserted an IV. Blood was drawn and the culprit, bacterial meningitis, identified.

The next twelve hours were dicey. As a medical team fought to reduce her brain swelling and suppress her seizures, Reesie's life hung in the balance. Fear filled Carol, possessing every part of her. But by the morning, Reesie began improving.

At twenty-four hours, she was out of the woods, awake and talking, able to move, albeit clumsily. Still, the doctors warned Carol there may be complications—returning seizures, a loss of hearing and/or muscle control, even brain damage. As feared, a complication did develop: hearing loss. However, a test forty-eight hours later showed improvement; Carol was told the odds were now very good for a full recovery.

What wasn't looking good, however, was the cost of the hospital stay, which was staggering—twenty-nine thousand dollars. And more bills were expected. Before taking Reesie home, Carol told the billing representative tearily that she couldn't pay any of it.

"Don't worry, Mrs. Pug, we can work out a plan," the rep had said.

"You don't understand just how *bad* things are," Carol told her. "I owe bikers money."

"Bikers? Oh dear!" the rep responded, thinking, *Apparently, I haven't heard it all.*

Carol stared at the thick envelope David had put on the counter. "I can't accept it," she said.

"Why not?" asked David. "Think of Reesie."

Honestly, David, when am I not thinking about her? Especially now!

Carol and David were in her kitchen. She'd just returned from checking on Reesie for the umpteenth time—her daughter was still sleeping. The adults were speaking quietly because Sunny was in the Pug family room playing with Legos.

"Carol?" prompted David.

"Oh, sorry," she said, refocusing. "With what happened to Reesie, I'm still a bit scattered. The offer's incredibly generous, David, but no. It's your money. Yours and Angie's. Does she even know you're offering this?"

"No," David replied awkwardly. "But now that I've defended my dissertation, Monsanto really wants me. They've offered me a huge signing bonus—thirty thousand dollars! I've accepted it. Fifteen of it's in that envelope for you, for the hospital bills."

"David, I *can't* accept money behind Angie's back, plus she's sure to find out, and then what?"

"True, Angie's a legal beagle, but she's terrible with numbers, so I run the checkbook," answered David. "She won't know Monsanto gave me thirty thousand. I'm going to tell her they gave me fifteen. She'll still be through the roof."

"It's dishonest, David."

"Carol, let me help you. You've been so good to me. To my family, I mean. Please, just take it." David nodded toward the envelope with its formal-looking bank logo.

"Even if I took it, I'd have to tell Trev," Carol said.

David looked worried, but said, "That's fine, I guess. But maybe you could wait until he's out?"

"I don't know," said Carol. "He's not coming home until March. Honestly, I don't know how he'll feel about this. And down the road, if he gets drunk again, there's no predicting what he'll say. Or do."

David had been so focused on hiding the money from Angie that he'd not thought through Carol's side of things. Sure, she was doing the Pug's bills *now,* but would Trevor take over when he came home? As well, it dawned on him: hospitals generated records—a *lot* of records.

Question: What doesn't have a paper trail?

Answer: Extortion.

"I've been so stupid, Carol. Pay off the bikers instead. Will fifteen thousand be enough?"

"More than enough, but it's just not right," said Carol. At greater volume: "Sunny, your daddy and I are going to check on Reesie again." Sunny, busily assembling a dinosaur, said, "Okay."

David followed Carol down the hall, pausing outside Reesie's opened door. The girl was still out like a light, as she'd been ten minutes ago and the ten minutes before that. Satisfied, they returned to the kitchen. "David, don't get me wrong. It's extremely generous of you, but let's be honest: you guys have your own bills, too—your mortgage, that business loan. And student debt, right?"

"Yes, but we make all the payments, and Angie's making real money now. We'll be out from under in a few years, even faster with me working for Monsanto. Believe me, Angie will flip her lid tonight when I tell her about the money. Who knows, I might even get lucky!" David's sudden exuberance caught Carol off guard, and she burst out laughing. Realizing what he'd just said, David laughed as well. The money tension, so palpable only a moment before, evaporated.

"What's funny, Daddy?" asked Sunny. The question had the adults trying to contain themselves, which made them laugh even harder.

"Nothing, Sunny," said Carol, guffawing.

Sunny looked up from his work, saying sagely, "Something *must* be funny, Mrs. Pug."

"Your daddy made, uh, a silly face," Carol managed to say. David did so now to add validity, which sent Carol into orbit. The boy put his half-assembled Lego beast down to investigate because Daddy rarely laughed like this. Seeing the child so concerned settled the adults down.

"Come on, Sunny," said David, "time to go home."

"But I haven't finished Dino."

"That's okay," said Carol. "Take him home with you. And the bin of Legos. You can bring everything back when you're done."

"But I like playing *here,*" Sunny responded. If the adults thought he was being pouty, they were wrong. Sunny just wanted to hear Daddy laugh that hard again.

"Sunny," said David, "you know Mrs. Pug's been through a lot with Reesie."

"Uh huh, hospital," said Sunny.

"Yes," his father said. "We should let her rest. I'll carry the Lego bin. You carry Dino, okay?"

Reluctantly, Sunny said, "Okay. Bye-bye, Mrs. Pug."

"Bye, Sunny. Reesie should be well enough to play on Saturday, okay?"

"Yay!" exclaimed Sunny.

"See you, David," Carol said. "We'll talk more about you-know-what later."

"Right," replied David.

"Take the envelope with you."

"Okay."

Carol checked on Reesie again, and this time she was awake, describing a dream she'd just had. Mommy had been imprisoned inside some weird cage in the center of a hospital room that was flooding with water. Daddy had a bunch of keys, trying each one on the cage's lock, eventually finding the right one.

"It's not too scary, I guess," said Reesie, "but I keep having it. Daddy takes longer and longer each time."

"Don't worry, Reesie," said Carol. "It's just a dream about your hospital stay. You're home now, safe and sound." Reesie didn't fully hear what her mother said, so Carol repeated it louder. When Carol returned to the kitchen, the envelope still sat on the counter.

Great, another errand. I'll return it to David tomorrow.

But the next day, it still lay there, and the next as well. After three days, Carol found herself depositing two thousand dollars at Maryland Trust, then calling Mullet, arranging a meeting for later that night in Hell.

David, I'll pay you back, she thought.

After the bank, she met with the Holy Cross billing rep, giving her a thousand in cash and setting up a payment plan to reimburse the hospital monthly at forty bucks a pop. In exchange, Holy Cross forgave sixty percent of what she owed. It would still take years to pay off, but they would be interest-free years.

She returned home, checked on Reesie, opened a bottle of wine, then began working on a short but very important speech.

Carol arrived at the Gates of Hell later that evening. She was alone, having not brought Sandy on purpose. *She doesn't need to know about this.* She took several breaths, then entered.

Mullet was at his usual table with the usual basket of fries and a pitcher of Budweiser. She sat down, passed a thick envelope to him, and told him it was the balance of her husband's "loan."

Mullet stared at it. "All of it? Luntz ain't gonna like this. You can't pay off early."

"Who are you, J. P. Morgan?" balked Carol. "For your information, I've already *been* paying off early. The rest of what I owe the club's in there. There's a note explaining the math. And by all means, count it if you don't trust me."

Who the fuck is J. P. Morgan? Mullet thought. He would have asked Carol directly but for some reason Carol seemed different tonight—ballsy. He also didn't ask because it would make him sound stupid, and he hated looking stupid, especially in front of a woman. *And it ain't the money, anyway,* he thought. He knew very well Christian's real objective: getting Trevor to run the club's books. He eyeballed New Carol suspiciously. "Luntz ain't gonna like this," he repeated.

Showtime, she thought. *Oh God, please don't let me be sick!*

"Well, Mullet, you tell Christian that if he doesn't like it, my mother will take Reesie out of state so I can go public. Ask him if he wants those TV people *Seven on Your Side* digging into Old Line's 'lending practices.' And I've written everything down. Got sealed envelopes in the hands of people I trust." (This was true.) "So take the money or go down in flames. Up to you."

Mullet stared at her, then slowly reached for the envelope, pushing it beneath his fry basket. Carol maintained eye contact for a moment longer, then left.

I don't like New Carol, Mullet reflected, putting a fry in his mouth. *Not one bit.*

Chapter 55: The New Bookkeeper

Saturday, 2 October 1999
La Plata, MD

TWO WEEKS AGO, the view from the Old Line compound farmhouse porch had been particularly bucolic, but Luntz had been in no mood to enjoy it. He was two guns short and furious. Angrily, he'd spat chaw at a Black-eyed Susan, nailing it. Normally, he considered his African-American DC gun buyers reliable, and therefore "Black," but when they weren't reliable—in this case, one of his Anacostia straws had disappeared with five hundred dollars meant to purchase a pair of Glocks—the straws were the n-word, which he'd used liberally that day.

"Now I have to send a goddamn message," he'd grumbled, and since Ward 8 wasn't exactly the club's stomping grounds, intermediaries would be needed to find the thief. That meant more money—another reason to be pissed.

The missing pistols had been promised to Sammy's Club, so their absence caused another problem. On top of that, ten days ago Carol Pug had paid off Trevor's loan, yet something else angering him. After serious thought, however, he decided that it wasn't worth crossing swords with her, a mamma bear ready to call Seven on Your Side. And she had, after all, paid in full. *A deal's a deal,* he'd told himself. For form's sake, he'd had Mullet get the woman to turn over her "in case of emergency" letters, warning her never to pull anything like that again.

Today wasn't bucolic—a cold rain—but for Luntz it was shaping up to be a good day anyway. Two days ago, agents of the club had found and appropriately retaliated against the Ward 8 thief. Two new straw purchases were made, allowing the club to fully deliver on Sammy's gun order this morning. But the best news? He was meeting a potential bookkeeper.

The candidate arrived at the compound at 3 p.m. Mullet and Rocker escorted him to the barn where Rocker searched him. The man submitted readily; obviously, this wasn't his first pat-down.

Christian, who was already there, asked, "You Perkins?" Rey nodded. "I'm Luntz. Sammy vouched for you. Said you and a buddy delivered hymnals to La Plata for him back in April. That true?"

"Yes, Mr. Luntz," said Rey.

"Just 'Luntz.' No 'mister.'"

Rey nodded.

Luntz knew that Sammy had had an actual family emergency that April night, some hillbilly cousin with angina, and had asked Rey for genuine help. While Luntz had no idea of Rey's initial suspicions, Sammy had not entrapped Rey. Neither Luntz nor Sammy knew about the traffic stop on Sunday morning and both assumed neither Perkins nor his buddy, Gary Graft, knew about the crate's false bottom.

"Curious, Perkins," Luntz continued, "you had your buddy Graft get them songbooks across the finish line. Why not you?"

Does he know that I know about the guns? thought Rey nervously. Hoping his anxiety didn't show, he responded, "Because I already had plans, and once Gary learned about the hymnals, he practically begged me to take them. He's a real 'God fearing' type."

"You had plans?" asked Rocker. "Like what?"

Rey, who had no ready answer, replied, "Getting laid." To his relief, the bikers laughed.

"Well, did you?" asked Mullet.

"Get laid? Ah, sadly, no."

More laughter. "Them's the breaks," said Rocker.

"Who told you about our job openin'?" asked Luntz.

"I used to work with Trevor Pug, before he lost his job. He's in prison now. DUI."

"So I heard," said Luntz.

"I know his wife," continued Rey. "She told me you guys wanted him to do your books." This was true—Gary had arranged for Rey to "bump into" Carol to establish a cover story.

"That's a nice Acura out there, Perkins," said Luntz, changing tack. "Your nine-to-five pay for it?"

"Yes. I'm a programmer. Y2K patches, mostly."

"Is that shit real?" asked Rocker.

"It is."

"So you make good money?" asked Luntz.

"I do okay."

"Then why ya need to moonlight?" Mullet challenged.

"I'm doing it for Carol," Rey answered, sticking to a script Gary had crafted.

"To get into her pants?" asked Mullet.

"I wouldn't put it that way," said Rey, "but, well . . . maybe." Gary thought potential infidelity would be the most believable cover story, and Rey hoped he was right. "Trevor doesn't need to know, by the way."

"I understand," said Luntz. "'Morality's a private, costly luxury.'—Henry Brooks Adams." Mullet fawned at Luntz—the boss's quote-bombs were the shit. "I don't care who you're puttin' it to."

"Or trying to," added Rocker, laughing snidely. Mullet brayed like an idiot.

Meanwhile, Luntz pondered the due diligence he'd collected on this tall pretty-boy. During the initial call, the subject of Rey's South American hostage fiasco came up. Luntz sent Wanda, his most bookish "sweet butt," to the library to follow up. She returned with copies of several old newspaper stories—Rey wasn't making anything up. Further, Christian's police mole confirmed that Rey wasn't in any state or federal database. The PI Luntz had on retainer checked out Rey's financials: he was a model citizen who paid his bills. Except for Inner Circle dealings, which Luntz would continue handling personally, the bookkeeper job was basically legit, so perhaps in Perkins he'd finally found his check cutter. But it paid to be thorough. "So you know Trevor from work?" Luntz asked.

"Yeah. And we attended the same book club."

This made Mullet laugh again. "Well *that* sounds gay," he said.

Rey clarified, "It's a book club for men who want to read books men actually like."

"Like I said, *gay*," replied Mullet.

Whatever, asshat, thought Rey.

"This that club meetin' at Shorties?" asked Luntz.

"Yes," said Rey. "I recognize you, sir—I mean, Luntz. You came looking for Trevor the night that homeless dude, Prophet, got murdered. Not that you had anything to do with that."

"Course not," said Christian. This was true, but a little innuendo never hurt.

"So, Rey," said Rocker, "bottom line is you wanna balance our books so you can tag your buddy's wife?"

"And get paid," said Rey boldly, hoping that was the right follow-up.

Luntz explored something else. "You bein' with Sammy means you're not too keen on the Heebs. Or the brothers."

"Jews, Blacks, they're fine. It's the spics I can't stand."

"Well, we like what we like, don't we?" asked Rocker.

"And we hate what we hate," said Mullet.

"True," said Rey, annoyed at having to agree with such idiots.

Christian gazed at him, measuring. "That jungle rumble of yours aside, you look like Polite Society. This ain't some biker wannabe crap, is it? Got no patience for that."

"No," Rey responded, genuinely offended. Realizing his tone was unnecessarily snarky, he pivoted. "Look, why don't you try me out for a couple weeks. See how it goes."

"How much?" asked Luntz.

"It's a favor for Carol. Not trying to get rich." Rey quoted an hourly rate.

Luntz thought it was a little high but accepted, considering it an investment: despite Perkins's Polite Society exterior, he likely had the moral flexibility Luntz was looking for. "Perkins, people think clubs like ours got a lotta illegal shit goin' on."

"Yeah, it's a painful stereotype," said Rocker melodramatically, which got Mullet guffawing again.

Rey responded, "For me it's simple. If there's stuff I don't need to know, then I don't need to know."

This answer was good enough for Luntz. He'd been concerned earlier when Perkins went a little white after being asked about the hymnal delivery, but not now. On balance, the dude was holding his own against three grizzled bikers on their own turf. *Guess those FARC fucks hardened him. Anyway, let's get him on board before he finds out Carol paid up and doesn't need his help saving Trevor.* "When can you start?" Luntz asked.

"Now, if you want."

Chapter 56: Manna from Heaven

Wednesday, 30 September 1999
Wheaton, MD

HELLO AGAIN, IT'S me, Trevor. I'm about to bed down for the night, but first, let me tell you about Maryland Central.

It's minimum security, not *The Shawshank Redemption*, so nervous newbies aren't marched past rabid catcallers. But we do wear jumpsuits. Your street clothes either get mailed home if you have the money or donated to charity. (The state gives you new duds when your sentence is complete.) I was given a jumpsuit and five underwear changes, plus a bag of toiletries.

On the first day, COs—corrections officers—led me to a "pod," an open area with ten attached lockups where I met my first "cellie," Greg. He asked if I wanted the bottom bunk, which he currently occupied. I said no, the top's fine. I didn't want to make waves, plus Greg, three hundred pounds easy, was no ballerina and wasn't going to fly there. I put my cardboard box under Greg's bunk. To avoid mix-ups and theft, everything's labeled with your prison ID, which is six digits. Mine has a lot of nines in it—easy to remember.

The rest of that day and most of the first week were dedicated to screening interviews, things like reviewing previous incarceration history, going over the code of conduct at MC (most guys call Maryland Central "MC"), setting up a commissary account—that sort of stuff. There was a thorough medical evaluation; they don't want you dying on their watch.

As you might imagine, seeking the right kind of incarcerated people is important. Prison is tribal; it's vital to be part of a group—going it alone looks weak. Tribes often break down racially, but not always. Age and life experience are important differentiators. I'm associated with eight other White guys (including Greg), a Black guy named Gerome, and, if you can believe it, father and son Samoans.

I've heard it said societies are judged by how they treat their least members. Inmates at MC are generally treated okay. The COs and counselors want us to better ourselves and then get the eff out (and stay out), but make no mistake—it's called prison for a reason. There's no giant stone wall surrounding the MC campus (yes, they call it a campus, which the cheekier types refer to as Harvard on the Yard), but there may as well be.

The COs make it clear: *Your wings are clipped.* At least at MC, COs use a few carrots. At the more secure facilities, I hear there's a lot more stick.

As you'd probably expect, the food's not great. But it's not horrid, like at County. Holiday meals are the best. Within the limits of prison food, they go the extra mile, especially at Thanksgiving, I hear. The best non-holiday meal is the baked chicken, once a week on Sundays. Everyone behaves well on Sundays, as no one wants to miss the baked chicken. The rest of the meals are hit-miss, the biggest miss being the lo mein, which is vile. Imagine the worst Chinese food you've ever had, double the celery, and add glue.

Cellies come and go. My current cellie is Tristian, an oral surgeon from Bethesda. He ran over someone in a blackout. He had a good lawyer, but Maryland's getting serious these days. Tristian's serving twenty-seven months for vehicular manslaughter. Like me, he has visitors every week (not everybody does). Last Sunday, a woman in the visitor's room approached him, thanking him for a free cleft palate repair he'd done for her son. Tells you a lot about Tristian, a standup guy respected by everyone . . . except the mother of the teenager he killed. As insane as me wrecking three police cruisers was, at least nobody died. Tristian's all smiles, but he's messed up inside.

Okay, moving on to something lighter. I've been writing love notes for Carol again—you know, the ones I like to hide around the house.

I've been working on some food and animal-themed ones:

> *What's the snuggliest fruit? Avo-cuddle.*
> *Muffin can come between us.*
> *There are a chameleon reasons I love you.*
> *There might be other fish in the sea, but you're my sole mate.*

Can't exactly tuck them under Carol's jewelry box at the moment, so I'm stockpiling them for future use. Got three months' worth so far, shooting for a year. Course that may not be enough considering I broke our eight-year sex streak. Good Lord Jesus, talk about a major screwup. I hope she forgives me and lets us start again. (We're still young. We can sail past eight years.) I'm not gonna lie to you: though I'm ashamed of putting the family at risk—who am I kidding? I put them in *danger*—it's breaking the streak that hurts the most. Lots of different glue will hold a relationship together, but sex glue's strong. I was toying with the idea of mailing a few of my better love notes to her, you know, to prime the pump (nothing sexual, just things like *You octopi my thoughts*), but it's probably not the time.

Her visits are a lifeline, but last Sunday she really scared me. Using her "everything's fine" voice, she told me Reesie had gotten meningitis. "It wasn't that bad, Trev," she said. Really? How can meningitis *not* be bad? Tristian the oral surgeon knew a case where the young woman was fine in the morning, sick by dinner, dead by midnight. Yeesh. After expressing how grateful I was that Reesie was okay, I asked about the cost.

"She was only in the hospital a few days, Trev. I've already worked out a payment plan."

"Yes, but how much was it, Carol?"

"Don't worry. Besides, what can you do about it from in here?"

Well, ladies and gentlemen, believe me, that stung. Regarding Carol, Cisco says *Ten miles in, ten miles out—re-establishing trust takes time.* He's right, of course. But just to give you some idea of how desperate I felt, I told her that no matter how badly the old goat would gloat, I wanted her to borrow the money from the monster-in-law.

"We don't need anything from Mother," Carol said. Normally I like her anti-Gladys assertiveness, but right then I didn't. "We need it," I insisted. "Blame me."

Carol gave me a look of *Duh, I sure do.* That also stung.

"Trev, relax," she then said. "I've got good news. Great news, in fact! We're free and clear from Old Line!"

For a moment, I was stunned, then, "How?"

"I've been paying more against the principal than I've been telling you. I've become quite the financial ninja."

"Really? That's fantastic!" I hugged her and got immediately reprimanded by a CO, but I didn't care. If I got written up, it would have been worth it. No more twenty percent monthly interest! No more pressure to run Old Line's books! But then I thought about the hospital again. "Listen, Carol, this is great news, but are you being straight with me? We owe Holy Cross a lot, don't we? If you don't want to borrow all of it from Gladys, then just borrow some of it."

"I can't."

"Yes, you can, Carol. I don't care what she thinks about me anymore, I just care about you and Reesie. I'll dance on the head of a pin if she wants. She can own me."

"It would be more than owning you, Trev," Carol said quietly.

"What does that mean?" I asked.

"I think you know what it means."

And I did know—a post-divorce two-bedroom apartment for me. "God, Carol, I hate her. And I'm so sorry."

"Hey, it's not your fault Reesie got sick," Carol said.

"It's my fault we don't have insurance."

"Don't dwell on that, Trev. Just do your time. Keep working with Cisco. And remember, we're done with Old Line!" She smiled then.

I smiled back, but last I knew, we still owed Luntz at least eleven grand. Given what Hallmark pays, no matter how frugal she's been, there's no way she scrimped enough for an early payoff. But I decided not to worry about it then. Manna from Heaven, right?

Carol moved on to other subjects, including Chin-chin, who will soon be Doctor Chin-chin. "Trev, don't say Chin-chin," she said. "It's childish. You should be grateful for all he does for us. I mean, the childcare *alone.*"

I know she's right, but it's hard to feel grateful when another man has to step in for you. And with his new job, who'll watch Reesie? Yeah, I know, I sound selfish. According to my annoying AA sponsor, an alcoholic's first thought is always selfish. I can hear Cisco now: *You should be expressing gratitude to David by praying for him.*

Okay, here goes: God, I'm grateful Ant-Man's got a job.

Okay, I admit it needs work.

Anyway, I'll be released on March 6, 2000: 172 days from now. I'm at least grateful for that.

Chapter 57: Falling Trees

Tuesday, 19 October 1999
Reston, VA

DARIUS KAY HATED Kent Ruger more than ever. However, it wasn't the real Ruger's sullen looks and vindictive Coventry Lane Christmas Carnival blog page entries that irked. It was a dream version, a bearded one resembling Mark Marks who cut madly at some backyard sequoia, doing his level best to kill D-Kay with it. The actual Ruger had tried railroading Christmas figuratively down Darius's throat, but Dream Ruger was literally trying to break his neck. *And the real Darius,* he thought, *is tired of it.*

D-Kay was anxious and sleep-deprived; Henry's death had hit him hard. He'd planned on giving Splash grief well into their assisted living years, but that wouldn't be happening now. *And I know it's got something to do with that grody curse-meister, Mark 'Prophet' Marks.* The manner of Splash's death bothered Kay. How could he have been driving fast enough to hydroplane with so much traffic? There was suspicion he'd been distracted (maybe Ken's call?), but his phone was lost in the floodwaters, so there was no way to tell. *And knowing wouldn't bring you back, buddy, would it?*

In addition to losing sleep, D-Kay was losing weight. After starting to refuse meals, Sandy, who pulled no punches, ordered an evaluation. "Darius, you look like a UNICEF poster child. Go to the doctor." At work, Danielle Trax remarked similarly, "Kay, you look terrible, and your work's suffering." Hearing the implication, he took the day off for an appointment.

D-Kay saw the doc earlier that day. Blood was taken, a lecture was given on reducing stress, eating better (eating anything, really), and getting more exercise.

You want exercise, Doc, you got it. When he got home, Darius decided to walk up Coventry Lane to the entrance of Governor's Landing, then across the main feeder into an older 1970s neighborhood called Hobbit's Glen, a collection of post-and-beams and one-story ranches with utility lines still above ground.

It was enjoyable at first, but he found himself dwelling on his vivid and quite awful Ruger/Prophet dream. *But you're taking precautions, aren't you?* he asked himself. This was true—he'd stopped going anywhere near

Ruger's fence because there actually were a few of his trees that, if cut just right, could conceivably crash through it and hit him.

Walking through Hobbit's Glen was relaxing because the neighborhood reminded him of the Morrisville, NJ community he'd grown up in. It also helped that his house was newer, better-looking, and larger than anything to be found in this older subdivision. The Glen had more trees, however, many more, most of which having already lost their leaves, which were now raked into tidy, gutter-blocking piles. Trees were on Kay's official worry list, but since Ruger didn't live in the Glen, he didn't worry about a Paul Bunyan death here. *It pays to be careful, however,* he thought, keeping his eyes out for anyone doing yard work. He saw one such man up on a ladder hanging a Halloween ghost display, so D-Kay crossed the street thinking, *This stupid dream owns me.*

The weather was lovely for October—cool, the heat of summer a memory. His stroll was noisier than D-Kay cared for—mostly leaf blowers. As well, some kid on a side street was gunning an old Trans Am's engine louder than God so he quickly hurried by. D-Kay reached the halfway point, then turned around to head home. As he passed the side street with the punk and his beater Trans Am, he was relieved: the kid was tinkering under its rusty hood now—no engine noise. *Another ten minutes to the highway.* A block before reaching it, D-Kay heard a distant roar behind him. *God, it's that piece of crap Trans Am, I just know it.* The roar got louder. D-Kay turned to look from the sidewalk, and sure enough, Herbert Hotrod was rocketing up the street toward the highway.

A block away, the Trans Am suddenly made a loud, lurching noise. Sparks began spitting from underneath it as if it were somehow dragging its own engine. As catastrophic as this likely was, the vehicle was still approaching quickly—the kid either wasn't using his brakes or they no longer worked.

At least it's not going to hit me, D-Kay thought.

And it didn't. Instead, it veered off to the other side of the street on its way to the highway separating Kay from the Hobbit People. He watched the Trans Am shoot past him, trailing smoke like a shot-up fighter plane. It clipped a parked car, then launched over the sidewalk and impacted a utility pole, shearing it two feet above the ground. The force of the collision carried the car and the pole into a parked minivan, totaling it.

At no point did the runaway Trans Am come within thirty feet of Darius, nor did it strike any tree. Yet a tree of sorts ended up killing him. The Pontiac's violent crash put such a strain on the lines attached to the utility pole that it pulled others connected to it, including wires spanning over to his side of the street. A pole behind Darius was snapped by the strain. It kicked out, crushing D-Kay's skull, then fell over.

Saturday, 30 October 1999

Darius Kay was put to rest two weeks later in Morrisville, NJ. It was a large funeral, though not quite as large as Haru Takahashi's due to the need for out-of-town travel. Trevor, still a guest of the State of Maryland, did not attend, but his wife did, along with the five remaining "evil men": Ken, Gary, Phillipe, Loo, and, surprisingly, Rey Perkins.

Even with valium, D-Kay's widow, Sandy, was a mess, barely able to follow the directions her girlfriends Carol and Cindy gave her. Every time she repeated the phrase "Freak accident," they rubbed her back, comforting her as best they could.

It wasn't known if the kid driving the Trans Am died impacting the pole or the minivan, but the strain transferred through the crosswires above D-Kay had pulled the murderous pole down so hard that its attached transformer exploded. Post-accident investigation revealed that below-grade rot infected the majority of Hobbit's Glen's utility poles. They were quickly replaced; it all made Channel 4 News.

The day of Darius's funeral was the same day the Alley Killer winnowed his "witness" list down to two men, one being Trevor Pug, currently incarcerated for a felony. He planned to approach the other man tonight after a meeting to determine if he could be "eliminated." If so, then that meant Pug was his man, and in that case, he would patiently wait for his release in March.

Chapter 58: The Keys Come Home

Thursday, 4 November 1999
Wheaton, MD

CISCO EXAMINED HIMSELF in the mirror. After a summer of looking better than he'd had in years, the haggardness he'd exhibited in the spring had unfortunately returned. And that wasn't the only thing. The Korean War dream of Jamie Took getting shot had also returned, Cisco still being the bullet's new target. In last night's dream, the angry hornet had nearly cleaved his skull.

Was this God's way of saying He's not forgotten the other thing?

In April, the last time Cisco had his evolving nightmare, he'd taken Trevor Pug's advice and written back to Mrs. Marks again. In his logical mind, the two things, the dream and corresponding with Prophet's mother, had no bearing on each other. *But summer was nightmare-free,* his illogical mind reminded him.

In his new letters, Cisco politely bragged about his wife, figuring that between expressing his fidelity to Maggie's memory and his age, Winnie would properly read between the lines. Mrs. Marks, however, ignored all references to age and prior devotion. Reading between *her* lines, what Winnie wanted was a gentleman caller.

Dating may have been a taboo subject, but Mark Marks wasn't. Though he'd told her previously he'd conveyed everything important, with each letter, Cisco discovered one more story, one more poignant example of how "Prophet" had touched the life of someone in AA.

On her end, Winnie kept it social, passing on all manner of small-town happenings, such as the goings on at Christ the Redeemer Church (pancake suppers, and Young Charlie replacing the retiring Old Charlie). Their commonality, both coming of age in the 40s, was helpful—Winnie's new pen pal knew Peggy Lee's biggest hits and Sid Caesar's funniest routines. Additionally, she described Cumberland's many social opportunities as potential dates: square dancing at the Y, the monthly downtown flea market, bingo at the Knights of Columbus.

Despite these thinly veiled invites, Cisco enjoyed her letters, keeping her abreast of his life as well: his trips to the hardware store, twice-monthly golf with his buddy, Reggie, and appropriate anecdotes from his AA work.

Over the summer, his program had been running on all cylinders. Though he'd taken on no new sponsees since Trevor, there were still several others he was working with, including Chico Rodrigez. Cisco still took men to meetings, picking them up from halfway houses. He met alkies for coffee and listened to their problems. In his basement, he worked them through the Steps. Trevor's original moral inventory, the precursor to the Fifth Step, was still locked safely away in one of the "mailboxes" attached to Cisco's cellar wall, as were many others.

Careful not to violate their anonymity beyond what Winnie already knew about "those two good-looking boys you brought to the funeral," Cisco kept her current on Chico and Trevor. She was crushed to learn of Trevor's imprisonment but hoped earnestly that he would discover Jesus and turn his life around. Though Jesus was, as the saying went, a good friend of Cisco Arkin, he explained to her that not everyone in the rooms believed in Christ, or God for that matter. Winnie would have none of this. *If a man accepts Christ*, she wrote, *then God will not give him a burden heavier than he can carry*, by which she meant alcoholism.

She prompted Cisco to keep busy. *My Theodore retired without a 'plan.' He just sat at the kitchen table drinking coffee. Six months later he was dead. Are you walking, Cisco? Are you eating well? Collard greens, dear man, collard greens!*

She was curious about the AA program. *Saving those men from Demon Alcohol must be exhausting, Cisco. Bravo! But after so many years without a drink, do you still need to go to those meetings?* He explained that even those with good recovery never graduated (and didn't want to), but he knew "normies" like Winnie Marks would never understand this.

Had Mrs. Marks confined herself to letter-writing, their correspondence could have gone on for years, but she overstepped. For ostensibly innocent reasons at first—seeing a relative, then visiting one of DC's many museums—Winnie began coming to town. That would have been okay, but before long, she began attending Wheaton-area AA meetings. After happening upon her at St. Paul's, Cisco, flabbergasted, did something he'd never done before: he used the "escape hatch."

To her credit, Winnie visited only open meetings where it was okay if non-drunks attended, but even so, she'd crossed a line. He composed a letter stiffly informing her that whatever this "field research" was, Cumberland was *not* located beyond the limits of the known world and had its own AA meetings; two hours' travel to visit the DC area was completely unnecessary, and let it not be forgotten that one of the *A's* in AA stood for anonymous.

For two weeks, Cisco had put off sending this letter, but yesterday, he'd mailed it. As he'd feared, the Korean dream returned. So scared was he during it that he attempted something new: altering the dream's outcome. As he and Corporal Biloxi pulled Private Took down the boulder scree to avoid the Chinese bullets, Cisco purposefully dropped his friend at the bottom and ducked, forcing Corporal Biloxi to take all of Took's weight. The corporal cursed his cowardice, but what upset Cisco even more was what Biloxi said next: "Arkin, that trick won't work forever!"

He'd fooled the dream once, but could he do it over and over? *What should I do now?* he asked himself. *Do as you'd have sponsees do—immerse yourself in Step Work.* But wasn't more AA just whistling past the graveyard? And really, what more could he do? He worked now with eight men, a lion's load. *But you've worked with twice that number, Arkin. Since Trevor, you haven't taken on any new sponsees. Why's that?*

He knew why. Despite correspondence with Winnie and full-tilt AA, both activities improving his health, there was still his dark secret, the *other thing*. It subconsciously controlled him, putting him in what Maggie would have called "buttoning up" mode. Looking back on one's life was an old man's prerogative, but whether he wanted to admit it or not, now that's all he was doing. He'd begun by checking on the sobriety of men he'd not talked to in years. He was also calling in his mailbox "markers," the keys for the basement apartment boxes where many sponsees kept their paperwork, knowing Cisco would take a bullet, or more accurately, another bullet, before letting anyone open them. Each man got assigned a box number, but many labeled their cubbies as well: DAVID L., CHICO R. Others used nicknames: DETROIT LEROY. COURT-ORDERED, and Cisco's favorite, THE SERENE MACHINE. Trevor Pug went by CODER MAN.

He'd begun asking for keys during late summer and had been receiving them all fall. Some keys would never return, their owners either having lost touch with him or abandoned the program altogether. Of this second group, most were in one of the three places Bill Wilson, AA's cofounder, promised untreated alcoholism led to—jails, asylums, graveyards. Those of whom Cisco knew had died had an "X" taped over their box, Arkin's way of spelling it out for his charges: *This guy did it his way.*

But most keys came back.

When asked why he wanted the keys returned, he claimed it was housecleaning, something like AA's Fourth Step inventory, only for his basement. "Making room for the new man," is what he said. But the *other thing* told Cisco there would be no new men. Trevor would be the last.

Chapter 59: The Last Supper

Saturday, 13 November 1999
Silver Spring, MD

TO QUOTE YOGI Berra, thought Loo, *it's déjà vu all over again.* A year ago, he and Rey had been walking to Shorties when Perkins went on a rant against three Latinos sitting in the back of a pickup. Tonight, he and Rey, who surprised him by attending, had parked at the same lot again and found themselves walking up the same sidewalk. Thankfully, there was no Bondo-patched Datsun pickup parked at the bodega. But, just as Loo realized this, a large Dodge pickup *did* pull in, giving him a bad feeling. *Oh no, it can't be!*

In the driver's seat, big as life, sat the Storyteller. Three of his friends were packed in with him, and four more sat in the bed. Blood drained from Loo's face as he watched Perkins once again stop to talk to them.

"Rey, don't say anything stupid!" he said, pleading. As if it wasn't obvious, he added, "There's more of them this time." It was the same crew who'd cruised into Shorties last March looking for Rey. *Perkins must be terrified,* Loo thought. As the men exited the truck, Storyteller pointed at Perkins. Loo whispered, "Let's go before we get our asses kicked!"

"Go if you want," said Rey levelly.

Storyteller was still an old man in painter's clothes, but the seven others were young and, "illegal" or not, didn't look like pushovers. Storyteller stepped up to Rey and Luigi as the others surrounded them.

And this is how I die, thought Loo.

During the eight-man bum rush in April, Rey's sphincter had seriously puckered. Tonight, however, he calmly, if palely, looked at Storyteller. A tense silence developed. At last, one of the seven confederates grew impatient, pushing Rey, attempting to provoke him. Rey ignored him. Motioning toward Loo, Perkins shook his head at the older man: *Just me. My friend's not involved.* Rey then pulled a twenty from his wallet, giving it to Loo. "Go buy a case of Modelo."

"Okay," said Loo, not needing to be told twice. He squeezed between two angry-looking men, then jogged to the bodega. He made his way quickly to the store's beer cooler, grabbing four six-packs of Modelo, placing them and Rey's twenty in front of a short, elderly Latina clerk. As she rang him up, two pot-bellied *señores* sitting at the store's lone table watched through the bodega's windows at the showdown.

This isn't going to end well, Luigi thought. He fabricated a plan: run to the truck, distract the compadres by tossing in the beer, haul ass to Shorties, hopefully with Rey in tow. The old woman had to wave to get his attention. With tax, it came to $22.43. Loo gave her one of his fives and headed for the door. In a voice unbecoming of her size, Tiny Bodega Lady called him back, insistent on giving him change. Meanwhile, the two señores went outside, joining the ring around Rey while Tiny Bodega Lady carefully counted Loo's change. He interrupted her—"Really, you can keep it!"—but she politely admonished him for making her lose count and started over. Another look out the window: the tall Rey's head was visible, but that was all. Tiny Bodega Lady finally finished, putting his change in Loo's hand, wishing him *buenas noches.*

He flew out the door. Rey and Storyteller were speaking animatedly in Spanish, the other men intently listening, their vibe hostile. *This is the part where you get a beatdown, Rey. You may tower over these guys, but that won't matter.* Loo, four six-packs stacked against his chest, yelled, "Hey! Here's your beer!" Everyone turned.

"Great," said Rey. "Put it in the truck." He then turned back toward Storyteller. Luigi wasn't sure which he liked less: Rey's dismissive *Put it in the truck* command or the Latinos' assuming Loo was Wally's manservant.

Rey wrapped up his spiel and there was a pause. Then Storyteller and the others nodded. This confused Loo: Rey now looked less like a potential hospital admission and more like some pep-talking football coach. As Loo very carefully put the beer in the Dodge's bed, all the men, including Rey, began laughing.

What the hell? "Hey Rey!" yelled Loo. "Let's go."

"You go on, Loo," said Rey, waving him off. Everyone laughed again.

Perkins, thought Loo, *you can kiss my shiny ass.*

Just like last year, Loo found himself incredibly torqued at Rey. Last time it was Perkins's unnecessarily insulting three Latinos. This time, Rey and his new Latino buddies were somehow insulting *him.*

Tonight's EMBC gathering was an "emergency" meeting—just original members, none of the new guys. It was Loo, Phillipe, Ken, Gary, and Rey, once he came down Shortie's stone steps a few minutes later. Trevor was still incarcerated; Splash and D-Kay were dead.

Though Loo had chosen a book, *Endurance* by Alfred Lansing, to discuss, no one, including Loo, had read it. Loo looked around: the other four looked as exhausted as he felt. Loo had called the meeting, but before he could get started, Rey took him aside, saying quietly, "Sorry about that, Loo. Thanks for grabbing the beer."

"You owe me five," said Loo stiffly.

"Here's ten."

"What the hell happened?" Loo was still peeved, but he was also curious.

"It's a lot to explain, trust me," Rey said. "But things are sorted out now." Rey's sincerity gave Loo pause, and after staring at him levelly for a second, Loo nodded, satisfied. They went back to sit down.

"Before we get started," Loo said, "I wanted to thank Rey for attending Kay's funeral in Jersey. When he was last here, things, ah . . . didn't go so well, so welcome back." Rey nodded without a trace of haughtiness. The others nodded back; the man was still no prince in their eyes, but he had shown respect by driving the five hours to the funeral, plus everyone knew Rey was up to his neck in this mess as much as they were.

"Guys," said Rey, "sorry I wasn't at Henry's service. No disrespect intended. I was . . ."—here Rey glanced at Gary—"dealing with some legal issues. Long story."

"Water under the bridge," said Loo. "Okay, let's jump right into it. Tonight's the anniversary of the meeting where Prophet—"

"Mark Marks," Gary corrected.

"Yeah, Mark Marks, died. Look, I don't wanna go all Stephen King on you, but before our street buddy 'Prophet' croaked out back, you all remember his curse: arrests, lost jobs, women 'going south' on us—not in a good way—and . . ." Luigi's breath caught here.

"Lost lives," Gary finished for him.

"Yeah," said Loo, taking a breath. "Okay, so out of eight members, including New Guy Gary, "the numbers really suck. Arrests: me, Splashdown—may he rest in peace—Trevor, Loo, D-Kay—may he also rest in peace—and Original Ken. That's six."

"Reymond?" prompted Gary.

"What qualifies as an arrest?" asked Rey.

"Getting fingerprinted," said Ken.

"Then make that seven," Rey said, looking uncomfortable. "But it's cleared up now."

"Leaving out the law-abiding Phillipe here, that's the *entire* club, right?" Everyone affirmed. We established a while ago that no one had been arrested before we were 'cursed,' so isn't it creepy that there've been so many arrests since? Then there's the lost jobs: Trevor, Loo, Splash—may he continue resting in peace—and Ken, making five. In the twelve working years before the curse, only two guys lost jobs, remember?" Heads nodded. "But in the last year alone, it was *five*?"

"Well," said Phillipe, "it's actually six. Southwest let me go." There was a rush of concerned voices. "It's okay, guys. The good news is I'm officially the Winsor Brother's full-time jet jockey. You can call me 'Johnny Pilot.'"

Emotions reversed and everyone cheered. What he didn't tell them, however, was that through Trevor's loose lips, word of his cross-dressing had reached his Hanger 18 crew. Management got wind of how Gallois's thirty-man crew was now shunning him, and quietly laid him off.

"Great news, Frenchie," Loo continued, but still, *six* outta eight when the economy's booming? Doesn't sound right." More nods of agreement. "Alright, moving on: women. For a while, it was just Phillipe and Estelle who, uh, broke up." Phillipe nodded absently. "Now I know this is an uncomfortable subject," Loo continued, "but has anyone *else* lost a woman? FYI, at the time of the curse, there were only five of us with women in the first place—me, Loo, Phillipe, Trevor, and Gary."

Gary slowly raised his hand. "My wife filed separation papers two weeks ago." The table went silent. Sure, Gary's facts-and-figures blathering was annoying at times, but he'd really grown on the group, even befriending Rey of all people. And didn't the man have kids?

"Holy crap, Gary, I don't know what to say," said Loo.

"I'd rather not dwell on it. Let's just move on."

But they didn't. Losing a job was bad, but losing a marriage was much worse. During an extended period of brotherly support for Gary, Loo quietly asked Rey, "So you're sure things are okay with the El Salvadorians now? And what were you guys talking about?"

Rey nodded, answering, "You wouldn't believe it."

"Try me," Loo offered.

"I asked for advice on getting green cards."

Loo looked at Rey skeptically. "What?"

"That was after apologizing for my rampage last year. I did that first."

"Holy hell, Rey, who *are* you?"

"Oddly enough, I'm not sure anymore."

Once everyone finished doing their best to prop up Gary's deflated spirits, Loo continued. "Okay, so that's Phillipe and now Gary the New Guy losing women, which is two out of five. Not terrible, I guess, but as for deaths . . ." Loo cleared his throat. "We're at two. Guys, one death in our age bracket: tragic and *highly* unlikely. A *second* one? Astronomically improbable."

"Agreed," said Original, "but what do we do about it? I mean, you called this meeting, Loo. Any ideas?"

"Yes, but first . . . has anybody been having weird dreams?" Four concerned faces looked back at Loo.

"Define weird," asked Phillipe.

"Weird as in repetitive, life-threatening, and getting worse."

Uncomfortable silence.

"Ken," continued Loo, "tell them what you told me you and Splash talked about, minutes before he died."

Ken relayed the phone conversation on the rainy night of the accident, describing the growing deadliness of Henry's "chicken" dream.

"Yeah, okay," said Gary, serving as group skeptic, "but didn't Henry hydroplane into a flooded creek? Just him. No one played chicken."

"True," said Loo, "but I'll get back to that, because listen to what D-Kay told me the morning he died." He related D-Kay's story about a dream where he kept dodging a tree Kent Ruger was cutting down.

"Okay," Gary said, a little less sure of himself. "But D-Kay died because some kid wrecked a Trans Am, not because some tree fell on him."

"True," said Loo, but you do know it was a collapsing telephone pole that killed him, right?"

"What?" asked Gary.

"A telephone pole. A former *tree*."

"I don't know," said Rey, "it sounds like a stretch to me." The others agreed.

"All I'm saying guys is this: Splash dreamed about dying in an auto wreck, and he died in an auto wreck. D-Kay dreamed about being killed by a tree and in a very technical sense, he did. It just happened to be a dead one with wires."

"Now you *are* sounding like Stephen King," said Gary.

"Look," said Loo, "I've been having this dream about a woodchipper. It started after Prophet died and it's been getting worse and worse." Spicotti relayed the details, including the mystery man who last night had been forcing Loo's arm into the woodchipper feeder's chute. "It hurt like hell. So, anyone else?"

They all broke down and told their stories. Phillipe went next, describing the thirty-foot fall from the ladder leaning against the 737, and how he originally fell toward the relative safety of six large cartons, but only one was left now, and as of two nights ago, the bearded man had begun pushing it away.

Ken relayed his nightmare about how a squabble at a high school football game led to his unceremoniously being shoved head-first into a bleacher. His last dream had been a week ago where his head had actually contacted the aluminum seat.

Gary related being drowned in his own bathtub but did not go into details. Curse or no curse, it involved a matter of national security.

"Rey, have you been dreaming?" Loo asked.

Rey hesitated. He wasn't unwilling to admit that he had, but condensing 87 days of terror into a few sentences seemed an impossible task.

But I guess I should try.

Rey spent the next ten minutes relaying the highlights of his Colombian experience, looking every so often at Gary, ending by recounting the gun dream, and how, Gun Girl, who now looked more like a Gun Guy, planned to shoot him.

The others stared at him, as did Gary, but Gary look concerned: *That's all they need to know, Reymond.*

"So that's why you can be such a dick, Rey?" Original asked. His question had been earnest, not sarcastic.

"To be fair to the FARC," Rey responded, "I was a bit of an asshole before ever getting captured."

Everyone, including Rey, began laughing—a much needed tension break. Without D-Kay around, they needed to work harder to keep things funny.

"Yes, agreed," said Loo. "And you're still quite the racist bastard."

"A subject for another day," Gary counseled.

"Good point," said Luigi. "Gents," he continued, "isn't it strange how each of us has some creepy dude in our dreams? And guess who my guy looks like?"

"Prophet," said Rey.

"Good God," exclaimed Ken. Phillipe and Gary agreed. Everyone looked at each other.

"Okay, since I don't want my brain splattered all over some aluminum bleacher," said Original, "what's the plan, Matlock?"

"Isn't it obvious?" Loo responded. "Prophet panhandled us for drinks, right? He didn't curse the other tables, just us. Why? Because we *humiliated* him."

"He kinda humiliated himself," said Rey.

"Let's not argue semantics, okay? We didn't show Prophet respect then, so we show it now."

"How?" Phillipe asked Loo.

"We visit his grave."

"What, pour forties on his tombstone?" Phillipe asked.

"*Exactly,*" said Loo. "Beer's what he wanted, right?"

"Technically he asked for money," said Gary.

"Jesus, Graft, stop harping on the details!"

"Sorry," he said. "Details are a bit of a curse with me . . . no pun intended."

"Yeah, okay," said Loo. "Sleep deprivation's making me snappy."

"Does anyone know where Prophet's buried?" asked Ken.

"Cumberland," Loo responded. "Admittedly not around the corner, but doable."

"Doable?" asked Gary.

"Doable as in let's go tonight," Loo answered. "Who's with me?"

The guys just looked at him. "So you think that's the solution?" asked Phillipe. "An 'I'm sorry' and some Old English?"

"Look, Phillipe, if you've got something better, I'm all ears," said Loo. "I mean 7, 6, 2, and 2? Those numbers suck. They are bad percentages, gentlemen, and let's be honest: are our remaining women really sticking with us? Is Carol really going to stand by Trevor? And if you want to move past that, let's just focus on what our two friends were dreaming about before they died, and what we're dreaming about now."

"What about Trevor?" asked Ken. "I mean he wasn't even there that night."

"Maybe," said Loo, "but Splash left before Prophet came to our table, and look what happened to him."

"Won't we need all of us?" asked Gary. "Trevor too?"

"Unless you can break the guy out of jail, I think he's on his own," Loo answered. "So again I ask, who's with me?"

"Can it wait until tomorrow?" Original asked. "I'd be leaving Sylvia in a lurch."

"I'm going to die tonight in my sleep, guys!" Loo yelled, starting to lose it. "Maybe you guys too! It *has* to be tonight."

"Look, I don't mean to give some séance mumbo-jumbo credence," said Phillipe, "what with the twenty-first century right around the corner, but I guess it can't hurt. I can take three."

"Way ahead of you," said Loo. "I rented a nice van."

Slowly, the others agreed. Loo looked around the table at his friends picking desultorily at their food. *The Last Supper,* he thought gloomily. *Witness, good citizens, the end of the Evil Men's Book Club.*

Chapter 60: The Grave

Saturday, 13 November 1999
En route to Cumberland, MD

LOO DROVE. NO one spoke for the first twenty minutes. Finally, Phillipe cleared his throat, breaking the ice: "Got a question, guys. How many deer did the Deerslayer kill *after* Loo here got arrested?" He put a friendly hand on Loo's shoulder. Numbers were thrown out between two and fifty—no one knew for sure. "It's seven," Phillipe said.

Loo, who'd been tracking the Deerslayer through the news for months, knew he was right. There was Big Stew, of course, found a week after Loo's February arrest, then a two months' pause, the period Loo had sweated the most. To his immense relief, during the following six months, Park and Rec Police found six more bodies. Except for Big Stew, Loo had always retrieved his quarrels, never leaving a bolt in a carcass. The copycat, on the other hand, purposefully left them in.

"Been six weeks since they found one," Phillipe continued. "Do you think he's done?"

"I doubt it," said Ken. "He's got a taste for it, plus he's a celebrity now."

"Heard they got the serial number for the batch of bolts the Deerslayer's been using," said Phillipe, looking at Loo. "He used to remove them, but since you got arrested, he's been leaving them in."

Loo nodded warily at him in the rearview mirror. *Where you going with this?*

"Seven corpses, one quarrel each?" asked Gary.

"Yup," said Phillipe. He'd removed his hand from Loo's shoulder.

"Well, what do *you* think, Gallois?" asked Ken.

"I think he's done," he said.

Loo now understood what he—could the copycat be anyone *but* Phillipe Gallois?—was driving at. Before Henry had patently refused to help him, Loo had told him the location where he'd left his buried quiver, and Splash must have passed this information along to Phillipe, who, for whatever reason, did what Splash wouldn't: save Loo's ass. *No more bolts, no more dead deer* is what Phillipe was saying.

"What do you think, Loo?" Phillipe asked, startling him.

"I'm just grateful people don't think it's me anymore," he said.

"Obviously," said Gallois, laughing dully. Phillipe leaned close to Loo, whispering, "Don't thank me, killer, thank Splash."

Chastised, Loo drove on.

"I still think Trevor should be here," Gary said.

"We don't have time to mail him a file," said Original, "plus he already went to the grave, to Mark's funeral in fact. Maybe he made his peace then."

"Dunno," said Rey. "Trevor's 'really bad shit'—him going to jail—that happened after the service."

"I got a bottle for him," said Loo, as if this solved the problem. "Splash and Darius too."

Due to darkness, it took time to find the church's tiny parking lot, but they did. Since the cemetery gate was locked, four men in their prime hopped the crumbling masonry perimeter wall, then waited for the fifth one, Loo, to pass a cooler to them before hopping over himself. The light was poor. Loo hadn't thought to bring a flashlight, so it took five minutes to find the grave. As the graveyard wasn't totally remote (a passerby could see five men skulking about Christ the Redeemer's tombstones if he or she was looking), they got right to the "sacrificial act."

Loo handed five bottles around. "Sorry Mark," said Loo. "We didn't know." He asked if anyone else wanted to say anything. No one did.

They poured their bottles out.

"We don't leave these here, do we?" asked Ken.

"No," said Loo, "put them back in the cooler."

"What about D-Kay's and Splash's beer?" asked Phillipe. "And Trevor's?"

Loo handed out the three remaining bottles. Original, Rey, and Phillipe each took one. Rey and Original poured theirs out while Ken said, "For Henry and Darius." Phillipe made ready to open the last bottle, but Gary stopped him. "Wait. Perhaps we shouldn't. I mean Trevor's not here to represent himself. Can we really do it for him?" No one said anything. Loo took it, putting it back in the cooler, saying, "Okay, I'll give it to Trevor when he gets out."

"A beer's the last thing Trevor needs," said Ken. As weird as the circumstances were, everyone laughed.

"Okay guys," said Loo, "back in the van we go."

Chapter 61: The Christmas Present

Saturday, 11 December 1999
Wheaton, MD

TREVOR HERE. IF my life's a sandwich, it's now splat on the floor. Today, Saturday morning, started off great. Fantastic, in fact. I was released today, December 11, instead of March 6, and believe me, I don't complain.

I overhear the COs—early holiday releases for guys with good behavior are common. Two days ago, I'm told to arrange transportation. I don't call Carol, figuring I'd give her and Reesie a surprise Christmas present. El Jefe Arkin would surely pick me up, but he's done so much, so I call my friends instead. No one picks up except Phillipe. I saved him for last as he's still probably sore at me about the whole cross-dressing thing, but he says yes. Lots of paperwork yesterday, including another health screening, confirmation that I have housing and that I know who my parole officer is. This morning I put on new prison-release clothes, including a coat, pocketing a check for laundry wages: $73.07. I can't wait to tell Carol I've learned to fold the hell out of a shirt.

I meet Phillipe in the MC parking lot. He shakes my hand firmly, which I thought meant no hard feelings. I offer gas money, but he refuses. I ask about Southwest and he laughs drolly. He doesn't work there anymore. He's now a full-time pilot for those rich kooks, the Winsor Brothers. Good for him.

Before home, we stop at his apartment, and thankfully, no giant dress. I sign my check over to him and he gives me seventy bucks. I joke, "Keep the change," and again, he gives the same droll laugh.

I hit the closest grocery store, buying the largest flower bouquet it sells. Carol will yell at me for spending money, but my early homecoming's something to celebrate, right? I bring Phillipe back some lunch—Quiznos. I wolf mine down, but he puts his in the fridge, saying he'll eat it later, which is weird as I've never known the man to pass up food. Feeling guilty, I volunteer to walk home from his apartment, but he insists on driving me. *Okay,* I think, wishing he'd be chattier. I force the issue, asking, "How's Estelle?" and then immediately feel like an idiot, remembering Carol telling me they'd broken up months earlier. *How could I have forgotten that?*

I didn't know it yet, but that's when my "life" sandwich began sliding off the plate. He didn't seem upset with my gaffe. Just said he's started dating someone new. "Cool, what's her name?"

"Steve."

Hold the phone, *what*? I ask, "Is Steve a dude?"

"Well, Trevor, you know I like drag," he answers. "You of all people shouldn't be shocked."

Well, I *am* shocked. Phillipe, the manliest member of the EMBC, gay? I'd never mentally unpacked cross-dressing into *actual* homosexuality. It must be a gag. I mean, my God, the way Phillipe looks at Estelle, or I guess "looked" at her—no way this guy's in the closet.

"Okay," is all I manage to say.

He grabs his keys. "Let's go."

It's a very quiet ride. Totally silent, in fact. We pull up to my house. The bushes look a little raggedy. There are no Christmas decorations up yet, but otherwise everything looks the same—no car in the driveway, but that's because we don't have one anymore. Phillipe gets out, grabbing the flowers I'd forgotten in the rush to see my girls, but he doesn't give them to me. Instead, he puts them carefully on the hood. Besides Phillipe's surprise gayness, I sense something else is wrong. I extend my hand to thank him for dropping me off . . . and out of nowhere he slugs me! I go down on one knee, wobbly. I'm confused. I spent my entire time at Maryland Central anxious about violence, and now that I'm out, my friend's trying to kill me?

"Because of your big mouth, Trevor, I lost my job," he says. "Lost the respect of thirty guys. *Thirty guys!* And it's your fault I lost Estelle, you asshole. We were talking about *marriage*. So I cross-dress Thursday nights at the Men's Lounge. Big deal. *Why* couldn't you keep that secret? You ruined my life! This ride home—it's the last thing I'll ever do for you. You're lucky I don't kill you." He hands me the flowers. "Say hello to Carol for me." Then he drives off.

Holy hell, what just happened? Sure, I discovered his closet full of dresses, but *he* never knew this, and I never told anybody. Okay, so I gave him some grief at club meetings, but solely based on the Sasquatch dress. And how could *that* have gotten back to his Hanger 18 buddies, none of whom I know? Well, I've blacked out more often than I've let on—it's *possible* I said something somewhere to someone, but I don't know anything about a "men's lounge." Is it a gay bar?

My eye hurts. Gonna have a shiner. Can't go through the front door like this.

Still wobbly, I head around back, grabbing some slush and putting it on my eye. I sit by my barbeque, mulling over what just happened. Do I owe him an apology for something I *might* have said in a blackout months ago? And this men's lounge—I thought he played poker with his Hanger 18 buddies on Thursdays. There's some explanation for Phillipe's actions, I'm sure, but I decide I need to patch things up with him later. Right now, I'm home!

I look through Reesie's bedroom window, but she's not there. I don't know why I expected her to be—it's not like she takes naps anymore. I hope she and Carol aren't home. I've got flowers to arrange and a pocket full of love notes to hide. I wipe the slush from my eye and enter the house through the backdoor. It still makes the *weesh, thunk* noises. The way the house is laid out, I can sneak past the common areas, straight to the bedroom to hide the notes. The girls aren't in the kitchen or living room. The house feels empty; even Kitty Batman is AWOL. Odd—no Christmas tree.

I take a minute to unwrap the flowers, cut an inch off their stems, and put them in a vase. I move some dishes and an empty wine bottle out of the sink to fill the vase with water. They look good if I do say so myself. I head down the hallway. No one in the guest room. Our bedroom door is closed. On the off chance she's napping, I open it slowly.

As long as I live, I will never be able to un-see what I saw: David Chin's eyes transition from ecstasy to horror.

My wife and Chin-chin . . . The betrayal is annihilating. I drop my notes. They flutter to the floor. My wife pops vertical, a frightened jack-in-the-box. She utters . . . wait for it: "Trev, this isn't what it looks like." Folks, it's *exactly* what it looks like. David, pants around his ankles, bolts for our French doors, which open out to the backyard. His pants trip him and he falls flat on his face, whacking his head on one of the doors. I certainly don't care. I've never wished for someone's lobotomy harder. But he's up quickly, fumbling with the door bolts, impatiently pulling them. He cuts his hand getting one open, then yanks his pants up and flees.

Now there's blood on the wall.

Carol looks genuinely terrified but I certainly don't care—I feel only fury. I plan to end her. But as horrible as this treachery is, it's prison that saves me. My self-preservation kicks in: if I assault her, and *definitely* if I kill her, it's goodbye MC, hello Jessup. Carol's chest is heaving violently. She's crying, talking—it's incomprehensible. I don't care. My feelings are now so far up my mental ass that I don't expect to ever see them again.

And Reesie, my daughter. *My* daughter. Already the language of divorce. Where did you nasty cheaters put her?

"Reesie?" I ask coldly.

"At Ci-Ci-Cindy's," Carol stammers.

On one bedside table, *my side,* sit two half-full glasses of wine. The bottle in the kitchen sink: my wife is whoring *and* day-drinking! Rage boils inside me again. The fury returns. I want violence.

But for Reesie's sake, I know I can't. I try distracting myself, imagining some court judge's voice, *Mrs. Pug, were you planning on wrapping up your affair* before *Mr. Pug came home, or* after *his return, which unfortunately for you, was today?* Nope, not a helpful thought at all. I'm staring at those half-full wine glasses, completely pissed off. Carol's yelling. I turn toward her, catching her saying, "Say something!"

No, Carol, you get nothing.

So I'm not talking, but what's my plan? If I take one step forward, she'll back away, maybe pick up a lamp to defend herself, or worse, run through the French doors after Chin-chin. Can my ego handle that? Apparently not, because I don't move. Instead, I stare at the teary snot my blubbering wife's wiping away with the back of her hand. Our eight-year marriage is over, but what am I thinking? *There's blood on the wall. No one buys a house with bloody walls.*

Don't just stand there, you stupid cuckold, a voice says, *do something!* I turn, showing her my back. "I'm leaving," I say—lame, but the best I can come up with. I stomp down the hall into the kitchen, taking the wine bottle and throwing it hard to the floor. It shatters. There's a gasp from the bedroom. I look at my coat but am too angry to pick it up. As I reach the front door, my fury demands a better parting shot than *I'm leaving*. Loud enough to carry, I say, "Cut the flower stems daily because I won't be around to do it."

I have to hand it to my nasty little id; the barb gets the desired response. From the bedroom comes this keening. It's an awful, gut-wrenching wail. I walk out of the house, leaving the door open. *You and Chin-chin can pay the heating bill.*

David Fucking Chin-chin.

At the sidewalk, I know that if I turn right, I'll eventually get to Cisco's house. But I turn left toward David Chin's house instead, two homes away. I don't know what I'm gonna do when I get there, burn it down?

From the sidewalk, I look through the Chin's mammoth front window. There he stands, Husband of the Year, backlit by an eleven-foot tree. It's well-shaped, well-decorated, and I hate it. *Cheaters don't deserve Christmas trees!* Odd logic, perhaps, but "odd" is the only logic I have left. My next move will be a beaut: run at the window, crash through it headfirst, knocking Chin-chin and his obscene tree over.

But I don't do this.

What stops me isn't realizing that I'd never survive diving into what is undoubtedly very thick glass. What stops me is who David is holding: his son, Sunny. Even at this distance, I can tell that the kid is tired, as if he's been woken from a nap. I'm *furious* that Chin's using the boy as some sort of shield because it works.

I pivot back the way I came, toward Cisco's. During the hour it takes to reach his house, the cold has completely penetrated my thin prison Oxford because I hadn't grabbed my coat. I arrive at Cisco's cellar door, pressing the buzzer repeatedly.

"Who is it?" Cisco finally says.

"It's Trevor."

"You're out early."

"Yes."

"Everything okay?"

I pause. "No."

The door unlocks remotely. I step in. It's warm inside, which is good because I'm as cold as a frozen turkey. Despite this, I have my game face on, ready to explain everything. He pads down the steps, then walks toward me wearing rumpled Dockers and an old sweater. As self-absorbed as I am, in that moment I think, *God, you look terrible.*

He regards me, looking concerned, knowing something is very wrong. I manage to get out, "Carol, she was on her knees," before completely losing it, sobbing uncontrollably. He bear-hugs me, holding me while my body wracks.

It's forever until the spasms subside.

When I'm ready, he leads me to the couch, sitting next to me, arm around my shoulder, implicitly understanding not to ask questions yet. I know he thinks a lot of Carol. I know he's disappointed in her and I know he blames me. Right now, however, I'm his sole concern—the world contains only me and him. I've always respected Cisco, sometimes begrudgingly, but as of this evening, I truly love the man. When I calm down, he asks about Reesie. Is she safe? Yes. Carol is safe, too—I tell him I got the black eye elsewhere. Though it's still the afternoon, Cisco suggests I lie down in the bedroom. I do that. I'm beyond tired. Eventually, I sleep.

In the morning, real life starts again. I'm totally numb but feel I can pretend to do the correct motions—I do not want to go back to prison. Cisco drives me to Carol's to pick up some clothes and my coat. He's called ahead; there's a suitcase by the front door. Over the phone earlier, I overheard her tearily trying to explain "her" side of things. God bless him, for I know she's the daughter he never had, Cisco responded politely but firmly, "Call Alice McGovern."

Next up, an 11:00 a.m. meeting. Yesterday, I barely noticed, but now I see how terrible El Jefe looks. I'm surprised—he'd looked reasonably chipper during his last prison visit. "Are you sick?" I ask. He says no, just not sleeping well. "Are you sure?" He says yes in a way that means *Mind your own business.* After the meeting, which I have no memory of, we go to one of his default lunch stops, TGI Fridays. He orders a sandwich and coffee. I'm not hungry and am pretty sure I'll never eat again.

He gets right to it. "Trevor, would Carol have done what she did if you didn't drink like you do?"

It's a straightforward question, but I can't answer it with words. The image of Carol and David together is just too painful. I answer by shaking my head no.

"Trevor," he asks, "with all that's happened, *now* do you believe you're an alcoholic?"

"Yes," I say. I think I'm crying.

I marvel at what finally convinced me. It wasn't the runaway bar tabs or Old Line buying my debt. It wasn't losing my job and then my license. It wasn't that spectacular auto wreck, being arrested, or going to prison. It wasn't the blackouts or my ruined reputation. *It wasn't even seeing my woman with another man.* No matter how hard Cisco had fought not to show it yesterday, it was the *pity* in his eyes. *You're a drunk, Trevor, and as bad as you've made it, you'll do it all over again, and worse, so you can keep drinking.*

I realize this is all another moment of clarity. Seeing my wife and Chin like that was wretched, but it represented a cold and viciously simple truth that I've now been forced to accept: if I wasn't an alcoholic, I'd have a faithful spouse. *The weapon may have been made by Anheuser-Busch, Trevor ol' boy,* I think to myself, *but you wielded it.*

I'm now ready to do the AA deal fully, no half measures, so we start again with Step One, me being powerless over alcohol, emphasizing the step's second part: acknowledging that my life is unmanageable—by me, anyway, and boy is that ever true. My life sandwich? Like I said: splat on the floor, with a boot print through it.

We make some progress, an hour's worth, Cisco drinking cup after cup of coffee. My cell phone rings.

"Hello," I respond.

"Trevor, it's Angie. Angie Chin. Where are you?"

"At a restaurant in Wheaton."

"I'm downtown at the Winsor Hotel. Can you meet me? We need to talk."

Chapter 62: My Ugly Higher Power

Saturday, 11 December 1999
Washington, DC

MEETING UP WITH Angie Chin is a terrible idea that I promptly agree to. I know it's just Satan wanting all 211 days of my current sobriety back, but I don't care. "I'll be there by six."

"I'll be in the bar," Angie says.

If I wasn't in the middle of step work, I would have lied about the call, but I tell Cisco the truth. He's obviously not thrilled about my dinner plan. "You're going downtown to meet up with the other wounded party, huh? You're gonna sit in a bar, commiserate, *drink*, then take revenge on your wife. That your plan?"

"What if it is?" I say defiantly.

Cisco looks pained. He's not mad, however. He quotes the Big Book of Alcoholics Anonymous: "'I vaguely sensed I was not being any too smart.' Well, Trevor, it's your business. But if you go, you'll need a new sponsor."

"Okay," is all I can say. I thank him for the lunch I didn't eat, then find the nearest bus stop.

I'm not thinking I'll hook up with Angie, who I'm sure is just as traumatized as I am, but I take Cisco's threat seriously. If I can't stay with him, where will I go? Not only do *'I vaguely sense I was not being any too smart,'* I also sense that I may soon walk the trail Prophet blazed for me: homelessness. What I'm doing is a terrible mistake. I know this, but I don't stop.

The bus comes. I have enough for the fare. I'm let off a few blocks from the Winsor. I enter the lobby, realizing that this DC landmark is like many others—one I've never visited before. There's no need to ask the concierge where the bar is. I gravitate to it naturally, like thirst to water. Angie's sitting in a booth, drinking wine. There's an appetizer in front of her but she's not touched it. She looks miserable. I sit opposite her.

She breaks the ice, pointing toward her plate: "Are you hungry?"

"No," I say.

She looks closer at me, scrunching her eyes. "Didn't know Carol had it in her."

I'm thinking *obviously* she did since I caught her and Chin-chin in the act.

"Your eye," she says.

"Oh," I say, realizing what she's talking about. "Someone else did that."

"I'm sure it wasn't David," she says with contempt. "Does it hurt?"

"No," I say. "Does it look bad?"

"Yes, very."

It's been a long time since I've spoken with Chin-chin's better half—I've forgotten how brutally honest she is. *Remember, Trev,* I tell myself, *she's been stabbed in the back too.* "How are you doing with this, Angie?"

"I'm not sure," she says guardedly. "David was pretty vague."

"I'm sure he was."

"What do you know?" she asks.

"I got out of prison yesterday, early release. Didn't tell Carol. Had a friend pick me up. He's the one that hit me. Long story. Anyway, wanted to surprise the wife. Turns out I did."

I get this all out quickly. She looks at me, unblinking. I'm wondering if she's a kindred spirit, one that compartmentalizes too.

"You wanna drink?" she asks, rotating a wine glass carefully by the neck. It's half full; she's half drunk.

"No thanks."

At this moment, I honestly think I don't want one. Maybe she doesn't know my stay at MC was alcohol related. After all, Carol's been tight-lipped outside the family. My evil little id speaks up: *But, buddy boy, she hasn't been tight-lipped with good-ol' Chin-chin, has she?* The double entendre nauseates me.

"How was prison?" she asks.

"Safer than the movies make it out to be."

Angie looks stern, which is typical, but despite her misery, she also looks good. She's dressed professionally in a smart-looking business suit. There's cleavage, but it's not overdone. I think she's recently gotten her hair styled and her jewelry catches the bar light. I wonder if she's already on the hunt. "Why meet here?" I ask.

"I've been here all day," she says. "Legal seminar."

I nod, asking how she found out.

"David called me. Said he was taking Sunny to stay with his mother for . . . I guess I don't know how long."

"That's all he said?" I ask. "You figured it out from that?"

"Yes," she says authoritatively. "I can read him like a book. He also said you were mad at him. Afraid you'd hurt Sunny."

I'm livid hearing this. "I would *never* hurt Sunny."

"I believe you," Angie says. The hand absently twirling her glass stops. Her other hand grips her cloth napkin, twisting it. "Trevor, did you . . . catch them in the act?"

I don't answer right away because I can't.

"Never mind," she says. "I don't want to know."

"Listen, Angie, how are you doing . . . for real?"

She stops wringing her napkin and composes herself, as if it's important to give a well-articulated answer, like she must do in court. "Not good," she says. "This is going to cost me." Now *this* is the Angie I've come to know, the one Carol loves to hate. She blushes, reading my mind. "I don't mean *money*, though that's going to be a problem too. I mean emotionally." She's said this stoically. I ask her if she's angry. She says she is, but there's no oomph behind her answer. Maybe she's still in shock. Or maybe she really is what Carol calls "a cold fish."

"Did you see this coming?" she asks.

"No." I add lamely, "I've been in prison."

She begins dabbing away tears, but her mascara stays intact. "What did we do wrong, Trevor?"

Isn't it obvious? We don't need Dr. Phil to know we took our spouses for granted. But I don't say this. "You didn't do anything wrong, Angie. It's my fault. I effed up and went to prison. If I was . . . around, this wouldn't have happened." But is this true? Even before the accident, the way I was acting, might it have happened anyway? Perhaps it's been going on for months, her weekly MC visits just so much smoke being blown up my ass.

Angie starts twirling her glass again. Its remaining content catches the light, glowing thickly, like some potion. *You're not a wine man, Pug,* I tell myself, which is true. But Angie's obviously a wine girl: this is the second glass she's polished off since I've sat down. Of course, who am I to judge, right?

She looks at me and orders another. What she's thinking now, I can only guess. No, that's a lie. I know exactly what she's thinking because I'm thinking it too. It helps that I've always found her cold assertiveness attractive. I'm normally turned off by ambitious women—sorry, wish I was more "liberated"—but right now I'm not turned off at all. I have one of those unhealthy, alcoholic "first thoughts" Cisco keeps talking about: does she ask for what she wants in bed or is the bedroom the last place her ambition has to conquer? "Angie, why'd you marry David?"

She considers, answering, "Because I deserve him." It's a statement that can be taken several ways. Given my opinion of Chin-chin, none of them are good. "Why do you say that?" I ask.

"You know why," she answers.

"Not exactly."

"Because I don't deserve a real man."

I'm genuinely surprised. "Come again?"

She empties her glass, catches the waiter's eye, then holds up two fingers. "I said I don't deserve a real man."

I've never thought much of Chin-chin—he's a pathetic douche, especially now—but Angie not deserving a "real" man? I don't believe it.

"Trevor, don't be stupid," she says, reading my thoughts. "I'm not *warm*. David's warm, inside and out, at least he was when I first met him. Now he's sad all the time . . . because . . . I *make* him that way." She segues, "He just started his first real job, you know. Great pay. Monsanto gave him a fifteen grand signing bonus."

"Great," I respond. "You can use it to pay for the divorce." Two glasses of wine arrive, one for her and apparently one for me. I don't protest. "Sorry, Angie. That was a rude thing to say. And really dumb since you're a divorce lawyer. I just don't like being called stupid."

"I'm sorry," she says. "I don't mean to be abrasive—I just can't seem to help it sometimes."

An elderly man approaches our table carrying a fancy bag. "Are you Miss Chin?" he asks Angie.

"I am," she says.

"Well hello, enchanting lady! My name is Adam Winsor. Cleveland, the concierge, said you needed a night kit, and since I was passing this way, it's my pleasure to deliver it." He produces an ingratiating smile.

"Thank you, Mr. Winsor. So, this is your hotel?"

"Yes, my brother and I have been running it since 1960. Our father, who built it, ran it before that. Is this your first time staying at our humble inn, Miss Chin?"

"Yes. I was at the *Women and Twenty-first Century Law* seminar held here earlier."

"Oh, how lovely," the old man says. "So, you want to be a lawyer?"

"I am a lawyer. I was giving the seminar."

Mr. Winsor's eyes pop, not with embarrassment, as perhaps they should have, but with recognition. "Damn my memory, Miss Chin! How could I forget? Your lovely likeness graces the brochure. So, is this your husband?" It's an innocent enough question as we're both wearing rings.

"No," she says.

I jump in with, "Sir, Mrs. Chin is my neighbor. Her husband watches my wife, I mean my daughter and her son. You know, childcare."

"That's wonderful," says Winsor, but his eyes say otherwise. "Will they be joining you?"

"No," says Angie. "They're both . . . watching the kids now."

"Oh, I see," says Winsor slyly. "Sir, do you need a kit as well?"

I can tell Winsor's getting off on us being some "scandalous" couple. I can't blame him. For starters, there's my black eye. Did her jealous husband do it or did Miss I'm-already-a-lawyer give it to me? *Better than a soap opera, Pops, isn't it?*

"No, I don't need a kit," I say, "but thank you, Mr. Winsor." I change the subject: "Sir, I believe you employ a friend of mine, Phillipe Gallois."

He looks at me uncertainly.

"Your jet jockey?"

"Oh, yes, Johnny Pilot! What a dear chap. Such a great addition to our family. So you're a friend of Johnny's, eh?"

I nod. *Yes, sir, he's the guy that gave me this beaut of a shiner.*

"Well, a friend of Johnny's is a friend of mine. Please continue enjoying our hospitality. And sir, don't hesitate to speak with Cleveland if you change your mind about that kit." With that, he winks lasciviously, then departs, buttonholing our waiter.

"He likes you," I say.

"Not my type."

"Ancient?" I was hoping for a laugh but don't get one. I examine the wine glass which has somehow jumped into my hand. "Angie, what is your type?"

"You mean, before David?"

"Yes, that's what I mean." But it's not exactly what I mean.

Her new glass is already half empty and she begins twirling it, the wine swirling evenly. She rubs the glass with her thumb, making the rim sing. It's alluring, sexy. She's wearing perfume. On her wrists for sure, maybe elsewhere too. Instead of answering my question she says, "Heard about your DUI. You're not driving tonight, right?" The message: *One glass won't hurt you*. Or perhaps it's a different message.

I nod slightly.

"Do you have a place to stay?" she asks.

The fact is, I don't. I burned a bridge with Cisco. None of my remaining friends will call me back, and I realize sadly that Henry and D-Kay can't because they're dead. "I'll be okay," I say. "But you . . . David's taken Sunny to his mom's. You can go home."

"But I don't want to," she says. "What type of women do *you* like, Trevor?"

"All kinds." *Including drunk, hurting ones.*

"You're not choosy?"

"Honestly, Angie, it's been a while since I've had to choose, and you didn't answer me earlier—the type of men you like."

"Complicated and unavailable, which never works out," she replies. After a pause to drink, she adds, "David was uncomplicated and available, so I jumped on him. I mean, I jumped at the opportunity to be with him."

"I know what you meant," I say. Since we're so chummy now, I ask, "When's the last time you guys slept together?"

Without hesitation, she says, "The night Sunny was conceived."

Wow, so it's basically been forever. Even though it's now permanently broken, I decide now's not a good time to bring up my eight-year sex streak. "Why the drought?" I ask.

Defensively: "Why'd your wife seduce my husband?"

For a moment, maybe two, I'm indignant. *Why do you assume Carol initiated this?* But in thinking it through, she has a point. Chin-chin, whose only passion seems to be fire ants, would never have worked up the nerve to seduce anybody. However, though I currently loathe Carol, I'm not ready to throw her under the bus just yet. "Honestly, Angie, I don't know who did what or when they did it. I've been in jail. Maybe you're right about Carol. Still, whore or not"—it's amazing how easy it is to use this term now—"it takes two to tango."

Angie's on the verge of tears again. "No, Trevor, this is all my fault. I work too much. I'm never home. I hounded him every day to finish his fucking dissertation. Two months ago, after Monsanto offered him a job, we did something rare—we went out to celebrate. I know deep down he hates me, but he was still, you know . . . *trying.* When we got home, he . . . made overtures, and I couldn't, Trevor." Fat tears well in her eyes. "I was a coward. I should have said yes." One of the tears rushes down her cheek. "It must have started then."

"You gonna stick with him?" I ask, amazed at how coherent she is after so much wine.

After a considered silence and another generous intake of wine, she says, "Probably."

"Why? I'm sure as hell not sticking with Carol!"

"Mine was already a loveless marriage, Trevor. David's cheating doesn't change that. He takes great care of Sunny, which is good because . . . I'm a bad mom. And honestly, we need the money."

We. She assumes they're still a "we." Good for her. But right now I can tell the only "we" she cares about is the two of us sitting at this table. Sure, she'll patch it up with Chin-chin after some suitable punishment period, say six months' separation to keep him on his toes, but tonight, it's written on her face: she wants revenge.

There's a soft lamp behind her. It's sending light through the whorls of her ears, making them glow—very attractive. There's longing in her eyes, calculated perhaps, but definitely real. There's longing in my eyes, too, I assume, but I wonder, *Does my black eye make me look stupid?*

Her desire coalesces in an intense stare. *Kit or no kit, Trevor, do you want to go upstairs with me?*

Of course I do. But I also want the wine in my glass.

The Devil speaks: *You can have both, you idiot.*

It's decision time.

I drink my glass, then order another. Angie's pleased. She asks if I want a third, but I'm no alcoholic, so I refuse. She attempts to pay the bill only to learn Adam Winsor has, in the words of our waiter, "excused it." A knowing look from the man—voyeurism on Mr. Winsor's part. *Winsor, you old letch.* I ask for a bottle to go. The waiter retrieves one.

We head to the elevator, standing close together, hands almost touching. The doors open. Our images appear in the elevator's reflective surfaces. She takes my hand, looks up at me, then places a slow kiss on my lips. It's wonderful and I will the elevator to rise faster. The doors finally open. We move with a comical casualness, not wanting to look like what we are: two lovers-to-be bolting for their room. She hands me the swipe card: *To cement the deal, you must be the one to open the door.* I do so.

We're inside, breathlessly looking into the foyer's full-body mirror. I think, *This is the last chance to call this off.* But I don't. My hands are on her neck and the small of her back, hers around my shoulders. We kiss again. Her tongue, thick with wine, searches for mine as we fall onto the bed's coverlet like a cataract.

I place the bottle carefully onto the rug, saving it for later.

In bed, whatever we lack in familiarity, we make up for with enthusiasm. I'm far from drunk and will most certainly climax. She's plastered, but that's helping her. She's passionately moaning, clawing my back for her orgasm.

But though we're coupled, we're not in synch, not *together,* as Carol and I call it. I look over my shoulder, worried that people—the bride's maids and best men from both our weddings, for instance—are watching, disgusted with what they see. Thankfully they aren't watching, but Adam Winsor is, and his licentious eyes speak to me: *Ah, friend of Johnny's, welcome to my world!*

Odd as it might seem, it's Old Man Winsor, the lecherous Ghost of Christmas Past, who ends up saving my sobriety. My Higher Power has, in a very ugly way, used his apparition to outflank Old Scratch, because Angie and I have not left the table yet. I look longingly at the undrunk wine in my glass, then put it down. I give Angie one last look, a combination of longing and sadness, then say, "I so very badly want to . . . but . . ."

Her eyes plead: *Trevor! I don't have the strength to rebel with anyone else. It must be you—it must be tonight!* I believe her.

"But I can't, Angie. I just can't." Her eyes well again. She closes them, squeezing out tears, then nods disappointedly. "Good night then, Trevor."

"Good night, Angie." In the lobby, I call Cisco. I explain and beg him to take me back. He's not happy. He tells me to wait outside—it'll be at least forty-five minutes. Ugly or not, he tells me to stand on the sidewalk and thank my Higher Power because, "Kid, you just received a whole lot of grace you didn't deserve."

Once again, Cisco is right, and I'm so relieved that he is.

Chapter 63: He Said, She Said

Monday, 13 December 1999
Wheaton, MD

STILL ME, MISERABLE Trevor Pug.

It's thankfully the next day, Monday, and my sponsor keeps me mercifully busy. First, El Jefe drives me to Rockville to meet my parole officer. She's a short, no-nonsense African-American woman named Lakeesha Knox. Mrs. Knox is middle-aged with brightly dyed hair. Though diminutive, I show her the appropriate amount of respect, which is to say a lot. *Confirm your address, Mr. Pug.* I give Cisco's, saying I have "marital problems." I don't get sympathy, I get *Do you have a job?* I tell her I'm in contact with my old boss, Frank Deguzman. This is mostly true: this morning, I left him a message. *There will be unannounced checks at work and at home,* she says. I nod, expecting this. *Fail to show for an appointment, back to Maryland Central. Fail a drug test, back to Central. Work no-show: back to Central.* I don't like her, but as Cisco reminds me, Mrs. Knox didn't put me at her desk, I did.

Jefe then takes me to an Oxford House, transitional housing for recovering drunks and addicts. (I can't stay at Cisco's as he's got a firm rule: no more than two consecutive overnights.) Chico Rodrigez lives here at this house, along with six other guys. If accepted, I'll make eight, a full house. They all see my black eye but no one asks questions, which is good because my mental walls are very thin: in the last two days, I've been conditionally released from prison, had my clock rung, witnessed my wife's infidelity, narrowly avoided "going back out" with Angie Chin in two different ways, met my county chaperone, and now I'm potentially moving in with seven other substance abusers. All in all, a big weekend.

As messed up as I am, there's still gratitude, especially for Arkin. He's really come through for me. I'm seven months sober now, and don't want to "go back out." I believe the AA maxim: It's easier to *stay* sober than it is to *get* sober.

I get accepted. Chico's great, shows me the ropes here at Mickey's Mansion. The house is nicknamed so because the front bushes resemble giant round mouse ears. Chico and I are going to be roommates. He apologizes for the tight quarters, but I remind him where I've been recently—this space is a huge step up. The Mansion has many rules, one being that everyone needs a reason to be out of the house during the day, a job being the best reason. There's this guy, Ricky, a sort of housemother, who runs things. Everyone's assigned a minimum number of AA or NA meetings to attend each week, plus chores. Ricky looks like he's worried I'll balk at scrubbing toilets, but I'll scrub as many toilets as necessary to stay out of prison.

It turns out I won't need to wander the streets during the day. With the Y2K meltdown eighteen days away, Frankie Deguzman returns my call. He's dealing with a last-minute work crush, so I'm hired over the phone, with conditions. I'm to be paid hourly, two bucks above minimum, with no benefits. "Screw up and you're out on your ass." I thank Frank and tell him I'll see him tomorrow.

Tuesday, 14 December 1999

The next morning, I return to Sim Systems. It's a madhouse, so crowded with coders that I'm put in the tiny kitchen to work. Frank brings me some truly bad coding—some of it I can fix, some of it I just redo from scratch. I don't mind. The work keeps my mind from *squirming like a toad* as the song says. Scooter, a guy at Mickey's Mansion, picks me up at 5:30 and we hit a meeting on the way home. Back at the Mansion, without work to do or a meeting to attend, thoughts of Carol's betrayal begin choking me. TV, talking with the guys—nothing seems to help. I skip dinner, taking my squirmy toads to bed with me.

Wednesday, 15 December 1999

I'm not sure who's more amazed that I show up to work the following day: Frank or me. I didn't want to get up, but Chico threatened to drag me out of bed. I threw some sandwiches together, then Chico dropped me off. So here I am again in Sim 2K's kitchen with my computer tower, a large screen (screensaver: HO HO HO BOY, IT'S Y2K), an ergonomic keyboard, a trackball, and dozens of red-lined computer printouts.

Being parked in the kitchen's no doubt a code violation, but the guys don't care about that. They care that they unfortunately now have a fulltime kitchen monitor. There's a sign above the sink—YOUR MOTHER DOESN'T WORK HERE, CLEAN UP AFTER YOURSELF. Before my arrival, people ignored it. There was soda stealing, dish dumping, and don't get me started on the asshat stirring his coffee with the communal creamer spoon. As head of the Food Police, or as Frank puts it, the Gazpacho Gestapo, I perform a necessary public service. There are no five-finger discounts anymore, and no one slinks away after exploding an enchilada in the microwave. I'm training them to identify and correctly use a sponge. Admittedly, as the new sheriff in town, I'm unpopular. However, since I have ten years on these buttheads and am a convicted felon in the best physical shape of my life, they're towing the line. What did Willie used to say? *Let them hate so long as they fear*. Right on, Willie.

Friday, 17 December 1999

Cisco's making me write a daily gratitude list. Things on it for today: I'm indoors. I'm out of jail. I'm out from under Old Line, though I shiver to think what Carol *really* did to get us clear. My nosy parole officer is satisfied.

And I've got a great sponsor. But I'm concerned about his health. He doesn't look well. He's been pushing the program hard on me (admittedly, what sponsors are supposed to do) but he has this almost unhealthy sense of urgency. I kid him about his girlfriend in Cumberland, Mrs. Marks, but he doesn't bite, saying he'd pulled the plug when she began attending his meetings (a big no-no). I tell him it's not her fault—she's in love. He tells me to buzz off.

I haven't seen my daughter, Reesie, since being released. I've asked Cisco to intercede with Carol, have her leave the house so I can visit, but he's refusing to referee. "When it becomes important enough to you," he says, "you'll pick up the phone and call Carol yourself," but I don't see that happening.

Christmas isn't too far off. I've picked up something for Reesie, which I guess I'll leave on my doorstep, Santa Claus-style. Speaking of yuletide, there's this box of ten thousand wooden coffee stirrers that's been sitting in the Mansion basement, apparently since the beginning of Time. The other night, Scooter, the guy who drives me home, brings the box up, produces an industrial-sized bottle of Elmer's, and starts gluing. Before long, the other guys, including me, join in (anything to keep my thoughts from Carol). It takes three nights but now we have a symmetric, nine-foot-tall Christmas tree made entirely out of stirrers, with lights and a star on top—truly a work of art.

With his creative gift, Scooter could really make something of himself. Ricky says that's true for all of us, but as housemother, he's supposed to say "healthy" shit like that. I get Reesie this nice teddy bear, a Gund, if you know what that is. The vest the bear wears has a pocket. I've stuffed it full of "love notes" for her, all G-rated, of course, but the real message is for Carol: *There's only my daughter now*. But if that's the case, why am I thinking about my wife constantly? The betrayal's still raw, of course, and oh how I still want to murder David Fucking Chin-chin, but there's something else. Scooter, who let me be the one to plug the coffee stirrer tree's lights in, says it's sadness. *You might be right, Scooter.*

I, Carol Pug, can't believe I'm ringing Alice McGovern's doorbell again, but I am. The door opens but instead of letting me in, Alice steps out, coat on, pocketbook in hand. "Hello, Carol," she says brightly.

"I don't understand, Alice," I say.

"We're going to a meeting."

I realize that going to a meeting is the price of re-connection. I'm tempted to say no, politely, of course, and drive home in Cindy Spicotti's car which I've borrowed yet again, but instead, I let her lead me to her Continental, obediently getting in. She backs the whale out a little too close to the mailbox for my comfort, but I say nothing, saving my energy for reciting my *This is how I'm going to fix things* speech, which I've been working on all week. Instead, I promptly start crying. Alice hands me a tissue. In addition to being a pretty good driver, she's a prepared one.

It's a quiet ride—there's no need to talk; I'd given Alice the rundown of my situation already over the phone. I'm scared, but it isn't the Al-Anon meeting that frightens me—the trips to Hell were far worse—it's this feeling that whatever advice these people have, it'll be wasted on me. She's just trying to help, but the next time Alice slows, I'm going to jump.

Reesie, you're all I have now. I'll be devastated when you learn that *not seeing Daddy* is my fault. As far as you know, he's still in prison. I threw away the flowers, swept up the notes. But I missed one and you found it: SO GLAD YOU ARE MY CELLMATE AGAIN. Cute, huh? But even a six-year-old knows it's a new note, not an old one. I lie like a champ, telling her Trevor gave it to me at my last prison visit—it must've fallen out of my purse. To this she says, "But it sounds like Daddy's already back home, Mommy." I say nothing. What *could* I say?

I elect not to jump from the moving Continental, so we both arrive at a community center with seatbelts on. The Al-Anon meeting is in an anteroom—twenty people: fifteen women, five men. I expect a circle of folding chairs, but instead, it's a bunch of couches set in a square, facing each other. They're huge; one couch has four people on it. One of the sitters is a very young woman with metal hoops through her ear cartilage. Oddly, she's knitting, such an old biddy pastime for someone so young. Most of the men look like they'd be hen-pecked even if their wives weren't drunks, but there's one confident, twenty-something named Brad who looks way too young to be married—but is. He's talking now, "sharing" in a calm voice like Mr. Arkin's.

Brad's a schoolteacher, part-time baseball ump, loves animals. And good looking. I'm not salivating here, it's just that he looks like the *last* guy you'd expect to see at a self-help meeting. What woman wouldn't straighten herself out for him? Apparently, his wife, Joan, an alcoholic trainwreck, is one such woman. Brad describes everything he's tried: hiding her alcohol, pouring it out, threatening to leave, then actually leaving. Nothing has worked. They're separated now. She's living in a motel with a guy named Dwight. Dwight has only one leg. They live off his disability money, which isn't enough to both drink *and* pay rent, so they panhandle at a freeway ramp.

Brad narrates his story smoothly, like a documentarian. The others are supportive, laughing at him—well, not *at* him, but with him—like they have their own versions of Joan. He talks about "detaching with love," which my mother, Gladys, calls tough love. He's found the strength to do this by attending Al-anon meetings and having a sponsor. I thought they only had sponsors in AA. Guess I'm wrong.

I realize that everyone's been "sharing" in order around the couches and my turn is next. I panic: the last thing I want to do is share my personal misery with complete strangers. Brad comes to my rescue: "Just tell us your name."

I try to speak, but nothing comes out.

"You can make one up if you want," says Brad. Everyone laughs at that, even me. Finally, I say my name but nothing else. After a polite pause, they thank me, and the next person starts—the wave of judgment I'd expected never materializes.

After the meeting, we returned to Alice's. This time, she invites me in. Mentally, I say *No, I've had enough for one day,* but in I go. The house smells like Pine-sol and good manners. I'm served the same wonderful coffee and we sit on the same comfortable furniture. She asks me what I thought of the meeting. I say it was educational. She asks what I learned, I say, "Alcoholism is a family disease," and then I wonder if that means Reesie will get it.

"So, Carol, tell me about yourself," asks Alice. "What brings you joy?"

Not a question I was expecting. My answer: "Writing."

I explain that I have a master's degree in English and, as cheesy as it sounds, want to write the Great American Novel. *Yes,* I chose to be a mom, and with that decision came responsibility and *yes,* I was okay with putting off the novel. I explain that about eighteen months ago, I felt I could start back on it, slowly, of course. I explain that Trevor's never been a big reader.

I then explain, in broad terms, the Evil Men's Book Club—how it was my husband's idea, oddly enough—and though the boys don't necessarily pick books *I'd* like to read, their selections are literature. Or at least literature-ish. Trevor read *Lolita,* liking it, and I recall the wonderful conversation we'd had about Nabokov. I explain finding a beautiful hardback of another Nabokov novel, *Ada,* in a secondhand bookstore. It was for Trevor's birthday, which he unfortunately spent in prison. I further explain that I'd gone to the trouble of unwrapping it, then re-wrapping it as a Christmas gift, even though he wouldn't be home for the holidays. Sweet, right? I then explain that the book never made it under the tree, however, because I didn't want my friends, or worse, my mother, to see it and feel sorry for me.

Then I tell her something surprising, even to me: I didn't want David to see it there, either. Why? I now realize that David, who gave me a book on Chaucer just because I mentioned Chaucer in passing, *might be jealous* if he saw it. This revelation stuns me.

Alice nods: *Go on.*

Back to the book. I describe how I've avoided putting *Ada* under the tree by not *getting* a tree, even though Reesie's been begging for one. We don't have the money is what I told her, even though, thanks to David, we do, but I don't tell Alice that. "Do you know what she wanted to do, Alice? Chop down a pine from the backyard by herself. Put a hatchet in the hands of a six-year-old? I don't think so. So she asks all pouty like, 'Why can't Mr. Chin do it?' I tell her it's Daddy's job. 'But Daddy won't be home for Christmas,' she says. I had no response for that, Alice. None."

I continue in this vein until Alice stops me: "Forgive me for being so blunt, Carol, but right or wrong, why did you sleep with David?"

An abrupt transition, but at least it's a simple question. Did I physically "want" him? I was lonely, sure, but I wasn't lusting after David. The way he sometimes looked at me, maybe he was lusting after me? *No, don't blame this on him.* "I must've wanted to, Alice, or I wouldn't have done it." Carol nods hearing this. I give her more information, including the fact that I initiated things.

Almost dismissively, Alice says, "It takes two and he didn't say no, did he?"

"At first he did," I say, "but we both knew that that's what you're supposed to say."

"Carol, never mind what he should or shouldn't have said. Again I ask: *why* did you sleep with him?"

I pause, shame welling in my throat, choking me, but I finally get it out: "David . . . lent me fifteen thousand dollars. No, he *gave* me fifteen thousand dollars."

"What for?" asked Alice.

"To pay off loan sharks."

"Okay," says Alice.

I have to say, she's not fazed by my answer.

"Let's put that aside for now," she says. "Carol, at some level, David, the prince in this scenario, understandably expects a kiss from the princess, right?" The question makes me sick. Then she hits me right between the eyes.

"Carol, I'm not going to lie to you. What you did, cheating on your husband, wasn't right. I don't have to tell you that it was a huge mistake."

I'm taken aback. Though we've been talking around it all evening, the words *cheating on your husband* and *it was a huge mistake* just shovels on the shame. But before I can sneak into her bathroom to die, she continues.

"Carol, it was more than the money and you know that. You and David were both lonely. The way you describe him, he may not be handsome or Mr. Personality, but he's a good guy, right?" I nod. "And David didn't just bail you out of a financial mess. David watched your child while you worked, sacrificing his own time. David listened to you. David played with your daughter. It's natural to want to reward him in some way."

I don't have anything to say.

"And Carol, you must sense that David, who bought you books on subjects you care about, is at least half in love with you. You must know that's true. Are you in love with him?"

Had she asked me before Trevor came home unexpectedly, I might have said yes, at least a little, but as much of a dumpster fire as my life currently is, the answer is no. I love Trevor. I also hate him. I tell her this.

"Makes sense to me," says Alice. "Another question. While Trevor was in prison, except for sex, was there anything David *wasn't* providing that Trevor used to?"

"Well, maybe lawncare—"

She looks—oh, what's the word?—cross. "Carol," declares Alice, "pre-alcoholic Trevor provided everything I mentioned, *including sex*, and *yes*, lawncare, not to mention writing love notes and chasing you around the bedroom every Thursday night for eight years, which, believe me, *is* some kind of record."

Wow, I have really set Alice off.

"But now, unfortunately, there's only Alcoholic Trevor," she continues. "Alcoholic Trevor will *never* provide these things again—not consistently, anyway. Once a pickle, always a pickle, never a cucumber again. But the good news, Carol?" she says, relaxing a little. "*Trevor's the alcoholic*, not you. Alcoholism is his problem to solve, not yours."

"Maybe you're right, Alice," I say. "He says he's going to leave me, so I guess he won't be my problem anymore."

Alice looks cross again. "Oh but he *will be your problem*, Carol. He's the father of your child. Even if he were the worst dad in the world, legally, morally, spiritually, he has a claim on Reesie, so even if you divorced him tomorrow and got re-married the next, he has rights. You'll need to co-parent. You'll need to meet and at least pretend to like his next wife—Reesie's future stepmom. Believe me, I've met the man, he's quite charming—he'll have one soon enough. So yes, Carol, you'll be dealing with Trevor, sober or not, for the foreseeable future."

And I thought I wanted to die before.

Alice smiles; it's genuine and disarming. "But you can relax tonight, Carol, because your only job right now is to understand that your mission is you, not Trevor."

I look at her like I'm not understanding . . . because I'm not understanding.

"You're here tonight for the same reason I first showed up at my sponsor's house," Alice continues. "I was doing too much, *being* too much. Too much was being asked of me. I get it, Carol. You work fifty hours a week. You're in debt. Your husband, now a parolee, has found out you've had an affair. You're raising a daughter, alone, which may or may not be a permanent condition. But saving your marriage, assuming you want to, and protecting your daughter—these aren't the reasons to work with me. I'm not a marriage counselor, I'm not a child advocate. But living one day at a time with the alcoholic in your life, Trevor—*that* I can help you with. That is, assuming you want my help. Do you, Carol?"

I nod.

"Good. Can you take direction?"

I say yes.

"Without 'improving' upon it?"

After pausing, I say yes again.

"Good," says Alice. "Well, I think we're done for the night. You look exhausted. And if you aren't, I am. Do you need to get home right away?"

"Reesie's staying overnight at Cindy's," I say. "I didn't know how late this would go."

"Do you want to watch some TV? Perry Mason's coming on."

"Sure."

We watch Perry Mason. It's an early one with dashing men in suits, women in full makeup, snappy dialogue. As usual, no matter how smart and determined Perry is, he can't close the deal without help from his trusty secretary, Della Street. They're a seamless team . . . *A seamless team.* This thought destroys me and I start bawling again, really wailing this time.

Alice puts her arm around me, handing me a Kleenex from a box I swear wasn't there a minute ago, and for the first time since that awful scene in my bedroom, I feel like I might survive this.

Chapter 64: The Bookkeeper

Saturday, 18 December 1999
Waldorf, MD

"GARY, IT'S TOO late," said Rey, "I already told Luntz. Yeah, yeah, I get it, you're not happy. Yeah, whatever. Just get here as fast as you can."

Rey disconnected, then put his cell phone, a tiny one that he was always losing, in his pocket. He looked at Christian Luntz, who was also sitting at Old Line's clubhouse bar.

"He's on his way," said Rey. Christian nodded, his face neutral, but Rey had learned well that Luntz was never neutral. Rocker was there, as was Rey's least favorite biker, Mullet, who was tending bar. All four had beers, but Rey was the only one drinking.

It was late on a December afternoon and already dark outside. *I should have left hours ago,* Rey thought, *but Gary wouldn't agree to come earlier, even though he knows I don't like being at the compound after dark. Teaching me a lesson, are you, Gary? Or perhaps you're preoccupied with your pending divorce. No, you never forget anything—this is spite.*

Rey's mental speech had not relieved his anxiety. Four bikers entered the barn to play pool. Rey pulled at his beer again. Luntz and his lieutenants still hadn't touched theirs. Perkins had never seen an Old Liner *not* drink something put in front of them, so he worried.

An hour and three beers later, Gary Graft pulled up to the barn in his no frills PROPERTY OF THE US GOVERNMENT Chrysler. He carefully parked next to Rey's car, then entered the clubhouse, wearing a worsted wool suit, a tie, and an *I'm here to help* grin. The pool players looked at him tetchily.

The balls on this guy! thought Rey. *It's like he* wants *these apes to mess with him. Graft, ol' pal, I'm sure you're somebody in whatever cube farm you work in, but believe me, you're nobody here.*

Gary passed the pool players, marching straight to the empty barstool between Rey and Christian. He ignored Rey and offered his hand to Luntz, who didn't shake it. Gary didn't seem insulted.

To Mullet, Gary looked like a whole lot of nothing. "So you're Graft?"

"Yessir!"

The man had responded chirpily, which Mullet didn't trust. "Wanna beer?"

"Please."

"There's a 7-Eleven down the road, Fed. Go. Don't come back."

"Mullet, give the man a beer," said Luntz. He looked at Rocket. "Search him."

Rocket searched Graft carefully, then nodded: *He's clean*. Mullet sullenly retrieved a beer, slamming it on the bar in front of Gary. It was still capped, so if opened, it would foam like a geyser.

"I'll just let that sit a bit," said Gary. "Gents," he continued, "you can be angry with me all you want, but you only have yourselves to blame." He turned to Rey. "And your new bookkeeper, here, Walter."

"I thought your name's Rey," Mullet said.

"It is," said Rey.

Eight more bikers entered the bar.

"Nope, Rey's an alias," said Gary. "It's Walter. Says so right on his birth certificate. Isn't that right, Wally?" Gary "playfully" punched Rey's shoulder hard enough to hurt, then turned toward Christian. "Mr. Luntz, is there somewhere we can talk privately?"

"It's just 'Luntz,'" said Christian. "Follow me." He stood, grabbed his beer, then glared at Mullet until he begrudgingly handed Gary a new one. "This way," said Luntz.

"Sounds good, but before we go, Wally, why don't you tell your two buddies here"—Gary pointed to Rocker and Mullet—"about your Colombian girlfriend."

Rey's eyes popped. He knew Gary would be upset about him going "rogue," but why was he throwing him to the wolves like this?

Gary continued, projecting his voice. "Luntz and I might be awhile, so, Wally, make sure to cover all the important details, like South America, the truth about the hymnals, your arrest, and the deal you made to save your terrorist girlfriend's life." Gary pointed at the lieutenants again. "I'm sure they'll especially want to know about your deal to spy on the Old Line so Uncle Sam would keep her in the good ol' US of A."

With that, Gary looked at Luntz: *Lead on, good sir*. The two left through the back and Mullet turned to stare at Rey as if the man had just wiped his ass with grammy's church dress. Rocker swiftly hopped from his barstool two seats away, landing deftly next to Rey, throwing his arm companionably—protectively—around his shoulders. It's obvious his job was to keep Mullet from killing him, at least for now. Rocker whistled for attention, motioning everyone in. Someone silenced the jukebox.

"Storytime, Wally," said Rocker. "Start talking."

If Rey was anxious before, he was terrified now, plus amazed that Gary had completely hung him out to dry. An audience gathered, a hostile one. *Well, if I'm gonna die, might as well get the facts out*. "So, ah, folks it's like this," Rey began. "In 1977, I was thirteen years old and won a trip to South America . . ."

Luntz led Graft between broken pallets, bags of trash, and old refrigerators. Fifty yards away, the farmhouse's windows glowed with the flicker of television. Once inside, Luntz directed Wanda to turn off the TV and fetch more beer. She did so. The men sat.

"You must really hate Rey," Luntz said.

Gary smiled. "I don't hate him, sir. But let's just say he deserves some sort of reckoning, for, among other things, trying to unilaterally renegotiate a deal. Plus, he's a dick." Luntz laughed despite himself. In addition to Graft's dorky swagger, he was funny.

"May I call you Christian?" Gary asked.

"Sure," said Luntz. "Just not 'mister.' Or 'sir.'"

"'Call me Gary. What's in a name, that which we call—" Gary started.

"A rose," completed Christian.

A Shakespeare-quoting biker? This revelation knocked him off his game for a beat, but Gary adjusted. "Christian, let's get down to business. This is what Rey told me earlier today."

Rey had that afternoon informed Gary that he, Rey, had let the Old Line in on the Fed's eavesdropping, and therefore the ATF would no longer be able to swoop up Old Line's gun operation. *Good God, Perkins!* Rey had worked an angle: in "exchange" for letting Luntz know, Luntz had agreed to entertain possibly rolling on the La Plata Patriots and, more importantly, not killing Rey. This was not the outcome Graft or Agent Feldman had wanted or agreed on, and underneath Graft's game face, which was a good one, he was livid.

"So, you'll give us Sammy's Club?" Graft asked, and Luntz nodded. "Incidentally, should I worry about Wally's safety?"

"You didn't seem concerned when you teed 'im up for my boys back there," Luntz responded.

"True," said Gary, nodding as if forgetting some important social nicety. "Your boys might rough him up, but I'm not too worried beyond that. Only the Inner Circle can approve a killing, and only with a majority vote, right Christian?"

Luntz didn't look pleased.

"What's more," Graft continued, "if you have a split decision, the president's vote, *yours*, carries."

Now Luntz *really* didn't look pleased. It was unlikely, but possible, that Rey, during his bookkeeping duties, had gleaned the existence of the Inner Circle, and further, had learned that a Circle majority must approve all deaths, but that parliamentarian bit about tie-breaking? Rey couldn't have known something like that. If Gary Graft of Government Land knew this, it wasn't good.

"It wasn't Rey who told me that," said Gary, reading his mind. "I have other sources."

Luntz squeezed the neck of his beer, making it squeak. *There might be an Inner Circle vote tonight about killin' you, Graft,* Christian thought.

Gary smiled again. "Relax, Christian. Your bylaws are public if you know where to look. I've strung other bits and pieces together and made some assumptions. Making assumptions is what I do for a living. You don't have a rat in the hold."

Luntz pulled his beer dry, then said, "Sounds like your assumptions about your wife didn't work out." *I know things about you, too, Graft.*

If Gary was affected by his statement, he didn't show it.

Wanda arrived with a bucket of iced beer. While she set everything out, Luntz eyeballed the wall standing in front of another wall that hid the club's gun safe. It contained papers, money, jewelry, a small amount of drugs—lots of things, *except* guns. It never did. On club property it was personal guns only, something spelled out in the bylaws that Mr. Graft had apparently read. Wanda left.

"Why do ya think Rey, or whatever the hell his name is, broke his deal to spy on us?" Luntz asked.

"The worst possible reason," said Gary.

"What's that?"

"Love."

Gary took out a pad of paper and a pen. He dropped his bland government pretense, showing his real annoyance. "Christian, whatever you got for me, it better be good. Give me the particulars. Everything."

When they were done talking, Luntz walked Graft back to the barn. From the clubhouse, distinct cries could be heard: either the bikers were torturing Rey or laughing at him—or both. As Gary re-entered, he noted the size of Rey's audience; the former tobacco barn was full, every chair and stool taken. Rey stood atop the bar, speaking animatedly. Whatever he was selling, they were buying.

He'd clearly just put a bow on it all, something to the effect of *Then I got wind of a government plot to shut down Old Line, so I warned Luntz about it.* Seeing Gary come back in, Rey jumped down, landing like he'd had a few, and approached Gary.

"And here, ladies and gentlemen, is Gary Graft from the Government, 'Doctor' Gary, the man I was telling you about. What do you say, Doc?"

It was obvious now that Rey'd had more than a few. "Wally," said Gary, "I've been waiting a long time for this." Rey, as if going along with a rehearsed gag, looked knowingly at his audience, putting his arm around Graft. *Ain't this guy a pistol?*

Gary was a pistol, all right. Swiftly turning, he hit Rey square in the jaw, knocking him back into the bar. Then he grabbed him before he could react, standing him up straight to fussily wipe off Rey's shirt as if he'd walked through cobwebs.

"Told you that would happen if you went rogue," Gary said. "We'll talk more later about how screwed you are." To the crowd: "Enjoy your evening folks! By the way, this guy's a lying sack of shit." Gary walked out, leaving Rey standing there.

Laughter erupted, mostly of the *what the fuck was that* variety, with Mullet's hyena-like bray being the loudest.

Rey, holding his jaw, looked petrified. Rocker, ever the more practical of Luntz's lieutenants, asked Christian, "What do we do with Wally here?"

"Nothing," said Luntz, who seemed pleased. He pounded Rey on his shoulders, yelling, "A round on the house and two for my bookkeeper." Everyone cheered.

Rey did not.

Chapter 65: The Favor

Sunday, 19 December 1999
Wheaton, MD

IT'S ME AGAIN, Trevor, six days before Christmas. All this week, El Jefe's been working me hard. Technically, I'm still on Step Nine, the "amends" step, the one where you apologize for all the bad things you've done to people in your life (drunk or sober), demonstrate you don't do these things anymore, then make restitution. I'd made a start on Nine while incarcerated. You're supposed to make amends in person, but the nature of some of the amends was such that, according to Cisco, an earnest letter would suffice. I pushed out five letters. One guy wrote back, telling me to keep up the good work (when you're in prison, encouragement's gold). Gratitude list item: no one told me to go to hell.

I had big plans for face-to-face amends after prison, but my wife's betrayal blew that up. Now I live at Mickey's Mansion where my daily mission, besides staying sober, is getting out of bed. I'm depressed, but I get up 'cause Chico, who's dragged me out of bed once already, will do it again, and nobody, especially the depressed, likes that. Chico continues dropping me off at work. Scooter keeps picking me up. Truth is, I'm dependent on the Oxford House guys. Chico says they're "carrying" me until I can carry myself so that down the road, I'll do the same for someone else—you know, all that AA happy crappy.

I'm not trivializing—it's just I'm dragging ass these days, going through the motions as best I can. Cisco says that's okay. Sobriety requires "practice." He also says that though my life may not seem to be getting better, my ability to *deal* with life is. Remains to be seen. Anyway, he says everything—prison and Carol's infidelity included—is part of God's "gift of desperation."

Some gift. That's what my alcoholism tells me. *Trevor, you've been treated terribly by mean people, particularly that whore, Carol. If you drink, you'll feel better.*

I know it's "drink poison and hope the other guy dies" logic, but sometimes I'm still tempted.

In addition to the daily AA meetings that Mickey's Mansion requires, I've been working with Cisco each evening. As wrapped up in my problems as I am, however, I worry about El Jefe. He looks really rough—eye bags, moves slowly, the muttering has really taken off. I catch words here and there: a Korean War flashback about a place called the Chosin Reservoir, and some guy named Took. When I ask him about it, he ignores me.

Another worry: my coffee-swilling sponsor is rushing me through step work, something normally unheard of for him. As I've said, I'm still technically on Nine, but for whatever reason, Cisco's pushing me through the last three steps: Ten, Eleven, and Twelve. These are the "maintenance" steps: if you're wrong, promptly admit it; pray and meditate; help others, especially alcoholics. Why's he fast-tracking me?

Maybe it's his health, like he's gotten bad medical news so now he wants to check items—like getting me sober—off his bucket list. There's something mental going on too. He keeps repeating versions of "worked at Nelson's" over and over. I've talked to other AAs, including his bestie, Reggie. He and others have noticed the changes; no one knows what's going on.

Most of the time, he's okay, still busting my chops, like three days ago: "So, Trevor, 'Cheapskate' Charlie's still living rent-free in your head, right?" I admitted it was true. I've seen the dude wearing three different business suits—he can *clearly* afford a dollar for the basket. Last night's meeting, for instance, I'm sitting next to him and the basket comes his way. Like always, he merrily passes it to me with a *This must be yours* expression. Drove me up the wall.

"Okay," said Cisco, "let's put this one to bed. Charlie doesn't put money in the basket because he doesn't have any."

"But he brags about his job. And those suits—"

"Hear me out. He's got a great job, but he never carries cash. Why? Because if he does, even one dollar, he'll spend it on booze. His wife handles all their money, as does yours, by the way. Charlie's been in and out of the program for years doing the best he can. Here's how you handle Charlie: when the basket goes around, don't look at him. In fact, don't look at anyone. What people put in the basket isn't your business."

"But Charlie really pisses me off, Jefe."

"In your case, serenity costs a dollar. Put a buck in for him and shut up."

Sometimes I hate my sponsor.

And now to the present: Sunday afternoon, 19 December. We're in the drunk tank. Cisco called me this morning, asking me to come over to discuss something "important." He looks especially bad today, the worst yet, which is saying something. It's obvious he's not been sleeping, perhaps not in days. I ask him if he's still dreaming about Korea. He looks at me a little funny but says nothing. *At least you're not dreaming about your wife drowning in a cage.*

I look around and notice his perpetually brewing coffee machine is empty. In fact, it's unplugged. Cisco without coffee is, well . . . I've never seen Cisco without coffee. I look around and see the whole cellar's been cleaned. He normally keeps it tidy, but today it's spic and span. The kitchenette table practically gleams. There's a manila envelope on it, along with some case the size of a large cigar box, and a glass of water.

We sit at the table and talk for a half-hour about a range of topics: his son, his deceased wife, guys we both know in the program, life at Mickey's Mansion. Cisco's present but a little foggy and I get the impression he's killing time. He asks about Reesie, but before I can answer, he suddenly smacks his head. "Jeez, kid, I almost forgot."

He goes upstairs, returning with a pint of whiskey, locking it in one of the mailbox cubbies. He keeps a pint in his coat and/or his car trunk during the day in case someone's got serious DTs, but he doesn't like to keep it upstairs at night. I've seen him lock it up before—it's not unusual. What is unusual is his opening the manilla envelope, one with a string you unwind, then putting the "whiskey" key inside it.

Cisco draws a breath like it's more work than it should be. "Trevor, before I discuss why I asked you here, I have one last AA question: You've done a good job preparing your amends list, but usually there's one or two 'take it to the grave' items that are so 'bad,' men don't include them. This is important: if you have anything like that, now's the time to tell me. I don't care what it is. I won't judge you."

At first, I think *no*, I've been thorough. Hell, a quarter of the people on my list Cisco had me take off, as I hadn't done enough "harm." Plus, it's not like I killed anybody. Then I think: *You did witness a murder, remember?* Did I do harm by not reporting it? This is something I've been agonizing over for months. On the one hand, nothing I could have done that night would have prevented what happened. And I did attend Prophet's funeral, but in my heart, I know I should have reported it. By not contacting law enforcement, Mrs. Marks was going to spend her remaining days not knowing who killed her only son. *Which is not right.*

I suck it up and tell Cisco that I witnessed, but did not report, a murder.

This somehow excites him. "Does the victim's family know?" he asks.

"That he's dead? Oh yes, his mother knows. And you know, too. It's Mark Marks from Cumberland. I was . . . in the alley the night he died. I was drunk, um, relieving myself."

Cisco, suddenly more interested, asks what happened next.

"His killer chased me but never got a good look at me. I was spooked for a few days but figured the guy didn't know who I was. Anyway, Mrs. Marks didn't get, you know, closure."

There's a pause. Cisco is staring at me now with this unnatural, almost unhinged look. "Kid, I'm *sure* the killer didn't get a good look at you."

"Why?" I ask.

But I realize I don't need him to answer.

Suddenly, I'm equal parts amazed and horrified. First, the site of the murder, the enclosed loading bay of the defunct paper company. *Worked at Nelson's.* Who was old enough to have retired from working there? One Cisco Arkin, that's who. It was Cisco arguing with Mark Marks that night! Now the argument makes sense. *Give it here! Give it to me!* What Mark wanted was Cisco's pint of rotgut and Cisco wouldn't give it up—*No, it stays in my pocket.* He probably thought Prophet wasn't bad enough to need it yet, but poor Prophet thought otherwise. They struggled and Mark got slammed against a wall. It was dark, so I heard this but didn't see it. But I *did* see the Alley Killer's boots and Cisco has a pair just like them.

Why hadn't I recognized the killer's voice as Cisco's? *Because that night, Cisco had had a head cold, a bad one.* I want to ask him, *If it was an honest accident, why didn't he report it?* There were mitigating circumstances and since the man has impeccable character, he surely could've explained things adequately to the police. *Or could he?* Could he explain meeting a troubled man inside a locked area of an abandoned building late at night? Had Cisco "lured" him there? And if so, for what purpose? And of course the only really important question of the evening occurs to me: *Is the Alley Killer going to kill me tonight?*

"Well, Trevor," says Cisco, "this revelation, you being in the alley with Mark and me that night, can't be timelier. And if you're curious, I've always suspected it was you."

"Why'd you kill him, Cisco?" I ask, pleading, because though I'm frightened, I'm also angry. "You could've just given him the bottle! It wasn't worth fighting over!"

"But it was, Trevor," he says. Suddenly, all animation leaves him. "Kid, it's all explained here." He pats the manila envelope.

"It was an accident, right?" I insist. "You didn't *mean* to do it, so why didn't you report it?"

"Like I said, it's all explained here." *Pat-pat.*

"You chased me, Cisco, you scared the hell out of me! I was looking over my shoulder for months!"

"Look, Trevor, I'm glad—relieved, really—that we've figured out who was who in the alley that night. But as crazy as this may sound, there's something more important to discuss."

I'm gobsmacked. What outweighs homicide?

"Oddly enough," continues Cisco, "it relates to Mark Marks. The Lord truly does work in mysterious ways, because I can't think of a better candidate than you to put things right."

"Put what right?" I ask, overwhelmed. I've just learned my sponsor killed someone right in front of me, then chased me for two blocks. Cisco sighs, gathering himself.

"Trevor, it's about a nightmare I keep having. My worst night of the Korean War."

"Okay, Cisco," I say, not knowing what else to say. "I'm listening."

He sucks in a breath, then starts telling me his Battle of the Chosin Reservoir experience. It takes a while because, for whatever reason, speaking is exhausting him, but I get the gist of it. What a story.

"But the dream's changed, Trevor, it's been changing all year. Now, instead of Took getting shot, *I get shot*. Last time I slept, two nights ago, or maybe it was three, was the worst. Before I get shot in my dream, which obviously never happened in real life, my buddy Jamie Took turns into Mark Marks and says, 'Next time you fall asleep, Cisco, you're gonna wake up and destroy everything you ever cared about.' Kid, I haven't slept since."

"But Cisco, it's just a dream—"

"Never mind what you think!" he yells. "It's real to me!"

Jumping slightly at Cisco's anger, I manage to ask, "But why Mark Marks? He wasn't even alive during the Korean—"

"Because, Trevor, the dream started changing the day I killed him!"

Though I can share my wife-in-the-cage dream with him, it's not the time. I'm not sure exactly what this all means, his dream, or mine, but somewhere down deep, maybe I do. "Okay, Cisco," I say, "it's Higher Power time. You need to call the police—now. Explain everything. I'll back you up. We can do it together. That's what you'd tell me to do, isn't it? Clean 'my' side of the street?"

Cisco, who looks like someone struggling to keep sane, says, "You'd be right, kid, *if* this was something in God's arena. But for the first time in my life, even fighting in Korea, I now know what it's like to be *outside* God's domain."

I'm stunned that a man like Cisco, so God-centered, so *rational*, would say this. But he did.

"Trevor," he continues, "what I'm going to ask of you now is unfair. Incredibly unfair, and I know that."

"What?" I ask nervously.

"You may need to kill me," he says.

What?

"I would never ask you to do something I should do myself, kid, but I'm Catholic. Suicide's a sin."

"And murder isn't?" I ask, my voice high.

"Suicide's an *unforgivable* sin, Trevor."

"But *why*, Cisco? *Why* do you need to die?"

"I may need to die, I may not," he says, becoming momentarily calmer. "You're my contingency plan. It's all explained here, Trevor." *Pat-pat*. "You can read it after we're done."

"Why don't you read it to me now?"

Cisco's face becomes unhinged again. He reaches for the metal case, unsnapping its lid. I'm mortified by what's inside: a revolver. Cisco flips the cylinder out and starts inserting bullets.

I won't lie, I'm terrified—my sponsor, the man I trust more than anyone in the world, has cracked up and is now loading a gun. I can't help looking at the door, wanting to be on the other side of it. "The door's got a new lock, Trevor," says Cisco. "I bolted the upstairs door too. Sorry, you can't leave yet." He snaps the loaded cylinder back, looking at me. "Relax kid, this isn't meant for you."

"Well, that's good news," I manage to say. "Can you put it away now?"

"No, but you can have it." He hands it to me. It's uncomfortably heavy. "I'm so scatterbrained these days, I wasn't sure it was loaded. Good thing I checked. Alright, Mr. Pug, this is what's going to happen. I'm gonna take something to help me sleep." He pulls two pills from his pocket. "These won't kill me. Well, they might, but anyway, if I wake up and I'm not . . . who I'm supposed to be . . . you . . . protect my world, do you understand? The thing in my dream, I call it the 'other thing.' It looks like Mark. *Exactly* like him. He's told me if I wake up, I'll be some sort of . . . maniac. That scares the hell out of me."

"Cisco, I'm not gonna shoot you," I insist. "That's crazy."

"Kid, *I'm* crazy," he says. "If I wake up some kind of monster, you're the safeguard."

"How will I know if you need to be . . . stopped?"

"That's easy, Trevor. I'll be trying to kill you."

Sorry for the sacrilege folks, but *holy fuck*. "Okay, Cisco. Specifically, what am I safeguarding?"

"Keep me from destroying everyone I love," he says.

"'Can you be more specific?"

"Sure, for starters, you, your wife, and your daughter. And my son, and about a million others. I can't let this happen, Trevor. You've gotta help me. I'm desperate!"

"Jefe, how about giving this one more day—"

"Trevor, *for the love of God, I don't have another day!* I need you to make sure there's going to be a *tomorrow* for everyone else."

"Dammit, Cisco, you're talking voodoo! What do you think you are, cursed? That Prophet cursed you?"

This is, of course, exactly what I'm thinking.

"Yes, Trevor," Cisco says.

Relax, I tell myself, *breathe,* and do so a few times. *I've got the .38. What am I worried about? All the man wants is for me to watch him sleep. I can do that, and while he's bedding down, I can call the police.* But there's never been a phone in the cellar, and Cisco cleverly told me to leave my cell phone at home. *Relax,* I think again. *I'll think of something.* "Okay, Jefe, whatever you say."

The look of relief in the man's eyes is so complete, it's pitiable. Such a strong man reduced to this. Cisco holds his manilla envelope, clutching it like it's the most important thing in the world, and maybe to him it is. He swallows his pills, washing them down with the glass of water that's been sitting there the whole time—however crazy he may be, the man's prepared.

"Trevor, after it's done—after I wake up . . . or not . . . sane . . . or not—read what's in the envelope." *Pat-pat.*

I look at him uncomfortably. No matter how many times I tell myself to relax now, it ain't gonna happen.

"Look, Trevor," he continues, "I said this was unfair to you, but it's also unfair to the program. Please don't hold this against AA."

"Okay, Cisco, sure, sure," I say soothingly. "You want to lie on the couch or go in the bedroom?"

He looks a little confused, like he'd not thought this particular part of his plan through. "Couch."

"Righty-oh," I respond. "You're gonna wake up tomorrow and be fine." He smiles at me, but it's not a smile of belief.

"Thanks, kid," Cisco says, reaching out to give a firm handshake. And a moment's eye contact. Is this the last time he'll ever look at me? He lies down on the couch and closes his eyes.

Twenty minutes pass. Whatever pills Cisco swallowed take effect. He looks drowsy. Unintelligible words drop from his lips like coins. His eyelids droop. He goes under.

During this time, I've decided to get help as I have no idea what those pills really are. Cisco, whether he meant to or not, may have poisoned himself. However, I can't make calls. I can't even leave. I search Cisco's pockets for a key, but he's planned this too well. I don't find one. I grab his wrist, checking for a pulse, and I can barely feel it. I'm no doctor but I don't have to be: Cisco is dying.

I scream at the door, which does no good. No one can hear me. I scream again, this time saying, "What do I do? What do I do?"

In my panic, I point the gun at one of the cellar's window wells and shoot at it. The gun is very loud. I'd expected the glass to shatter, but I've just punched a hole through it, that's it. But maybe someone heard it? I check Cisco's pulse again—I can't find one.

The neighbor, I think. I take the gun to the window well and take a risk. I aim through the hole at the neighbor's house, specifically at what turns out to be a living room window and shoot at it. Again, loud gun, small hole. I scream through the hole but it's not necessary; the neighbor's already turning on all his lights. But he won't venture out of his house no matter how much I plead. I hope he's called the police. That was my goal—that and not accidentally shooting anyone.

I check on Cisco again. Definitely no pulse and he's not breathing. I think about CPR but worry it won't help because it's some type of poison. Surely the police will come but they'll have to assess things, then call an ambulance, and by then it will be way too late. I need to get out now.

Then it comes to me: I can shoot my way out. I jog over to the cellar door in front of the steps leading up to the back yard. Four bullets left. I squeeze the trigger three times until the door jamb around the lock gives. I start picking out the busted bits with my fingers, but it's not enough. One more round. I cock the revolver and put it very close to the lock. I fire.

There's a terrible burrowing in my skull, and my left eye goes dark. Intense pain. A brief burst of nausea, then things soften.

My very last thought: *Not what I expected.*

Chapter 66: The Funeral

Saturday, 20 January 2000
Wheaton, MD

CAROL PUG AND her daughter Reesie sit in the front row. The chair where Trevor Pug, husband and father, would normally have sat, is empty. Mother and daughter wear black, and along with hundreds of others, face a stage with a speaker's podium, a large picture of the deceased, and flower arrangements.

The gymnasium can accommodate three hundred, but nearly twice that attend—it's packed, standing room only. Carol's mother, Gladys Edock, isn't there, but two of Carol's sisters are, as well as Trevor's mother and stepdad. The five remaining "evil men" are there: Gary, Phillipe, Loo, Ken, and Rey. Several dozen friends and neighbors are present. Trevor's boss, Frank Deguzman, is there.

The AA, Al-Anon, and NA communities have come out in droves, at least four hundred, an incredible number. Alice McGovern is there, sitting behind Carol. Reggie Davis sits next to her. To the discomfort of some, every member of the Old Line has attended—full colors—including Blister, who stands next to his sponsor, Thumper. Rocker has brought five barrels of cider for the reception. The Vee Sisters and their father, Poland Manchester, are there. Even Estelle Largo is there, on the arm of her friend, Marco, three rows behind Phillipe and his new girlfriend, "Steve." Winnie Marks attends in a full mourning outfit, including a veil. She cries through the entire ceremony.

Carol looks behind her, amazed at how the dead man could have so many friends. A Catholic priest and the funeral home director have already given opening remarks. Selected family members and friends will share their thoughts, but due to the circumstances of the decedent's death, it makes sense for the man now stepping up to the podium to speak first. He wishes to "explain" things.

He starts with Cisco Arkin's recent history, describing the deterioration of the man's mental state—the depression after his wife's death, the doubts about being an effective sponsor, the nightmares about the Korean War. The speaker says Arkin, by his own written account, admitted to killing Mark Marks. He'd claimed that prior to his death, Mark had gone out on a three-month bender and had called Arkin that 1998 November night, begging to meet him. "Prophet" had suggested the loading bay of the now-defunct Nelson's Paper Supply Company, as he, Mark, had a key for the gate from previous employment. According to Cisco, Mark was so desperate for alcohol that he'd meant to take the "medicinal" pint Cisco carried in his coat by force. Arkin refused to give it up. A struggle ensued and Mark fatally hit his head on the loading dock wall. According to what Cisco wrote, it was an accident.

Attendees could be forgiven for doubting Arkin's account. If it was an accident as he claimed, why hadn't he reported it right away? And why did he chase Trevor Pug, a witness to the incident? Fair questions. Cisco admitted to worrying that the witness, who he hadn't seen, would alert the authorities and that Cisco might look understandably guilty. Arkin claimed to only want to "talk" to Trevor Pug, unknown to him at the time. Cisco claimed to have called 911 about two hours after the incident to report a body. This was probably true—records indicated someone did call from a local payphone. Though Cisco knew his sponsee's death was accidental, it caused him incredible remorse, something he called the "other thing." This *other thing* hounded him, making his service nightmares even worse. Oddly, they abated once he started sponsoring Trevor Pug. It was a tall order to believe Cisco didn't know he was sponsoring the only witness to Mark's death, but this is what he'd claimed. Unfortunately, the nightmares returned, but after meeting Winnie Marks at her son's funeral, the *other thing* quieted again after he began writing her. But the guilt still hounded Arkin: how could he correspond, telling her everything he knew about her son *except* how he died?

The speaker then discussed the circumstances of Trevor Pug's "accident," including Arkin's sleep-deprived delusions that he, Arkin, was turning into some sort of monster. Why the man had thought a gun was necessary to "protect society" from him was something his written account didn't describe, but the speaker did, in some detail. The speaker explained how Pug, worried that his sedated sponsor was dying, had foolishly tried to shoot his way out of the cellar, and that a lock fragment had very unfortunately penetrated his eye.

The speaker concluded by saying, "You may not believe Cisco, or me, either . . . but . . . I have no reason to lie."

He began crying, softly at first, then louder, finally ending in sobs. One of the officiants helped him off the podium. The man, wearing an eyepatch, accepted assistance—it was still difficult for him to navigate. The officiant almost escorted the speaker past his seat, but his daughter grabbed his hand, gently pulling him down. His weeping wife, two seats away, couldn't bear to look at him and excused herself. Now on the podium, Reggie Davis, Cisco Arkin's best friend, began eulogizing him.

"Those were nice things you said about Mr. Arkin, Dad," Reesie said once he was seated.

He removed his eye patch, revealing scar tissue from the original damage plus a subsequent surgery. With a handkerchief, he gently dabbed his damaged eye, saying, "He was a nice man, Reesie. Troubled at the end, but still a very good man who saved my life."

Chapter 67: New Dresses

Saturday, 25 March 2000
Wheaton, MD

SO IT'S TREVOR, one final time. Obviously, that was Cisco's service, not mine. Now I *did* get shot, sort of, and it was dicey—a large metal piece hit the corner of my eye, detaching it. It's been re-attached. I can see with it and the docs say with time and rehab I'll look less and less like Igor. The fragment scooted around the inside of my skull, luckily not through my brain proper. Still, there's damage, things I can't remember. I get confused sometimes, but the docs say that's likely to improve, and other than having a hole drilled through my skull, removing the fragment was straightforward.

An inquest was held on the manner of Mark's passing. The panel ruled that his death was accidental based on my eyewitness testimony (they were nice enough to gloss over the fact that I was drunk and really couldn't see anything). I was able to describe most details, however, everything from Arkin's rawhide laces to the critical dialogue. They really did believe me. Importantly, Mrs. Marks also believed me, and even more importantly, she didn't blame Cisco for her son's death. She blamed the real villain, Mark's "craving."

It's been two months since Cisco's service, and I still live at Mickey's. Chico's moving out. His new sponsor, a guy named Craig, gave him his one-year chip three months ago, by the way. A Jefe High graduate.

Reggie comes to see me after my surgery, and I ask him to sponsor me. He says between shuffleboard and wood-duck carving, he might not have the time. "I should run this by my sponsor first," he further jokes, "but unfortunately Cisco, may he rest in peace, accidentally overdosed, so I'll just say yes." It's not really a funny joke. He knows that. I know it. Which kind of makes it funny.

Reggie's been checking on his ex-sponsor's house while Cisco's estate's being settled (first thing Reggie does is pay for replacing the neighbor's shot-out window). Sixty percent of Arkin's assets will go to his son, who is serving as his father's executor, and the remainder's earmarked for his home group. A club independent of AA is being formed to purchase the building they meet in—no more renting. Word is it'll be called Cisco's House.

A surprise bequest: El Jefe willed me his truck, which is funny since I'm not allowed to drive.

Phillipe visits the hospital with Steve, whose real name is Claudia, which no one uses. I tell him I really like "Stevie," which makes her blush. Personality-wise, she's night and day to Estelle, so the women shouldn't hate her. She's gonna attend next month's book club meeting as we have a new rule, Rule #3: "Chicks can join." She promises to tell me all about it. Phillipe's "come out" to the guys, telling them how he met Stevie, so everybody knows about the dresses now. The good news for me? Estelle figured out Phillipe's "hobby" all on her own—it was she who leaked it to the guys at Hanger 18.

Phillipe apologized for hitting me. "We're good," I told him, "Just don't hit me again—I really need to reduce the eye injuries."

Speaking of Estelle, don't count her out. Word got back to her about the real deal at the Men's Lounge: an old boy network with cigars, liquor, and, yes, dresses. She understands now she's misjudged Phillipe. To her credit, she fessed up to him about calling Hanger 18, begging his forgiveness—that's how he found out. She must want him back. Hard to imagine that happening, but never underestimate a Largo.

Loo stops by too. I'm worried about him. Deerslayer-wise, he's got Park and Rec fooled, along with everyone else, but he's still not told Cindy the truth. It'd be one thing if they were on the same page—"Yes, I'm the Deerslayer, Cindy, and *yes*, it was stupid, but for the sake of the children . . ."—but they're not. As you obviously know by now, I'm no nuptial expert, but having to lie all the time, publicly *and* privately? That'll kill a marriage. He and Cindy are on my prayer list.

Loo brings me up to speed on the curse dreams, which I hadn't known about, and the guys visiting Prophet's grave. When I tell him about my cage dream, Loo looks frightened.

I say, "Hey, relax, the bad stuff's stopped, right?"

"Maybe you should go to his grave too," says Loo. "Just in case. Get rid of the bad juju."

"I can't drive," I tell him.

"I'll drive you," he offers.

"I've already been to his grave."

"Yes, but did you give him a beer? We saved one for you, figured you'd want to do it yourself."

"I honored him at his service," I say, "then apologized to his mother after my sponsor's funeral for not reporting her son's death. She hugged me. It was . . . cathartic. I haven't had the cage dream since. And beer, Loo? Really? I'm in AA."

"Suit yourself," he says, but I can tell he's unhappy. It's been over four months since his Cumberland trip, and all the remaining guys are dream-free, but Loo, he's been having nightmares about *having* nightmares. There's something he's not letting go of—I think it's his lying to Cindy. He continues pushing me—he'll drive, he'll pour, he says, I won't have to touch the bottle. I won't even have to look.

"I'm not going, Loo," I tell him flatly. "And dude, what's really going on?"

He looks at his feet. "Trev, those dreams were . . . they were *awful*. I felt my arm being forced into that goddamn woodchipper—smelled my own blood, smelled like a thousand pennies. I can't go near anything remotely mechanical. It's a problem!"

"But the curse is lifted."

"Yeah, it's lifted, alright," he says, "but those dreams . . . You gotta understand—*I was a day from dying, I'm sure of it!* I know it's been months, but I still worry all the time: will the woodchipper dream return? Or one like it? You and me going back to Cumberland, that's *insurance*. It can't hurt, right?"

I keep refusing and finally have to say, "I'm in a goddamn hospital bed with brain damage, Loo! Leave it alone."

He apologizes, then leaves. I'll try and patch it up with him later, but honestly, what he really needs is help, *professional* help, because my best friend's developed a for-real *phobia*, something way above the friend paygrade.

Angie Chin makes an unannounced visit. She's chatty at first. They've sold the house. David's still with his mom, but she picks up Sunny on weekends. She's moved into a condo close to her office. David commutes to a technology farm in Beltsville where he toils to defeat fire ants. I get the impression that when the punishment period's over, she'll have him and Sunny move into the condo with her and then pretend nothing's happened. May they have better luck than the Spicottis are having hiding from the truth.

"Trevor," she says, "I'm glad now we didn't . . . take our revenge. Are you?"

"Yes," I say. "At the time I felt they had it coming, but fortunately for me, *for us*, I mean, grace stepped in." I leave it at that, along with a look that confirms her suspicion—sack-wise, it would've been fantastic.

"Trevor," she then says, "There's more. You're not going to like it."

First, she explains the whole setup of David having given Carol his "signing bonus money"—*so that's how Carol paid off Old Line!*—but then David admitted he hadn't given Carol his signing bonus money but rather *Carol's mother's money*, a favor good ol' Gladys forced on the weak-willed

Chin, telling him to call it a bonus. The news stuns me. She told me I'm the second person to learn this. Much to her credit, Angie had called Carol first. I bet that was a fun call.

Before leaving, Angie leans over me, kissing me near my damaged eye. "Goodbye, Trevor," she says.

Original Ken and Tori Bora visit later that day. I really like Tori. Ken's never looked happier, and man, she just *beams* being around him. Original's straight as an arrow—*duh*—and much to his delight, so is Tori, he thinks. I laugh learning how they met at their therapist's office, how she had the female version of Ken's "jinx." Jokingly, though not completely jokingly, they've both given each other a get-out-of-straight-free card, in case one (or both?) need it later. Sylvia approves, and Gee and Gree are equal parts afraid of, and in love with, Tori—for their age, it's the perfect fraction. Tori and Ken joke about everything, including some inside gag about handbags. I wish D-Kay was alive. He'd pile on some Babble rabble, something like "Hand-bag-istan."

On the night before I leave the hospital, I get one last visitor: Death Rey Perkins.

He starts with, "Hello, Trevor, glad you're improving." While we exchange pleasantries, I notice there's something different about him, but I'm not sure what. "So, I'm leaving Sim Systems," he says. I'm taken aback and ask if something happened. "No, just moving to Texas." He spends some time relating his 1977 jungle trauma to me. I'm *floored* by his story—it doesn't explain everything about him, and it's still no excuse for the way he acts sometimes, but it explains a lot.

"Trevor, I told you what I told the guys about Colombia, but there's more. Can I trust you not to pass it on?"

"Yes," I say, which I mean. He hesitates, then explains the events leading up to and beyond Beer Can Beach. I continue to be floored. He plans to relocate close to where Tatiana Ruiz, the Colombian "terrorist," is being held—the Fed's Three Rivers facility south of San Antonio. Just when I think I can't get any more floored, he announces his intention to . . . wait for it . . . marry her! He further explains that Garrulous Gary worked some government magic to get Tatiana a better plea deal. (Gary? *Our* Gary?) She's serving time concurrently for her Colombian and U.S. charges and won't be extradited. Marrying Rey, becoming an American citizen, has something to do with it. In exchange, she's providing information on the rebels because she holds no illusions—today's FARC wasn't the FARC she'd originally signed up for.

I ask Rey a question that I think matters: Do you love her?

"Don't know," he says, "but that's not important."

"What?"

"Trevor," he says, "listen to me: I've been carrying the FARC around my neck for twenty-two years now, specifically the fear, no, the *hatred* of our brown neighbors to the south. All this craziness I'm doing now, it's my last chance to get right with things, otherwise all I'm left with is Sammy's bullshit."

He then explains Sammy's Club to me (I'm appalled to learn he fell in with them, but not surprised). Then he roundabout implies he'd spied on the Old Line bikers for Gary Graft, apparently *secret agent spy* Gary Graft—who in turn offered Old Line some deal where the Feds forgave their past sins in exchange for them rolling on the La Plata Patriots, something they very reluctantly did. Some ATF agent named Feldman—that Rey sounds hot for—and her fellow agents executed a warrant at some hunting club near Waldorf, discovering an arsenal under the floorboards. According to Rey, the Sammy guy took the fall for everything because the other guy, Miles Jacobsen, had kept his hands clean. It's very complicated—I don't follow all of it.

Rey's current plan (Texas) will ask a lot of Future Rey, who, in my opinion, still has a "dick" problem. I don't share this, however. I'm sort of proud of him. It's then I recognize what's different about him since he'd arrived: Rey looks happy.

"So Reymond, this plan, what sold you on it?"

"Tatiana's boy," he says. "Is it fair he grows up the son of a pariah in *two* countries?"

Wow is all I could think. "Will her prison allow conjugal visits?" (As a member of the EMBC, I can ask such questions.)

"Once we're married, yes." He explains that the longer Tatiana cooperates, the more her multi-year sentence will be forgiven.

I want to ask if the boy likes him, but instead I ask, "Do you like the boy?"

"I didn't at first, but he's growing on me."

As someone with a stepdad, I ask Rey if he truly understands what he's signing up for: a lot of responsibility with little authority. "And Rey, what if it the marriage doesn't work out?"

"She's signed a prenup," he answers. "And if she wants a divorce the day she leaves prison, so be it."

More wow. I take a moment to recover, then say, "Well, I wish you luck, Rey. Really. And if you wanna keep me posted on how it all turns out, that'd be cool." I'm sincere about this.

He nods, then adds, "Oh, I recommended to Frankie that you take my position."

I'm wowed once again—all this wowing, by the way, is tiring me out. "Thanks, Rey, but I'm a parolee with no license living in a group house. Not sure I'm ready yet."

"Well, you got four weeks to get ready—that's my last day at Sim 2K." He pauses. "Pains me to admit this, Trevor, but when you're sober, you code pretty well."

Another wow—I hadn't seen that coming. (Yes, I will be sleeping deeply very soon.)

"Also, thanks for inviting me to your book club," he adds.

Considering how generally negative the experience had been, for him and for us—never mind the curse—could he really mean this? "Okay. You're welcome." I ask if he's going straight to Texas.

"No, got someone to visit in Australia first."

I assume he means the Jack Sparks boy he'd been kidnapped with. "Okay, Rey, best of luck with everything."

He shakes my hand, then leaves.

I immediately add "Happy Rey" to my prayer list, worried that his newfound altruism might kill him.

New sponsor Reggie says I'm not ready to be around alcohol yet, so I gave up being EMBC co-chair. Loo did too—those home troubles with Cindy I told you about, plus the woodchipper nightmare business. Gary the New Guy stepped into the power void. He still goes off on serious tangents if not watched—the guys say they unfortunately know more about Phoenician dietary habits than the Phoenicians did—but Gary's got time to run the club because he quit whatever super-secret government job he had. The good news is that he's back together with his wife, at least on a trial basis, and Original said Gary seems optimistic. Was his needing to quit his job another notch on Prophet's curse belt? Who knows. Says his new nine-to-five's boring, and it's obvious he misses being a secret agent or whatever the hell he was, but he's at least having fun with the club, and it shows—more new guys (and at least one gal, Stevie) are joining.

I talk with Reggie about Prophet's curse. On the one hand, I wasn't at the meeting where the guys insulted him, so despite the Carol-in-a-cage dream, I really hadn't been taking it seriously because I had way too much other stuff—like jail—going on. I hadn't felt the terror the other guys had. I've thought about it since though, and I wonder: if I'd called the police that night before getting in my car, would I have avoided the curse all together? Putting myself in Prophet's spirit shoes, that's what I would have been mad about. *Why didn't you call the police, Trevor?* Cisco did, sure, but I was the *witness,* and isn't that what witnesses are supposed to do? And even if I'd waited till the next day, things might have still turned out differently. But wishing doesn't make it so.

It's entirely possible that this curse and the dreams are totally coincidental. It's also possible, because anything's possible, that the curse was real. I lay it all out for Reggie because I guess Loo isn't the only one worried—I am too, not about the curse, which I feel is genuinely over, but about there having been an otherworldly pox in the first place, one stamping out Cisco's belief in the absolute power of the Almighty. Anyway, I explain everything the best I can to him, from that night in the alley at Shorties to my last conversation with Loo. When I'm done, I can tell that though Reggie's bothered by what he hears, he doesn't believe me.

"Trevor," Reggie says, "you never had a chance to meet Mark when he was working a good program, right?" I nod. "You heard the stories at his service, his commitment to the AA fellowship. Can you imagine *that* Mark wishing some evil curse on anyone? Even drunk, would he sell his soul to curse some yuppies who insulted him?" I think about it, then say no. "Mark was so in withdrawal, he did something he *knew* was shameful, panhandling inside a bar. He must have been terrified to do it, and sure, you guys were rude to him, but he was used to that. Let me ask you: in the worst of your drinking episodes, would you sell *your soul* to punish some bar rats calling you names?"

I know I wouldn't, and neither would the Mark Marks I learned about at the funeral, the one with the same disease I have. I tell Reggie I'm adding Mark to my prayer list, and that makes him smile. Mark is on my list for the right reasons, but also for a "wrong" one. Sorry, but I don't believe it was all coincidence, because I'll never be able to forget the fear in Cisco's eyes the night he died.

I pray, earnestly, that there is no such thing as a bogeyman.

All the big stuff is over and dealt with now. I'm still living at Mickey's and am back working for Frankie.

At this very moment, however, I'm fifty feet from a house I haven't been inside since December. Carol brought Reesie once to the hospital, waiting in the lobby while a nurse took her up. Haven't seen Carol since Cisco's funeral. We talked on the phone yesterday, and she asked if I could come by today and see Reesie. Of course I said yes. She thanked me for the money I've been mailing her (I'm still hourly, but Frankie gave me a nice bump).

There's a lot of divorce rigamarole left to talk about, probably best done through lawyers, but we can't afford them, so I've pushed off dropping papers on her. It's just not the time. There are other practicalities, too: additional hospital bills (mine), a court date to set up a payment plan to reimburse the County for the cruisers I destroyed, and my weekly parole meetings.

I start walking toward my house again, thinking, *How stupid I am for not asking Carol if she'll be home!* Am I gonna keep it together if she is? I feel terrible: Reesie wants to see *me*, not the two adults responsible for her upbringing frostily staring at each other, or worse, fighting. I still want to vomit thinking about what happened inside that house between Chin and my wife. I'd discussed seeing my daughter with Reggie, and he agreed it would be great idea. He thought it might not be a good idea to talk with Carol yet, however; he suggested I pray about it. Reggie's "suggestions" aren't quite the edicts Cisco's were—he gives me his honest opinion, then wishes me well. I prayed last night for over an hour, putting the outcome in God's hands, as the word is He's big enough to handle it. Hopefully He nudges me when I need nudging.

I slowly walk up my driveway, past Cisco's old truck. Carol said she appreciated having wheels again. She's put in her notice at Hallmark. I give her 80% of my paycheck, and with Frankie's bump, plus overtime, she's better off staying home right now anyway. And if I can keep my nose clean for the rest of the year, Frankie says he'll put me back on salary. I told him about the thirty-two-thousand dollars I owe him. "That's all water under the bridge," he said, but I convinced him that to stay well, I *had* to pay him. He'll keep my bonuses until it's paid off—a good deal for both of us.

Twenty feet from my door, I stop to recite the Serenity Prayer.

Reesie pokes her head out, then runs at me like a rocket, wrapping around me, screaming, "Daddy! Daddy!" She's wearing a new dress, obviously Mommy's doing. Carol's at the door as well, wearing a matching one. She looks incredibly nervous. Reesie talks a million miles a minute: "Kitty Batman's inside! Did you really make a Christmas tree out of sticks? Mommy and I cleaned the whole house! Will you have to wear an eyepatch forever?" The whole time, she's leading me by the hand toward the door, toward my wife.

I lose it, hot tears leaking from my eyepatch. So does Carol.

"Why are you crying, guys?" asks Reesie. "We're back together!" To Carol's credit, though Reesie suspects something *uh-oh* happened between Mommy and Daddy, she doesn't know what. It helps to know that the monster-in-law had put her meaty thumb on the scales of our imbalanced marriage, but the simple truth is the adultery's on me: *If I didn't drink like I did (and still could), it wouldn't have happened. None of this would've happened.*

After we settle, which takes some time, Carol, white as a ghost, asks: "Trevor, what do we do now?"

My first thought is, *That's a question with a million answers.*

I pause at the door, hoping God will nudge me.

I think of Cisco, then wait for my second thought.

Finally, it arrives.

How about we go inside?"

Getting help

If you need help with your drinking:
aa.org

If you need help with someone else's drinking:
al-anon.org

Acknowledgments

Thank you for reading.

There was an EMBC in the DC Area in the late 90s, but to my knowledge, we didn't get cursed, at least not like Trevor and crew. Some episodes, dialogue, and character references in this novel are loosely inspired by experiences from 1998 through 2000. The portrayal of Washington, DC, and surrounding geography is also loose. My apologies for the graffiti humor; I couldn't help myself.

I got considerable help sorting out my mental monkeys through the efforts of the following beta readers: Alison McDonald, Daniel Ryder, Chris Hartstein, Brian Rooney, John Barber, Eric and Maryann Plummer, Lori Schueler, and especially Mr. Bryan Bellec.

This novel is a level above my writing ability due to careful and thoughtful editing by Heather Ryder.

To contact the author: www.tcschueler.com

Made in the USA
Middletown, DE
08 April 2024

52629470R00281